PRAISE FOR *THE WELL OF SHADES*

"A fine example of literary Celtic knotwork: twists and turns, bright threads, and unexpected shadings contribute to a satisfying whole. Fans of the series will not be disappointed with this installment."

—*Romantic Times BOOKreviews* (4 stars)

"Another page-turner with wonderful characters and superb storytelling."

—*VOYA*

PRAISE FOR *BLADE OF FORTRIU*

"Lush detail, lyrical writing, and stirring characters make this story memorable. . . . Readers will rejoice in their triumphs and mourn their losses."

—*Romantic Times BOOKreviews* (4½ stars)

"Skilled world-building and characterization set Marillier's historical fantasy at the head of the pack."

—*Publishers Weekly*

PRAISE FOR *THE DARK MIRROR*

"Marillier excels at breathing life into the past. Possessing the charm and sweetness of the very young, Bridei and Tuala keep their golden glow to the last page."

—*Booklist*

"Fans will be enthralled, and the happy ending—all too rare in first volumes of series—will encourage new readers to seek out both future installments and past publications."

—*Publishers Weekly* (starred review)

"Marillier does her usual masterful job of storytelling."

—*VOYA*

The

Well *of*
Shades

Book Three
of the
Bridei Chronicles

JULIET MARILLIER

TOR®
fantasy

A TOM DOHERTY ASSOCIATES BOOK
NEW YORK

THE WELL OF SHADES

Copyright © 2006 by Juliet Marillier

First published in Sydney, NSW, Australia, in 2006 by Pan Macmillan Australia Pty Limited

A Tor Book
Published by Tom Doherty Associates, LLC
175 Fifth Avenue
New York, NY 10010

www.tor-forge.com

Tor® is a registered trademark of Tom Doherty Associates, LLC.

ISBN-13: 978-0-7653-4877-7
ISBN-10: 0-7653-4877-2

First U.S. Edition: May 2007
First U.S. Mass Market Edition: November 2008

Printed in the United States of America

0 9 8 7 6 5 4 3 2 1

In Memory of

JANA KOUDELKA

1985–2005

A girl who lived every day to the full

ACKNOWLEDGMENTS

My thanks to all those who helped with the development of this book: my peer support group, Fiona, Satima, and Tom; my editors, Brianne Tunnicliffe of Pan Macmillan Australia, Stefanie Bierwerth of Tor UK, and Claire Eddy of Tor Books; my Australian copy editor, Julia Stiles; my agent, Russell Galen; and my family.

Cast of Characters

ERIN

Dáire Líobhan Áine	} Faolan's sisters
Fionn Fergus	} sons of Echen Uí Néill
Donnan	Líobhan's husband
Conor	Faolan's father, the brithem at Fiddler's Crossing
Phadraig	son of Líobhan and Donnan
Faolan's grandfather	

Brennan Donal Aidan Conor Ultan Oonagh	} villagers, Cloud Hill

Anda	sister of the deceased warrior, Deord
Dalach	her husband, a farrier
Eile Saraid	} other members of their household

Maeve	housekeeper at Blackthorn Rise
Orlagh	her assistant
Seamus	head guard, married to Maeve
Conal	guard
Enda	guard

Colm (Colmcille)	charismatic monk and leader
Suibne	scholar, cleric, translator, and observer
Seosabh	ancient monk

Éibhear — novice, son of a sailor

Lomán
Sean
Tomas
} monks

FORTRIU

WHITE HILL (COURT OF FORTRIU)

Bridei — king of Fortriu
Tuala — his wife, queen of Fortriu
Derelei — their son
Broichan — the king's druid
Aniel — councillor
Eldrist — Aniel's bodyguard
Tharan — councillor
Dorica — Tharan's wife
Imbeg — Tharan's bodyguard
Faolan — Bridei's chief bodyguard,
a Gael
Dovran — Bridei's new bodyguard
(in training)
Garth — Bridei's second bodyguard
Elda — Garth's wife, an herbalist
Gilder
Galen
} twin sons of Garth and Elda
Rhian — widow of the former king,
Drust the Bull
Garvan — royal stone-carver
Wid — ancient scholar
Tresna — wet nurse
Kennard — gate guard

Ban — the king's dog

RAVEN'S WELL

Talorgen — chieftain
Brethana — his second wife
Bedo — his elder son
Uric — his younger son

Warrior Chieftains of Fortriu

Carnach of Thorn Bend	Bridei's chief war leader
Morleo of Longwater	
Uerb	
Wredech	
Umbrig of Donncha's Head	
Fokel of Galany	
Mordec	
Loura	widow of Ged of Abertornie
Aled	her son
Amnost	druid from Abertornie

Banmerren

Fola	senior wise woman
Ferada	Talorgen's daughter; head of secular school at Banmerren
Sudha	midwife

Pitnochie (Broichan's Household)

Drustan	chieftain of Dreaming Glen and Briar Wood
Ana	princess of the Light Isles, betrothed to Drustan
Mara	housekeeper
Ferat	cook
Cinioch	} men-at-arms, survivors of battle for Dalriada
Uven	
Fidich	farmer
Brenna	Fidich's wife
Cloud	a guard dog

CIRCINN

Court of Circinn

Drust the Boar	king of Circinn
Bargoit	councillor
Garnet	} brothers of Drust the Boar
Keltran	

THE LIGHT ISLES (ORKNEY)

Keother	king of the Light Isles (vassal king to Bridei)
Breda	his cousin; Ana's younger sister
Cella	daughter of Keother's first adviser; maid-in-waiting to Breda
Cria	
Amna	} maids-in-waiting to Breda
Nerela	
Evard	Breda's favorite groom
Orina	Keother's wife
Dernat	Keother's second adviser

THE GOOD FOLK

Gossamer
Woodbine

The
Well *of* Shades

1

WINTER WAS COMING. Faolan saw its touch on the land as he traveled southward out of the province of Ulaid toward a place called Cloud Hill. In the mornings the grass was crisp with frost and a shroud of mist hung low over the hills, wrapping itself around barn and stable, cottage and byre. The fields held only stubble, among which crows made leisurely paths, exchanging occasional sharp comments. The skies were uniformly gray. So long absent from his homeland, he had forgotten the rain; how it came every day without fail, gently insistent, penetrating cloak and hat and boots so a wayfarer could never be entirely dry.

He reached Cloud Hill in a fine, drenching drizzle. The tiny settlement huddled under the sudden rise of the hill, low stone huts clustered in a scattering of leafless rowans, geese gathered in the shelter of an outhouse with only half a roof, a larger hall standing square, with smoke struggling up from the thatch and a skinny gray dog skulking in the doorway. The rain became a downpour; Faolan decided it was time to put aside secrecy, and made for the entry. The dog rumbled a warning as he approached, and a man twitched aside the rough sacking that served as a door, peering out into the rain. The growl became a snarl; the man aimed a kick at the creature and it cringed back into the shadows.

"What's your business?" The tone was both surly and defensive.

"Shelter from the rain, no more."

"Not from these parts, are you?" the man muttered as Faolan came in. "Hardly a day for traveling."

There was a small crowd within, gathered around a smoky hearth, ale cups in hand. The wet was an excuse, maybe, for a brief respite from the work of smithy or field. A circle of suspicious eyes greeted Faolan as he made his way toward the fire, his cloak dripping on the earthen floor. He could not tell if this was home or drinking hall; the atmosphere was hardly convivial.

"Where are you headed?" asked the man who had let him in.

"That depends." Faolan sat down on a bench. "What's the name of this place?"

"What place are you looking for?"

He'd need to take this carefully. Deord's kin might be among these wary-looking folk, and he would not come right out with his bad news in public. "I'm seeking a man named Deord," he said. "Big fellow, broad shoulders; from over the water in Caitt territory. I'm told he has kin in a region known as Cloud Hill."

Muttering and whispers. A cup of ale was slid across the table in Faolan's direction; he took it gratefully. It had been a long day's walking.

"What's Deord to such as you?" asked a tall, thin man with calloused hands.

"Such as I?" Faolan kept his tone light. "What do you mean?"

"You've a look of someone," the first man said. "Can't quite put my finger on it."

"I've been away. Years. Deord and I share a past; we were guests in a certain place of incarceration. You'll know where I mean, perhaps. There's a name associated with it, a name folk in these parts will be familiar with."

Another silence, then, but with a new feeling to it. The cup of ale was joined by a hunk of bread and a bowl of watery soup brought in by a woman from another chamber behind. She stopped to watch him drink it.

"You and Deord, hm?" the first man said. "He's not here, hasn't been these seven years or more. Not that there aren't folk nearby would be wanting news of the man. By the Dagda's bollocks, that fellow was a fighter and a half. Built like a prize boar, and light as a dancer on his feet. When did you last see him, then? What did you say your name was?"

Faolan thought of lying and decided it would make things too difficult later. "Faolan. Yours?"

They introduced themselves. The spokesman, Brennan. The tall man, Conor. The woman, Oonagh, wife of Brennan. And others: Donal, Ultan, Aidan. Someone threw another log on the fire, and the ale jug went around again.

"I saw Deord last summer," Faolan said. "We met in Priteni lands." *He was hacked apart and died in my arms. He honored a vow and was slain for it.* "A good man. If he has kin in these parts, I'd welcome the chance to speak with them."

Brennan glanced at his wife. Conor exchanged looks with Ultan. The gathering was suddenly full of something unspoken.

Aidan, a lad of sixteen or so, cleared his throat. "Were you really in Breakstone?" he asked in a whisper. "And you got out, just like him?"

"Hush, lad," said Brennan. "If you'd your wits about you, you'd know men don't like to speak of such things." He addressed Faolan again. "You know Deord came back? Lasted from plowing to harvest; couldn't cope with it any longer. The time in there scars a man. Only the strongest make it out, and only the strongest of those pick up the pieces of what they had before. He came home and he left again. Where did he go? What's he doing?"

Sleeping a sleep of no dreams, and the forest creeping

over to hide him. "I'd best pass my news to the family first, that's if there is one," Faolan said. "He mentioned a sister."

"You got the Breakstone mark?" someone asked in a rush. "Show us."

It was, Faolan supposed, necessary to prove he was not lying. He obliged by turning his head and lifting his hair to show the little star-shaped tattoo behind his right ear.

"Just like Deord's," said the man called Ultan. "And yet there's a look about you that suggests captors rather than captives. You mentioned a name that goes with talk of Breakstone. Your face puts me in mind of that name; an influential one."

"It's like a basket of eggs or a creel of shellfish," Faolan said smoothly. "There's good ones and bad ones. Every family has both. I was—I am a good friend of Deord's. The men who escape Breakstone Hollow are bonded for life. So, his sister? She married a local man, I understand?" He drained his cup. "This is uncommonly fine ale, Brennan."

Brennan favored him with a cautious smile. "My own brew. Deord's sister is Anda. They live around the hill in a hut on its own. We don't see much of them. Her man, Dalach, is a farrier; follows the horse fairs. He might be away. You should find someone there. It's wet out; why don't you leave it till the morning? We can find you a pallet in a corner."

"Thank you," Faolan said, taken aback that the mention of Deord and Breakstone had turned deep suspicion so quickly into welcome. "I'd best be getting on."

"The offer stands," said Brennan, glancing at his wife. "If you find you need a bed, there's one here. It's a fair walk over there. Aidan will go with you as far as the stile and point out the way."

Aidan grimaced, but went for a piece of sacking to put over head and shoulders.

"You got a knife on you?" Donal asked, offhand, as Faolan was heading out the door.

"Why do you ask?" Faolan turned a level stare at Donal, and Donal gazed at his own hands.

"What he means is, can you defend yourself?" Brennan's tone was diffident.

"I think I should be able to manage," said Faolan, who had been not only translator and spy to two kings of Fortriu, but assassin as well. "Difficult, is he, this farrier?" It was not quite a shot in the dark; he was expert at reading faces and voices, at hearing the words not spoken.

"You'd want to be on your guard," Brennan said.

The rain continued. They reached the stile and the boy pointed out the way, a muddy track barely visible in fading light and persistent downpour. His job done, Aidan fled for home. Faolan climbed over the stile and headed on, boots squelching. He had an odd sense that someone was following him. The dark forms of cattle could be discerned here and there in the gloom, but nothing could be heard but the rain and his own footsteps. Nonetheless, he looked back and looked back again. Nothing; he was being foolish, taking those men's warnings too much to heart. No self-respecting vagrant would choose such a day to lurk by the road for easy pickings. No sensible traveler would be out in such a deluge. He should have taken up the offer and stayed in the settlement overnight. All the same, the news he bore was bad, and he owed it to Deord to make sure it was his family who heard it first. He just hoped they were home; it would be a long, wet walk back.

The hut was a poor thing, a low construction of mud and wattles, with the water streaming off the thatch to pool around the base of the walls. Here and there the fabric of the place was crumbling; farrier this Dalach might be, but he was evidently not handy around the house. Someone had made an attempt at a vegetable plot; a low stone wall surrounded a dug patch in which a few cabbages grew, and a row of stakes stood ready for peas or beans. In a corner Faolan thought he saw lavender, its gray-green spikes bowing under the rain.

As he came up to the doorway, he had the eerie sense again of an unseen presence behind him. Not being a man much given to superstitious fears, he turned calmly, reaching for his knife as the gray form of the emaciated dog came into view, slinking low, ears laid back in anticipation of a blow, coat bedraggled. It had followed him all the way.

"If I had a crust on me, I'd give it to you," Faolan murmured, slipping the knife back in his belt. "But I'm all out of provisions. It wasn't worth your while." He drew a deep breath. There was a dim light inside the small dwelling; someone was home. And he had the worst kind of news to give them, news that would be hard both in the telling and the hearing. Ah, well; best get this over with.

He lifted a hand to knock on the door frame; only a strip of stained felt covered the entry. An instant later, the tines of a pitchfork were a handspan from his eyes.

"Get out, or I'll push this through your head!" snarled someone, and the thing jerked forward.

Faolan's knife was in his hand again. He calculated the position of the speaker's arms and shoulders as he replied. "I'm a friend. I mean no harm."

"Friend, huh! I know that trick. Now get out or I'll set the dogs on you!"

Faolan did not look behind him. The cur that had tailed him from the settlement was silent; if there were indeed dogs within, they did not seem to be causing it concern. "Are you Anda?" he ventured. "I'm seeking a woman of that name. I'm a friend of her brother's. I've come a long way to speak with her."

There was a silence. The dog came up to the door, stationing itself beside Faolan, ready for admittance. The pitchfork wavered.

"It is the truth. I mean no harm to anyone here. My name is Faolan."

"Never heard of you. He never said anything about you." The felt curtain moved a fraction away from the door frame, and Faolan found himself looking down into a face that was angry, scared, and much younger than he expected. Green eyes blazed defiance against grubby pale skin. He revised his guess. This was not much more than a child.

"Is your mother home?"

"Huh!"

"A reasonable question under the circumstances. It's very wet out here. We're getting soaked. Do you think you could put that thing away?"

"*We're* getting soaked? You and who else?" The pitchfork was back in his face. For such a small boy—girl?— the wielder was exceptionally strong.

"Me and the dog. I'd introduce you, but I don't know his name."

The curtain twitched farther. The green eyes looked down and the dog looked up, mangy tail wagging. The curtain came aside at the base, aided by a foot, and the dog slipped into the house. Faolan made to follow, and the girl—he had seen the long, unkempt hair tied back with string—spoke again. "Not you. You're a liar. Deord went away. He never came back. Why would he send you?"

Because he was dying, and could not say good-bye. "What I have to tell is for his close kin," Faolan said levelly. "When will Anda be home?"

"Soon. Any time now."

"Then might I come in and wait?"

"No. Take one step and I'll whistle for my big brothers. They'll make you wish you'd never been born. Go home. Go back where you came from."

"I do have news. She'll want to hear it."

"Go away and take your poxy news with you. If he's not coming back, he needn't think sending his friends here with messages is going to make up for it."

Faolan was thinking hard, but he could not place this

girl anywhere in what he knew of Deord. The sister's child? She did not speak as a serving girl would. There was something there that curbed his tongue; he saw the longing in her eyes, for all the furious words.

"I won't hurt you," he said. "I give you my word."

"You'd be better to give me your weapons," the girl snapped.

"That's before or after you set the dogs and the brothers on me?" he queried, and instantly regretted it. Her small features tightened; there was a look on her face that sat ill in one so young, the look of a person who is accustomed to betrayal. He could not quite judge her age, but she was surely no more than thirteen or fourteen. An image of Áine came to him, and he willed it away.

"Don't you dare mock me!" the girl hissed. "I know how to use this and I'll do it. You'd better believe that. Now go. I'll tell her you came. When she gets back. Aunt Anda, I mean." Then, seeing some change in his face, "What?"

Let this not be. Let me not have to tell her now, alone, at night. "Forgive me," Faolan said, "but does that mean you are Deord's daughter?" And, before she could reply, he saw that it must indeed be so; it was in the square stance, the hard grip on the too-large weapon, the way she held her head, proudly for all the filth and the fear. Deord had never spoken of a wife, of children. Only the sister. Gods, this girl must have been the merest infant when her father went into Breakstone. She would have been five or six, perhaps, when he came home and lasted only a season. "Is your mother still living?"

"None of your business, but yes, that poxy wretch is my father and no, she's not. He broke her heart. She strung herself up from one of those oaks out there. When you go back to wherever he is, you can tell him that."

"I'm sorry," Faolan said inadequately. "Is there nobody home but you?"

"If you think I'm going to answer that, you're even

stupider than you look. Go back to the settlement. I'm not letting you in." And, as he turned away, "What is this news anyway? Tell me." He heard it again in her voice, a trembling eagerness she was fighting hard to hide. His heart clenched tight. He had viewed this as the easiest of his three missions. At this moment he would have given much not to have to reply. "Go on, tell me," she said. "Just say it. He's not coming home, is he?"

Go back to Brennan's, Faolan told himself. *Wait for morning. See the sister alone and tell her first, not this quivering bundle of defiance and need. You can't tell her, not here, not now.*

"Tell me the truth!" she commanded, and in that moment he saw Deord's face, dying, and the strength in the lone warrior's eyes.

"It's not something I'm willing to say out here," he told her. "You need to be inside, sitting down. Here, take my knife. Hold on to that if you must have a weapon. Just put away the pitchfork. If it helps, you might notice the dog seems to trust me. Dogs are astute judges of character. Is he yours?"

She had paled at this speech; the girl wasn't stupid. Now she leaned the fork against the wall and backed into the house, holding Faolan's knife in front of her, point aimed accurately at his heart. "Sit there and don't move. Now tell me."

"You should sit down. What is your name?"

"Eile. I'll stand. Just say it, will you? What? He's not coming? Could have guessed that. He's hurt? Not much I can do about that, since he never bothered to let me know where he was . . ." She faltered to a halt, eyes on Faolan's face. "Just tell me. Please." She sat down abruptly, and the dog came to stand by her. It was hard to say which was the more pathetic specimen; both were disheveled and looked half-starved. The fire in the rudimentary hearth was barely alight, the wood basket near empty. Faolan could see no sign of food or drink in the place, just empty crocks on a shelf and a bucket of water.

He cleared his throat. "It's bad news, I'm afraid. I had hoped to tell your aunt first."

She waited, utterly still.

"Deord—your father—I'm afraid he's dead, Eile." Not a flicker on the neat features, not a twitch of the thin lips. "He was killed in early autumn, up in the north of Priteni lands. There was . . . a battle. I got there too late to save him, and he died of his wounds. I buried him in the forest. Eile, he was a good man. A brave man." No words could capture Deord's transcendent valor or his deep serenity.

Eile bowed her head a little. One hand went out to touch the dog, moving against its neck. Her fingernails were bitten to the quick, the hands raw and chapped. She said nothing.

"He asked me, when he was dying, to come here and break the news. It was a heroic end, Eile. He gave his life so that I and two friends could escape from certain death. If I say I am sorry, I don't expect you to believe it. You don't know me, and you can't know how it happened. But I am sorry; sorry at the waste of such a fine man. He loved you. I am certain of it." That part was a lie.

"That's not true." Eile spoke in a whisper. "If he'd loved us, he would have stayed. He wouldn't have just . . . gone."

"I don't know how much you were told about his past. Perhaps there were reasons for what he did."

Abruptly, the anger returned to the girl's eyes. "If he was going to leave, he never should have come back," she said. "It's cruel to let people think everything's going to be all right again, and then take that away. Then Mother went, too. Never mind. That's of no possible interest to you. You've told your news, you can go now."

Outside the rain was hammering down. Faolan observed three different places where drips were coming through the roof.

Seeing him looking, Eile laid the knife on the table, got

up and moved automatically to set vessels beneath them. "I never did learn to mend thatch," she said shakily.

"Doesn't your uncle do that kind of thing?"

She gave a snort. "Uncle? Oh, you mean Dalach?" She spoke this name with chill distaste. "He's got other interests. Didn't you hear me? I said you can go."

"If that's what you want. I would like to speak with your aunt; tell her what I know. Perhaps in the morning." Faolan rose to his feet. "You shouldn't be alone in the house overnight."

"Why not?" Her expression was bleak, resigned. "They go away all the time. I'm used to it. I prefer it. Except when strangers come knocking, and I can deal with them."

"Yes, I'm sure you can." Faolan thought of the pitchfork. "I don't think Deord would be happy if he knew your circumstances here. I'm sure some arrangement can be made . . ." He had not thought this would be necessary. He had assumed Deord's sister would be comfortably settled, and that he'd need only to tell his tale and move on. But this was pitiful. Something was wrong here, surely; something more than poverty. Brennan and the other villagers had seemed good enough souls. Why had this girl been allowed to dwindle to skin and bone, a frail creature who seemed held together only by her desperate anger? The circumstances of Deord's death had meant any savings the man had were inaccessible. Faolan, however, had wealth of his own, accumulated through years of working at kings' courts. There had been little to spend his silver on. He had neither wife nor children; his parents and sisters he had never expected to see again.

"What?" Eile was staring at him. "What is it?"

"Nothing. Eile, I'm certain Deord would want some provision made for your welfare. I can discuss it with your aunt—"

"Huh! Discuss all you like, it'll never change a thing for us."

It was like holding a conversation with a stone wall. "A small amount of silver could pay a thatcher, or even someone to rebuild the whole hut," Faolan said, calculating whether he had carried sufficient funds with him. "It could provide warm clothing and fuel. It could ensure you are adequately fed."

"We do all right. Not starving, am I? I know how to provide. We don't need anyone." The look in her eyes was the bleakest he had ever seen. Her hand went down to fondle the dog's ears. For all the aggressive thrust of the chin, the defiant words, he wondered if she was waiting for him to go so she could weep alone.

"I'm sorry I brought such ill tidings," he said simply. "I can help you, if you'll let me. Deord and I both spent time as prisoners in Breakstone Hollow. Men who escape that place of captivity are bound for life to help one another. There aren't many of us. Deord took that bond to an extreme. In view of that I consider myself bound to aid his family."

"We're past aiding," Eile said flatly. "Silver won't mend us. You'd best leave me to deal with this myself. You'd be wasting your money. That's the truth."

"How old are you, Eile?"

"How old are *you*?" she snapped back.

"Old. I've lost count."

"I bet you haven't. Let me guess. Five and thirty?"

Gods, his sojourn in the lands of the Caitt must have taken a heavy toll. "Not quite so old as that. I'm not yet thirty. You?"

"What are you asking? Am I still a child? The answer's no. I've been old since I was twelve. That's four years now. Don't take that as an invitation. Not unless you want a knife in your belly."

Faolan was seldom shocked, but her speech startled him, and he was lost for a response.

"If you'd asked them, down at Brennan's, that's what they would have said. *The girl's up there on her own, and she's no better than she should be, filthy little slut.*

The word's been put about so often they all believe it now, not that they come up here and try anything; when *he's* home they give us a wide berth, and when he isn't, I know how to see folk off."

"Believe me," Faolan said wearily, "there is no need to fear such attentions from me. That's the last thing on my mind. I've two more missions to undertake after this and they crowd all other concerns from my thoughts. Besides . . ." He pictured Ana by a mountain lake, wading in the shallows as the sunlight touched her hair to shining gold. Ana looking up, dazzled, not at Faolan but at the tall, bright-eyed figure of Drustan.

"Besides what?" asked Eile, crouching to put the last log on the fire.

"It could be said I've been unlucky in love." He did not want to tell that story.

"Love?" Her brows went up. "I don't think that's what Brennan and the others had in mind."

He smiled. "I've put aside the other thing, too. It makes life a great deal less complicated."

"Yes, well, you're a man." Her voice was muffled as she reached to poke the struggling fire. "When things get difficult you can put a bundle on your back and just go. That's what he did. My father. A woman can't do that. Not even with silver. Someone'd take it off her before she got as far as the next settlement. Someone'd go after her and make her come back . . ." Her voice trailed away. Faolan saw her take a deep, unsteady breath and square her shoulders. "I really want you to go now," she said. "I know it's wet, but I want to be by myself. Oh, drat!" The iron poker had toppled with a clang from where she had leaned it against the wall. An instant later, a small voice came from another chamber behind.

"Eile?"

"Curse it, now I've woken her up!" Eile's voice was a fierce whisper. "Go, will you?"

"Are you sure? Who is that?"

"Go. How hard is that to understand?" And, as a small

figure appeared from the inner chamber, rubbing its eyes, "Now, Faolan. Before she has a chance to get scared. Hush, Saraid, it's all right. Did you have a dream?"

He went. This time, the dog did not follow. One image stayed in his head all through the decidedly uncomfortable walk back to the settlement: the child, whose age he could not guess, not being familiar with children, clad in a much-mended nightrobe, long brown hair ruffled from sleep but healthy and clean, eyes big and dark from her sudden waking. Little, certainly, and skinny like the other one, but surely well loved; he'd heard the change in Eile's voice, as if she became another girl entirely in this small one's presence. How old was Bridei's son, Derelei? Somewhere between one and two. This child was bigger, perhaps a year or so older. For her aunt and uncle to leave Eile alone in that isolated, near-derelict hut was bad enough. To leave their own small child there as well was quite unacceptable. He hadn't seen a scrap of food in the place.

Faolan sighed, pulling his wet cloak more tightly around his shoulders. He was making too much of this. It was poverty. It existed, and folk did what they could to survive. His own upbringing had been one of privilege by comparison, food on the table, a loving family, a household where smiles were common currency and the talk flowed freely. Until that day when he destroyed the very fabric of it. There had been poor people at Fiddler's Crossing; there were poor people in the settlement near Bridei's fortress at White Hill. But folk helped each other. Food was shared; a man chopped a neighbor's wood in exchange for a share of nuts harvested or shellfish gathered. His mother had taken remedies to the sick. Faolan himself had played for village festivals, long ago, before his hands turned themselves to the occupation of killing. His music had been free; rich and poor alike had shared it.

So, it was simple poverty. But Eile was Deord's daughter. Faolan was bound to help her. She'd scoffed at his silver, and he did not understand that, for it was plain she needed money. It was all he had to offer, anyway. He'd go back in the morning and give a sum to the aunt, who'd likely be less hostile. He'd request that part of it be spent on the girl's welfare: perhaps she could be taught some skill whereby she might achieve a position beyond those crumbling walls, sewing maybe. Faolan grimaced, remembering the expert grip of her small hands on the pitchfork. She'd learned that somewhere. Maybe, in his brief sojourn home, that peerless warrior Deord had begun to teach his daughter how to protect herself.

Well, tomorrow was a new day. He'd get this thing done and be on his way. Faolan had embarked from the shore of Dalriada with three missions to fulfill. In the epic poetry of his homeland, much of which he'd memorized during his bardic training long ago, things had a tendency to come in threes: three blessings, three curses, three wise sayings. The first mission, for the king of Fortriu, was to locate a certain influential cleric known as Colmcille, find out what he was up to, and carry a report back to Bridei. The second he had just attempted: to break the news of Deord's death to his kinsfolk. The third . . .

The third mission would carry him home; home to Fiddler's Crossing to face the unthinkable. It was years now since he had walked away from his birthplace with his harp under his arm and a bundle on his back, never to return. He had left with his brother's blood on his hands, the beloved brother he had killed in order to save the lives of his parents, his grandparents, and his three sisters. Three . . . Dáire, a widow at twenty, aged beyond her years; Líobhan, fourteen years old and full of defiant pride; Áine, the youngest, Áine whom his act of murder had not saved after all. He could still see her eyes, dark and terrified, as Echen Uí Néill's henchmen dragged her away. His sisters would be older now, of course, Líobhan a grown woman. He had never been able to imagine them beyond that night. Now every part of him shrank from going home. As a young man he had acted to save his family. He had not known until it was too late that, although they had lived, he had destroyed them anyway.

It would have been better to come in summer, but Bridei was astute. He had known Faolan could not secure safe passage back to Fortriu now before next spring, and still he had let him go. That meant a whole winter to be spent in Erin. A winter for three missions; that had seemed ample time. See Deord's family in Cloud Hill; investigate Colmcille in the north; confront his own past. The first had proven awkward thus far, but a few incentives should smooth the way for Eile. The second would require skills of a kind Faolan possessed in abundance, having worked as a spy and translator for two kings of Fortriu and done it expertly. The third was another matter. A lifetime would not be sufficient for him to summon the courage for it: to find out what had happened to his family since he walked away. To look in their eyes as they saw him and recognized him. He would perform that mission last. If it should chance that he ran out of time before spring opened the sea path to Fortriu once more, so be it. And if he had promised Ana, what of it? She was marrying another man, the altogether too perfect Drustan. Her way and Faolan's had parted forever. That was just as well, for she had peeled back the protective layers he had set around his heart and when it was exposed, raw and tender, she had broken it. That was entirely his own fault; Ana was a woman of honor and goodness, and all she had wanted to do was help him. When he got back to Fortriu, she would likely be gone. Who would know whether he had confronted his demons or failed to find the courage?

Up until now he'd been cautious, sleeping in barns and hedges and avoiding attention. The nearer he came to his home settlement, the more likely it was folk would know, if not his identity, at least his ties of kinship. He'd never asked to be born an Uí Néill. It was more curse

than blessing. In Fortriu he had worked hard at being unobtrusive, the kind of man folk's eyes passed over. Here
on his home shore his features were distinctive. It was
unfortunate that the mission laid on him by Deord had
happened to bring him so close to Fiddler's Crossing;
more than odd that Deord, a man of Priteni blood, had
kin among the Gaels here in Laigin. He'd only expected
the sister; she was the only one the dying man had mentioned. Deord hadn't even given her name, just the district and the fact that she'd wed a Gael. Nothing about a
daughter or a wife. He shivered, seeing again that girl's
desperate eyes. The mission had proved to be a little
more difficult than anticipated. Never mind that; he had
silver on him, and he'd use it to make things more comfortable for Eile. Then he'd move on. North. Almost certainly north.

(from Brother Suibne's Account)
*I begin this account in the house of prayer in Kerrykeel,
where we are housed until Brother Colm chooses to move
on. When he goes, I go, for he is a man great in faith and
in goodness, a man strong of mind and radiant with the
love of God, and I cannot but follow him.*

*It seems to me that great matters are afoot, and there
is a strong will in me to set them down in writing. It is
a time of change; a time that will influence not simply
the small men and women who play their parts in the
story of Brother Colm's journey, but generation on generation of folk who follow. Thus my account. It is for my
own record; I do not intend that others should read it. As
a scribe, I am better suited to the copying of manuscripts
in a fair hand, for that is a safer occupation than the
composition of scholarly or didactic pieces. Too often
my mind finds conformity a challenge.*

*This is a difficult time for Brother Colm. He is a son of
the Uí Néill, the warlike family that wields such influence*

in the north of our land. Colm was never warrior or secular leader, but the Uí Néill blood runs true in him and he cannot escape it. No matter that he put aside worldly ambition long ago to serve the Holy Cross in true humility. I see his breeding in his proud stance, his keen eye, and his commanding voice. I see it also in his impatience with fools, for all his efforts to moderate that.

There is a tale associated with this good priest, a dark tale that explains his urgent quest to quit our home shore. Some say all that drives him is the fire in his belly to spread the faith in the lands of the Priteni. The tale suggests otherwise.

There was a great battle in the north of our homeland. Cúl Drebene, the place was called. North fought south; that is to say, northern Uí Néill fought southern, for are not all the most warlike chieftains and petty kings in that part of Erin descended from the same stock? The High King himself is one of them. Their common blood does not hold them back from warring among themselves, and Cúl Drebene was just one blood-soaked example of their territorial struggles.

It was fought on a plain in early autumn. At the time I was far away, over the sea in the kingdom of Circinn. I had not yet encountered this man of God who would so profoundly influence the course of my life. A missionary monk, I was, not an exile but a standard-bearer. The folk of that land were but newly come to knowledge of God's word, and my task was to strengthen that knowledge; to nurture the small flame of belief in their hearts. I met two kings in the lands of the Priteni, and one was to the other as a great eagle is to the least of finches, but that is a different tale. I met a king with faith in his gaze and strength in his heart, and that king was no Christian. Bridei of Fortriu presented a puzzle; an enigma. It exercises me still.

To Colm, then, and the field of Cúl Drebene on a drizzling, clammy autumn morning. The armies were ranged, ready to march forward into combat. No less a man than

*the High King led the forces of the south. The northern
army was led by Colm's close kinsmen. No sooner had
the leaders called their warriors to advance than a thick
mist descended on the field, so that no man could see beyond the end of his own arm.*

*Horses whinnied in confusion; men cursed; the chief-
tains muttered accusations. It was the southerners who
had done this, their druids being known for a capacity to
call up freakish weather in times of difficulty. No, it was
the Christian northerners who had done it, through the
power of prayer. Warriors clashed on the field and did
not know if it was the enemy or their own comrades they
smote. Their leaders called:* Retreat! Fall back!, *but the
curtain of vapor muffled their cries. The battle descended into screaming, bloody chaos.*

*Fionn of Tirconnell sent a messenger to his cousin
Colm, who was then lodged in a house of prayer but a
stone's throw from that field of battle. In response, the
holy brethren saw the devout monk fall to his knees in
prayer, remaining thus a goodly while. By the time Fionn's
messenger came back to Cúl Drebene on a panting,
foam-flecked horse, the mist had lifted, its blinding blanket shifting in the way best calculated to give the northerners the advantage. They moved, closing in on the flanks
and squeezing the southern forces tight. Many men fell.
The High King was among the wounded. War is no re-
specter of birth or blood.*

*Now, whether the holy man Colm caused the defeat
of the High King of Erin and the rout of his forces, or
whether the whole thing was no more than a fortunate
coincidence, is not for a lowly cleric to express in words,
let alone set down in writing. Suffice to say there were
those who believed Colm responsible. In time he was
called before a synod, to which he offered a most fluent
and powerful defense. It was not sufficient. The bishops
made it clear to him that he was no longer welcome on
his home shore. It was not quite excommunication, but it
was plain that, if he were to remain in Erin, Colm could*

neither preach the word of God nor live his life in the example of Our Lord. The taint of his kinsmen's disputes
and the stain of the blood apparently shed through his
own request for divine intervention must always hang
over him. The field of Cúl Drebene would always lie between him and his yearning for a life lived wholly in god-
liness.

It was during that time of uncertainty that I met the
man and found my life transformed. I saw in him a power
beyond the earthly, a faith beyond the saintly, a voice
and a presence that spoke to the place deepest in every
man's spirit. I had believed myself devout. He awoke in
me a joy in God's word I had never before dreamed of.
My time at the court of Circinn was over, and I expected
a long and peaceful stay in my homeland, exercising my
wits on scribing and scholarship and avoiding the other
activities that had become part and parcel of my existence in such a place of plotters and schemers. I wished
to stay with Colm; to join the small band of brethren
who shared his vision for the future.

He had by then formed a profound desire to quit the
shores of our homeland and not to look back. From the
Dalriadan king, Gabhran, he had obtained a promise of
a haven: an island known as Ioua, off the western shores
of the Gaelic part of Fortriu, on which he might settle
with a small band of brethren and found a monastic center. It would be a new land: a new beginning, where a life
of simplicity and obedience might be lived free from the
dark cloak of the past. Before them lay a realm in which
the light of Our Lord had barely begun to shine: Fortriu,
heartland of the Priteni.

As it fell out, I found myself called away from home
once again, this time to serve as translator and spiritual
adviser at King Gabhran's court. Colm approved the
venture, saying it could only benefit our cause for me to
have the king's ear and keep him mindful of his promise.
So I traveled to the Gaelic territory of Dalriada, in the
west of Priteni lands. No sooner had I arrived than the

tide turned. Fortriu moved on Dalriada. Bridei's tactics were brilliant; even a man of limited military knowledge, such as I am, could see his flair. The advance took place far earlier than anyone expected. It was on a grand scale, with a multitude of separate forces converging by land and sea on our countrymen and almost annihilating Gabhran's army. Nobody had believed Bridei of Fortriu could do it without the support of Circinn, the southern counterpart of his own country; but he did. To me it was less surprising. From the first I saw something exceptional in Bridei. Whether that quality can be exercised for pursuits other than war is still to be proven, but I believe it can. Whether that passionate faith will ever veer from the ancient gods of the Priteni, those in whose laws Bridei has been steadfastly nurtured from infancy by his mentor, Broichan, remains to be seen. That is a higher mountain to climb.

So, Dalriada is lost to the Gaels, for now at least, though our presence remains; folk do not inhabit a land for three generations to be entirely cast out, not when the conqueror is as just and wise a man as this young king of the Priteni. Gabhran is a prisoner within his own fortress at Dunadd, and his territories now fall under Priteni chieftains, all answerable to King Bridei. But those communities, those outposts and villages are full of a new folk, bred of both Gaelic and Priteni blood. And, for all Bridei banned the practice of the Christian faith in Dalriada, it still goes on in lonely cave or on windswept island, in smithy or barn or on the deck of a small boat plying the choppy waters of the west in search of codfish. As they spin and weave, women sing of Mary, Mother of God. The Lord's flame flickers; the coming of this man we call Colmcille will fan it to a great blaze.

We have not yet sailed. Gabhran promised a sanctuary, but it is no longer his to give. Bridei told me once that I am everywhere. Not possible, of course; but the skills God has granted me have certainly led to extensive travel. I was there when Bridei became king of Fortriu. I

was present when Gabhran ceded the kingship of Dalriada and Bridei pronounced sentence of banishment, a
sentence commuted to a period of incarceration in recognition of the Dalriadan king's poor health. On that field
of war, with the Gaelic dead lying in their blood, I spoke
of Colm and of his mission. I spoke of the place called
Ioua, Yew Tree Isle, and of the making of a promise.
Bridei heard me and understood. I believe his messenger
will seek us out.

We wait, meanwhile; winter is coming, but in spring
God will send us a fair wind and a fortunate tide. Colm
will not give up the promise of a haven in that realm,
even though the one who gave it no longer has the power
to grant us our island. We will sail for the Priteni shores
regardless of that; if need be, Colm will petition Bridei
to grant us the land. In doing so he will be swimming
against a mighty current, for the taking of Dalriada has
shown Bridei of Fortriu to be a leader of immense
power, and I know he is devout in his adherence to the
old faith of his people. I believe the meeting of these two
men will be extraordinary.

SUIBNE, MONK OF DERRY

AT WHITE HILL, it was raining. The days had grown
short, dusk settling early over the high walls and orderly
stone buildings of King Bridei's hilltop fortress. The
gardens were drenched. Water gurgled busily into drains
and, below the walls, the stream coursed brimful down
the pine-clad slopes of the hill.

Derelei had spent the afternoon with Broichan, making boats from twigs and leaves and sailing them on the
pond. Observing from a distance, Tuala had noted the
capacity of each of them, infant and druid, to maintain a
dry area around himself no matter how heavy the downpour. She'd seen also how the small craft moved, pursu-

ing one another, making a steady course without need of
wind or oar, in a game of maneuvering that owed far
more to the art of magic than to luck or physical skill.
She hoped Broichan would remember how young her
son was and that, for all his exceptional talents, Derelei
tired easily. As for the druid himself, his health was
much improved since his sojourn among the healers of
Banmerren, but Tuala knew he was not infallible. He,
too, needed to husband his strength.

Derelei was indoors now, eating his supper in company with his nursemaid. Today his small vocabulary
had been augmented by a new word, *boat*.

It was time, Tuala had decided, to broach a particularly delicate subject with the king's druid. She had
avoided it up till now, lacking the courage to confront the
man she had feared since childhood, when he had bent
all his considerable will on ensuring she and his foster
son did not form too strong a bond. As a child of the
Good Folk, Tuala was an unlikely wife for a king of Fortriu. If Broichan had had his way, Bridei would have wed
a far more suitable girl, someone like Ana of the Light
Isles, for instance. Tuala and Bridei, between them, had
won that battle and in time Broichan had become almost
a friend to her. He had saved Derelei's life when fever
nearly took him. Tuala had helped Broichan battle his
own long illness. She had agreed to let him tutor her
gifted son. Now, with a second child expected and Bridei
away seeing to a matter at Abertornie, it was time to confront Broichan with an event in his past. She did not expect him to welcome it.

For a long time Tuala had struggled with the mystery
of her identity in silence. She might never have acted on
what little she had discovered if she had not observed
her son's talent developing in all its confident precocity.
She had seen Broichan watching Derelei; seen the
watchful love in the druid's eyes. If what she believed
was true, the two of them should know it, Broichan now,

her son when he grew older. There were some painful truths, Tuala thought, whose importance was such that they must be exposed to the light.

She willed herself calm as she made her way to the druid's private chamber. Even now her heart thumped and her palms grew clammy at the prospect of raising such a matter with her old adversary. What if she was wrong? This was conjecture, after all, based on her own interpretation of a vision in the scrying bowl. One of her very first lessons at Banmerren, the school for wise women, had been how deceptive such images could be and how easily misinterpreted. The gods used them to tease and to test, and the seer walked a narrow path between giving good counsel or ill.

Tuala used her skill rarely; there were those who would seize any opportunity to point out the strangeness of her origins, seeking thus to weaken the foundations of her husband's kingship. For a while she had not used her craft at all. She had come to it again after a vision of hers helped save Bridei's life at the time of the great battle for Dalriada. She had known then that the risk was worth it. Today she planned to scry again.

She knocked. Broichan opened the door, showing no sign of surprise when he saw who it was.

"I need to speak to you in private," Tuala said. "If you will."

"Of course, Tuala. Come in."

She thought perhaps she had interrupted him in prayer, for two candles burned on a shelf and before them a thin mat was laid on the stone floor, a small concession to his illness. The chamber was orderly. Shelves were neatly packed with the accouterments of his calling; an oak table held a jug of water and a single cup. From the rafters hung plaits of garlic and bundles of healing herbs. His scrying mirror was nowhere to be seen.

"Please sit. You wish to discuss Derelei's progress? His welfare?"

"Not today. I see that he is doing well, though he does get very tired. I have a difficult matter to set before you, Broichan. You may have some idea what it is; I've heard Fola refer to it once or twice, obliquely."

Broichan waited, a tall figure, dark-robed. His hair was more gray than black now and fell in a multitude of small plaits across his shoulders. In the candlelight the moon-disc, a circle of pale bone he wore on a cord around his neck in tribute to the Shining One, gleamed softly. His deep-set eyes gave nothing away.

"It would be easier for me to show you this in the water of a scrying vessel," Tuala told him. "I feel a certain reluctance to put it straight into words; I'm afraid it will offend you."

"If you wish." His voice was at its most constrained. Tuala suspected he knew what was coming. "You are confident you can summon what you need and reveal it in one form to the two of us? That's a prodigiously difficult task, Tuala."

Not for me. "If the Shining One wishes us to see this, we will see it. Have you a bowl we can use?"

He fetched a vessel without further comment, uncovered it, and poured water from a ewer. "You prefer this to the mirror," he said. It was not a question.

Tuala nodded, not speaking. Already the water called her, too powerful to resist. She stood, and Broichan, opposite, reached over to take her hands. They faced each other across the bowl. Tuala felt his hands, strong and bony, relax in hers as he looked down. He was expert in the seer's art, as in all branches of magic. He knew without the need for telling that, in order to grant Tuala control over the vision, he must submit his formidable will to hers. And indeed, for all his long years of training and discipline, it was she, the child of the Good Folk, who had the greater facility in this branch of the craft. Perhaps it was not so surprising that some folk distrusted her.

The water rippled, shimmered, and was still. The vision came: the same Tuala had seen once before. That first time neither Broichan nor the wise woman Fola, both of whom had been in attendance, had discerned it. Now she felt Broichan start. His hands gripped tightly for a moment, then relaxed again as he forced his body to obey his will.

In the water a younger Broichan, clad in a white robe, walked a forest path in springtime. Another figure shadowed him, a slight, lovely woman whose fey eyes and milk-pale skin marked her out as one of the Good Folk, that diverse band of Otherworld people who inhabited the woodlands of the Great Glen and beyond. This person was one of Tuala's own kind, akin to the two beings who had shown themselves to her in her childhood, interfering in her life and Bridei's, tempting her with promises to reveal her true identity and always holding that knowledge back. She knew only that she'd been a foundling, an abandoned infant. If she had parents, they had never come forward to claim her, not in all the nineteen years since they had left her on Broichan's doorstep.

In the water, the white-clad druid looked around; he had sensed he was not alone. A voice seemed to speak, though in the candlelit chamber where Broichan and Tuala stood all was silent. *Come, my son. Come and honor me.* And, when the younger Broichan hesitated, suddenly very still on the sunlit path amid the dappled greens and golds of the springtime forest, *Come, faithful one. I require this of you.*

Tuala did not doubt that the goddess spoke. The fey woman was only a messenger. Perhaps, for this one day, she was an avatar: the earthly embodiment of the Shining One, whose own presence was ever veiled in the daylight. The white-clad druid saw the woman. His face paled and his jaw tightened. Obedient he might be, but this was plainly difficult for him. The woman smiled. She was beguiling, her lips full and rosy, her slender figure shapely and enticing beneath the sheer fabric of her floating gown. She reached out a hand toward the druid.

Go, my son. The voice again, not that of this charming creature but a deep, strong one that made every tree in the wildwood shiver. *I call you to my service. Do you hesitate?*

The druid took the proffered hand in his. Tuala could feel his reluctance and, along with it, the coursing pull of physical desire in his body. It was customary for his kind to perform a solitary three-day vigil to mark the festival of Balance, when day and night were equal and spring stirred even in the north. If the Shining One required of a believer, at such a time, a devotion expressed with the body rather than the mind, how could a faithful man hold back? If such an act felt wanton, abhorrent, lacking in self-control, he must still perform it, for at the heart of spiritual practice was the love of god and goddess, Flamekeeper and Shining One, and perfect obedience to their will. Indeed, he must exercise mind and body to perform it in a spirit of good faith, for to practice a rite reluctantly was to cause the goddess most bitter offense.

The woman stepped closer. Her free hand slipped down to touch the front of the white robe, between the druid's legs; if he was shy, she most certainly was not. Caught as she was in the vision, Tuala found herself sufficiently aware of the here and now to hope profoundly that the goddess would draw a veil over what was to come. She had called this up to illustrate her theory to Broichan, not to embarrass and shame him.

The water swirled; the image broke up into brief glimpses, snatches of sight: here a white hand on the plane of thigh or back or chest; here a sensuous mouth, lips parted, tongue moving to lap and lick, to taste and tease; here muscular buttocks clenching and unclenching; here long fingers stroking, playing, clearly not fettered by lack of experience. They were in a grove. They lay on the druid's white robe, which was spread in a grassy hollow. The woman's gown hung from a willow branch, its gauzy fabric as insubstantial as cobweb. Their bodies moved, at first slowly, with sensuous delight in every moment of their concourse, then more quickly as urgency overtook them, until their hearts surely shared the same desperate drumbeat. It was the oldest dance of all, beautiful, powerful, over all too quickly, leaving forest woman and druid lying together on the grass-stained linen, bodies sheened with sweat, chests rising and falling fast as the pounding heartbeat slowed and the fierce breath calmed. A cloud darkened the sun; a shadow passed over the little grove. The vision dissipated and was gone.

Broichan drew his hands away from Tuala's. There was a silence as each returned slowly to the shadowy chamber. A practiced seer allowed such a vision to release its hold gradually. To hasten the process led to dizziness, nausea, and distress. Tuala blinked, moving her fingers, stretching her arms. Broichan reached for the dark cloth that had lain on a shelf beside the scrying bowl and draped it over to conceal the water. When he spoke, his voice was tight with constraint and decidedly chilly.

"I cannot imagine why you would wish to view such images in my company," he said. "This was unseemly. Distasteful. I had thought us almost friends, Tuala. I had come to believe we trusted each other; to think my first assessment of you, long ago, was incorrect. I believed you dangerous: to me, to Bridei, to all you touched. This makes me suspect I was right."

Tuala felt his words like a blow. For a moment she could not speak. Then she reminded herself that she was queen of Fortriu and that, as Derelei's mother and Bridei's wife, she had power over the king's druid whether he liked it or not. It didn't help much; she was amazed at how her heart shrank before his repudiation.

"Please go now," Broichan said, walking to the door and holding it open.

"If that is your preference, of course. I'll ask you a question first."

He waited, eyes cold and remote.

"I don't imagine such events occur often. Very likely, a man experiences them only once in his life, and therefore may have an excellent recall of when they happened. I must tell you that when I saw this before, the vision was far briefer; I did not expect such . . . I did not call this up to shame you, Broichan. The goddess showed far more than I anticipated."

"Please leave now, Tuala."

"It was springtime, wasn't it, at the feast of Balance? Was that the spring before my own arrival at Pitnochie? Was the winter after those events the one when unknown hands delivered me to your doorstep as a newborn babe?"

"I will not discuss this." His voice was hard as iron. "I will answer no questions."

"There's no need to answer them," said Tuala, walking past him and out into the passageway. "All I request is that you give them consideration. The idea must have occurred to you. Or is the possibility that I might be your daughter so painful to contemplate that you have closed your mind to it and thrown away the key?"

He shut the door in her face. Tuala stood outside, working on her breathing, willing back tears, slowing the painful thudding of her heart. She had known Broichan a long time. Part of her had anticipated this rejection, this refusal to acknowledge any error. And yet, the wave of sorrow that swept through her was so profound that for long moments it paralyzed her there on his doorstep. Her father. Her own father. How wonderful it would have been if he had offered a little, a wary trust, a tentative recognition of that bond. She realized that, in her heart, she had hoped for more: an embrace; words of affection; perhaps a guarded apology. That had been foolish. Even if he had been prepared to acknowledge the possibility of blood kinship, the closest Broichan ever came to an expression of feelings was a wintry smile or approving nod of the head. Only with Bridei, his foster son, had he ever come close to revealing what was in his heart. And with Derelei because, after all, Derelei was Bridei's son.

She had wanted to ask, *Does it mean nothing to you that this would make you Derelei's blood kin? That the infant mage whose rare talents you nurture with all your skill might be your own grandson? Do you not long to acknowledge him?* How could she say those things when she herself stood in the way? The thought of her as a daughter was abhorrent to him. That had been in his affronted eyes; it had been in the tight distaste of his tone. He would never tell the truth about this. He would never accept it. Apart from his deep distrust of her, which had existed since the moment he first set eyes on her as a tiny babe, to acknowledge her as his daughter was to admit shutting his own kin out for all the years of her growing up. He had provided her with food and shelter. At the same time, he had made no secret of his hostility toward her. To admit the truth was to recognize the greatest error of his life: an unforgivable insult to the Shining One. And is not a druid's whole existence bent to the goddess's service? Dashing the tears from her cheeks, Tuala forced herself to walk away. Maybe her own father did not want her, but she was still queen of Fortriu, and there were things to do.

2

Soon after dawn Eile heard them coming and the familiar feeling gripped her, cold and tight in her chest. Saraid was awake, sitting up on the pallet with her shapeless cloth doll in her arms, whispering to it. Fear gave speed to Eile's limbs, though it was bitterly cold in the tiny lean-to where they slept. She was fully dressed already, that being the only way to stay at all warm at night, but she always made Saraid put on her nightrobe, giving her the second blanket to compensate. She encouraged Saraid to wash her face every day and sit up nicely to eat as well. If Saraid didn't learn to be a lady she'd be doomed to a life like Eile's own, an existence of squalor and slavery. Someone had to make sure Saraid escaped before she got too old. There was only Eile to do it.

"Get dressed, Saraid. Can you manage by yourself? They're home and I need to tend to the fire."

Saraid nodded, solemn and silent, as Eile put the little gown, the shawl, the apron, the stockings, the boots on the bed next to the child, then scraped her own hair back and tied it with a length of string. She pushed her feet into her worn boots, an old pair of Aunt Anda's, and stumbled through to the main room. Fire; light; hot water. Quick. Never mind that it was cold enough to freeze a pig's tail off and that she had spent more of the night crying than sleeping. If things weren't ready, Dalach would be angry.

Her hands were numb with cold. There was no wood left beyond a few sticks of kindling. The dog had crept out of the bedchamber after her and now stood by the ashes, staring up at her. He only stayed when Dalach and Anda were away. Those nights were better. The hound made a warm and undemanding third in the bed.

The woodpile; everything would be soaked after last night's downpour. A pox on it. There was no way to avoid a beating. She could hear them coming into the yard now, Dalach's voice already raised, Anda's barely audible.

Eile pushed the door hanging aside. "Go," she said, and the dog obeyed. It was more biddable than that man, Faolan, had been. Chances were he wouldn't come back today. Men were like that: full of empty promises. Like Father.

Eile closed her eyes a moment, feeling the banked-up tears behind the lids and knowing she must let no more fall, not now, not when Dalach could see. She had longed so for the day when Father would come home again, big and quiet and strong, and take her in his arms as he had the last time, after that place, Breakstone. She had dreamed she would whisper the truth to him, and he would take her away, her and Saraid, to somewhere safe where he could protect the two of them and the child could grow up happy and well-fed and unafraid. Where she herself would not have to endure the constant clutch of dread, nor the terror that, one day, she would no longer be able to keep Saraid safe. *Father, oh Father, why couldn't you have come home?*

Eile took a step outside the door and saw that someone had brought a small load of logs up from the saturated woodpile and placed them in a neat stack beside the doorway, where the overhanging thatch sheltered a dry-ish patch. The wood was still damp, but perhaps she could coax it to burn. A kindness; she wondered what Faolan had been after in return. She wondered if he had heard her crying, after she thought he was gone. She loaded the basket, heaved it inside, and was crouching to stir up last night's embers when Dalach strode in, Anda a meek shadow in his wake.

"What, no fire? Get moving, you scrawny sluggard, I've come a long way and I'm frozen to the marrow. Where's my breakfast?"

He expected, perhaps, that she would conjure it from nothing.

"You didn't leave us much, and it's all gone, all but a handful of oats." *And please, please let Saraid have that, she needs it.* Eile was shivering; it was a walk on eggshells whenever he was home, a constant guessing game. She felt anger, but could not let it show, for the child's sake. If not for Saraid, she'd have done the man serious harm long ago and taken the consequences.

"You should have managed better." Anda put down

her bundle and stood with her hands on the small of her back. She looked worn out, but Eile could not find a shred of sympathy. It seemed to her a person who stood by and let evil things happen was as guilty as the person who performed them. "You should have made it last."

Eile thought of the times she had not eaten, so that Saraid could be adequately fed. She said nothing.

"You're a slut and a wastrel," Dalach said, walking over. He was a big man, tall and broad. Strong as an ox; Eile knew just how strong. She felt his fingers in her hair, then a fierce pain as he jerked her upright. She put her teeth through her lip, so as not to cry out. She wouldn't give him the satisfaction. "Just as well there's one thing you're good for," Dalach went on, "or you'd be out on your ear, and no two ways about it." As abruptly as he had seized her, he let go, and she collapsed back beside the hearth. "That supposed to be a fire? Get on with it, wretch. I'm wet through." He turned toward his wife. "You'll have to go down to the settlement. See what you can scrounge. Here." He took a handful of coppers from his pouch and gave them to Anda. "Don't rush home."

His eyes were back on Eile; she felt his gaze on her as she fanned the embers and fed on the last sticks of kindling. *Burn, please burn.* "I can go, if you want," she said, heart thudding. "I can take Saraid. The rain's stopped. You've already had a long walk, Aunt Anda."

"Who asked you for your opinion?" snarled Dalach. "Go on, Anda, I'm hungry."

"There was a man here yesterday." Eile had not planned to tell them until later, but the words came out in a rush. She so much didn't want to be left with Dalach, especially not when Saraid was awake. The child was in the inner doorway now, a little shadow, staring. "He brought news of Father."

Instantly she had their attention.

"A man?" asked Dalach, glowering. "What man?"

"What news?" Anda's voice was hesitant.

Eile chanced a bigger branch on the fire; it hissed as

the flames licked it. "Bad news. He's not coming back. He was killed not long ago in some place over the water. A heroic death, that's what the man said."

Anda sank down on a bench. She said not a word.

"So he's not coming back for you," Dalach said heavily, subsiding on the bench, eyes fixed on Eile. "He's leaving it to us to provide for you. Typical. He always was a fellow who walked out on his responsibilities. He's left us with you and the brat both." The eyes flicked across to the silent Saraid, and the child shrank back behind the door frame, thumb in mouth.

"The brat, as you call her, is your own kin." It was unwise to challenge him, but Eile could not keep the words in.

"She's another mouth to feed. A man can't afford kin if they can't earn their keep."

"She's three years old," Eile said as the fire began to crackle, defying the odds.

"Three years old and growing." Dalach's lips stretched in a humorless smile. "She'll have her uses before long."

In that moment, Eile knew it was time to act. Father was dead; there was no point in hoping and dreaming and wishing, not anymore. It was up to her now. She had run away before, in the days before Saraid, and Dalach had come after her and dragged her back every time. This time she was going to make sure he couldn't follow.

"Where is this man now?" asked Anda wanly. "Did he bring anything for us?"

"Don't be any more of a fool than you are already," snapped Dalach. "When did Deord ever show generosity to us? As a provider he was worse than useless. He'd have died without a copper to his name. Got into a brawl at a drinking hall, is my guess, and fell foul of a bigger man than himself."

"The man—his name was Faolan—said he was coming back to see you today. He did mention silver. And it wasn't a drunken brawl. My father died in battle. He sacrificed himself so others could live. And he *was* a provider." Eile swallowed her tears. "Back before, we had a good house and food on the table. Maybe you think I can't remember, but I can. We were happy then—"

Dalach's fist came out and struck her on the jaw. Her teeth rattled; a spear of pain went through her neck. She fell silent. It was true; a hundred blows wouldn't alter that. Maybe she'd been only little, Saraid's age, but she *did* remember. The house on the hill; the garden with vegetables and flowers, lavender, rosemary, some kind of tall lilies by the wall. A cat; she remembered the cat, a stripy one that brought in mice and laid them at Mother's feet as if they were priceless gifts. Mother laughing; Mother spinning and singing. Father was not always there, for he used to go on voyages, but he always came home, and when he did the whole house lit up with his presence. Father telling her stories at bedtime, stories about the strange places he'd sailed to and the exotic folk who lived there. Father with that look in his eyes, the look that made her feel safe. Back then they had not lived with Anda and Dalach. Back then she had believed her life would be full of good things.

"What's this, tears?" Dalach scowled at her, and she scrubbed her cheeks, not knowing if she wept from the blow or because the past was gone and could never be re-made. While she had knelt there dreaming, Anda had slipped out of the hut, and now she was alone with the person she hated most in the world.

"Get that fire built up, then wash yourself," Dalach said. "You stink like a midden. I don't want that all over me. When you've cleaned yourself up, get in the back."

"Saraid's there."

"The brat can watch. Not too soon for her to learn a few tips. Hurry up, Eile, I've been ten days on the road and I'm itching for it. You don't think that dried-up stick I'm wed to is able to satisfy me, do you? It's like rutting with a scarecrow."

It was only possible to make washing last so long before he would grow impatient and snatch the scrap of cloth from her, or kick over the bucket of bracingly cold water. Dalach didn't wash. It was immaterial to him whether Eile cared for his smell, a rank, sweaty odor deepened by his days and nights on the road, coming home from the last horse trading of the season. The winters were the worst time. With nothing to set his hand to, he divided his days between drinking away his meager savings and tormenting the rest of them.

She wiped her face and hands, then hitched up her skirt and sluiced between her legs. Beside her, Saraid stood silent. She had dipped her own cloth in the bucket first and washed her face, dabbing behind her ears and around her neck. She had washed her hands and dried them on her apron. *I'm not having her in there with us. I'll never, ever do that.* "Saraid? Take my shawl, here, and go out the front. Sit on the step until I come out for you. Don't go off anywhere. Aunt Anda will be home soon with something for breakfast. You can look out for her. I know it's cold."

The child nodded and slipped away, as obedient as the dog. Eile wasn't sure how much Saraid understood. She suspected it was more than such a little girl should, and she hardened her will against what she must do next. Just once, just one last time he'd do it to her, and she'd have to let him, and then . . .

While he was grunting and thrusting inside her, off in some trance of his own, Eile had become accustomed to shutting off her mind. She would think of how it had been before: before Saraid, before Dalach's house, before she found Mother hanging from a tree. Before the eve of her twelfth birthday, when her aunt's husband had come in the dark, pinned her down and robbed her of her innocence. Now, as he satisfied himself in her with an urgency born of the days away, she thought of the time when her father had come back, after Breakstone Hollow. Eile had been eight years old. Perhaps she'd been too young to realize how much Deord had been changed by his imprisonment. He'd been quiet; but he'd always been quiet. There had been no bedtime stories. When she'd asked, he'd said he only knew sad ones now. So Eile had told him tales instead, the ones she could remember from before and some she made up. Sometimes her stories made him weep, and she would climb on his knee, put her arms around his neck, and press her warm cheek against his wet one. Yes, he had been different that time. But he'd still been Father. When he'd gone away again, she had seen the hope gradually leach out of her mother. Every day, every single day Eile had prayed that he would come home. After her mother died, after Dalach, the prayers had become no more than desperate, unformed longings. Now, even those were pointless. All that she had was this moment, the straining, red-faced Dalach with his ever-ready manhood deep inside her, and the knife Faolan had left behind clutched in her hand, under a fold of blanket. Her grip tightened; she drew a deep breath.

Voices came from outside: her aunt's, and, replying, a man's. Faolan. He had come after all. He must have met Anda on the way, making it necessary for her to accompany him back empty-handed. Eile pushed the knife under the old sack that served as a pillow, and Dalach, unwilling to relinquish the opportunity his wife's brief absence had provided, thrust hard and fast and spent himself inside her with a muffled groan before rolling off the pallet and hastily pulling up his trousers.

"Make yourself decent, slut," he hissed, and went out.

Eile did not go out straightaway. Surely her father's friend would smell Dalach on her. Surely he would hear her hammering heart, for she had been so close, a hair's breadth from thrusting the weapon he had so conveniently left her deep inside her tormentor, giving Dalach a taste of his own medicine. The first time he'd done it to her, it had hurt a lot. It had never stopped hurting; she'd just become used to it, and learned that it was more bearable if she breathed slowly and let him get on with it. If she fought, it made him rougher, and got her a beating later. Dalach needed little excuse to use his fists; she and Anda both bore their share of bruises. Not Saraid; not yet. Saraid was so silent, so obedient. She had learned to make herself invisible.

Eile straightened her clothing and spread the thin blanket neatly across the pallet, making sure the knife was quite hidden. She waited until her breathing was under better control. In the outer chamber they were talking.

"I've brought a few supplies." That was Faolan. "I hope you don't mind. I'm heading across country as soon as I leave here, and I haven't had breakfast. Some fresh bread, a little cheese, and there's a handful of dried plums here; the child might like those. I'm happy to share."

"Eile!" It was *his* voice, shouting as if she were a servant; he who had just taken her with casual indifference. To him, she barely existed save as a receptacle for his lust. "Get out here and serve our guest! We need clean platters, and the fire's smoking."

She did as she was told. There would be another time, another opportunity. Nothing was more certain than that. As long as Faolan did not ask for his knife back. Tomorrow, the next day, she would do it. Even servants got wages. She would take hers in blood.

Faolan divided the bread. He cut the cheese, not with his own knife, but with a blunt one Eile passed him. Under his penetrating look she was aware of her chilblained hands, her gnawed nails, her unwashed hair and ill-mended gown. Saraid had come in to stand by Eile's skirts, big eyes on the food. Faolan could not know that this was a feast such as none of them had seen in many turnings of the moon.

"Can I give her some?" Eile asked Faolan direct.

He said nothing, simply cut a slice of cheese, placed it on a portion of bread, and offered it to the child. Saraid had been taught to sit up; to eat slowly. Eile had tried her best. Now, overwhelmed by such bounty, the child snatched bread and cheese from Faolan's hand and bolted for the inner chamber, clutching the food to her chest.

"I'm sorry," Eile said. "She's hungry."

"Your aunt tells me you've broken the news," Faolan said. He watched as she served Dalach, putting a generous portion on his platter, as she then served the guest himself. The bread smelled like all the best things of summertime put together. Her mouth was watering. Eile cut cheese for Anda, then a sliver for herself. The crust was red as crab apples, the cheese itself as golden as the sun. She divided the last of the small loaf between her aunt and herself, glancing sidelong at Dalach. If Faolan hadn't been there, she knew Dalach would have denied her so generous a portion. Now he simply tightened his lips. Eile took one blissful mouthful of bread; one salty, wonderful bite of cheese. Then, when nobody was looking, she slipped the remainder into the pocket of her apron. Saraid was little. She didn't eat much. There were two good meals in this.

"Not eating?" Faolan asked her.

"I'm not very hungry. But thank you for bringing it."

"Forget the pleasantries," Dalach said, wiping his mouth. "What about Deord? What provision did he make for his daughter here? You know we've been supporting her out of the goodness of our hearts these seven or eight years? We can't keep the girl forever. Duty only carries a man so far. Times are hard. You'll know. Or maybe you won't." He looked Faolan up and down. "What's your trade?"

"Dalach—" hissed Anda, but it was a halfhearted effort; she lived in fear of her husband's sharp tongue and punishing hand, and seldom remonstrated with him.

"I have several," Faolan said, frowning. "I see your circumstances here and they concern me. Is work hard to find?"

"You making some kind of comment? What, you think I can't provide for my family?" Dalach glowered, clenching his big fists. There was good reason why folk did not come up to the hut very often.

"I don't know you," Faolan said levelly. "I did know Deord. Whatever may have happened at this end, I know he would want Eile to be given the chance of a good life, one in which she's well provided for and able to make something of herself."

"If he wanted that, why didn't he stay and look after her and her mother himself?" Anda's voice was shaking. "There was need for him here."

"You must understand," Faolan said, "that what Deord went through in Breakstone Hollow was an extreme kind of punishment. That place destroys the strongest of men. Few come out. None at all come out unchanged by it."

"How would you know?" challenged Dalach. "Man like you, soft-spoken as a bard, in your good clothes— never had a day's hardship in your life, I'll wager."

It occurred to Eile that he'd be better to feign politeness; to convince Faolan that he'd like nothing better than to keep on supporting her and Saraid forever. If he wanted Deord's friend to demonstrate generosity beyond the provision of a single breakfast, the way to do it wasn't to antagonize the man.

"I know because I was an inmate of Breakstone myself," Faolan said. "Not with Deord; earlier. A man comes out of that place unfit for the company of wife or child, incapable of living as other men do. He loses his bearings; he loses his faith in gods and in humankind. If his wife speaks to him unexpectedly, when his mind's on something else, he's as likely to grab her by the neck and squeeze hard as to give a civil response. If his child jumps onto his bed in the morning, he may strike a lethal blow before he comes back to the here and now. It's no wonder Deord didn't stay. The pity of it is, such a man still longs for the old life; to be as he was before. It just isn't possible."

"You seem normal enough," Eile said. In fact, he was utterly ordinary; the kind of man you wouldn't be able to describe later, because he had so little about him that was remarkable. Middle height, spare, athletic build; dark hair of medium length, slight beard, plain good clothes. Thin lips, well-governed expression. If she had to pick out something, it would be the eyes. Guarded as they were, she had caught them once or twice with a complicated expression in them: when he looked at Saraid, and when he'd spoken to her last night about trying to help her. There were things in there he didn't want anyone to see. Maybe they were what he'd spoken of, from Breakstone; the things that made a man turn his back on his kin.

"I manage," Faolan said. "My stay in that place was far briefer than your father's. It may interest you to know that after Deord left here for the last time he spent seven years guarding a prisoner at a place called Briar Wood, in the lands of the Caitt. That is to the north of the kingdom of Fortriu, across the water. The captive was a man of exceptional qualities who had been wrongfully incarcerated. As a warder, Deord showed humanity, patience, and kindness as well as extraordinary strength of both body and mind. In the end he was instrumental in assisting his prisoner to escape. I never found him anything but utterly strong, dependable, and good. I am sorry about your mother, Eile. I'm sorry your father could not come home. He did die well. It was a shining example of selfless courage."

"Selfless courage never put bread on the table," said Dalach. "Didn't the man leave anything?"

Faolan seemed unperturbed by his rudeness. "The circumstances were such that I had no access to what he may have put aside," he said. "As his friend, I wish to assist Eile. I'll leave some silver with you." He made it clear it was Anda he was speaking to. "You must use it as you think best, for whatever is the greatest need. You should give Eile herself a say in the matter. There's sufficient to allow some improvements to this cottage and to see you through the winter. My advice would be to put aside half of this sum for Eile's future. There's a community of

Christian women not far west of here, at least there was in times past. They might perhaps take her in and teach her some useful skills."

If only that were possible, Eile thought. She'd be prepared to believe in any god they liked, just so long as she could escape from here. But not without Saraid. She couldn't leave Saraid behind. Besides, Dalach would have the money off Anda almost before the giver's back was turned, and it would all be drunk or wagered away before there was a chance so much as to think of other possibilities. There was no point in trying to tell Faolan this. He'd just leave and take his silver with him, and she'd get the worst beating of her life for robbing Dalach of his windfall. Dalach didn't care about any of them. All his mind could span was the next drink, the next brawl, the next time he'd bed her. Anger and resentment had eaten away any finer feelings he might once have had. She'd never understood why Anda stayed loyal to him.

Anda sucked in her breath, feeling the weight of the little bag Faolan put in her hand.

"This is generous of you," Dalach said. "Most generous." His hand twitched; Eile saw him force himself not to snatch the prize. "We'll put it to wise use, you can be sure of that."

Faolan gave him a penetrating look. "See that you do," he said. "The situation here disquiets me. I'd be happier to see Eile with the nuns. Indeed, if you wished it, I could escort her there myself. I've business to the west as well as in the north; the order in which I attend to it is immaterial."

"No!" Eile said quickly. "Not now. Don't think I'm not grateful. But I can't go."

"The girl's an extra pair of hands," Dalach said smoothly. "We need her here. She has her particular duties. Besides, it wouldn't be seemly for a young girl to travel with just a man, and a stranger at that." If this was somewhat inconsistent with his earlier talk, he did not seem to notice.

"Well," Anda said after a little, "you'll be on your way, then. West, did you say? Where are you headed?"

"You wouldn't know the place."

"You'd want to take care if you're going over by Three Oaks," put in Dalach. "We've just come back that way; there's a bridge down. All this rain. It's passable as far as the crossroads."

"Ah, well," said Faolan easily, "I expect I'll manage. Uí Néill lands beyond the river, aren't they?"

"You'd know."

"I've been away for some time."

"Beyond the river is Ruaridh Uí Néill's," Dalach offered, glaring in distrust. "You've such a look of that family yourself, I'm surprised you need telling. Ruaridh's got far more interests up in Tirconnell. It's the woman looks after the territory here. He's prepared to let her hold it for her son."

"Woman? What woman? I thought those were Echen Uí Néill's lands." Eile heard an odd change in Faolan's tone. She could not quite work it out.

"Where've you been? Echen's been dead these four years. His widow controls it all. She's a hard thing; rules as tightly as any man. Still, sooner her than that wretch. She's evenhanded. Not that it's a job for a woman. She's held on longer than anyone expected. Her brother-in-law just left her to it."

Faolan breathed out. Eile saw him relax his shoulders, a conscious attempt at self-control. "So Echen's dead." That was all he said.

"Good riddance," muttered Anda. "There were tales about that man would curdle your blood."

"I'll be getting on," Faolan said, rising to his feet. "When I reach the crossroads I'll make my choice of ways. Eile, think about what I suggested. Whatever your own beliefs, I think the nuns would treat you well, especially if your aunt made a gift to their establishment. Their life is not luxurious, but it is orderly and serene."

Eile nodded; she could not find the right words. To be

so close, to have escape at her fingertips, and not to be able to go . . . It was too cruel. *Take me with you.* The words hovered on her lips. She clamped her mouth shut.

"Got everything?" Dalach was affable now it was clear their guest was off and leaving his bag of silver behind.

"I think so. Oh, there was a small knife . . . I can't quite remember where I left it . . ." He did not look at Eile direct, only let his glance travel over her, brows lifted. She said nothing.

"Ah, well," said Faolan, "maybe it's in my pack somewhere, or back at Brennan's. I may pass here again on my way home to see how Eile is getting on and whether she's changed her mind. For now, I'll bid you farewell. I wish I'd brought better news. Deord was a fine man."

"So you keep saying." Dalach's mouth twisted. "Never saw it, myself."

"Some see only what they choose to see. Farewell, Eile. He would be proud of you."

Tears spilled. She dashed them away with a furious hand. Deord, proud of his slut of a daughter with her filthy hair and her ragged clothes and the disgusting things she had to do to survive? Hardly. "Farewell," she mumbled, looking at the floor. *Take me with you, anywhere, just away from here. Take me away so I don't have to do it.*

Saraid had slipped back in. Her small hand clutched a fold of Eile's apron. Her eyes were on the man who had brought a feast. "Say good-bye, Squirrel," Eile whispered. But the child buried her face against the coarse homespun and said nothing at all.

BRIDEI WAS AT Abertornie to attend to the welfare of Ged's family. A flamboyant chieftain who had been one of the young king's most stalwart supporters, Ged had fallen in the last great battle of the autumn, dying even as

Dalriada was won back for the Priteni. He left a young widow, a ten-year-old son, and three tiny daughters. Bridei spoke to all of them, making sure they understood their husband and father had died a hero; carrying them certain last messages.

While the king was thus occupied, his chief councillor, Aniel, who had accompanied him, performed a discreet investigation as to the state of fields and buildings, and together they put in place some arrangements to ensure Loura could look after the holding while young Aled grew to manhood. Bridei invited the boy to spend time at court next summer; the lad thanked him soberly and said he would if he could, but he thought he might be rather busy.

Then Bridei and Aniel rode to the coastal fortress of Caer Pridne, for a council had been called, not an open meeting of the kind convened at White Hill, but a small, particular, and private one.

It was almost too late in the season to travel so far. Gateway was past; the first snows had fallen. The king and his councillor rode with an escort of five, one of whom was Bridei's personal guard, Garth, and another Aniel's man Eldrist. Faolan's lengthy absence had put a heavy load on Garth, who was now the only one of Bridei's experienced bodyguards left. The training required was lengthy and rigorous. Back at White Hill, Garth had a new man in place, Dovran, who was proving his worth. Bridei believed Faolan would not be back before next summer.

"You need at least three men," Garth had protested. "Four would be better. What about Cinioch?"

"Faolan will return. He can't resist the poor pay and the sleepless nights," Bridei had told him. "Cinioch belongs back at Pitnochie. I want him and Uven to go home and forget battles for a while." It had been a season of blood and death, of the loss of many good comrades, the loyal Breth among them. It had been a victory: a great triumph. The Gaels were driven back, the lands of the west reclaimed for the Priteni. Now, Bridei's heart held a powerful wish for peace. His people needed that. They needed time to till their land and sow their crops, to raise their children and to celebrate their love of the gods. No more war; the borders must simply be held, and within them the fabric of community made whole. Spear must become scythe, staff turn to oar, dagger to adze or awl. The men who had risked all for their king, their land, their faith must have time to weave anew the threads of their lives.

The massive promontory fortress of Caer Pridne, on the northeast coast, had once been the seat of Fortriu's kings. This stronghold now formed the headquarters of Bridei's fighting forces, led by Carnach of Thorn Bend. Caer Pridne was quiet tonight. It was winter. The massive army that had been assembled for the many-pronged attack on Dalriada was disbanded, its men departed for their home territories while the roads were still passable. A force remained, made up of the most expert warriors, those who had no other trade. They were quartered here year around, ready for whatever might come. Families lived within the high walls; the stronghold housed a whole community. Caer Pridne provided the guards for White Hill, a force rotated every season to keep the men sharp.

Bridei's most trusted warrior chieftains, Carnach and Talorgen, were newly arrived back from Dalriada. Both leaders had remained there at the war's end to oversee the departure of the Gaelic leaders over the sea to their homeland. The Dalriadan king, Gabhran, had fallen gravely ill not long after the last great battle, and had been allowed to remain in his fortress of Dunadd, along with his immediate household. A force of Priteni warriors was quartered there to guard the place and its occupants.

Bridei had already had his chieftains' news, for they had visited White Hill on their way back, to great acclaim. But not all news can be shared openly. Tonight, in the small, private chamber Bridei had chosen for his council, red-haired Carnach and the older Talorgen sat at the long oaken table with Bridei and Aniel, in company with a small, white-haired woman in a gray robe: the senior priestess of Fortriu, Fola, whose establishment of Banmerren lay just along the bay. Save for Garth, the personal guards remained outside the bolted door. Niches set in the stone walls held oil lamps. All was orderly and quiet.

"Thank you for being here, my friends," Bridei said. "I regret the need for such secrecy. I've news on which I require your counsel. Once you have given it, we will decide together how much further this news can go, and when."

"Bridei," interrupted Fola, her sharp dark eyes on the king, "why is Broichan not present? Was he too unwell to travel? I had thought his health greatly improved when last I saw him." She was an old friend and did not stand on ceremony.

"I could not be at Caer Pridne for Gateway this year," Bridei said, choosing his words with care; this would be difficult to explain. "I did not conduct my usual ritual at the Well. Tonight, when we are done here, I will keep vigil until dawn. Had Broichan accompanied me, he would have insisted on performing the rite with me. The ride from White Hill, he might just about manage. The vigil would tax his strength beyond endurance."

There was a brief silence.

"There's more to this, isn't there?" asked Fola, raising her brows.

"Broichan is not yet party to this news," Bridei said, and saw a look of surprise pass over the wise woman's serene countenance. "He will hear it as soon as I return to White Hill. I want your opinion first. Your good advice, all of you."

"The business of this council is secret until the king

chooses to have it spread more widely," said Aniel, steepling his fingers before him on the table.

"That's understood already," said Talorgen of Raven's Well, a handsome, open-faced man of middle years. "What is this news?"

"The king of Circinn is dead," Bridei said quietly, and a gasp of shock went around the table. This was momentous; Circinn, the southern kingdom of the Priteni, had become Christian under Drust the Boar while Fortriu had remained staunchly true to the old gods. An election must now be held to determine which man of the royal line would become king. "We did not have this from a messenger; one of our spies brought the news just before Aniel and I left White Hill. With winter setting in hard, it's our belief Circinn will not call the election until season's end; they'll have remembered how difficult it was last time. On the other hand, they may try to do it by stealth; just put their man in as king and present it to us as a final decision in springtime."

"Exactly," said Aniel. "They may conveniently overlook the fact that the chieftains of Fortriu are entitled to a vote. You know Bargoit and his fellow councillors. They'll be all too ready to bypass correct procedures if it happens to suit them."

Carnach whistled under his breath. "Drust the Boar dead, eh? I wonder which of his weaselly advisers slipped a little something in his stew."

"We should say prayers for his passing," said Fola with a reproving glance at the red-haired chieftain. "We may not have had a high opinion of the man, but that should not prevent us from doing what is right."

"It's Christian prayers he'd be wanting," put in Aniel with a twist of the lip. "Are you able to turn your hand to those, Fola?"

"Drust may have been baptized in the Christian faith," the wise woman retorted, "but I've no doubt the deity he called on at the last extreme was Bone Mother. There's no wrong in wishing a man a safe journey. I don't sup-

pose Drust was bad, just weak. Too weak to be a king."
As an epitaph, it had a sorry ring to it.

"A quandary," said Aniel. "Who would the chieftains
of Circinn see as the strongest contender? What candi-
dates do they have to offer?"

"None, surely, who could hold a candle to Bridei,
fresh from his stunning defeat of the Gaels," said Carnach bluntly. "We need to ensure they hold the election
fairly, as we did ours on the death of Drust the Bull. If
Bridei could be elected king of Fortriu on the vote of
representatives from all the Priteni realms, then the same
process should apply now the kingship of Circinn is in
question. It's the opportunity we've been waiting for:
Broichan's dream. Within a season, we could see Fortriu
and Circinn united under a single leader. You must stand,
Bridei. You can do it." Carnach's features were flushed
with zeal, his eyes bright. He was a generous man. He
himself had been eligible for the kingship of Fortriu,
nearly six years ago, and had stepped down to lend his
support to Bridei's claim.

"Broichan will be of the same mind, I know," Bridei
said. "But this is not so simple. There's the question of
faith; the will of the folk of Circinn and the chieftains
who represent them. It may lie just across our border, but
whether it pleases us or no, Circinn is a Christian kingdom now."

"Besides," said Talorgen, frowning, "there's the west
to consider. Dalriada may be won, but a newly conquered territory needs careful handling. I have no doubt
at all the Gaels will be back, in three years, five, ten,
however long it takes them to regroup. We will have
continuing dissent in the region, for there will be those
who want the old rule returned. We've done our best to
weed out the likely troublemakers, but a strong Gaelic
presence remains. You don't just ride in and occupy a
place, then expect the conquered residents to get on
with their lives as if nothing has happened. I hate to say
it, but this may not be the best time for Bridei to take on

the leadership of Circinn alongside that of Fortriu. He'd be pulled two ways. We all would."

"How often does an election come along?" asked Carnach. "What if a young man gets up, one even younger than Bridei? This could be the only opportunity we get in a lifetime, Talorgen. It would be madness to let it pass by!"

"Fola," said Bridei quietly, "what is your opinion?"

"You consult me, and you have not yet passed the news to Broichan, your lifelong mentor?"

Bridei had expected this from the wise woman. To shut Broichan out of such an important decision was unprecedented; even now, he wondered if he had acted correctly. "You know him. You know why. It is his passion to see Fortriu and Circinn reunited in the old faith. Do not doubt, any of you, that I share that dream. If you had asked me, in the first days of my kingship, whether I would seek to add Circinn to my realm at the first opportunity, I imagine I would have said yes with not a shred of doubt in my mind. Ask me today and I will tell you that what I want for Fortriu now is a time of peace. A time of rebuilding. A time for reflection."

"There is much at risk here," Fola said. "I'm aware that you've sent Faolan back to the heartland of the Uí Néill leaders. I know part of his mission is to ferret out information about these Christian clerics who seek a foothold in our western isles. I must interpret that as an indication that you are not fixed on giving them an outright refusal. Not yet, anyway; not until your spy returns, and that cannot be before spring. I know your attention is still upon the west. A resounding victory on the field does not necessarily mean continuing peace. The Uí Néill will always be a threat, and you do right to remain aware of that threat. Circinn also knows where your priority must lie. My feeling is that by springtime the southern kingdom will have chosen its own king without troubling to include Fortriu in the process. We all remember Bargoit. Officially that man is only a councillor,

pursuit and demands for justice. This would not be quietly and conveniently forgotten.

"She loved him," Eile said as if reading his thoughts. "Funny, isn't it? After everything he'd done, to her, to me, after all of it, she still wanted him. People are strange. Or maybe that's normal, her and him. Maybe I'm the odd one."

"Maybe," Faolan said. "Drink the rest of that, Eile."

"I don't really want to sleep."

"You need rest. I'll think of a plan. I'm good at them. And I'll wake you, I promise. There are men coming to mend the bridge in the morning. If we can't get across here, we'll find another place."

"I'm not going to the priory." The hackles were up again. "I told you. I'm not going."

"I heard you," said Faolan, and took a considered breath. "I've somewhere else for us to go. It'll be safe. My father's a brithem."

"What?"

"Not the kind who hauls young girls up to answer awkward questions. The kind who understands real justice. They live at Fiddler's Crossing; it's not too far for Saraid to go if we take it carefully. I think they'll shelter you. If not, we'll go farther." He did not tell her he had only known since earlier today that his father still lived, and was still a lawman. He did not explain that, for him, going home was like plunging into a well of shadows.

"We?" Her voice was the merest wisp of sound.

"I said I'd look after you. I'll do so until I know you're safe. I'll stay with you until you don't need me anymore." He waited for a crisp reprimand, a snapped denial of any such need or a withering statement of disbelief. But Eile said nothing. She gave a little weary nod, then lay down behind Saraid with her arm curved over the child.

He waited until he thought she was asleep, then laid his own cloak over her.

Eile's eyes opened. "What did he do?" she murmured. "That man you say wronged your family?"

"It's not a good story for bedtime," he said shortly. *It's not a story I choose to tell.*

"Nor's mine."

"Mine is old history. Let's just say I've been away a long time and I'm sure my family will be pleased to see me. Like you, I left home with blood on my hands." *Enough; no more.*

"But then—" She half rose, voice tight.

"My father may not welcome me, but he's a man of strong principles. That won't have changed. You'll be safe there."

Eile looked less than convinced.

"Rest now," Faolan said. "I'll wake you as I promised. Believe me, this will look better in the morning, after a night's sleep."

BROICHAN WAS GONE. Between dusk of one day and dawn of the next the king's druid had packed a little bag, slung a cloak over his shoulders, and ridden away from White Hill without a word. Bridei's second councillor, Tharan, alerted to the early departure, had come striding down to the stables to express his concern and to question the wisdom of a solitary journey so close to Midwinter. The words had died on his lips as he met the druid's stone wall of a stare. Never mind that Bone Mother's grip now tightened on the land, lengthening the nights and filling the days with flailing winds and bonedeep chill. Never mind the frost, the snow, the long, weary ride down the glen to Pitnochie, which was Broichan's home. Never mind that others were in residence there now, the king's druid having moved to court six years ago when his foster son became monarch of Fortriu. Meeting Broichan's eyes, Tharan knew such arguments would be like chaff before the wind, dissipated without purpose. He had known the druid a long time.

After Broichan was gone, the councillor paced rest-

lessly until it was no longer too early to disturb the
queen's slumber, then presented himself at the door to the
royal apartments. The new bodyguard, Dovran, had been
on duty all night, but his sharp eyes and capable hands on
the spear were not suggestive of weariness. Garth had
chosen him carefully and trained him expertly.

Tharan was admitted and stood in the anteroom waiting. He had barely time to take a sip of the ale a maidservant brought him before Tuala was there, fully
dressed and wide awake, her large eyes wary. She was always pale, but this morning the whiteness of her cheeks
spoke of a terrible fear; what but the worst kind of news
would bring her husband's councillor to her quarters so
early in the morning?

Tharan hastened to reassure her. "My lady, I regret the
intrusion. No cause for alarm. It's about Broichan . . ."

Tuala heard him out in silence. When he was done she
said, "Thank you for bringing this to me so promptly,
Tharan. Do you think he was heading for Pitnochie? Going home?"

"That seems likely."

"He cannot have forgotten he lent his house to Ana
and Drustan for the winter." Tuala was thinking aloud.
"Pitnochie isn't a place designed to hold both Broichan
and others beyond his crew of loyal retainers, at least not
for long. It could be awkward. I know Ana does not wish
to impose a return to court upon Drustan; he finds it difficult. I wonder if Broichan does intend to stay there."

"Where else would he go in this inclement season?"
asked Tharan. "He's not well, and he's no longer young."

"He'd have been better to retreat to Fola at Banmerren if
he wanted to avoid us." Tuala seemed to be talking to herself; Tharan could not grasp what she meant. "I can't believe it," she went on. "To go away, just like that. To leave
without saying good-bye to Derelei. To abandon so abruptly
the work he was doing. Not to be here when Bridei gets
home." She seemed to remember, belatedly, that she was
not alone. He thought she swallowed further words. "It is

strange, Tharan. I think we should send someone after him; someone discreet, who can watch from a distance. It would be a job for Faolan. I'm much surprised by the number of times I've wished my husband's right-hand man was back here. There are certain tasks that only he can really be trusted with. I will leave you to find a man, someone with the skill to do this undetected."

"Not such an easy job, spying on a druid," commented Tharan.

"It's not so much spying we need, more of a protective presence. Let me know when you've chosen someone, Tharan. We should move quickly. You understand why, I'm sure."

"Yes, my lady." Neither the queen nor her husband's councillor would say a word on the topic of Circinn and its kingship, though each of them had, in fact, been advised of the death of Drust the Boar before Bridei and Aniel left White Hill. There were levels of secrecy and of trust: levels within levels. Such is the nature of a royal court. Each understood the need for silence, especially now, with Broichan gone, Broichan who was the only member of Bridei's inner circle who had not yet been told this momentous news.

WHEN THARAN WAS GONE, Tuala went out to the garden, where a cold morning mist hung over straw-covered herb beds and plots of winter vegetables. All was shrouded in white. She could not see the pines on the hillside below the fortress walls, nor the track that snaked around the rise, leading to a choice of ways: southwest down the Great Glen to Pitnochie, east to Banmerren and Caer Pridne, north to Abertornie and, beyond it, the wild lands of the Caitt. Ana's journey there had furnished her with a lover who would soon be her husband: Drustan, that enigmatic, beautiful chieftain with his eldritch ability to shift between the forms of man and bird. They were at Pitnochie over the winter, the inclement season making travel back to Drustan's home territories near impossible. In spring they would journey north and face the daunting prospect of reclaiming what Drustan's brother had stolen from him on the basis of a lie. Until then, they had withdrawn to Broichan's isolated holding to recover from the ordeal they had faced in the autumn. They wouldn't be expecting the druid home.

Tuala walked along the parapet wall, deep in thought. Broichan was not stupid. He'd have no desire to get in the way of a pair of lovers enjoying the privacy of his domain. No, he wouldn't be planning to stay there. She thought she knew where he would go: off into the forest, somewhere Bridei couldn't find him. On his own? She hoped not; Broichan was physically frail still, not fully recovered from his long, draining illness. To the forest druids in the nemetons? Maybe. Perhaps, after her revelation, he simply needed a time to reflect, to pray, to reassess his position. There, at least, he would be provided with shelter, sustenance, and companionship.

Tuala sighed. She was trying to make sense of it, but there was no sense. The king's druid had behaved like a spoiled child. The unwelcome news she had given him had, in effect, made him stamp his foot and run off to hide. He wasn't trying to comprehend the fact that he had a daughter and a grandson. He was still trying to deny it.

The hardest part to understand was that he would choose to leave Derelei. Perhaps he didn't realize how a little child could be wounded by the sudden absence of one he had loved and trusted and come to rely on. How could she explain this to her son, who could barely talk yet, for all his masterly skills in magic? *Broichan's gone away* was woefully inadequate when the druid had been spending part of every afternoon closeted with the infant, guiding Derelei's first steps on the journey to discovery of his astonishing abilities.

What now, with Broichan gone? Stop the training? Teach her son herself, a path fraught with risk for, as the king's wife, she had striven long to divert attention from her difference? She did not know. Perhaps the Shining One would have answers.

As for the question of Circinn and another looming election for kingship, Tuala's mind wanted to shy away from that, but it was all-important; a major challenge of Bridei's leadership. If the timing of her revelation had denied Bridei the opportunity to discuss his decision with his foster father, she had made a serious error of judgment. It was vital that Bridei put the matter to Broichan as soon as he and Aniel got back from Caer Pridne. Should Bridei decide as she believed he would, it would be a double blow for the druid: not only would his foster son fail to seize the great opportunity they had both long planned for, but Broichan must face the fact that, of all Bridei's close advisers, he himself had been the last to be told of Drust's death with its monumental implications. Broichan must see this as a betrayal.

As for Tuala's own feelings, they must be set aside. Broichan was her father. Of that she was becoming increasingly certain. If that was not the truth, all he had needed to do was to say so; to provide some other explanation for the vision the goddess had shown them. Instead he had closed in on himself, as if the truth were still too repulsive to contemplate, let alone accept. It hurt. For so long, nearly all her life, she had longed to know who she was, who her father and mother were and why she had been left on the druid's doorstep for Bridei to find. But she thought she would sooner have no father at all than one who shrank from the very idea of their kinship. Broichan's love for Derelei could be seen on his face whenever he was with the child; it was in the gentleness of his hands and the softness of that compelling voice. It was in his patience as tutor to such a tiny student. The druid must hate her powerfully to turn his back on Derelei rather than accept their bond of blood. He must still fear her influence on Bridei, as he had done from the first.

The child in her belly kicked, stretching its limbs, testing its strength. *My daughter,* Tuala thought. *By spring the druid will have two grandchildren.* If he did not come back, in time she would have two to teach, and still the need to keep it covert, for Bridei's sake. "Come home, stubborn man," she muttered. "My son needs you." It was cold out there, and the druid was more vulnerable than he would ever acknowledge.

Right now, she could use some advice, but there was nobody to give it. Bridei would not be home for a few days yet. Fola was at Banmerren. Nobody else knew Broichan's secret; there was no one she could talk to. The scrying bowl might have answers, but Tuala was not at all sure they were ones she would welcome.

4

(from Brother Suibne's Account)
We are building a boat. A farmer has given us use of an old barn, and no questions asked, although he looks at us strangely as we labor, thinking it no doubt an odd occupation for winter. Brother Colm, eager for new shores, sees in the work of our hands and the sweat of our brows a way to draw our whole community into his vision. On the far shore of his dreams a life can be lived wholly in contemplation of God's love, each moment a prayer. It can also be lived wholly away from his troublesome kinsfolk. I would not put it thus bluntly in his hearing. Were this account intended for eyes other than mine alone, I would choose more circumspect language. I mean no criticism of the man. His situation is difficult; a lesser

soul might snap under the strain. God's love puts iron in Colm's sinews; God's breath moves in his lungs and fills his voice with a fervor that cannot fail to carry the rest of us along with him, lacking though we may be in the skills of carpentry and tanning, of caulking and rope making and the hundred other trades a man must ply to construct a seaworthy craft.

I hope it is seaworthy. My stomach clenches when I contemplate that choppy passage between the two lands named Dalriada, one in my homeland and the other in Fortriu: the waves; the swell; the endless soaking spray. My heart quails to contemplate another trip so soon. God tests me. I do not fear powerful men, or new experiences, or challenges of the mind. Indeed, I relished my dealings in the courts of Circinn and Fortriu, and my experiences in the last days of the Gaelic court of Dalriada. My fondness for such work is perhaps greater than is altogether appropriate for a man of the cloth. So God, in His divine wisdom, does not place before me the obstacle of a difficult chieftain to placate or an awkward dialogue to render into a foreign tongue. He faces me with a wooden boat, twelve clerical companions, and an expanse of storm-tossed sea. I praise Him for His perspicacity and thank Him with all my heart that we need not go until spring.

I feel some relief that, this time, the vessel is being built from solid wood and not from ox hides stretched over withies. I wish, all the same, that I were the son not of a scholar but of a fisherman, for then I would find the surge of the sea not sickening but soothing: the rocking of the world's great cradle.

My hands ache. They are all blisters and cannot hold the quill steady. Let the work be done soon. God grant my spirit obedience and my body strength.

Young men come here from time to time, seeking to join us in our temporary shelter. We have had two in the last seven days. One was clever, keen, well spoken. I would have welcomed the skills he had in reading and

*writing, for such abilities are rare. The young man, in his
eagerness, let his words spill too freely, and mentioned
Cúl Drebene—a miracle, he said. Colm was severe. He
bade the youth finish his growing up and come back in a
few years' time. By then, if the boat does not sink, we will
be far away in Fortriu.*

*The second youth was a quiet, lumpish sort of lad,
steady-eyed. He gave his name as Éibhear, and said he
was the son of a sailor. We took him.*

SUIBNE, MONK OF DERRY

EILE AWOKE FROM a dark dream in which she was
reaching for the hidden knife and could not find it; a
dream in which Dalach was laughing and raising his fist
and Saraid's small face was shrunken with terror.
Blood . . . so much blood . . . She sat up, breathing hard.
A cold light was coming through the unshuttered window space of the ferryman's hut. It was morning, and she
was freezing. Saraid. Where was Saraid?

Eile leaped to her feet, looking wildly around. The
fire had gone down to ashes. Not only was the child
nowhere to be seen, but both dog and man were gone as
well. Faolan's pack was still there, by the hearth; her
own bundle lay by her makeshift bed, and she'd had
Faolan's thick cloak over her. No wonder she'd slept so
soundly.

Her heart was thumping. He'd taken Saraid. Where?
What had he done? Eile ran to the door and wrenched it
open. After this, after all this, how could she have stayed
asleep and not kept the child safe? It was true, what
Anda had said. She would never be a good mother, she
just didn't have it in her.

Eile took two steps outside and halted. Saraid was sitting on an old bench, legs dangling, looking down toward the bridge. The dog crouched by her, chewing on
something it had caught. Above them gulls flew in crying

chorus toward the east. The constant voice of the river came close to drowning their calls. As Eile came out, the child turned her head and put a finger to her lips.

Eile crouched beside the bench and whispered in her daughter's ear. "Where did the man go? Faolan? Where is he?" They could not afford to waste any time. They must be over the river and away before pursuit could reach them.

"Shh." Saraid touched her mother's lips this time.

"Did he tell you—"

"Shh."

A moment later, Eile saw Faolan coming along the path by the willows, an old sack held up to keep his head dry. Of course, he had given her his cloak.

"Inside," he said, coming up to the door, and they obeyed. He sounded calm, but Eile's stomach was churning with anxiety, the need to move clawing at her. It was morning; they must pick up their things and cross the river. They must go on the rope again.

"What?" she hissed as soon as they were back in the hut. "What is it?"

"We have company." Faolan sounded like a man who is used to convincing others that all is well when, in fact, the sky is about to fall. "Seven or eight of them, all armed after a fashion and, I'm sorry to tell you, speaking of a violent death and the need for the perpetrator to account for herself. Take a deep breath, Eile, and stay calm. We'll get out of this."

Eile gulped in air, aware of Saraid's eyes on her. "I am calm," she said. "You'd better go on without us. No point in you getting in trouble as well."

Faolan grimaced; she could not tell what he was thinking. "I have a better suggestion," he said. "We brazen it out. They didn't see me, I made sure of that. We wait until the fellows come to mend the bridge. Then we lie. At least, I do. You don't say anything. I didn't see Brennan or any of those men from your settlement out there. I'll say you're with me."

The man was more of a fool than she'd thought. "They're searching for me and her. A girl and a child. Who's going to believe you? Anyway, they'll come up here looking and find us before the bridge gets fixed. It's a stupid idea."

Faolan looked at her. He did not seem upset or angry. "You think I should fight them all at once? I did say seven; perhaps you didn't hear that."

"My father could have done it." She could remember him practicing. Back in those days, Father had been like a warrior from a story, a hero who could never be defeated. It must have taken a remarkable man to kill him.

Faolan's eyes had gone strange; he was seeing something she couldn't. His mouth had become a thin line.

"We're going." Eile picked up her bag, reaching out the other hand to take Saraid's. "Up the river, away. You don't need to fight anyone. I'll cope."

"You won't get two miles before they catch you, Eile. Is that what you want for your daughter, a chase, a violent ending to this, perhaps confinement among strangers? You said you didn't want her taken away; that was your reason for refusing the priory. Do this, and you'll lose her before midday."

She hated him for speaking the truth. "Nobody's going to believe you," she said. "What were you planning to say, that I'm your little sister? Your daughter?"

"Neither. Folk will know me once we're over the river. They'll know I have—had—three sisters in Fiddler's Crossing. But I've been away a long time. More than long enough to have acquired a wife and child."

Eile said nothing. The idea made her feel sick. The need to repudiate it warred with the realization that it might possibly get them over the bridge. "So long as you don't expect anything," she said.

"I told you," said Faolan mildly, "I've given it up for the sake of my peace of mind. Eile, I can hear someone shouting out there. I think you were right; they're coming closer. I want a promise from you."

"I don't do promises."

"Listen to me. When it's my plan, it's my rules. When it's your plan it will be your rules. Agreed?"

"What, then?"

"Don't say anything and don't throw anything. Look after Saraid, keep her quiet and do what I tell you."

"Huh!"

"Just until we're across the bridge and out of earshot. A silent, submissive wife, that's what's required."

Eile glared at him. The voices were nearing the hut; there didn't seem to be any choice. She felt Saraid's arms around her leg, clutching, and bent to reassure her. "It's all right, Squirrel. Nobody's going to hurt us. Now be quiet, hold Sorry tight, and stay close to me. Faolan's going to look after us. We're going over the river to a new house. A nice one."

"Sorry?" Faolan murmured.

"That's what she calls her doll. It was how she used to say her own name. Hush now!" she hissed as the dog began to bark in warning.

It was clear that Faolan was not the type of man who waited for trouble to find him. He picked up the pack, threw open the door, and strode out, and the dog went after him with hackles up, hurling its challenge at the approaching group. Saraid's grip tightened on Eile's thigh. The child was trembling. *I'm not afraid,* Eile told herself. *I'm all she's got. I can't be afraid.* In her mind, her hand thrust and thrust until knife and fingers were sticky with blood; until Dalach was so limp and heavy on her she thought she might never struggle free of him. She'd believed that once it was done the dark things would flee from her dreams, but they were still here. They hovered close even now, when she was wide awake.

". . . sheltered for the night," Faolan was saying. "Not safe for my wife . . . expecting a child, sick all the time . . . you know how it is . . ."

"Shut your dog up, will you? Can't hear myself think," someone said.

Faolan snapped an order at the dog, which continued to bark. He looked over his shoulder. "Wife's creature," he muttered. "Won't obey me. My dear . . . ?"

Eile called the dog back to the doorway, quieted it, held on to the frayed piece of rope that was its collar. She took the opportunity to glance quickly around the circle of faces. One or two of them were familiar from the market at Cloud Hill. She lowered her eyes. Submissive was easy. She just had to act like Aunt Anda.

"We're looking for a girl," one of the men said. "Young woman with a child. You seen them?"

"The only woman and child I've seen are my own," Faolan said easily. "We're on our way to Fiddler's Crossing; just waiting for the bridge to be made safe."

"You might have a long wait."

"Only if the men I saw here yesterday are liars," Faolan said. "I'm supposed to help them this morning, as soon as they bring the materials. Then we'll be on our way. Sorry I can't assist you."

"Bid this wife of yours come out where we can see her properly." A new voice, this, one with more authority. "And the child. We're seeking a fugitive. We can't take your word that she's not in there."

"Search if you want. As for my wife, she's poorly, I told you. And I don't take kindly to orders where my family's concerned."

Eile took Saraid's hand again and moved out of the hut to stand by Faolan's side. They'd know her, she was sure of it. How could they not know? If her face didn't give her away, her shaking hands surely would.

"What's your wife's name?" the man snapped, eyes narrowed.

"Aoife," said Faolan without hesitation.

"And the child?"

"We call her Squirrel, mostly. I think I see someone at the bridge. I promised to help, as I told you. We'll look out for this fugitive on the road. Is she dangerous?"

Eile set her teeth in her lip. He kept on frightening her,

with his stupid names and his foolhardy questions. Her feet wanted to run; she could feel the same restlessness in Saraid's small body. A sob of sheer panic was welling up in her; she fought to suppress it.

"Excuse us," Faolan said. "My wife is quite unwell, as I said . . . Best you let us pass, unless you want her breakfast all over your boots."

A joker as well. Gods, she felt so sick right now she might do a very good imitation of an expectant woman, not that there was much in her stomach to bring up.

"You sure she's your wife?" The leader of the group had motioned his men into the hut to search, while he himself moved closer to Eile, scrutinizing her face. "Looks the right age for what we're seeking, and the child as well, three-year-old girl, dark hair . . . Where are you from? What's your business in these parts? Why is she wearing men's clothing?"

The questions had been thrown at them like knives. Eile cleared her throat.

Faolan took a step back. His arm came around her shoulders and she felt him draw a long breath.

"I'm the son of the brithem from Fiddler's Crossing, Conor Uí Néill," he said. "The surviving son."

The strangest thing happened. The man's face changed before her eyes, a look of fascinated horror crossing his features. He said not a word.

"I've been away a long time," added Faolan quietly. "I had neither wife nor child when I left these parts. I made my home far from this shore. Folk who remember me will tell you I'm a bard, and a bard travels. I thought it was time to introduce Aoife here, and my daughter, to the family. Now we'll be on our way, if you please."

They stepped aside and let him pass. She was certain, almost certain, that at least one of the men must recognize her. She'd been at the market now and then, though Dalach preferred Anda to go. He had his reasons for wanting Eile to stay at home. Besides, Anda refused to look after Saraid unless she absolutely must—"It's the girl's by-blow, let her tend to it"—and Eile didn't trust her aunt to be kind to the child. Anda was jealous. So foolish, as if Dalach's attentions were something to be coveted.

Well, it was over now, that part of it, at least, and it looked, incredibly, as if Faolan had just talked them out of trouble. She gripped Saraid's hand, fixed her eyes on the ground and moved forward, keeping pace with him. No choice in that; he still had his arm around her. His touch made her edgy and afraid; she wanted to break free, to push the arm away, to be her own self again. He'd better not think he was going to step into Dalach's shoes, with his talk of wives. Given it up, huh! Men didn't give it up. They took it when they wanted, they didn't know how to go without. Faolan was a liar like the rest of them. Like Deord, who'd probably never intended to come back.

"All right?" Faolan murmured as they reached the willows and the knot of men behind them broke into rapid, muted talk, of which nothing was clear enough to understand.

"Mm."

"Keep moving. I'll carry Saraid if you want."

"No. You need your hands free. She can walk."

"If you say so. Keep quiet until we're over the bridge. We'll have to wait until the wood's in place. The child's not going over that rope, nor am I."

They emerged from cover. There was a clear view of the rushing river and the broken span of the footbridge. On the other side a group of men was gathering, and materials had arrived on a cart: lengths of wood, coils of rope, tools. As Faolan and Eile walked along the river path, a party of riders appeared behind the laborers, a group of ten or so clad in tunics and breeches of blue and black. Their clothing seemed of fine quality, their shirts of pale linen, their boots well polished. Here and there a silver chain, a hat with a plume or a bronze sword hilt showed their status as members of a great household.

They must be waiting to cross the other way; perhaps that explained the workers' early start.

The wait was long. Faolan made play of finding somewhere for her and Saraid to sit, and she swallowed a curt denial that she needed his help with anything so simple. They sat. Faolan coerced a couple of their pursuers to help with the bridge. It looked tricky, grabbing the planks as the men on the other side slid them out, lining them up, then fastening them with more ropes on this side. She watched her father's friend as he leaned out over the rushing water, and pondered what her next move would be if he fell in and drowned. She'd probably give herself away the moment she said anything; he was the one who could tell lies and make them sound like the truth. He was the one with authority. Maybe she could fall down screaming and weeping, as Anda might have done, and get them to take her to this brithem, somebody Uí Néill. That name she knew; everyone did. They were big people, landowners, chieftains and kings. Eile could imagine the look in their eyes if she and Saraid turned up on the doorstep. Besides, what could she say? "I'm your son's wife?" That was a joke. Anyway, she couldn't scream and cry, even if Faolan drowned before her eyes. She couldn't do that to Saraid, who was already like a little ghost, silent and scared.

The rest of the men were talking. Two conversations: she could hear bits of both as she sat huddled in her cloak, with Saraid leaning up against her and the dog at her feet. One of them was about her.

"I'm sure it's her."

"But he said . . ."

"Take a look. You can see what he is: wealthy, highborn, speaks like he owns the place. She's a scrawny bit of nothing; roadside rubbish. Wife? I hardly think so."

Eile tried to scrunch up on herself; to make herself beneath any kind of notice. She prayed. *Let us get away. Please, oh, please.* She fought the urge to jump up, grab

Saraid and run. His plan; his rules. She'd probably been stupid to trust even for a moment.

The second conversation was about Faolan, and made her wonder.

"You know what he did, don't you?"

"Doesn't bear thinking about. Bet his father never thought he'd come home."

"Don't know how the fellow can live with himself."

"Looks normal enough."

"You reckon?"

"Wonder where he went, all those years."

For all the difficulty, the bridge was serviceable before morning was well advanced, and the men on the far side invited Faolan to be first across, since he had helped them while under no obligation to do so. The mounted party had tethered their horses and waited at a distance while the work was done. Now they moved up, and Eile could see a cloaked and hooded figure among them, someone who seemed to be giving all the orders.

At last they could go. She put Saraid in the sling and lifted the child onto her back. Faolan came over to them, his hands bleeding, his good tunic somewhat the worse for wear.

"Ready?" he asked, as if this were an everyday sort of journey, and the three of them a small family going to market or to visit kinsfolk. Those were the sorts of things ordinary families did together. Maybe she had done them with Father and Mother, long ago when she was little. She wished she could remember.

The rope remained as a handhold, but now the planks made a secure, though narrow, purchase for feet. Below, the river coursed in frothy white around the bridge supports. Faolan stepped onto the timbers and turned back to face her, extending his hand. "One hand in mine, the other on the rope," he said. "One step at a time."

"Shut your eyes, Squirrel," Eile said, pitching her voice above the noise of the rushing water. "Count up to ten, as slowly as you can, and then again, and we'll be on the other side." Clenching her teeth, she took the first step.

"You know," Faolan observed, walking backward, "that child is the best behaved I've ever encountered. You've done a wonderful job with her. Where I come from, there are several little boys, and they seem to run about yelling quite a bit of the time. I think Squirrel there would be quite taken aback by it . . ." He kept on talking, and leading her forward without once looking where he was going, and before he had finished they were on the other side. She had not once thought of falling.

Eile stepped down off the bridge and heard him say quietly, "Well done." A moment later a sharp voice snapped out, "That is the man!" and, before Faolan could so much as turn around, a pair of the blue-and-black-clad fellows had his arms pinned behind his back and were marching him away from her.

He fought. He fought quite well, in Eile's estimation; the two men were joined by two more, and then by another, before they got him trussed up, a gag over his mouth, and threw him across one of the packhorses. One man's nose was pouring blood; another was groaning, a hand to his head. A third lay sprawled on the ground, clutching his knee. Saraid had started to cry. Eile could feel it. The child wept soundlessly, a skill she had learned from her mother.

My plan; my rules. The plan had gone wrong now and the rules had to be broken.

"Let him go!" Eile shouted. "He hasn't done anything!" But there was so much noise, what with the blue and black people cursing and shouting orders, and horses everywhere, and the voice of the river, that nobody seemed to hear her. She was standing in the middle of someone else's place, someone else's business, and it seemed she was invisible at last, just when she didn't want to be. "Listen to me!" she yelled. "You! Listen! He's innocent, he didn't do anything!"

Someone lifted a hand, and there was a sudden stillness. Voices hushed; animals were quieted. A horse moved up beside Eile, a big horse with silver on its harness. The cloaked rider looked down.

"And who are you?" The voice was a woman's, sharp, impatient. It was the same voice that had been giving the orders.

Eile drew a deep breath and looked up. The woman was straight-backed and proud, as she imagined a great queen might be. Her hair was entirely covered by a veil and neck-piece of deep blue, like the evening sky, in some gossamer-fine stuff. Rich people's clothing. The eyes were grayish blue and hard as iron below the elegant brows. The woman did not look angry; she looked as if she was in a hurry and couldn't be bothered listening.

"Please," Eile said, forcing her voice steady as her heart raced. "He hasn't done anything wrong, he's just a traveler. Please let him go."

"What concern is this of yours, girl?" The tone was crisp. "Conal, deal with this person, will you?" The woman began to turn her horse away.

"Please! You're in charge, make them release him! This isn't fair—"

The poised head turned back a little. "What are you to him?" the woman asked.

I'm his wife. No, not that; Faolan's plan was for the other side of the river. "I'm his friend," she said, wondering what it was that had made her stay and speak, when it seemed she could have simply walked away amid the chaos and been free. "Where are you taking him?" She could see Faolan's face, upside down over a horse's back; she could glimpse his furious eyes, see the labored movement as he continued to struggle while tied at wrists and ankles. Then a man with a club came up and hit him on the head, and the eyes closed. "Stop hurting him!" Eile screamed.

A hand clapped itself over her mouth and a large arm came around her waist. She felt Saraid stiffen with fright.

Eile used her teeth. The hand let go. A moment later a searing pain went through her ear as the man cuffed her. Tears sprang to her eyes, tears of pain and of outrage, tears of sheer terror. No pitchfork; no knife; nothing but her bare hands.

"Gently, Conal," the veiled woman said. "There's a child there." Her voice held not a trace of softness. It was more the tone of someone who sees the wisdom of safe-guarding a new possession until its value is properly assessed. "Girl! Where were you headed?"

"Fiddler's Crossing."

"Oh? For what purpose?"

None of your business. "Visiting kin, my lady." Torn between fear and fury, she forced the title out.

"And what kin would that be?"

What now? An outright lie? Or tell the truth, the truth that had for some strange reason got them away from those first pursuers? "His kin, my lady. The family of the lawman in that settlement. My friend is his son."

The woman regarded her. The air seemed to go chill. "And your name is . . . ?"

Eile bobbed a curtsy, hating herself. "Aoife, my lady."

"Aoife, I see. Like the fairy woman in the ballad. How inappropriate." The cold blue eyes raked Eile up and down; she saw herself reflected there, from lank hair to bitten nails, from grimy face to worn boots. Her too-large clothing, a man's garments; the child's small hands clutching her.

Eile squared her shoulders. "I suppose my mother and father thought me fair, as an infant," she heard herself say. "We can't all choose what we become." Wrong, all wrong; she sent a mute apology to the unconscious Faolan. Silent and submissive, he'd said. With those sharp eyes on her, she couldn't manage that.

"This girl is of no interest to us," the lady said. "Leave her; ride on."

"No!" They were ignoring her; moving off, one man leading the packhorse with Faolan limp over the saddle.

"No! You can't take him!" This wasn't right. Someone had to make them understand.

"My lady?" A man spoke from behind her.

"What now?" The woman halted her mount once more.

"I've had a word with those fellows on the other side. This girl—she's under suspicion for an unlawful death. A man stabbed: her uncle, not two days since. They want to take her back to Cloud Hill, deal with it properly."

"Then give her to them and let us be on our way. I've no time for this."

"The only thing is," said the man, "the story the girl gave, and the fellow," he nodded toward Faolan, "is that she's his wife and the child his daughter. If not for that, they'd have taken her back straightaway. I thought you'd want to know, my lady."

"It's all right, Squirrel," muttered Eile. "Don't cry; it'll be all right." She had promised a new home; a nice one, if only Saraid crossed the river. She had lied to her own daughter.

"Are you his wife?" The words were like drops of ice; Eile could not tell if the woman was angry or amused or playing some strange game beyond other people's understanding.

"We're traveling together. The three of us. Please don't lock him up. We need him." Let this proud creature make what she wanted of that.

"They're being quite insistent," the blue-and-black-clad man said. "They want their own people to handle it. Shall I take her back over, my lady?"

No, please, no. Let him go and let us go. Somewhere far away. We will never trouble you again.

"I've changed my mind, Seamus. These travelers are on my land now, and under different jurisdiction. Tell those fellows we will deal with the matter under due process of law. Tell them to go home. Conal! Find this girl a mount. If she won't keep her mouth shut, gag her. We've delayed long enough here; let us ride for home."

"My lady, the child—and there's a dog—"

"For pity's sake, Conal, do you need step-by-step instructions? Put the girl and the child on the other packhorse and forget about the dog. If it wants to follow us, it will."

A horse was found. A man tried to help Eile up, but she snarled at him when he put his hands on Saraid. She untied the sling, lifted the shivering child to the creature's back, then allowed the fellow to cup his hands for her foot. Every part of her was strung tight. She wasn't going to say she'd never been on a horse before. She had to keep up. She had to watch out for Faolan, since there was nobody else to do it.

The lady rode over to him now and got down from her horse. As Eile watched, she took hold of Faolan's hair and pulled his head up so she could gaze into his white, unconscious face. Her eyes were strange; Eile thought for a moment that this fine lady was about to spit, or slap the stricken man, or scream a curse. Instead, the ring-decked fingers let go the dark hair abruptly, and the woman turned away to mount her horse once more.

"To Blackthorn Rise," she called. It was a command. The group rode forward, away from the bridge. Balancing Saraid in front of her and gritting her teeth, Eile rode with them.

⟋⟍

THE GREAT GLEN was in Bone Mother's grip. It was close to Midwinter and the pines spread dark under a sky of slate. The waters of Serpent Lake lay sullen and dangerous from shore to shore, criss-crossed by changeable currents. Beneath the surface, unseen presences lurked close in the hungry season.

I will be a swallow, Broichan thought, *winging to warmer climes on the breath of the storm.* He walked on, regretting his decision to test himself by leaving the horse at a local farm and continuing to Pitnochie on foot. His sandals were heavy in the saturated mosses, his robe damply clinging. And he thought, *I will be a deer, running swifter than the sunlight, sheltering in the birch thickets.* Here the lake shore was broken by a number of sharp indentations. The water swirled in sudden small bays, cut deep in the thickly wooded hillside. There had been rock falls, earth falls. The serpent had swallowed chunks of the land. Here and there the path disappeared entirely. Broichan sought new ways, climbing until there was a fiery ache in his thighs. *I will be a salmon,* he thought, *and swim the length of this great water in powerful surges; my scales will throw back the silver gleam of the Shining One like a melody of bright notes. I will be a bee, a snake, a moth . . .*

When night fell he sought the hollow of an ancient oak well known to him and sheltered within, folded in his cloak. A druid has many techniques for slowing the body's workings the better to endure privations. Of these skills he still had the mastery, even if the power to travel in forms other than that of man had left him as he fought the long illness for control of his body. The wondrous changes, the creature shapes, were now no more than vivid memories, a level of the craft of magic that would never more be within his grasp. His legs ached. His back hurt. His joints were stiff in the damp cold of the season. He was not such an old man in years, but tonight he felt old.

Rain came. The Shining One was veiled by clouds; the night was dark. Broichan made himself breathe in a steady pattern; his heartbeat slowed, his blood ran less swiftly, his body stilled within the swathing cloak, within the sheltering tree. He was a whisper of breath in the night; a pair of dark eyes amid the great shadow of winter. He prayed without a sound. *I seek wisdom. I need a path. What is required of me?*

And it seemed to him, after an endless time, that the

answer was there in the wash of the lake waters against the shore, and in the sigh of the wind in the pines: *Acknowledge your weakness. Learn acceptance. Open your heart to love.*

But when he asked: *Is it true? Is she my daughter?* the voice was silent. The only answer was the slow beating of his own heart.

THERE WAS WORRYING news. Not long after Bridei's return to White Hill, Carnach had sent a messenger to say that he was going home to his holdings at Thorn Bend over the winter, and was as yet uncertain when he might come back to Caer Pridne and to his duties as the king's chief war leader. The forces in the northern fortress being much reduced already, he had left things in the hands of his deputies for the time being. The message was of concern not for this statement, but for what it did not say. Carnach had made his bitter disappointment at Bridei's decision quite plain when they had met at Caer Pridne. Now, in effect, he was withdrawing his support as a result.

In the judgment of Bridei and his councillors, Carnach had not been serious about contesting the kingship of Circinn himself, although he was qualified by blood to do so, since his mother had been a woman of the royal line. But it seemed clear that, in deciding to let the opportunity pass him by this time, Bridei had lost a powerful ally and a friend. Carnach's lands were strategically situated on the border between Fortriu and Circinn. Six years ago, his decision to support Bridei's bid for the kingship of Fortriu had been critical; as an ongoing ally, he was invaluable. He would make a formidable enemy. Steps must be taken to win back his trust.

As for Broichan, Bridei wondered if he had misjudged his foster father. He missed him; he feared for him out in the wet and cold, on foot, alone and in precarious health.

On the other hand, Broichan possessed an iron discipline, a core of strength Bridei understood all too well.

It had been a shock to find the druid gone from White Hill, and to know he had lost the opportunity to break the news of his decision to Broichan before announcing it to the court. That had filled him with misgivings. It had seemed a betrayal. Now, on the eve of the assembly at which he must make public the news of Drust's death and his own intentions, what he wanted most of all was his foster father's wise counsel.

Bridei had learned early that getting a man like Broichan to accept unwelcome news was a matter of presenting it in a certain way, clearly and honestly, with logical arguments to support it. If his foster father were here now, he would explain his reasons: the desire for peace, the need to heal his wounded country after the time of war, the urge to build alliances and strengthen borders. The inner conviction that, although it was the will of the gods to see Fortriu and Circinn reunited in the ancient patterns of faith, now was not the time for it.

Bridei sat alone in his small council chamber, pondering these things and considering the fact that leadership in time of fragile peace might be still more challenging than it was in time of war. Conflict drew folk together; it tended to make them follow willingly, provided they believed in the cause. It was when the danger was past that folk began to question. When not united against a common enemy, they invented their own disputes and disagreements. He would have welcomed his foster father's observations on this. He would have enjoyed debating it with Faolan.

Bridei sighed. The longer his right-hand man was away, the more he seemed to need him. Faolan could have sought out Broichan. He could have gone after Carnach and assessed the risk in that quarter. Most of all, he could have served at White Hill as the king's protector and sounding board. Faolan was as unlike Broichan as anyone could be, but the man had a particular wisdom that cut through irrelevancies like a knife through soft butter. Nobody knew what lay in Faolan's past. He never talked about it. No, that was not quite true; it seemed that, in their long and arduous journey across the north last autumn, Faolan had unburdened himself to Ana and to Drustan, but neither would betray his confidence, and that was as it should be. Whatever the man's history, it had made him strong. By the time Faolan returned to Fortriu in spring, Bridei judged, he'd have recovered from his broken heart—that had been a startling development—and be ready to resume his duties at White Hill once more. Meanwhile, the one who must receive Bridei's confidences and help him through his quandaries was Tuala.

As if in answer to his thoughts, Bridei's wife came in now, tapping gently on the door then slipping through. Although they had known each other since he was a child and she an infant, Bridei's heart still turned over each time he saw her afresh. Tonight Tuala was wearing a tunic the hue of violets, cut wider to accommodate the growing child in her belly, over a skirt of gray wool and soft kidskin slippers. Her dark hair was plaited down her back, but wisps escaped around her pale face to form a soft halo, and her ribbon was half untied. Her eyes, turned on his as he came across to embrace her, were troubled.

"Oh, Bridei," Tuala said, "you're sitting here in the dark again, worrying. I'm so sorry. If I'd known Broichan would react this way I would have waited to confront him with it until after the crisis was over, Drust and the election, I mean—"

"Shh," Bridei said, putting his fingers gently against her lips then bending to give her a kiss. Although her pregnancy was well advanced now, the swell of her belly was small; she had ever been a slight girl and this infant seemed likely to take after its mother in stature, as Derelei did. "Don't apologize. Who among us would have predicted that Broichan would take such drastic action? He's not known for being impetuous. I have been sitting in the dark, as you put it, planning exactly how I will explain my decision to him when he returns." He detached himself and moved to light a lamp from the single candle on the table beside him. "I'm wondering if the future of the Priteni kingdoms may pale into insignificance for my foster father beside the news that he may have fathered the queen of Fortriu. I still find it hard to comprehend that it never occurred to him before."

The lamp's glow spread across the small chamber, making Tuala's large eyes shine like an owl's. "I hope he is safe," she said soberly. "It's so cold out there."

They both fell silent, remembering a past winter, one in which Broichan's determined efforts to shut Tuala out of his foster son's life had seen her make her own desperate journey down the glen through the snow. If he were indeed her father, he had a great deal to come to terms with.

"You know—" began Tuala, then stopped herself.

Bridei waited.

She twisted her hands together, a small frown creasing her brow, then spoke again. "You know when I ran away from Banmerren with those two?"

She meant the boy and girl of the Good Folk, Otherworld guides who had aided her flight and come close to coaxing her away from the human world forever. Bridei could not remember that night of fear and wonder and death without a shudder. "Mm," he said.

"You remember what I told you, how I got down from the wall by believing I was an owl? I must have changed, the way Drustan does, but only for a moment. I must have flown. But there was no spell, no incantation, nothing. I had no awareness of using magic. I did it without thinking. Bridei, I suppose I could do that again, or something like it, if I chose to."

He was not sure where she was heading, only that she was deeply uneasy, pacing, fidgeting in a way quite unlike her. She had ever been his still center, his anchor and his repose. "I imagine you could," he said. "And I understand why you have never attempted it since."

"I just thought . . . I suppose I've been thinking about Derelei and what will happen with Broichan gone. Our son is too little to understand the concept of *never*. He looks for Broichan every afternoon. He sits and waits, more patiently than is natural for any child of his age, and when Broichan doesn't come he curls up and puts his thumb in his mouth like a baby."

"He still is a baby. Didn't you say he is too young for such intensive study? Perhaps this will allow Derelei to spend more time being a child before he must become a mage or a druid or whatever future awaits him."

"I do let him run about with Ban, and kick a ball, and play with Garth's boys," Tuala said, an edge in her tone that was unusual. "And he enjoys those things. Not long ago I would have told you that is quite enough for any child of his tender years. But Broichan was right all along: Derelei's precociously talented. He can't help what he's inherited, from me, from you, from Broichan himself. He savors his tutelage in the craft. He craves it. Already he misses his lessons terribly. It would be so much easier if we knew how long Broichan planned to be gone."

Bridei grimaced. "From the sound of things, there wasn't a lot of planning in it. All I know is that, if he does not wish to be found, it will take a person of remarkable skill to track him down. I doubt the ability of Aniel's man to do it."

"Agreed," said Tuala. "But I think I could. Not by scrying; Broichan will be using all his craft to block such seeking eyes. There is another way."

"Wh—?" Bridei bit back his response. Tuala was not given to statements of the foolish or ridiculous kind. In that, she took after Broichan. "That fills me with trepidation," he said. "If you mean what I believe you mean, it would be fraught with risk on so many levels I could barely start to list them. Broichan has acted unwisely. He doesn't deserve such a response, Tuala. Besides, there's the child."

"This one, you mean?" She laid a white hand on her belly. "Breeding does not stop a vixen or a hart or a she-badger from traversing the wildwood, Bridei, whatever the season. As for deserving, if he is my father I'm bound to care about his safety whether he deserves it or not. You've gone white as fresh cheese, dear one. Don't be alarmed, I'm not planning precipitate action, all I'm doing is thinking aloud. Perhaps we'll get a message soon to tell us he's arrived at Pitnochie and that there's no cause at all for our fear. My mind turned to that partly because of Derelei. I think I may need to continue what Broichan began with him. He had learned some tricks now, some skills that could prove perilous if left to develop unguided."

Bridei nodded; this, he had been expecting. Not the other. "Set safeguards in place," he said. "Take Aniel into your confidence. He is completely to be trusted and thinks highly of you. Wid could be useful, too. I'm confident you have the goodwill of everyone at court now, but those who come and go are less of a known quantity, and we're heading into a difficult time, thanks to Drust's demise."

"I'll be careful," Tuala said. "I wouldn't do anything to undermine you, Bridei. I hope you know that." She sounded suddenly close to tears.

"I didn't mean that—Tuala, don't cry, please. Of course that wasn't what I meant." He wrapped his arms around her, aware of how slight she was, unborn child and all. "If I speak of safeguards, it's because I fear for you, not for myself, dear one. I won't have you hurt, not by the least cruel word. You know the way some folk think. They'll seize on the slightest oddity in the king's personal life if they think it's a means to discredit him. In the light of my decision not to stand for the dual kingship, we'll be under ever closer scrutiny."

"Oddity. I don't think I've ever been called that before." Tuala grinned through her tears.

"I didn't mean—"

"I'm joking, Bridei. I seem to weep over the silliest things these days; I put it down to having a child on the way. Once she's safely born, I trust this weakness will cease. And don't worry about my other suggestion. If I take it into my head to attempt a magical transformation I'll warn you first, so you know that beetle on your pillow may actually be your wife."

"Just as long as you can change back again," Bridei said lightly. The terror that clutched his vitals at the very thought of her trying such a thing, he kept entirely to himself.

A REGULAR, JARRING pain. A horse, cantering, each step another stab through his neck, another jolt of his lolling head. He was over a saddle, head down. They forded a stream and it wet him up to the eyes. All he could see was the horse's side and a leather strap with a buckle. Gods, this hurt.

Eile. Where was Eile? Nobody was talking; this was serious riding, swift and purposeful. If he'd been unconscious a while, those fellows back at the bridge might already have her and the child well on the way back to Cloud Hill and punishment. Curse it! Why in the name of all the powers had Echen's people taken it into their heads to apprehend him now? At least, Faolan assumed they were Echen's people, though their chieftain was said to have been gone these four years. He'd know that blue and black gear anywhere. He'd been seeing it in his dreams since his last night under his father's roof, a night whose restless sleep had been preceded by another sharp tap to the skull.

Maybe the chieftain of Blackthorn Rise was dead, but his men hadn't changed their methods. Surely the old feud wasn't still alive, after all that had happened? Surely there was nobody, on his side at least, with any will to keep it going? Only himself; and his quarrel had been with Echen, not with the man's kinsfolk. Now it was too late for vengeance.

Eile. Saraid. He had to get out of this somehow and go back for them. For all her bravado, the girl was scared, and with good reason. What she'd done had to catch up with her sometime, and in the face of formal justice she'd be powerless. Chances were the child would be handed over to the aunt, and not receive a kindly welcome. As for Eile, he was not certain what penalty she would face, but he could think of several possibilities, none of them pleasant. He couldn't let that happen, not to Deord's daughter. The girl was frail; skin and bone. He had to get her, get *them,* to safety.

The horse was going uphill. Faolan's head was jolted about, his teeth biting involuntarily into his tongue. He tasted blood and caught a glimpse of other riders, black boots, blue shirts, and the glint of silver on their harnesses. A hill with birches; a tower. He thought he recognized the place. A dog. He knew that, too. Persistent creature. Its flanks were heaving and its tail was down, but it kept pace. So maybe she was here. Why? Why take her?

The muddy track turned to gravel and then to flagstones. They had reached somewhere. The horse halted; rough hands untied Faolan from the saddle and dropped him to the ground like a sack of turnips. The dog licked his face, above the gag. He sought Eile with his eyes but could not see her, only a circle of male faces.

"Take him in, lock him up," a woman's voice said. "Don't untie his hands and feet until you have him secure. He has a reputation for getting away. Don't dawdle, move."

A large man who smelled of garlic picked him up bodily. He was conveyed over this person's shoulder to a stone building, dumped on straw and then, mercifully, bonds and gag were removed by the big man while two others held thrusting spears with the tips uncomfortably close to Faolan's chest.

"After that ride," he croaked, "believe me, I haven't the inclination so much as to attempt a crawl to the door, let alone make a bolt for freedom." Gods be merciful, could this be the prelude to another sojourn in Breakstone Hollow? His skin crawled at the thought of it. *Deord, my friend, what have you done to me?* "Don't tell me my informant's got it wrong, and Echen Uí Néill's not dead after all?"

"Shut it, will you?" muttered the big man. "It's the Widow gives the orders here, and it's not for you or me to question them. Now don't try anything stupid or we'll have those bonds back on before you can so much as blink. Here." Another man, perhaps a groom, had appeared with a blanket, and the big fellow tossed it into the straw where Faolan half crouched, half lay, willing some feeling into his cramped limbs. There was no point at all in trying to resist. It would only get him spiked. The blanket seemed a positive sign.

"Thank you," he muttered, pulling it closer. "There was a girl. And a child. Did you—?"

But, at a word from their leader, his guards had backed out of the room. "No funny business," the big man said from the doorway. "There's an armed man up the end and more outside."

"I wouldn't dream of it." Then, as the fellow moved away, "I don't suppose you can tell me why I'm here? What is it she thinks I've done, this widow?"

"No idea. We just do as we're told. Looks as if you've offended her somehow. She'll tell you when she's ready."

"Now why don't I find that reassuring?" Faolan murmured, wrapping the blanket around his shoulders.

The big man folded his arms, leaning on the door frame. "She can be tough," he said. "As tough as any man. But if you've a clear conscience you've nothing to worry about." The grilled door closed; Faolan heard the bolt slide home with a clang. Footsteps retreated.

What now? It seemed an interrogation was coming. He was practiced at those. It would help to know what this woman wanted with him. Who was she? The Widow; it had been spoken like a title. He had to assume that meant Echen's widow, though he did not remember the fellow having a wife back in the old days. Someone had said, across the river, that she held the lands for her son; that Echen's brother, who'd stood to inherit them, wasn't interested. So she was powerful; her husband all over again? Faolan caught himself shivering and forced himself to stop. It had been years since the summer his brother had led a local resistance against Echen's cruel chieftaincy and paid, not just with his own life, but with the very fabric of family.

Did this widow know who Faolan was? One of those fellows at the bridge last night had seemed to guess at his identity. Could his return have been of sufficient interest to spark an urgent message to this lady, precipitating her appearance on the riverbank this morning? Surely not. She'd know the story, of course; everyone in these parts had to know, it would be part of local legend now. But nobody had confronted him with it in her hearing. He had not had time to give his name before they disabled him. Maybe this was a simple case of mistaken identity.

There was another possibility. She was an Uí Néill, by marriage at least, kin to the High King and to Gabhran, deposed monarch of Gaelic Dalriada. And he was on this shore as a spy. He was in the pay of the enemy: Bridei of Fortriu, the very man who had just scored a stunning victory over a force rich in Uí Néill princes. He didn't think she could know this; he was expert at covert missions. They'd taken his bag, but very fortunately had not asked him to strip. They did not know, therefore, the amount of silver he carried, nor the full extent of his concealed weaponry. He could deal with this.

Faolan made an efficient examination of his place of imprisonment. The last time he'd been locked up, in Alpin's fortress at Briar Wood, a bird had come to fetch him the key. That wasn't going to happen here, nor was a more ordinary kind of escape, for the single window was

sturdily barred, the door was strong and, short of starting
a tunnel under the stone walls, there was not much he
could do. An image of Eile and the child was in his mind,
captive and marching back to the scene of that bloody
killing. That bloody and altogether justified killing. It
disgusted and repelled him to think of it, that wretched
lump of a man forcing himself on her, stealing her childhood, making her a kind of slave, using her love and fear
for the little girl to keep her compliant . . . The aunt was
no better: too weak to do what was right. Eile had only
survived, in Faolan's estimation, because she was her father's daughter. Strong; indomitably strong, for all her
waifish build. He must hope she would be safe until he
could reach her. He must hope she wouldn't do anything
foolish, like try to fight or make the wrong people angry.
In Fiddler's Crossing, long ago, he'd been robbed of the
opportunity to try to save his sister. But he could save
Eile. He could save her and her daughter, and he would,
no matter what it cost him. They were survivors, the two
of them; he would help her. He lay down on the straw,
the blanket over him, his eyes narrowed to slits. Whatever might come, he would be ready for it.

"No!" EILE PROTESTED, her voice rising to a shriek despite her efforts to control it. "She's frightened! Don't
take her away, please—"

"She can't stay here the way she is, and nor can you,
girl." The speaker was a large woman in plain, good
homespun, a snowy linen apron wrapped around her
waist. "I can see the vermin crawling in your hair. Nobody's putting her head on one of my mattresses in that
state."

"Let me go with her—"

"In the name of Brighid, girl, stop your caterwauling,
will you? It's only a bath. The nursemaid will tend to the
child and I'll keep an eye on you. Anyone would think

the two of you had never seen hot water before. Now hush your mouth and come with me. The girl's not crying, is she? Good as gold, quiet little thing. And if she's not upset, why would you be?"

Saraid was in the arms of a sweet-faced young serving woman, being borne away to some other part of this enormous dwelling. She was silent all right; she had learned the necessity for that over three years in Dalach's cottage. Eile hesitated a moment, then wrenched free of the large woman and darted across the chamber to snatch her daughter back before she could disappear forever.

"No!" she said. It was not quite a shout. "If we have to wash, we will; but together."

The two serving women seemed perplexed, but something in Eile's face stilled their protests.

"Come on, then," said the older one. "Aoife, is it? Funny name for a girl like you. And what's your little sister's name?"

"Squirrel."

The woman eyed her strangely. "Oh, yes? Poppet, isn't she? So quiet. Can she talk?"

"She's three years old. Of course she can talk." Eile gritted her teeth. "She's scared, that's all. Where is this bath?"

The woman led the way into a chamber that seemed to be a scullery or wash room, though it was bigger than the whole of Dalach and Anda's place. There was a fire burning on a hearth. There were buckets and brushes and cloths, racks for drying things, pots and bottles and crocks on shelves. A large pan stood in the center of the flagstoned floor; vapor arose from it.

"I'm Maeve," the large woman said. "The housekeeper. Take off your things. The child, too. Then get in. We'll have our work cut out, Orlagh. You'd better find some oil of rosemary for the hair. And ask one of the maids to seek out some fresh garments for both of them. What's this you're wearing, anyway, lass? Some fellow's trousers?" Her nose wrinkled.

"None of your business," muttered Eile, eyeing the steaming tub. She could not remember the last time she had bathed in hot water. It had been before she came to live with *them,* certainly. Anda had only allowed cold, except for Dalach, and he didn't wash much anyway.

Saraid had a fist to her mouth and the doll clutched in her other hand.

"All right, Squirrel," Eile murmured, crouching beside the child. "We're going to take off our clothes and have a wash, and these nice ladies are going to help us. Put Sorry over there; let me take her. See, she can sit up on the chest and watch us. Now I'll take off this shirt and you do yours . . ." She tried to let neither her daughter nor this alarmingly capable woman see that she was afraid. Nobody had said who their captor was or what was to become of them. These folk knew what she had done; that man back at the bridge had told them. They might take Saraid away any moment. They might lock Eile up and throw away the key, and she would never see her daughter again. There was no knowing. Since they had come here, nobody had said much at all except orders like: *Through there! Give me the bag! Sit down!*

"Do you know . . ." she began, shivering as she slipped Faolan's shirt over her head. "Yes, that's good, Squirrel . . . I wonder if you know where the man is who came here with us. The one they slung over a horse. He's our friend."

"Can't tell you." Maeve was waiting, arms folded, foot tapping. "Quick now, get those things off, I don't have all day. Orlagh! Where's that oil?"

But Orlagh wasn't moving. She was standing there staring as Eile stripped off the trousers and her ragged smallclothes. For a moment Eile could not understand why; it was bad enough having to be naked in a house of strangers without some woman gawking at her. Then she realized it was the bruises. She was so used to them, old ones fading to gray and yellow, new ones blue and purple, she'd never really thought how many her body wore, or that perhaps women like this well-fed housekeeper and her inquisitive assistant did not have men who held power over them; men who beat them as a matter of course. Anda had bruises, too. Being on Dalach's side had not spared her his fist. Eile tried to cover herself with her hands, feeling a sudden sense of shame and, with it, a curious defiant pride.

"It's all right, lass," the housekeeper said quietly. "Orlagh, I said get the oil."

Eile took Saraid's hand and stepped over to the tub. The child stiffened; a tiny whimper emerged from her.

"It's not as hot as it looks," Eile said, dipping in a cautious hand. "See, nice and warm. Come on, Squirrel: one, two, three."

A little later, sitting in the warm water and feeling the comfort of it seeping through her weary body, Eile wondered if the whole thing was some kind of strange dream. Maybe she would wake up and be back in the hut with Dalach, and she'd have to do it all over again. But this time there would be no knife . . . She jerked back to reality. The woman, Maeve, was scooping water over her hair, then rubbing something in with vigorous fingers.

"You do the child," Maeve ordered. "The whole scalp, mind, we want every one of these creepy crawlies out before either of you sets foot in the rest of the house. This'll take a lot of combing. Brighid save us, girl, who's been looking after the pair of you? This is criminal."

"We look after ourselves," Eile retorted, stung by the criticism. "She's well enough, isn't she? What's a few bugs?" She saw Orlagh exchange a look with Maeve; there was no reading it.

The housekeeper's fingers made their painful way across Eile's scalp; a sweet herbal smell filled the steamy air. Saraid was up to her neck in the bathwater, sitting between Eile's knees; she submitted silently to the hair wash, but Eile could feel the anxiety in the small body, the same restless urge for flight that she felt in her own limbs, for all the delight of being warm again. She was naked, wet, and among strangers. She did not know what was coming. And she was full of questions, but they were all ones she couldn't ask. *What will she do to me, this fine lady? They'll punish me, won't they—lock me up, hurt me? Don't let them take Saraid, please, please . . .*

"Where must we go, after this?" she asked. It seemed reasonably safe.

"I'm bid get you clean, suitably dressed and fed, no more." Maeve was rinsing off the oil now, a hand keeping the water out of Eile's eyes. "You can have a pallet in a corner for tonight, if she doesn't send for you before then. The two of you look as if you could do with a good sleep."

"Send for me?" Eile made sure her voice sounded strong.

"Stands to reason, doesn't it? The law's after you, and in these parts the Widow *is* the law. She'll expect you to account for yourself, and then she'll decide what's to become of you. Don't look like that, lass. She's no reason to be anything but fair with you. Here, use this scoop to rinse the poppet's hair, then we'll get dry. She can't keep this thing here, it'll be crawling with vermin."

The housekeeper walked across and picked up the rag doll gingerly between thumb and forefinger. She turned toward the crackling hearth fire.

Saraid screamed. The sound tore through Eile like a knife, and she jumped from the bath, sending a wave over the clean floor.

"No! She needs it!"

Maeve had blanched. Silently, she held out the limp scrap of cloth with its dark staring eyes, and Eile snatched it.

"Saraid, shh, shh. See, I've got Sorry here, she's safe. Hop out and let the lady dry you, and then you can have her. She's fine, Saraid. Hush, now."

There were thick cloths to get dry with and then garments to wear, not as fine as Faolan's things, but of good quality, with hardly any patches or mends. Saraid got a little gown and stockings and a woollen shawl in which she cocooned the doll tightly. Eile donned a shirt, a skirt, a kind of overdress. It was a long time since she had felt so warm, and her skin was tingling and strange from the hot water and scrubbing. She felt tired, as if she could sleep right now, although it was still day.

They were led to a different chamber, and while Orlagh combed out Eile's long hair with painstaking thoroughness and a considerable amount of muttering, Eile tended to Saraid's, an easier task by far since the child was used to having her dark curls brushed daily. It came to Eile how short of the mark her pitiful attempts to maintain standards at Cloud Hill had been. It was plain to her that these women, servants themselves, thought her and Saraid wretched, weak, and filthy. The shame of that was hard to bear. She had tried to keep Saraid nice. She had done the best she could.

"You don't need to stare," she snapped, intercepting Maeve's look as the housekeeper came back in with a tray in her hands. "We're not wild animals!"

"Is it true what they're saying?" Orlagh's voice was tentative. "That you killed someone?"

"Orlagh!" Maeve's tone was a sharp warning.

Eile pulled free of the comb, wincing. "If you think I'm going to answer that, you're stupid. I'll do this for myself, thanks. I don't need folk tending to me. If this lady of yours thinks we're not good enough to be in her fine house, maybe you can just let us out the back door and you never need clap eyes on us again. Nobody asked for a bath."

"Orlagh, we don't need you any longer." Maeve set down her tray and the younger woman withdrew at the frosty look in the housekeeper's eyes. "Lass, maybe you don't understand. Come, sit here by the fire, get some food into you, and I'll try to explain it. I'm sure the little one would like a bowl of soup and a bit of bread. Come on, now." She might have been coaxing a wild creature out of hiding.

Eile remembered something. "Our dog; the dog that was with us. Where is it?"

"Dog? I couldn't tell you. I suppose it'll be in the yard somewhere, if it hasn't wandered off."

"Could you find out?" The soup smelled wonderful; as good as the breakfast Faolan had brought them, two very long days ago. "You can eat it, Squirrel. Sit up straight and take small mouthfuls."

"A dog's the least of your worries, lass. What I've been told is that you're accused of an unlawful killing. You'll need to explain yourself to the lady first and then, depending on what she decides, you may have to go up before a brithem, a lawman."

"I know what a brithem is. I'm not ignorant."

"Eat up, girl. You look half starved."

Eile broke her bread into four pieces and set one back on the platter, then hunted for pockets in her borrowed garments; the three remaining bits would last Saraid a day or two. She looked up and met Maeve's sharp eye.

"No need for that," the housekeeper said. "We feed folk properly here. There'll be supper later. This is for now. Your little sister has pretty manners. I couldn't have trained her better myself."

Sudden treacherous tears sprang to Eile's eyes and she sniffed, willing them not to fall. Why would this stranger decide to be kind unless she wanted something? "I'll answer this lady's questions," she said. "But only if you let Saraid—Squirrel—stay with me. I'm all she's got. I can't let her be frightened."

"There are children here in the house; playthings; nursemaids. No need for her to—"

"Nobody's taking her." Eile had set down her spoon with the delicious soup, full of grains and vegetables, barely begun. "I don't go anywhere or do anything without her. And I want to know where Faolan is. They hurt him. I didn't like that."

Something suspiciously close to a smile was hovering on Maeve's lips.

"Don't laugh at me!" Eile lost her precarious control.

"Eat your soup, child. One word of advice. It's best to hold on to your temper with the Widow. She admires strength. She likes it even more when it's properly harnessed. You may find her intimidating, but you'll do all right if you're courteous and honest. That's what will help you most. Come on, eat that, it's good for you. Your sister's already finished and she's only half your size."

"She's my daughter," Eile muttered. If she was supposed to be honest, this seemed a good place to start.

"Brighid save us," said Maeve mildly. "You poor little thing. Now listen. I'm going to stand here and watch until you finish every scrap of that, and the bread, too. Then I'm going to tuck the two of you in bed for a rest. The lady won't want to see you until later; there's time."

Saraid's eyelids were drooping. Before the fire, her hair was drying to glossy curls.

"Will you ask about Faolan? Please?"

"We'll see. Come on now, do I have to spoon-feed you like a baby?"

Not long after, Eile was conveyed to a bedchamber that seemed to her quite grand, with pallets in rows and chests for storage. A ewer and bowl stood on a side table, and there was a window with blue-painted shutters.

"This is where Orlagh and the other maidservants sleep," said the housekeeper. "You take this bed, pop the child in the next, and I'll make sure you're left alone awhile. You look worn out and she's half asleep already. Here, give her to me, I'll tuck her in—"

"She can go in with me." Eile held the child firm. "That's what we're used to. Are you sure—?" She could not quite name what she feared: the sudden coming of strangers less kindly than this one, curses and blows, folk who would take her away from Saraid. It did not seem safe to sleep; not without Faolan to watch over them.

"I'll call you in plenty of time. You won't be disturbed."

When Maeve was gone, Eile put Saraid in one of the beds and sat by her, humming while the child fell asleep with the shawl-swathed Sorry held in a tight embrace. She could remember making Sorry from one of her mother's old gowns, and how cross Anda had been at the waste of materials. Eile thought maybe she could remember a doll of her own, from long ago in the house on the hill. Woolen hair long enough to plait; little shoes made from scraps of leather; green eyes like hers. Maybe it was only in her imagination. Sorry was a poor thing, bits and pieces stuffed into coarse homespun, and getting less and less like a human shape the longer she survived. To Saraid, she was the most beautiful doll in the world.

Maybe she'd lie down for a bit. She could stay alert and still rest. Her back was aching from the ride and her head was spinning. She lowered herself to the bed beside the slumbering child. A warm blanket; they treated their servants well here. A soft pillow, which seemed to be stuffed with feathers. No wonder that woman hadn't wanted Eile's filthy head on it. She observed, with detachment, that her hair was drying out quite a different color from its usual muddy hue. It seemed to have all shades of red in it, from fox fur to autumn beech leaves. Back in the old days, Father had had red hair. When he came back from that place, Breakstone Hollow, it had gone white, and he'd shaved his head. Mother's hair had been soft brown, like Saraid's.

"Father," Eile whispered, "I'm afraid. But I'll do my best. Mother, I'll look after her. I promise." And she was asleep.

5

❧

ARE YOU SURE you want to take the child in with you? The lady will be expecting a full account of what you did. You wouldn't want the little girl to hear that, would you?"

They were outside a grand oak door with a heavy bolt and two guards. Maeve stood frowning, hands on hips. Eile, jittery with nerves even after her long sleep, held Saraid's hand tightly.

"She can sit in a corner, somewhere she can see me but not hear. She'll be good."

Maeve sighed. "I'll ask the lady if that suits. Are you ready now?"

She'd never be ready for this, Eile thought. She was strung up tight enough to snap at the least touch. "Mm," she managed.

"By the way, that dog you asked about is still here. Hanging about the kitchen door making a nuisance of itself."

"And Faolan?"

"I can't tell you about him. You could ask the lady. Not straight out; later, when you've answered her questions. Remember what I told you."

"I'm not an infant." Eile made herself take a deep breath. If she wasn't careful she might cry, or make a bolt for it, or do something else that was all wrong. "My mother did teach me good manners." It was true, though there hadn't been much call for them in Dalach's house, where threats and blows were the main currency.

They went in. This house was full of huge chambers, and this one was the biggest Eile had seen so far. The walls were hung with tapestries of men on horseback hunting deer and wolves. The hearth was broad, fashioned of a greenish-colored stone, with a warm fire glowing; these people clearly didn't see the need to conserve their wood supply. A little dog ran toward them, yapping. Saraid shrank back against Eile's skirts, then, as the creature came closer and the shrill greeting turned to tail-wagging and snuffling, the child reached down a hand to touch its head.

At the far end of the big room a woman sat in a tall chair. The light from a western window shone on her face, making it an oval of stark white against the dark hangings on the wall behind her. Armed guards stood on either side of her chair. The lady remained utterly still and completely silent as the housekeeper led Eile and Saraid, with the little dog prancing around their feet, all the way along the flagstoned floor to stand before the thronelike seat.

Maeve bobbed a sketchy curtsy. Eile copied her, trying to summon up the proper attitude of respect owed to highborn, powerful folk and failing utterly. Instead, fear and resentment churned within her. These people had been kind enough to her. But they'd hurt Faolan and taken him away. Now this lady was looking at her and Saraid as if they were rats in her kitchen or beetles under her mattress.

"My lady," Maeve's voice was apologetic, "this is the young woman, Aoife. The child is her daughter. She wouldn't let me take her away."

Blue eyes bored through Eile; passed briefly over Saraid, who had crouched down to pat the dog. The Widow was young. Eile judged her to be less than thirty, though the veil that covered her head and neck, concealing her hair, made it difficult to tell. Her features were neat and small, her mouth hard, her brows artfully shaped. The eyes gave away nothing at all, save that this woman knew she was in control. It was clear she took that as her right. *Don't get angry,* Eile warned herself, but it was already too late.

"Take the child over by the fire," the Widow ordered

Maeve. "Keep her occupied. Step up closer, girl. That's better. You understand why you're here?"

Eile met the challenging eyes full on. A large part of finding courage was not letting your fear show. What to say? How to do this? They knew who she was; of course they'd believe those men at the bridge, not a—what was it they had called her—a piece of roadside rubbish? On the other hand, perhaps Faolan had already told them his lie, and by contradicting it she'd get all of them in more trouble.

"No, my lady. We were on our way to Fiddler's Crossing when your people attacked my friend and took him captive. What have you done with him? Where is he?"

A calculating look entered the well-guarded eyes; the lips tightened. Eile glanced over her shoulder. By the hearth, Saraid was sitting on the floor playing with the little dog, while the housekeeper had seated herself on a bench nearby.

"Maeve!" the Widow called. "I asked you to explain the situation to this young woman."

"I did, my lady."

The dark eyes returned to Eile, assessing. "You are fond of risks?" the Widow asked.

"No, my lady. I take them when I have to."

"You should learn to guard your tongue more skillfully. Do you know who I am?"

"You're a landholder; the widow of a great chieftain. You have a grand house, men-at-arms, servants. You have power. That's all I know. Power over folk like him and me."

There was a brief silence. Then the lady said, "What are you implying, exactly? Is that what you admire, power? Is it what you would wish for yourself?"

No time to weigh her answer, to calculate what might serve best. "Not power over other folk, to put them in fear, to twist and turn them. Only enough power so I can protect her properly." Eile glanced toward the fire. "My daughter."

"Who did you say you were?" The question came smoothly, like an expertly cast line.

"I didn't, my lady. My name's Aoife."

"Maeve tells me someone's abused you, Aoife. She says your body bears a record of many beatings, not to speak of the fact that you seem half starved. On the other hand your child, though thin, has evidently been well looked after. Are you sure you've told the truth? Is she really yours? She isn't perhaps the offspring of a cruel mistress, whom you stole for reasons of your own? This doesn't add up, Aoife. I know Maeve's told you what you've been accused of. Unless you're half-witted, and I can see that's not so, you must surely realize how serious this matter is. Telling lies cannot aid your cause. If you have been ill-treated, you should give me the details. If you have taken a man's life, you must confess that also. Account for yourself, and make it the truth! Lies do not win power; that path is sure to see you lose your child. Don't waste what strength you have in fighting me, young woman. Use it to make your case."

"I'm not in a court of law now," Eile said, lifting her chin. "Give me one reason why I should trust you." She heard Maeve's gasp of horror behind her. Saraid was murmuring to the dog.

The Widow sighed, leaning back in her grand chair. "Your existence up till now has not given you great cause to trust, I imagine," she said levelly. "In fact, I do not require trust from you, only the truth. Folk do not customarily demand that I prove my goodwill. I stand as chieftain of this region in my late husband's stead. I have the power to decide your future. You will be fairly treated if you are honest, Aoife. I know that is hard to believe, but it is true, in my territories at least. If you conduct your business with the attitude of a wildcat shut up in a little cage, all snarls and biting, you make it hard for folk to help you."

"He helped us. Faolan. All he got for it was a beating. You still say I should trust you? Show me that he's all right and I'll answer all the questions you want." Eile was pleased with her tone. It sounded bold and challenging; the lady could not know how she was quaking inside.

"Maeve," said the Widow, "take the child away."

"No!" They could not do this, it wasn't fair, she must stop them. "Leave her alone!" As Eile spoke, one of the guards moved down to position himself beside her, spear across to block her path. Beyond that barrier she saw the housekeeper take Saraid's hand and lead her toward the doorway. The child looked back, big eyes anxious, but kept her silence. The little dog pattered after them. "You can't take her!" Gods, it was happening, what she feared most. Saraid would vanish out that door and she'd never see her daughter again.

"You think not?" the Widow said. "It's as easy as one, two, three. Don't look like that, girl, we treat children kindly here. Indeed, I think your daughter, if such she is, may be better off at Blackthorn Rise, growing up among the children of my household and, in time, being trained in skills that will provide her with a home and a living, than wandering the byways with her mother, never more than half a step from trouble."

Eile made a dash for the doorway. Before she had taken three steps the guard had dropped the spear and grabbed her around the arms, halting her flight. She tried to fight him, but he simply held on as she struggled and kicked, and the Widow watched in impassive silence. "It's not fair!" Eile shouted. "She's only three! She won't understand! What have we ever done to you?"

After a time it became apparent that all her efforts would change nothing. The second guard had stationed himself in front of the door, and there was no other apparent exit. Saraid was gone.

The Widow waited. Eile drew a sobbing breath, then said, "Tell your henchman here to let go. I need to wipe my nose. Then ask your poxy questions. She'd better not be harmed or—"

"Enough!" said the Widow. "No threats. Seamus, let her go. Fetch a stool; the girl needs to sit down. And some water. Compose yourself, Aoife. Or would that be Eile, by any chance?"

Eile wiped her nose on the sleeve of her borrowed shirt and stiffened her back. "How much do you know already?" she asked.

"I want you to tell me all of it. Who is the child's father?"

Eile flinched. Where had this question come from? "I'm not saying that. I'll tell about what happened. The other doesn't matter. Saraid's mine. Her father's dead."

"I see. And what about your father and mother? Where are they? What are their names?"

"Do you think I'd be here like this if they were still alive?"

"Their names?"

"Deord. Saraid. My daughter's named for her, but my mother never knew I had a child." No tears. She had to get this right from now on, win Saraid back, and then, at the first opportunity, they'd be out of this cursed place. How dare this woman play games with little children as the pieces?

"What was your father's trade, Eile?"

"He was a mariner. A traveler." That barely touched it: the epic adventures, the wondrous tales. The shell of a man that came home from Breakstone. It did not encompass the love, the hope, the shattering of her fragile dream that everything could one day be all right again.

"Sit down," the Widow said as the guard set a stool beside Eile. "Now give me a simple, truthful account of the last few days."

Eile drew a deep breath. "I stabbed my aunt's husband in the heart," she said. "He was . . . hurting me. When I knew Father wasn't coming home, I had to do it. For her; for Saraid. Then we ran away. If you want me to say I'm sorry, I can't; not if you expect the truth."

The Widow nodded, features composed. "When you knew your father wasn't coming home?"

"I thought he'd come back someday. I hoped he would.

But he died. He never did come." Eile paused to get her voice under better control. "That's all I have to tell. Let Saraid come back in. She's not used to strangers."

"The man who was with you; the one you call Faolan. He said you were his wife, and the child his daughter. Was that a lie?"

"He was trying to protect us. To get us safely away."

"Why would this man lie for a girl who had just murdered her kinsman? Is he well known to you?"

"My father's friend. At least, that's what he said. I only met him two days ago." A curious feeling was coming over Eile as she watched the woman's face: the feeling that the Widow was not interested in her or Saraid at all. The growing conviction that the one she'd been wanting to know about all along was Faolan. There was something wrong here. Eile could see it in the Widow's eyes when she spoke his name. He was in danger.

"Answer the question!" the Widow rapped out. "Why would he lie for you? What promise did he extract from you in return?"

Eile stared at her, bemused. "Promise? I don't know what you mean."

"Don't be disingenuous, girl. The fellow's a stranger to you; he could be anyone. You have no money, no resources; you have only one thing a man's likely to want, and evidently you're not reluctant to offer that. Why else would this Faolan take up with you?"

Eile felt the blood rush to her cheeks, then as swiftly ebb. It didn't seem to matter that insults were more or less her daily bread; that did not make them any the less hurtful. "Think what you like," she said, quite unable to summon a pretense of civility.

"What I think is that you've been ill-treated and that it's very fortunate you now find yourself at Blackthorn Rise, where we can provide shelter for you and your child. If we'd handed you over to those fellows from Cloud Hill you'd have had far rougher handling, I assure you. How old are you, Eile?"

"Sixteen. And, before you ask, my daughter's three, and no, I didn't have her because I was wanton, but because a man forced me. If I'd had a knife and a little more courage back then, I'd have spared myself four years of bruises and worse. And if I had to kill him all over again I wouldn't hesitate."

"And Faolan?"

"I told you. He's my father's friend. He didn't ask me for anything. He brought breakfast, and he left me his knife."

"And that was the best gift you ever had," said the Widow with a strange little smile.

Eile did not answer. This was an odd game indeed.

"I'll need more," the Widow said. "More details; more of your background. But not now. Go to your daughter. My guess is that she'll be in the kitchen with a lot of folk fussing over her. She's a pretty little thing. It takes a lot to bring out Maeve's motherly streak. Go on, now."

"I—I need to know about Faolan. Where is he? Why did you let them beat him and tie him up? He had no part in what I did. He's just a traveler."

"Didn't you say it was his knife that struck the fatal blow?"

"He didn't know what I was going to use it for. I want to see him."

"He's not here, Eile. Far from proving a friend, it seems he couldn't wait to see the back of you. Such men have no time for women and children. Your Faolan moved on today, while you were sleeping."

The flat statement hit her like a fist. This could not be true, surely. "But—" Eile faltered, "you arrested him, your men attacked him, why would you just let him go?"

"I made a mistake. After all, he was not the man I was looking for. We offered to wake you; he said not, he'd be best on his own."

Eile was shocked into silence. She had imagined all manner of terrible fates for Faolan, but not this. Not the familiar old pattern. "I can't believe it." The words were a forlorn whisper. She despised her weakness; this should not matter at all.

"It's what men do," the Widow said. "They just pack up and go when it suits them. Forget Faolan. He's not worth your tears."

"What tears?" Eile scrubbed a furious hand across her cheeks. Hearing her own theory about men from this lady's lips only seemed to make things worse. Foolishly, she had begun to believe that this man might be different.

"You're dismissed." The Widow rose to her feet; she was not very tall. "Find your daughter, reassure yourself that she is safe and so are you. We will shelter you and deal with the law on your behalf. You'd be surprised what can be achieved by a word or two in the right ear."

IT TOOK MANY days to reach Pitnochie, far more than it should have done. Broichan walked in rain, in sleet, in snow; his sandals splashed through streams and sank into mud, slipped on wet stones and slid in gravel. The cloak was less than adequate as protection from the weather, and he would not squander his strength in magic merely for the purpose of keeping dry. Back at White Hill, he had performed such small feats only in order to teach Derelei. Out here in the forest there was no tiny apprentice to crouch by his side, sharing a wondrous journey of discovery. Derelei had been left behind, and Broichan knew a piece of his own heart had been left in the child's keeping. More than aching limbs or uneasy belly, that wound pained him.

Each night he prayed. *You said I must open my heart to love. I did that long ago. Bridei is as dear to me as a son; his child also. Your meaning is obscure to me.* And if this last was not quite true, he refused to acknowledge it, even to himself.

Sometimes he sensed responses to his questions, but more often the gods were silent, and this he understood.

It was a druid's way to learn by seeking his own answers; a good teacher provided only the questions, and the means to discover what answers might exist. For a long time, most of his life, Broichan had studied the druidic lore and the craft of magic, the stars and the elements, the patterns of the seasons, the mysteries of the plant and animal kingdoms. As king's druid, he had also been intricately involved in matters political; he had been power broker and peace maker, tactician and arbiter. It had been he who had labored, over fifteen years, to prepare Bridei for the throne of Fortriu. Bridei: the perfect king. Broichan had seen the first part of his long dream come to fruition. He'd been right about Bridei. His solemn little fosterling had grown up to be the finest leader of men any kingdom could wish for.

Unfortunately, Broichan had also been right about Tuala. He'd known from the first that she was trouble. She'd been the unpredictable element, the one factor that could spoil his plan. He had tried to remove her from her position of influence, but by then she had already worked her Otherworldly charms upon his foster son, and it had been too late. Bridei had refused to give her up. He had made her the price of agreeing to be king.

It had been a bitter defeat, for all the joy of seeing his protégé crowned and Fortriu victorious over Dalriada a mere five years later. Those five years had seen a shift in the druid's dealings with Bridei's wife. He accepted, now, that she loved her husband and wanted only the best for him. Her intentions were all good. He recognized that she loved her child, as indeed did Broichan himself. They had exchanged gestures of wary trust. There was respect between them now; respect and understanding. Or rather, there had been. Then she had shared her vision, and he had been struck by doubt all over again. Why do it? Why meddle? What was it she wanted from him?

At length Broichan reached the place where, looking down from the fringe of the forest, he could see the broad valley of Pitnochie below him, the bare-limbed birches, the dark bones of the oaks and, half screened by them, the long stone house with smoke rising lazily from its hearth fires. The rain had cleared and the day was bright and cold. The druid stood awhile watching, and there was nothing in his body but a longing to be warm and dry, and nothing in his head but, *Home. I'm home.*

He could see folk about, his own folk: Fidich and his sons moving sheep into the barn, with dogs pacing the back of the flock, all bunched muscle and intent eyes; Brenna hanging washing on a line between bushes; a child squatting to stroke a cat. He imagined others inside his house: Mara grim and capable as ever, Ferat clattering things in the kitchen. There was a new cottage taking shape beside the one where Fidich and Brenna lived with their children. That would be Cinioch's. Cinioch, a man of middle years who had never been other than a warrior by occupation, had requested permission to marry and turn his energies to farming. Pitnochie had seen heavy losses in last autumn's conflict. Cinioch's closest friend had been among the fallen. It was good for these survivors to come home. That was what Bridei wanted for all of them: a season of peace.

With that sentiment Broichan had been surprised to find himself entirely in agreement. He had not let folk know that, of course; it was essential that he be seen to show strength at all times. His position as king's druid made him pivotal in the affairs of Fortriu, for all Bridei was a man who made his own decisions. People would expect Broichan to want the advantage pressed hard; they'd anticipate his advising the king to push borders farther south or to challenge Circinn openly on the issue of Christian missionaries preaching the new faith in that land. But something had changed in the druid while his foster son was away at war. He knew, from the moment Bridei rode safely home with banners flying, that the young king needed time, that Fortriu needed time before its sons were sent again to the slaughter. There had been grievous losses. Victory did not change that. And Bridei, for all the near-godly status bestowed by kingship, was only flesh and blood. He must have time to make a settled land, to build his alliances. He must have time to see his children grow. There were still territories to be won, barriers to be pushed back. But not yet. For now, for the next few years, winning Dalriada was enough.

If his own motives for wishing this were selfish, Broichan thought, if his personal affection for Bridei weighed as much in the balance as the desire to see Fortriu's king fulfill his destiny, so be it. Peace was good for the Priteni. His own folk at Pitnochie, down the hill there, had lost two and seen a third severely wounded. Enough. The gods were surely satisfied, at least for now. Let there be no more untimely deaths.

For a moment, the druid wondered if he was growing old, for he could remember a time, not so long ago, when his burning ambition to see the lands of the Priteni united in adherence to the ancient gods was so strong he would not have brooked any delay; he would have urged Bridei to drive ahead, expanding his borders and punishing those who brought new gods and new ways. Bridei could do it; last autumn's move on Dalriada had proven that. This king was both visionary and man of power. In time, it would happen. Something had changed in Broichan; he knew he was prepared to wait. He could be patient, as the rocks and trees are patient, knowing all things come in their right time.

He gripped his staff and began his walk down the hill. He was pleased to observe that Uven, whom he'd placed in charge of security here, had guards on duty where fields met forest. Go a little farther, and someone would look across and see him; they'd call, and he'd raise a hand in greeting, and before long he could be in his own house again and let his own folk tend to him.

Of course, Ana and Drustan were there. That was a little awkward. Never mind; Mara would fit them all in somehow. And this would provide him an opportunity to talk at length with Drustan, whose unusual gifts interested him. The Caitt chieftain's mastery of shapeshifting went far beyond that of the most adept druid. There would be plenty to keep them occupied until . . . until . . .

Broichan halted. His breath caught in his throat. Before his eyes, the landscape was changing, as if a veil were being drawn across it. The plume of smoke dissipated and vanished. The tiny figures of man and woman, the moving shapes of dog, sheep, horse winked out like doused candles. Snowdrifts lay suddenly around house and barn, as high as a man's shoulder. The barn doors, which had stood open to admit the flock of privileged sheep as Fidich herded them to their winter quarters, were now shut and bolted. Strangest of all, where the bare limbs of birch and oak had formed a sheltering network around the stone and thatch of Broichan's dwelling, now stood a thicket of bristling thorn, a menacing barrier to any traveler who dared approach. Shade hung over the valley. Nothing stirred.

He felt defenseless. He felt like a little child whose prize has been snatched from his hands. It was more than uncomfortable. He could in no way summon the self-control proper to a king's druid. *Why?* he asked without a sound, but the answer was already in his mind. He saw another day, long ago: the day when Tuala, on the eve of her fourteenth birthday, had reached this very spot after a desperate, solitary journey through the snow in search of shelter; a day on which he, a figure of authority, the man responsible for her upbringing, had cast a spell to keep her from reaching home. Pitnochie had stood open that day, its fires burning, its folk busy preparing the Midwinter feast. They could have offered her shelter; they could have received her. But Broichan, fearing her influence on his foster son at the critical time of the election, had used his craft to disguise the house. He had set bars on doors and drifts against walls; he had used a charm of glamour to conceal his folk from her eyes, and to make the place appear empty of life. So Tuala had turned away. She had made her lonely walk to the Vale of the Fallen. That night she had almost died, and it had not been Broichan who had saved her. He had never told a living soul what he had done. And if Tuala had been right in her interpretation of the vision . . .

Good. A voice spoke from behind him. He recognized its nature, and did not turn. *This is the first step.*

His bones ached for home. The longing tugged at his heart and weakened his limbs. He could not give in to it. He would not beg.

Come, said the voice. It was melodious and deep. He thought it was a woman's, but this was no earthly woman. *You know what you must do.*

He did know. It was clear. He must finish Tuala's journey; go to the lonely vale and seek his answers in the seer's pool, the Dark Mirror. Seek the forgiveness of the goddess and, if the Shining One could not pardon his insult to her Midwinter child, could not overlook his refusal to recognize his own, he did not know what he could do.

Broichan turned away from the valley and began to climb again, under the shelter of the forest fringe. A figure moved with him, a form cloaked and hooded, a shadowy outline. *Walk,* the voice said. *With every step, remember. Remember your pride. Remember your ambition. Remember your cruelty.*

"All I have done," Broichan said, "was done for love of the Shining One and of the Flamekeeper. I have been obedient. All my life I have followed the path of the gods and respected their laws."

Look in your heart, whispered the voice. *Examine the past. Turn the sharp eye of scholarship on your own actions. Apply your own oft-stated dictum: there is learning in everything. Yes, even in the recognition that you have failed your own daughter. For how can you profess*

*obedience to the gods' will when you proved unable to
recognize their most precious gift?*

჻

THEY'D GIVEN FAOLAN two regular guards, one for day,
one for night. He didn't see them much. They brought
food and water, took away his bucket and returned it
sluiced. Neither was prepared to talk. Neither would tell
him how long he'd have to wait, or what exactly it was he
was waiting for. The big man, the one from that first day,
had not come back. Faolan regretted that, for it had
seemed to him there was something there he might work
on, some spark of fellow feeling. These two were just
plain dull.

He hid his silver before anyone decided to take his
clothes. He hid his loop of wire and his very small dagger, his spiked iron ball and his vial of poison. The other
things, including sword, knife, and gear for the road, had
all been taken away. He bore no written messages, nothing to identify him as a Priteni spy, a man who had
turned against his own. What he needed to do for Bridei,
the questions he must put concerning the influential
cleric, Colmcille, he carried in his head.

He was equipped to attempt an escape, but for now he
judged it unwise to do so. The only way would be to overpower one of the guards, to take the second man he'd been
told patrolled the hallway, then to fight whatever forces
stood between him and the outer wall of this Widow's
compound. He'd seen, coming in, that the place was heavily fortified and solidly manned. Echen had always kept it
that way, and it seemed his wife had not let standards slip.
In Faolan's estimation, his chances of getting clear did not
outweigh the very real possibility of dying within moments of leaving this room that had become his cell.

Besides, there was Eile. He was duty bound to survive
long enough to find her, whatever had happened, wherever
they had taken her. He had already broken his promise.

He must not do so again. It was odd, Faolan mused as he paced out the endless hours from sunup to sundown, or scratched the mark of yet another day on the stone wall of his prison, that his promise should matter so much. Last autumn had changed him. Deord, dying in his arms, had laid a load on him. Now, his own vow was strong in his mind: *I'll look after you until I know you're safe. I'll stay with you until you don't need me anymore.* Eile hadn't believed him, of course; her past had hardly prepared her to trust. He must find her and prove that those had not been empty words. He hoped it would not be too late.

Each day he expected a summons; each day none came, only the two guards with their bread and meat and watery soups, and the sounds of the household faint outside the high window. The little row of scratches on the wall became a tree, a grove, a small bare-limbed forest. Thirty, forty, forty-five. By all the powers, what was this? Did this Widow plan to send him crazy, not from torture or hardship, but through sheer boredom and frustration? Fifty, he thought. At fifty he would take action if she did not call him. Let it go too much longer and the winter would be over. If he delayed until then, the vital mission, Bridei's job in the north, could not be fulfilled in time. This Colm might act, and there would be nobody to warn the king of Fortriu. Fifty, then. He'd use the wire and take his chances with the guards.

ANA HAD NOT realized quite how sick she would be. She had planned to keep her news from everyone except Drustan until the shape of the child in her belly became obvious, but between the constant retching and the exhaustion that went with it, both the housekeeper, Mara, and the farmer's wife, Brenna, began plying her with cordials and herbal brews within the first turning of the moon.

"This won't last, my lady," Brenna assured her, wiping Ana's brow with a damp cloth. "By the time your belly starts to swell out, the sickness will have passed. I was just the same with my youngest."

Drustan was worried about the need to make the journey north in spring, and the risks to Ana and the unborn child in such a trip. Neither he nor Ana suggested she stay behind while he went on; they could not bear to be apart even for a day. But Drustan could not wait beyond the spring. Already, in his absence, unscrupulous chieftains might have tried to seize the territory left leaderless by the death of his brother last autumn. Bridei had sent a messenger on Drustan's behalf, laying formal claim to Briar Wood and stating his intention to set things right there. Another messenger had gone to Dreaming Glen, with the news that once his brother's business was settled, Drustan was coming home. But a whole winter was a long time. Anything could happen. As soon as he could go, he must.

"We could travel the other way," Ana suggested one day as they sat before the fire in the hall of Broichan's house, a game board on a little table between them. "Down the lakes by boat and through the pass by Five Sisters. Folk say that's far easier."

"It is still long and taxing," Drustan said, moving a tiny bone druid on the board. He refrained from mentioning that, if he went alone, he could use his other form and be there in a day or two. "It won't be safe for you to ride. We can't risk our child, Ana."

She imagined a time when he and his son or daughter might soar into the sky together; that would be both wondrous and terrifying, for a bird faced dangers a man scarcely thought of. If their children were gifted with Drustan's uncanny abilities, she thought she might spend a great part of their growing years paralyzed with fear. She did not tell Drustan this. "The baby won't be born until next autumn," she said. "By spring I should be able to ride safely, if we take care how we go. We should ask

Broichan to conduct our handfasting soon. Folk here will expect it now the child is coming."

"I wonder if he would come to Pitnochie to perform the ritual."

Ana glanced at him. She knew his reluctance to go to court; he was uncomfortable among folk. Long periods within walls made him restless and wild. That was something that would probably never change, but when they reached Dreaming Glen he would be safe in his own place again. In that remote spot, her children would be free to exercise whatever skills the Shining One might choose to grant them. "We can ask," Ana said.

But events overtook this plan. A day or two later a rider came in from White Hill, one of the men-at-arms from Bridei's court. His purpose was simple: to discover whether the king's druid had made his way to Pitnochie. For Broichan was gone from court, gone suddenly and without explanation. Drustan and Ana offered the fellow a good meal and a bed for the night. Then he went back to tell the king that, wherever Broichan had taken himself, it was not home to the house under the oaks.

THERE MUST BE something wrong with her, Eile thought. For so long, in Dalach's house, she had dreamed of a place where Saraid could be warm and well fed and safe; a place where there would be no more fear. That vision, that hope had kept her going through the dark times. Now they were at Blackthorn Rise and there was a proper bed, warm clothes, and two good meals a day. There was work to fill Eile's time, work that was easy compared with her duties at Anda's. There was no doubt they were safe, with guards constantly patrolling the walkways atop the walls and standing about the gates looking grim. She should be happy. Instead she was full of a restless discontent, a sense of wrongness that disturbed her sleep.

Eile recognized, with mixed feelings, that the dream of warmth and safety had always included a cozy little house on a hill, with a garden full of herbs and vegetables. It did not belong in a highborn lady's grand compound swarming with servants. The place of her vision was nobody's but theirs: hers and Saraid's. It was her childhood home made anew, complete with a small hearth fire and a striped cat and a savory smell of bread baking. There, the sun was always shining. There, she was answerable to no one but herself.

Maeve was kind, of course; she didn't scold folk unless they deserved it, and as Eile always got her work done promptly, she rarely incurred the housekeeper's displeasure. The other serving women were different. Word had quickly got around about what Eile had done and why she was at Blackthorn Rise, and their attitude to her was at once wary and contemptuous. Maybe they thought she'd be all too ready to stick a knife into anyone she didn't fancy. She tended to get jobs like washing, with nothing sharp involved. That suited Eile fine. The feel of a knife in her hand would bring it all back. Think too much about what she'd done, and about the years that came before, and she'd be curled up in a little ball in a corner and no use to anyone.

So, it was all right here, on one level. But she was worried about Saraid. The child would crouch nearby watching as Eile worked, or she'd wander around the edges of the courtyard like a little shadow with the gray dog from Cloud Hill following after her. Occasionally the Widow's terrier would come out with a ball in its mouth and Saraid would play a game of fetch with the creature. Sometimes the Widow's sons, sturdy boys of eight or nine, would come out, too, and Saraid would slip away silently, pretending she was invisible.

The daughter of a serving girl didn't play with a chieftain's sons, that was understood. Besides, these boys were intimidating with their forthright manner. Big for their age, they had an air of privilege, as if they owned the place and everyone in it. Eile had heard them giving orders to Maeve and Orlagh and the others, and had itched to deliver a few sharp words herself. Maybe the Widow was wealthy and powerful, but it was clear she didn't know the first thing about raising children. The elder one, Fionn, would probably grow up just like his father, what was his name, Echen? The Widow's husband had done something terrible to Faolan's family; he'd been a cruel man. This lad had the same kind of disregard for people. Eile tried to stay out of his way.

She'd kept a count of the days since they arrived here. She scratched them on a stone out by the clothesline, with an iron nail she had found. It was a long time. The feast of Midwinter was over. Here in the Widow's house she had witnessed it with amazement: so much food, so much mead and ale, so many folk behaving the way Dalach did when he'd been drinking, as if all the rules in the world had been swept away. That night Eile had kept the rusty nail under her pillow, for lack of a better weapon, and avoided being where any of the men might corner her alone. Some of the other maidservants did not sleep on their own pallets that night, and most of the household yawned its way through the next day. Eile wrapped up the best part of her festive supper in a cloth and stored it in the box she'd been given for her meager possessions. Old habits were hard to break; she would never get used to waste.

Now Midwinter was well past, and the record of days stood at almost fifty. She made Saraid count them, then collect pebbles to match. As she heaved the wet sheets over the line, fearing rain would come before supper-time, she tried to make the learning into a game. "Ten white ones, ten black ones, ten gray, and ten brown. Then six more, Saraid, any colors you like. How many does that make?"

Saraid was engrossed in selecting her stones; Sorry sat propped against the pole that held the washing line.

"Count them on your fingers. Ten, twenty . . ."

"Thirty, forty, and six more," Saraid said, holding up a white stone. "Little moon." She began to set her pebbles out in rows, the tip of her tongue between her teeth.

Eile's back was aching. The sheets were heavy, and the prop that ensured the hems did not drag in the dirt must be shifted across to hoist the line higher. She gritted her teeth and took hold of it with both hands.

Splat! A clod of mud landed in the center of a freshly washed sheet, clung a moment, then fell, leaving a dark loamy residue. Eile gasped with outrage and released the prop. The line sagged; the edges of both sheets dropped to the muddy ground. As she cursed, another lump of mud sailed through the air to strike Saraid on the cheek, hard enough to knock the crouching child over. Saraid lay immobile a moment, hands to her face, then scrambled to her feet and bolted toward her mother. She made no sound, but Eile saw the look in her eyes and, all at once, muddy sheets were the least of her concerns.

She'd learned to be quick, over the years. A dive into the bushes and she had Fionn by the right arm and his younger brother Fergus by the left.

"Let me go!" shrieked the scion of Blackthorn Rise, surely loud enough to bring an army of folk running. "How dare you touch me, you filthy slut! My mother will have you whipped! Let go at once!"

Eile hung on grimly.

"I didn't do anything!" screamed Fergus. "It was him that did it! It's not fair!"

Saraid had retreated to the shelter of the bushes as the two boys struggled and kicked and shouted in Eile's grip.

"Try that again and you'll really be sorry!" Eile's voice cut through both the children's. "Now find something better to do with your time than picking on hard-working people and scaring little children!"

"Take your filthy hands off me!" shouted Fionn, hitting her arm with his free hand. "You're a whore and a killer, and she's an idiot! She can't even talk properly." He made a ferocious face at Saraid.

Fergus was crying. Eile let him go, and he bolted. She grasped hold of Fionn's shoulders, holding him at arm's length. "Maybe you think calling people names is funny," she said. "Let me tell you something. I don't care who your mother is. I don't care how much of a little lord you think you are. Lay a hand on my daughter again and I'll thrash you. I mean it."

The boy spat in her face. She felt the spittle running down her cheek, and a moment later she slapped him, hard enough to leave a red mark on his face. Folk would be coming; if the indignant Fergus didn't fetch them, the noise surely would. "You only get one warning," she hissed. "I'll do it, believe me." Then she let him go. Bolder than his brother, or more sure of his ground, he stood there glaring, hands on hips.

Someone shouted. Not folk coming to investigate the hubbub; a voice from somewhere beyond the drying green, beyond the vegetable garden and washing area, over on the far side by the men's quarters. Someone had called her name. She held her breath, straining to hear over a new sound of approaching footsteps from the other direction, accompanied by Fergus's dramatic sobs. If the man called again, she did not hear him. Had she imagined it? She didn't think so, and her heart went cold. She could have sworn the voice was Faolan's. The welcoming house, the safe haven had been built on a lie.

A high-pitched scream pierced her skull, and she whirled around. The boy had moved to the clothesline. He was bent over with Sorry's woolen hair in one hand and her rudimentary feet pinned beneath his boot. His free hand held a knife; he was sawing at the doll's neck. At Saraid's shriek, Fionn gave a little cold smile; in the time it took Eile to stride over to him, he had severed the small head and dropped it in the mud. His boot heel ground down.

Somehow, Saraid was there before her mother, reaching, grasping, small hands wrenching at the boy's leg. Fionn kicked out; Saraid clung on grimly and used her teeth. As the figures of two maidservants and a guard appeared, with the weeping Fergus between them, Fionn gave a yelp of pain and fell to his knees, clutching his thigh. Saraid grabbed her prize and, hiccupping in distress, buried her muddy face in her mother's apron.

"She bit me!" Fionn's finger pointed accusingly at Saraid. "The little savage bit me! And the whore struck me in the face! Tell my mother! Have them punished! Shut up, Fergus, stop being such a baby!"

"He threw mud at my daughter and destroyed her doll. He spat at me. I don't care whose son he is, he's the one who deserves punishment—" But nobody was listening to Eile. Fionn, busily talking, was leading the guard away, righteous purpose in every corner of his nine-year-old being.

"You're a fool," said one of the maidservants, eyeing Eile sideways. "You don't cross Master Fionn, not unless you want a good beating. His mother's convinced the sun shines out of him."

"Best get those sheets back on the boil," said the other. "I reckon you've got just enough time to wash them again before she hears the story and sends for you. Watch that child of yours. Biting, eh? Little wild thing. I don't know why the lady ever took the two of you in."

The first maid whispered something and the two of them giggled. Then they were gone. Eile knelt down. "Saraid?"

The child was shaking with sobs; she would not take her face out of the apron.

"Saraid, listen to me. It will be all right. I won't let anyone hurt you again."

Words between the sobs, the tone full of woe. "Sorry's dead."

Eile's heart turned over. "No, she isn't." She wrapped her arms around the weeping child. "I can clean her up and stitch her back together. She won't be exactly the same. She'll have . . . honorable wounds. Saraid, you mustn't bite people. It hurts them." She wondered what

she would say if the child pointed out that Eile had hit
Fionn, and that hitting people hurt them, too. But Saraid
put her head against Eile's shoulder, pressed the two
parts of the muddy plaything against her chest, and said
nothing at all.

SOME TIME LATER, Eile stood before the Widow in her
great room, with Maeve silent by her side. Saraid had
cried herself to sleep and, reluctantly, Eile had left her in
the bedchamber.

"My son will be chieftain here one day," the Widow
was saying. "What he may or may not have said or done
is immaterial. You struck him. Your child sank her teeth
into his leg; I saw the mark she made. Such acts of violence against his person cannot be tolerated."

Eile had given the most honest accounting of events
she could, and the lady's response startled her. She had
expected better. What she had done today was, in her
view, entirely justified. "My lady," she protested, "your
son insulted me. He ruined my morning's work. He destroyed something Saraid loved—"

"Enough." There was not the slightest spark of compassion in the Widow's eyes. "We spoke of power once,
young woman. It's plain to me that although you crave it,
you do not understand its nature. Power bestows privilege. It bestows the right to make decisions. I learned
that lesson early; I was far younger than you. Tell me,
does it not concern you that your child is acquiring bad
habits from her mother? A bite one day, a knife in the
heart the next?"

Eile was outraged. The fact that there was a grain of
truth in this statement did not diminish its hurtfulness.
"She retaliated; defended her own. That's only natural."

"Her own? Oh, you mean the doll." The lady gave a
mirthless laugh. "Your daughter's better off without it. A
filthy old rag, was the way my son described it."

Eile clenched her fists. "Tell me," she said, "does it not concern you that your son may be growing up just like his father?"

Maeve sucked in her breath. The Widow rose to her feet. Her features were as well governed as ever, but something dangerous had stirred in her eyes.

"I had thought we might make something of you, Eile," she said in ominously quiet tones. "I sheltered you out of a certain fellow feeling; your circumstances were pitiable, and your act of violence, while ill-considered, could be seen as self-defense or even as just vengeance for the wrong your uncle did you. But you've disappointed me today. You seem to imagine I can allow an assault on the future chieftain of Blackthorn Rise to go unpunished. My power is absolute here. It remains thus because of the steps I take to maintain discipline within my household and within my territories. Maeve, the girl is to have a whipping. Ten strokes will suffice. And three for the child. I'll expect your report in the morning."

"No!" Eile threw herself forward, not sure what she intended but desperate to make this woman hear her. Maeve's strong hands restrained her as the Widow departed the hall, back straight, head high, a somber figure in her elegant dark gown. "No!" Eile screamed again. "Not Saraid, you can't—" The lady was gone, and her guards with her. "Let me go! Maeve, let go!" Eile fought, twisting and kicking.

"Shh!" Maeve's voice was almost inaudible. "Shh, now, lass. Stop fighting and listen to me, will you? We don't have much time."

Eile's heart was pounding, her palms were sweaty, her skin crawled with terror. A whipping. Saraid. They couldn't, they just couldn't. She'd die before she let them touch her daughter.

"Eile! Listen!"

Through her terror, she registered Maeve's expression; she felt the restraining grip on her wrists change to a supporting arm around the shoulder.

"Pack up your things during supper," the housekeeper whispered in her ear. "Don't let anyone see you doing it. Bring the child to my quarters. Be angry; be afraid. Let everyone think I'm going to go through with this."

"You . . . you won't hurt her?"

Maeve's jaw tightened. "I've disciplined a wayward maid or two in the past. The lady's testing me; testing my loyalty. Well, she's got it wrong this time. That little wretch Fionn . . ."

"But she'll know. Everyone will. You'll get in trouble."

"You'll have to go away, lass. You're right, she will know, and if you stay here she'll get someone else to carry out her whipping. Once you're outside the walls, you and Saraid, you'll be on your own. I can get you out, give you a few coppers and a bite of food for your journey, but that's all. Go now," in the face of Eile's whispered thank-you. "Make it convincing. After supper I'll show you a way out. Good thing the moon's full. You'll need to cover as much ground as you can before morning. She'll send men after you. She doesn't forget easily."

"Maeve?"

"What?"

"Faolan. You know, the man who was with me. I thought I heard him today. Surely she can't still have him locked up, after all this time?"

"I've some advice for you. You're in deep enough trouble already; don't go out of your way to make it worse. That's a dark story, him and her, and folk who know what's good for them stay well out of it. Now go, before someone hears us."

BY NIGHT, EILE stood inside an unobtrusive doorway cut in the stone wall, a bundle on her back. Saraid, warmly cloaked, was clutching a little bag of her own, a receptacle Maeve had given her to hold the two parts of Sorry, for there had been scant opportunity for sewing.

The gray dog had gone out ahead of them and was sniffing about in the bushes. A mist hung low. It would obscure their way. At the same time it would help conceal their flight.

"You're a good girl," Maeve said soberly. "If I had a daughter, I wouldn't mind if you were her. Take care, now. Those fellows from Cloud Hill will be after you again once she tells them you're gone."

"But—"

"She never called in the brithem," Maeve said. "Never did the formal process. That means once you're out of her protection, you're still accountable for the killing, under the law. You'd best run as far away as you can."

Eile nodded, knowing that if there were any chance the Widow had lied about Faolan, running away was not an option until Eile had ensured he was all right. This was not something she could explain to Maeve. "Thank you," she said. "If you were my mother, I'd tell you to move away from here and find someone else to work for."

Maeve sighed. "I've been with her a long time," she said. "Since before she wed Echen. She's got her reasons for being the way she is. I couldn't leave her now. All folk need love, Eile. Even the ones that don't seem to want it. Off you go, then. Good-bye, poppet." She bent to kiss Saraid's cheek, and Eile thought she saw the glint of tears in the housekeeper's eyes. Then the door swung to behind them, and they were on their own again.

Eile crouched to whisper. "It's an adventure, Squirrel. In the dark, with only the moon to light our way. We're going to be as quiet as mice. Better take my hand; it might be a long walk. We're going to Fiddler's Crossing."

6

ON THE FIFTIETH day, in the morning, the big guard came and let Faolan out with his ankles hobbled, so the best gait he could achieve was an old man's shuffle. They searched him first, and he was glad he had not yet begun to put his escape plan into action, since its initial step would have been to take his smallest knife out of its concealment in his cell.

"Where are we going?" he asked, and heard the hoarse croaking of his voice, as rough-edged as a weapon left too long idle.

"The lady sent for you."

"I see." Faolan was struggling to keep up with the other man's walking pace. He had done his best to maintain his body's fitness during the long, empty days, but the chamber where he had been confined was not spacious, and these leg restraints did nothing to help. It came to him that only someone familiar with his life after he left his homeland would think it necessary to curb him thus. In the old days here in Laigin, he had been young and harmless, a bard in training, a second son who never lifted a weapon until the day he was forced to slit his brother's throat. Even when Echen put him in Breakstone Hollow, it was not for fighting or intrigue or treachery, but for simple defiance. He'd refused to work for a man he despised. It was enough to earn him a season in that hellhole. It was only on quitting his home shore that the young bard had begun to make his living with fists, weapons, and a newfound talent for duplicity.

There had been no music after the night Echen came to Fiddler's Crossing. Faolan had not touched a harp again until last summer, when circumstances had required him to play the part of a musician. How word could have reached Blackthorn Rise that the unobtrusive traveler at the bridge was a spy for Fortriu, he could not imagine. Surely, if folk here recognized him, it would not be for that, but for his family's dark tale. No doubt that had provided years of fodder for local storytellers; it was the reason why people spoke the name of Fiddler's Crossing in a special tone, a tone guaranteed to put folk off going there if they could avoid it. Echen had given the place its own special nightmare.

They halted outside a formidable oak door.

"What does she want?" Faolan ventured. "What am I supposed to have done?"

"I'm not the one you need to ask." The big guard glanced at him with a certain sympathy. "The Widow makes her own rules; often they're beyond folk like you or me." He rapped at the door, then opened it. "Go on, then."

The Widow was seated in state, her grand chair placed on a dais. She was a small woman, but the position of her seat was one of authority. It was necessary for Faolan to perform his ungainly shuffle down the full length of the spacious chamber, between armed guards, narrowing his eyes against the bright lamps that stood by the raised platform. He was dazzled; his cell had been a dim place even on winter's rare sunny days. After so long confined, the broad space and the light were unsettling. He schooled his features and came up to the high seat.

His vision was disturbed by the lamps, and the Widow sat behind them. All he could discern was the pale heart shape of her face, the dark swathing folds of her head scarf. He held himself still, waiting. Let her speak first. Let her tell him what in the name of mercy she was up to, and why, through the tiny window of his cell, he had heard Eile screaming out in the yard. Let her explain what she knew of him and then he would decide what to tell.

"Faolan," said the lady.

He gave a nod.

"Was it a long time to wait?"

She sounded young; young and chilly. He squinted and made out a pair of emotionless blue-gray eyes in the pale face.

"I cannot say, my lady. Until I know my misdemeanor, I cannot tell you if the penalty was appropriate." He strove to match her cool tone, but his voice let him down; he could not disguise the rough edge.

"Was?" Her tone was light. "Oh, I'm not finished with you yet, Faolan. That was just a taste. I can test your patience far more severely than that, and if I choose to, I will. I wonder what would be apt? A season? A year? Two, perhaps. You might be a little less facile in your comments after that."

Faolan did his best to maintain a steady gaze. "When I play games," he told her, "I prefer to know the rules in advance. It's so much fairer. What am I charged with? And what have you done with my companion, Aoife?"

"Companion. What a bland word. I thought you said she was your wife."

"I heard her calling out, not so long ago. She sounded distressed. I heard a child scream. If you are the lady known locally as the Widow, it is your responsibility to ensure folk you shelter within your walls are fairly treated."

"Twice you've spoken of fairness. I should have thought you, of all people, would have learned that life is essentially lacking in that quality. Life is full of inequities, of cruelty and grief and abandonment. It abounds in folk who turn their backs when they should hold out their hands to help. Fairness exists only in the minds of those who have lived solely in the shelter of some haven where folk cling to notions of ideals. There is no fairness. The only things that matter are survival and power. It amazes me that you have not learned this."

A curious feeling was coming over Faolan; the sensation of familiarity, as if he had met this arrogant woman before, in very different circumstances. He breathed deep; he blinked, trying to get his eyes to focus properly. "Do I know you?" he asked. "It seems you know something of me, though perhaps less than you imagine."

"I know you inside out," the Widow said, her voice small and cold. "I know you better than you know yourself. I'm the voice that is never silent; the one you hear in your dreams. I'm the nightmare that never goes away. Or maybe not. Maybe you did forget. Perhaps you put it all behind you and moved on to a new life, one in which your past could be reconstructed to be more pleasing, more palatable."

"I have no idea what you're talking about." He found himself trembling, and clenched his fists to force his body still. "Tell me where the girl is, and the child. They were under my protection. I'm concerned for their well-being."

"Answer a question. Why did you choose that name for her? Aoife?"

"It is her name."

"Don't lie to me! I know who the girl Eile is, and what she did. Why the name?"

"It was the first one that came to mind," he said lightly.

"For *her*?" He saw the Widow's brows lift in scorn. His eyes were working better now, and he could make out the straight, short nose, the guarded mouth, the delicate contours of the face. The tight, implacable jaw. She was familiar; her features teased at him, stirring old memory. "For that wretched little thing with her straggly hair and her stinking, abused body?" the lady went on. "You named her for a great beauty of the *daoine sidhe*? What kind of a man would do that?"

"A man who was once a bard," Faolan said. "Eile has her own kind of beauty. Her father was the same. They're a rare breed."

"Really? Well, she's gone now. You asked about some noise in the yard. Your rare beauty attacked my son, who is barely nine years old. The child marked him with her teeth. I ordered a beating. The two of them ran away rather than remain here within my walls and under my protection. The girl's not only violent, she's a fool."

"When? Where did she go?"

"Ah; a spark of feeling at last. I don't think I much care for that, Faolan. It disappoints me that you have become the kind of man who attaches himself to vulnerable young girls for no good reason. Why so concerned? Are you upset that your newly acquired property has escaped you? What's the matter, don't you fancy a cold bed? Don't look down your nose at me like that; you did say the girl was your wife. It doesn't take much imagination to guess what you expected in return for your offer of protection."

With an effort, Faolan swallowed his anger. "I traveled to Cloud Hill to bring Eile some news. Her father died in the autumn. I was not instrumental in what happened after I left that house. I seek only to establish that she is safe and well provided for. That is the very least I owe Deord."

"Oh, she'll be back at Cloud Hill by now," the Widow said casually. "She had charges to face. I can't protect her any longer; she hit my son."

"What is this? Why are you doing this? You know who I am, that's clear enough. Do you plan to carry on your husband's feud with my family even now? Will you pursue his mindless drive to punish us until we're all in our dotage? Why are you holding me prisoner? And how dare you beat Eile and expose her to that rabble from Cloud Hill? She's not much more than a child herself, and she's been badly hurt by that wretched uncle of hers. Imagine how she feels—"

He fell abruptly silent. The Widow had risen to her feet and stepped forward. The lamplight shone on her face, and Faolan's heart stopped. He waited to wake up, but the nightmare continued.

"Seamus, Conal," the Widow said, "I wish to interrogate this prisoner in private. Bind his hands, then leave us. Wait outside the door."

"My lady." The guards obliged, the big one coming up with rope to tie Faolan's wrists together behind his back. Briefly, Faolan considered putting up a fight, then abandoned the idea. What he needed were answers, not a beating and a prompt return to his lonely cell. Who knew how long this madwoman would leave him there next time?

"Very well, Faolan." The Widow stepped down from her dais and came to stand before him. She had to look up to meet his eyes. His breath caught in his throat; his heart hammered.

"You asked me how I think your Eile feels," she said. "I know exactly how she feels. Abandoned; disillusioned; betrayed. The poor wretch made the error of trusting you, based, I imagine, on your tale of being the father's friend. She expected rescue; she anticipated that you would be there when she needed you. I told her that was foolish. I told her men do that, make women trust them, then simply vanish when they can't cope with a challenge. I should have explained more clearly, since the girl isn't educated. Eile, I should have said, if you wait for that man to come and rescue you, you'll wait forever. You'll wait and wait, and every day you'll shed one less tear, and your heart will grow just a little harder, and when ten years have passed, give or take a little, you'll find there are no more tears to weep. You'll discover your heart has turned to flint. You'll realize there's no need to wait any longer, because you've stopped caring. I know it's the truth, Eile, I should have told her. I know because they did it to me: my father, and my brother."

Ten years had passed. Not Dáire, who would be over thirty by now; not Líobhan with her big brown eyes. His heart reeling, his head spinning, Faolan fought to guard his expression and failed. The Widow's small features grew pinched with strain; her eyes narrowed.

"Why did you come back?" she asked him. "All that time, all that endless time of waiting, and now you come, and the only gift you bring me is your contempt. If you can't manage a show of relief that I am, after all, alive and well, you might at least try to conceal your disgust."

The lights danced before his eyes. It was hard to draw breath. "You married him," he whispered, the flood of horror drowning his ability to choose his words, to soften the blow. "Echen. The man who destroyed our family. You married him. After he took you, after he . . ."

"I see you haven't been home yet." She began to pace, arms tightly folded, head down. The longer he watched her, the more he saw it: it was in the delicate hands, the shape of the brow, the way she held her head. It was Áine; Áine, his youngest sister, taken by Echen and his men on that terrible night. Áine, whom his father had believed beyond rescue.

"What do you know of the story?" she asked him.

A torrent of words fought to spill, and he choked them back. *I would have come for you, I wanted to, but Father made me flee Laigin. He ordered me to go away and not return. If I had known . . . I was only seventeen . . .* There was no point in saying this; it was ten years too late. His beloved little sister, his sweet, lovely Áine, had become a hard-faced, cruel autocrat. To his shame, he recognized that it had been easier to accept her death than this hideous reversal of what should be. Between them, all of them, it seemed they had turned her into another Echen.

"I don't know any of the story," he croaked. "I never went back. Your husband's kinsmen threw me into Breakstone Hollow. I escaped. I left my home shore. I came back only to bring Eile her news. But I was going to Fiddler's Crossing. I was taking her there. What . . . ?" Behind the word lay an unknown world of possibilities: their father and mother, their two sisters, their grandfather, all those who had survived that night. If the others had come out of it with wounds as deep as his own, with scars as ugly as Áine's, he did not think he wanted to know.

"Your eyes are so cold, Faolan," Áine said. "Your face is so harsh. You think I should have done as the girl Eile did, and knifed my assailant in the heart? You'd have felt better about the blood on your own hands, maybe, if I had shared it, even if it led to my own swift demise? You don't need to say it. You'd rather I was dead."

"I—"

"I don't want to hear your answer. You know, I never saw what you did that night. Echen told me later. He respected you for it, did you know that? Admired your capacity to carry out his order, even as he knew he'd succeeded in destroying you. I never saw our brother lying on the floor with the blood pumping from his throat. I only saw you and Father standing there staring; standing still while I was dragged away by strangers. Nobody coming after me. Nobody saying a word. You just let me go."

There was no possible comment to make. There was no point in telling her she had misremembered, though he knew he had screamed abuse; he recalled hurling himself after her, and a blow to the head turning it all to darkness. She had her own particular set of memories, and before them his heart trembled like grain under the thresher's flailing.

"The only one to show any compassion that night was the one you've dubbed the archenemy. Echen took pity on me. He liked me. So I kept my maidenhood and my life, and instead of using me and sharing me, he sent me away. I didn't know where I was going. I didn't know why. An escort took me to Echen's mother in Tirconnell. Two years I spent there, learning how to be a suitable wife for a chieftain of the Uí Néill. She made sure I learned quickly. She punished me if I made mistakes. I had never dreamed I could be so alone. Every night, for two years, I begged the gods to let you find me. Every night I dreamed of the day when you or Father would come for me. But you never did come."

"I thought you were dead. I was gone from this shore; far away."

"I came to rely on Echen's visits, more frequent as I grew older. He brought gifts: a pony, a gold ring, a little dog. He was kind to me. I even came to like his mother, once she thawed toward me. On my fourteenth birthday, Echen married me and we came back to Blackthorn Rise. I gave him a son within the year, another a year later. I had no need to knife him; no compulsion to slip poison in his drink. He always treated me well. I learned to help him; I learned the knack of ruling folk, of wielding power. Well, he's gone now. And I'm repaying the favor by raising our sons and governing his territories until the boys are old enough to assume control in their own right. I see from the naked distaste on your face that this tale sickens you. Your head is still in Father's world of lofty ideals, notions of justice and selflessness and compassion. That world is not real, Faolan. It's a phantom. In the real world, power is the only key to survival. I've survived. I've made something of my existence. I've stepped out of the nightmare Dubhán created for us and achieved wealth, family, position. You should not despise me for that. You should learn from me. What is your life?"

For a moment he could not speak. Somewhere, deep within him, there was still love: love for the old Áine, the one who existed in his memory, his baby sister, a sweet, rosy-cheeked innocent. At this moment, facing her excoriating stare, he could not find it.

"I went on," he said simply. "Some time I wasted, some I used well. I remained my own master, after Breakstone. I have no desire for wealth or power. Only for freedom. The freedom to make my choices, for good or ill."

Her smile was grim. "You have lost your freedom here at Blackthorn Rise. You've lost your friend's daughter as well. A poor job you've done of protecting her. You never were very practical, were you, Faolan? Once a bard, always a bard. Giving a girl a pretty name doesn't go far toward keeping her safe."

So she did not know what he was now; not unless she was still playing with him. "True freedom lies, not in being outside walls, but in the heart and the spirit," he said. He felt numb, bruised; as if he had received a beating. "You said Dubhán created our nightmare; you laid the blame on him. What Dubhán did was speak out for the oppressed, those who have no power. He was a voice for those too frightened to open their mouths. His resistance to your husband's cruel practices was a shout of freedom, a song of defiance. Dubhán did not die because Echen ordered me to cut his throat, Áine. I performed that act because, at the last, our brother bid me do it. He gave his life willingly to save his family. Only once, since that night, have I seen such a shining act of courage. It was Dubhán I obeyed. Maybe Echen was kind to you, to the extent that such a man is capable of kindness, and I can only be glad of that for your sake. But I do not know how you can reconcile being his wife with the foul acts he perpetrated that night, and in the time before. Echen was evil. He set a darkness not only on our family, but on the whole community at Fiddler's Crossing. I don't understand how you can live your life as you do, knowing that." Some part of him was struggling to say what he knew he should: *I am so glad you are alive, I am happy to see you, I missed you so much. My sister; my little sister.* But he looked at her, and all he could see was Echen Uí Néill.

"I suppose, then," said Áine, her voice clear as tinkling ice, "that fifty days' confinement was not long enough. I have been too kind; perhaps, after all, I was not entirely successful in forgetting what our father taught us as children." She raised her voice. "Seamus!"

"Please," Faolan said, "let me go. Let me find Eile and the child. I made a promise. I'll stay away after that. You need never see me again. Just let me out."

"Your urgency for this quest baffles me," said Áine as

the big guard, Seamus, came back into the chamber. "This Eile is not your blood kin. She's a pitiful thing born to poverty and has a nasty streak of aggression to boot. She's murdered a man and she's run away from just punishment. Yet you're all on fire to race off and save her. Why her, Faolan? Why can you do this for her, when you couldn't for me, your own sister?"

"I cannot answer you."

"Cannot or will not? You feel shame? Or would that be too much to expect?"

"I feel . . . confusion. All I can tell you is that the man who stands before you now is not the same man who stood in the brithem's house in Fiddler's Crossing and drew a knife across his brother's throat. If that night changed you, Áine, it surely changed me. I've spent every moment of these ten years trying to understand it."

"Until you know what I felt, the terror, the helplessness, the sense of being utterly alone, you can have no insight into what that night meant. Fortunately, I can help you. I plan to keep you here until that insight comes to you. It is no less than you deserve. Lock him up again," she ordered Seamus. "Leave his wrists bound, he's not to be trusted."

"Wait!" Faolan said. "Just tell me, what of the family, Mother and Father, Dáire and Líobhan? How have they fared? Are they well?"

"Hah!" The sound was an explosion of scorn. "Now you ask, as an afterthought. Perhaps that is apt, since the last thing the family would wish is for you to return to Fiddler's Crossing. Your name is not spoken in that household. Since that night, it is as if you had never existed. All trace of you was wiped away; all thought of you forbidden. Your deed caused a widening ripple of destruction for your kin. Mother is long dead; she never recovered. Father is a shell of himself, barely able to put two thoughts together. Dáire fled to the Christian sisters; she never knew the fulfilment of husband and children, but lives in silence and sorrow there. Líobhan is full of bitterness at her lot, obliged to remain at home to keep house for her shattered, incapable father. Grandfather has not long to live; he was never strong. That is what you have done. Do you regret asking, now? If you expected to walk home to some kind of forgiveness, Faolan, you were a fool. Some acts can never be forgiven."

He found himself unable to speak. The guard, Seamus, was staring at the floor.

"Farewell, now," said Áine. "I intend to be generous and give you plenty of thinking time. Perhaps you could make up some songs while you're in my custody. Oh, and don't concern yourself with Eile. That girl's a survivor. She's like me. She doesn't need you."

Faolan's voice returned. "Oh, no," he said as Seamus took him by the arm to lead him out. He saw the frail figure of Eile stepping onto the rope bridge over that surging wash of water, her straight back, her terrified eyes. He saw the tenderness in the soft mouth, the gentleness in the work-roughened hands as she laid a cloak over her sleeping child. "She's not like you at all."

DERELEI HAD TAKEN to sitting at the very edge of the pond. The nursemaid fussed, fearing he would catch cold or topple in and drown. Tuala, observing from a distance, knew her son was not seeking out fish or dreaming of sailing boats under Broichan's watchful eye. The water called him; he was drawn to look. Watching him, she felt the same compulsion.

She had anticipated that the seer's gift would be as strong in her son as it was in her. She had hoped it would not develop so early, before Derelei had much facility with words. It could be a frightening phenomenon even when one was adult and had some understanding of its nature. For a child of two, it might prove overwhelming.

There was no point in wishing Broichan home. She had done that often enough, and he showed no sign of appearing, either in the flesh or in the visions of the scrying bowl. Nobody knew where he was; nobody knew where his journey had taken him. He had not been seen at Pitnochie, nor at Banmerren, nor at any other place Tharan's messenger had visited on his search. Perhaps he had slipped away to join the druids of the forest, who were only found when they chose to be. Tuala hoped he was with them, for in their remote dwellings there would be food, shelter from cold and storm, folk to tend to him if he took ill. There was guidance, too; perhaps he needed that most of all.

She and Bridei had discussed asking Drustan to perform a search in his hawk form, and had discarded the idea. It was unfair to expect it of Drustan. His ability was such that, all too easily, he might find himself in constant demand as messenger, tracker, or spy. In autumn, at some personal risk, he had flown the length of the Great Glen to save Bridei from an assassin. They could not ask him again. He and Ana should be left to enjoy their season of peace at Pitnochie.

"Broichan may be perfectly well," Bridei had said, "and simply tired of court. We must give him time."

"He was always such an assiduous teacher, for you, at least," Tuala had said, remembering the endless times of waiting for Bridei to finish his lessons. "It is so unlike him to leave Derelei right in the middle of everything. It's as if he rowed a boat halfway to an island, then dived overboard, leaving his passenger stranded."

"I suppose you must pick up the oars," Bridei had said with a smile.

That afternoon Tuala dismissed the nursemaid and went to sit by her son in the garden. All was quiet. Under the rosemary bushes, Ban was fossicking in the muddy soil; today he was not so much a white dog as a creature patched in various shades of brown. Garth was on watch, discreetly, down beyond the archway. The old scholar, Wid, sat at the other end of the garden, a shawl around his shoulders, enjoying the rare winter sun. Tuala had asked him to cough loudly if anyone came out, but she didn't think they would; Aniel had promised to ensure mother and son were undisturbed.

How to begin? How to teach a child who combined a dazzling raw skill in magic with the limited vocabulary and volatile emotions of his two years? Already, under Broichan's tuition, Derelei had begun to manipulate the weather, to perform small transformations, to play with light and shadow. Somehow, she must teach him to be cautious, to be covert, to limit his boundless abilities. He must learn to see the unthinkable and to hold on to his courage. The task was monumental. It was by no means certain to Tuala how far her own talents in the craft of magic extended. Only in the art of scrying had she ever given them full rein. Best start small and work gradually up.

Not the pool; therein lay peril for the two of them. She could not afford to be pulled into a vision with the child by her side, for she might lose the awareness of him and so leave him in danger.

"Derelei?" she asked him quietly. "Take my hand; that's it. Look at Ban; doesn't he love digging? Have you ever pretended you were a dog?"

They worked hard. These were not bodily transformations such as Drustan performed with such apparent ease, but a lesser step, the melding of one's own mind with that of creature or growing thing, gaining the awareness of its movements, its thoughts, its feelings, while one remained in one's own form.

Once or twice, as the afternoon wore on, Tuala felt her son's mind pulling against hers, as if he wanted to do more than she was permitting. She saw that he wanted to *be* a dog, chasing sparrows across the grass, drinking from the pond, rolling in the leaves and mud. But he held back from changing his form. Whether her skill was enough to prevent him from taking that last step, or whether it was the child's choice to obey his mother, Tuala could not tell. They tried *beetle* as well as *dog,* and Derelei wanted *bird,* but Tuala shook her head.

"Not yet. That one's too dangerous. When you are older."

Derelei gave an uncharacteristic squeal of complaint and lay down on the damp grass, rubbing his eyes.

"Time to stop now," said Tuala firmly. "Let's take Ban to the kitchen. Maybe there's cake."

The child squirmed away from her, protesting. He was overtired; she must make this shorter next time. He was at the rim of the pond again, his head almost in the water. Tuala moved to pick him up and bear him indoors, but her pregnancy made her slower than usual and by the time she reached him, Derelei was on his belly, staring at the still surface with a familiar intensity. "Bawta," he said. "See Bawta."

She'd been unable to avoid a glimpse at the water, and there had been a vision forming there. Such images came for her even when she didn't want them. "Broichan's gone, Derelei," she said, kneeling beside him. "You know that."

"Bawta in there." He was emphatic.

She looked. There were trees and shadow: not a reflection of this orderly garden with its paved paths, its leafless plums and lilacs, but a forested place dark with pines and mazed with little twisting footways. A thick mat of decaying leaf matter covered the ground, and on the massive trunks of the trees mosses glowed eerily. In the crooks of bare oaks sprouted a multitude of little ferns and creepers, and Tuala could see something moving among them, perhaps birds, perhaps something a great deal stranger. The light that filtered here and there through the dense canopy was white and chill.

Keep hold of his hand, she warned herself. *Don't let go.* The power of this was strong; she might soon be oblivious to the here and now. It did not take long for a child to drown. It could happen in a heartbeat, silent from start to finish.

"Bawta," Derelei said again, and there the druid stood, a dark figure under the darker trees, obsidian eyes in marble face, his breath a cloud in the winter air. He did not open his mouth, but Tuala heard words nonetheless. *A season of penitence. Guard him well.*

Questions trembled on her lips: *Where are you? Are you all right? Can you see us?,* but the edges of the vision were already breaking up, and she knew there was not sufficient time to ask. Only a moment; only an instant . . . No time to think. She touched the tip of her fingers to her lips, then held her hand out toward the image in the water. She thought maybe Broichan's mouth twisted a little, its customary severity turning to a self-mocking smile. Then dark forest turned to still pond water, and the vision was gone.

Derelei sat frozen a moment, then began to cry. Piteous tears: the utter woe of an exhausted and disappointed infant. Gathering him into her arms, Tuala shed a tear or two herself. One could not reassure such a little child by saying: *At least he is alive,* or, *I think he will be back in springtime.* His beloved mentor, his grandfather, had been here only an instant before vanishing, and it was as if the child had lost him all over again. "There, there," Tuala murmured. "There, Derelei, it's all right."

"All gone," he sobbed.

"He is alive and well," Tuala said, talking more to herself than to her son, who was momentarily beyond comforting. "He has revealed himself to us. It's a great deal better than nothing. Derelei, you know what we're going to do? Give Ban a bath before he gets his supper. Wash doggy?"

Through his tears, Derelei showed a spark of interest. He stretched out to dip his hands in the pond, an inquiring look breaking through the woe. Thank the gods little children were so easily distracted.

"Not in the pond," Tuala said firmly. "In the kitchen,

in a tub. With lots of bubbles. I'll hold him while you scrub."

"I'M TOO TIRED to carry you anymore," Eile told Saraid. "I know it's dark, but it's not much farther. Look, I can see lights down the hill there. That must be the place."

Saraid took three steps, stumbled, and sat down on the muddy path. It was so dark, Eile could see her daughter only as a small, exhausted shadow.

"Oh, come on, then. Not the sling; hold on to my shoulders and put your legs around my waist." Eile gritted her teeth and heaved the child up, then rose slowly to her feet again. Her knees ached; she was so tired that each breath was an effort. *Let this be Fiddler's Crossing,* she thought. *Let me find them; let them not take one look and turn me away.* She made herself move on, the dog plodding behind her, tail down.

The settlement was bigger than the one at Cloud Hill, the cottages gathered around a grassy square. Lanterns shone here and there, illuminating whitewashed walls and neat patches of garden. A man was walking along the path. Eile cleared her throat nervously. "Where is the brithem's house?" she asked him.

"Conor's? Down there, across the little bridge and up the bank—see the big place with the wall? That's his house. It's late to be knocking on doors. You in some kind of trouble?" He eyed her curiously.

"We're fine. Thanks." Eile turned her back and walked away quickly. No questions; no delays. *Let them open the door. Let them listen.*

The brithem's house was surrounded by a substantial stone wall, in which was set a heavy gate of ironwork. A leafless creeper grew extravagantly on the stones, branching here and there in a complex pattern of its own; in summer the place would be mantled in green. A lantern burned not far inside the gate, and Eile could see lights in the house. The gate was locked. Eile rattled it, reluctant to shout, and somewhere inside a dog began to bark, setting their own companion growling in response. This lawman was evidently wary of intruders.

The watchdog kept up its alarm, but nobody seemed to be coming. Eile contemplated a third night spent in the lee of a haystack or behind a pig pen, and raised her voice. "Is anyone there? Hello?" A pause; the barking had quieted. "Hello? Can someone let me in?"

A woman was coming down the gravel path with a lamp in hand. By her side padded a big hound. The gray dog moved up to the gate, hair bristling, a rumble in his throat.

"Hush," said Eile.

A pair of beautiful brown eyes examined them between the bars of the gate. The woman was youngish and not very tall. Eile felt a chill run up her spine. Even in the fitful lantern light, she could see that this woman bore an uncanny resemblance to the Widow. That was wrong. These were supposed to be Faolan's kinsfolk. They were meant to be friends.

"Who are you?" the woman asked. "What do you want?"

"My name is Eile. This is my daughter. I need to see the brithem. It's urgent. Is he here?"

"I'm afraid not. He's in another settlement hearing a case. Can you come back in the morning?"

Gods, another night in the open. Eile hitched Saraid higher on her back. "I've walked all the way from Blackthorn Rise," she said, annoyed that her voice was not quite steady.

The brown eyes sharpened. "Carrying the child? Is it just the two of you?"

Eile nodded. "And this dog. He's harmless."

"Blackthorn Rise. From Áine's house?"

"Who?"

"My sister. She's more commonly known as the Widow."

"Your *sister?* But—" Something wrong here; something askew. "Maybe I've made a mistake. The man I'm looking for is Faolan's father."

The eyes went wide. The face paled. The woman looked as if she might faint from shock. "You know my brother?" she breathed. "You've seen him?" The lamp shook in her hand.

"If you mean Faolan, I have news of him. Wait a bit. Are you saying the Widow is Faolan's sister, too? That's impossible. She never—I mean, she—" What kind of tangled web had they fallen into?

"Down, please?" Saraid's little voice, through a yawn.

The woman moved swiftly to unlock the gates, using a key from a big bunch at her belt. The hound stood by her, watchful and obedient, as Eile, Saraid and the gray dog slipped through and the gates were secured behind them.

"I'm Líobhan," the woman said. "You look exhausted. Come inside; I'll call the others. You really have some news of Faolan? He's still alive?"

"Alive?" Eile was taken aback. She surely hoped he was. "He was a few days ago. But he may be in trouble. I really need to speak to the brithem—"

"Tell us tonight." Líobhan's voice, mellow and warm, was shaking with emotion. "Please. We've heard nothing of my brother since he left Fiddler's Crossing ten years ago. No news at all. This is—it's unbelievable. You said a few days—does that mean he's close at hand somewhere? That he's coming home at last?"

She did not wait for an answer. Leading Eile along a covered way and in a door to a warm room with a big table and a broad stone hearth, she called out, "Donnan! Grandfather! There's a girl here who's seen Faolan!" At the same time she was seating Eile on a bench by the damped-down fire, helping Saraid out of her cloak, filling a kettle; from a nook by the hearth a brindled cat emerged, stretching. The gray dog went under the bench.

"You're freezing," Líobhan said. "Let me stir up the fire, and I'll find you something to eat. Your tale can wait until my husband's here, he was just finishing some work . . ."

Cautiously, Eile looked about her. This was the coziest chamber she had ever seen, the firelight supplemented by various lamps set about in corners, the furnishings of mellow wood, the walls softened by hangings embroidered in bright wools: she saw Saraid eyeing the scenes depicted there, a bard playing a harp and people dancing in a line, hands linked; folk with pitchforks loading a cart with hay; a child feeding chickens, with a dog standing watchfully by. Strings of onions and garlic hung from the ceiling and on a side table stood stacks of earthenware platters and bowls, as if this household were used to providing for unexpected guests. In a jug was a collection of winter twigs and foliage, silver and gray and black, lovingly arranged. A striped rug lay before the hearth, fiery red, golden yellow, earthen brown. The cat had moved to sit in the very center of this, the firelight setting a mellow glow on its fur.

Líobhan was bustling about. At top speed, a basket of bannocks and a dish of preserves appeared on the well-scrubbed table, along with cheese, onions, and a useful knife.

"Can I do anything?" Eile felt uncomfortable. This lady should not be waiting on her.

"Sit and warm yourself. If I don't keep busy I'll burst into tears or swamp you with questions before the others get here. I can't believe we've heard from Faolan at last. It's been so long. Oh, here's my husband."

A thickset man in his twenties came in, wiping his hands on a stained apron.

"Donnan, this young woman says she's seen Faolan. She has some news for us."

Donnan gave Eile a nod and seated himself by the fire. The cat jumped immediately to his knee. Saraid's attention was captured by the creature. Eile could feel her quivering to go and touch, but shyness held her by her mother's side, all big eyes and silence.

"Her name's Patch," Donnan said to the child. "Would you like to stroke her? She doesn't bite."

But Saraid shook her head and buried her face in her mother's sleeve.

Líobhan had poured some kind of cordial into a jug and was topping it up with hot water. "This will warm you up, Eile," she said. "My own brew: blackcurrant and crabapple."

"My wife's a cook of some renown," observed Donnan with a smile.

"Thank you," said Eile, accepting a cup. This was overwhelming. The kinder they were, the more desperately they sought news, the harder it would be to tell the truth. "I should tell you first . . . I need to be sure you will still receive me in your house when you know about me . . ."

A tall old man with a shock of white hair entered the room, and after him a boy of six or seven, wearing a cloak over a nightrobe.

"Phadraig," said Líobhan, frowning, "what are you doing out of bed?"

"You did shout, Mama." The boy came over to the fire, scrutinizing first the shrinking Saraid, then Eile, who met him in the eye. "And I wasn't asleep, Great Grandfather was telling me a story. That's our cat." He addressed this straight to Saraid. "She's having kittens soon; see her big belly? I'm going to keep one. I'm calling it Cú Chulainn, because he was a great fighter, and my cat's going to be one, too, and catch all the rats in Father's workshop. If you put your hand on Patch's stomach you can feel the kittens moving around. Want to try? Here." And, without further ado, there was Saraid, putting her small hand beside Phadraig's slightly larger one. Eile saw a smile of complete delight illuminate her daughter's wan features. It seemed a small miracle; she had to blink back tears.

"Tell us now, Eile." Líobhan had seated herself by her guest's side, a cup of the spicy brew between her capable hands.

"Let the lass eat, Líobhan," said the old man mildly.

"I'm sorry. You must be starving, Eile. Phadraig, Saraid hasn't had supper yet. Can you put some things on a platter for her? Yes, you can have some, too. You're growing so fast, I don't think a second supper will hurt you."

"First I have to say . . . You need to know . . ." Eile glanced at the two children. The boy was assembling bread, cheese, preserve on a small platter while Saraid remained by Donnan's knee, fingers gentle against the cat's soft fur.

"Phadraig," said Líobhan, "why don't you and Saraid take that over to the little table in the corner? I think her dog needs feeding, too. Maybe there's a bone somewhere. Saraid will help you look."

Impossible, thought Eile. In yet another houseful of strangers, Saraid had done well to venture three steps from her mother.

"A dog? Where is it?" inquired Phadraig, squatting to peer under the bench. "Oh, I see. What's his name? I bet he's hungry. Come on, good boy. Come on." Carrying the platter and talking all the time, the boy drew both cowering dog and shy child after him all the way across the chamber and out through a small door. Saraid did not even look back.

Eile felt a tremulous smile curve her lips. "She's usually very wary of strangers."

"Phadraig has a way with him," said Líobhan, her tone matter-of-fact. "What is it you need to tell us, Eile?"

Eile swallowed nervously. Blurting out the truth in all its violent, bloody detail felt wrong here, among these peaceable, courteous folk. These people did not seem to belong in the same world as Dalach and Anda, a world of curses and threats, of blows and bruises and silent endurance. What if Líobhan heard this and set them both outside the gate to spend another night in the cold? Folk suffered harsh penalties for far less than Eile had done.

"I killed someone." There, it was out. "A man who had

been hurting me for a long time. I was afraid for my daughter. I did it a while ago; more than fifty days, by my count. The lady at Blackthorn Rise took me in. She said she'd deal with everything for me, but she never did. She just kept me there. I still have to face charges; I still have to be punished. I don't want to lose Saraid. I ran away from Cloud Hill, after it happened, and then I ran away from Blackthorn Rise."

Brown-eyed woman, quiet man, and grave grandfather looked at one another in silence, weighing this. The fire crackled; the cat stretched, luxurious on Donnan's knee.

"You've come to Fiddler's Crossing to ask Father to deal with this matter?" asked Líobhan.

"That's not why I came. But I suppose he will, now I'm here. I don't want to be locked up. There's nobody else to look after Saraid. I never hurt anyone, except him. Well, that's not quite true. There was a horrible child at Blackthorn Rise, his name was Fionn, he was cruel to Saraid and I slapped him. That's why we left there. But I won't hurt anyone again."

"Faolan," said the old man. "What can you tell us of Faolan?" His knotty hands were clasped tightly together.

"He helped me." As swiftly as she could, Eile told the story; her audience of three sat silent and still, hungry for every word. "So," she said at the end, "I thought he was gone, because that was what the Widow told me. But I'm sure I heard him calling my name. Certain of it. If he's her brother, why would she do that? Why would she lie to me? I'm nothing to grand ladies like her. Me and Saraid, we're the dirt under her boot sole." Belatedly, she remembered whom she was talking to. "I'm sorry," she added. "She's your kinswoman; I didn't mean any offense. But she was unkind, and she lied to me. She played games with us. She said I'd be safe there, and I wasn't; she never settled things with the law. She would have had my daughter beaten. Saraid's only little."

Líobhan sighed. "Gods," she said as if to herself, "he came back at last and this was what he walked into."

Donnan reached over and took her hand. "He did come back," he said. "Hold on to that. We can sort this out. Your father and I will have to go there. We'll have to confront Áine openly."

"Young lady," said the grandfather, "Faolan is lucky to have such a friend as yourself. It took courage and strength to make your way here to us, when most other folk in your situation would have seized the opportunity to flee the district. My son-in-law, the brithem, is a just man, and wise. He will settle your case. You should not be afraid."

Eile gave a nod, sudden shyness robbing her of speech.

"I'm sure this all seems very odd to you, Eile," said Líobhan. "Did Faolan tell you anything of his past? Do you know what happened to us here before he left home?"

"Not much. He spoke of your family being wronged, and how it was too late for vengeance because the man who did it was dead. There were folk talking about it at the bridge we crossed. They said Faolan had done something so terrible it didn't bear thinking about."

Donnan exchanged glances with the old man. "They must have gone straight to Áine," he said. "It explains how she knew, how she was there the next morning to take him. She must have offered incentives for silence, or we'd have heard before now that he was home."

"You wonder, perhaps," Líobhan said to Eile, "why we are not more shocked to hear of your own violent deed. Of course, we are a brithem's family, and that must count for something. But what happened that night, long ago, changed all of us. It took a heavy toll, and we've been a long time recovering. Faolan was forced to kill his elder brother, Dubhán, before the eyes of our whole family. The choice offered to him was to do that or see the rest of us die as well. Dubhán bid him do it, and he obeyed, though not until after the perpetrator's men had killed my grandmother."

The old man bowed his head.

"We were spared, the rest of us," Líobhan went on,

"but the men who had invaded our house did not leave empty-handed. They took our youngest sister, Áine. She was twelve at the time. They laughed, leaving, about what they would do to her that night. My father believed her beyond saving; he was certain she'd be dead before rescue was possible. Indeed, he thought that if any of us tried to intervene we, too, would be killed. The man who did this, Echen, was a powerful chieftain. To resist him, as Dubhán had done, was to invite a violent end. It happened right here in this room."

Horrified, Eile stared at the flagstoned floor, imagining the blood; seeing a young Faolan with the knife in his hands.

"For a long time, we couldn't bear to come in here," the grandfather said. "My daughter, Conor's wife, lived only a season after that night. She never recovered from what she witnessed; the first winter chill carried her from us as easily as the breeze gathers up a dandelion seed. Líobhan's eldest sister, Dáire, went to the priory at Winterfalls, not far from here. She found solace in the Christian faith, and is content with her life of seclusion. She had lost husband and unborn child before that night. It was Echen's cruelty that took them both. Dubhán sought only a just vengeance."

"Two years after it happened, we were still reeling from the blow," said Líobhan. "Then Donnan came courting me, like a bit of sunshine in a dark place. He'd long been close to the family; my brother, the one who died, was his friend, and Donnan had been part of the resistance that sparked the whole thing. We decided we didn't want Echen's victory over us to be complete, as it would be if we let this destroy us. We decided it was time to start healing ourselves. We made this chamber into the warmest, most welcoming place in the house. We said prayers here, lit lamps, sang songs, and told stories. We cooked meals to share. We invited folk to visit."

"What about Áine?" asked Eile, thinking this tale was one of the strangest she'd ever heard.

"It was a shock," said Donnan softly. "We had done our best to avoid Echen's notice, all of us who'd been involved, for those two years. We'd abided by his rules, and Líobhan's father had not practiced as a brithem during that time for fear of antagonizing his enemy again by pronouncing an unfavorable judgment on one of his favorites. For those two years after the night it happened, we had believed Áine dead. Attempts to get information about what had happened were fruitless. Then we heard that she was, after all, alive and well; that she'd been in Tirconnell, and that now she was Echen's wife."

"It couldn't be a happy ending," said Líobhan. "Not with that man as her husband. But we wanted to see her, to be reassured that she had not been ill-treated and to know the marriage was her own choice. She refused to see us. Even now, with Echen gone, she has nothing to do with us. She was displeased when Father resumed his role as a brithem after Echen's death. He'd been giving people advice on matters of law all the while, unofficially; folk knew to keep quiet about it. Because the local community had sore need of a qualified lawman, my sister could hardly raise objections when he took up his formal duties again. We do meet her occasionally; it's inevitable our paths will cross from time to time. She avoids it if she can. She despises us. She loathes us. This has changed her more profoundly than it did any of the rest of us, save perhaps for poor Mother, who never recovered from losing both her sons in one night. Áine's mind has been somehow twisted. She may be a powerful and competent chieftain in her husband's stead, and far more just with her folk than he ever was. But she's erratic. She's dangerous."

"She blames Faolan for what happened to her," said the grandfather. "Him most of all, because he was a man, and young, and she thought he should have saved her. If she has him prisoner, he's in real danger. What time do you expect Conor home, Líobhan?"

"Early," said Líobhan as the back door opened and the two children came in, followed by the gray dog with a meaty bone in his mouth. "He said he'd be back here for breakfast."

"We must wait for his decision, of course," the old man said. "But this is what he'll want to do. We must ride there tomorrow and confront Áine with what we know."

"Ride where?" asked Phadraig. "Can I come?" A look from his mother silenced him. Saraid had climbed onto Eile's knee.

"What if she says I was mistaken? That Faolan's not there?" Eile asked them. "If what you say about her is true, she's not just going to let him go, is she?" She felt a chill, thinking of that place, Breakstone Hollow, and what it had done to her father.

"Conor's a good talker," said Donnan. He did not sound completely confident.

"We must wait until morning," Líobhan said. "She hasn't let any of us in the gates of Blackthorn Rise in all the time she's been head of that household, and it's very possible tomorrow may be no different. As brithem, Father does have great authority in the district. He's widely respected. But Blackthorn Rise makes its own rules. We're not welcome in Áine's house and perhaps we never will be. She can't see the irony of it: that the husband whose sons she's dedicated to raising, the one whose lands she puts her life into governing, was the man who set this darkness on us all in the first place. I don't think she'll ever understand."

"Who won't understand?" asked Phadraig.

"Your aunt Áine, the one who doesn't come here," his mother said. "What's in the little bag, Saraid?"

Saraid turned her head into Eile's shoulder.

"It's a doll," said Phadraig. "She showed me. Only it's broken. A boy sawed its head off. It's called Sorry. I told her you would fix it, Mama."

"I'm sure I can manage that," Líobhan said with a wry smile. "We'll do it in the morning, shall we, Saraid? Maybe Sorry would like a ribbon around her neck, or a little frill. You can help me sew it on."

"I can do it." Eile heard the combative tone of her own voice and hastened to add, "But thank you for the offer. If I could borrow a needle and thread . . . We're used to fending for ourselves, Saraid and me. I do know how to mend."

"I'm sure you do. Now, it's time for bed, Phadraig, and I think Eile and Saraid need somewhere to sleep. Let's go and see where we can squeeze them in."

MORNING BROUGHT THE brithem, a gray-haired, clean-shaven man with Faolan's thin lips and wary eyes. It was plain from the moment he walked in that he would be the one who made any decisions required. Despite his reserved manner he was the kind of man, Eile thought, who was accustomed to taking charge.

Over breakfast, the others told him the tale of an unlawful killing and the story of Faolan's capture. Conor was adept at concealing what he felt; the more Eile watched him, the more of Faolan she saw in him. It made her wonder about her father and about herself.

Saraid had slept well. She sat up next to Phadraig to eat her breakfast, and Líobhan, with a glance at Eile, complimented her on her good manners. Dismissed from the table, the two children headed straight out into the yard with the gray dog loping after them.

"She's not scared here," Eile said in tones of amazement. "Your son is a good little boy. I think she knew that straightaway."

"Children know who they can trust," said the grandfather. "Conor, I have some misgivings about this plan. We don't want to inflame the situation. Have you considered asking a druid or a Christian cleric to go with us?"

"Áine won't want that," the brithem said. "She has her reputation to consider in the district. It's one thing to lock her brother up in secret with only her own household knowing. It's quite another for all and sundry to be made aware of it. We can use that, if we manage to get in. If she has no legal reason for holding Faolan, she's committed an offense. Our difficulty is getting her to admit to it. Faolan will be helpless in there. He was never a fighter."

"Helpless?" Eile was taken aback. "He seemed very capable to me." She fell silent as the brithem turned his stern eyes on her. She was not afraid of Líobhan or Donnan or the old man; but she was afraid of him. He did not look like the kind of man who would bring breakfast when you were hungry or tell a lie to keep you safe.

"Tell us," Conor said.

"He had traveled a long way by himself to bring me the news of my father's death. He spoke to my aunt and her husband as if he was a person of authority. He gave them silver, but he didn't just hand it over, he told them they had to use it for me, for my future. Not that it did any good." She grimaced, remembering how quickly Dalach had taken the little bag off his wife, once the visitor was gone. "And Faolan fought the Widow's men when they laid hands on him. It took five of them to overpower him. He only stopped struggling when they hit him over the head." She bit her lip. "I'm sorry," she added.

"Are we quite certain this is Faolan?" the brithem asked, and this time Eile heard a new note in his voice: that of a man whose iron self-discipline was no longer quite concealing the turmoil of emotions beneath. "We must not antagonize Áine still further by going to her with false accusations of wrongful imprisonment."

"It is your son." Eile put a hand over his, then removed it quickly. He was someone; she was a piece of rubbish who'd knifed her own uncle. He administered the law; she was a miscreant. In this hospitable house she had come close to forgetting. "He spoke of you. He said you were wise and just. He told me you would help me, and that I mustn't be afraid." She glanced around the family. "Faolan said this was a house of good people, and I see that it is."

For a little, nobody said anything.

"I have an idea," Eile told them, wondering what was making her bold enough to suggest it and crazy enough even to consider leaving Saraid for a day, or however long it would take to get to Blackthorn Rise and back again on horseback. A strange conviction had come to her along with the scheme: the certainty that this was what her father would expect her to do. To be bold and resourceful; to aid his friend; to put her own needs last. "Let me explain."

THE PARTY OF riders, three men and a girl, reached the gates of Blackthorn Rise in early afternoon. It was raining again; the travelers had a bedraggled look about them. Challenged by the guards, the youngest man moved forward. He looked slightly familiar, but neither man-at-arms could quite place him. The other men were hooded against the rain, their faces concealed. The girl the guards knew well.

"We're here to see the Widow," the youngest man said. "We're returning this young woman, who ran away from this household. We understand she's facing serious charges at Cloud Hill."

"And what's that to you? Give us your name."

"Donnan. I'm a harness maker, from west of here. Picked up the girl on the road. I heard the lady's offering a reward for her return. Two silver pieces, that's what folk are saying."

"First I've heard of it," one guard muttered to the other. "What do you think?"

"Could be true. Seamus might know. You there! Hand the girl over and wait out here while we check this. Two silver pieces sounds a lot for a scrawny thing like her. And where's the child? She had a child before."

"They took her away." The girl's voice was a tremulous whisper; she looked terrified. There were tears of fright on her cheeks. It seemed wrong to bring her in, in a way; everyone knew she was due a beating, but that was nothing beside what she'd get for unlawful killing.

"Ask the Widow if she'll see us," said Donnan. "If she promised silver, she'll deliver."

"The lady's out riding. You'll have to wait."

"We're not sitting out here cooling our heels all afternoon," said Donnan. "It's raining. If you won't let us in, we'll go on to Cloud Hill and hand the girl over direct to her kinsfolk. You can explain that to your lady when she gets in. I know I'll get a reward there. They've put it about that they want this girl punished."

"You'll be lucky if the folk of that settlement can put together two coppers between them, let alone a bounty in silver."

"We'll put that to the test." Donnan turned his mount. "Come on, we're wasting our time."

"Just a moment!" called the guard. "She might want the girl here. I'll ask my superior. Wait right there."

The head guard, Seamus, was engaged in an activity he saved for times when the Widow was unlikely to walk in: checking on the welfare of his prisoner. Now that it seemed the lady's brother was to remain in custody for an indefinite period, he felt duty bound to take what steps he could to stop the fellow from going completely crazy. They'd talked about the situation, he and Maeve; they'd wondered if, at long last, things at Blackthorn Rise had reached a point where it was time to pack up and leave, since both of them would get work easily in other households. Loyalty was a strange thing, loyalty and pity. They'd been with Áine a long time. When it came to it, neither of them was prepared to take that final step. Chances were Áine would find out they'd been breaking her rules and throw them out anyway. There was the little matter of Maeve helping that red-haired waif and her child escape; and there was Faolan. Seamus had let his underlings manage the prisoner until the Widow finally called her brother in to see her. Everyone had expected she'd let Faolan go after that. Fifty days was a long time for a man to be locked up alone.

After what he overheard that night, and the order to keep Faolan in custody, Seamus had assumed personal responsibility for the prisoner. He wasn't following the new rules, which demanded wrist shackles as well as the hobbles, and only one meal a day, delivered in silence. That was stupid. Apart from the initial struggle, the prisoner had been a model of good behavior, polite and reasonable. The shackles stayed off, though Seamus kept them ready in case the lady took it into her head to visit. Faolan got his meals when the guards did, and while he was eating, or more often staring at his platter, Seamus stood in the doorway and talked to him. He wished Faolan would talk back; he seemed an interesting sort of fellow, a man who had traveled. The Breakstone Hollow story was evidently true; Seamus had seen the tattoo. But since Áine had spoken with him, Faolan had gone silent. Most of the day he spent sitting on the ground, arms around his knees, head down. Seamus hoped the lady would decide to let him out soon. This felt wrong.

He'd just locked the door again when Enda came hurrying along the passageway, babbling about the girl from Cloud Hill and a bunch of men waiting at the gate. Seamus made him slow down, ascertained one girl, three men, something about a reward. He weighed up the possibilities and tried to remember where he'd heard of a harness maker by the name of Donnan before. It rang a bell; something to do with the old days, the Echen days. Something they'd all tried hard to forget.

"Let them in," he said.

THERE'D BEEN A pattern of activity, before, a variation of the one he had invented in Breakstone to keep his mind and body active. Bending, stretching, pacing, jumping. Inventing escape plans. Telling himself stories, playing games in his head with numbers. For fifty days it had been possible to maintain that, to keep eating, to achieve tolerable sleep. For fifty days he had been able to believe that when he left this cell he would rescue Eile and see his family, for good or ill. He had convinced himself that there might be time to put things right before the next mission called him. To try, at least.

Then he'd seen Áine and that hope had vanished like fertile soil washed away in violent storm. The damage he had wrought was irreversible. Each item in her passionless catalogue of ills had been a further blow to his heart. His mother, his father; Dáire, Líobhan. Áine herself, so cruelly changed, Áine whom he could not forgive, for all the ill he had done her. Dubhán, the brother the young bard had so worshipped. Grandfather, who had always been so strong, so ageless; Grandmother, knifed to death before his eyes. How had it ever been possible to delude himself into thinking, somehow, he might go to Fiddler's Crossing and make his peace with them? That was like expecting the dead to get up and dance: nonsense.

Nothing seemed important anymore. Why go through the motions of exercising, of swallowing food, of playing the game of survival? Bridei's mission, the visit to Colmcille, had lost its meaning. Bridei was a distant figure, someone who had wanted to befriend him, a good man. Bridei would find another spy.

A part of Faolan made him test himself; called him to account for the offense of despair. He had survived Breakstone Hollow. To end it all now made a mockery of that, since the men who came out were as scarce as dry days in autumn. He touched the little star tattooed behind his ear. A survivor. If he was that, he hardly deserved it. Better if Echen had made an end of him that night. Then, at least, he would never have known the full extent of the harm he had done.

Ana: a reason for going on, a reason for not giving up. He thought he could remember, vaguely, making some kind of promise to her. It was difficult to picture her face; all that would come was a haze of gold and a pair of searching gray eyes. Not liking the look in them, Faolan put her out of his mind. He took off his shirt and began to tear it into neat strips, using his teeth. He assessed the height of the window bars. Doing this would require a high degree of will, since they were not quite far enough from the floor. He would do it. Not yet. Later, after Seamus had brought the supper. He must make quite sure there were no interruptions.

It did not take long to knot and twist his pieces into a serviceable kind of rope. There was one voice muttering inside his head, a voice he failed to silence: Deord's. He could see the broad-shouldered, bald-headed form of the warrior in his cell, standing with legs apart in the shadows. Cursed place. *Don't let me down*, Deord was saying. Faolan blinked, and the phantom was gone. The voice remained. *Keep your promise. Live the life I won for you. Live it for the rest of us; the ones who couldn't go on.*

Faolan fastened his rope around the bars and tested it for strength, trying his full weight on it. The thing held firm. Perhaps, after all, he would do it now. If he waited, he might weaken. He might listen and be swayed. Chances were Seamus wouldn't be back for a bit. It didn't take long to die, when you were set on it.

He made a noose; slipped it around his neck. Best not take time to think. Best just get on with it . . .

"Faolan!" A voice from outside, shrill as the call of a sea bird. It was Eile. "Faolan, where are you? Your father's here! We've come to get you!"

Gods. His hands on the noose, he filled his lungs and shouted back. "Here! Eile, I'm here!"

"Just hold on—" She fell suddenly silent. He thought there were other voices out there, though he could not distinguish the words. Seamus's, perhaps, and those of other men.

His body was possessed by a violent shaking. Slowly, carefully, in the manner of a man who is accustomed to exercising the utmost control over his thoughts and actions, he loosened the knot, removed the noose, took down his makeshift rope and, subsiding to the floor, began to unmake it. In his hands, the instrument of death became a bundle of fraying rags, which Faolan used to wipe away his tears.

7

I NEED TO put something to you, Eile," said Conor, his expression serious.

"What is it?" Eile asked, knowing it must be something to do with laws and offenses and punishment. Yesterday, the day they'd brought Faolan back home, had been the wrong time to speak of such matters. She'd seen Faolan kneel in Áine's hall, tears flooding his cheeks as his father laid a hand on his head in blessing. She'd seen Áine's frozen features and heard the cold rage in the Widow's voice as she ordered the lot of them from her house. She'd seen Líobhan fold her brother in her arms, welcoming him like a lost child found again, to the accompaniment of Phadraig's volley of excited questions. Today the other sister had come, the one who was a nun, and they were all gathered together in the chamber that had once been a place of death and was now a haven of love and family. All except Eile and the brithem. He had called her to a smaller chamber, where a table held writing materials and the walls were fitted with shelves full of scrolls; it seemed to Eile a magical domain, rich in possibilities. To be able to read and write must be wondrous. To set down tales; to interpret maps of exotic places; to hold in your hands the very words of the ancients . . . "Tell me," she said.

"The law is clear on the matter of unlawful killing," said Conor. There was compassion in the gray eyes; Eile shivered, wondering if he was about to tell her he had no choice but to hand her over to the folk from Cloud Hill. "I discussed your case with Faolan last night," the brithem went on. "It kept us up very late. Most folk would agree that there were strong mitigating circumstances. Unfortunately, those make no difference to the law's perception of this as wrongdoing. You did not act in self-defense. You planned the deed, executed it, and fled. The kinsmen of the dead man are entitled to apprehend you and to keep you in custody indefinitely and, as you are without resources, it is possible a far graver penalty could be imposed."

Eile waited.

"A penalty of death," Conor said. "It's not likely, but I do need to make you aware of it. Faolan told me you would want the full truth."

Eile nodded, feeling a sense of distance, as if the whole world had retreated and she was all alone in a little space of her own where nobody could really see her. "Saraid," she whispered. "What would happen to Saraid?"

"We need not look so far ahead," said the brithem. "Tell me, have you any blood kin besides your aunt? Did your mother have brothers?"

She shook her head. "Mother never spoke of any family."

"You're certain? I ask because there is such a thing as *éraic,* the body-fine, a sum payable for unlawful killing. What you need, Eile, is wealthy kinsmen. From what Faolan has told me, I think your aunt would be willing to accept the *éraic* payment in lieu of seeing you incarcerated or executed. You are young; you have your child to raise. The circumstances of your action were such that it seems clear you are no threat to the community."

Her heart was beating again; the fog was clearing

from her head. "How much is this *éraic*?" she asked. Hope. You had to hold on to hope.

Conor named a sum so large that she couldn't get her head around it. Perhaps she gaped; in any event, the brithem said, "It would not be beyond a man of status to raise such a sum. It would provide security for your aunt for a good many years; allow her to re-establish herself. She must agree to it, I believe."

"I have no silver and I have no kinsmen," Eile said. "Me and Saraid, we're on our own."

The brithem nodded. "I have something further to tell you," he said. "Before I do, I must explain to you that, once a person pays the *éraic* on behalf of a killer, the latter enters what is called debt-bondage to the payer. He or she is required to remain in the ransomer's service until such time as he can buy himself out by paying the sum in question. Of course, if family members pay the *éraic,* it's relatively simple. But if a person who is not a kinsman of the offender should choose to pay the body-fine, for whatever reason, the expectation is that he takes control of the debtor's person and possessions until paid out. I need to be sure you understand this, Eile."

"Why?" she asked blankly, as the chamber began to recede again, leaving her alone on a little island, apart from the rest of the world. There were shadows all around. She would not shed tears. "Nobody would ever pay that for me, it's enough money to . . . to buy a castle. The law's unjust. This means rich people can go free and poor people can't. I . . ."

"What is it, Eile?"

"How . . . how would they do it? Execute me, I mean? What do they . . . ?"

Conor's hands came across the table and fastened around hers. "Eile," he said, "Faolan has said he'll pay the *éraic* for you."

"What?" That couldn't be right.

"Faolan has sufficient funds to pay it, and he will, if you agree. He wasn't sure how you'd feel about it. If you're prepared to consider his offer, he'll talk to you about what it would mean."

"Faolan has that much silver?" Eile had begun to shake. "Where? How?"

"You can ask him. The silver went to Blackthorn Rise with him, and it came out with him. My son has learned some surprising skills in the years since he left home."

"I don't like the idea of being some kind of slave."

"He predicted that would be your response. You must at least consider the offer. Indeed, you should make a decision as quickly as you are able."

"Make a decision?" Eile stared at him. "I may be a bit stubborn sometimes, but I'm not pigheaded enough to choose death or imprisonment just because I don't want to be beholden to anyone. I've got my daughter to think of. Of course I'll accept. But I need to talk to Faolan. I need to make it clear—" She stopped herself. She wouldn't be laying down any rules. Once he paid this fabulous sum, he would own her.

"Very well." Conor smiled, and it seemed to Eile the smile was as much sad as happy. "I'll fetch him."

"Don't interrupt them now." The family had so much ground to make up, mourning those lost, celebrating survival, exchanging ten years' news; she had no part in that and did not want to get in the way. Her head was still reeling. At the same time, she knew a great weight had fallen from her shoulders. They'd be safe. Saraid would be safe. As for herself, maybe she'd never have the little house of the dream, but that was a selfish wish, anyway, one she didn't deserve to have granted. If she had to work her fingers to the bone to pay Faolan back, she'd do it.

She went to find Saraid. The weather was dry today. The gray dog and Líobhan's hound were both sunning themselves in a corner of the courtyard and Phadraig and

Saraid were busy setting something out on a bench. As Eile stepped outside, Saraid ran over to seize her hand.

"You mend Sorry now," she ordered. "Ribbon. Frill. New clothes."

"Mother's got all the things ready," said Phadraig, motioning to the bench. "She made the gown, it's from an old one of hers. We watched her. But she wouldn't fix Sorry, she said you'd want to."

"Fix Sorry now," said Saraid.

Everything was there, needle and thread, the promised ribbon and frill, extra cloth that almost matched, and a diminutive rose-pink gown finished with minute neat stitches for Sorry to wear once her two parts were joined together again. It would be a little like putting a queen's robe on a scarecrow.

"We washed her while you were away," Phadraig said, "and Mother dried her by the fire. But she still looks a bit dirty."

"Honorable wounds," Eile said, smiling. "Now, Phadraig, you pass me the needle, and Saraid, you hold Sorry's head in place while I get started."

"Be brave, Sorry," Saraid whispered. "It won't hurt much."

The delicate operation was carried out in near silence, its only interruption the arrival of the dogs to investigate. Phadraig took them off to chase a ball, and Eile slipped the little gown over Sorry's head, did up the fastening at the neck, and put the doll in Saraid's waiting arms.

"You could go and show Phadraig's mother," she suggested.

Saraid wavered; pride and shyness fought a small battle in her eyes.

"Phadraig will take you in." Eile could see Faolan coming across the yard. He was in clean clothing, gray wool trousers, a blue shirt somewhat too big for him, a tunic over the top. He'd shaved off the dark beard acquired in captivity, and Eile observed his unhealthy pallor and a shadowy look around the eyes. Coming home, she thought, was not all hugs and smiles and happy endings. And now he was going to be poor as well, all because of some promise to her father. He was probably cursing the day he met Deord.

"Take this basket with your mother's sewing things, Phadraig. It was very kind of her to lend them, and to wait for me to do the mending."

Phadraig touched the row of stitching around Sorry's neck, peering close. "It's *quite* good," he said. "Come on, Saraid."

They were gone. Faolan sat down on the bench beside Eile, stretching out his legs. "Father told me he's explained the body-fine to you, and that you've agreed to let me do it," he said, not meeting her eye.

"I could hardly not agree." There was a constraint between them; this was their first conversation alone since before Blackthorn Rise. During the time apart, Eile had come to think of him as a friend; the closest thing she had to family. Now she was uncomfortably aware that he was almost a stranger. "Your father said that unless this bond is paid, Anda could ask for my death. I've got Saraid to consider."

Faolan nodded.

"I mean," Eile blundered on, "I don't want her growing up as a sort of slave, but at least she'll be with me. I love her. Nobody else cares about her. This will keep her safe. I suppose. I don't really know what it means, only that I'm not going to be locked up, and I'm not going to die before she grows up."

Faolan smiled. Like his father's, his smile looked sad.

"I'm sorry," Eile said. "I forgot to say thank you. You've saved my life. I can't imagine why you would hand over so much silver on my behalf. Being Father's friend doesn't bind you to impoverish yourself because of me. I'm nothing. I'm not really worth it."

"Isn't Saraid worth it?" He was looking at her now; she had no idea at all what he was thinking.

"To me, of course she is. She's the most precious thing

in the world. I'd die for her. But I'm her mother; of course I think that. You're not even blood kin."

He looked down at his hands. "Eile," he said, "I've no intention of keeping you as a slave. The very idea makes my skin crawl. I'm just paying the *éraic*, that's all. Can you really not understand why I'm doing that?"

She shook her head. "I know you believe you owe Father something. But this . . . It's too much, surely."

"You're asking me to retract the offer?" His brows lifted; for a moment he looked like his old self.

"What do you think?" she retorted.

"I think you're too wise for that. Eile, your father saved my life at the expense of his own. That, on top of the natural bond between Breakstone men, would be sufficient to oblige me to do this for you. But in fact that is not the only reason for my offer. You seem to have forgotten yesterday. It was your shout that saved my life, not to speak of your plan to gain admittance to Blackthorn Rise. I'm deeply in your debt. I'm happy to have this opportunity to repay that."

Eile was confused. "Saved your life? Me? You mean your sister was going to kill you?"

"I don't know what Áine planned or what she plans now. Her mind runs on paths incomprehensible to ordinary folk."

"Ordinary? None of your family is ordinary." Eile thought of lovely, giving Líobhan and her quiet, strong husband; inquisitive, kind Phadraig; honorable Conor and the grave, good old man. And Faolan, the man who had got himself captured and locked up trying to help a blood-soaked fugitive most folk would have shrunk from. "If anyone saved your life it was your father. He talked us out of there."

"Father doesn't know the full story." Faolan was avoiding her gaze again, staring at the ground by his boots. His voice had gone quiet.

"What story?"

"As I told you all last night, Áine waited fifty days before she saw me. I'm used to captivity. I know all the tricks for keeping fit and staying sane, and I used them. Then she called me to her hall and . . . and I discovered not just who the Widow was but how deeply she still loathes me for what I did. She can't forgive me for failing to rescue her that night."

"I understand that part. What was it you couldn't tell your father?"

"Before she sent me back to the cell, Áine uttered some terrible lies; all too believable lies, for I had been seeing my family in my dreams for ten years, Eile. I had seen what might have become of them. She painted me a picture far crueler than the truth. By the time I got back to my solitary chamber, I believed I had destroyed all of them in one way or another: my mother dead—the only truth—my sisters bitter and sorrowful, my grandfather deathly sick and my father . . ."

Eile took his hand. "You can tell me," she said, feeling suddenly much older than her sixteen years.

"She said his mind had been destroyed; that he could no longer put two thoughts together. That seemed the most grievous news of all. You've met him. He was always our rock, our shelter, our reassurance that we could be brave and just and walk straight paths in the world. Always, Eile, always over those ten years, however deep my despair, I refused to take the easy way out, the quick, merciful ending, though the trade I ply now taught me a hundred ways to do it. Always, I'd been strong enough to keep going. But after those revelations, after seeing what Áine had become and finding myself unable to forgive her, despair overwhelmed me completely. Nothing made sense to me; there seemed no longer any point to things. Didn't you ever feel like that? With Dalach, and what was happening to you?"

"No," Eile said. "I had Saraid. I couldn't give up. Anyway, I always believed Father would come and fetch us one day. When you told me he wasn't going to come, I did what I had to do. I knew it was up to me. I'm sorry that's meant you had to save us after all. I'd much rather have done it myself. Are you saying that when I yelled your name in the courtyard, you were about to kill yourself? Truly?"

Faolan nodded. "My neck was in the noose. Your voice was the loveliest thing I ever heard in my life, Eile. Your words told me I had a future. All the silver in the world can't pay for that."

They sat in silence for a little. Líobhan came to the kitchen door, looked across and went in again.

"What does this mean, then?" Eile asked him, pleating a fold of her skirt between her fingers. "This *éraic* thing? What do you plan to do about it?"

"It's difficult. Saraid seems like a different child here; even I can see it. Líobhan would be happy to have the two of you stay. The problem is Áine. She won't forgive us for this. Both of us represent a danger to this household because of what she might do. I can buy your freedom, but I can't buy safety from the Widow. She knows she has you to blame for coming here to tell Father where I was, and for bringing the rescue party. As for me, my sister will never cease her attempts to punish me, as long as I remain within reach."

"Oh." This was a lovely house, full of kind people, warmth and courtesy. For the first time in longer than she could remember, Eile had felt she could really breathe. "So we have to go away. How soon?" How to tell Saraid again: *We're leaving, Squirrel. An adventure.*

"Soon. I'm sorry."

"It's worse for you. This is your family. You only just found them again."

"I was never planning to stay here long. Indeed, I only came because of you. I'd made up my mind to bypass Fiddler's Crossing because it was too difficult."

Eile nodded. "Are you happy now you've done it? Despite what happened with your sister? Despite having to give up all your money?"

Faolan smiled. "On balance, yes. Another reason I am

in your debt. And it isn't quite all my money. There'll be enough left to get by on."

"You said you weren't planning to stay. But this is your home. You shouldn't let Áine force you to leave, that isn't right."

"I've a mission to perform in the north before spring. After that I must take a ship back to Dunadd and points beyond. I'll need to go on earning my keep, not to speak of yours and Saraid's."

She looked at him.

"It isn't safe for you here, so close to Blackthorn Rise," he said. "Áine has a great deal of power. Not only are you and the child at risk, but my family remains vulnerable if we stay. I want them to be able to return to the wary truce they had with Áine. It's the best that can be achieved."

"I see. So you do want a slave after all?"

"To be honest, my journey would be accomplished far more easily alone. I'm accustomed to that. On the other hand, the presence of an instant family should help me remain relatively inconspicuous, and that can only stand me in good stead."

"Family." Eile's voice became a growl. "You mean the wife and child thing again? I don't like that. You know why."

"I refuse to identify you as a bonded slave, Eile. That sits very ill with me. I've explained this to you before; you should know you can trust me. And if it feels wrong to you that I should sleep on the floor and give my slave the bed, then we can take turns. Both of us have lived rough before. What we need is honesty. I won't lay a hand on you, I swear it. I won't expect more of you than common sense and discretion. In return, I offer my protection. I realize it hasn't helped you much up till now but, believe it or not, I am highly skilled in that field, and I will prove it to you. You want Saraid to be safe. I'll keep her safe."

Eile said nothing. Although she was pretty sure he

would keep his word, the idea repelled her. She could not get Dalach out of her mind, heavy, stinking, thrusting, grinning Dalach.

"The place I need to visit in the north is a community of Christian monks," Faolan told her. "I don't wish to create the wrong impression by arriving with a young woman whom I cannot identify as wife or sister."

The obvious question, Eile thought, was why, if he didn't fancy a slave, he didn't take her and Saraid somewhere far enough away and simply leave them to fend for themselves. She didn't ask it. Faolan might not think it important that she repay this massive debt, but she disagreed.

"Did you say Dunadd?" she asked him. "Isn't that over the sea?"

"It certainly is," said Faolan. "How do you feel about boats?"

This time, Eile thought, she wouldn't have to lie to Saraid. This time it really would be an adventure. "I don't know," she said, remembering Deord's tales of epic voyages and strange new realms. "I think I might quite like them."

⌇⌇

A FEW DAYS later, they left Fiddler's Crossing. It was early, the horses' breath smoke-white in the morning chill and Saraid and Eile standing pale and silent, wrapped up in the good, warm clothing Líobhan had provided. Faolan swallowed a multitude of regrets: that he could not allow them to stay here where they might be happy; that he must bid his family farewell so soon after finding them. That he had not been able to forgive poor, damaged Áine, and must leave others to deal with her twisted desire for vengeance. But he had laid his other ghosts to rest. So quickly, the wounds deep inside him had almost healed. His family's forgiveness was a powerful salve, but he did not forget that, without Eile, he would not have been here to receive it.

Now his father stood before him. Conor's eyes were both stern and loving as he set his hands on Faolan's shoulders and gazed at him. "Go with my blessing," he said. "A safe journey." He touched his lips to his son's brow. Then his glance went to Eile, who was bidding a grave farewell to Donnan and the old man. "That's a fine young woman," the brithem said. "Or will be, once she learns the whole world isn't against her."

Faolan held back tears. He had shed a few since he came home, over swift-passing days and nights into which they had done their best to cram ten years of vanished time. Today, it was not possible to stand here without remembering that other departure, the morning after Dubhán's death: the drained face of his mother as she'd given Faolan a little bundle of food for the road; his father's helpless despair; the fact that his sisters had not come out to say good-bye. He looked into Conor's eyes now and saw the same memory; he saw the same unshed tears.

"Faolan," the brithem said gravely, "never forget that you are my son, and that I love you. Even in the darkest moment, that was always so. Wherever you travel, and I think that will be far, you carry your family with you. Keep us in your heart, and make your way home to us one day."

At that moment control escaped Faolan long enough for a single tear to fall, and he embraced his father, saying something, he didn't know what, some kind of promise. He hugged Líobhan, who was managing to smile.

"You'll come back, Faolan," his sister said, holding him tightly. "I know it. There'll be a time."

He took his farewell of his grandfather, and Donnan, and Phadraig, who had gone uncharacteristically quiet. He thanked Donnan for procuring the horses that would take them quickly beyond the borders of Laigin. He had told nobody, not even his father, where they were going; it was safer that way.

It was time. He helped Eile onto her horse. His father was right; she was becoming a fine young woman not just in her honesty and strength, which Faolan had seen from the first, but in other ways, too. A little good feeding and a temporary sense of security had begun to turn the half-starved wretch of Cloud Hill into a thin but healthy-looking girl with a long sweep of glossy hair the hue of oak leaves in autumn. The green eyes were bright, though still wary; her skin had a better color now. She was quiet this morning. He knew she would have liked to stay.

"Saraid ride horsey?" a small voice asked. "Please?"

He lifted the child onto the saddle in front of her mother. "All right?" he asked Eile. "Just follow me; we'll take it slowly."

"Mm."

"Look after him, Eile," said Líobhan.

"Well, then," Faolan said, "I suppose it's time to go." His voice was less steady than he had intended. He took one last look at his family. It was nearly his undoing; if his father had asked him at that moment to stay after all, he knew he would have been hard put to say no. He mounted in a rush, turning his horse so the others could not see his face. "Come, then, Eile," he said, and they rode away to the north.

AT WHITE HILL the festival of Maiden Dance, celebrating the very earliest stirrings of spring, passed by with no more than token observance. A severe storm had blanketed the region in heavy snow. Chill, flailing winds made venturing beyond the shelter of homes and walled gardens a test of endurance; stock not housed in the safety of barns was at the mercy of Bone Mother's last assault for the season, and early lambs perished in their dozens.

Within the king's household the atmosphere was tense; there was a threefold sense of expectation. Tuala's baby was due within a turning of the moon. Nothing had been heard from Broichan since his precipitate departure some months earlier. Word about the household was that, if he planned to return, it would surely be as soon as the weather cleared and blessed All-Flowers breathed the warm air of spring through the Great Glen once more. If the druid did not walk into White Hill as the first flowers peeped out beneath the budding trees of the forest, then perhaps he would not return at all. Some believed he had gone out of his wits, as druids were inclined to do sometimes, and had perished in the dark chill of the winter woods. Tuala had shared her vision only with her husband and Aniel. In her opinion, what happened next was Broichan's choice, and it fell to his family—that, it seemed, was what she and Bridei were—to be patient about it.

The third cause for the edgy sense of anticipation was Carnach, and a growing rumble of unrest that made itself known to Bridei through the spies he sent out to glean what they could in village drinking halls and the gathering places of powerful men. Carnach himself had sent no messengers. Bridei knew his kinsman had spent the winter at his home in Thorn Bend, far to the southeast. His spies had brought him the news that Carnach had not made a claim for the kingship of Circinn; the best intelligence was that it would go to one of Drust the Boar's brothers, as Aniel had anticipated. But Carnach was too quiet. By now he should at least have let the king know his intentions for spring and summer; for the conduct of the garrison at Caer Pridne and for the ongoing defense of Fortriu's borders. Leave it too long, and Bridei must seek another man to be his chief war leader. To do so would be the equivalent of slapping his influential kinsman in the face. He did not wish to be forced into it.

Meanwhile, the weather prevented much movement in and out of the king's stronghold and the children who lived there, deprived of their usual outdoor activities, were driving everyone crazy. Tuala kept Derelei's lessons brief and to the point, for she was often weary now in the last days of her pregnancy. They had learned much together, but she felt, always, that insistent tug at the limits she set for her son, the urgent need to delve deeper. He wanted to cross boundaries and she refused to let him. Without her controls to guide him, Derelei had the capacity to cause havoc. It was exhausting. Once the new baby arrived, she thought she might not have the energy, or the will, to keep it up.

Thus, when there came a day on which the air seemed a touch warmer and the wind a little less biting, the queen sent a messenger to Fola at Banmerren, requesting the wise woman's presence at court as soon as convenient. The official reason was the imminent arrival of the king's second child. Banmerren could furnish midwives, since this was a function the healer priestesses of the Shining One performed regularly in their neighborhood. Fola knew Broichan better than almost anyone now living, and she would understand that Tuala needed counsel as well as midwifery.

It was still too cold for the children to be long outdoors. The three little boys, Garth's twins Galen and Gilder, with Derelei, had taken to running along the passageways of White Hill at top speed, hurtling up and down stairs, barreling into anyone who might be in the way and erupting into ear-splitting squeals of overwrought laughter at the least provocation. The nursemaids were tearing out their hair. Garth's wife, Elda, who was expecting another child herself, could be heard lecturing her sons from time to time, after which all would be quiet for a little before mayhem broke out again. Derelei tended to have scraped knees and bruises on his arms and legs, and a wildness in his eye that Tuala did not much care for. Whenever she could, she took him to play with Ban in the garden, or to watch the men at wrestling games in the hall. But Derelei's restlessness went beyond the forced inactivity of winter. Tuala wondered if Broichan had been right when he had first raised the subject of the child's special talents. Perhaps her son should be sent away, baby as he was. Perhaps he did belong with the druids of the deep forest, who could tutor him with wise discipline, free from distractions. Her heart quailed at the prospect.

Help for the immediate problem came in an unlikely form. The warrior chieftain of Raven's Well, Talorgen, was both old friend and trusted supporter of Bridei and had recently arrived at White Hill with his two sons. One morning, Bedo and Uric came to see Tuala in her private apartment. The inquisitive lads she had known when they were seven or eight and she a shy thirteen had now grown into lanky, red-haired young men with grins every bit as disarming as Talorgen's own.

"Bedo, Uric, how good to see you! I would say, 'How you've grown,' but I'm sure you must be tired of hearing that. Is your stepmother here, too?"

"Yes, Brethana came. She didn't really want to, but Father said she'd like court when she got used to it." Bedo, the elder of the two, came into the chamber and, at Tuala's nod, seated himself by the fire. His brother leaned on the chimney piece, a picture of studied nonchalance.

"I'll look forward to meeting her when she's got over the journey," Tuala said. "It's good to see your father so happy." Talorgen had recently remarried; the story of his first wife was not aired in public. Dreseida had been set aside by her husband and banished from Fortriu over a plot to put her own eldest son on the throne in place of Bridei. That son, Gartnait, had died in the strange course of dark events that followed. It had been largely through the courageous intervention of Tuala's close friend Ferada, Talorgen's daughter, that Bridei had survived to become king. "I'm hoping your sister will be here at court soon," Tuala said. "I've invited her to keep me company when the baby's born."

"Ferada hates babies," Bedo said with a grin. "You'll

be·doing well if you can prize her away from her new project. Everyone's talking about it; the first secular school for women in all Fortriu. Trust my sister to take on something nobody else would touch. She misses bossing me and Uric around, you realize, that's the only reason she's doing it."

At that moment there was a roar of children's voices outside the door, and a sound of running footsteps accompanied by hysterical barking.

"Derelei!" Tuala's tone was unusually sharp; she was feeling queasy and uncomfortable today, and it didn't help to be constantly worried about her son either bothering folk or managing to hurt himself again.

"Mine!" a twin shouted, beyond the door.

"No, mine!"

"Is not! Give it to me!"

A wail: Derelei. He still had few words, and this made it difficult for him to hold his own with the twins, a year older and not only bigger but much more fluent.

A scream. Tuala was on her feet and wrenching the door open before she could think, for the sound had indicated utter dread. She stepped into the hall, Uric and Bedo at her shoulders.

Derelei was standing with his back to the wall and his hands outstretched in front of him. Opposite him, pressed against the other wall, was Gilder, preternaturally still and very red in the face. He couldn't move; his eyes were terrified. The screams came from Galen, who stood a little way off, a straw-packed leather ball in his small hands. Ban stood stiff-legged, his barks escalating.

"Derelei, no!" Tuala snapped, her heart thumping.

Derelei moved his hands, closing them into loose fists. Gilder's rigid form relaxed; he fell to the flagstones, a sob of fright breaking from his lips. Tuala stepped forward.

"Doggy," said Derelei calmly, and in an instant Gilder had disappeared, and there were two dogs in the hallway.

It was as if Ban had spawned a twin. There was no telling them apart. A new frenzy of barking broke out as they circled each other, hackles up. Galen had wisely backed away, still clutching the ball.

Uric gave a long, slow whistle.

"Holy hailstones," said Bedo in what seemed to be awe.

"Derelei!" Tuala's voice was close to a shout. "Bring Gilder back! Now!"

Perhaps she had been too angry. Derelei looked up at her. His mouth crumpled; his eyes brimmed with tears. At once, he seemed no more than an overtired two-year-old. It was unusual for Tuala to reprimand him; he was always so good.

"Do it now, Derelei. No doggy. Bring boy back."

"Ball," Derelei said tremulously, glancing at the other twin, who hugged the disputed item to his chest.

It would be an easy matter to take the ball and give it to her son. The less Bedo and Uric saw here, the better. But she could not allow that; Derelei must not learn that he could use magic to get his own way.

"No," said Tuala. "You can't have the ball. Derelei, bring Gilder back."

Derelei brushed past her and went into her chamber, where he could be seen retreating to crouch under the table. Uric bent down to separate the two dogs, which were snapping at each other in preparation for a serious encounter. Bedo had picked up the frightened Galen and moved him out of harm's way.

Someone was approaching; Tuala could hear voices, probably Elda in search of the twins. "Ban!" she ordered crisply. "Sit!"

After a moment's hesitation, one dog lowered its rump obediently to the floor, a resentful growl still issuing from its mouth. Uric grasped the other by the scruff of the neck, wincing as the snapping teeth came close to removing a finger.

This had better work. Tuala pointed in the small dog's direction, closed her eyes, and whispered a few words. There was a moment's hushed silence, then an ear-splitting wail. As Elda and a maidservant came around a turn of the hallway, Uric crouched down beside the hysterical Gilder, holding him firmly by the arms.

"You're all right," he said. "You're not hurt. Be a man."

"What's wrong? What have they been up to this time?" Elda sounded as exhausted as Tuala felt.

"Just a fight over a ball," said Bedo calmly. "We've sorted it out. I think."

"It was Derelei's fault," Tuala told the twins' mother. "I'll be having a few words with him. Maybe you should take the twins away for a bit, Elda. They're quite upset." She hoped very much that any small tales of turning into creatures would be dismissed as the products of an overwrought imagination.

When the sobbing Gilder and the sniffing Galen had been borne away, Tuala looked at Talorgen's sons, and Uric and Bedo looked back at her.

"I won't lie," she said. "I'd have been far happier if you hadn't seen that. Folk know Broichan's been training Derelei. But none of us knew he could do that."

"Remember that time when we were little," Bedo said, "and you told me you were going to turn me into a newt?" After a moment he added, "My lady."

"I did no such thing," Tuala said repressively. "You asked if I could, and I said I'd try if you wanted. And you went green in the face. I remember it well."

Uric chuckled. "But you could have, couldn't you? Like you undid the dog thing. Just as well Bedo didn't ask to be a monster or a powerful sorcerer or something. What if you did a spell and couldn't reverse it?"

"Or wouldn't," commented Tuala grimly. "Now, boys, you must understand something."

"Don't tell anyone?" Bedo was smiling.

"I'd be most grateful if you kept this to yourselves.

This kind of thing doesn't happen often here. What these little boys need is diversion. They need to be kept so busy they have no opportunity to get into mischief."

There was a brief silence.

"Don't look at us," said Uric.

"I don't know." There was a distinct glint in Bedo's eye. "It does get pretty boring here in bad weather. I wonder if those carts are still here somewhere, you know, the ones we brought from Raven's Well a couple of years ago? They'd go well on the slope down to the main gate, don't you think? And we could show them dodge-the-ball." He turned to Tuala. "The carts have iron wheels. We got the blacksmith at home to make them for us. They're good for races."

"As long as nobody gets hurt," Tuala told him firmly. "No broken bones, no serious bruises. And no annoying other folk about their daily business. Ferada was full of stories about you two. I've heard them all."

"We're not so bad," said Bedo with a crooked grin. It seemed to Tuala that, for all Uric's practiced air of coolness, it was this brother who would have all the girls after him in a year or two.

"And you let me know straight away if there are any . . . problems."

"Yes, my lady."

These boys had surely changed during their years under their older sister's guidance, Tuala thought as the two of them strolled away, all relaxed good humor. Ferada had made fine young men of them; she seemed to have wiped away the shadow that had touched that family at the time of Bridei's election to kingship. Ferada would be coming to White Hill for the birth of the royal baby. Tuala must remember to congratulate her friend on a job well done.

Right now there was Derelei to deal with; Derelei who was curled in a tight ball under the table, silent. Tuala walked into the room and closed the door quietly behind her. She moved across and seated herself on the floor, a little awkward with the bulk of the unborn child to balance.

"Derelei?" She kept her voice low. "I'm not cross anymore. Gilder's all better. Come out now."

No response. She could feel the tension emanating from her son, even from two arm's-lengths away.

"Derelei, you mustn't use magic when you're angry. It hurts people. Gilder was scared. He didn't like being a dog." Gods, if only he were a little older, a little more able to talk and to understand. "Come out, sweetheart. Mama isn't angry."

Ban went under the table and began to lick the child's face. Nobody could stay still long under such vigorous attentions. Derelei uncurled, whimpering, and crept out. Tuala had no lap left to sit on; she gathered him to her as best she could. "Who taught you that?" she asked him. "Boy into dog? We never tried that, and I'm sure Broichan never did, either." Then, after a silence, "Derelei?"

"Doggy." His tone was mutinous.

"No doggy. You mustn't scare your friends. Mama says no."

Silence.

"And Broichan says no." Or would do, she was certain, if he were here. Today's small drama had opened possibilities that filled her with dread. Keeping her child's untapped powers under control could consume her every waking hour, her every last scrap of energy. That was not possible. There was a baby coming. And there was Bridei, who needed her.

The quiet was broken by a little, forlorn sound. Her son was weeping. "Bawta," he whispered. Ban pushed his nose against the child's leg. Clearly, the dog had forgiven the earlier affront.

"I know, sweetheart," Tuala said. "I miss him, too." She would not say, *he will come back*. This child could not be pacified with less than truths. "If you are good and don't do this again, the big boys are going to play with you and the twins tomorrow. They've got a cart that you can have rides in. With wheels. Go fast." She would not think of broken limbs and cracked heads. Children must be allowed to play. Even children with a terrifying facility in the craft of magic.

"Whee," said Derelei half-heartedly, moving his hand through the air in the motion of a swooping bird. Tuala thought she could see an image of wheels, and sparks flying, and trees and bushes moving crazily past. She blinked and it was gone.

"That's right," she said. "But you must be good. No doggy. No magic at all, unless Mama is there. Promise?"

He made a little sound, not a word, but perhaps an indication of agreement. It would have to be enough, for now. Sooner or later, Tuala thought, her son was going to cast a spell she lacked the power or the knowledge to undo. She hoped he would not reach that stage before he had a better mastery of words, before he could learn the perils his ability carried with it. As for today's episode, it had made her wonder. Broichan had tutored Derelei wisely and carefully; she had done her own share of teaching in the same spirit. But what he had done this afternoon, the complex transformation performed without visible effort, had not been learned from either of them.

(from Brother Suibne's account)

God be praised, we touched the shore of Priteni lands this morning, our boat intact, our crew untouched by storm or sea serpent or freakish current, our hearts still full of zeal for the new life that awaits us in this far land. Not all of us are sailors. My guts feel as if they have been pummeled and twisted and hung out to dry, and it is a blessing to have solid earth under my feet once more. Our landfall was close to Dunadd, thanks to Colm's sound navigation, the expertise of our young novice, Éibhear, and the assistance of our unexpected passengers. The traveler, Faolan, who was familiar to me from the court of Fortriu—I never forget a face, however unremarkable— proved expert with oar and sail; that was no surprise, as I had already assessed him as a man of many parts. His little wife, so silent and compliant, proved more of a revelation. My fellow brethren were less than happy to take a woman as passenger, especially one accompanied by a girl-child; there are many tales of boats sunk and voyages beset by ill fortune because of a female presence on board. Once under sail, with most of us bent over the rail in the throes of acute seasickness, it became apparent the woman was an asset. Colm, brought up among sailing men, was unaffected; Éibhear has salt water in his veins. Faolan helped them, and so did the girl Eile, doing her share willingly and with every appearance of enjoyment. Indeed, a grin of pure pleasure spread across her face at the heaving movement of our frail craft through the endless waves of that wretched strait. As for the child, she sat quietly, hugging her doll and eyeing the monstrous seas with perfect equanimity. When we saw great, gray creatures leaping from the waters, she showed not a trace of fear, but smiled and pointed.

They make an odd little family. Faolan does not seem the type of man to travel with a wife and child; he has the air of a loner, wary and deep. Colm was struck by him and by what he had to tell of the court of Fortriu. We performed certain inquiries while we waited for spring; it would appear this man's ancestral roots are in the same patch of ground as Colm's own, but his life has not followed a straight course. He has his own pressing reasons to make a home away from the shores of Erin. The three of them, Faolan and his wife and child, were lodged at a farm near our house of prayer for a good part of the winter, and Faolan made it clear to us that he needed to return to White Hill as soon as the season made it possible. Thus the offer of a passage. It was in Colm's interest to aid him, woman, child, and all.

Not the dog. There was a dog, a poor, thin thing that came into our yard with this trio of wayfarers and headed straight for the refectory door to stand waiting outside with hopeful eyes. There was no way the dog could accompany us in the boat. The little girl wept to hear this; she was attached to the wretched creature. During the time they spent quartered at the farm a solution found itself. We had a very old and venerable brother among our number in that house, Brother Seosabh, whose mind had begun to wander amiably; he spent his time sitting by the fire, or in a sunny corner outside, mumbling to himself and nodding at anyone who was prepared to stay by him awhile and talk, though there was no saying how much made sense to him. The dog took a fancy to Seosabh, and he to the dog; they seemed to understand each other. At any time of day the dog might amble over from the farm and be found sleeping at the old man's feet or sitting by him while the ancient fondled its ears and muttered endearments. When we took Seosabh his bowl of broth, the dog tended to get a scrap or two at the same time, since we were unable to harden our hearts to the reproachful look the creature turned on us if its own portion was forgotten.

Seosabh, of course, was not among the volunteers for Colm's expedition. There are thirty brethren in the house of prayer at Kerrykeel; only twelve volunteered or were chosen for the mission to Fortriu. Others will come later, when we have built a house and a church and all we need for survival on our island. We are the spearhead; the bright torch to light the way. When we launched our boat and set out for new shores, the child farewelled her dog with tears, but her mother's reassurances that the creature had found his true home, and the old man's gentle hands touching the child's as if she were the most precious thing on God's earth, provided the little one with some comfort.

So, our landfall, and a walk to the fortress of Dunadd, which now lies in Priteni hands, although the deposed king of Dalriada is still resident there. Gabhran is in his last illness; it was deemed too risky to send him back to his home shore by sea. Had Bridei's men slain him in the great battle of Dovarben, it would have been deemed acceptable. To have him perish during an enforced voyage of exile would not sit well with the king of the Priteni, who has a reputation for fairness and justice along with a strong grasp of strategy. Gabhran renounced the kingship of Dalriada; his household is overseen by a Priteni chieftain. Nonetheless, Dunadd is full of Gaelic speech and Gaelic customs. It has not changed so very much since my last visit.

We bade Faolan and his little family farewell this morning. He said his wife had no desire to spend time in grand establishments such as this fortress that was once the Gaelic court of Dalriada; her origins meant she had scant time and patience for such halls of the wealthy and powerful. In fact, Faolan had pressing business at the far end of the Great Glen. There was no need for him to tell me this, nor to tell Colm. It goes without saying that he will bear a message to the court of Bridei, king of Fortriu, asking if that powerful monarch would be prepared to receive a delegation of Christian brethren. The name of Ioua will be mentioned; Yew Tree Isle, the place the Gaelic king promised Colm as his sanctuary from the political dealings of his kinsmen. Ioua is no longer in Gabhran's gift. If we want to stay, it is Bridei who must approve our settlement in that place.

Perhaps, if I had not been among Colm's small flock, Faolan would not have chosen to identify himself. His mission may have been to spy rather than to negotiate. But I knew him; he could not conceal the nature of his quest from me. That is a good thing, I believe. Matters should move more quickly as a result, and that will please Colm, who dislikes this shadowy half-court where we are housed, and chafes at any delay in seeing us lay the foundations of our new home on Ioua. There are armed men everywhere here. Some are Gabhran's own, *and some belong to a chieftain named Umbrig, who is apparently in control of the fortress and its inhabitants on Bridei's behalf, though he resides elsewhere and they say he visits seldom. The guards are huge and fearsome in appearance. I do not rate very highly our chances of coaxing them to join in our morning prayers. On the other hand, Colm needs only to open his mouth to make folk listen. Under the light of his powerful faith, perhaps even these shambling bears of men can open their ears to the word of God.*

SUIBNE, MONK OF DERRY

8

FAOLAN WAS TENDING the fire, nurturing it against a moisture in the air that he hoped would not develop into rain. They would be sleeping under the moon again tonight; there were few places within Dalriada where he was prepared to seek shelter beneath another man's roof. The Gaelic presence remained strong in this territory newly regained by Bridei, and Faolan's own face was known to more than a few of the influential locals. Since Alpin of Briar Wood had unmasked him as a spy, a man who used his lineage as an entrée to Gaelic courts and his close bond with Bridei as the currency by which he made his way in Fortriu, it did not seem safe to come out from cover, so to speak. Not until he must. He had apologized to Eile, surprising himself. The farmhouse in Kerrykeel where they had spent the best part of the winter had provided comfortable lodgings, warm, secure, and private; neither of them had needed to sleep on the floor, for there'd been three shelf beds in the chamber they were allocated. It seemed wrong to expect her and the child to lie on the ground with only bracken to keep out the wind. Not that she complained; there was never a word of criticism. Somehow, that made it worse.

"Faolan?" she asked now.

"Mm?"

"You know you said these folk speak a different tongue? At this place we're going to, White Hill?"

"Mm." The fire was catching now; he blew on the licking flames.

"They're going to think I'm stupid," Eile said.

"No, they won't. It's a king's court. They're used to all kinds of folk coming and going. Some people speak a little Gaelic."

She sat silent, her hands stilling in their task of scaling the fish he had caught earlier. Saraid was crouched nearby, holding her doll up to see.

"You'll manage, Eile."

"I should have asked you to teach me the language over the winter, when we were at that farm. Will you teach me some words while we're traveling, enough so I don't make a fool of myself? It's going to take a while to get there, isn't it?"

Faolan did not answer. The fact was, slowed by woman and child, it would take a lot longer than he was happy with. That man, Colm, burned with a missionary zeal that set warning bells ringing loud. They needed to get to White Hill soon and advise Bridei to be ready for visitors. In Faolan's estimation, this Christian cleric wasn't going to sit quietly at Dunadd and wait for the king's invitation. He wanted his island, and he wanted it soon. He believed this god of his had somehow ordained that Ioua be his servant's sanctuary. If the fellow wasn't up the Glen and knocking on Bridei's door before Midsummer, Faolan would be greatly surprised.

"Faolan," said Eile in a different tone, "you can just leave us behind, you know. If you really need to go quickly, tell us the way and we'll follow at our own pace."

She brushed a strand of hair away from her brow, leaving a shining smear of fish scales. "We'll be all right."

Things had changed between them over the winter of enforced companionship. She had begun to show a wary trust, while he was becoming accustomed to the presence of the two of them and developing skills he had not possessed before, such as knowing how to cajole Saraid out of her tiredness and how to allay her small fears.

"Here, let me do that." Faolan reached for knife and fish.

"I can do it perfectly well!" The knife flashed down, brutally efficient.

Of course, he did still get things wrong sometimes; she hated to be thought incompetent. "I know that. Eile, it's a long way up the Glen. Many days' travel. The paths are difficult even in summer. And there's Saraid to think of. I'm sure you are completely self-sufficient. On the other hand, I think I've demonstrated that I can be useful catching fish and trapping rabbits, so you need not do those things and watch over her as well. Besides, if we part ways, who's going to teach you the Priteni tongue?"

She eyed him suspiciously. "That's a joke, yes?"

"Is that fish ready? I'm getting hungry, and this fire seems to have decided to burn. Here, pass it to me."

She handed it over. "I can look after myself," she muttered.

"Maybe so. And maybe I am in a hurry. Never mind that. I don't want you and Saraid at the mercy of any unscrupulous wanderer you might meet on your way."

"Who'd be interested in me?" Eile folded her arms and hunched her shoulders. "Only some freak like Dalach. We'd be perfectly safe without you."

Faolan glanced at her, taking in the creamy pallor of her skin, the bright sheen of the red hair, the figure that was changing now with good food and less anxiety.

"Don't look at me like that!" Eile glared at him.

"How? As if you were a woman?"

A flush rose to Eile's cheeks. "I'm not a woman, I'm roadside rubbish."

There was a little silence.

"Rose-dye rubbige," echoed Saraid, trying out the words.

Faolan balanced the skewered fish over the fire. "Who told you that?" he asked after a little.

"Someone. It's true. After Dalach I'm no better than some slut who sells herself for a copper or a bannock. I'm nothing. I'm invisible. Her and me, we can slip by anywhere. You don't need to worry about us."

"You know," Faolan said, sitting back on his heels, "for a girl with so much common sense, you have quite a few blind spots. Here you are, alone in the world with a little daughter you love dearly and guard fiercely, and you dismiss my offer of protection as if it were worthless. This journey is full of dangers. Perhaps I should mention that my official job at court is as the king's personal bodyguard, so I am something of an expert in these matters. You've accepted my help thus far. What makes things different now?"

Eile stared down at the ground, her long hair falling forward to frame her face. "It's not that," she said. "I do value it. It's what I dreamed Father would do; come back and look after us. But it's different. I can't afford to get used to it, because I know it can't be forever. Besides, he would have done it because he wanted to. You're doing it because you think you have to. I know you need to get to White Hill in a hurry. Now we're over the water, Saraid and I are slowing you down. I'd rather do this on my own than start feeling like a burden."

He looked across the fire at the two of them: Eile sitting cross-legged in her borrowed gown, an old one of Líobhan's, with her hair touched crimson by the firelight and her green eyes forbidding him to be sorry for her; Saraid with the shapeless doll cradled in her arms. "You're not a burden," he said. "Eile, I want you to promise me something."

Her eyes took on the wary expression of a creature scenting danger. "And what would that be?" she asked.

"I want a promise that from now on you won't call yourself roadside rubbish or slut or any such name. If your daughter hears that often enough she'll start to believe it, not just of the mother she loves and trusts, but of herself. I don't want to hear it ever again."

Her features tightened. "So you're telling me how to bring up my child now, are you? What gives you the right to do that?"

He drew a slow breath and let it out, reminding himself how young she was. "If I wanted to be cruel," he said, turning the fish over the flames, "I'd answer that a substantial payment in silver gives me the right to tell you anything I like."

"So what am I?" Her response was quick as a slap. "Your slave or your friend?"

"I would not make such a suggestion to anyone but a friend," Faolan said. "To Saraid, you are the best person in the world, good, brave, beautiful. I expect we all believe that of our mothers when we are small. She doesn't have much, Eile. Let her keep that."

He expected another reproof, another challenge, but she was silent. When he looked up from his cooking, he saw to his amazement that she was crying. Saraid edged across to lean against her mother, mouth drooping in sympathy.

"It'll never be all right," Eile whispered. "Sometimes I forget to think about it, like on the farm when it sometimes felt like we belonged there, and when we were on the boat. I liked that. It made me feel like a new person. Then it all comes back. He sullied me. Dirtied me. That's never going to wash away."

"Dalach's dead," said Faolan. "That time is over. Some things you never forget, however hard you work at it. But you can put them behind you. You can say, yes, it was bad, so bad it nearly made me give up. But I didn't give up. I'm strong. I'm alive. And then you can go on and make something of the rest of your life. Not easy, but possible for someone like you."

"Is that what you did?" She scrubbed a hand across her cheeks. "After your brother died?"

He thought about this. "Not exactly. I tried to block it out; shut it away. For ten years I thought I'd done that. I lived a life, performed certain tasks, honed certain skills. Earned my silver. In all that time I never told the tale of Fiddler's Crossing. Until last autumn. Until I met your father."

"You told him?"

"Not exactly. I told . . . someone else. Someone who challenged me to confront the past. So, you see, I've only been following my own advice for a short time. I may be ancient in your estimation, but in this matter of starting life anew, I'm not far ahead of you."

"Feeler," said Saraid, "Sorry's hungry."

"It's almost ready, Saraid." Let Eile not ask him about Ana. Not now, sitting here by a little fire in the darkness; not now when the sweetest and most bitter memory was stirring deep inside him. "Deord did have advice for me," he said. "He challenged me to live my life well. He told me not to waste the opportunity his bravery had won for me. I'm still not sure what that meant. I had thought survival was good enough. I had thought it the best I could manage." He lifted the fish from the fire, laid it on a flat stone, divided it with his knife. "Careful, Saraid," he said. "It's hot."

Over the makeshift meal he taught Eile the words for *fish* and *thank you* and *knife* in the Priteni tongue. Saraid wanted to learn, too; he taught them *doll* and *eat* and *good night.* When the child was asleep, rolled in her good woolen blanket from Fiddler's Crossing with Faolan's cloak over the top, he and Eile sat by the fire while the moon rose into the velvet dark and stars emerged on the high arch of the night sky. It was bitterly cold; beyond the circle of firelight things stirred and rustled in the dense undergrowth.

"Everything's big here," said Eile, huddling deeper into her cloak. "Tall mountains, huge trees, lakes that take all day to get across. It makes me expect to meet giants."

Faolan wondered if he should mention the Good Folk, and decided against it. "The folk at White Hill are quite normal," he told her. "There's nothing to be afraid of."

"I didn't say I was afraid!"

"My error."

"All the same, kings and queens . . . I'm not accustomed to grand folk like that. Your sister Áine was bad enough. I didn't seem to be able to open my mouth without saying the wrong thing."

He did not answer.

"Faolan?"

"Mm?"

"What am I supposed to do when we get there? Be a servant? Scrub floors, wait on tables?"

Faolan was reluctant to confess that he had not really thought this out. "It won't be like that," he said. "As the king's bodyguard, I suppose I could be called a servant of sorts. I do a job; he pays me. But I'm also . . ." He would not say, *I'm his friend.* To do so was to acknowledge something he had long deemed an impossibility. "Bridei trusts me," he said. "I'm close to him."

"You haven't answered the question."

"It depends on what you want for yourself and for Saraid. Education; training in some kind of work, maybe. A place to settle. I have a couple of possibilities in mind." He had thought Drustan and Ana might take Eile in, along with the child. She was Deord's daughter, after all, and Deord had been Drustan's only friend for the seven years of incarceration. They would want to help, if they were still at court. Part of him hoped profoundly that they were not. Still, it would solve this problem neatly. "I have some friends I believe would welcome you into their household. Or there's a school for young women, not very far from White Hill. You could go there, if you wanted. The third possibility is that Tuala—the queen—could find you a position at court."

"What about you? Where would you be?"

He stopped himself from telling her that was irrelevant. His bag of silver had made it relevant, whether he liked it or not. "I'm at court sometimes. More often I'm away. My duties require me to travel."

"Guarding this king, you mean?"

"I'm one of three personal guards. I do other things as well."

"What things?" She fixed her gaze on him. The firelight flickered in her green eyes.

"Things. I don't discuss them."

"Uh-huh. I guess those extra duties wouldn't include being a bard. That's what Líobhan told me you once were. It's a bit hard to believe."

He felt his mouth twist in a smile. "You won't hear me singing at White Hill. These days, I turn my talents elsewhere."

"Mm. I don't suppose you earned all that money as a musician, unless you were really good." Then, after a silence, "You know you said once you were unlucky in love? Who was the woman? What was she like?"

"It's old history. I don't talk about it."

"Was she the person you told your story to? The one who made you go back to Fiddler's Crossing?"

"It's none of your business, Eile. We'd best get some sleep; if the rain holds off, we'll make an early start in the morning."

"Your voice goes different when you talk about it," Eile said quietly, moving away to lie down beside Saraid. "As if it still hurts. Was she beautiful?"

He settled on his own side of the fire. Eile was too acute. Her questions were like little knives. Best give her some answers now, if only to stop her digging deeper. "Like a princess in a song," he said. "In fact, she really is a princess, cousin to the king of the Light Isles. She was a hostage at the court of Fortriu for a number of years.

That's not as bad as it sounds; she was there to ensure her cousin's loyalty to King Bridei, who is his overlord. Ana was treated more as an honored guest than as a prisoner. Last summer I escorted her on a journey to marry a chieftain of the Caitt. It all got very complicated. Now she's betrothed to someone else, a highly suitable man whom she loves. And that, as far as you're concerned, is the end of the story."

"It doesn't sound as if it is," Eile said softly. "You're still angry and hurt, I can hear it. You still love her. Did you and she—did you ever—?"

"That's not the kind of question a young woman asks a man who's nearly old enough to be her father," Faolan said repressively.

"I'm just asking because . . . well, I . . ."

Something in her tone, reticent, delicate, made him ask, "What's wrong, Eile? What is it?"

"I just don't understand how . . ." The words seemed to escape her lips in a rush. "It's just that . . . well, it's so vile, brutal and hurtful, what men and women do together, I can't understand how it can go with . . . with what you call love. Surely as soon as you lie together, as soon as you do it, it must destroy those tender feelings. It can't be otherwise. Yet I remember Father and Mother . . . They were always so kind to each other, even after Breakstone when he was so changed . . . Maybe I'm trying to remake the past, so it's the way I wish it had been. I'm sorry, I shouldn't have asked you that. It was wrong. Forget I said it."

Gods, how could he respond to this? What did he know of such matters, with his own twisted history following him like an unlucky shadow? For a little, confusion and embarrassment halted his tongue. Then, glancing at her tight, wounded features, he found words. "What was between you and Dalach wasn't the usual way of it, though there are plenty of men like him who'll take their satisfaction when and where it suits them, with no regard to a woman's feelings. That's why I don't want you traveling on your own. You're prey to the unscrupulous. But it's not always that way; there are other folk like your mother and father, Eile. Folk like my sister and her man. Some young fellow will come courting you one day, and you'll discover that for yourself. It can be a . . . a loving thing, a thing folk take pleasure in." It felt completely wrong to be offering her advice on such a matter. But there was nobody else.

"I don't believe you," she said. "How could any woman enjoy that? I expect if you were fond of the man you could put up with it, but that'd be all. It's repulsive. It makes you feel unclean."

"I'm telling the truth, Eile."

"You're a man. What would you know?"

Her tone was bleak. It made him feel old and tired. "Good night, Eile," he muttered, settling as best he could on the hard ground. He did not expect to sleep, but after a long time sleep came, and with it a tangle of disturbing dreams.

WITH THE CLEARING of the weather White Hill began to fill up with visitors. Bridei had called a great gathering to thank and reward the chieftains who had played a part in last autumn's victory. Such formal recognition was necessary to maintain balance and unity within the kingdom of Fortriu. Songs must be made, gifts given, each carefully selected according to the recipient's social standing, contributions, and character. Bridei's two councillors were busy. Aniel was working on the gifts while Tharan and his wife, Dorica, ensured the practical arrangements for the anticipated influx of guests were flawless.

Meanwhile Bridei considered the issue of what to do if Carnach failed to appear. To have his chief war leader and close kinsman turn against him would be not simply distressing but dangerous. It would open possibilities for the future that were unthinkable. Carnach was popular, successful, influential. He bore the blood of the royal line. Should anything happen to remove Bridei from the kingship of Fortriu, nobody was in any doubt as to who his successor would be.

Chieftains from every corner of Fortriu began to arrive with their wives and sometimes their children. Morleo and Wredech, Uerb and Fokel, all were there by the time the buds began to open on the beeches.

A messenger rode in from Caer Pridne one afternoon. Seeing him coming, Garth sought out the king, who was closeted with Aniel and Tharan.

"Thank the gods," Tharan said. "Word from Carnach at last."

But when the fellow came in to deliver his message, it was to announce the imminent arrival, not of the chieftain of Thorn Bend, but of another, still more powerful leader: Keother of the Light Isles, Bridei's vassal king and cousin to Ana. Keother had made landfall at Caer Pridne that morning and would be riding for White Hill in a day or two, when the women in his company had recovered from the rigors of the sea voyage.

"Women?" queried Aniel, gray eyes sharpening. "What women?"

"There were several, my lord. I wasn't given all their names; some are serving maids. One is the Lady Breda, Keother's cousin."

"I see." Bridei considered the issues this news raised, not least the fact that Ana's kinsman was unaware she had spent the whole winter at Pitnochie with Drustan, and that the two of them were not yet handfasted. "Thank you for bringing this news to us so promptly. There will be food and drink for you in the kitchens and a bed for the night in the men's quarters."

The messenger dismissed, the three men exchanged looks that spoke more than words could convey.

"Why would Keother bring this young woman?" Aniel murmured. "She's Ana's sister, I presume. It's as good as asking us to take her hostage, especially after his failure to provide so much as a single warrior for our endeavor against the Gaels."

"Keother is no fool," said Tharan. "He's up to something. What's his motive? Is he trying to placate you, Bridei?"

"We'll be in a better position to assess that when we meet him face to face," Bridei said. "He'll have to be received with appropriate formality and allocated the best chambers. Tuala will have to move Talorgen and Brethana. And there's the question of Ana."

"Mm," said Aniel. "I wonder if the young lady's come simply in hopes of attending her sister's wedding? We'd best dispatch a messenger to Pitnochie."

"Indeed," Bridei said. "With Keother on our doorstep, a wedding is most certainly called for. I don't imagine Drustan and Ana will have any objections. The current situation cannot continue indefinitely, or we'd give her cousin entirely reasonable grounds for complaint. That the formal handfasting has been delayed while Drustan and Ana live in every other respect as man and wife is . . . unconventional. Unexpected visit or no, they must marry before they travel back to Briar Wood."

"We'll be needing a druid," said Tharan. "Do you believe Broichan will return in time, Bridei?" His tone was delicate; it was a difficult issue. Theories abounded at court on where the king's druid had vanished to, and why. Some of them were foolish, others verging on scurrilous. The longer Broichan stayed away, the more imaginative the gossip grew.

"We must summon another druid. There's a man at Abertornie, a lone mage by the name of Amnost. He should be prepared to travel if we provide safeguards." Bridei did not mention Broichan. Nonetheless, his foster father's absence loomed large. Tuala remained confident Broichan would return when the time was right. It seemed to Bridei there could be no better time than this, and that if his foster father did not come now, perhaps the rumor that he had perished alone in the forest was true. It had been a harsh winter.

"Very well," Aniel said. "A written message to Lady Ana, I think. Tell me what you want in it, Bridei, and I'll do the scribing and dispatch it with a reliable man today. A verbal message to Loura at Abertornie, asking her to bring this Amnost when she and her children come to court." The recognition due to Ged of Abertornie, who had fallen in the last great battle for Dalriada, was to be given to his wife and son. There was still time to get a message to them before they rode out from home.

"And I'll warn Tuala to expect still more visitors," said Bridei.

It was not a good time. Occupied as he had been with preparations for the gathering, the king was well aware of how exhausted his wife was and how Broichan's absence had given her an additional burden in the final stages of her pregnancy: dealing with Derelei's budding abilities. Bridei felt a constant, nagging ache in his belly that he knew was worry about his wife. He feared the rigors of childbirth, the poisonous tongues of visitors to court, the weight Tuala carried as mistress of the royal household at such an important time. The look in her eyes concerned him more than he would ever tell her. He saw that she felt tired, anxious, perhaps guilty. That this last was without foundation made no difference. Broichan was a grown man. The decision to leave had been his alone. That did not stop Tuala from believing it was her fault for confronting the druid with her unwelcome vision of kinship.

Let her be well, Bridei asked the gods as he made his way to his private quarters with his guard Dovran an arm's length behind. *Let her come through this safely. Let the child be born whole and sound. That is all I ask.* He knew in his heart the power the dark god held over him; his own past disobedience and the penalty that might at any time be demanded in compensation. *Not now,* he thought. *And if it must come, strike me, not them. Not my dear ones.*

He had hoped to find Tuala resting, but she was in the small reception chamber with two older women: Tharan's wife, Dorica, and Rhian, widow of the previous king, Drust the Bull. Dorica stood as the king came in. Rhian inclined her head.

"Bridei," said Tuala with a wan smile. "We've just been making some plans, moving folk around a little and ensuring everything's in place for such an influx of guests. I have a feeling I won't be able to help for much longer."

"What are you saying? Have your pains begun?" He was alarmed.

"Not yet, but I think it will be within a day or so. Elda has predicted it will be tomorrow night. I hope Fola will be here in time."

"Now, my lady," Dorica said, "you just forget about supplies and bedchambers and keeping folk entertained, and concentrate on yourself for a little. We have everything under control, and more helpers coming in from the settlement. You're not to worry."

"Indeed not." Queen Rhian rose to her feet, a plump, dignified figure. "I've done this more times than you can possibly imagine, Tuala."

"I have to tell you the king of the Light Isles is on his way," Bridei said, "and with him Ana's younger sister. They're at Caer Pridne. It looks as if a wedding's in order." He saw Tuala's brave attempt at a smile, and went to sit by her side, holding her hand. Dorica and Rhian made their farewells and left the royal apartments. Dovran pulled the door closed. He would remain on duty outside.

"I'm sorry, Bridei," Tuala said, touching her husband's cheek. "I want to be more help. This is such a difficult time for you. But I'm so tired. And worried about Derelei. Thank the gods Bedo and Uric have turned their hands to a spot of nursemaiding, if it can be called that. We owe those lads a great deal. The little ones are so exhausted at the end of the day they fall into their beds the moment they've finished their supper. Derelei is simply too weary to think of attempting more perilous pursuits than running, climbing, and riding down steep slopes on makeshift vehicles. Still, with the weather improving, Talorgen's sons are going to want to return to more manly pursuits such as hunting and practicing their combat skills, I imagine."

"Derelei will need careful watching with so many folk here," Bridei said. "I won't express a wish that Broichan return, though I know he's the one we need. We should speak to Fola of our concerns when she comes."

Tuala nodded gravely. "I shrink from the idea of sending our son away," she said. "He's too little. But he's a danger to all of us until he's old enough to understand the need to curb his gift. If he can turn his friend into a dog over the temporary possession of a ball, what havoc could he wreak in a hall full of the most powerful folk in Fortriu, should something happen to displease him?"

"Worse," said Bridei, "what might the unscrupulous seek to use him for, should they witness the raw power at his disposal?"

"I've tried to show him how to harness it." Tuala sounded miserable. "My lack of formal training makes it difficult, as does the need to keep what we're doing relatively covert. I'm barely beginning to learn the extent of my own abilities. No wonder I cannot exert proper discipline over Derelei's."

"With both Fola and Ferada coming to court," said Bridei, "you'll have expert advice and practical help. Leave the household arrangements to Dorica; between them, she and Queen Rhian can cope with whatever is required. You need not do anything but rest, keep well, and prepare for our child's birth. Tomorrow, you said? Do you think the prediction is accurate?"

"Apparently Elda's never been wrong before," Tuala said. "I'm sorry, in a way. I'd have liked to take an active part in planning Ana's wedding."

Bridei smiled. "If this visit by Keother means Ana and Drustan are handfasted and away from White Hill before Faolan gets back, it can only be to the good. I gave him an undertaking that I'd try to ensure they were gone before his return."

"Poor Faolan. It would be altogether too sad if he arrived at White Hill just in time to see his beloved wed another man. He was not at all himself when they came back from the north. I had never thought to see him so unmanned."

"I don't expect him back so soon," Bridei said. "His missions were various and complex, his return to this shore dependent on clement weather and the availability of passage. As for his devotion to Ana, I saw how that had changed him, and I think what awaited him on his home shore might have wrought still more changes. There was a dark secret there, something only Drustan and Ana were privy to."

"Is it possible he, too, will not return?" Tuala's voice was small; she leaned her head on Bridei's shoulder, holding his arm, and he was reminded of the way she had embraced him when they were children and sharing bedtime stories.

"He, too?" he queried. "I thought you possessed an unshakable faith that Broichan would stroll up the hill one day, cloak swirling in the breeze, ready to pick up the tools of his trade as if he'd never been away."

"I do," she said simply. "What I don't know is how long it will take. I see him sometimes in visions. He is always in the woods and always alone, though I think voices speak to him. I see in his eyes a longing to return to his family and an acknowledgment that, until the gods give him leave, he cannot. As for Faolan, he has made no appearance in my visions, but I believe we need him back as urgently as we do Broichan. It's a time of risk. Nobody deals with the protection of the king as well as Faolan does."

"I have Garth and Dovran, and many good folk who watch out for me," he told her.

"All the same, there are dangers. Bridei, what about this girl, Ana's sister? What do you plan to do? She'd be about sixteen or seventeen, wouldn't she?"

"I'll have to keep her here. I'm sorry, I realize it's distasteful to you, but I see no choice in the matter. Her cousin's behavior has been such that I'd be a fool not to make her a hostage. Indeed, I believe it possible that Keother has anticipated such a demand and forestalled it by bringing the girl before we asked for her. Why else would they come?"

"Perhaps to see how Ana is," Tuala said. He heard the disapproval in her tone, and it wounded him. "They've received your message about her betrothal to Drustan, I presume, and have journeyed here to acknowledge that. It's years since Ana saw them. How can we watch that reunion and then present them with the news that Ana's sister is to replace her as your hostage? It's like slapping your close friend in the face, Bridei. I understand the need for safeguards. I know why hostages are necessary. But this is a cruel sort of wedding gift."

He sat silent a little. Then he said, "You think that? You think me cruel?"

"No, dear one. It is the decision that is cruel. If there is some other way, you should find it. At least wait until we meet Keother and the girl, and assess their reason for making this long journey. You owe that to Ana. After all, your first choice of husband for her proved to be quite a misguided one. It's fortunate both for Ana and for you, as king of Fortriu, that she did not wed Alpin, but came home with his brother instead."

"Very well; I will delay my decision until we speak with Keother. As for Ana and Drustan, a message will go to Pitnochie today. Ana's not stupid, Tuala. She's going to know what's coming."

"All the same," she said, "let us delay the decision until

there is no other choice. Who knows what travelers may make their way up the Glen this spring? My mirror has shown me many images: a bright light, a billowing sail, a little child with a doll made out of rags. All coming from the west. I saw the great serpent, too, raising its head from the lake to watch them pass in wonder. Our little daughter here," she laid a hand on her swollen belly, "will see strange sights before summer is over."

"WELCOME, KEOTHER." BRIDEI stood on the steps before White Hill's main doorway as the king of the Light Isles rode into the courtyard with his entourage. Keother was a tall man with thick fair hair and impressive shoulders. He had brought a great number of attendants; Bridei wondered how many vessels had been required to carry the party from the islands to the shore of Fortriu.

His eyes moved to the women. There was no question which of them was Ana's sister. Breda had the same flawless features and rippling golden hair, though there was a subtle difference in the expression. She glanced at him, eyes cool, and favored him with a slight, formal nod.

"Lady Breda," Bridei said, "welcome. You'll be weary from the ride, no doubt. Please come inside. I regret that my wife is unable to greet you now. The arrival of our second child is imminent."

Folk craned their necks for a better look as the party from the Light Isles dismounted and swept indoors, surrounded by their own guards and the dignitaries of Bridei's household. Everyone knew the risk this vassal king was taking in presenting both himself and his young cousin at the court of the monarch of Fortriu. The relationship between overlord and island king had long been awkward, though Ana's time as hostage had kept Keother in check during the early years of Bridei's reign. Now Ana was to be married, and to a chieftain of the Caitt, a tribe that, for all it bore the same blood and spoke the same tongue as both Fortriu and the Light Isles, had ever been a law unto itself. With Ana out of the picture, Keother appeared to be stepping into an open trap.

The travelers had arrived just in time for supper and, in anticipation of this, the repast was a fine one: pies of mutton and leeks, seethed fish, puddings with nuts and spices. Keother was seated on Bridei's right, Breda on his left.

"All right, my lord?" Garth, standing behind Bridei's chair, leaned over to address him in a murmur.

"Mm," said Bridei. "Make sure someone brings news promptly."

"Dorica's maid has instructions to keep us informed. It's early times yet."

"Forgive me." The king of Fortriu addressed his guests. "I'm a little distracted. We're expecting a new arrival in the family before morning. Lady Breda, you may be pleased to know I've sent word to your sister of your visit here. I'm anticipating Ana and her betrothed will arrive within days."

Breda turned a small, cold smile on him. Her beauty had something unsettling about it; it seemed almost too perfect. Or perhaps it was simply the sense of both familiarity and unfamiliarity: she was so like her sister. "Oh, Ana," she said. "It is so long since I saw her, I can hardly remember her."

"She speaks fondly of you," Bridei said. "I'm sure Ana will be delighted to see you again. And her cousin, of course." He gave Keother a polite nod. "She'll be happy to introduce you both to Drustan. You'll like him. He's a fine man." He'd leave Ana to explain her betrothed's highly unusual qualities to her family.

"A chieftain of the Caitt," observed the king of the Light Isles, glancing up from his fish. "And not the man you originally chose for my cousin, I understand."

"His brother. It's a long story, which we'll give you in due course. When the spring is further advanced, Drustan and Ana will be returning to his holdings in the north, which are extensive. It's likely they will be handfasted here at White Hill in the near future. My wife and I are delighted to have you with us for that joyful occasion."

"I bet," muttered someone from a lower table, causing Garth to grip his spear and scowl in the general direction of the comment. There was no telling who had spoken.

"Time enough to discuss these matters when all are rested from the journey," Aniel put in smoothly from his position on Keother's right. "We hope you will be able to stay for some time."

Breda looked at him, brows raised. "I imagine I may be here awhile," she said. "Longer than my cousin, I expect."

Keother shot her a warning glance and she fell silent. An awkward pause followed.

"You enjoy hunting?" Tharan asked the royal guest. "We can offer opportunities here that will not be open to you at home, I imagine, since your isles lack forested areas. Later in the season there will be fine quarry farther down the Glen. I'm sure Talorgen would be happy to ride out with you."

"Fishing, as well," offered the dark-bearded chieftain Morleo. "The trout in some of our more secluded lakes are of great size and uncommon cunning; they provide excellent sport."

"Thank you," said Keother. His light blue eyes bore a calculating expression; Bridei could see he was weighing up each speaker and each comment. "I would be more than willing to participate, as would my men, but my cousin does not much care for such sports. You must find gentler occupations for Breda."

"Several other women usually join us at the king's table," explained Aniel. "Tonight they are attending the queen as she gives birth. If you enjoy music, my lady, or womanly crafts such as weaving, you will find many compatible friends at White Hill."

Queen Rhian was seated farther down the table; she leaned forward to catch Breda's eye and smiled. "Lady

Breda, your sister is something of a scholar; I'm told she did very well during her time at Banmerren. And she shares my interest in fine handiwork. Ana's embroidery is exquisite."

Bridei recalled Ana as she had been on return from her journey north: lean, brown, her flowing hair cropped short, her manner turned from that of sensitive court lady to decisive, no-nonsense traveler. In company with Faolan and Drustan, the royal hostage had witnessed murder, battled wolves, saved a man's life at risk of her own. "You'll find your sister much changed," he said.

"Of course," Tharan put in, "we can also offer an education superior to that generally available for girls. Banmerren provides tuition not only for future priestesses of the Shining One but for young women of high birth. Ferada, daughter of our chieftain Talorgen, has recently instituted a new branch of that well-respected establishment. You will not be bored, Lady Breda. Indeed, we have both Ferada and the senior wise woman, Fola, in attendance at White Hill; they arrived here earlier today. They are with the queen now, as is my own wife. Dorica will ensure you are introduced to everyone tomorrow."

"Thank you." Breda's tone was lukewarm. Whatever it was she needed for amusement, Bridei thought, it evidently hadn't been mentioned yet. Perhaps he was being unfair. The girl was very young, and she'd had a long journey. Maybe she was simply tired.

It was one of the requirements of kingship that a man be able to conduct a conversation with powerful visitors, assessing each nuance of tone, noting each change in the eyes, each movement of the hands, even when his mind was on other matters entirely. Bridei wanted nothing more than to stand outside Tuala's door, to be told of any progression in her labor immediately, to be able to reassure her with his voice, even though the mysteries of childbed meant he would be denied admittance to his wife's chamber. Kingly status made no difference to an event that was so much a women's province. He worried. Tuala had not had an easy time of it with Derelei for she was slight of build and, although the infant had been small, her labor had been long. Elda had said it was sometimes quicker with the second one. He hoped that was so.

As soon as he could extricate himself from this supper and hand the care of the royal visitors over to his councillors, he would go to pray. He would make a formal request of the gods, not the desperate clamoring that seemed to pour from his heart at such times, but a reasoned, courteous plea that Fortriu's queen and her new infant be spared Black Crow's touch. Measured; dignified; kingly. There would be no giving in to his emotions tonight. He could not afford that. Besides, there was nobody at White Hill before whom he was prepared to reveal such weakness. Broichan had vanished. Faolan was away, Faolan who had witnessed more than one of Bridei's dark times of doubt. To Tuala herself, should he be allowed to see her before the child was born, he must present a face that showed no trace of disquiet; his voice must betray nothing of his terror. All the same, Tuala would know what he was thinking. She knew him better than anyone.

"I had been hoping to see our kinsman Carnach here at White Hill," Keother was saying. "I've met him before on several occasions and have been much impressed by his forthright manner. Is he expected for your gathering, my lord king?" He did not quite manage to conceal the fact that he knew this was an awkward question.

"I hope very much that Carnach's commitments in the south will not prevent his attendance," Bridei said, phrasing his response with care. "I intend to acknowledge every chieftain who contributed to our victory last autumn. Carnach played a major part in it; he serves as my chief war leader. If he can be here, he will be."

"After a season of conflict," said Aniel, "our chieftains have pressing duties in their own territories."

"All the same," the king of the Light Isles cast his pale blue gaze up and down the hall, "I see many are already in attendance here."

. "Indeed," said Tharan smoothly. "But we have many days yet. Now that the season is more clement, travel should be easier for those located farther afield. Umbrig, for instance; you may not be aware that our Caitt ally stayed on in Dalriada as custodian of the captured king of the Gaels and chieftain of the southwestern region. It's a long distance, but we're hopeful of seeing him here. And Carnach, of course."

DERELEI'S PASSAGE INTO the world had been long and difficult. His sister was in more of a hurry. With a circle of capable hands ready to ease her from her mother's body, Anfreda arrived in such a rush that the midwife, Sudha, nearly dropped her. The child did not complain; indeed, she was so quiet Sudha put a finger in her mouth, then dangled her upside down just to be sure she was breathing.

"She's white as a ghost," the midwife muttered, turning her head so Tuala could not hear. "Quick, pass me a blanket."

Fola, who had known the queen of Fortriu for a very long time, remained unperturbed. "No cause for alarm, Sudha," she said, reaching to fold the infant in a length of fine woollen cloth. "Tuala, you have a healthy daughter. Hold her a little now, then I'll take her to meet Bridei while Sudha deals with the afterbirth." The wise woman's eyes were very shrewd as she laid the tiny girl in her mother's arms. Within the folds of the snug blanket, Anfreda's face was a circle of flawless ivory. Her large eyes were open, their color so light it could hardly have been called blue. The mouth was a tight rosebud, the little head fuzzed with dark hair. Anfreda bore none of the characteristics most newborns share: wrinkles, blotched skin, temporary deformities of the skull after the tight passage out of the mother's body. This infant was tiny, pale, perfect. A single glance would tell the least observant of people that she was descended from the Good Folk.

Tuala smiled, wept a tear or two, kissed her daughter and relinquished her to the wise woman. "Take her to Bridei," she said. "I know he's just out there, worrying."

Fola bore the precious bundle out into the anteroom, which seemed full of men, though in fact only four were present. Bridei's companions for his anxious wait were his bodyguard, Garth, the chieftain Talorgen, and Aniel, who was concealing a yawn as Fola entered the chamber. It had been a long day for all of them.

"Your daughter, my lord king," the wise woman said, placing the baby in Bridei's arms. "Tuala's well; tired, of course, but cheerful. There were no complications." Fola glanced around the chamber as the king cradled his daughter, murmuring to her. "Who was that?" she asked, looking at Talorgen. "Was someone else here?"

"No, my lady." Garth stood by the door, tonight fulfilling the dual role of king's guard and companion. "Not that there weren't more wanting to share the king's wait, but Bridei said he was content with the three of us."

"Odd," said Fola. "I'm sure I saw someone. Out of the corner of my eye . . . Ah, well, perhaps I'm starting to show my age." She would not tell them the figure she had half-seen had been clad in garments of leaves and crowned with twists of ivy.

"You'll never do that, Fola," said Aniel. "You're always a step or two ahead of the rest of us. Congratulations, Bridei! So it's the girl Tuala expected."

"I understand she's to be named for your mother?" Talorgen bent to take a closer look.

"Anfreda, yes." Bridei held the tiny girl as if she were a basket of eggs, and he a little boy doing his best not to break them. He was beaming.

"Though, clearly, it is her mother's side of the family

she favors," said Fola drily. "If I ever thought Derelei fey of appearance, I take it back. Beside this scrap of a girl, your son seems all miniature warrior of Fortriu, Bridei. I'll wager little Anfreda is the image of Tuala as a newborn."

Bridei, who long ago as a child had found Tuala on the doorstep of Broichan's house when she was about the same size as this infant, nodded his understanding. "She's so small," he said. "I'd forgotten how small they are. When can I see Tuala?"

"Soon," said the wise woman. "Let me take the child back; it's warmer in there. Certain matters must still be attended to, but it won't be long. Then you'll all be wanting your beds, I imagine. At this hour only martens and owls are astir."

"You'd be surprised," Aniel said, putting a hand up to screen another yawn. "Half the household's still awake, waiting for news. I'll perform that duty, then I'll take your advice, Fola. I'm certain Tharan will expect me to be up bright and early to help him entertain our guests. I'd best attempt to be at least half awake. Bridei, please convey my warmest regards to Tuala. This is joyful news."

When he went out, Talorgen followed. They walked a little distance along the passageway and out to a secluded corner of the garden, where a torch still flared to light the path for anyone foolish enough to be wandering outdoors in the middle of the night. After a little, Fola emerged to join them, wearing a hooded cape over her gray robe.

"Bridei is with his wife and daughter," she said, casting a glance around the paved pathways, the neat plantings of lavender and rosemary. "There are plenty of skilled hands to do what must be done. I have a suggestion, before you share this news further."

"I believe I can anticipate it," Talorgen said. These three knew one another well; all had been part of Broichan's secret council, the council that had worked since Bridei's childhood to ensure he would one day take the throne of Fortriu. "We inform the household of the safe delivery of the king's daughter. We let them know the name: Anfreda, a fine old Priteni name, demonstrating Bridei's love for his mother and reminding folk of his impeccable bloodline. We advise them that, as mother and infant had a difficult time of things, neither will be receiving any visitors other than the queen's personal attendants and friends for the foreseeable future. We don't say this ban will continue until certain guests are gone from White Hill; to maintain it so long would arouse more distrust than putting this extremely unusual infant on show might do. However, we'll keep her out of sight until we get more of an idea of why Keother's here."

"Not just Keother and the girl," said Aniel, "but others, too. We have many folk in attendance who do not know Tuala well, folk who may be ready to use any tool they set hands on to strike a blow at Bridei. I wonder if mother and babe might be better at Banmerren awhile, Fola? Not yet, of course; but when they can safely travel."

"Bridei would never agree to that." Fola was glancing around the garden as if unseen presences lurked there. "You saw the look in his eyes; utter devotion at first sight. It is his family that keeps our king strong. I will speak to him and to Tuala. Not tonight. Let them enjoy this new gift from the Shining One in peace for now. Tomorrow I will suggest some safeguards."

"Make use of Ferada while she's at court." Talorgen gave a crooked grin. "She'll be here awhile; I understand her fellow tutors are capably maintaining the course of instruction at Banmerren. My daughter can be relied upon to see off any unwelcome visitors."

Fola smiled. "I know that very well, Talorgen. Don't forget she and I work closely together. Oh, by the way, is it true the royal stone carver is due back at court soon?"

Aniel looked surprised. "Garvan? I imagine so. We've work for him here over summer. Why do you ask?"

"No reason." Fola was looking into the corners of the garden again.

Talorgen followed her gaze. "What is it?" the chieftain asked.

"Nothing. I keep thinking I see someone, but it can only be shadows. It's late. Look, the Shining One is peering out from the clouds in recognition of her fine new daughter. Prayers seem to be in order; I hope the goddess will forgive me if mine are somewhat brief. Let folk know, but be careful. Broichan would agree, I'm certain."

"Ah, Broichan," said Aniel quietly. "Would that our druidic friend might walk back into White Hill tomorrow, full of wise advice. Maybe he has terrified me occasionally, and irritated me frequently, but I recognize how sorely we need his counsel."

"Do not underestimate Bridei and Tuala," the wise woman said. "They may be young, but they are strong partners and the gods have always smiled on them. As for the child, be glad she is a girl. My sisters at Banmerren will be overjoyed to offer her a home and a calling when she's a little older. Their attitudes have undergone some changes since the time we had Tuala as a student."

"Perhaps you're right," Talorgen said. "Maybe there is no real cause for concern. The royal household has long supported Tuala, for all her difference; she's proved herself more than capable as queen. As for our visitors, they are here for a turning of the moon, perhaps two or three, a brief span. How much can go wrong in a single season?"

⁂

As is common at such turning points in human existence, birth, death, handfasting, neither Tuala nor Bridei slept much on the night of their daughter's arrival, though both were bone weary. After reassuring himself that his wife was well and in good spirits, Bridei allowed himself to be shepherded away by Garth, the influx of

women to the royal apartments meaning he must seek
his rest elsewhere for now. The king of Fortriu was
lodged in his chief druid's quarters, with his guard in the
anteroom, and before Bridei put his head down on
Broichan's narrow bed, he knelt before the druid's stark
shrine, two candles and a white stone on a shelf, thanked
the goddess from the depths of his heart, and pledged his
obedience anew.

Tuala lay in her bed with the tiny bundle that was Anfreda tucked in beside her; she had refused to let Sudha
put the child in its cradle. The midwife and a maidservant slept on pallets across the chamber. Dorica and the
other assistants had long since gone to their beds. Candles burned and the fire was banked up to stay warm
until dawn. Derelei, tucked up in his own bed in an adjoining chamber with a nursemaid to watch over him,
had slept through everything. He would awake to a surprise. Tuala had prepared him as well as she could, explaining her increasing girth and talking about the
arrival of puppies and foals as well as human babies, but
she could not be certain how much of it her son had understood. Besides, no amount of careful preparation can
ready a child for the moment when he is no longer his
parents' only treasure, but one of two.

Fola had gone off to rest in the women's quarters; she
made few concessions to her age, but she had looked
tired tonight, once it was all over. Ferada had washed her
hands, commented on what a messy business it all was
and how happy she was that she had decided to forego
the delights of husband and children herself, given her
friend a quick embrace, and taken herself off to her family's quarters.

"And now," Tuala whispered into the semidark of the
candlelit chamber, "you can tell me why you're here;
why you chose tonight to come back."

The shadowy presences she addressed formed themselves into more discernible shapes: a woman with a
cloud of silver hair, clad in a smoky, shifting robe; a man

with nut-brown skin, wearing a crown of ivy twists. They were not quite as she remembered them. The Good Folk did not age as human folk did. Nonetheless, these two had altered their outward manifestations to reflect the passage of a number of years since they had last appeared to Tuala. She had not seen them since the night they led her into the forest above Pitnochie and urged her to leap from Eagle Scar, to fly across to another world or die on the rocks below. They'd never come when she wanted them and now, unexpectedly, they were back.

"Tell me," she murmured, conscious of the sleeping women just across the chamber and her son in the next room. "And don't ask to hold Anfreda. You know I'm not so foolish."

Gossamer seated herself on the end of the bed, her garment moving about her like cobweb in a breeze. "You think we would take her and give you a little turnip baby in her place?" she said in a voice like the tinkling of eerie bells. "We will not harm the child, Tuala. She's one of ours."

"Will you answer questions?"

"We cannot say until you ask them." The man of the Good Folk, whom Tuala had always called Woodbine, seated himself cross-legged before the hearth. The firelight made his cheeks shine like polished chestnuts.

"Is Broichan my father?" It was only the first of many questions that tumbled in Tuala's head. Knowing the capricious nature of such visitors, and recognizing her own weakness on this particular night, she was trying to ask the most important ones first.

"If you need the answer to that," Gossamer tossed back her shining hair, "you are less clever or less decisive than you should be."

"That is a yes, I take it." Tuala shifted a little on the bed; her body was full of aches and pains. The soporific draught Sudha had brewed stood untouched by the bed. She would not dull her senses for one instant while these two were here. Her arm tightened around Anfreda; the infant gave what sounded like a sigh. "Then I will ask you, where is my father? Who has him and when will he return?"

Her visitors turned their large, dispassionate eyes on her. "He is in the forest," said Gossamer. "He will return when he is ready."

"Ready for what?"

"Ready for the challenge that awaits him. Broichan's craft has made him stronger than is customary for human folk. His human clay renders him weaker than a great mage must be."

"He's been ill," Tuala said. "But he was getting better; regaining his strength. I don't see how a winter in the forest could help that. He's no longer young, and it's cold out there."

"A druid is accustomed to hardship and privation," said Woodbine. "It strengthens him in mind and body. Without this season of penitence, of learning and recognition, your father will be unable to meet his greatest challenge."

"Tell me," Tuala said. "What is it Broichan must do?"

They looked at her, vague smiles on lips that were pleasing in shape, if not quite human.

"What is it a druid must do?" Gossamer asked. "What is his purpose?"

"To love the gods," said Tuala. "To obey. To be their voice for those who cannot open the ears of the spirit. In the case of the king's druid, it is more. He must serve Fortriu with all his faith and all his energy. He must love and honor both gods and king. There is no need to ask me this. I've known it since I was five years old. Tell me what this great challenge is that will bring Broichan back to court at last. We need him here soon. There's my son . . ."

Woodbine's smile broadened. His dark eyes seemed to warm a little, though perhaps it was only the candlelight glinting in their depths. "We will teach your son." His tone was soft, almost tender; it made Tuala's skin crawl. "Derelei needs no druid. He can learn without Broichan. So small and so clever."

"If you think using dangerous tricks of transformation on other children is clever, then perhaps I was wrong ever to believe you had the best interests of the king and of Fortriu at heart," Tuala said. "I want you to leave my son alone. He needs Broichan, not you."

"But you are not averse to teaching him," said Gossamer slyly. "In what way is your own facility in scrying, transformation, and mind-reaching so different from ours, Tuala? You possess the same unfettered talents as your son. You do not tutor him in Broichan's mode, structured, cautious, hedged about by rules and restrictions. You share with Derelei your joy in the freedom this craft allows; you dance with him through the doorways it opens. And now," the silver-haired woman reached out a finger toward Anfreda's dark, fuzzy hair, and Tuala shielded the infant with a quick hand, "you have this one as well. Two to teach, two to guard. How much can one woman do, be she queen of Fortriu or no? Broichan is occupied; you are tired, and wish to assist your husband in this season of challenge. We can keep Derelei busy and content. We can ensure he continues to develop his powers. All we want is to help you, Tuala. To help our sister . . ."

"Sister? Maybe my next question should be, who is my mother?" It had once loomed large; now it hardly seemed to matter.

"One of us," said Woodbine. "Which one doesn't matter. A daughter of the Shining One: a chosen daughter."

Tuala nodded. "Chosen to take the goddess's place in a kind of ritual, yes, I've seen it in the scrying bowl. So the union between my mother and Broichan was planned by the goddess herself. Why?"

"So you would be born, and your children after you. You have your part to play in the great scheme of things, Tuala. Already you walk that path. Without you by his side, Bridei would be crushed by the weight of kingship."

"What do you see for my children? Can't they be left to make a free choice of ways?"

"Are you saying your own choice was not freely made, Tuala?"

"I can't answer that," Tuala said. "There is no telling how much was my own choice and how much the goddess governed. I've tried to follow the paths I believe she intends for me. But it scares me that Derelei and Anfreda, small as they are, may already have some grand plan unfolding for them. They need time to grow and play and be unafraid. They need time to be children."

Gossamer swept a long-fingered hand through the air; a cloud of tiny stars seemed to trail behind it. "A child with such abilities as your son's," she said, "can never be quite as others are. You will always fear what he might do and what others could do to him. It is that, perhaps, which will at last force you to utilize your own powers to the full. The ward you have set over your daughter tonight, to prevent us from touching her, is stronger than any I have yet encountered. You hold that in place, and another over your son, and yet you lie there talking to us as if there were no drain at all on your powers. We know you are gifted with uncanny skills, your mother's legacy. We know the strength and self-discipline you have inherited from your father. Once or twice, as tonight, you use a little of that potential. It makes us wonder why you do not employ what you have to further your husband's cause: to rout out enemies, to destroy attackers, to frighten opponents into submission. It would be so easy."

"The new faith creeps closer to Fortriu," said Woodbine, now sprawled on the floor by the fire with his head propped on one hand. "In nearby lands it has weakened the goddess; it has driven out her wise women and put her druids to flight. It takes little to send human folk running. From fear or hunger or ignorance, they will turn their backs on all that is ancient and good. Soon your husband will face a great test of his kingship; a deep trial of his obedience. He will need Broichan, for one comes to confront him who is Broichan's equal in strength and in faith. Bridei will need you, Tuala."

"I will be here," she said, somewhat perplexed. "I vowed to stand by his side and help him be strong, and I've no intention of breaking that vow. Now I'm tired; I must try to sleep."

"You misunderstand us." Gossamer was starting to fade around the edges, a sure sign that she was about to depart. Tuala wondered if it would be another six years before she saw them again. There were so many questions she hadn't asked. But she was tired . . . Gossamer was right; maintaining the spell of protection over the two children was hard work. She would not release it until she was certain her visitors were gone. Fortriu was full of stories about changeling babies, little figures of sticks or coals or vegetables left all tucked up in bed for parents to find in the morning.

"You will need to use all the abilities you possess," Woodbine said. "The threat is powerful. Only by utter obedience and selfless courage can it be countered."

"Selfless courage?" Tuala stared at him. "Of all the qualities I might expect you to recommend, that is one of the least likely. I doubt your kind has much idea of what the concept means." The two of them began a rapid fading. "I'll consider what you've said," she added hastily. "I'll do all I can. Just leave my children alone, for now at least."

There was no reply; the Good Folk had dwindled to faint outlines that winked out as a sudden draft blew down the chimney, setting a momentary glow on the coals.

"Was that a yes or a no?" Tuala whispered to her daughter. "Those two always did talk a lot of rubbish. In the old days I was more inclined to believe it. The trouble is, one has to listen, because there's often sound advice hidden in there. The immediate problem is your brother. I'll worry about trials of obedience and selfless courage later. Anfreda, I do wish two-year-old boys were just a little wiser . . ."

9

"FEELER?" SARAID'S LITTLE voice was hoarse. "My head hurts."

Eile was outside preparing the rabbit Faolan had trapped for supper. The child lay within the shelter of the disused hut they had made their temporary home when it became apparent Saraid had a fever and could not go on. With the clearing of the weather had come bitterly cold nights, with a thick mist that hung low over the forested slopes until well after sunup. They had reached the waterway that separated Maiden Lake from the broad expanse of Serpent Lake, which stretched all the way north to White Hill.

"Drink some of this, Squirrel," Faolan said, supporting the child with his arm so she could sit and take a sip of the herbal draft he had brewed. There was a small hearth inside the hut, and they were keeping a fire burning there in addition to the outdoor cooking fire. Saraid was sometimes hot, sometimes cold; he put a hand to her brow, seeing the flush in her cheeks. Hot; too hot. Yet she huddled under the blanket as if frozen.

Perhaps they should backtrack and take her to Raven's Well. It seemed likely Bridei would have invited Talorgen and his wife to court by now, since he'd be needing to hold a ceremony of thanks and recognition before long. But there would be folk at that house, women who understood how to nurse a sick child. There might be a healer. His own skills in herb lore were limited to what might keep a man up and moving when there was a job to be done, and provide sleep even on the hardest bed. All his concoction would do was grant Saraid a short respite from the fever. He did not like the rasp of her breathing. From outside came the sound of Eile coughing.

Saraid had closed her eyes. Faolan took the cup and went out.

They'd been traveling together a long time now. He would not have thought he could become accustomed to the constant presence of others, especially a woman and child who were vulnerable and, in Eile's case, somewhat volatile. But the fact was, right now he found himself far more concerned about Saraid's breathing and the exhausted look on Eile's face than he was about the pressing need to get to White Hill. At the rate they were going, Colmcille would be passing them on the road. It didn't matter. Eile and Saraid were everything to each other. He had promised to keep them safe, and that was what he had to do.

Faolan set a mask of calm on his face and went out to the cooking fire. Eile was crouching to turn the rabbit on a rudimentary spit. The enforced stay of several days in this lonely hut had led them to invent some improvements in their domestic arrangements: as well as this means of roasting meat, they had gathered bracken to lay on the remnants of the old place's shelf-beds and had mended the roof to keep out leaks. It was hardly luxury but it was more comfortable than their nights spent on the ground under the stars, coming up from Dalriada.

"You're limping again," Eile said, sitting back on her heels to watch his approach. "The cold makes your knee hurt, doesn't it? Here, stand closer to the fire. Is she asleep?"

"Not quite. I gave her some more of the draft. I'll need to forage for herbs again: wild endive, tansy, perhaps holly leaves. What I brewed is almost finished." He bent to rub his leg, wincing. Eile had quickly discovered this weakness; there was no point in pretending it did not slow him down. The knee ached at night and it was stiff in the mornings. When he had told Eile he got the injury fighting a pack of wolves she had refused to believe it.

"I'll go," Eile said, coughing again. "Where are they? How far upstream?"

"No, I'll go. I want you to keep warm; to stay well. Eile, some friends of the king live not far from here. It would be half a day's travel back the way we've come, then up a branching track to the east. There would be proper shelter there; warm beds, women who could help."

"Is that what you want to do?" The look in her eyes was wary.

"It is a possibility. Once there, she'd have a better chance of recovering quickly. But we'd have to take her out in the cold to reach Raven's Well. If we stay here and wait, we can keep her in bed and out of the chill air."

Eile nodded. "Are you asking me to choose?"

"To consider it. We'll decide together."

"You could go there and fetch help," she said, giving him a sidelong glance from where she squatted by the fire.

Faolan was astonished at the strength of his own reaction to what he knew was, on some level, an entirely reasonable suggestion. "Absolutely not," he said. "I'm not leaving the two of you on your own." His mind showed him, one after another, all the ills that might befall them in his absence. Each was darker than the last; all were unthinkable.

"We've come through some hard times already, Faolan," said Eile quietly. "I think we could manage a day on our own. We have food and shelter. We have fire."

"I'm not doing it. I won't discuss it further."

"Oh." She gave the rabbit an experimental prod. "Well, it's too late for us to start back for this place today, so we may as well wait and decide in the morning. Perhaps she'll be better."

Faolan heard the fear in her voice despite her efforts to sound calm and capable. He did not think the child would die; she was healthy, though slight. He was more concerned by Eile's rasping cough. But what did he know? Only last summer, they said a malady had swept through White Hill and carried off several children like newborn lambs in a sudden cold snap. The amenities of court and the attentions of no less than the king's druid had not been able to prevent that. Saraid was as small and vulnerable as a new violet. Eile was frail; her fierce will could not disguise the translucent pallor of her skin, and her eyes still seemed too big for her face, despite the better diet of recent times.

Faolan put a hand on her shoulder and, feeling her flinch, withdrew it. "I'm no expert," he said. "Right now, I'd prefer the two of you were warm and dry, here where I can keep an eye on you. It's best if we don't travel until both of you are well again. Tonight, I want you to take the herbal draft, too."

Eile made a face. "It smells like dog piss," she said, reminding him that she was only sixteen.

"And tastes worse, no doubt. But it's good for you. Now I'm going to get those herbs. If I can find some wild onions to go with the rabbit, I'll bring them. I won't be far off, Eile. Stay alert, and shout if you need me."

Her smile was hard to read. He deduced it was a good sign that she would smile at all. Then she began to cough again, and Faolan headed off up the stream, hoping she had not seen the alarm in his eyes before he turned away.

He'd gathered most of what he needed when he heard Eile's voice raised in a defiant challenge. He ran. The ground was muddy and studded with mossy rocks and tangles of vegetation. His foot slipped, causing him to half fall, jarringly, against a tree stump. He regained his balance, pain lancing through the injured knee, and forced himself on, the knife he had used for cutting herbs ready in his hand. After that single cry, she had not called out again. He reached the clearing where the little hut stood. There were men, horses. Eile was in the doorway; the point of her knife was steady, aimed in the general direction of the three men who stood in front of her. Her eyes were big with shock.

"Come one step closer and I'll stick this in your guts," she hissed in Gaelic.

Faolan raised his arm, positioning his own knife for

flight. He pitched his voice to be quite clear to them and spoke in the Priteni tongue. "Lay a finger on her and you're dead. Turn around slowly and put down your weapons."

They turned, and he saw that none of the three had weapons in hand. He saw that they were familiar. His pose did not change, nor did his tone. "Step away from her," he said.

"Faolan!" exclaimed one of the men, a tall, square-shouldered individual with close-cropped hair. "Put down that thing, will you? We mean no harm; we were offering to share our provisions in return for a chance to warm ourselves by the fire. The girl was the one who started flashing knives."

Faolan lowered his hand. "She doesn't understand this language," he said, limping across to the hut and positioning himself between Eile and the travelers. "And you're hardly a reassuring sight, the three of you." They were men of Broichan's household: tall Cinioch, sturdy Uven, and a younger fellow whose name he could not recall. No threat, certainly; not to him. He could see how their grim demeanor and warrior tattoos would appear to Eile, not to speak of the array of bows, knives, and swords hanging about their persons. He reminded himself that, household guards as they were, these fellows had all served in Bridei's army last autumn.

"There's no cause for alarm," he told Eile in the language she understood. "I know these men; they are friends and may be able to help us. I'm sorry I took so long to get back." He would not say, "I'm sorry you were frightened," though he could see the terror in her eyes.

"Your leg's hurt." Her voice was shaking.

"It's nothing. Eile, I'll have to let them share our fire. They may have useful news."

She gave a tight nod. "Just tell them not to try anything."

"I said I'd kill them if they did."

Eile gave him an odd look, then vanished inside the hut. Faolan sheathed his weapon.

"Who's the girl?" asked Cinioch.

Up till this point of the journey, Faolan had introduced her, where necessary, as his wife, and Saraid as his daughter. He was too close to White Hill for that to be appropriate any longer. He did not especially care for *the daughter of a friend;* coupled with the ache in his knee, it made him feel old. "Eile's a friend," he said simply. "From home. She and her child are traveling to court under my protection. You'll treat her with respect."

"As Cinioch said, the girl was the one who wanted a fight, not us. You have a child in there as well?" Uven's brows were raised.

"They needed help. I was the only one offering. Enough of that. Share our fire if you wish. Eile and the little girl are sick; a fever and cough. We're camped here until they can go on. Unpack your gear, then give me what news you have. If you've food to share, we'd welcome that."

The three were on the way back up the lake to Pitnochie; they'd been to Raven's Well with messages, and to seek out news of Broichan. Over a supper of fish caught by Cinioch, the roasted rabbit, and an oaten gruel, they provided Faolan with more news than he had expected to hear, a great deal of it unsettling. Eile had chosen to eat her food in the hut with Saraid. Distrust had been written all over her features.

Faolan listened intently and chose his questions with care. The alarm bells were at full peal. The king of Circinn dead. Bridei deciding not to contest the kingship of the southern land. Broichan not at court; Broichan gone away somewhere, leaving no idea of when or if he might return. That was not just odd, it was disturbing. When the Christians came up the Glen, and Faolan thought that would be soon, the king of Fortriu was going to need his druid.

"We heard another strange thing," Cinioch said. "Something you might want to pass on at White Hill, though it's only rumor. A fellow who was passing through Raven's Well had it from another man who'd been traveling near Thorn Bend; he'd been up and down the Circinn border. You know how Carnach went home for the winter?"

"I didn't know, but that's not so surprising," Faolan said.

"The word is," Cinioch went on, "he's been talking of rebellion. Unhappy with the king's decision about this election, and speaking to all the chieftains of his own region about mounting a challenge to Bridei. Carnach wouldn't put his hand up for the kingship of Circinn, though he could have, seeing as he's of royal blood. What Carnach wants is Fortriu. He thinks Bridei has gone weak. The word is, there are others who agree with him."

Faolan felt a cold sensation in his spine. "What others?" he asked calmly.

"The fellow didn't say. We challenged him for proof and he went quiet. He did hint at help in high places; I've no idea what he meant. But I didn't like what I heard. I'd have taken it straight to Broichan if he'd been home. Even if this is no more than malicious tales, the king should know."

"I'll tell him," Faolan said, his mind working fast. While he had been taking his time to travel, going at a pace suited to Eile and Saraid, it seemed all manner of potential disasters had been closing in on Bridei. If he'd been on his own, he could have been at White Hill by now. "Spring's been here awhile; shouldn't Carnach be at Caer Pridne, where the king can simply ask him the question outright? Who's in command of Fortriu's fighting men?"

"He could be back for all I know." Cinioch sucked appreciatively on a rabbit bone. "I'm out of it, myself. Getting married soon, settling down to help my cousin and her man look after the Pitnochie farmland. I don't care if

I never see another Gael in my life." There was a pause. "Present company excepted, of course," he added, glancing from Faolan to the hut and back. Inside, Saraid could be heard coughing, and Eile speaking to her in a low voice.

For a little, nobody spoke. Faolan's reputation meant the Pitnochie men-at-arms would not engage him in idle conversation or tax him with obvious questions such as, "When were you planning to move on?" or "How can we help?" Most folk were afraid of him; all were wary in his presence. His sudden unlikely acquisition of a woman and a small child did nothing to allay their natural caution.

"Cinioch," Faolan asked after a while, "with Broichan gone, who is currently in residence at Pitnochie?" Broichan's house was the next logical stop on the trip up the Glen; a fair way, but a house of friends, well able to provide everything needed for Eile and the child, and inhabited by folk who understood discretion. It was quiet and secluded; less frightening for Eile than the grand establishment at Raven's Well would be. But . . .

"The lady from the Light Isles is still there," Uven said. "Her and her betrothed. They've been in the house all winter. Lovely folk to look after: quiet, courteous, no airs and graces. Even Mara likes them. But they'll be off soon."

Faolan ordered himself to breathe slowly. "Off?"

"To the north, to Drustan's lands," said Cinioch. "They were waiting for Broichan to conduct the handfasting, but now it seems they'll be married at White Hill, with another druid performing the ceremony. News of that came just before the three of us headed off for Raven's Well. They could be already gone when we get back. You want to ride with us?" He glanced around, apparently for horses.

"We're on foot," Faolan said. "Eile's not much of a rider. I'd hoped to secure passage up Serpent Lake by boat, if there's anything going that way. Right now the two of them are too sick to be moved."

"And you're in a hurry," Cinioch ventured.

"You could say that."

"You want us to take the girl and the child back to Raven's Well while you go on? We can lend you a horse and replace it with another from Talorgen's stable. We're not in such a hurry that an extra day would make much difference."

"No." It was an effort to get the word out. Bridei needed this information; it could be vital. This was Faolan's job, his mission. Take one of these sturdy mounts, and he could be at White Hill in a day or two. "Eile would be frightened; she doesn't know the language. And the child's too sick to go even as far as Raven's Well. I'll wait until they can go on."

"Suit yourself." Uven gave him a searching look.

"You can help me by letting the household at Pitnochie know we'll be coming; we'll avail ourselves of at least one night's shelter there. If Eile and Saraid can't travel further, I'll leave them in Mara's hands. Do you have sufficient oatmeal to leave us a supply? That will be welcome. The child needs good plain fare."

"You can take what we have," Cinioch said. "Our bread as well. It's not as if we've far to go, and we can hunt easily."

Faolan could see a bemused look in the three men's eyes; this encounter would likely be the cause of much speculation when they moved on. He cared nothing for that. Let them think what they liked.

He'd had to go back for herbs, since he'd dropped what he'd gathered when Eile called out. With the Pitnochie men settled in their cloaks by the fire, he took his fresh harvest into the hut.

Saraid was asleep, snuggled deep in her blankets. Eile sat cross-legged on the floor by the hearth, staring into the fire. Her supper had barely been touched. The look on her face disquieted him; even her daughter's illness had not brought such shadows to her eyes.

He squatted by her, herbs in hand, and reached for the little pot of water.

"What am I going to do?" Eile's voice sounded as if she'd been crying. "I can't understand what anyone's saying here; the words you've taught me are no help at all. How am I going to get on? Those men, I thought they'd come to kill us or to . . . to make use of me the way Dalach did . . ."

"I won't let that happen, Eile. I promise you."

"What were they telling you? It was something important, wasn't it? You need to go. To go on ahead."

A tear escaped, running down her cheek, catching the firelight. Not letting himself think too hard, Faolan set down knife and herbs, reached out a hand and wrapped it around hers.

"We're staying here until Saraid's well," he said. "I wouldn't dream of going on without you."

She had not snatched her hand away. It was the first time, and that seemed a small miracle. He found that he was holding his breath.

"But you want to." Her tone was flat.

"I made a choice. These men offered to take you back to Raven's Well while I went on. You're right, there are urgent messages to deliver, messages that only I can carry. I declined the offer. They're leaving us some supplies and heading on in the morning. I won't lie to you, part of me wants to be at White Hill as soon as I can. It is important. But another part of me knows I have to wait. I made a promise."

"I told you we could cope without you."

"Then why are you crying?" he asked her quietly.

The response was instant. "I'm not!" A moment later, she put her head against his shoulder and dissolved into convulsive, silent sobs. His heart thumped; this was completely unexpected, and he did not know what to do. This was not a woman who could be comforted by an embrace; she had made it clear such closeness was repugnant to her.

And yet his instincts made him put his arms around her shoulders, awkwardly, and lay his cheek lightly against her hair. She wept; he held her. All the time his heart beat a kind of warning, but of what he was not certain. He had not held a woman in his arms since he said good-bye to Ana. Ana . . . Gods, Pitnochie was not far up the Glen, and she was still there. He longed to see her, and yet he wished with every fiber of his being that he need never see her again.

"Hush," he whispered. "Hush. You can trust me. Believe it. I won't let anything happen to you, or to Saraid."

"I'm scared, Faolan." For all the childlike statement, the tone was a woman's. The fear he heard in it was a grown-up fear, the terror of yet another move, yet another loss, yet another betrayal. "I'm tired and sad and scared of what's to come. And I'm angry. Angry with myself for being so weak. I should be happy. Grateful. I could be still in Dalach's hut; so could Saraid. I could be facing execution. I'm sorry. You've done so much for us. I don't know what's wrong with me." She seemed to notice, at last, that he had his arms around her, and disengaged herself, pushing back her hair then scrubbing her cheeks.

"You're tired and sick, and you've got Saraid to look after. Don't be so hard on yourself."

"You're tired, too, and your knee's hurt. But you just seem to keep going."

"If you think I've never suffered from despair, you have a very short memory," he said. "Eile, I want you to eat that supper."

"I feel sick. I don't want it."

"You need it. Just the oatmeal, if that's easier. And drink some of this when it's ready." After a moment he added, "Please."

She drew a shuddering breath. "If you want. I wonder if I'm always going to be like this."

"Eat it, Eile. Like what?"

"Always remembering. So that, as soon as things go wrong, I feel like I'm back in Dalach's hut, and my belly goes tight with terror, and I have to force myself to do what needs to be done, when all I want is to be a little child again and have Mother and Father come and make things better."

"I don't know. I think it's the way I said before: the memory's still there, but it fades so you can bear it. Going back helped me. I didn't think it would, but Ana was right to make me go. To see my family well and content . . . that healed a wound for me, even though my mother is gone, even though Áine is no longer herself. But it didn't wipe out what I did to my brother. I still dream of the blood. I still wish, every day, that I could change the past." He realized this was not at all what he had intended to say to her. "You're young," he said. "It will get better."

"I don't think I'll ever be able to trust anyone," Eile whispered. She had eaten one mouthful of the oatmeal and set the platter down. The steeping herbs began to fill the air with a pungent aroma.

Faolan thought of the way she had let him touch her. He said nothing.

"Tell me about Ana." It came out of the blue, like a blow.

This was not a moment to go tight-lipped; to refuse a confidence. "I've told you the bare bones of it."

"Tell me more."

"As I said, it was my mission, last spring, to escort her to Caitt lands to wed a chieftain there. She'd never met him. It was a strategic alliance. Various disasters befell us. We met Deord, and when we were in trouble, he saved us, and died. The man Ana's to marry now is the brother of the chieftain Bridei intended for her. His name is Drustan."

"Not much of a story." Eile's green eyes scrutinized him closely.

"The whole tale would take all night. There were wolves; that is the truth. There was the spectacle of the king's emissary acting the part of a court bard."

"But you were a bard."

"It had been years since I played or sang. I did manage a convincing show at Briar Wood. Ana was amazed. I won't do it again. It hurts too much."

"Singing hurts?"

He nodded. "It's too close to the heart. It stirs things up. Everything started to go wrong the day I sang a little snatch of a song . . . I was carrying Ana across a ford on my horse. What came over me was worse than any fairy curse. It was unwelcome, destructive, inconvenient, and pointless, since she was on her way to make a strategic marriage and it was my job to get her there safely. Besides, I was the last man to put himself up as a suitor for a princess."

"Why? Your kin are highborn, aren't they? Princes and chieftains of the Uí Néill? Don't Priteni princesses marry such men?"

He'd distracted her from her misery; he told himself that was a good thing, and went doggedly on. "Not when their employment includes the roles of assassin and spy. Not when they're Gaels."

"Oh."

"Keep that to yourself. It's best if you consider me only a bodyguard; I am that as well."

"An assassin. Really? So I'd never have got near enough with that pitchfork to do so much as scratch your pretty face?"

"I'm glad we never put it to the test. You're not going to eat that, are you? Here, drink the draft instead. I intend to sit here watching until it's all gone."

"Faolan?"

"What?"

"It's not too late, you know. I mean, this Ana's not married yet, is she? Why don't you do something about it? Things don't change unless you're brave enough to change them yourself."

The suggestion filled him with a chilling mixture of longing and dread. "That's a really bad idea," he said, "for more reasons than I could possibly list. To start with, nobody at White Hill knows what family I belong to. Ana does, but she won't tell. Even the king is unaware that his chief bodyguard is kin to Gabhran of Dalriada. Besides, Ana loves Drustan. If she married me everyone would be unhappy."

"Even you?"

"I want her to wed her chieftain and go away. I can deal with it as long as I don't have to see them together. I know I'm not the man for her, Eile. I've always known that."

She sat silent, the cup between her hands.

"Anyway," Faolan said, "I don't make it my business to tell you who you should marry. Why would you take it upon yourself to suggest such a thing to me?" He tried to keep his tone light, inconsequential; it was not quite successful.

"But you did," Eile said quietly. "A nice young man of my own age who'll come courting one day and make me forget Dalach, and the years in that hut, and the fact that a man's touch frightens and repulses me. You had it all worked out."

After a little he said, "I'm sorry. I didn't mean it to sound so . . . facile. I understand that you've been terribly hurt. Such wounds take a lot of healing. What I wanted to say was how much I admire your strength of will, your courage. And that I am certain you can do it: be healed, be happy, make a life. I see that in you."

"You do?" The voice had changed again; now it held a fragile hope.

Faolan nodded, meeting her eyes. "You are your father's daughter. If Ana and Drustan are still at Pitnochie when we get there, they can tell you more about him.

About his bravery and his goodness. He was Drustan's only companion for seven years."

Eile's mouth twisted. "All the years I waited for him to come back."

"I'm sorry. I'm sorry the only one who came was me."

Saraid stirred, drawing a wheezing breath, and muttered something. Eile went to lift her higher on the rolled-up garments that served as a pillow, murmuring soothing words.

"She feels a bit cooler now."

"Good. Can you get her to drink?"

"She's still asleep, really. Talking in her dreams."

"You should sleep, too. Have you finished that draft?"

"Most of it." She returned to the hearth, dropping to sit cross-legged and straight-backed. "I want to ask you something."

"Ask, then."

"You know what you said about a nice young man my own age; what you said about men and women, and how what they do need not be like it was with Dalach?"

"Mm?" Faolan felt uneasy about this turn of the conversation, especially with three men lying out there by the fire. Still, he did not think any of them likely to know Gaelic. There was a manner of talk between himself and Eile that had grown up on their journey, a familiarity born of long days on the road and nights in whatever shelter they could find. It owed something to what they had shared back in Laigin.

"If I asked you . . . if I asked you to show me, to prove to me that you were telling the truth, would you do it?"

His jaw dropped. *"What?"* he blurted out before he had time to think. He was unable to school his expression. Eile's eyes changed. Her lips pressed into a hard line.

"Are you saying what I think you are?" He found words, knowing he must speak before she took his silence to mean something other than he intended. "That I should give you a practical demonstration to prove that all men are not like Dalach?"

"More than that." She was very serious; her voice quivered despite her evident efforts to control it. "I need you to show me he hasn't ruined it for the future; to teach me how to . . . how to feel pleasure, not pain. Joy, not fear. If anyone can do that, it's you."

"Me? A battle-scarred bodyguard with a faulty knee? A man who's earned a reputation for being incapable of feeling? You must be crazy."

"The thing is," Eile said very carefully, "you are the only person I can even half trust. I think you could help me not to be scared. Maybe. I mean," she was turning the empty cup around and around in her hands, "what if this nice young man came along, and we played the game of courtship, and when it came to the point, the touch of his hands made me sick?"

"I can't believe we're having this conversation," Faolan said. "What you suggest is . . . is . . ."

"If you hate the idea so much, just forget I ever mentioned it." Eile's voice was tight; she would not meet his eyes. "Someone like you and a—and someone like me, of course it wouldn't be acceptable, I must have been stupid to think you'd ever consider it." She slumped her shoulders, staring into the fire.

It seemed to Faolan that what was unspoken filled the little hut with a sadness that was almost palpable. He'd managed to hurt her badly. Try as he might, he could not think of the words to make it right again. "I'm too old," he said. "Old enough to be your father. Well, maybe not quite, but too old anyway. And . . . Eile, do you want an honest answer?"

"I don't know," she muttered. "I suppose it depends what it is."

He chose his words carefully. The confusion of feelings she had awoken in him made this necessary. "I think I've got to know you reasonably well over our journey. Right now you're sick and dispirited, worried about Saraid, doubtful about how you'll cope in a new land with a new language. I'm certain you are not ready for an . . . experiment . . . such as you've suggested. Give yourself time."

She glanced up at him. "Aren't I the one who knows if I'm ready or not?"

Gods, this was like crossing a raging torrent on wobbly stepping stones. One error and the two of them would go under. "I'm sure of one thing. I'm the wrong man for the job. You're asking me because I'm all you have for comparison. Much safer if you see me as your father's friend, someone who's helping you get to a place of safety and set your life to rights again. Anyway, I've given up this particular activity, I told you."

"You mean you're incapable?"

"Eile!" He lowered his voice, remembering the travelers by the fire. "No, of course not."

"So it's just me that's the stumbling block. The piece of rubbish. I bet you'd have done it with Ana if she'd asked you."

"Ana's a lady. It would never occur to her to make such a request." The words were out before he could stop them, and he saw her flinch. "Eile, I didn't mean it to sound like that."

"Don't lie to me. It's all over your face. She's a lady, I'm a slut. Don't pretend. You're disgusted by the very idea."

"Eile, this is crazy."

"Oh, so I'm a slut *and* crazy. Forget I ever asked, Faolan. I'll find some other fellow to practice on. I expect I'll work out the right way to ask them if I try a few."

Suddenly he was angry. He swallowed the other emotion that welled up at the same time, something that felt like a kick in the guts. "If I didn't know how much you hate to be touched," he said, "I'd give you a good shaking for that."

"For what?" Her voice was harsh with furious hurt.

"For that—that threat."

"Threat? What do you mean?"

He made himself take a steady breath. "All right," he said, trying to think like a father, calmly and capably. "First, I thought you promised not to use those terms for yourself: slut, rubbish. If you expect me to keep promises, you should do the same."

"I forgot." Now she was sitting hunched on herself like an old woman, the challenge gone from her voice.

"Don't forget again."

Her head bowed lower.

"Now I want another promise from you," Faolan said.

"What?"

"Don't ask anyone else what you just asked me."

Eile was silent, apparently giving this deep consideration. Then she said, "What gives you the right to stop me?"

"Since you ask, there's the *éraic,* among other things."

Another silence.

"How am I going to find out unless someone shows me?" she asked eventually. "You just said you were helping me set my life to rights. This is part of that."

"It's . . . it's inappropriate, Eile. Your own introduction to such activities has been cruel and brutal. I understand that you may not . . . that perhaps you're not aware . . ."

"You already said I'm not a lady. Tell me something I don't know."

"The promise I want is that you'll wait. That you'll give this more time. That's all."

"Wait how long? You mean until this nice young man makes an appearance?"

"Wait, and talk to me again before you do anything about this. And promise me you won't offer this . . . invitation . . . to anyone else in the meantime. You'd be putting yourself in danger."

"You think I'm stupid, don't you? Why do you think I asked you and not one of those fellows out there? Because I know you won't hurt me, that's why."

In the silence that ensued, Faolan thought the beating

of his own heart was loud enough to fill the space between the two of them; fierce enough to drown rational thought. "I'm sorry," he said. "I've failed your test. If you want to know what I felt when you asked me, it was . . . I was honored that you would trust me with something so important. And terrified."

"Why?" It was a whisper.

"That I'd get it wrong. That I couldn't give you what you needed. It's too soon, Eile."

"You didn't really think I'd go out and offer myself to any man who happened to be passing by, did you? Is that how little you think of me?"

"I thought Dalach might have warped your judgment. That wouldn't be so surprising. After all, you did tell me you believed all men must be like him."

She looked down at her hands. "I don't think you would be," she said. "But if you don't want me . . ."

Another cautious breath. "I didn't say that."

"A man like Dalach would have seized the opportunity before we were one night out of Fiddler's Crossing," she said flatly.

"I undertook to keep you safe, Eile. There will come a time when you'll understand why I said no."

Eile lifted her head. The green eyes met his, searching, perplexed. "Honored," she said. "Do you really mean that?"

"That, and a confusion of other things," said Faolan. "Now I'm going to lie down on my bed, and you're going to lie down on yours, and we're going to forget this ever happened."

"Huh!" said Eile quietly, getting up and moving to her usual spot beside Saraid. "How are we supposed to do that?"

"Try to fix your mind on something else."

"You could sing a song," she suggested.

"Is that supposed to be a joke?"

"Only half. I'd like to hear your voice some time. Saraid loves lullabies."

"I'll teach you some words in the Priteni tongue instead."

"All right."

He heard the bracken rustling as she settled by the sleeping child, huddling under the blanket. She coughed, muffling the sound with her hand.

"What do you want to learn?" Faolan asked.

"Kindness," she said. "Hope."

He translated them.

"Strength," Eile said. "Love."

Faolan cleared his throat, then gave her the words. "I'd be better to teach you, *Which way is the settlement?*, or *May I have some more bread?*" he said into a silence as deep and dark as the cold forest outside the hut.

"I want these words now. They're like—like—I don't know how to say it. A powerful thing that keeps you safe. A special sort of gift."

"A talisman," said Faolan.

"Mm-hm. Kindness, hope, strength, love. Like magic. Magic to protect us."

"I wish you all those things, Eile."

"And I wish them for you."

"I've no trust in talismans; no belief in gods or in magic." Briefly, he thought of Drustan, the man he had witnessed transforming into a creature with wings and talons and a breathtaking ability to fly. "I've found it much simpler to rely only on myself."

"That's . . . sad." Eile's voice was a little remote as if, against the odds, she was already falling asleep. "So lonely. At least I've got Saraid. If I was all by myself, I don't know how I could go on."

Faolan did not sleep for a long while. He lay by the fire working on his thoughts; making them comply with a more manageable pattern. He divided the immediate future into a set of tasks, a priority of missions. Ensure Eile and Saraid got well again. Escort them safely to Pitnochie. Ask Ana and Drustan to take responsibility from that point. After tonight it was better, surely, if Eile was with other folk; with a family and a household, not in this odd, push-and-pull arrangement with him. She expected something from him that he could not give. If she stayed with him, it was inevitable that he would disappoint her in one way or another. He would let her down as her father had done. She'd be far happier with Drustan and Ana. They would welcome her; she was Deord's daughter.

The next mission was White Hill and Bridei. A double warning: Colmcille and Carnach. He would deliver his news, then ask the king to send him out in search of these plotters. No other man at court could perform that kind of covert surveillance quite as effectively as Faolan could. Besides, such a mission would take him away. When he got back they'd all be gone: Ana, Drustan, Eile as well . . .

You're a craven coward, a voice said inside him.

"Shut up," he muttered.

On the pallet Saraid was asleep, and so was Eile, her long hair spread over the pillow like a river of dark flame. Out by the fire the Pitnochie men lay silent, rolled in their cloaks. There was nobody to hear him but the shadows.

IT HAD NOT taken long for Breda of the Light Isles to set her stamp on the court at White Hill. She moved among the chieftains, the warriors, the councillors, and household retainers like an exotic pale butterfly with an attendant flock of plainer creatures. She dabbled in embroidery or music, she stroked a cat or admired a flower while seemingly unaware of the impact her presence made. Men could not take their eyes off her; she drew the gaze of all from the ancient scholar, Wid, to the twelve-year-old sons of visiting chieftains. Wid's comments were wry and to the point: "Trouble, I see it in every hair on that creature's head." Younger admirers were dazzled and confused. Several well-connected older men made tentative enquiries of Keother as to whether his young cousin had received any formal offers of marriage. Some bolder individuals made it their mission to win Breda's friendship.

Uric and Bedo had been unable to think of much else since the first moment they clapped eyes on this shapely, golden-haired vision. They had decided their self-appointed task of entertaining small boys was sure to get in the way of their chances with Breda. For several days, therefore, they had been too busy to play with Derelei, Gilder, and Galen. Instead, they'd hung around the great hall listening to tedious harp music and trying to look as if they had some meaningful purpose there. Neither had managed more than a brief word before Breda's eyes passed over him and on to someone more interesting. Finally their father had told them to stop mooning about and find themselves a useful occupation or he'd pack the two of them off home to Raven's Well. Talorgen was testy right now; his sons put it down to annoyance at being moved to less spacious quarters to make room for the royal visitors.

At last Bedo managed to engage one of Breda's handmaids in conversation. As Breda's entourage swept across the courtyard, it happened that the king's dog, Ban, was passing, and the dark-haired girl stopped to pat him while the others went on.

"You like dogs?" Bedo had been close by and seized the opportunity.

She nodded. "I have one at home; a terrier. I really miss her."

"We have mostly hunting hounds at Raven's Well. This is King Bridei's dog, Ban. He's quite friendly. Oh, my name's Bedo, son of Talorgen, by the way."

"Cella. My father is one of King Keother's advisers. I know who you are. You and your brother introduced yourselves to Lady Breda the other day. Or tried to."

Bedo grinned. He had his father's infectious smile, and

the girl smiled back. "Uric and I would be happy to help entertain the lady, if we could discover what amuses her," he said. "Riding, maybe, or playing games?"

Cella's look was assessing. "I did hear Lady Breda say she'd like to see the royal baby," she said. "That seems difficult to arrange. Of course, it's early days, I know."

Bedo thought fast. "My father's a close friend of King Bridei's," he said. "Uric and I see a lot of little Derelei; we've been helping to keep him busy with one thing or another. Later on today I expect we'll be in the garden with him. Maybe we could . . . ?"

᧟

TALORGEN'S DAUGHTER FERADA had been acting as the queen's watchdog. She was a tall young woman with sleek auburn hair, known for her immaculate grooming and excellent deportment, and her position as educator of the daughters of Fortriu's noble families meant she carried a great deal of authority. With Ferada guarding the door, the only visitors admitted were the tried and true ones.

Thus far Anfreda was proving an easy baby, placid and quiet, feeding well and sleeping soundly. When first allowed to see his sister, Derelei had spent quite some time standing by her basket, examining her gravely; he had reached to touch the dark wispy hair, the snub nose, the neat rosy mouth. He had moved his hand in the air above the cradle, making a flock of tiny, sparkling birds appear momentarily over Anfreda's sleeping form, and Tuala, watching, had seen Ferada's eyes widen, though her friend had made no comment.

"Nice baby," Derelei had pronounced, and bent to give his sister a kiss. Then he was off to seek other amusements.

Today the nursemaid had taken Derelei out to the garden. Ferada was sitting with Tuala in the royal apartments while the baby slept nearby. The wise women had retired to a grove below the walls for private prayers and, as Ferada put it, a break from the overwhelming nature of family life.

"It is so much quieter at Banmerren," Ferada remarked to her friend. "Even in my part of that establishment, which as you know is full of girls all missing home and wanting to tell one another about it, there is a great sense of peace and order. With babies and little children, one has to *be* there all the time, to feed them, or wipe some portion of their anatomy, or tend to their noisy woes."

"You and I, of course," Tuala said with a smile, "can always get helpers to do those things. I have a bevy of folk here who are only too glad to take care of the children for me. I do far more of it than people think quite proper for a queen. But the fact is, I don't entirely trust other folk to do the job adequately. Not with these particular children. And I suspect I'd be the same even if Derelei and Anfreda were quite ordinary."

Ferada regarded her friend, a smile passing over her severe mouth. "You know, you still look about sixteen," she said. "It seems extraordinary that you're a mother of two. I admire you for doing so much of the hard work yourself, when you need not. I find tending to infants quite exhausting. Give me a little scribing or reckoning any day."

"Oh, but I do it because I want to," said Tuala. "They don't stay small for long. Besides, other people do help. Your brothers, for instance. And, of course, Broichan, when he's here."

"You're looking washed out." Ferada's tone was firm. "I think you should accept more help. I can stay awhile longer; my work is in capable hands."

"And Garvan's due at White Hill any time now," put in Tuala with a grin. Ferada's friendship with the royal stone carver was not a public matter. It had grown up quite unexpectedly during a time when stone masonry was being carried out at Banmerren, and Tuala knew references to it were likely to provoke a sharp denial from Ferada herself. How she and her lover would manage things in the far more public setting of White Hill was interesting to consider.

"Don't worry, Tuala, we'll be discreet." Ferada's lips twisted in a self-mocking smile. "I don't wish to cause any offense to you and Bridei, or to my father and stepmother. Besides, it's most important, in view of my new role as educator of the daughters of the highborn, that I be seen to be a model of good behavior."

"Only *seen* to be?" queried Tuala.

Ferada, usually a confident woman, was reluctant to meet her friend's eye. "We're grown-up people," she said. "What we do is our own business. What folk don't know cannot offend them. That is my belief." And, after a lengthy pause during which Tuala simply fixed her with her large, questioning eyes, "These things just come out of nowhere, Tuala. I didn't expect it; I didn't really want it, it's awkward and inconvenient. But there it is. I do like him. I like him a great deal. He's so . . . so strong and deep. And quiet. Like a slow-flowing river." Abruptly she fell silent.

"You're happy with this the way it is?" Tuala's question was tentative. "Seeing each other only from time to time, when Garvan's work brings him your way? Keeping what you feel for each other secret?"

"It can't be any other way, Tuala." There was an edge to Ferada's tone now. "As a craftsman of low birth, Garvan would be considered unsuitable for me. I might persuade Father to agree, given sufficient time. But I see no reason to formalize our relationship with a handfasting. I intend to stay at Banmerren and make a success of my project; there's so much more to do there. The nature of Garvan's craft means he must travel widely and spend much of the year away from home. Besides, the main purpose of marriage is children, surely. I've never wanted them and I don't now. I've made that clear to Garvan and he understands."

Tuala's gaze was searching. "Ferada," she said, "have you asked Garvan what *he* wants?"

Ferada was spared from replying by a tap on the door: one of the maids, perhaps, carrying a basket, or Fola returned early and not wanting to walk straight in.

"Think about it," said Tuala as her friend went to open the door.

"See baby!" First in was Derelei, making his way on small, confident feet straight over to his sister's cradle. "Bedo 'n' Uric see!"

Ferada's brothers were on the threshold, Bedo flashing an apologetic smile, Uric leaning against the frame as if, at fourteen, he was really too much of a man to be interested in babies, but would tag along in case there proved to be some amusement in it.

"What are you two doing here?" Ferada made no secret of her displeasure. "It's too soon for visitors; the whole household was given that message."

"I don't mind, Ferada." Tuala smiled at the two lads. "Uric and Bedo may have a quick look if Derelei wants to show them his new sister. Tread softly; she's sleeping."

Ferada stepped back and the boys came in. A moment later, it became apparent that they had not come alone. A vision appeared in the doorway, all shimmering golden hair, wide eyes, and figure-hugging sea-green gown. Tuala saw Ferada open her mouth to say, "No visitors," and bite back the words. One could not risk offense to this particular visitor, who stood in the delicate position of potential political hostage and possible bearer of tales to her influential cousin Keother. Although Ferada remained silent, she failed to keep the annoyance from her features. Her sharp eyes went first to Bedo, who at fifteen should have known better, then to his lounging brother.

Tuala rose to her feet. "You must be Ana's sister," she said. "What a surprise. You're very like her." This seemed both true and untrue. Ana had been a close friend of both Tuala and Ferada, sharing their education and spending five years at court under Bridei's kingship. This girl, thought Tuala, was physically similar: shapely, though shorter than her sister, possessed of the same breathtaking head of hair and the same beauty. The eyes were different. In place of Ana's serene gray, these were blue and seemed to be defying the queen to question Breda's presence here. Something else as well; a subtler difference Tuala could not quite put her finger on. She was staring. "I'm sorry I could not be in the hall to welcome you on your arrival," she went on hurriedly. "Anfreda is only a few days old. It will be some time before I am ready to appear in public again. Indeed, we are not receiving any visitors other than the wise women who attend to us and the queen dowager, Lady Rhian. You've met Ferada, daughter of Talorgen? She is my close friend, here at White Hill to assist me for a while."

Breda gave the queen a deep, graceful curtsy that fell just short of mockery, then turned to Ferada and gave her a perfunctory nod. Perhaps she did not know that Ferada, too, was of the royal line of the Priteni. "I'd like to see the baby," Breda said.

"Baby," echoed Derelei, who was on tiptoes peering into the cradle where Anfreda lay wrapped in layers of fine wool.

Tuala avoided Ferada's eye. This was precisely what they'd been trying to prevent. Well, Breda was here now, and there was nothing to be done but pretend the situation held nothing untoward. "You may look at her, of course," the queen said. "She is very young yet and needs her rest, as do I. We must keep the visit brief."

Bedo was crouched by Derelei. The smile on the young man's face was good to see, a spontaneous grin of delight at something so tiny and perfect. In her sleep, Anfreda had wrapped her hand around one of her brother's fingers. Derelei stood extremely still, as if the baby might break if he moved. By the door, Ferada was now conversing with Uric in an undertone. Tuala was certain a lecture was being delivered, and justifiably so.

Breda stalked across to the cradle. She stood there a good while, staring down at the infant form. Tuala watched a series of expressions cross the lovely, discontented features, none of them reassuring. It was plain Breda was thinking hard. There was a powerful urge in Tuala to offer some placatory, apologetic statement such as, *I know she looks a little unusual, but she's quite ordinary, really.* She did not speak. She would not apologize for her daughter who was, by many measures, quite perfect. Breda was only a girl; barely seventeen. Her interest was probably superficial and in no way dangerous. What Bridei had told his wife of this visiting princess was that she seemed very young for her age and had less grasp of the niceties of behavior than her sister. It was foolish to be afraid of what she might do. Yet as the girl stared down at Anfreda, Tuala saw something disturbing in her eyes, and a shiver ran through her.

"May I hold her?" Without waiting for a reply, Breda reached into the cradle as if to scoop up the sleeping baby. Tuala moved swiftly to stop her, but someone else was quicker.

"Oh!" exclaimed Breda, flinching away before her fingers could touch the infant. "What was that? That hurt!" Suddenly pale, she stared at her own hands, which were shaking violently.

Derelei had taken a step back. He was looking anywhere but at his mother. Tuala made a subtle gesture, and the charm of ward that her small son had thrown over his sister was undone. "Were you bitten, Breda?" she asked, forcing her voice to be quite calm. "I'm so sorry. We are having quite a problem with insects now the weather has turned so warm. Ferada, perhaps you could take Breda down to the stillroom and see if Elda has some lotion? A mixture of wormwood and lavender is very effective."

Ferada stood by the door, her eyes conveying a firm message that the visitors had outstayed their welcome. Reading their sister accurately, Uric and Bedo headed out.

"Wait." Breda's tone was cold. "That was no midge or fly, I'm sure of it. It was more like—like a kind of . . . wall. As if the child were encircled by a solid but invisible barrier. And it was somehow alive. It sent a shock into my hands. That's very odd. I don't know how that could happen. Or who could do it." She glared at the queen, then at Ferada.

"How strange," Tuala said mildly. "I suppose, when we are a little tired or lonely or out of sorts, we can imagine all kinds of things. Breda, the baby is waking up; we've made too much noise. I think you must go with Ferada now. When Anfreda is a little older, I will be able to bring her out and let folk admire her. If you are still here at White Hill, of course you can see her then."

"I see." Breda's tight voice registered her understanding that she had been dismissed.

"Come," said Ferada. "Elda's good with healing herbs; I'll show you her quarters. They'll likely be full of small boys. But then, you like children, don't you? Tuala, shall we take Derelei with us?"

"Derelei will stay here awhile. Please find Garth and ask him to come and see me straight away. Thank you, Ferada."

When she was alone with her children, Tuala called Derelei and lifted him onto her knee. Anfreda was barely stirring; it would be some time before she needed feeding. Tuala addressed her son quietly, although what he had done had alarmed her.

"Derelei? It's all right now. The lady's gone, and Anfreda is quite safe."

"No hurt baby." He seemed to be aware that he had done something that was both necessary and, at the same time, wrong.

It was impossible to explain to him. The situation was far too complex for his limited understanding of language. And yet, instinctively, he had done what was required to protect his sister. Somehow, without really knowing what this was about, he had used his craft at precisely the right moment. Perhaps all Breda had intended was to cradle Anfreda a little, as girls like to do with babies. All the same, Tuala herself had sensed peril in that moment.

"Derelei," she said, "no charms when other folk are here. No magic, understand?" And, as his mouth drooped and his head bowed, "You were good, Derelei. Good boy. You helped Anfreda. But from now on, let Mama do it. You can use your magic with Mama and with Broichan. That's all. Do you understand, Derelei?"

He was only two years old. "No hurt baby," he said again, glancing over at the cradle.

"Next time, wait for Mama."

The large eyes turned to her. "Bawta home?" he said hopefully.

Abruptly, Tuala felt herself on the verge of tears. "I hope so, Derelei. I hope Broichan will be home very soon." She imagined the druid back at court, surely changed by his winter in the woods, but still devoted to her son and ready to resume the education without which, she realized more strongly as each day passed, Derelei's startling abilities could quickly turn from gift and blessing to danger and burden. "You miss your lessons."

"Bawta home." It was by no means certain whether this was a statement of foreknowledge or simply one of hope.

Tuala cuddled him awhile, then put Anfreda to the breast while Derelei played on the floor with the little stone horse Garvan had made for him. Later, Ferada returned with Bridei's bodyguard Garth, and Tuala formed with him a plan to ensure that, even when her attendants were absent, no visitor save those previously approved by name might approach within a certain distance of her door. She was reluctant to do it, since it would mean at least two of Bridei's best men were removed from other duties at a time when the influx of powerful guests meant every guard was constantly busy. But she knew Bridei would agree. If both she and Derelei had felt that sense of danger, then the threat was real. Unfortunately, there existed dangers of a kind even the most expert of guards was helpless to combat.

10

❦

"THERE'S THE HOUSE," Faolan said, pointing ahead to an impenetrable tangle of dark oak branches hazed with green.

"I don't see any house." Eile was tired and out of sorts. Her chest was aching and her head was dizzy; she had lied to Faolan about being well enough to travel, and now she was paying the price. As soon as Saraid had been running about again and eating with enthusiasm, Eile had declared herself fully recovered. There was no way she was going to hold Faolan back from getting to White Hill and delivering his urgent messages. She'd delayed him too long already. She'd cost him a fortune and embarrassed him with her proposition. He didn't want her. It was becoming evident, as they neared King Bridei's court, that Faolan had important things to do, a life in which she could take no part. She knew better than to expect anything of him. So why did it hurt so much? Since Mother died, she'd always been alone. She'd always done things on her own; she'd always coped. She didn't need anyone. Not even Faolan. She had to stop feeling let down. She couldn't afford to be sad. There was Saraid to think about.

"There, between the oaks."

"I can't see it."

"Cat!" exclaimed Saraid, wriggling to be let down from Faolan's back. "Little cat!"

The striped feline shot off into the undergrowth with a flourish of its bushy tail.

"Down, please?" Saraid requested.

He set her on her feet. They had come to Pitnochie on a barge ferrying logs; with nobody on the jetty, they had walked up to Broichan's house.

"Stay close!" Eile warned her daughter. "If the cat wants to be found, it'll come out. It's probably half wild."

Faolan set a hand on Eile's shoulder and pointed ahead again, between the branches. "Bridei used to say Broichan—the druid who owns Pitnochie—had set a spell on the trees so they moved about to conceal his dwelling," he told her as Saraid crouched in the ferns calling to the cat.

Eile regarded him skeptically. "Why would he need to do that?"

"To protect Bridei while he was growing up. There were plenty of folk who didn't want him to become king. Fortriu has its own share of plotters and schemers. In that, it's not much different from home." His smile was grim. He did not seem happy to be back. But then, that woman, Ana, was probably here: the one he loved and didn't want to see.

"If Bridei is king now, why are the trees still shielding the house? I can see smoke rising, but no buildings."

"Broichan has his own enemies. Those men said he's gone missing. That's another thing I need to investigate."

"Makes me wonder how this king ever managed without you."

He eyed her narrowly. "That's a joke, yes?"

"I don't know. I've never met him."

"Bridei's highly capable, virtuous and clever. But a king can't perform his own self-protection. He can't be invisible when it counts most. He can never be anonymous. There are other good men to watch over him. I expect, if I were not here, someone would step into my place."

"You sound doubtful." Eile was getting better at reading

his expressions, guarded as they were. "You don't really believe anyone else can do it."

There was silence for a little, punctuated only by Saraid's, "Here, kitty," and an occasional rustle in the bushes, indicating that her quarry was at least half tame.

"Come," Faolan said. "We'd best get up to the house. The two of you need a rest. They'll be expecting us."

As he spoke, a figure appeared ahead of them, striding forward under the trees: a tall man with flaming red hair and unusually bright eyes. He was dressed in a russet tunic and trousers of fine quality, with good leather boots. By his side padded an enormous gray dog. Saraid retreated behind her mother's skirts; Eile herself felt her stomach clench with a familiar fear. Strange men were threat enough. Strange men who dressed like lords and spoke a language she could not understand were still more alarming. This smiling nobleman made her feel dirty and pathetic. She squared her shoulders and lifted her chin.

"Faolan!" The red-haired man came up to them and put his arms around Faolan's shoulders as if they were best friends or brothers. Faolan greeted him more soberly, though he returned the embrace. He said something in the Priteni tongue; Eile heard *Drustan,* and later *Ana.* He was asking questions; perhaps where was Ana, and was she well.

The other man gave an answer, brief, somber. Eile saw Faolan's features change; a look of deep concern came over them. Then he seemed to remember she was there, and reached to take her hand. She let him; she felt very alone, and his grip was reassuring. He said something else; something with Eile and Deord and Saraid in it.

Drustan's eyes went still brighter as he gazed at her. He was a strange-looking man. Eile saw a wild kind of knowledge in those starlike eyes, a thing that was entirely at odds with his nobleman's clothes and soft voice. Then he said in almost unaccented Gaelic, "Welcome,

Eile," and reached out a hand toward her. She could not stop herself from shrinking back. Faolan's fingers tightened around hers.

"This is Drustan," he told her.

"He speaks Gaelic," Eile whispered, then collected herself. She had to be polite, to speak appropriately. This was Faolan's friend, and a person of consequence. "I'm Eile," she said. "Deord's daughter. Faolan told me you knew my father."

"He and I were companions for a long period behind bars," Drustan said, his eyes still fixed on her in what seemed wonderment. "Please, come up to the house. Ana hasn't been well. I just explained that to Faolan. But she will be eager to meet you. The three of us owe our lives to Deord."

Eile nodded, a sudden lump in her throat. "The language," she said, "did he teach you? My father?"

Drustan smiled. "He liked to keep me busy. He found all sorts of ways."

"Come on, Saraid. Not much farther." Eile knelt to hug her daughter, who had gone very quiet. Another new place; more tall strangers.

"I expect there are cats at the house," Faolan said, squatting down beside Saraid. "I bet Sorry would like to see them. And there used to be a man who cooked very good pastries. Shall I carry you?"

As they went up the path and the oaks seemed to edge aside to let them through, Eile caught an expression of wonderment on Drustan's face as he watched Faolan. There was something like delight in his eyes. She was not sure why Faolan's actions should inspire this. When a child was scared you reassured her. When she was tired you carried her. That was all Faolan was doing: the right things. He'd been doing them all the way from Fiddler's Crossing, and even before. What was so surprising about that?

The house manifested bit by bit: a thatched roof with little straw birds woven here and there on the surface, stone walls, small windows with their shutters open to admit the spring sunshine, a big door with iron reinforcing. The door stood open; folk were moving about within. Somewhere farther away sheep bleated, a dog barked, voices called. There were woods up the hill behind the house, a thick blanket of oak and ash, elder and rowan. As they came up to the doorway, Eile saw a pair of birds, real ones, fly down from the roof to settle on Drustan's shoulders: on the right a hooded crow, on the left a strange little thing with red feathers and an odd-shaped beak. Neither Drustan nor Faolan expressed any surprise at these arrivals. Saraid smiled, reaching out toward the creatures, then flinched back as Drustan looked at her.

"Eile and her daughter have made a long journey and seen many changes since winter," Faolan told Drustan, speaking in Gaelic so she could understand. "They're not used to being among folk, nor to staying in a druid's household. May I explain to Eile about Ana?"

"Of course," Drustan said soberly. "It's best if she knows from the start."

"What?" asked Eile, not sure if she wanted to know what had turned both men pale and tight-lipped.

"She lost a baby," Faolan said. "It was early times; it would not have been born until the autumn. She's recovering, Drustan says, but very downhearted, as is he."

"I'm sorry," Eile said, looking at Drustan. "Does she want people to talk about it, or is that too upsetting?" So sad. So terribly sad. Even from the first she had wanted Saraid; even in the face of Dalach and the unthinkable future, she had loved her unborn child from the moment she felt the stirring in her womb. She had thought she might not like Ana much, perfect Ana, Faolan's princess. This changed things. Suddenly, Ana became real.

"The child was taken before we could really know him, or her," Drustan said. "All the same, our infant was well loved. To talk of these things helps us heal. Best to be open with it; shutting sorrow inside only allows it to eat at us. Come in, please. We've prepared sleeping quarters for you. Our cook, Ferat, will have food and drink ready. We knew you were on your way, of course; Broichan's men brought the news. The big surprise was to discover Faolan's companion was Deord's daughter. I never knew—" He stopped his words a moment too late.

"He never told you he had a daughter?" Eile halted on the steps by the door, hearing the wounded, tight note in her own voice. "He never mentioned me? Not even once?"

"Eile," Faolan said, "it's a long and complicated story, best not told in the young one's hearing. Don't be hurt. We'll talk about this later."

"I'm not hurt. I've learned not to expect anything. That way I don't get disappointed. He went away. He forgot us. Simple story."

"Impossible," Drustan said. "He could not have forgotten you, Eile. He chose not to speak of you, nor of your mother, for his own reasons. Sometimes a man needs to hold his dearest things to himself or he will lose his way completely. This is for later. We should eat, you should rest, then I will take you to meet Ana. We'll have time to talk."

Pitnochie was not like the brithem's house at Fiddler's Crossing. It was darker, quieter, altogether more somber. Folk did welcome them. The housekeeper, a grim large person, showed Eile a little chamber she and Saraid could have to themselves. The cook brought out soup and bread and promised to make pastry cats for Saraid. Drustan translated everything in his soft, courteous voice. The dog watched them all, quietly alert. But Eile felt frozen. She felt as if there were a wall between her and the rest of them. Here, there was no Líobhan, quick with smiles and warm words, instantly accepting her as an equal with no need for questions. There was no Phadraig to charm Saraid with his easy kindliness. Saraid was tired and scared. She sat between Faolan and Eile on a bench and sucked her thumb. She would not touch the food, though they had not eaten since early morning. Eile could see the lost look in her eyes.

Drustan was doing his best, that much was plain. He made sure she understood what folk were saying. But he was preoccupied, and he was not the only one. Eile had never seen such a tight mask of control on Faolan's features. He was counting the moments until he could see Ana, she deduced. And Drustan was worrying about his wife.

At a certain point during the meal Faolan asked Drustan a question in the Priteni tongue, and they began a rapid dialogue in which all Eile could catch was an occasional word from the list Faolan had taught her: king, danger, ride. And names: Bridei, Broichan, Carnach, Colm. She stared into her empty bowl, wondering if she could ever learn the language well enough to get by here. Without it she felt entirely excluded.

"Eile," Faolan said, halting in midflow, "I'm sorry about this. Drustan and I need to exchange a lot of information quickly: political talk. Fluent as he is in Gaelic, he'd struggle with this kind of conversation. I've been finding out what he knows about the state of affairs at court and beyond, and letting him know that we took passage with the Christian missionaries on their way to Dunadd. If I speak of you I will do so in Gaelic, I promise. Drustan says he's going to see if Ana is awake, and ask if she's ready to receive us."

"Thank you. Can Saraid come, too? She's upset, I think. Too many changes." His words had reassured her to a degree; she thought, not for the first time, what a kind man he was, and how well he seemed to read her moods. Better than she wanted him to, sometimes.

"Saraid is Deord's grandchild," Faolan said. "Ana will want to meet both of you."

They were called in straightaway. Ana was in bed; her loss must have been quite recent. When she was well,

Eile thought, she must be strikingly lovely, like a lady from a heroic old tale: rippling wheaten hair, big gray eyes, perfect pale skin. Right now there were shadows under the grave eyes and it was plain she'd shed bitter tears. Eile stole a glance at Faolan. He'd let the mask slip. There was another new expression on his face, one composed of love, longing, and pain. Seeing it, Eile felt a curious aching in her chest. She was not sure which was stronger, the wish somehow to make things better for him, or the recognition that, oddly, she shared his unhappiness.

"Faolan!" Ana's voice was low and warm. She continued in the Priteni language, her gestures summoning him to sit by her bed on a stool. She put both her hands around Faolan's; the bond between them was quite evident. It had been too much to hope that Ana, too, would speak Gaelic.

For a little, these two might have been alone in the chamber. Their voices, pitched at intimate level, spoke vividly to Eile without the need to understand their words. Drustan did not seem at all disturbed by this. He seated himself a little farther away, eyes tranquil, pose relaxed.

"They are old friends," he murmured to Eile. "They've been through some hard times together. Faolan is dear to both of us." He turned to the child. "Saraid? See what I have in this bag."

Saraid hung back, eyes dark with distrust.

"You see," Drustan went on, "how this game has little men and women, creatures and trees and other things? They go on this board with the squares."

Saraid stared, owl-eyed, as he unfolded the inlaid game board. She made no move.

"I'll put them on the little table," Drustan said. "You can move them about if you like. They used to belong to an old man who lived here. They're old, too; old and precious. Only very special visitors, such as yourself, are allowed to play with them."

"Drustan!" called Ana from the bed. Then she said something with Eile in it.

"Ana speaks only a few words of Gaelic," said Drustan. "I'll translate, or Faolan will. Ana bids you a warm welcome to Pitnochie, you and your little daughter. I told her Saraid likes cats; she says you will find several in the barn. The farmer's children can show you where."

"Thank you. Saraid's very shy. She's had too many changes. And we don't speak the language. I am trying to learn. Faolan's teaching me."

Ana smiled as her husband translated this.

"Please tell Ana I'm so sorry she lost her baby. That's such a sad thing. There will be others, I'm sure. But that cannot make up for the one who was taken too soon."

Drustan translated; Faolan was regarding Eile curiously, as if her words surprised him. Ana's eyes were warm as she nodded her thanks.

"Bridei has requested that Ana and I travel to White Hill," Drustan said. "He did not know of Ana's illness when he asked us, and we don't intend to make it public. We'll tell our friends, and, of course, the folk here at Pitnochie know. There's no need for others to share it."

Faolan translated for Ana and rendered her reply. "Ana says she is much better now and will be ready to set off for court in seven days or so. It's best if she doesn't ride. The journey is quite short by boat. She suggests that you and Saraid travel with her and Drustan. It will be far more comfortable for you than either walking or riding."

More changes, Eile thought. Maybe the rest of her life would be like this. Maybe there never would be a time when she reached home. Home: what did that mean, anyway? The sunny cottage of her earliest memories was gone forever; the house on the hill with the garden and the striped cat was a dream, a nonsense conjured up from loneliness and desperate hope. Home was a place like Líobhan's house, a place full of warmth and love, a place of family. This house at Pitnochie probably felt like that, too, for those who actually belonged here. She wondered if she and Saraid would ever truly belong anywhere.

"There's a grand celebration planned at White Hill soon, in formal recognition of the contributions of Bridei's chieftains to last autumn's victory against the Gaels," Drustan said. "It's something he needs to do, although these rumors about Carnach and a rebellion, not to speak of Broichan's strange absence, must be causing Bridei to regret the need to spend time on speeches and gift giving and the entertainment of a large number of guests. What you tell us of the arrival of Colm's band of Christians in the west adds yet another complication. The situation is quite volatile."

"Disturbing, yes," said Faolan absently. It seemed to Eile that he was thinking fast.

"Ana and I intended to have Broichan perform our handfasting in early spring. We'd planned to depart for the north straight afterwards," Drustan went on. "But Broichan is nowhere to be found, and spring is almost over. Bridei suggests our wedding be held as part of the festivities. We received word that Ana's sister is at court, along with Keother, king of the Light Isles. Ana has not seen Breda since they were children. We'll go as soon as she can travel safely. As for the trip north, that may need to be delayed. Ana should not go until she's fully recovered."

"I'll be fine," Ana protested when this was translated. "We need to go, Drustan. The longer we delay, the more difficult things will be at Briar Wood. Besides, I'm longing to see Breda. She was only seven when I left home. She'll be a fine young woman now."

"You understand," Drustan said to Eile, "we left my brother's lands in awkward circumstances. There are those in that place who believe me out of my wits and dangerous. Now that my brother is dead, I must reclaim that territory and prove my ability to govern it."

He seemed to Eile the kind of person who must instantly be recognized as more than capable. This was not something she could say aloud. Such a man as this would hardly care about her opinion.

"Faolan?" she ventured. "You'll need to go on straightaway, won't you? You'll need to ride, since that boat will have already left. You can't wait seven days."

Faolan smiled. He looked sad and terribly tired. "Yes, I should leave as soon as possible. Drustan and Ana are my friends, Eile. You'll be safe with them. Staying at Pitnochie for those seven days will give you and Saraid a chance to get some proper rest." He sounded as if he was trying to convince himself; as if he did not quite believe his own words or, at least, as if he did not expect her to believe them.

"Of course," Eile said. Chin up, back straight; she would not let him know that her stomach was churning with alarm at the thought of being left here, where only the imposing Drustan spoke the tongue she understood. She would not reveal to Faolan how badly she wanted him to stay. *Expect nothing,* she reminded herself. *It makes life far easier.* "We'll be fine, won't we, Saraid?"

Saraid, her doll clamped under one arm, was studying the game pieces Drustan had left on the small table. Thus far she had not ventured to touch. She glanced at Eile and said "Yes," in her tiniest voice: an automatic response to a question whose implications she had not fully understood.

"We can look for the cats, and eat nice food, and cheer Ana up."

"Mm," said Saraid, eyes full of doubt.

One day, Eile thought, *one day I'll be able to tell her, We're really home now, and it'll be the truth. One day I'll be able to say: This is our house, and this is our cat, and this is where we're going to make our garden with rosemary and lavender and good things to eat. It can't go on being like this forever. I won't let it.*

"You're not fine at all." Faolan was scrutinizing her face. "You're upset. We'll speak about this later."

"Don't be stupid. You have to go. I understand. There's no need to speak about anything." She tried to sound calmly accepting.

"I'm not going on until the morning, anyway. If you and Saraid could ride quickly enough, I'd take you."

Oh, yes? "Forget it, Faolan," Eile said. "Do what you have to. If you've learned anything about me, you'll know I can look after myself. And her."

"Later."

Drustan had watched this interchange with the same expression of wonder that Eile had seen on his face before, in the woods. No doubt he would translate it all for his wife later. No, not his wife; it seemed these highborn folk had not been wed when they lay together and made a child destined to perish before it could ever be born. Not only that, but the irregularity of their situation didn't seem to trouble them; they had been quite open about it. She must ask Faolan why that was so, and why his friends kept looking at him as if his words and actions were utterly astonishing. She must ask . . . No, she would not ask. In the morning Faolan would be gone. Chances were he'd be off on some mission or other before she ever reached White Hill. Handy for him that Drustan and Ana were in a position to escort her the rest of the way. It relieved the king's assassin and spy of an awkward responsibility. As for Eile, she'd need to get used to being on her own again.

"You've changed," Ana said softly, looking into the dark eyes of her friend as he sat by her bed later in the day. Drustan had persuaded Eile and the child to venture out walking with the guard dog, Cloud, looking for cats. "Something's happened on that journey, and I think it's for the better." She made no comment about the fact that he had not come back alone; she did not ask him if he had seen his family, or indeed anything at all. If he wanted to tell her, he would. As for what lay between them, she'd best not speak of that unless Faolan broached the topic himself. There had been more than enough hurt inflicted already.

"Mm," Faolan murmured. "I did what you bid me do; went home and faced it all. I will not tell you the whole story. I have my father's forgiveness. I underestimated my family's strength, Ana. There have been grievous losses, and the trouble is not entirely past. But they are doing well enough; far better than I imagined would be possible."

"Were you tempted to stay? Not to return to Fortriu at all?"

Faolan shook his head. "I had a mission. Besides, Eile and I were in trouble; we had to move on."

His tone forbade further questions on that topic.

"She seems so much Deord's daughter," Ana said, smiling. "Underneath that fragile exterior, I can see something . . . dauntless. I wish I could speak Gaelic properly; I'd so much like to have a proper conversation with her. If she stays awhile, Drustan can help her with the Priteni tongue. She'll need that, whatever happens. And he could do with a diversion; this inclement weather restricts his flights."

Faolan regarded her for a while, expression quizzical. "You've simply accepted it, haven't you?" he said. "His difference, his strangeness; I doubt you even think about how much that marks him out. He is a lucky man."

Ana felt a flush rise to her cheeks. "I know it makes him vulnerable in the company of powerful men, or prejudiced ones," she said. "That's why we had hoped to avoid court. But we must go now; I want to see my sister, and the handfasting may as well be done while we are at White Hill. In the long term, I think we will stay mostly at Dreaming Glen. It sounds safe there. A good place for children." She could not keep her voice from cracking. It had seemed so real, the images of Drustan walking in the forest with a flame-haired infant in his arms, of herself singing the old songs of her home islands to rock a tiny babe to sleep. As soon as she had known she was with child she had begun sewing baby clothes, little soft garments with birds embroidered on them. Only yesterday she had put them away, deep down in a corner of an oak chest.

"I'm so sorry." Faolan's voice was tight. "Truly sorry, Ana. I do want you and Drustan to be happy, believe me. I hope Eile is right; that you will have another child."

"I believe you, dear friend. Faolan?" She hesitated, thinking she might risk putting the most delicate subject into words.

"What is it?"

"This feels different. You and me, talking. Not as difficult as it was at White Hill, before you went away."

His voice went very quiet. "If you are asking me whether my feelings for you have changed, I cannot tell you I no longer love you. But the nature of that love is different now. I cannot explain exactly why. A great deal happened over the winter, things that could have broken my heart. I came a hair's-breadth from ending it all, Ana. I tell you that in the knowledge that you will not speak of it to anyone, not even Drustan. When a man allows himself to sink so far into despair, yet survives it, the only way out is upward. Last autumn, I told you I was happy for you, that you had found love with Drustan. When I said that, I suppose I was just speaking the words. Now, when I say it, I feel it in my heart. I speak in the sure knowledge that I can move on; find my own path. That does not make my bond with you, and with Drustan, any the less. We went through the fire together. That will never change."

"Does Eile know?" Ana asked. "That you nearly killed yourself?"

Faolan's lips curved in a sweet smile, an expression of

which she would not previously have believed him capable. "Oh, yes," he said. "Most surely, she knows."

MUCH LATER, AFTER a hearty supper of which neither Eile nor Saraid ate much, and after Saraid had cried herself to sleep, inconsolable and incapable of explaining precisely why, Faolan sought Eile out, tapping on her door.

Don't wake up, Eile willed the child; it had been a distressing time and all she wanted was to climb under the covers herself and release the tears that had been building behind her eyes as she failed to comfort the child's woe.

"It's me," came Faolan's voice. "Is Saraid asleep? I need to talk to you."

Eile opened the door a crack. "She's only just gone to sleep. She was upset. She cried and cried. I need to stay here in case she wakes again."

"All right, we'll talk here. If you'll let me in."

"I don't think so."

He gave her a direct sort of look. "I thought I heard you say not so long ago that you half trusted me," he said. "It's this or have our conversation out here in the hallway where it's cold and anyone passing by can hear us."

"There's no need for a conversation. You're going and we're staying. That's it. Good night."

She made to close the door. Faolan's foot was suddenly in the gap.

"You know that's not it. Please, Eile. Let me in just for a moment. Surely you can't think I . . . ?"

"In fact, no. I saw the look on your face when I made my ill-considered suggestion."

"Please. This won't take long."

"If you wake her up I think I might hit you. She was so upset I nearly cried myself." Eile opened the door and retreated to sit on the bed, her hand on the huddled form of the child. Faolan came in to stand with his back against the stone wall. Eile noticed that he had left the door slightly open. "That's to protect your reputation, is it?" she queried with a grimace.

"No," said Faolan. "It's to stop you feeling trapped."

She did not reply. Then, abruptly, words welled up that she could not stop. "This would be a whole lot easier to cope with if you weren't so nice to us," she said.

"Nice? Me? You've got the wrong man."

"You understand things without being told. I was starting to get used to that." *And I can't afford to do that, because sooner or later you'll be gone forever.*

"It's only for seven days." Faolan's voice sounded a little odd. "And I do have to go, Eile. I thought you understood that."

"I do," she said as a new misery settled over her. "This is what you are; what you do with your life. All the time. One mission and then another. Always going somewhere, doing something important."

After a moment he said, "What are you saying? That you think I'm running away?"

It jolted Eile's heart. She had been thinking only of herself and of Saraid. She looked him in the eye, seeing the pain there. She reminded herself that Ana was in the house: Ana who was dear to him, Ana who was lost to him. "No," she said. "Maybe you've done that in the past. But you went back to Fiddler's Crossing, didn't you?"

"If it had been up to me, I'd have skipped that and headed for the north. The only reason I stopped running, the only reason I saw my family, was you. You and Saraid."

"A lot of help we were. Got you locked up, then cost you all your money. Now we've delayed you on your important business. You'd better be on your way out of here in the morning or I'll really start feeling bad."

His eyes warmed a little, but he said nothing.

"You look tired." Eile scrutinized him closely.

"I don't need much sleep." The eyes went bleak again.

"Rubbish. You look washed out. Go on, go and get some rest." He was upset; brooding over something. "I'm really sorry about Ana," Eile added, making a guess. "She seems so nice. You must be worried about her."

"Mm," he said absently. "I planned to go early tomorrow. At first light. Will you tell Saraid I said good-bye, and that I'll be at White Hill when you get there? Or should I delay setting off until she's awake?"

Eile turned her head away so that he could not see the tears welling in her eyes. "I'll tell her," she said. "I'm hoping she'll sleep late to make up for tonight. Will you go now, please?"

There was a silence. Then he said, "Don't forget to talk to Drustan about your father. He'll have much to tell. Better to ask him here than at White Hill. He's ill at ease there; like you, he doesn't care for crowds."

"All right."

"Don't worry about the language, Eile. Deord spoke both Gaelic and the Priteni tongue ably. So will you in time. This will get easier. I'm sorry you are unhappy. On the voyage over, in that wretched boat with its motley crew of clerics, I thought you were enjoying yourself. I saw a look on your face then that I've never seen again: confident and happy. I wish I could—"

"Please go, Faolan. I want to sleep."

A pause. "Good night, Eile. I'll see you in seven days." His voice was very quiet.

"My father was a sailor." She felt obliged to say this. "Maybe I'm like him. The only thing is, I think voyages should end at home. That's hard when you don't know where home is."

"You're not the only one. Sleep well. Don't forget to tell Saraid—"

"I'll tell her. Good night, Faolan. Ride safely."

Eile heard the door close softly. He was taking care not to wake the child. She found that, after all, she wasn't going to cry. She wrapped her arms around her daughter, shut her eyes, and made an image of the house on the hill. There was the striped cat, there the rows of herbs and flowers fresh and bright in the sunlight. Someone was singing and there was a sound of Saraid's laughter. In that place, it was always summer.

THE MEN AT White Hill were all too old or too young, too plain or too stuffy. The tediousness of it was driving Breda crazy. Keother hadn't brought any of her favorite attendants here from the islands. It was as if her cousin had deliberately chosen to leave behind Breda's comeliest groom, her most muscular bodyguard, her wittiest musician. What did he expect her to do, spend her time putting tiny stitches into useless bits of linen and practicing pretty table manners? Did he imagine there was any real satisfaction to be had in that?

Perhaps, thought the princess of the Light Isles, resting her chin on her hands as she stood by the parapet wall atop White Hill and gazed northward, this visit so long promised as a treat by her cousin was in fact a punishment. Perhaps, that time when Keother's busybody of a councillor had caught her in the stables with Evard, doing a little more than feeding the horses treats, someone had gone running to the king with tales. Keother hadn't said a word and neither had the councillor. All the same, Evard hadn't come to White Hill, even though he was head groom. Her cousin's choice of companions seemed weighted toward old men or ugly ones.

Gods, if this went on things were going to become quickly intolerable. There was absolutely nothing to do here. Her maids were out of sorts and squabbling and she had nobody at all to talk to. If this was the thrilling life that Keother had promised her at the court of Fortriu, she didn't think very much of it at all. These folk had no idea how to have fun.

Breda paced the walkway, lifting her skirts out of the

way of debris blown up there by Fortriu's fierce winds, and making sure her ankles showed. The guards stationed nearby kept their eyes grimly trained on the hillside below the walls. Someone had had a word to them. She blamed the queen, that odd woman with the pale skin and weird eyes. Not a woman, really; something else. As for the children, they were downright unsettling. There was an uncanny strangeness about the little boy that made Breda feel unsafe. The baby looked like something that should have been drowned at birth. Something that had come out wrong didn't deserve to live. Breda couldn't understand how folk could tolerate such oddity. On a farm, if a lamb or a kid or a calf was born deformed you put it down. It was the only practical thing to do. Merciful, really. It eliminated later complications. The royal baby might be pretty in a bizarre kind of way, like its mother, but it looked just . . . wrong.

Breda sighed. If nothing interesting happened here soon, she'd have to make it happen herself. There was Ana's wedding, of course, but it was hard to get at all excited about that. She did remember her sister vaguely. They used to do things together: walking on the beach, singing songs, working on embroidery. The aunt who had raised them had never punished Ana; Ana had been the good sister. Breda's palms had been criss-crossed with welts; Ana's had stayed soft and white. Aunt's approach to punishment had been imaginative. The burning of favorite toys; periods shut up in the woodshed, where large beetles lurked in every corner. Beatings and scaldings. The withholding of nice things, the pretty ribbons and shoes that Breda so coveted. The banishment of certain playmates. Ana was well behaved and quiet; she'd always been able to avoid Aunt's cruelty. Then, at ten years old, Ana had gone to Fortriu and never come back. It sounded as if Ana had never grown out of sewing and music. This fellow she was marrying was sure to be another boring middle-aged chieftain like so many of the men here at court. Where were the warriors? Where were the risk-takers? Where was even one fellow who could prove himself a real man?

The king's guard, the younger one, Dovran, was a good specimen; broad shoulders, long legs, abundant brown hair. Thus far Breda had barely got him to look at her, but she was working on it. The other one, Garth, was married with children. That in itself was no obstacle, but Garth was too old; pushing forty, Breda estimated. And those two lads, with their pathetic eagerness to please, were much too young. They'd be good for novelty, a quick—probably all too quick—encounter. Bedo was the elder; that she'd seriously considered him even for a moment showed how desperate things were getting. But Bedo had disappointed her. Since the little episode with the baby, he seemed to have ceased pursuing her. In fact, she had found him several times in smiling conversation with her attendant, Cella. Cella! Who'd look at her when Breda herself was in view? Cella was a nobody, plain, boring, utterly ordinary. Cella shouldn't be flirting with a chieftain's son, a boy whose mother had been a princess. It was completely inappropriate. The girl must be punished. Not in the usual way; something more entertaining was called for. It would be fun deciding exactly what.

Breda smiled. Court need not be so tedious. All that was needed was enterprise and a touch of imagination. And the raw materials. Those were all around her. She'd see what she could do with them.

SEVEN DAYS HAD sounded long when Eile had learned Faolan was going on without them. It passed all too quickly. Drustan and Ana were keen to give Eile her father's story, and there was a lot of it, far more than she'd expected. They spent long hours talking, first in Ana's bedroom, later before the fire in the hall, where they were left in privacy by Broichan's servants, folk who had evidently been well trained in courtesy and discretion.

Eile had a strong urge to make herself useful. It felt inappropriate to be sitting with this chieftain and his lady, whom Faolan had told her was a real princess, rather than helping Mara wash sheets or scrubbing pots in the kitchen. There was no need for a common tongue when performing tasks such as those, and once or twice she caught Mara glancing at her as if about to suggest she stop sitting about and do some real work. But Drustan and Ana made it clear, without quite saying so, that she was their guest, a friend, and that she was to spend her time accordingly. It felt odd; not quite right.

As the days passed the three of them, with Saraid, took gentle walks around farm and woodland, Ana working on regaining her strength, Drustan supporting her and telling Eile his tale all the while.

The farmer's children were all much older than Saraid, and though the farmer's wife, Brenna, was a kind soul, everyone was busy and Saraid was overwhelmed by the constant activity. When the weather was inclement, she played with the game pieces Drustan had brought out for her, her small fingers careful. Once or twice the cook, Ferat, coaxed her into the kitchen to make rabbits or cats or little men out of dough; he seemed well-practiced at this. She made friends with the big dog, which seemed to like children.

Outside, Ana and Drustan accommodated the child's slow pace and spoke quietly to her. She walked at Eile's side, making small forays away to investigate toadstools or hedgehogs or interesting rocks with patterns on them. While the dog, Cloud, always stayed close to Ana, Drustan's two birds followed Saraid. It seemed to Eile, oddly, that they were watching over the child.

As the days passed, Eile learned of Deord's strength and endurance. She learned of his heroism. She discovered that her father, half destroyed by his own time in prison, had made the most humane and compassionate of jailers. She began to wonder about him, for what Drustan told her did not suggest someone who had chosen to forget his family. This was not a man whose dark experiences had erased from his heart the capacity to love.

"I wonder why he didn't talk about us," she mused to Drustan, toward the end. "He did love us. I remember that. Surely it doesn't just go away. Even when he'd been in Breakstone, when he came home so sad, he called me his little flame, his bright light. Because of my red hair. At least, that was what I thought. Maybe it meant more than that. He loved Mother. He was sweet to her, even then. He used to wake up crying. He had terrible nightmares. I can remember hiding under the covers, but I could still hear him. I heard her singing him back to sleep as if he was a baby." She wiped away tears. "I so wish he'd stayed. But then you'd have had some other guard, and you wouldn't have been saved."

Drustan nodded gravely. "Without Deord I would quickly have run mad. I don't know if Faolan told you, but . . . there is a particular reason I find confinement hard to tolerate. I possess the ability to go between forms; to transform from man to bird and back again. These creatures are, in a sense, parts of me." He indicated the crow and the other bird, which he had told her was a crossbill, foraging in the undergrowth close to Saraid, who was showing Sorry some beetles. "It is both a gift and a curse. It was through this oddity that my brother was able to accuse me of a crime I had not committed and label me mad. Ana and I have still to confront the shadow of that when we return to the north."

"You're the least mad person I've ever met," Eile said. "Apart from Faolan, that is."

Ana grinned as her betrothed translated this. She spoke softly to him. The sunlight, filtering down through the canopy of new spring green, touched her golden hair to a brightness that seemed almost magical. Her voice was low and gentle, her gray eyes full of a deep calm. Eile wished she could talk to her directly, without the need for translation. Ana might be of royal blood and dauntingly beautiful, but there was a realness, an honesty about her that suggested they could become friends. It was ever clearer to Eile why Faolan loved this woman; who would not?

Drustan said, "Ana says you seem unsurprised by what I have told you. Some folk find it unsettling."

"That you are a—what's the right word?—a shape-shifter? I think it's wonderful. I would so love to be able to fly. That's a kind of freedom I can hardly imagine."

Ana said something to Drustan. Her tone alerted Eile to a change in the conversation. She heard the other woman say her name.

"What?" she asked sharply.

"Ana says it's time we put something to you, Eile, and I agree. We wondered if you had given any thought to the future."

"What kind of question is that? I have a three-year-old child. Of course I've considered the future."

"What path do you see for yourself and Saraid, after White Hill?"

"After . . ." Eile felt a chill creep over her, the familiar cold breath of change. "I'm not sure. I'd have to talk to Faolan."

Drustan and Ana exchanged a glance.

"What?" demanded Eile, aware of something unspoken, something she wasn't going to like.

"Eile," said Drustan, "if you wished to come with us to Caitt territories, Ana and I would be very happy to take you. You're Deord's daughter; we both had the deepest respect for him. You and Saraid could have a permanent home with us at Dreaming Glen. That is my own land-holding on the west coast, a remote and beautiful location. It is a fine place for a child to grow up in, quiet, safe, full of good people. My brother changed it somewhat with his boats and his warriors, but I will restore it to its old peace. Ana and I have decided to travel down the lakes and up the coast to Dreaming Glen first, to settle in there and establish a strong base. Only then will I venture to what was my brother's holding and set that household to rights. We'd like you to come with us. Ana would welcome the companionship. I'd be honored to have this opportunity to repay the debt we owe your father."

"Oh." Eile had not expected this, even though Faolan had once or twice referred to some arrangement of the kind. "It's a lot to offer. You don't even know me." There was a confusion of feelings in her. Not so long ago she would have thought this a wonderful dream come true: safety, an end to arbitrary changes, friendly people, no more desperate struggles to keep her daughter fed and warm and secure. A future: a real one. She knew these were good people; they were Faolan's friends, weren't they? All the wise arguments pointed to *yes*. Yet there was some part of her that said, instantly and without logic, *no*. It was a part she could not disregard. "Thank you," she said. "Your generosity is . . . overwhelming. But I can't."

Neither Drustan nor Ana said anything. It was obvious that Ana had understood the negative without need for translation. They looked rather sad but not surprised.

"I'm sorry," Eile said. "I can't even say why; I can see this would be good for Saraid. But I know I can't do it. You talked about repaying debts. I've got one of my own; if I go away, I can't ever repay it." She knew Faolan did not expect his silver back; she had hardly thought of the *éraic* in recent times. But going off and leaving him behind felt profoundly wrong.

"You might perhaps take time to consider it," Drustan suggested. "We'll be staying at White Hill a little so that Ana can see her sister."

"And for the wedding," Eile said, thinking how painful that was going to be for Faolan.

"That, too, although I believe we may disappoint some

people. We intend to keep our handfasting small and private. Bridei and Tuala will understand. Ana and I have no liking for grand celebrations." And, translating when Ana spoke, "We seem to have moved beyond the need for such events. Besides, in our own eyes and in those of the gods, we know we are already true husband and wife."

Eile nodded, thinking what unusual folk they were and how it was a shame she would not have time to get to know them better. "I don't need to consider it," she said. She hoped they would not think her ungrateful. "I can't come."

"That's what we expected you to say." That was Ana. Drustan smiled as he rendered the words into Gaelic. Then Ana said something else to him and his smile faded. They seemed to dispute whatever it was; Eile heard Ana say Faolan's name.

"Tell me," she said. "What about Faolan? He did speak of the possibility that Saraid and I might stay with some friends of his; maybe it was you he meant."

The two of them were looking at her now. She wasn't sure what those expressions meant. They were sorry for her? They didn't want to upset her? They weren't sure how much to tell? With a tight feeling in her belly, Eile glanced at Saraid to make sure she was out of easy earshot, then said, "Tell me, whatever it is."

"This will be best back at the house," Drustan said. "Ana and I need to discuss it first."

"Now, Drustan," said Ana in Gaelic.

"Very well. Eile, Faolan asked us if we'd assume the role of guardians to you. He wanted us to take you north with us. He pressed us to give him that assurance before he left. He's very concerned for your welfare."

Eile was momentarily unable to reply. She told herself this was entirely reasonable; that it was much better than she should have expected. She stared at the ground, willing herself to act as Ana would do under the same circumstances: like a lady. "Thank you for telling me the truth," she said. Her voice came out tight and wounded;

she couldn't control that. "So you said yes. An obligation to my father. Faolan's done his share and he's passing over the responsibility."

"Our offer was made in a genuine wish to welcome you and your daughter into our household," Drustan said. "Certainly we owe Deord a debt none of us can ever fully repay. But once we met you and once we knew your circumstances, Ana and I would have made our offer whether Faolan had asked or not. We thought highly of your father. We like and respect you."

Ana put in a few words, her grave eyes all the while fixed on Eile. Not pitying; more assessing. Eile liked that look much better than the earlier one.

"Ana says you assume we said yes to Faolan. In fact, we gave him no answer. Ana told him the decision must be entirely up to you. If you chose not to come with us we would respect your choice, and so must he."

"Oh." Eile considered this. Faolan was not the sort of man folk gave orders to. Perhaps Ana was the one exception.

"After he left, Ana and I discussed this at some length. Ana says we should tell you that both of us believe you've made the right decision."

Ana was stamping her foot in frustration, gesturing, unable to find the words she wanted.

"She says it's annoying she cannot talk to you woman to woman, in private. I believe she wants to tell you something out of my hearing. I'm afraid it must wait; nobody else here is fluent in Gaelic."

They began to walk back toward the house. Eile was feeling very odd, as if she'd been on the verge of falling and had been saved by something quite unexpected. As if she'd been picked up and set back on the path, although perhaps it was a different path now. She had no idea where it led, and yet she felt better.

"You said you'd learned about my circumstances," she said. "How much did he tell you?" Let him not have spoken of Dalach. Or of the *éraic*. Or, most treacherously, of the request she had made of him, the one he said had made him feel honored. Almost certainly that was what had tipped the balance and made him decide to get rid of her.

"He was tight-lipped with the details," said Drustan. "It is plain you were very young when you had your daughter. Faolan told us both you and he had to leave Erin because of an ongoing threat to your safety. He told us your mother was dead; that you had experienced great hardship and dealt with it bravely, as he'd expect from Deord's daughter. That was as much as he was prepared to tell. He believes you and Saraid will be better off with a family; with someone who can provide stability for you. He's told you what his profession is, I imagine?"

Eile's lips twisted. "Officially, the king's bodyguard. Unofficially, a bit more, but I'm not going to talk about that. A family, eh? It *sounds* sensible. Like the nice young man he keeps talking about, the one I'm going to meet some day."

Drustan glanced at her with a smile. Ana had bent down to admire some flowers; Saraid was counting the petals. "Look, Sorry," the child said, "little stars."

"Drustan," Eile said, "why do you think it's the right choice? I don't even know what's going to happen at White Hill. I can't speak the language. I can't really do much except look after Saraid and perform servants' work. Why bring me all the way here just for that? I mean, he did make a promise, but there'd have been easier ways to fulfill it."

Drustan translated for Ana; her reply was a question. "Will you tell us what the promise was?"

"That he'd stay with me until I didn't need him anymore." She could not keep the regret from her voice. It was plain to her, now, that Faolan's understanding of the promise had not been the same as hers.

Ana spoke again.

"She says," said Drustan, "it's a pity you cannot ask Faolan whether he believes he needs you. Being that man's friend is like watching over a person lost in a maze. The turns are many and complex; he is surrounded by shadowy corners, by dead ends, by tricks and traps. Some of them are of his own making. If you would be his friend, you need to stay by him even when he orders you to leave him. It's not an easy path. Far simpler to bid him good-bye and go your own way."

It made an odd sort of sense to Eile.

"He did tell us," Drustan added, "that you were not the kind of girl to choose the easy path."

THEY HAD TESTED the druid beyond pain. Day and night had blurred into a single, continuous waking. His eyes fell on the familiar and found it alien. He lost names; objects no longer made sense to him. Sound was ephemeral and insignificant, or immediate and terrifying. The call of a forest creature became a dark summons to death; the trickle of a stream echoed the draining away of intellect, of consciousness, of self. He was a stone rolling before the inevitability of the river. He was a feather borne here and there by random winds. He was a bough of rowan awaiting the touch of devouring flame. At the last, when bone and sinew had been driven and stretched and hammered, when eyes and ears no longer perceived shape and sound as before but knew only a wild continuum of being, when from a winter's torment his mind emerged, swept clean and bare, he was a still pool: a vessel for the will of the Shining One. *I am ready,* the druid said.

BRIDEI AND FAOLAN were standing on the parapet wall at White Hill with Garth keeping watch at a discreet distance. The sun was setting over the Great Glen, edging a tumble of clouds with rose and crimson. It was a measure of Faolan's particular place in the king's circle that

Bridei had excused himself from the company of Keother, among others, to seek an immediate and confidential meeting with his newly arrived bodyguard.

There had been no embrace; Bridei knew better than to offer one, though he considered Faolan his closest friend. Greetings were exchanged, the wish that each was in good health. Bridei provided the news of Anfreda's arrival; Faolan offered congratulations. Then it was down to business.

On both sides the news was worrying. Colmcille was already on the shores of Dalriada and, in Faolan's considered opinion, likely to head for White Hill sooner rather than later. Carnach was apparently plotting some kind of coup, or at the very least a serious challenge to the king. Broichan absent; Keother and his young cousin at court. The most experienced of jugglers finds so many extra balls a challenge.

While Faolan talked, Bridei wondered how much he could ask about his right-hand man's journey. Had Faolan seen his family? Resolved whatever it was he'd had to deal with there? Faolan's expression was a well-governed mask. His dark eyes were guarded. Whatever had occurred during the time away, his self-control appeared intact.

"We must choose our priority," Bridei said. "You and I, that is. I'll have Aniel call a select meeting for tomorrow. Fola's here; that's fortunate in view of Broichan's continuing absence. We'll put this to them. Faolan, my instincts are pulling me in a certain direction. I want to know if you agree."

"Before I give you my opinion, tell me what the situation is with Broichan. If the Christians decide to make you a visit while these other issues remain unresolved, you'll need your druid to deal with Colm. I understand Broichan disappeared, leaving no word of where he was headed."

"We've heard nothing. He seems to have vanished from Fortriu entirely. Were it not for Tuala's visions, we'd have believed him dead. She remains confident that he'll come back."

"He'd want to hurry," observed Faolan drily.

"Tuala's instincts are sound. He'll be here in time, unless these Christians possess wondrous powers of transportation."

"Colm knows how to sail. I can't say the same for the rest of them."

Bridei folded his arms, leaning his back against the wall. "If you were in my shoes, what would you do first?" he asked quietly. "Speak freely."

For the first time Faolan seemed hesitant.

"What is it?" Bridei asked.

"Nothing. I believe we have a little time, not much, but perhaps sufficient for your druid to make his way back to White Hill before Colmcille decides to head up the Glen. Keother we can deal with; he's here, right under our noses, and that should keep him out of trouble. The girl probably isn't important. Keother knows she may be the next hostage. He knows we expect his best behavior. Let us hope it shames him to be the only leader not recognized for a contribution to last autumn's war. You must still hold your victory feast. Cancel that, and you offend your chieftains and disappoint their families. It would be taken as a sign of indecision. In view of your choice not to seek the crown of Circinn, it could be seen as weakness."

"Go on." Thank the gods for Faolan, Bridei thought. There was nobody else so astute, or so prepared to advise his king in total honesty. He realized anew how badly he had missed his friend.

"I see the matter of Carnach as the greatest threat," Faolan said, "the one crying out for our immediate attention. When I first heard of this rebellion I found it hard to believe. Carnach a traitor? Carnach whom we know and respect so well? If he's done this, it must be with a heavy heart; he loves Fortriu and I would have sworn his loyalty to you was unflinching. But now you tell me there have been other rumors along the same lines as the one I heard, tales brought from many quarters. Someone must go and find out the truth. Not a large party of armed warriors; not an official emissary such as Tharan or Aniel. Someone who can slip by unnoticed."

Faolan stood relaxed, features calm. All the same, there was a tension there that Bridei could almost feel. The silence drew out.

"Is something wrong?"

"Wrong? You mean, other than the weighty matters we've just set out?" Faolan's brows lifted.

Bridei spoke carefully, choosing each word. Negotiating a conversation with Faolan on personal matters required a degree of skill that was often beyond even him. "I notice you don't immediately volunteer your services. Both of us know this requires your particular expertise. I recognize that you've only just returned from a lengthy absence. But the need to go straight from one mission to the next has never stopped you before."

Faolan did not respond. He was staring into the distance as if he had not heard.

"Perhaps you're not aware," Bridei went on, "that Ana's and Drustan's wedding is to take place in the near future, just before the victory feast. Broichan's absence delayed it. I imagine, based on your attitude last autumn, that you will not wish to be at White Hill for the handfasting."

"I know about the wedding. I saw them at Pitnochie." Faolan's expression forbade further probing. "I'll go, of course. How soon?"

"I want you here for tomorrow's meeting," Bridei said. "It will be small. Only those men and women in whom I have unconditional trust. You'll need a couple of nights' rest before you leave. One of the fellows who brought news is still here; you may wish to hear his account."

"I don't require rest. I'll go as soon as you need me to go."

"Very well. I value your loyalty, Faolan. And your honesty. Make no doubt of that."

Faolan gave a stiff nod.

"Tuala would like to see you." Bridei gestured to Garth that they were going indoors. "I think it's important you hear what she has to say about Broichan, for that matter is equally significant, if perhaps less urgent."

"If you wish." Faolan's voice sounded tight.

"To be quite honest," Bridei said, masking his concern, for something was wrong, that was plain, but he could see his friend had no wish to speak of it, "I can't wait to show you my new daughter, although I know you have no interest in little children. She's the image of my wife as an infant." For a moment they were two equals, not Priteni king and Gaelic guard. "You set hard rules for yourself," Bridei added. "Too hard, sometimes."

"An essential part of the job. So I remind myself."

Bridei headed down the stone steps toward the garden. Near the bottom, he heard Faolan's voice from behind him, the tone quite different.

"Bridei—?"

Bridei turned. Faolan was in the shadows near the top of the steps; he had barely moved.

"What is it, Faolan?" There was something there, an unease, a reservation.

Garth loomed behind the Gael, a watchful presence, spear in hand.

Faolan shook his head, not in a negative, but as if to clear his mind of unwelcome thoughts. "Nothing," he said, descending the steps. "Nothing at all."

11

(from Brother Suibne's Account)

We have visited the island. Another voyage; another test of faith and fortitude. Ioua is a place of deep calm, for all its winds and tides. Walking on that pale shore, I felt my soul swept clean of sin, my heart relieved of all burdens. Colm said, This is an isle of new beginnings, *and our spirits knew it for truth. God wants us here; it is His place.*

The fisherman who brought us across—we did not take our own boat, for several of our brethren had not the will to sail again so soon—let us wander at length. He followed us with eyes like the sea, deep and watchful. When it was time to leave, he took us to the larger isle off whose coast Ioua lies, and thence back to Dunadd.

If Brother Colm chafed before at the need to stay here in this half-court with its ailing monarch and wary guards, it is nothing to his mood now. He questioned me again about Bridei and his druid. He quizzed me on the faith of the Priteni, their deities and rituals. I have spoken to him on these matters many times, but I told it again. This time I spoke of the Well of Shades and the ceremony that required the sacrifice of human life to a god who remains ever nameless. Colm heard me out in silence. For once he asked no questions. Those will come later.

Tonight, I examine my heart to discover why it was that I felt such reluctance to divulge that final dark truth about the folk of Fortriu. Perhaps I recognized that, after a certain point in the narrative, even the most perspicacious and balanced of listeners would cease to hear my words. It is too shocking: a thing brought forward in time from a primitive existence based on fear. I do not think

Colm heard me tell him that Bridei had forbidden the practice, or that this king had only ever participated once. Perhaps that is why I never put it into words before. The king of Fortriu is a good man, a man of sound principles. To tell this tale is to seem to discredit Bridei. I would rather he and Colm met without prejudice and without illusions.

Arrogant soul! I read my words fresh on the page and cringe in mortification. Who am I, that I would order the lives of king and priest to a pattern that happens to please me? Who is this lowly scribe, God's servant?

After reflection, I pick up the pen again. Like each and every one of my brethren, I am indeed God's well-beloved child and servant. He will light the way for me, for Colm, for each of us. I wonder who lights Bridei's way?

We have Ioua in our eyes now, those of us who made the trip there. Colm has sent Sean, who was raised on a farm, and Tomas, who was a carpenter, across to the larger island to make the acquaintance of folk in the settlements there. When the time is right they will see about the acquisition of building materials and livestock. We will need a dwelling house, a small church, places for stores, a barn, a byre . . . My heart shrinks as I contemplate the conveyance of cattle by sea.

The island is not ours; not yet. It is in Bridei's gift. Before we can begin our new life on that lonely, peaceful shore, there must be a meeting. Bridei has forbidden the practice of our faith in these parts. He has banished many souls back over the sea to our homeland. There is no reason to assume he will look on Colm's request favorably.

I remember the druid, Broichan, a man with authority stamped on every corner of his being. He is a figure much feared even among his own. Broichan is not simply Bridei's spiritual adviser, but also his foster father. He is skilled in magic, so they say. Colm asked about that. He said, So this man is impressed by tricks, shows of power? Demonstrations of the wondrous and unnatural? *I do not know what Colm plans. His own power is in his voice and in his eye; it comes from God. Broichan must see in Colm an adversary, a threat to his own dominion. He will come to the council table with eyes and ears already closed. As for Colm himself, I regret my honesty in giving him the account of the Gateway ritual in all its cruel detail.*

God requires of me truthfulness; openness. That is what I have given. Perhaps, in the end, these two powerful men, each staunchly adherent to his own beliefs, may prove to be opposing forces of equal weight. How, then, can either prevail?

I think this journal must at some point be burned, or shredded and fed to goats, or cut into pieces and tossed out into the waves west of Ioua to travel where it will. On occasion my musings disturb even myself. I have a theory about Gateway. I do not believe in Bridei's Nameless God. The well, I believe, represents our past. The shadows it contains are those of our own misdeeds, and those of our ancestors since a time before memory. For a man who knows not the Lord God, the burden of his failures, his omissions, his errors and blunders can in time become intolerable. A man's heart can break under the weight of it. So the sacrifice. The dark deity accepts; the burden is lifted for another turning of the wheel. I think there is some truth in it, a bleak sort of truth. Even without the well, and the god, and the ritual, a man can become a slave to his own past. Its entanglements can be a net holding him fast. If he does not break free, he will drag it along with him all his life. That is like walking in fetters, and blindfolded. When we go to White Hill, and the look in Colm's eye tells me that will be soon, I must discuss this with Bridei. If he will.

Enough of that. I am in danger of overreaching myself once again. I think I will entreat Colm for a little scriptorium on the island; a meager hut will suffice. There I will be still and quiet. I will copy those passages of scripture

I most love, or, better still, those likeliest to lull to sleep all perilous thoughts and dangerous philosophies. On the other hand, it has always been plain to me that a man's faith must grow stronger when put fully to the test.

SUIBNE, MONK OF DERRY

EILE WAS IN the garden waiting. Saraid crouched to look in the pond, then stood by the lavender bushes, showing Sorry the feathery gray-green leaves, the spikes of fragrant flower heads. It was a good place, sheltered by high stone walls and warmed by the afternoon sun. They'd not long arrived at White Hill. In the courtyard a confusion of Priteni folk had greeted them, people who seemed to know Ana well, people whose glances touched Eile and Saraid without much curiosity. Perhaps it was only when she opened her mouth that they would know she was a Gael. Eile reminded herself that there had been a war not long ago, and that the Gaels had been the enemy. She had not anticipated this would be a difficulty. In all her imaginings of White Hill, Faolan had been somewhere close at hand. He was a Gael, and he was the king's trusted guard; at least, that was what he had told her. Thus far there had been no sign of him.

Down at the far end of the garden, Drustan was talking to a broad-shouldered man with a sword and two knives at his belt. Ana had gone to see the queen, who was apparently an old friend. Old friends were the only ones allowed in, since Queen Tuala had a very new baby. Eile wondered how Ana would feel about that. Sad, of course; but maybe comforted as well, if the two women were close. An infant was an assurance that, despite all, life went on. In time, Ana and Drustan would surely have another child.

"Bee," observed Saraid, pointing. "Bzz."

"Mm." Eile was glad that Ana had left them to wait here, not in the parts of the house that were swarming with alarmingly grand-looking folk. It was surely only a matter of time before she said something wrong, offended someone, got in trouble as she had at Blackthorn Rise. Where was Faolan? Busy, she supposed. Occupied with his mysterious duties, plotting and planning. She'd thought he would be here to greet them. That was unrealistic, of course. Still, she'd hoped.

Time passed. Drustan and the other fellow were still down there, out of earshot, deep in serious conversation. What would Ana say to the queen about her? Would she even mention her? *There's this girl Faolan picked up on the road; he doesn't know what to do with her . . .* No, not that; Ana was kind. She wanted Eile to stay at White Hill. At moments like this, the thought of volunteering to be Ana's maidservant and travel north with them after all had strong appeal. She'd probably been stupid to say she wouldn't go.

"Look, a lady," said Saraid, pointing to a half-concealed bench at one side of the herb patch, by the wall. "And a cat."

There was a cat, a little stone one in a niche, with a smug expression on its carven face and one paw raised for washing. Eile looked again. There was also indeed a lady; a real one. She was so like Ana that she could only be the long-lost sister the princess of the Light Isles was to meet at last on this visit to court. If the girl had noticed Eile and Saraid, she showed not a sign of it. She was standing by the bench, as still as a hunting creature sizing up its prey. Her sharp blue eyes were trained down the garden toward the tall, flame-haired figure of Drustan. The expression on her face took Eile aback. She looked hungry.

"He's taken," Eile said before she could stop herself.

The fair-haired girl started; clearly, she'd been unaware she had company. She snapped out a challenge, both guilt and offense in her tone.

"I only speak Gaelic." Eile had memorized this statement in the Priteni tongue. She'd worked hard at Pitnochie under Drustan's tutelage, suddenly desperate to keep afloat once she reached this place full of alien speech.

"Really? Who are you?" The girl's Gaelic was almost flawless. Her eyes traveled from Eile's head of dark red hair across to Drustan's tawny locks. "His sister?" She glanced at Saraid, who was looking on solemnly. "No, I suppose you're a nursemaid. Or a slave? You are a Gael, I see it now. Something in the eyes."

Eile swallowed her irritation. She'd endured worse insults before. Besides, if the *éraic* was taken into account, she was a kind of slave. "I'm . . ." What could she say? Ana's friend? Perhaps Ana would have it thus, but to say so felt presumptuous. A traveler? True, but insufficient here, under this girl's probing gaze. "I'm a friend of Faolan's," she said. "I traveled here with Ana and Drustan. I think you must be Ana's sister. You're very like her." She was pleased with the confident sound of this.

"Faolan?" The girl lifted her brows. "Who's he?"

"The king's bodyguard. Like me, a Gael."

"Bodyguard? I thought Bridei only had the two, Garth there and a handsomer one, Dovran. I've never seen a third. Is this Faolan young?"

"He should be here," Eile said, a chill coming over her. "You should have seen him, I think. He's . . ." Words fled. There was a perfect image of Faolan in her mind, correct in every detail: his strength, his kindness, his courage. His reticence; his wariness. Those things were the essence of the man. But they were not what this girl wanted. "Dark hair," Eile went on. "Medium build, rather a forbidding look about him. About Drustan's age, but he looks older. He should have been here several days. But then, it seems rather a busy place."

"Maybe I overlooked him," said the girl lightly. "Who's this little thing? Not Ana's, I assume, since my sister apparently isn't wed yet. I gather Ana's been living with her betrothed all winter. Strange; she was always so prim and proper, even as a child." She looked over at the two men again and her eyes narrowed. "Wait a bit. You're telling me that's him? My stuffy sister is marrying that splendid specimen?"

Eile wondered greatly at the girl's manner of speech. Surely this was not the usual way of things at court. Perhaps it was the opportunity to speak in Gaelic, a language it was likely few here understood, that had loosened this young woman's tongue so alarmingly.

"This is my daughter, Saraid," Eile said. "And yes, the red-haired man is Drustan. We all traveled here together. My name is Eile."

"I'm Breda." The girl looked from Saraid to Eile. "I see my sister's not the only one to flout convention. You got busy early, didn't you? How old are you, exactly?"

It seemed princesses were not always taught good manners. "About the same age as you, I imagine. My lady."

Breda grinned. "No need for formality. It's just the two of us, after all. None of the other girls speaks Gaelic. That could be fun. A secret language."

Eile wondered if this girl was younger than she looked. "How did you learn to speak it so well? Ana has only a few words."

"We have a bunch of Christians in the islands, countrymen of yours. They wander about telling stories and trying to convert us. We have slaves, too, not all of them wretched and ignorant. But mostly I learned from my Gaelic bard." An odd little smile. "He's very talented; magic fingers. He's taught me all manner of things. It can be quite tedious there. One has to fill in the time somehow."

"I see." Alien indeed, for all the common tongue. Eile thought of Dalach's house and the aching, wrenching labors that had begun at sunup and ceased only when she was beyond exhaustion.

"You're judging me. I see it in your eyes." Breda was suddenly severe.

Eile bit back an automatic denial. She would not tell lies just to be polite.

A peal of laughter rang out, causing the heads of the two men to turn in Breda's direction. "You should see yourself!" Ana's sister spluttered. "What an expression! Oh." Her tone changed abruptly; her eyes darkened. "Garth's noticed we're here. Look, he's stamping across to order us out of the queen's private garden. That's so annoying. It's a stupid rule, and making someone of my status comply with it is downright offensive. There's so much here that just isn't *right*. Someone needs to fix it."

The large, well-armed Garth strode up, Drustan a pace or two behind with his birds on his shoulders. The bodyguard spoke briefly and firmly. Nobody offered Eile a translation. Breda scowled at Garth, offered Drustan a lopsided smile and a flutter of her lashes, and was gone. Eile took Saraid's hand, intending to follow. If this garden was forbidden to a princess, Ana must surely have made an error in suggesting Eile wait here.

Garth spoke again, putting out a hand. Eile stepped back before he could touch her.

"Not you, Eile," Drustan said. "You and I can stay here until the queen is ready. Was that Ana's sister? Silly question; the resemblance is clear."

"Drustan?"

"What is it, Eile?"

"Could you ask this man . . . He is one of the king's guards, isn't he? . . . Could you ask him . . . No, never mind."

"I have asked," said Drustan gravely. "Faolan has left White Hill, Eile. Garth is not at liberty to tell me where he's gone. He's been away five or six days."

"Oh." Another promise broken. Thank the gods she had decided not to pass Faolan's message on to Saraid. There was no way she would have her daughter clinging to false hope and continually disappointed. If you set your expectations low, there was less hurt in having them shattered.

She had questions. Most of them could not be asked. Faolan's business was not her business. That had never been clearer than now. He would have left no message. He thought he'd tidied her away; that Ana and Drustan would take up where he'd left off.

"I don't suppose anyone knows when he's coming back?" she ventured.

A door opened at the far end of the walled garden and an elegant, auburn-haired woman of perhaps three-and-twenty came out. She spoke briskly; Garth retreated to his earlier post and the woman motioned Eile and Saraid toward the doorway.

"This lady is the queen's friend Ferada," Drustan said. "The queen wants to meet you. I'll wait here for now. The only male admitted to Tuala's quarters, apart from her son, is King Bridei. That rule applies until the baby is old enough to be out in company."

"But—"

"Tuala has some Gaelic," Drustan said. "Don't look like that, Eile. You can do this. Use the words we practiced." He headed away toward the steps that rose to the high walkway where guards patrolled. Eile saw him go up in three long strides, as if near-weightless, his bright hair a flash of flame; she remembered his oddity, his wondrous talent. Hoodie and crossbill arose from his shoulders as he went, winging up, then settled again on the rampart by his side.

"Come," said Ferada in Gaelic, and Eile followed her in.

She had expected someone grand, someone like the intimidating Áine, but taller, older, and more richly dressed. Queen Tuala was not like that at all. She was little and pale, with pretty, untidy dark hair and huge eyes. She seemed not much older than Eile herself, and her smile was warm, if guarded. Apart from the friend, Ferada, who had an alarmingly severe look to her, the only other people present were Ana and a tiny boy, smaller than Saraid. And a baby. The boy was standing by a cradle, but when he saw them come in he walked straight over to Saraid and reached out to grasp onto her shawl.

Saraid used Sorry to hit him on the hand, and he let go. It did not seem an auspicious start.

"I only speak Gaelic, my lady," Eile said, curtsying to the queen and remembering the last time Saraid had attacked a nobleman's son. "I'm sorry; my daughter gets frightened. We've seen so many changes . . ." She fell silent as Saraid released her grip on her mother's skirt and followed the small boy over to the cradle. The boy said something like *Fayda,* and the two of them peered into the little bed together. Saraid's features were suddenly illuminated by a brilliant smile. "Baby," she said, reaching a gentle finger to touch.

"Come, sit by me." Queen Tuala's accented Gaelic was easy enough to understand. "Ferada and I can put together enough words to talk to you, I hope. You've had a long journey, Eile."

Eile nodded, keeping her eyes on the children. "She's usually very well behaved," she said.

"And so is my son. Sometimes he forgets the proper way to do things. He's proud of his new sister, and protective. He seems to like your daughter. Saraid, is it?"

Ana must have told her. Eile nodded, wondering how much more Ana had told. She could think of no reason why the queen of Fortriu should show any interest at all in a wandering girl and her by-blow. No; not that. She'd promised Faolan not to say that sort of thing. "I saw your sister, Breda," she told Ana, remembering and thinking this should be passed on. "Just now, out there." She would not say that Breda had been banished from the garden, or that she had shown little interest in meeting her long-lost sister. She would not comment on Breda's distinctly odd manner of speech.

Tuala spoke to Ana in the other tongue; the fair-haired woman jumped up, eyes alight, and excused herself.

"Hmm," commented Ferada when Ana was gone. "An interesting reunion. I wonder what they'll think of each other." Her Gaelic sounded remarkably competent.

"We won't speak of that now." Tuala's voice was soft;

nonetheless, Eile was reminded that she was queen. "Eile, Ana tells me you are a good friend of Faolan's."

"We traveled together. He helped us, me and Saraid." Then, after a pause during which she tried and failed to suppress the words, "Do you know when he's coming back, my lady?"

"I'm afraid not. Faolan works for my husband, not for me. Bridei speaks very good Gaelic, and I know he will want to talk to you. I also know the nature of Faolan's work is such that even Bridei will not be able to tell you where he's gone or when he will return."

Eile nodded. The king, wanting to talk to her? Not likely. Even if he did, she'd be so scared of saying something wrong she'd be wetting herself every time he asked a question.

"We can find accommodation for you and Saraid here at White Hill," Tuala said. "For now I'll ask Dorica, who's currently in charge, to put you next to Ana and Drustan."

"Thank you."

"Ana tells me they don't plan to stay long. I understand you've chosen not to go north with them."

"That's right."

The two children had settled themselves on the rug before the hearth. They seemed to be exchanging words, though in what tongue it was by no means clear. Saraid had Sorry sitting up on her knee. The little boy was holding a horse made from carven stone; a royal sort of toy, Eile thought, beautifully detailed. She started as it seemed to move a miniature hoof and toss its tiny aristocratic head. She must be far more tired than she thought.

"Did Faolan speak to you much about court?" The queen's tone was gentle.

"Just that there were good people here, my lady, and that we'd be safe. He did say that perhaps a place might be found for me. Or at a school; he did mention a school, but I won't go anywhere without my daughter. Besides, I don't think I would fit into such an establishment. I imagine it's all fine embroidery and singing."

"I imagine so," said Ferada gravely.

"Eile," said Tuala, "what do you think Faolan had in mind for you?"

Eile felt a flush rise to her cheeks. "I think he expected me to stay with Lady Ana. I don't think he considered things much further than that. The fact is, the only skills I have are for servants' work: scrubbing floors, washing clothes, plain cooking. I like gardening. Oh, and looking after children. I am quite good at that." She glanced at Saraid and her companion. Her daughter now had the stone horse between careful hands, examining it closely. The boy cradled Sorry, scrutinizing her painted eyes and battle-scarred neck. Eile's astonishment must have shown on her face. Even the charming Phadraig had not been allowed to hold Saraid's only treasure.

"Derelei can be very . . . persuasive," Tuala said, smiling. "Eile, Ana believes Faolan did not mean you to be given a servant's position, and indeed, we would not offer you that."

"Oh." Was she to be sent on again? Sent away before she even got the chance to say good-bye?

"If you are his friend, and that in itself is surprising for all manner of reasons, then you must be treated appropriately. I want you and your daughter to make yourselves at home here. To feel safe. You must stay at White Hill as long as you like."

Tears pricked Eile's eyes. She reminded herself of Blackthorn Rise and Áine. She must learn to be cautious; warm welcomes did not necessarily translate into happy futures. "Thank you, my lady. I do want to work. I want to earn my keep and Saraid's. Anything else would be wrong." She considered the *éraic,* the phenomenal sum that would take a lifetime to pay back.

"I'll talk to my husband. You and Saraid need time to rest and recover. There are several children here at court of about her age. All boys, I'm afraid, and quite loud ones. Your daughter seems a quiet little thing."

"She's had to be." All those times with Dalach, and Saraid sitting out on the step, still as a mouse, waiting. Eile shuddered as it came back.

"Maybe she will set a good example here," Tuala said. Her eyes were on the two children, who had their heads together, whispering. Derelei was helping Sorry pat the stone horse.

"There are some rules you need to understand." Ferada had said little; her voice, now, was like a dash of cold water. "They've had to be put in place to keep the queen and her new daughter safe. Only a handful of people are admitted to these quarters and the part of the garden that adjoins them. There are two guards on duty to enforce that at all times. Court's very full just now. The rules will be relaxed somewhat when the visitors are gone. We did consult Faolan during his brief stop here. He approved."

"Oh." That explained what the girl Breda had said, about being asked to leave the private garden. It did seem odd that the prohibition should apply to Breda herself; she was Ana's own sister. "I suppose we should go, then. Is that what you're saying? Saraid, come with me."

"Eile—" Tuala began, but Ferada said with a frown, "You'll be tired. I'll call someone to show you—"

"No need," Eile said, hearing the tight sound of her own voice. "Drustan said he'd wait for me. I'll stay out of the garden, don't worry. We're used to keeping out of folk's way." Then, as the two of them looked at her, "My lady."

"That wasn't what Ferada meant, Eile," said the queen quietly. "You are Faolan's friend. I'm sure in time you will become our friend, too." Her eyes went to the children, Saraid now back at Eile's skirts, Derelei looking crestfallen. "My son already wishes that were so, I think. But you're right, it is time to go. You need to settle in. Ana tells me you're a little concerned about your inability to understand the Priteni tongue. We have an old scholar who would enjoy teaching you the language;

he's a lot less terrifying as a tutor than Ferada here, and he gets wonderful results. I'll have a word with Wid. He could do with something to keep him busy."

"Thank you, my lady. Before I go, may I look at the baby? Fayda, is that her name?"

She could see Ferada was about to say no, and Tuala herself seemed hesitant, but Derelei heard the name and jumped to his feet. "See Fayda," he said, holding out a hand to lead Eile to the cradle. That much in the Priteni tongue Eile understood.

"Anfreda," Tuala said. "She's named for Bridei's mother, who wed the king of Gwynedd. Derelei's learned her name quite quickly. He's over two, but he doesn't talk much."

"He will learn in his own time, I'm sure," Eile said. "Children are all different. Oh, she's lovely! So like you!" She took in the translucent skin, the long lashes, the coal-black hair. Abruptly, the infant opened her eyes. They gazed up at Eile, big, deep, strangely knowing. "So beautiful. And so . . ."

"Unusual?" Tuala's tone was light. "My mother was of another race. Did Faolan mention this?"

Eile shook her head, stepping back from the cradle. If they were worried enough about personal safety to keep folk out of the garden, they wouldn't want a perfect stranger like herself close to the baby. "We talked mostly about home; about how things had been for us before. And about my father, whom he knew. Then there were the day-to-day things, getting food, keeping the fire going, tending to Saraid." They were looking at her strangely again, as if she were a curiosity. It made her feel edgy. "When he spoke of you and of King Bridei, he just said you were good people, wise and kind. Nothing about birth or breeding."

"Such things shouldn't matter," said Ferada. "But here in Fortriu they do. For me and Tuala, for Bridei, for Ana, they are all-important. Some of us make a choice to ignore that, and our lives become complicated as a result."

"I don't understand."

Tuala said, "My mother was . . . Tell me, in your own country, have you a race of people who belong . . . who dwell in a realm outside the human world? Whose homes are deep in the forest, or in wells and caves, places beyond an invisible margin? My mother was of such a race. Here in Fortriu we call her kind the Good Folk, though that term cannot adequately encompass such a widely varied array of beings."

Eile sensed Tuala was a little afraid of what her response might be. It startled her to think the queen of Fortriu might be in fear of her, a mere . . . No, she wouldn't even let herself think it. "We call them Fair Folk," she said with some hesitation. "I was never sure if they were real or just a story. This is a very strange land." Wondrous, really. If a man could be talking to you one moment and turn into a bird the next, and folk accepted someone who was only half human as their queen, perhaps there was a place here even for herself. "Your father must be a man of some consequence, for you to have risen so high. I'm sorry, that sounded discourteous—"

"Oh, he is." Tuala's smile was a little odd, as if she felt both sad and happy at once. "And please don't apologize. You'll understand the need to be discreet about what we discuss here, I'm sure. I have spoken to you of this only because Ana assured me both she and Faolan consider you entirely trustworthy. Ana is a good friend of mine and I know her judgment is reliable. Faolan is never wrong in his assessments of character."

Eile could not stop her voice from wobbling. "Thank you, my lady. I will not betray any confidences."

"Fayda hungry," Derelei said, and it was indeed so. Ferada ushered the visitors to the door, her expression stern.

"Bye, Derry," Saraid said, hanging back and waving.

Derelei looked as if he were about to burst into tears. His mother said something to him and he brightened.

"I told him he can play with Saraid tomorrow, if you

agree," Tuala said. "Go now, rest well. I'm happy to have met you. And extremely surprised. We've never met any of Faolan's friends before. He always told us he had none."

ᔥ

"WHAT DID YOU make of that?" the queen of Fortriu asked her friend a little later, when Anfreda was suckling and Derelei had gone off with his nursemaid.

"That you are too trusting," Ferada said. "You don't know this girl. She could be anyone."

"I trust Ana. She says Eile is her father's daughter, and he, I understand, was courageous and noble to a super-human degree. Didn't he sacrifice himself for the three of them, Ana, Drustan, and Faolan? This girl seems genuine. I like her honesty. She's mature beyond her years."

"Use that argument and you might deduce our friend Breda must be gracious, wise, and honorable simply because she is Ana's sister."

"There's Derelei. He was instantly on guard against Breda. This girl he allowed to approach, to admire the baby. He took her hand."

"Tuala," said Ferada, "your son may be a highly re-markable boy, but he is only two. His attention was prob-ably caught by Eile's daughter. I expect he never even thought about danger. The little girl is a delightful child."

"She is, isn't she?" Tuala regarded her friend owlishly.

"I didn't say I wanted one," retorted Ferada, raising a hand to smooth her already immaculate coiffure. She had taken to dressing more plainly now, in keeping with her new role as head of an innovative school for young noblewomen. But she had never swerved from her natu-ral elegance of garb and deportment. "Tuala, in such a time of danger you must stick to your own rules. Eile's a complete stranger."

"You weren't on hand when Ana and Faolan came home last autumn. He was quite damaged by what had

happened on their journey, and I don't just mean his man-
gled leg. He was . . . somehow lost. Bereft. Ana and Drustan care about him deeply. So does Bridei. Ana wants the
girl to stay here until Faolan comes back, at least. She believes it's somehow important. I don't know Eile's past
history and nor does Ana. Apparently she's as buttoned up
as Faolan himself. Ana believes she's had a difficult time.
I want to trust Eile, Ferada. My instincts tell me I can."

"I'll grant her one point. She didn't blink an eye when
you spoke of your origins. The girl's hard to surprise for
one so young."

"We don't know how old she is."

"I'd put her no older than seventeen; about Breda's
age. I can't for the life of me see Breda raising a child.
Hers certainly wouldn't be smiling at babies and sharing
its toys."

Tuala grinned. "She did whack Derelei on the hand."

"That was the part I liked best," said Ferada. "A man
must learn to ask permission before he touches."

"Speaking of such matters," Tuala said, "your brothers are growing up quickly. I don't just mean their will-
ingness to help entertain the little ones. Queen Rhian
tells me Bedo is showing a great deal of interest in one
of Breda's handmaids, a girl named Cella. Very charming, Rhian said, and of good character. Their behavior
is perfectly discreet, of course; little chats in the Great
Hall, glances when they think nobody's looking, a particular kind of smile. I do tend to think of Bedo and Uric
as children, but of course they are young men now."

"Hmm." Ferada's thin lips twisted in a smile. "I
worked hard enough to ensure they'd grow up well. Yes,
they're good boys, I have to agree, for all the headaches
they've caused me. Of course, it won't come to anything,
Bedo and this girl. He's too young. Tuala, about Eile.
Promise me one thing."

"What?"

"Talk to Bridei before you decide to make a friend of

the girl. She's a Gael, after all, and that's going to look odd to many folk. You're not supposed to be drawing adverse attention right now. See if Bridei agrees with this theory of Ana's. For such a dour, shuttered individual, Faolan seems to have a lot of people looking out for his welfare. I'd have thought a man like that more than capable of running his own life."

"You heard Eile," Tuala said, shifting the nursing infant to the other breast. "She traveled with him all the way from home. They talked about the past. They looked after a three-year-old together. This is Faolan we're speaking of."

"Perhaps that's evidence that this girl is lying."

"You're so cynical, Ferada. Ana spoke to Faolan himself, remember. He wanted Eile looked after."

"If he cares about her, why did he move on before she got here?"

"Because he had no choice." Tuala was suddenly solemn. "His reticence has done neither Eile nor himself good service. I'll talk to Bridei, of course. We talk about everything. Don't you and Garvan do that?"

※

DRUSTAN HELPED EILE and Saraid settle into their quarters, then went in search of his betrothed. He sent the hoodie ahead and, when it flew back to him, all he had to do was follow it across the garden to a small upper courtyard protected by a creeper-covered wall. There was a round stone table here, and a view over the parapet to low hills and the distant sea. Ana was standing very still, one hand on the table, the other curled up against her mouth. Halfway up to the court, Drustan realized she was crying.

One long stride carried him up the remaining steps; he moved to enfold her in his arms. "What's wrong? What has happened?" he asked her, his lips against her hair.

"I'm all right," Ana said, wiping her eyes. "I'm sorry if I worried you."

"You don't look all right, dear heart. Tell me. What has made you sad?"

"I met my sister. Breda. You know how much I've been longing for that; looking forward to seeing her again now she's grown up." Her voice was shaky.

Drustan kissed her brow but did not speak.

"She . . . When I saw her, I threw my arms around her and held her close. I could feel her stiffen all over, as if she found my touch disgusting. It was odd. Odd and terrible. I thought, maybe she's afraid; she must know she could be the next hostage. And then I thought, she's still young. This must be very strange to her, meeting me after so long; perhaps she doesn't know what to say. I tried to talk to her; to begin telling her how much I regret those lost years, and how much I missed her and worried about her. She just looked through me, Drustan. She didn't seem interested in anything I had to say. She was . . . coolly polite. As if I were a stranger, and rather a tedious one at that."

"I'm sorry," Drustan murmured. "You don't deserve this, on top of everything else. Perhaps Breda simply needs time."

"Maybe." Ana sounded doubtful. "I hope it's only that. She was . . . I can't quite say what it was, but she made me uneasy. And . . . this is going to sound silly, but she was quite impolite, as if she had never learned the appropriate way to behave in company. But she's been at our cousin's court for some time now. She must know these things. It's as if she doesn't care. I didn't say anything about the baby." The tears began to fall again, wrenching at Drustan's heart. Her sadness made him feel helpless.

"Come," he said. "Are you ready to go in? We are housed in your old chamber, I understand; a very comfortable one with some beautiful embroidery on the walls. It was not hard for me to guess whose hands had fashioned that. Eile and Saraid are next door. If you don't want to talk to Breda anymore, you need not."

"Of course I want to," Ana said as they made their way down the steps. "But I'm not sure I know how."

REALIZING THAT SHE had been offered an opportunity at White Hill, Eile determined to swallow her doubts and misgivings and make the most of it. The old scholar, Wid, was both strict and kindly. He seemed to spend a lot of his time seated in a strategic position just where the queen's private garden met the broader expanse of the general garden with its vegetable and herb beds, its substantial ponds, its small statues, its myriad places to walk or rest or, in the case of dogs and children, run about and chase things. Observing the pattern of guards, the fact that either Garth or Dovran tended to be on duty here along with any of a small group of other men who took it in turns, Eile deduced that white-bearded Wid with his ferocious hawk nose was an unofficial member of the team, his role to alert the others with a cough or a movement if he spotted anything untoward.

Wid was a good teacher. She spent part of every morning with him, and in less than one turning of the moon she had grasped enough of the language to try out her basic skills on others, starting, at her tutor's suggestion, with the king's bodyguards, often conveniently present just across the garden. She'd been shy of both at first. Garth was a big man, the kind of man she shrank from instinctively, but he had a nice smile, and she had seen how gentle he was with his little boys. Dovran was stern and solemn; he took his duties very seriously. She had not thought he would deign to talk to her. As it was, her halting efforts elicited friendly responses from both men, and she managed a brief conversation every day with whichever was on duty. It tended to be restricted to remarks on the weather or a polite inquiry as to their family's health but, as the days passed, she became more and more adventurous in her use of words. When they understood and replied, keeping their own speech simple so she in her turn could follow, it warmed her. Wid expressed his satisfaction by pushing her harder.

Saraid was learning still more quickly. While Eile studied, her daughter played with Derelei, who had attached himself to this new arrival to the exclusion of all else. Perhaps *played* was not quite the word. The two of them could generally be found sitting quietly in a corner, with Sorry an inevitable third, examining some object of mutual interest—a feather, a leaf, a stone with patterns on it—and whispering in a language that was somewhere between those of the Gaels and the Priteni. This friendship had quickly won Saraid and Eile access to the private part of the garden. To her surprise, Eile on occasion found herself trusted to watch over the two of them, though never quite on her own; there was always a guard somewhere nearby. Saraid was now a frequent visitor to the queen's apartments; Tuala said she was exceptionally good for Derelei. Eile found it hard to believe that, before her arrival, the king's son had apparently spent his days running about with Garth's energetic twins, the three small boys driving the household crazy with their exuberance.

She'd had her own run-in with the twins. One rainy afternoon she had volunteered to look after all four children while Elda rested. Garth's wife had a baby due in less than two turnings of the moon, and her boys did wear her out. Eile had taken a set of rolling balls and led her small troop to a covered courtyard, out of the wind. She marked goals with chalk, and they took turns to get as many balls through as they could. The man-at-arms whose job it was to keep guard nearby was coaxed to take a turn, but was laughing so hard he missed the goal by a handspan. The whole thing was loud, competitive, and chaotic; the twins grew red-faced, trying to outdo each other, Derelei retreated to a step nearby to watch, and Saraid, to her mother's surprise, played a little, observed a while and then took charge.

"Gilder, put the ball down. His turn."

"*My* turn!"

"I said no. Galen's turn." She stood with hands on hips, a miniature commander, and Gilder, round-eyed, surrendered the ball.

"Now Derry's turn. Come on, Derry."

Derelei got up, obedient to the voice of his new soulmate, and bowled his balls across the flagstones, each one neatly passing between the chalk marks. For this perfect result to be possible, one ball had to change direction sharply as it rolled. Saraid glared at him; he had the grace to look a little abashed.

"Not that one," Saraid declared. "Roll again."

So it had gone on, orderly and civilized, until the twins' mother, refreshed from her rest, appeared to fetch them and offered an invitation for Saraid to play with Gilder and Galen any time she liked. Elda spoke slowly, using gestures; Eile was delighted to find she could understand, and had sufficient words for a polite acceptance.

"Saraid play *Derry,*" said Derelei, a frown on his infant features.

"You, too," Elda told him quickly. "And you are welcome, too, of course," she added, smiling at Eile. "I could show you the stillroom, if you're interested."

There was a lot that interested Eile: Elda's herbs and potions, the wonderful music played in the great hall after supper, the stories Tuala told the children, which reminded her of her father's tales, long ago. It came to her that, when she was a tiny girl, she must have heard the Priteni tongue at home, for her father and Anda had their origins in Caitt lands, the northern realms where Drustan came from, and must surely have spoken their native language together from time to time. She wondered what use Anda had made of the fabulous sum Faolan had paid for her freedom. She wondered if Anda had the capacity to use it wisely, or whether her aunt would let herself fall victim to another man like Dalach, a man who saw women as possessions to be used and exploited and cast aside. She recognized, to her surprise, that a trace of pity had crept into her feelings for her aunt. She hoped Anda had forgiven her. She began to think that maybe, some day, she in her turn would be able to forgive.

They had provided her and Saraid with a little chamber next to the one shared by Ana and Drustan. It had a comfortable bed, a small table, a chest for storage, in which their possessions filled only a corner, and a window looking out over the garden. Shutters could be closed to keep out the chill wind and opened to admit the sun. There was a green-dyed blanket on the bed and a green felt mat on the floor. It was not the house on the hill, but it was a good place. Eile ordered herself not to like it too much; not to start taking it for granted. Allow herself to do that and, inevitably, it would be taken away.

Ana and Drustan would be leaving soon. She could see the restlessness in them, the profound desire to be away on their new journey. It had occurred to her that, once she was no longer under their protection, her place at White Hill might change. Ana treated her as a friend, if a rather perplexing one. Drustan's attitude seemed part that of older brother, part wise adviser. His fluency in Gaelic had made him the recipient of certain confidences she could not express directly to Ana. She would miss the two of them badly. Because of them, it seemed to Eile she had not sunk to her natural position in the hierarchy of the court, which would have been at the bottom scrubbing floors, washing linen, and taking her meals in the kitchen, not at the board in the great hall with kings and princesses. Without the patronage of Drustan and Ana, she would have fallen far below that middle level of folk, the one inhabited by people like Garth and Elda, who came somewhere between servants and leaders. Leaders had two levels as well: there were councillors and chieftains, druids and wise women, and, above them, those of royal blood. Of course, at White

Hill there were places where that order became jumbled. Tuala treated Elda as a friend; their children played as equals. Eile suspected Faolan would be another piece that would not slot neatly into the puzzle, and perhaps that was the reason why she herself had unexpectedly become a friend to the folk at the very top, welcome to wander in their garden and learn from their old teacher.

She had met the king. It had been necessary, intimidated as she was, for he had asked to see her quite soon after her arrival. Bridei was not a physically formidable man like Garth; he was not strikingly handsome like Drustan. Nonetheless, he was unmistakably a king. Eile sensed his innate authority from the first moment she saw him, a square-shouldered, upright figure moving among his attendants and bestowing a grave smile here, a considered word there. When she was called to see him, alone save for Tuala, she had taken a while to conquer her nerves, but she had found him courteous, direct, and perceptive. He had spoken to her as if she was an equal; she had liked that. She sensed he had questions about Faolan, questions he was not quite prepared to ask. She gave him the same account as she had given Tuala, brief, accurate, lacking in detail.

At the end of the meeting, after explaining the nature of Faolan's work and his frequent need to travel at short notice, Bridei had said something she almost missed, for her mind had been on Saraid, under Ana's care and perhaps fretting for her.

". . . oddly reluctant to go. I've never seen him hesitate before," Bridei was saying.

"I'm sorry?" Eile snapped back to the here and now. "Could you say that again, my lord?"

"Faolan knows when a mission requires his own particular skills. This was one such. He's always ready to volunteer promptly and to depart quickly. He is the best man I have. This time was different. I sensed he had reservations; something he wanted to tell me, but could not find the words for. You know how he is, I imagine."

Eile found herself smiling; ridiculous, he would think her a halfwit. She thanked the king and excused herself, fleeing back to her little chamber with the words hugged to her, an unexpected and wondrous gift. Perhaps, after all, Faolan had not set her aside as unimportant. Perhaps he had not forgotten that little children expect promises to be kept. She did know how he was. He would have wanted to be here; would have wished, at least, to leave a message. He had tried to put it into words, perhaps, and failed, knowing his first duty was to his king: a fine, good man deserving of loyalty. What that meant, she was not sure. She only knew it kept a tiny, fledgling warmth alive in her heart.

THE KING OF Fortriu had never cared for hunting. He had the skills; they formed an essential part of any Priteni nobleman's education, along with unarmed combat and horsemanship, the ability to conduct a logical debate, and an acquaintance with music and poetry. Being druid-raised, Bridei had received a somewhat more extensive training in which knowledge of lore ran deep, and love of the ancient gods of his homeland still deeper. Along with that came the awareness that the life of the Glen and of the wider kingdom was like a great net, intricately interwoven and finely balanced. Humankind, creatures, and the folk beyond the margins all played a vital part in it. To take a deer for food was one thing. The gods accepted the need for blood to be spilled as long as the huntsman performed the killing in the right spirit, with gratitude and respect. To chase and kill for sport was another matter and, where he could, Bridei avoided it.

There were times when one had to grit one's teeth and do what was required. He'd been neglecting Keother. The king of the Light Isles was a man of status and had the capacity to become a significant ally or powerful enemy. Bridei could only leave his entertainment to Aniel and Tharan for so long before an insult might be construed in the king's constant occupation with other matters. As for Breda, it had been indicated to Bridei that she was a difficult girl, restless and awkward. While Dorica and the other senior women of the household would not say so, he had grown aware that their young guest was getting on everyone's nerves. Seeing her sister after so long apart had done little to settle Breda. Tuala had told him Ana, in her turn, seemed saddened by the meeting and had not deviated from her fervent wish to be married and away from White Hill as soon as that was possible.

Ged's widow, Loura, and her son had arrived from Abertornie, bringing their local druid, a shy man called Amnost. Other guests trickled in from their more distant bases, among them the Caitt chieftain Umbrig, as huge and bearlike as ever. But not Carnach. There was no word from him and, as yet, none from Faolan, who had been gone twenty days. The feast of Balance was long past and it was almost summer. They could wait no longer. Bridei set the handfasting of Ana and Drustan for full moon, in two days' time; the victory feast would be held the following night. Then he took his royal visitors out hunting.

It was an expedition on horseback with hawks and dogs, appropriate to the rolling coastal lands between White Hill and the king's fortress at Caer Pridne. In these parts the likeliest quarry so early in the season would be small: rabbits and hares, a fox or two, and, closer to the sea, great flocks of marsh birds. The party was a large one, for most of the warrior chieftains had welcomed the opportunity to give their horses a good run and to escape the confines of court awhile. Seeing them ride forth laughing and joking, Bridei remembered last autumn and the field of Dovarben where so many good men had fallen under his banner. He saw among the healthy, smiling faces of his chieftains a ghostly interweaving of riders, those loyal men he had lost in the quest to regain Dalriada: his guard and friend Breth; flamboyant, cheerful Ged who had lain in his blood and breathed words of joy and pain; the men of Pitnochie whom Bridei had known since he was four years old and sent away to be fostered by a druid. Others rode here too; the Priteni had sacrificed generations of men to win back their territory and their pride. *I will not think it,* Bridei told himself. *I will not ask myself the question.* But it was in his mind, always. *I paid a monstrous price for my victory. Was it worth it? If those who fell could speak now, perhaps I would hear them say: You did not pursue the crown of Circinn; you wasted the advantage we won for you.*

There were few women in the party. Breda had brought three of her attendants. Some of the wives had accompanied their husbands; most had remained behind. Both Ana and Drustan had compelling reasons for not wishing to watch animals being flushed out and slaughtered. There had been no need to issue them an invitation, only to warn Drustan of the hunt so he and his creatures would not inadvertently set themselves in peril.

Talorgen's sons had both ridden out. They were handsome young men now. Bridei could not look at them without seeing Gartnait, their elder brother who had been his close friend. Long ago, Gartnait had been embroiled in his mother's plot to kill Bridei and had paid the price for that treachery with his own life. The past held many shadows, dark rememberings that hung over the sunniest days, the most joyful occasions. Good men turned to ill deeds; loyal friends rewarded by death. Doubts that threatened to paralyze the hand that must move decisively to rule. If he had no news of Carnach soon he must appoint another in his war leader's place. If Faolan brought word of an uprising, he must act

swiftly against a man who had been his staunch supporter since the very first day of his kingship. It felt
wrong. Instinct urged him to hold back. But he could not
wait long; they were all here, at court, and as soon as
Faolan returned Bridei must make the decision. He was
king. He must lead.

The hunt went well. A full and healthy mews was another essential part of the trappings of a royal court.
Guests were allocated a bird and local chieftains brought
their own. Keother's hawk took a fat hare, Talorgen's a
fox. Others, too, were successful. Aled, the young son of
Ged, brought down a pigeon with the goshawk he'd carried from home. Bridei flew a bird, not wishing to draw
attention by refusing to join in, but his hawk struck nothing; it was the gods' will that the king take no life today,
and he thanked them for it.

Breda did not hunt. She rode well, holding herself
straight, her figure shown to advantage by her plain-cut
tunic and skirt of dark blue. Her abundant fair hair was
caught back in a cunning sort of beaded net. She
watched as one of her handmaids flew a small merlin,
which took a smaller marsh hen. She watched as Talorgen's elder son, Bedo, congratulated the handmaid and
dismounted to help her extricate the prey and put the
hood back on her overexcited bird. She watched Uric,
who was looking at her under his lashes. And she cast
a number of glances in Bridei's general direction, but he
suspected it was not him, six-and-twenty years of age,
married with children and of only middling looks, that
she had her eye on. He'd brought Dovran as his personal
guard today and left Garth on duty with Tuala and the
baby. Dovran was young and well built; he tended to
draw the ladies' glances in a way no previous bodyguard
of Bridei's had done. The discipline instilled by Garth
meant Dovran was doing a creditable job of not noticing
Breda was there. They had their own designated watchers, she and Keother; Bridei had made sure of that.
Dovran's sole duty was to ensure the king's safety. He

would not have kept his job long unless he had been good at it.

It happened out of the blue. The young lady's bird was being troublesome, lifting its wings and trying to bate from her gauntlet; both of Talorgen's sons were now occupied in helping the girl hood it securely. Others sat their horses, hawks quiet in hand, talking of this and that; it was almost time to ride for home and a congenial supper. The sky was scattered with dimpled clouds, tinged gold by the afternoon sun; the voices of geese, disturbed by the hawks, babbled restlessly across the marshlands.

"My lord king," said Keother, riding up alongside Bridei, "what do you think of—"

Breda screamed, a sudden piercing sound of utter fright. Her horse reared up, leaving her clinging precariously with her feet out of the stirrups and her hands twisted in its mane. The creature's front hooves came down hard amid a crowd of folk, and then it bolted.

There was no time to think. Even as Bridei glanced at Dovran, the two men urged their mounts after the panicked mare with its dangerously clinging rider. The terrain was undulating, grassland pocked with unexpected holes and studded with great rough-surfaced stones. If Breda fell or was thrown, she could break her neck or smash her skull. The girl had got a knee over the saddle, but most of her weight still hung from the clutching hands. She could not last long. Shouts and screams behind them faded fast; there was only the thud of hooves, the honking of the birds, and the distant wash of the sea.

"Help!" shrieked Breda, and the mare took fright anew, swerving abruptly to head for the wetlands. Bridei knew this place well. There was sucking bog close by; the marsh that would slow the panicked flight might as likely swallow horse and rider together.

He kicked Snowfire's flanks; Dovran urged his own mount on, keeping pace on his left. These horses had seen battle after battle. They were as one with their riders.

Long ago, a man called Donal had taught Bridei certain tricks of horsemanship, and he had passed them on to each of his guards in turn. The mare tossed her head as they came up on either side; the foam of her spittle flew. Breda's hair had escaped its neat confinement and streamed out in the sea breeze, a golden banner. As the two men closed in, each spoke to his mount then slid sideways in the saddle, leaning in toward mare and rider. Dovran stretched to snatch the mare's bridle, maintaining momentum forward. Bridei grabbed the easiest part of Breda to lay hands on: her hair. "Ow!" she screamed. He edged Snowfire in closer as Dovran began to slow his horse's pace, easing the terrified mare gradually back. Bridei leaned across the gap between Snowfire and the mare, the weight of his upper body holding the gasping Breda safe from falling. The desperate flight became a gallop, a canter, a faltering, exhausted stumble. They halted.

What the rescue had lacked in dignity and comfort it had certainly made up in efficiency. Bridei disengaged himself and helped the girl to the ground while Dovran stood murmuring to the mare and checking her over for damage. Their ride had carried them a long way. The rest of the hunting party could be seen only as a distant jumble of small figures moving about. Nobody had followed them, and that seemed rather odd. A sense of foreboding came over Bridei. The girl was shaken but unharmed, save for a few bruises. Dovran declared the mare sound of limb, though severely scratched by the bushes she had brushed on her headlong flight. But something was wrong.

"You take Lady Breda with you," Bridei told his guard. "I'll lead the mare."

Dovran obeyed, cupping his hands to help Breda to the saddle.

"Best for you to ride again straightaway," Bridei told her. "It will help you regain your confidence." He kept his tone brisk but watched Breda closely nonetheless. Although breathless, she was remarkably composed after her adventure. As Dovran vaulted to the saddle behind her, she turned her head to look at him admiringly, a becoming blush rising to her cheeks. Dovran set his gaze sternly ahead.

"Very well," said Bridei, one hand holding the mare's reins and the other on Snowfire's neck. "Keep the pace steady; this creature's had a severe fright."

As they crossed the uneven field, the little figures grew larger and their activities clearer.

"Flamekeeper help us," muttered Dovran, "what's happened? What damage has been wrought?"

But Bridei said not a word as they discerned each cruel detail in turn: men improvising a stretcher, folk clustered around someone sitting on the ground, a man kneeling with his hands over his face. Keother was giving orders and Bridei's own folk were hurrying to obey. And, as the riders reached the edge of the hunt party, where grooms held several horses and dogs milled about, he saw a cloak laid out on the sward, and under it a still shape. One foot protruded from the covering; a smallish foot clad in a lady's riding boot. The weeping man was one of Keother's.

"Oh no, oh no, oh no . . ." Breda began to gasp.

"It's all right, my lady, don't distress yourself," Dovran said awkwardly. But the princess of the Light Isles slid down from his horse and stumbled forward to crouch by the prone form and draw aside the gray wool of the covering. The afternoon sun fell on the blanched features and staring eyes of her dark-haired handmaid, the one whose father was Keother's adviser, the man crouched by her waxen-faced and shaking. There was a crimson stain all across the girl's left temple and in her hair.

Breda said nothing. She pulled the cloak back over her handmaid's body and stepped away. "She's dead," she said in a flat voice. Bridei put her blank expression down to shock. "Cella's dead."

Bridei dismounted. It seemed clear that in its plunging descent the rearing mare had wrought terrible damage here before its flight. "Keother," he said with what control he could summon, "this is an ill end to our day's sport. I'm more sorry than I can tell you. Your cousin has escaped harm. But this young woman—"

"Struck by the animal's hoof." It was Talorgen's voice; Bridei spotted him now, at a short distance, kneeling beside his son Bedo. The boy was sheet white, his jaw set against pain, his eyes fierce. His father was fastening a rudimentary sling around an arm that was, without a doubt, broken between wrist and elbow. Uric, equally pale, stood beside them with the dead girl's hawk, hooded and quiet, on his glove.

"She—" Bedo began, then drew a hissing breath as Talorgen eased the sling into place. "She screamed—"

"Hush," his father said. "Later. Bridei, as you see, my son, too, was injured. Uric was thrown to the ground but is unharmed. We have men making stretchers to bear the poor lass back, and for Bedo here."

"I can walk," Bedo snapped. His tone spoke as much of fury as of pain.

"I'm sorry," Bridei said again. It was woefully inadequate. The gods, after all, had chosen to be cruel today. "Bedo, listen to your father. The sooner you get that to a bonesetter, the better your chance of mending well enough to use sword and bow once more. Keother? We must say a prayer over the young lady's body; then we will convey her back to White Hill as gently as we may." He knelt by the girl's father. "I offer you my respects, friend, and my deepest apology that this has occurred on your visit to Fortriu, and on my territory. No words can express my sorrow. Come, let us join in a prayer, then make our sad way home."

MUCH LATER, WHEN all had returned to court and Cella's body had been washed and wrapped for burial, Bridei stood in the small upper courtyard with its round stone table, watching the moon rise and trying to set his thoughts in order. He had spoken to the assembled household; let them know that it was his own wish and Keother's, as well as that of Cella's father, that her funeral rite be held promptly here at White Hill, there being insufficient time for her mother to travel from the Light Isles to bid her only daughter farewell. By the time news of the tragic accident reached home, Cella would have been dead two turnings of the moon. Summer flowers would be growing on her grave. If she had stayed at home, she might be playing with her dog now, or watching the moon come up over the sea, or strumming her harp. Through his tears, her father had mentioned her exceptional talent for music.

Bridei had announced that the victory feast would go ahead as planned, since so many had traveled so far to be present. The celebrations would be tinged by sadness. This new tragedy could only remind folk of how many had been lost in last autumn's war. Victory came hand in hand with sorrow.

He stood alone now, save for the undemanding presence of his dog Ban at his feet and Garth's solid form on guard a short way off. Soon Bridei would go down to Tuala. He would talk it through with her, just the two of them, seeking comfort in the calm and balance she brought to the most challenging situations. He would find solace in the sweet forms of his sleeping children, for whom life, so far, had been mercifully free of cruel complications.

Today's death was sad; it was all too easy to put himself in that man's shoes, the man whose daughter Bone Mother had snatched, in an instant, quite arbitrarily out of this world. If it had been Derelei or Anfreda, Bridei doubted his own capacity to act with such dignity and restraint. He thought he would scream, rail at the gods, prostrate himself on the earth. At such an extreme he knew the king would take second place to the father.

Ban whined and Bridei bent to reassure him. "It's all right, good boy."

"Who's there?" Garth's stern voice, breaking through his own. "Identify yourself!"

"Talorgen. I'm alone." The chieftain of Raven's Well sounded desperately weary.

"All right, Garth," Bridei said. "Come up, Talorgen, I'm here by the table. How is your son doing?"

"The bonesetter is cautiously pleased," Talorgen said, coming across the little courtyard to stand by the king's side. The moonlight rendered his handsome features into a grim mask; there was no sign of the ready smile folk knew so well. "Only one bone snapped. It's possible Bedo will regain full strength in the arm, as long as he heeds the physician's advice, which includes the unwelcome instruction to rest for two full turnings of the moon and keep the limb strapped. Bridei . . ."

"Out with it," Bridei said. They were old friends; Bridei had spent a good portion of his years, as he grew from child to man, in this tall chieftain's household. At Raven's Well he had learned skills he could not have developed in the scholarly realm of the druid's house at Pitnochie. "Something's wrong, isn't it? I feel it."

"We're all unsettled." Talorgen leaned back against the stone wall, folding his arms. "That was an ill chance."

Bridei waited, offering no response.

"My son," the chieftain said, lowering his voice, "strapped up and resting, with a herbal posset by his bed and a court physician scowling at him if he so much as twitches a finger . . . Bedo's making some very odd accusations, Bridei. I feel distinctly unsettled by this whole episode. Of course, we're all on edge over this matter of Carnach. We sorely need word from Faolan, if not from our missing chieftain himself. If rebellion is brewing, we must be ready for it."

Bridei traced a pattern on the table's stone surface with his finger. The moonlight sent the shadow of his hand across the wall like a giant, clutching claw. "What exactly has Bedo said?" he asked quietly.

"He seems to believe what happened was not entirely an accident," Talorgen murmured. "That there was something odd about the way Breda's horse reared so suddenly, for no apparent reason. The boy's wound tight as a spring. This is especially distressing for him, since he and the girl, Cella, had become friends. I know what it's like to be a lad just becoming a man. Bedo's a mass of confused feelings. The sudden death of a girl his own age must make him question the gods, if not the workings of our day to day lives. All the same, he's a steady boy, reliable and calm. Mature for his years. Not that he's gone to pieces; not exactly. The pieces are inside. He's holding them together by sheer effort of will. Uric seems to share the same suspicions: that perhaps somebody caused the whole thing; that someone wanted the girl harmed. That seems less than likely to me; this was a handmaid, after all, even if her father was quite well connected. All the same . . ."

"Say it, Talorgen. Nobody can hear us save Garth, who is the soul of discretion. By the way, where is your own guard? You should not come out alone."

"I left him with the boys, watching their door. Maybe I'm growing old, Bridei. Tonight I find myself beset by irrational fears." He drew his cloak around him.

"Let me ask you a question."

"Ask it."

"What did make Breda's mare bolt? Did a bird fly low? One of the hawks startle? Someone make a loud noise? That horse is one of ours, chosen for our royal guest because of its equable temperament. Queen Rhian used to ride it for hunting."

Talorgen remained silent.

"Your sons were helping Cella settle her bird. The merlin may have made a sudden movement. All the same, the young men are right in thinking such a small thing should not set a well-behaved horse in a panic."

"Perhaps Breda is a less experienced rider than most highborn girls her age." Talorgen sounded unconvinced by his own words.

"She hung on quite tenaciously when the creature bolted, even if she could not arrest its flight," Bridei said.

"True. Your rescue was an act of great skill and courage, Bridei; in the horror of the aftermath, nobody remembered to mention that."

"It was nothing. We merely acted as the circumstances required. Thank the gods for Donal's tricks in horsemanship. Without those, Breda would have a broken leg at best, or at worst be drowned in the bog along with the wretched horse. Talorgen, in a way I understand your sons' concern, but I cannot think there is much real foundation for it. An attack would hardly be aimed at the unfortunate girl who was killed. If it was intended to harm Keother's young cousin, I cannot think of a good reason why."

"I can think of several," Talorgen said drily. "To create instability for you; to drive a wedge between yourself and Keother, with whom cordial relations are essential. To remind Keother how easily death can strike in the middle of a pleasurable activity on a sunny day."

"You mean, to keep the king of the Light Isles compliant?"

"It is one theory."

"Talorgen," Bridei said, "were that the reason for this act, then surely the most likely perpetrator would be me. Or my agents. I am Keother's only overlord. With Breda as my guest, placed perfectly as a potential hostage against her cousin's good behavior, I hardly need to kill a young lady to make a point."

"Nobody in his right mind could suspect you, Bridei."

"You know me. Others do not."

"We must also consider that Keother may have developed new alliances." Talorgen glanced about and lowered his voice still further. "This matter of Carnach, for instance. If it's true he's setting up against you, and he has already canvassed Keother for support, the two of them could mount a challenge from north and south. Or Keother may be in league with the Caitt chieftains. We know little of the allegiances of those in the far north, just a hop and a step across from Keother's home islands."

"My friend," Bridei said, "I know you're concerned for your son; such an injury is a serious matter for a young man whose future must include service as a warrior. I believe it highly likely that what you said earlier is the key to this; Bedo's feelings for the girl who died and his confusion and distress that violent death has come so close to him. These boys suffered a grievous loss when they were younger; the death of an admired elder brother must leave a deep scar. I hope it does not offend you that I mention that; it may play a part in the way Uric and Bedo deal with this. I am reluctant to consider theories of conspiracy. I am still more reluctant to discuss them with Keother; that could be extremely awkward. I suppose Breda could be questioned. When she's recovered from her shock, perhaps she may recall what alarmed the mare. We can't do that now; I've been told she's tucked up in bed. I will have a word to Keother in the morning; it may be more appropriate for him to question her. He conducted himself well today. The circumstances have been difficult for him; the girl's father is distraught. We must allow them all a little time."

"I expect you're right," Talorgen said quietly. "Perhaps I'm simply suffering a bout of fatherly anxiety. It distresses me to see my boys hurt. They're good lads, the two of them."

"Indeed. Advise your son from me to obey his physician and rest that arm. I'm inclined to believe this was no more than it seemed: an unusual accident with tragic consequences. But you can also tell Bedo I will consider folk's accounts of what occurred to see if there is any foundation to his theory. Gods aid us, we have a funeral, a wedding, and a celebratory feast to endure in the space of a couple of days. I pray that we are sent no more catastrophes until those observances are over. As for Carnach, I will seek the wisdom of the gods once again. Perhaps I can persuade Fola to cast an augury." There was another avenue of guidance, a far more potent one, but he would not mention that even to Talorgen, close friend and trusted adviser. Tuala could scry for answers. She could seek news of Carnach in the water of a seer's vessel. If Bridei asked her, it must be in private and the vision must be sought behind closed doors. "If that fails to provide answers," he said, "I suppose we must wait for Faolan."

12

HIS HANDS CURLED around a beaker of ale, Faolan sat in a shadowy corner of the drinking hall at Thorn Bridge, watching and listening. His mission had carried him far to the southeast, near Carnach's home territory of Thorn Bend and even closer to the Circinn border.

He knew the man who ran this hostelry; long ago, he had seen the advantage of befriending the fellow. Each time he passed this way, he made sure he carried a small payment in silver.

There was no settlement here, just the bridge and the inn, with a farm or two close by. It was pleasant, rolling country dotted with trees; the sheep that grazed in these fields looked fat and healthy. Through the strath ran the river Thorn, a broad watercourse that marked, roughly, the split between the two major kingdoms of the Priteni, Fortriu and Circinn.

Three ways met at the bridge. One ran southward to Thorn Bend, one north and west toward Caer Pridne.

The third took an easterly course and led into Circinn before joining a road to the court of Drust the Boar. At least, it had been his court; there was a new king in that realm now, Drust's brother Garnet. That much Faolan had gleaned from the travelers who passed this way and paused for a drink, a bite to eat, and a chance to rest weary feet or worn horses. The inn at Thorn Bridge was the perfect place for gathering information. He had been here several days now, sometimes giving the innkeeper a hand with this and that to earn his bed in the stables—the payments in silver were more for keeping quiet than for food and lodgings—sometimes, as now, just sitting. He'd cropped his hair ruthlessly short and avoided shaving since White Hill. He wore plain worker's clothing. He could have been anyone. When required to speak he used a neutral accent based on Garth's, a voice that identified him as a man of Fortriu, with nothing particular to indicate his home territory or family status. Thus far, nobody had asked his trade. Folk's eyes tended to pass over him. It was a well-practiced invisibility.

There had been small bands of armed men on the roads, traveling here and there. From those who were not too tight-lipped to talk, and from cottagers and traders, Faolan had learned that Garnet was now king of Circinn, and that Carnach had passed this way some time ago, heading for the new king's court. To do so openly was uncharacteristic, for Fortriu's chief war leader was a subtle man. Something did not add up.

Faolan stared into his untouched ale, watching the patterns as he turned the cup between his palms. He needed more. Another day, he'd stay here one more day, and if nothing conclusive came in he was going to have to cross the border and head into Circinn himself. There was a dark possibility in the rumors, and if it proved to have foundation, he must make certain of it before he took it to Bridei.

Faolan shivered, pushing the ale cup away. A rebellion; perhaps another war. If it happened, it would not be like last time, when the king had sent him away as escort to Ana so he would not have to fight. That journey had proved so dark and dangerous both he and Ana had emerged as different people. And then Bridei had sent him home. Home. Another adventure, strange, terrifying, full of surprises. He found himself smiling. Eile and her pitchfork; Eile on that wretched bridge, clinging. The smile faded. Eile all over blood. Saraid flushed with fever, her breath harsh in her small chest. Eile asking him . . . No, he would not think of that. It had haunted his dreams for more restless nights than he cared to remember and he wanted rid of it. She'd be gone when he got back to White Hill; nothing was surer with this mission carrying him so far south and the information so slow to come. She'd be gone and so would Ana. That was what he wanted. That was best for everyone. If there was war again, this time between Fortriu and Circinn, there could be no possible reason for Faolan not to stand at his patron's side to protect him. He could use his skills with the best of them. If he went, this time, Garth might yet again stay behind and survive; Garth who had a wife and children who needed him. Nobody needed Faolan. He could be a perfect warrior, with no reason at all to fear death.

For a moment he allowed himself to imagine it: dying heroically as Deord had done, surrounded by fallen enemies. Then something made him look up, and he saw Deord seated opposite him at the rough inn table, muscular arms folded, serene eyes fixed on Faolan in question. *Have you forgotten?* the spectral warrior whispered. *You owe me. You know the payment. Live your life. Live it for all those who never left Breakstone.* And, as the figure faded, he heard Eile's voice in his head, raised in a scream: *Faolan! We've come to get you!* Tears pricked his eyes. If there had once been a hero hidden somewhere in him, that man was surely gone. He did not want to go to war.

"I've done poorly thus far, friend," he whispered to the vanished Deord. "I broke a promise. Two promises." He'd told Eile he would be waiting when she and Saraid reached White Hill. Then he'd left her on her own yet again. What was it he'd told her back in Erin, *I'll be there as long as you need me*?

Still, they would be safe with Ana and Drustan. Eile would be happier, with a surer chance of making something of herself. What else was he supposed to do? He was Bridei's man; this was his life, one mission after another, an existence of journeying, of risk, of sudden death and perilous chances. It was what he did. It was the only thing he did, and he was good at it. Bridei needed him. He could not let Bridei down.

Faolan sat awhile longer, staring blankly across the dim expanse of the drinking hall, which was empty save for the hostelry's proprietor sweeping. He tried to stop his mind from turning in unproductive circles. Right now, the only important thing was Bridei's mission. He'd made his choice back at Pitnochie when he spoke to Ana and Drustan. He'd made it again when he couldn't summon up the will to leave Eile a message at White Hill. Such a simple thing. *I've been sent away; I'm sorry I was not here as I promised.* And perhaps, *I hope you will be happy at Dreaming Glen.* He'd had it in his head, all ready. But who could he tell? Faolan, the king's assassin and spy, the man so secret and private folk thought him incapable of human feelings, suddenly acquiring a young woman and a little girl as traveling companions? Leaving personal messages for them? He could imagine the raised brows, the knowing smiles, the conjecture. Even Bridei, he could not bring himself to tell, Bridei who had long tried to convince him that he was not that hard-shelled, impervious professional. To go on, to do what his job required of him, he must be that man. To do the things he had to do, he must put away all notion of a different kind of life. Softer feelings made a man vulnerable. They gave him weak spots that could be

exploited. A man whose trade was all in plots and sub-
terfuge, in trickery and sudden death must, in the end,
walk on alone. To attempt otherwise was to put those he
loved at terrible risk. If he had not known this, perhaps
he would have stayed at Fiddler's Crossing. Eile had
been happy there.

The smile came back as he remembered her at the
table, her red hair freshly washed and shining in the sunlight from the big window; he pictured her in the blue
gown Líobhan had given her, the bright color emphasiz-
ing her pallor. "Eat slowly, Saraid," he heard her saying,
and saw the child, large eyes solemn, breaking her bread
into tiny, even pieces.

Faolan got to his feet and walked over to the doorway,
suddenly unable to be still. Logic had no place in this argument. Logic could not account for the aching empti-
ness inside him. It could not explain the dreams.

࿐

WHEN ANOTHER NIGHT had passed and no fresh news
had come in, Faolan left Thorn Bridge and headed for
Circinn. He did not take the road, but went by covert
ways, sometimes walking, sometimes getting a lift on a
cart, always traveling roughly southeastward. The news
by the way was full of contradictions. He hoped he
would not have to infiltrate the southern court itself; this
was taking too long, with the influential Christian, Colm,
expected at White Hill before midsummer and the king's
druid still absent from court. Faolan wanted this matter
of a rebellion out in the open before that new challenge
must be faced. If Carnach planned a revolt, let him declare it. If he was in league with Circinn now, having decided to throw in his lot with this new king, let them
announce that for all to hear. If there was to be war
again, let these plotters at least have the decency to allow
Fortriu to draw breath before the first blow.

He put Eile away in a corner of his mind, and Saraid

with her. He found he could not banish them completely; they had a habit of reappearing from time to time in a small, intense image or a snatch of words. He let those moments pass and tried not to think too much of them. Nights were the worst. He dreamed. Often he awoke, uncomfortably, with his body hot and hard with desire, requiring a sudden dip in a cold stream or a bout of furious physical activity to quell it. There had been a time when the image of Ana had tormented him thus, a time when his golden-haired princess had walked regularly through his sleep, as lovely and untouchable as a fairy woman of ancient story. To his astonishment, that had changed from the moment he saw her at Pitnochie, saddened by her recent loss but profoundly content in the choices she had made. What had once been a passion that threatened to possess his very soul had become, without his being aware of it, a quieter, less dangerous feeling: a lifelong bond of deepest friendship.

The dreams persisted, full of sensual delight and tormenting choices. But Ana no longer had a place in them. On this journey, the woman who lay with him by night was younger, slighter, with hair like dark fire and pale skin dotted with freckles; her touch was sweetly hesitant, her body a wonder to explore, lithe, fresh, giving. Sometimes he got it right, and pleased her, and heard her little sound of satisfaction; felt her move above or beneath him, sighing; saw her smile in surprised delight. Sometimes he got it wrong, and sent her back into the nightmare of Dalach, the pain, the powerlessness. Waking from those dreams was a tumult of guilt and sorrow, tempered by profound relief. Thank the gods that he had refused her offer.

Once inside the borders of Circinn, Faolan took a more cautious approach to his task. He could not afford to be apprehended; he must get back to White Hill as soon as he had what he needed. For two more days he traveled, stopping here and there for directions, chatting casually to farmers who gave him lifts, visiting a dwelling of

Christian monks, where he was offered bread and parsnip wine and the advice that he should go carefully, as the roads in the district were not considered safe at the present time. He asked why this was so; the cleric whispered that there had been talk of parties of armed men on the move, of ambushes and general unrest. Faolan did not think he could ask any more questions, so he bid the fellow farewell and went on his way.

He had never been much of a sleeper; the nature of his work meant his nights were often spent on watch, listening for sounds in the darkness. It was his practice to make do with brief or broken rest, taken only when all was safe. Now his dreams were coaxing him out of that long-held discipline. At day's end he found himself sinking into a well of sleep from which he did not emerge until near dawn. The dreams enmeshed him; sometimes they felt more real than the daily world of crossing ground, finding cover, gleaning the scant harvest of news. When it was the good dream, often enough he would half wake, then dive again into the secret, tender world of his imagining. A man on a covert mission cannot afford such indulgence. Such a slipping of standards can only lead to disaster.

Thus it was with Faolan one morning on his journey farther across Circinn. He lay in the shelter of a straw stack, his cloak wrapped around him. A drystone wall kept the wind at bay. She was in his arms, not sighing and moving in an act of passion this time, but sleeping curled against him, her arm across his chest, her head in the hollow of his shoulder. He pulled the quilt up over her, his hand lingering on the long, silken strands of her hair. It was almost dawn. It seemed a miracle that she lay there thus, skin to skin, the soft touch of her breath against his body, the warmth of her filling him like a blessing, the depth of her slumber telling him that, against the odds, he had won her complete trust . . . A little voice spoke up, right next to the bed. *Get up, Feeler. Sorry's hungry.*

He opened his eyes. There was a spear point not far from his face, and an armed man behind it. "Can't you understand a simple instruction?" asked the man with the spear. "Get up! Come on, step out where we can see you, and keep your hands open. Move!"

He moved. There was not just one man but a whole group, seven or eight at least. No time to snatch his weapons; the small knife was on his person, but the assailants were too many. Getting himself killed was not going to help anyone. As they dragged him forward, pulling his hands behind his back and binding his wrists together, he observed that they were not a rabble of wayside thugs but a disciplined team, clearly sent on a mission to apprehend him. "Who are you? What am I supposed to have done?" he ventured, and was silenced immediately by a gag, slipped on from behind and promptly tightened. This wasn't looking good. Never mind that; he would get information from this one way or another, and then he would give them the slip. He still had his knife.

"Search him," someone said. "Be quick. We're too near the road here."

They took the knife, as well as his bag of traveler's supplies. His other weapons and his silver, concealed in the straw, they did not find. Then he was marched along the edge of the field, through a gate, and into the darkness of a shadowy wood.

THERE WAS ONLY one thought in the druid's mind: *Home.* What it meant was hazy still: a house wrapped in oaks, a whisper-quiet chamber of stone, objects set out in orderly fashion . . . He ran, his bare feet knowing the changeable nature of the forest floor as part of himself, his breathing at long last strong and easy, his body bursting with the joy of freedom. *I'm going home.* The trees made a wondrous, changing tapestry as he passed, bright beech, silvery birch, dark pine, the soft fronds of ferns beneath, the spiky guardian hollies. His feet touched the crunching softness of fallen leaves; they trod on needles of pine, releasing a pungent aroma; they slid over gravel and splashed through streams, knowing each rolling pebble, each great lichen-crusted stone, each touch of sun or shade. From his high throne in the sky, the Flamekeeper smiled down on him.

As he drew close to the margin of the great forest, his pace slowed. Memory stirred, seeping into the great bright spaces his winter journey had opened in his mind. One by one they came back: a child, his pupil, his dear one . . . brown curls, blue eyes, a tiny, solemn boy who spoke like a sage . . . his son . . . no, not his son, but dearer than any bond of kinship could make him. Bridei. But Bridei was a man now; a king. Yet still he saw the child . . . a different child, a boy of exceptional talent, of prodigious promise, an eldritch, precious child . . . the child of his own blood . . .

"Derelei," whispered the druid, his voice harsh and strange after a season's silence. Once he had given a name to the image, others flowed after it: Bridei the man, strong and grave, and Tuala . . . Tuala, the daughter he had wronged, the daughter whom he must learn to know all over again, this time with love and trust and an open heart. He thought that he could do it; he thought that he could try.

He halted in a clearing fringed by drooping willows and spreading elders: a place of the Shining One. Here the streamlet whose course he had been following flowed into a round, deep pool edged by moss-cloaked stones; small fish darted there, hiding in the fronds of underwater plants, and above the surface dragonflies made zigzag paths, their wings a wonder of transparent grace.

The druid knelt on the rocks by the pool. *Home.* It had a wealth of meanings. Perhaps, after all, for him home was not a place, but a state of mind. Perhaps it was forgiveness; acceptance; belonging. Was that simple message the sum of his winter's hard-won learning?

He looked into the water. For a man long practiced in the arts of divination, augury, and prophecy, to do so was instinctive. If the Shining One had some final wisdom for him before this journey was ended, she might reveal it to him here in this still place, his last resting place before he walked out of the wildwood and returned to the realms of men.

A face looked up at him. At first he thought it a vision, an image from beyond death, for surely this was his old friend Uist, a solitary druid of the forest, who had long been considered half-crazed; the hair was wild, its long strands thick with scraps of foliage, twigs, and mosses; the eyes were mad, seeing and unseeing; the figure was smeared with filth, and underneath, completely naked. The druid lifted a hand, and the madman in the pond lifted his own as if in ironic greeting.

He made himself look again; struggled to analyze. The unkempt hair was of every shade between black and white; it was not Uist's, but that of a younger man. The eyes were dark as polished obsidian; they had not the pale clarity of the ancient sage's. The body . . . He did not want to look down, to recognize that wrinkled, pallid, scrawny nudity as his own. *But I feel young,* he thought. *I feel sound. I feel more alive than I have ever been. I want to run, to shout, to sing, to work marvels.* And heard an inner voice reply: *So did he.* It was true; Uist had been rich in both a young man's vision and an old man's wisdom even to the moment he slipped away from this world.

The druid did not look down. He laid a hand on his ribs, feeling the prominence of the bones and how the flesh had shrunk away during his time of privation. He touched his elbow, his knee; he touched his neck and cheek and looked again into the water. He tried to see the image as a child might, or a woman, or a shepherd grazing his flock at the forest's edge, glancing up to see a figure walking out under the oaks.

"Is this the sum of my learning?" he whispered. "That in the space of one season, I am shrunk to a shadow of myself?" The figure in the water looked up, eyes bright with madness, hair like a rat's nest, body exposed in all its gaunt and filthy wretchedness. The druid stepped back from the forest pool, retreating into the shadows under the sheltering trees. "What are you telling me?" he asked the Shining One, and sat down on a mossy rock to reflect on the answers already beginning to unfold in his thoughts. He reminded himself that outward appearances did not necessarily signify truth; that oftentimes the meanings of things lay deep within. Perhaps the journey must be slower; perhaps he must walk, not run.

"I am reborn," he murmured, not sure if the words were his own or those of another voice. "An infant. I must learn it all again; how to walk, how to speak, how to listen." He saw himself back at Pitnochie, long ago, with a small, grave boy by his side, and a lesson to teach. *Step with care upon the path,* that younger man said. *Let your feet be part of the earth they tread. Know the thoughts of owl and otter, beetle and salmon. Speak the truths of the heart.* It came to him that he had lost touch with the simple wisdom he had imparted to the child Bridei. There was another child to teach now, a perilously able child who needed him still more than that fledgling king had done. So, he would go on, but slowly. He would walk each step of the way with the love of the Shining One in his heart and his senses awake to the winter's great lesson. That lesson was a beacon to show him the way forward. He thought its name was love.

"I WANT . . . SAY a thing, Eile," Ana said in her halting Gaelic. The wedding would be tomorrow. Despite the tragic death of Breda's handmaid, it had been decided not to delay the ceremony. Eile was helping the bride with some final adjustments to the outfit she would wear, a plain tunic and skirt in fine cream wool with little birds embroidered in a band around the hem. "The handfasting . . . I wish you . . . with me . . . not sister. Sounds bad, but true. You . . . at ritual . . . for Faolan. We . . . very fond . . ."

Eile did not reply; there seemed no right response. Very probably she had misunderstood, though if Ana did indeed mean she would prefer that Breda not attend the ceremony, she thought she knew why. Breda's behavior was decidedly odd at times, and one could never be sure what outrageous statement she would come out with next. The young noblewoman had sought Eile out on many occasions since their first meeting, as if to make a special friend of her, but Eile had not been able to warm to her. Breda could be amusing in an edgy, barbed sort of way but, beyond their age, they had nothing at all in common. Yet Ana was such a good person, so wise and gentle; it seemed possible she had not meant the words in the way Eile understood them.

Saraid had made herself at home on the bed, surrounded by the contents of Ana's sewing box. She held up one scrap of fabric after another against the shapeless form of Sorry, who was still clad in the pink dress Faolan's sister had made for her. "New clothes?" the child inquired hopefully.

"One piece," Ana told the child. "You choose. Eile sew for Sorry."

"There's no need. She shouldn't ask—"

Ana put a hand on Eile's shoulder. "I want to," she said. "So little . . . how can she know? A gift. A farewell. Sad . . . we will miss you . . . Sad you not come with us." Then, seeing Eile's expression, "You stay here. Faolan needs . . . you wait. You here when he comes home."

Again, Eile wondered if she had misunderstood. "Waiting is not a happy thing," she said carefully in her new language. "My mother . . . she stopped waiting. I

would not . . . be my mother . . ." The words began to
spill out in Gaelic, "Father never came home. We waited
and he never came." She struggled with sudden tears;
perhaps she would be an old woman before she could tell
this tale without weeping.

Ana crouched beside her and hugged her. It felt good,
but made the tears come more quickly. Aware of Saraid's
big eyes and trembling chin, Eile made herself draw
breath and be calm again.

"Forgive," Ana said. "You must forgive him. Your father. A good man. He tried. And . . . Faolan is not Deord."

"I know that." Eile got up and began to help Ana out
of the wedding clothes. "I'll just put in a stitch or two
and this will be ready. What will Breda be wearing?"

Ana grimaced. "I do not know. She is . . . not interested. I wish . . ."

"Blue." Saraid had chosen her piece of fabric, a sweet,
warm color like the sky on a hot summer's morning.
"Make clothes now." Then after a little, "Please."

"Later," Eile said. "Fold it up neatly as I showed you.
Maybe we can find a strip of braid for the hem, so it's
like Ana's pretty skirt." She moved to collect the discarded wedding clothes as Ana got back into her everyday outfit. She thought about Breda, Breda who waited
for her often in the outer garden, Breda who was not allowed to visit the queen although she herself was of
royal blood and Tuala was not. For all her bevy of attendants and her place at the king's table, Breda seemed
lonely. "Maybe your sister is missing home."

"I . . . hostage . . . eight years," Ana said softly.
"Breda . . . maybe next."

"Yes, Drustan explained it to me." It seemed odd to
Eile that Ana, so plainly an honored guest here, so
clearly one of Tuala's closest friends, had only come to
court in the first place as surety of her cousin's compliance with Bridei's rule. She felt a new surge of sympathy
for Breda, odd girl as she was. Perhaps there was not so
much difference between a bondwoman, bought with the

payment of an *éraic,* and a hostage held as political leverage. Each had sacrificed her freedom; each had been robbed of the power to determine her own future. And yet, of the two, Eile was certain she was the better off. Maybe the *éraic* did make her a kind of slave. In some people's eyes, perhaps she would always be one. But she wasn't restless and discontent like Breda. There were so many good things here: warmth, safety, friendship, learning . . . It felt like the beginning of something new and fine. She must be careful. She must remember how easily things could change.

"Come, Saraid," she said, reaching out a hand. "You can tell me what kind of gown Sorry wants, and I'll make a start on it."

"Wedding gown," said Saraid. "Blue. Bray. Pretty, like Ana."

"Braid," Eile corrected, grinning.

Ana smiled and held out a length of ribbon embroidered with butterflies in gold thread and tiny amber beads.

"Oh, we couldn't—" Eile protested.

"Only a scrap. Sorry should be beautiful. Faolan say heroic . . . Like you and Saraid."

♒

AFTER THE ILL-FATED hunt, Eile had done her best to stay out of everyone's way. She had known Cella slightly, for Breda's attendants thought Saraid as sweet as a little doll, and often stopped to pet her on their way past, not without a curious glance or two in Eile's direction. Breda herself had two faces where Eile was concerned; when accompanied by her maids, she ignored her completely, but when the two of them were alone, she seized the opportunity to release a flood of gossip about everyone at court, especially the men. An odd young woman indeed.

Cella, by contrast, had been one of the friendlier girls.

It was impossible to imagine her dead: so young, younger than Eile herself. As for Talorgen's son, if he wanted to emulate his father's prowess as a warrior chieftain, he was going to need all the luck the gods decided to bestow on him now his arm had been broken.

On the morning of the handfasting Ana and Drustan called Eile in early. She had only just finished dressing, and Saraid's gown was half unfastened. Eile knelt to do up the ties at the back as Drustan spoke.

"Breda has sent a message to tell us she's not well enough to take part in the ritual later today," he said. "We don't wish to delay it; already it has been too long for us."

Eile nodded. She knew how he hated court; how he longed to be free to take his other form and fly off over the forest, seeing with bird-eyes. The restlessness that had been building in him, visibly, must soon have its outlet or it would become intolerable. She thought of the low, dim place he had described to her, the place where his brother had imprisoned him for seven years. For seven years Deord had stayed by him, kept him active, held despair at bay, risked everything to allow his charge brief flights into freedom. Drustan had been at White Hill now for almost a turning of the moon. He had told her he would not effect his transformation here, while the court was full of guests who might see and not understand. But he must change soon; he was strung tight with the need.

It came to Eile that Ana, too, would have a life of waiting. Ana had made the choice herself, and was content with it. Perhaps love made that possible. They were blessed, these two; blessed to have found each other.

"We want you to take Breda's part, Eile," Drustan said. "We'd be honored if you would agree."

She felt herself flush scarlet. "Oh, but—" she began.

"Bridei and Tuala have approved our choice. There are only two brief responses for you to give, and plenty of time for you to memorize them. Wid will help you.

The druid understands you are new to the language. This seems entirely right to us."

"Please, Eile," said Ana, using her limited Gaelic. "Tuala lend gown. Same size."

Thus it was that, at dusk, Eile found herself clad in a queen's gown, soft violet with gray borders, with a little wreath of flowers in her hair, in the middle of a handfasting ceremony held under the dimming sky in the small upper courtyard. Torches burned around the flagstoned space with its central table. It was nothing at all like her imaginings of the wedding of a princess, and yet it seemed to her utterly perfect. For Faolan's sake, she tried to notice everything. Perhaps he had said that he did not want to be here, but she knew in her heart that he would be hungry for her description, if ever she got the chance to give it. Ana was his beloved and he was losing her. That would not make his feelings for her any the less.

A small circle of folk was in attendance. There had been no public announcement of time and place, and the stalwart Garth and Dovran were stationed where steps came up from the lower courtyard, ensuring there were no uninvited guests. Ana was a vision in her plain cream with her golden hair loose over her shoulders; Drustan wore a russet tunic and trousers over a snowy shirt, and had his wild mane tied at the nape, though strands escaped like licking flames at his brow. The crow perched on one shoulder, the crossbill on the other. Their eyes were bright, but Drustan's were brighter, fixed on Ana with such love and tenderness that Eile began to think, just possibly, that certain things Faolan had told her about men and women might be correct after all. There was a sweet trust between these two, and a shy passion that showed itself in their every touch, their every glance. She could not for the life of her imagine Drustan treating his wife cruelly, or requiring her to endure anything she feared or disliked. That was not possible for a man so gentle, so courteous, so selfless. Ana had been carrying a child; Drustan's child. Did that mean it was indeed possible to lie with a man and, if he was the right one, actually find pleasure in the act? Could it really be true?

If there had been time, a great deal of time, perhaps Eile would have learned enough words to ask Ana this question in the Priteni tongue. But Ana was leaving; she and Drustan were not even staying for the victory feast. After tomorrow, Eile would not see them again. Forever was a long time. Likely they would visit White Hill again in two years, three years, perhaps with their children. The pattern of her own life thus far suggested that, wherever she was by then, it would not be here.

The druid, Amnost, spoke the ritual words quietly, with reverence. Much of it Eile did not understand, but Wid had explained, while coaching her in her responses, that the handfasting was sworn by the powers of earth, water, fire, and air, and that the Shining One, most revered goddess of the Priteni, was asked for a special blessing on husband and wife. Ana made her responses softly, from the heart. Drustan spoke his with ardor, his voice shaking.

Bridei and Tuala watched on, hand in hand, more like a pair of young lovers than monarch and consort. Ana's cousin Keother was there, a king in his own right, a silent, imposing figure. Tall, severe Ferada stood across the circle, Ferada who, Eile had learned, was head of the school for young women that she had dismissed so lightly in their first conversation. A scholar; a woman who had defied convention and made her own choices. By Ferada's side was a very large, very plain man whose place here Eile could not work out. The two of them did not touch; they hardly looked at each other. Yet there was something between them; something powerful. As if aware of Eile's thoughts, Ferada looked across the circle into her eyes, and her well-shaped brows lifted.

There was a wise woman, a priestess, assisting the druid with the ritual. Fola, her name was, a white-haired personage of diminutive size with piercing dark eyes and a big nose. She passed Amnost the ritual foods: bread, honey, herbs, and water. She spoke the prayer to the Shining One, her features calm, her eyes showing clearly her affection for the bride and her approval of the bridegroom. A wave of anxiety came over Eile. What was she doing here among such clever folk, kings and queens, druids and priestesses? If they knew the things she had done, if they knew the dark and bloody path she had traveled . . .

There was an awkward silence. All eyes were on her where she stood a little behind Ana. Eile realized she was supposed to speak now. For a moment, the words she had practiced over and over during the day fled entirely from her mind, leaving only a space full of terror and shame. She looked down, and her eyes fell on the embroidered border of Ana's skirt. *Pretty, like Ana.* In her head, someone said, *Heroic, like you.* The words came back. She lifted her head and took a shaky breath.

"Step forward on your new path with love and courage," she said in the Priteni tongue, moving forward to light a candle from the lamp on the stone table and place it in Ana's hand, then do the same for Drustan. "Honor the gods and be true to each other." As she stepped back she saw Tuala smile and Bridei nod approval. Ferada had unbent sufficiently to bestow a little smile of her own; as Eile watched, the red-haired woman slipped her hand through the arm of the lumpish man standing by her side. He put his big hand over hers, engulfing it, and Ferada's pale cheeks turned pink.

Wid's earlier explanations allowed Eile to understand the general meaning of the words now spoken to conclude the ceremony. Fola invoked the blessing of the Shining One, and called down her light to illuminate the pathway ahead for the new husband and wife. As the wise woman spoke, the moon sailed up above the dark outlines of the pines, full and perfect in a sky deepening to dusky violet.

Then the druid called on the Flamekeeper to brighten the lives of Drustan and Ana with courage, and to bless them with the gift of children. Eile saw the sorrow pass over Ana's perfect features; she saw the shadow in Drustan's eyes. It was only a moment. Now she had to speak again. "Blessed All-Flowers fill your home with joy, and keep you and yours safe from the storm," she said, her voice steady. She took up the handful of petals set by and cast them across the stone table. It was a pity Saraid was already tucked up in bed under Elda's watchful eye; she would have liked that part. Now it was done, and the handfasting was over.

She could tell Faolan how beautiful Ana had looked; how the moonlight had touched her lovely face to pale purity. She could tell him how Drustan's love for her could be heard in his every word; how he touched his new wife as if she were at the same time lover, best friend, and goddess. Maybe Faolan wouldn't want to hear that part. But she'd tell him anyway. He loved Ana more than anything in the world. He'd loved her enough to let her go, even though it had broken his heart. He would want to know that Drustan recognized the value of that selfless gift. He would want to be certain that Drustan would make her happy.

They said their good nights. There would be no feasting or celebration to follow the handfasting. In the morning the druid would conduct a funeral rite for the young woman who had been killed. And Drustan and Ana would set off down the lake, taking the easier route back to his home in the west, Dreaming Glen. Tomorrow night, Bridei would hold his victory feast. It must be difficult to be a king, Eile thought. With a tiny new daughter and a son of barely two, he had scant time to take a breath and watch them grow; scant time to come to terms with one challenge before another loomed. They said he'd been very brave and skillful when Breda's horse bolted. Maybe a king needed to be able to do everything.

It was a pity if that meant Bridei had no time to be a husband and father, Eile thought. She had never really considered, before, that kings and queens were real people like herself underneath.

Time to go; the others were talking among themselves, King Keother congratulating Ana, the druid and Fola in intense debate, Drustan speaking to Bridei. She muttered a farewell and made her way down the steps. As she crossed the lower courtyard she found she was being shadowed by the tall form of Dovran, the king's bodyguard. He said something which she interpreted as an offer to escort her to her chamber.

"No, I'm fine," she said, his presence by her side at night making her acutely uncomfortable. "I can go by myself." Then, as he kept walking, she struggled for words to say it politely in his own tongue. "No, thank you," she managed.

Dovran kept pace; when she glanced up, his handsome face—long, straight nose, fine gray eyes, firm jaw—bore a slightly awkward look. He said something more; it had Bridei's name in it. Perhaps the king had ordered him to do this, though why she would need a personal guard to help her find her way along a couple of passages and down a flight of steps she could not imagine. Eile walked on, and Dovran walked with her. When they got to the steps he offered his hand to help her down. It was quite silly. What did he think she would do, trip over her skirt and fall in a heap? Since refusal would seem ill-mannered, she let him do it. At his touch, her body tensed with fear. She hoped he could not tell that panic was making her heart thud; that cold sweat was breaking out on her skin. At the foot of the steps she withdrew her hand, forcing herself not to snatch it away.

They reached the door of the chamber she shared with Saraid. Elda would be within, watching the child; the twins were in the care of a maidservant.

"Thank you," Eile murmured, holding on to calm. "Good night."

"Good night." Dovran was not a man given to smiles; right now, he was even more serious than usual, and had his gaze fixed on the wall above her head. He said something else, then turned on his heel and marched off without another word. Eile stood there a moment, putting the words together and wondering if her interpretation could be right. Surely he hadn't said, *You look beautiful tonight*? Perhaps it had been an expansion of their weather conversations, the far more innocuous, *It's a beautiful night*. She didn't think so. He'd looked embarrassed; bashful but determined.

Saraid was fast asleep, tucked up with Sorry, whose blue wedding dress lay half completed on the little table. Eile thanked the yawning Elda and saw her out, then undressed and got into bed, blowing out the candle. She couldn't stop shivering. Her head was full of images that didn't seem to go together but, in an awful, inevitable way, did so all too well: Drustan and Ana, eyes locked, faces radiant with happiness; Bridei and Tuala with hands clasped, like a pair of inseparable children; Ferada blushing as that big man wrapped his gentle hand around hers. Dalach. She tried to force Dalach out of her head but he wouldn't go. He was still there; he'd always be there. And Dovran: a nice young man, comely, unwed, with a good position at court; Dovran whose courteous touch had made her blood run cold.

Eile found that she was crying; she kept it silent from long practice, not to disturb Saraid. This was such a good place. It was a haven. But . . . but . . . Watching Drustan and Ana was like looking in a window at something bright and precious, something she would never have for herself. Something Dalach had ensured she could never have. The two of them seemed to Eile deeply pure and innocent, and their love for each other true and selfless, a thing of wonder indeed blessed by the gods.

The tears flowed in a hot river. *You'll never have that,* she told herself. *Never. No matter how much you want it, he's made sure you can't reach it.* Saraid stirred, making a little sound, and Eile ordered herself to be still, though her nose was blocked by tears and her eyes stung. She knew she should be happy, grateful, astonished at the good fortune that had brought her to this house of kindly, generous folk. The remarkable fortune that had seen her put on a queen's gown and take part in the wedding of a princess. The wondrous fortune that had seen Saraid blossom into a different sort of child, one with the confidence not just to make new friends, but to take charge of them . . . And she *was* grateful; she understood how far they had come from Cloud Hill. But the tears still flowed. Her heart was a tight core of misery. It wasn't right. It still wasn't right. She tried to fill her mind with a picture of the house on the hill, the cat, the garden, the savory smells, but tonight it would not come. She was cold all through; her body felt the touch of Dovran's fingers and remembered Dalach. She curled herself into a ball, pulling the green blanket up to her chin. In the darkness her lips formed words in silence: *Where are you?*

13

INTERROGATION. BEATING AND being left for dead. Summary execution. A combination of these. As Faolan's captors hurried him into the darkness under the trees, he considered the possibilities and how he might deal with each one. They had not blindfolded him. He assessed their clothing, their weaponry, the way they carried themselves, and deduced they were a chieftain's household men-at-arms or warriors from the court of Circinn. An organized fighting force. Not Carnach's unless his troops had put off their chieftain's colors, for these wore anonymous garb, brown, gray, nothing to draw attention. If they were the new king's, they showed no particular sign of that, either. Drust the Boar had borne his emblem on a red background; one might have expected the same from his brother. The gag made questions impossible. Instead, Faolan observed the way they followed, the twists and turns traversed with ease despite the dense shade under the old oaks; wherever they were leading him, the path was so familiar to these men they trod it without needing to think.

They halted at the foot of a natural stone wall higher than a man's head. The trees grew close, but more light filtered down here, illuminating the mosses and tiny ferns, the fungi and creepers that occupied each chink and crevice in the rock.

"Through here," someone said, pulling Faolan by the sleeve.

There was a narrow gap in the stone, well concealed by the undergrowth, hard to spot unless a man knew what he was looking for. They sidled through in single file, Faolan awkward with his bound hands. The chink opened to a sheltered space bordered by great stones and floored with grass. Here horses stood hobbled and men were packing up gear in apparent preparation for a move. Beyond this scene of activity two men stood together talking. As the tall, red-haired man turned to look in his direction, Faolan made his features impassive. He made sure he gave no sign of recognition. Carnach's eyes rested on him thoughtfully. Then the other speaker turned his head, and Faolan's hands clenched themselves into fists behind his back. The dark-eyed, grim-featured man by Carnach's side was Bargoit, chief councillor from the court of Circinn.

Faolan was good at what he did. He stood calmly while one of his captors walked over to Carnach and gave what he assumed was a quick report. Then he was led forward to stand before the chieftain of Fortriu and the weaselly councillor of Circinn. The gag was removed. The rest of the men turned their attention to horses and gear.

Silence was the best course initially. This looked bad; it looked like a conspiracy. Carnach, then, would have to choose interrogation followed by summary execution. On the other hand, it seemed Carnach had decided not to recognize him. Faolan kept his breathing steady. *Wait; do not speak. Be ready for whatever they may throw at you.*

"State your name and your business in these parts!" rapped out Carnach. "Be quick about it. We've had reports of a man asking questions. Too many questions. If that's you, you'd best ask them now, and tell us who sent you here to gather information."

Faolan thought very fast indeed. A game; a perilous game with Bargoit standing there. He must play as cleverly as Carnach, and hope he had guessed the rules correctly. "My name's Donal," he said, aiming for a tone of innocent confusion. "I'm a farmhand, my lord, looking for work to tide me over. Things are not so good at home. My father-in-law threw me out. You know how it is."

Carnach regarded him thoughtfully. "And where might home be?" he asked.

"Place called Fiddler's Crossing, my lord. Other side of Pitnochie, in Fortriu, far to the west." He did not think Bargoit would remember him. It was six years now since the last time the councillor could have seen him, when Bridei was elected king, and Faolan was expert at the art of blending in. Besides, his appearance had changed; hadn't Eile said he looked at least five-and-thirty now?

"What's this father-in-law's name?" Bargoit snapped, quick as a snake. "If you're a farm worker, where are your tools?"

"Garth," said Faolan. "I made the error of getting too friendly with a certain lady; my wife didn't take too kindly to it, and her father's got a heavy hand. She'll have me back. She always does. I didn't bring tools. It's a long way to carry a pitchfork."

Carnach took a step forward and hit him on the jaw, hard. "Hold your tongue," he said, mildly enough. "Don't waste our time with your rubbish about wives and dalliances. What are you, a fool?"

Faolan said nothing. What was the truth here? Guess wrong and Carnach must kill him to stop his mouth. Guess right and he might not, after all, need to find some way of evading a large number of armed men in a confined space with not even a knife to his name.

"A pitchfork?" Bargoit's suspicious eyes narrowed still further. The snake seemed ready to strike. "Since when do folk stack straw in springtime?"

"In fact," Faolan looked at the ground, "he took my things. Father-in-law. Locked them up. Didn't leave me so much as a—"

"Yes, yes," said Bargoit in irritation. "Why come so far? Pitnochie's halfway down the Glen. Surely there's work nearer home?"

Faolan fixed a dull gaze on him and did not attempt a reply. Carnach and the councillor exchanged a glance.

"Now—what did you say your name was? Donal?— now, Donal, I will put a question to you," Carnach said with a slight curve of the lips, giving the impression that he found the hapless farm hand something between amusing and tiresome. "Why should this father-in-law take you back, eh? Indeed, why should your wife do so, if you've a habit of straying? Maybe you should be seeking new pastures. Circinn has fine farming land; opportunities for a fit fellow such as yourself."

Bargoit was getting bored; his gaze had moved to the men-at-arms, and he gestured to someone, indicating a certain horse should be saddled.

"He'll take me back because, underneath it all, he trusts me, my lord," Faolan said. "And my wife will take me back because there are certain activities I've a particular talent for. Why would she want to put another fellow in my place when I give her perfect satisfaction?" He looked into Carnach's eyes, but kept his tone light. Sniggers arose from the men standing closest.

"My advice to you, then," Carnach said quietly, "is to be off home without delay. Be there by Midsummer; get your back into your work and show your wife and her father that you have at least a scrap of loyalty left. You're a fool and, I suspect, a braggart; don't make things worse by wasting the goodwill of your family. If they'll have you, you're a luckier man than you deserve to be." He turned to Bargoit. "This fellow's a halfwit; he's of no account."

"Mm?" Bargoit had not been listening; now he fixed his penetrating stare on Faolan once more. "A fool deserves a beating. You, and you!" He jerked his head at two of the men who had brought Faolan in. "Take him back to the place you found him. Teach him a lesson, but don't take too long over it. We'll meet you where the path branches north."

So it would be beating and being left for dead after all, Faolan thought as they retraced the way through the forest. He wouldn't be able to fight them, even though there were only two; attempt that and they'd know instantly that he was no farmhand. Trying to escape carried the same difficulty. He did not care to submit to a thrashing; it went against all his instincts. Not hitting back was one of the hardest skills to master.

They threw him down in the straw by the wall, his wrists still bound. Fortunately they were in a hurry; less fortunate was their decision to use their boots. He was still conscious when they left; still able, vaguely, to recognize that this morning's episode equated to good news for Bridei. His leg, the one already damaged from last autumn's battle with wolves, was full of a stabbing pain, a pain that made his breath falter in his throat. As the sun rose higher and the day warmed to a hint of early summer, he curled himself on the straw and observed with detachment that there was a fair amount of blood. Then he surrendered to the dark.

BREDA WAS NOT sufficiently recovered to attend her handmaid's funeral rite, a small private ceremony. Only those closest to the girl were present: Cella's father, of course, as well as Keother and the young women who had been her fellow handmaids. Bridei and Tuala were both in attendance. The official confinement period following Anfreda's birth was not quite over, but the queen of Fortriu had made it known she felt great sorrow for this loss, and wished to acknowledge the fortitude of the young woman's father by offering her sympathy in person.

Eile knew this because she had been asked to stay with Derelei and Anfreda while Tuala was at the ritual. Dovran was on guard and one of the nursemaids was also in attendance, but Tuala had said she felt most confident that Derelei would stay out of trouble when Eile and Saraid were there. It was a warm day, the garden full of sweet scents, the flowering lavender and rosemary alive with bees and butterflies. Eile busied herself pulling out wild grasses from the beds; Saraid and Derelei were lying on their stomachs, side by side, staring into the pond. The nursemaid sat outside the door to the queen's apartments with Anfreda beside her in a basket draped with fine lawn to keep out insects.

It felt good to be asked to help; good to be trusted with the royal children after so brief a time at White Hill. The sorrow was still there underneath. It surfaced every time Eile saw Dovran walk past the foot of the private garden, sometimes with eyes sternly ahead, once or twice with a glance in her direction and a hint of a smile. At least she hadn't offended him. It wasn't his fault that she couldn't bear his touch.

She was sad for Cella, too, though it was probably too late for that. Whatever happened when a person died, it had already happened for Breda's handmaid. Either she was in some other realm, or her spirit had been reborn as a new baby, human, or creature, or she was just beginning the long, gradual crumbling away to dust and the thing inside that had made her eyes shine and her skin flush pink and her body run and dance and ride was gone altogether, snuffed out as easily as a little candle.

Eile pulled up a root of wild endive that had sprouted between the lavender bushes and put it in her basket. Weeding was an odd occupation. What was a weed, after all, but a perfectly good plant that had simply decided to grow in a place somebody happened to have chosen for something else? Endive had a medicinal use; Elda had told her so when she was revealing the secrets of the stillroom. It seemed a shame to pull these up, really. By setting root here they had shown enterprise and strength. They had shown they were survivors. Eile glanced at Saraid again; she was up on her elbows, looking at Derelei, who lay utterly still with his gaze on the water. *We're like weeds, her and me,* she thought. *A couple of scrawny little grasses, sticking our heads up in a bed full of grand, blooming flowers.* The idea made her smile.

A polite cough from a short distance away. She straightened. There was Dovran, standing a few paces down the garden. Eile got to her feet, heart hammering foolishly.

"Good morning," the bodyguard said.

"Good morning." Best think of this simply as an opportunity to practice her new language. No reason for fear; none at all.

"You are well?"

"Er—yes. You?"

Dovran smiled. It was possible to see how, to some other woman, he would appear charming, kindly, and handsome with his long brown hair and his good teeth.

"I have a message for you." He was speaking slowly

so she could understand. "Lady Breda wants to see you. She sent a maid."

"Lady Breda?" That didn't sound likely; not at the very time of the funeral the princess had been too unwell to attend. Eile sought for words to say, *Are you sure?* or, *That can't be right.*

"She asked if you would go to her chamber now. I told her maid you were watching Derelei. She wishes to see you as soon as you are free."

"Oh. Thank you."

He smiled, shuffling his feet a little. His awkwardness was incongruous with his impressive stature, his leather breast-piece and array of weaponry, sword, knives, crossbow on his back. "Will you . . ." he began, then stopped to clear his throat. "Will you be at the feast to-night, Eile?"

It was the first time he had addressed her by name. For a moment she was too surprised to reply. Then she said, "Perhaps . . . be with children again. King and queen . . . must go feast."

Dovran gave a nod that could have meant anything, then headed off on his march around the garden. As Eile watched him go, she thought of Faolan, who had asked her not to put her proposition to any other man without speaking to him first. Well, he wasn't here, was he? He showed no sign of coming back. If he never came, what was she supposed to do? She could see that Dovran was interested. She could see that he was eligible. He was precisely the kind of young man she probably *should* ask, as he had revealed a reticent kindness that suggested he would not be a selfish lover. Eile grimaced. She'd never ask him; not in a hundred years. One touch of his hand had been enough to tell her how impossible that was.

She shivered, drawing her shawl tighter around her shoulders. Drustan and Ana were gone. They had left early, making no secret of their longing to be away. It had been hard to say farewell. She had not known them long, but they had become dear friends. Before they left Ana

had asked her, in halting Gaelic, to tell Faolan she hoped
he would be happy. Drustan had bid her remember she
was her father's daughter, and that Deord would be proud
of her. He had added that they hoped to see both Eile and
Faolan at Dreaming Glen some day; that Saraid would
like the garden and the two small lakes that lay by his
house there, Cup of Sky and Cup of Dew. No words had
seemed adequate to thank them for their kindness.

"We must go now," Drustan had said. "Tell him . . ."

Ana had said something in the Priteni tongue, too difficult for Eile to follow.

Drustan had looked Eile straight in the eye; she would
always remember the bright intensity of his gaze, like
that of a wild creature. "There will come a time when he
must stop running," he had said. "Every being has its
need for shelter, every man his desire for home."

"But," Eile had asked, "what if you can't find home?
What if you don't know what it looks like?"

"The search needs patience. Endurance. Keen eyes
and a strong heart. He will recognize it before too long."

Eile had offered no reply. In her mind, still, was the
response, *But what if* I *don't?* The safe walls of White
Hill, the comfortable chamber, the hand of friendship
extended even by kings and queens, that was shelter, of
course. But it was not home. It was not her own little
house, Saraid with the striped cat on her knee, Eile cooking with her own pots and tending to vegetables in her
own garden. It was not . . . Somehow it was not complete. *You want too much,* she told herself. But this morning she had nodded to Drustan, blinking back her tears,
and waved farewell as the two of them made their way
out through the gates of the king's stronghold with their
modest escort, and off down the Glen.

"Eile?"

Her daughter's voice broke into her reverie, and she
moved over to the pond. Saraid was sitting up now, Sorry
on her lap, while Derelei did not seem to have stirred at
all. His eyes were fixed on the still water.

"Derry's sad," said Saraid.

Perhaps he was; more alarming to Eile was his preter-natural stillness, uncanny in so small a child. For a moment she wondered if the boy was in some kind of fit, and reached down to touch him, but something held back her hand. She perceived that he was finely balanced, his energies entirely concentrated on what he saw, his ears deaf to the world that held herself and her daughter, the nursemaid, the baby, the bees buzzing in the garden. He was behind an invisible wall; he had one foot in another world.

"He's fine, Saraid," she said quietly. "We need to watch over him and wait." She hoped she had got this right; Tuala had left her in charge, and the boy's behavior was quite odd. But then, Derelei and Anfreda were not like other children. With them, she supposed one must expect the unexpected.

Eile seated herself on the flagstones two paces from Derelei, and Saraid edged in closer. They waited. Saraid sang softly to Sorry, a little lullaby Eile had learned somewhere long ago, and had hummed in an undertone night after night in that wretched hut at Cloud Hill, soothing her troubled child to sleep:

> *Cow in meadow, sheep in fold*
> *Sun is setting, red and gold*
> *Babe in cradle, bird on nest*
> *Moon is rising, time for rest.*

"That's lovely singing, Saraid," Eile said. "Is Sorry asleep now?"

Saraid shook her head solemnly. "Sorry's sad. Crying." She held the doll against her shoulder, patting its back.

"Oh. Why is she sad?"

"Sorry wants Feeler come back."

It was like a punch in the gut. She had thought Saraid had forgotten him; she had assumed new friends and a safe haven would drive the memories of that long journey across country, just the three of them, from her daughter's mind. Foolish. The images of that time were still bright and fresh in her own head; she dreamed of them every night. Why should Saraid be any different, just because she was small? Eile wondered what else Saraid remembered.

She wanted to say, *Faolan will be back soon,* but that was to raise false hope. Saraid must not endure what she had, the endless years of waiting for a loved one who never came home. That was too cruel. "Faolan is on a journey," she told her daughter.

"Feeler lost?" inquired Saraid.

"I don't know. I don't know where he is."

"Feeler coming soon, Sorry," the child whispered to her doll, rocking it in her arms again. *"Cow in meadow, sheep in fold . . ."*

"He *might* come." Eile felt obliged to offer this correction.

Derelei stirred at last, blinking, stretching, getting up with such an odd expression in his big, pale blue eyes that Eile felt a prickling at the back of her neck. For a moment he looked quite Other. He put both hands up to rub his eyes. A moment later his chin wobbled, his lips trembled and he began to cry.

"Derry's sad." Saraid clutched Sorry to her chest, staring.

The sobs were piteous, heart-wrenching. Eile gathered the small boy in her arms, hugging him close, her heart thumping. What might be the cause of such sudden, acute misery? "It's all right, Derelei," she said helplessly. "We're here, you're all right." It seemed to her this was the kind of crying that followed a nightmare, part confusion, part fright. After a while she could detect speech in Derelei's weeping, though for his age he had few words. He kept repeating something that sounded like *border,* or *border loss.* What that meant, she had no idea.

"Eile sing," Saraid suggested. "Dog song." Her small

voice was shaky; she seemed on the verge of bursting into tears herself out of sympathy.

It seemed a reasonable idea. The dog song had helped them out of a few tricky situations before.

> *"Doggy's got a bone; Doggy's got a bone;*
> *Doggy's going to eat it up and run back home."*

Saraid put Sorry down and got to her feet, ready for action. Derelei still heaved and hiccupped in Eile's arms.

"Ready?" Eile said. "Doggy's got a—" *stamp!* "Doggy's got a—" *stamp!* "Doggy's going to eat it up and run back—" *stamp!* Very good, Saraid. Now Derelei and I will join in." She stood up with the boy in her arms; the sobbing had died down a little. "Doggy's got a—" *stamp, clap!* Managing this while supporting Derelei's weight required a certain agility. "Doggy's got a—" *stamp, clap!*

After a little, when the number of required actions had grown to five, Eile noticed that she had an audience: the nursemaid with Anfreda, now awake, in her arms and, more embarrassing, Dovran watching her from down the garden, a wide grin on his face. Ah well, at least Derelei was over the worst of his sudden sadness. He wriggled to be put down, then stood watching as Eile and Saraid finished the dog song with an energetic sequence of stamp, clap, turn around, shake, jump, bow.

"Sorry's better now," said Saraid, who was not at all out of breath. "Derry all better now?"

Derelei said nothing. An occasional leftover sob shook his tiny frame, but his eyes no longer saw into that other world. Eile crouched down to wipe his nose with a handkerchief. It was hard to know how to comfort him; the simple words she would use with her own daughter, the hugs and kisses seemed to help, but she sensed a depth in this scrap of a child that went far beyond anything in her own experience. There was no knowing what it was he had seen.

Tuala returned from the funeral rite looking sad and tired, and Eile felt some reluctance in reporting what had happened. She did so anyway, putting herself in Tuala's place and recognizing that she would want to know. The queen seemed to take it with equanimity.

"Yes," Tuala said, "he sees things ordinary folk cannot. The water is a strong lure for him, and he is too young to know that he should look away. All you can do is make sure he does not fall in, and wait for him to return to himself. You've done well, Eile. I should have warned you about this."

"He kept saying something. Border, I think it was. Border loss. I couldn't understand."

Tuala was taking off her good shoes and settling on a bench to feed the baby. "Broichan," the queen said. "He speaks often of his . . . his tutor and friend, the king's druid. Broichan left court before the winter; nobody knows where he went. Derelei still misses him. Border loss . . . Broichan lost."

"It seemed far worse than mere sadness. He was distraught. What does he see, a vision of another place? Things to come?"

Tuala took Anfreda from the nursemaid's arms and put her on the breast. "I can't tell you," she said. "For every seer it is different. I think Derelei sees Broichan, yes. He wants his teacher home. Whether the visions are random or whether my son can summon what he most wishes to be shown, only Derelei can tell you. Or could, if he had the words."

Eile felt something cold run through her, like a breath of winter. "He's so little," she said. "So young to have such power. If I were his mother I would be so scared . . . I'm sorry, my lady, I shouldn't have said that."

"Not at all, Eile. I appreciate your frankness. My son does scare me at times, but not as much as the thought that unscrupulous people might recognize his rare talent and seek to exploit it. Derelei will have much to offer

Fortriu as a man, if he can be kept safe until he learns to harness his power."

"Much to offer—as king, you mean?"

Tuala smiled. "My son can never be king of Fortriu, Eile. For the Priteni the royal succession runs through the female side of the family. Kings are selected from the sons of those women. Bridei's mother was a cousin of the last king, Drust the Bull. Ana's sons would be eligible; so would Breda's. And also those of my good friend Ferada, whose mother was another kinswoman of Drust. Of course, Ferada swears she will never marry or produce children, but I'm not convinced."

"There was a man with her yesterday, at the handfasting," Eile ventured. "They seemed . . . attached to each other, I thought."

"Garvan, the royal stone carver, yes. An unlikely pairing, you might think. They are friends, that's all. Or so Ferada would have us believe. She's a determined woman and is making up for lost time. Her own school; it's her long-held dream to make a success of that, and to produce young women who know their own minds and are not afraid to speak out. It is a difficult path; she must swim against a strong tide, for many of our men find her project odd, even threatening. I admire her greatly."

Eile did not reply. A woman who had the strength to do such things against the opinion of powerful people was a figure of awe.

"Each of us has her strengths, Eile," said Tuala. "Now I should let you go. Will you leave Saraid here with us awhile? Derelei has need of an understanding playmate today."

EILE MADE HER way to the part of White Hill where Breda and her cousin, the king of the Light Isles, were housed with their substantial entourage. These apartments were at the far side of the kitchens and great hall. She walked along a broad passageway with an arched roof and through a big doorway into a chamber hung with bright woven pictures, where several of Breda's attendants were clustered by a little hearth, conversing in low voices. All of them fell silent as Eile entered. For a moment she wished she had not agreed to leave Saraid with Derelei; if her daughter had been present, these girls would have smiled and shown pretense of welcome, at least. On the other hand, she assumed they had but recently come from Cella's funeral rite. Perhaps sorrow had frozen their smiles and robbed them of polite words.

She hated this kind of thing. Part of her knew she was a Gael and a bond-slave and had no business here with these people; their eyes told her she was so far below them they could not even despise her. Another part of her said, *I am my father's daughter; strong; a survivor. What's a few snobbish girls?*

"Lady Breda, ask to see me?" She used the words she had prepared, making her voice steady. "I . . . sorry . . . Cella. Very sad."

One of the girls spoke, so rapidly there was no way Eile could follow. Others joined in. She stood with hands clasped behind her back, trying to look calm. She waited until the interchange, complete with whispers and giggling, had finished, then repeated into the silence, "Lady Breda, ask to see me?"

"Eile!" a familiar voice called from an inner chamber.

"Go on, then," said someone ungraciously. When none of them moved to accompany her, Eile put her chin up and walked across the chamber on her own, stopping to tap on the open door leading to the room where, it seemed, Breda was lodged.

"You're here at last! What took you so long? Come in and shut that wretched door, the girls are driving me crazy with their moaning." The flood of Gaelic was music to Eile's ears; now that Drustan was gone, there were few left at White Hill who could speak her tongue with complete fluency. She could hardly go to the king or queen when she needed someone to talk to, and Wid insisted she use the Priteni language in his company. She obeyed Breda's command.

The fair-haired girl was in bed as Eile had expected. She was sitting up with a small mountain of pillows behind her back and a jug and goblet on a little table beside her. The bedchamber was large, far grander than the one Ana and Drustan had shared, which had once been Ana's own room at court. This place had a closed-in feeling; only a slit of a window let in the sun, and there were numerous candles lit on shelves along with an oil lamp that cast a mellow light on the embroidered hangings, scenes of folk picking berries, hunting deer, sailing in a squat little boat. Eile smiled, remembering that choppy sea voyage in the company of monks. It had felt so good to find she could help; to know she was not just useful, but an essential part of a team. She had landed in Dalriada with honorable blisters and a backache that was almost welcome. She could still feel the ropes in her hands. She could still see Faolan's smile as he watched her, a rare, sunny smile, and Saraid's gaze of wonderment as the sea surged all around them.

"Sit down!" Breda ordered, patting the quilt, and Eile sat.

"Are you feeling better?" she asked politely. In fact, Breda looked rosy and comfortable; if she was distressed about Cella's death, she was hiding it well. Her eyes were sparkling, but her hands were restless; she picked at the bedding and twisted the silver rings on her slender fingers. "I'm so sorry about your handmaid," Eile added. "What a shocking thing to happen."

"I was nearly killed myself," Breda said. "That poxy horse they gave me almost threw me. I've never been so scared in my life."

"I heard the story," Eile said. "King Bridei saved you.

He must be a very good horseman, and brave as well. I'm glad you weren't hurt. That boy, Bedo, broke his arm quite badly."

"It was Dovran who did most of the rescuing," Breda said with a crooked smile. "He's so strong; he picked me up as if I weighed nothing at all." Her cheeks were pink. "Of course, the king's bodyguards are handpicked warriors. They are all well-built men. But he's . . . I could feel the raw power in him, Eile. He's something special. It set me thinking . . ."

Eile refrained from comment.

"Oh, well," sighed Breda, "it was an adventure, I suppose. I could do without the bruises. Bridei made me get straight back on a horse. Quite inconsiderate, I thought."

It was not up to her, Eile thought, to suggest to the princess of the Light Isles that it might be appropriate to express sorrow at the death of her handmaid or concern at the serious injury to a young man of the household. Often Breda seemed like a child of nine or ten, who believes the whole world centers on herself and acts accordingly.

"I don't suppose Bridei would have made you ride if it wasn't safe," Eile said. "He seems a very wise sort of person. I wonder why the horse did bolt. Did something startle it?"

Breda shrugged. "How would I know? Everyone seems to think I've got the answers to everything; there's been one person after another wanting to come in here and make me tell it over and over again. It was probably Cella's stupid merlin flapping about. She never controlled the thing properly. It needs its neck wrung. Now, Eile. I have something to ask you. I think you can probably guess what it is." The big blue eyes fixed themselves on Eile's; the well-shaped brows arched above them.

"I can't imagine."

"Really? You disappoint me; I thought you were a clever girl. Well, I see I must set it all out for you. I know you've had a difficult time, so young and with a daughter to look after, and so far from home . . ."

For one horrified moment, Eile wondered if Ana or Drustan had revealed some part of her history to this odd young woman; she herself had told nobody at White Hill of her origins, or how she had met Faolan, or the dark reason the king's chief bodyguard more or less owned her. Then common sense asserted itself. Even Ana and Drustan didn't know those things; Faolan had told them she'd had a bad time, that was all.

"So I thought someone should give you an opportunity," Breda went on. "A chance to make something better of yourself."

Eile waited. Breda seemed to be expecting her to guess. She was not sure she wanted to guess. *I don't need to make myself better. I'm fine just as I am.* She held her tongue. Offend this willful young noblewoman and things were sure to go awry.

"You really can't guess? Well, Eile, with Cella gone I'm going to need another handmaid, aren't I? I always keep five. You seem ideal for the position. It's not a servant's job, you understand; it's somewhere between personal attendant, confidante, and friend. You're young, you're presentable without being too . . . You speak Gaelic, so I can talk to you without the others understanding. I see that as a strong point in your favor. And I like you already. You're not scared to speak up. I hate those demure, quiet little girls, they're such a bore." Breda babbled to a halt, then looked at Eile, all expectation. It did not seem possible to answer with a bald refusal.

"You're forgetting," Eile said, keeping her tone politely respectful. "I have Saraid to look after."

"The child? Oh, that's no problem. There are heaps of servants here, and they like the little girl, she's such a poppet. Anyone could watch over her. And when we get home there are plenty of folk to do it."

"When we get home?" Eile's stomach dropped.

"To the Light Isles, of course. I don't think I'll be staying here after all; I hate it. Just think, a whole new start for you. The place is full of lusty fishermen." Breda's grin seemed almost predatory. "We'll have you married off within a season, mark my words. I've a talent for matchmaking. A new father for little . . . what's her name again?"

"Saraid. Thank you, Lady Breda, I'm . . . honored. But I can't accept your offer."

A pause. The expression in the blue eyes changed. "What?" There was an edge in Breda's tone now.

"I don't wish to offend you. The fact is, I couldn't leave Saraid's care to other people. Not all the time. She's my daughter. I have to make sure she's raised the right way. Kindly. Fairly. With love. So she learns how to live her life well."

"You're not the only person who can do that." Breda's tone was crisp. "Most highborn children grow up seeing little of their mothers. Mine died when I was two. Then Ana went away. I had nobody."

Eile could have sworn she saw tears in Breda's eyes. She bit back a remark along the lines of, *And look how you turned out.* "That's very sad; I lost my own mother early, too. That is why I must be there for Saraid."

"But you're still young!" exclaimed Breda. "Don't you want to enjoy yourself before you get wrinkles and a pot belly and nobody will so much as look at you anymore? I bet the only man you ever lay with was this Faolan of yours. He's the child's father, yes? I have to point out that he seems in no hurry to come back here. Couldn't care less, I'd say. You can't waste what good years you have left on lullabies and nose wiping. Come on, Eile. This will be fun!"

"The thing is," Eile said, feeling suddenly as if she were swimming through something thick and ungiving, such as mutton-fat porridge, "I don't look after Saraid myself just because I have to. I do it because I love her; because I want to. And I can't go away. Not so far, across the sea and everything."

"Why not?"

There was no good answer to this; none she was prepared to put into words. She could not claim Fortriu was home. The only family she had here was Saraid. She could not claim she had a real position at White Hill, not with Drustan and Ana gone. The best she could hope for was to become one of the permanent team of nursemaids and attendants who helped Queen Tuala and watched over the royal children. However kind and friendly the king and queen of Fortriu might be to White Hill's workers, that was indeed a servant's position. "I can't explain," she said. "I just know we need to stay here, Saraid and I. For now, at least."

"I see." Suddenly there was something frightening in Breda's eyes, and Eile felt a shiver run through her.

"I'm sorry," she said, wishing profoundly that she were somewhere else. "Very sorry. I do understand how generous your offer is. Your sister was very kind to me, too. A lovely woman."

"Oh, Ana." The tone was dismissive. "Well, Eile, you must go, I suppose. You'll have important things to attend to. Picking up after little children and wiping their bottoms."

Eile managed a smile. "It's not all hard work," she said, getting up and smoothing the quilt. "It's fun and laughter, too. Hugs and kisses and good times. You'll change your mind when you have children of your own." She could not for the life of her imagine this girl as a mother. Breda was more like a willful child.

"Good-bye, Eile." The words were coolly distant. "Thank you for coming to see me. I want to rest now." Breda sank back on the pillows and closed her eyes.

For a moment, Eile felt genuinely sorry for her. The girl had lost her mother early, then her sister. Perhaps there had been nobody to teach her; to ensure she grew up properly. Eile made a silent promise to herself that she would never, ever let that happen to Saraid. "Good-bye,

Breda," she said. "You understand, I just can't say yes. I hope we can still be friends."

Breda's big blue eyes snapped open, making Eile jump. Her mouth curved in a knowing little smile. "But of course," she said. "Of course we will be friends."

THE CHILD WAS calling him. There was a catch in the little voice, as if tears were not far away; there was a pleading in the strange, light eyes. The druid saw the dear familiar face in every forest pool; he heard the words in the song of a thrush, the warble of a wren. *Come home.*

He moved to the northeast, keeping to woodland by day, crossing open ground as a thief would, by night. Indeed, he became a thief, stealing a garment from the washing line of a low cottage, a shapeless, much-mended shirt that covered him to the thighs. Close to a smithy he found a rusted knife lying on a bench. The next day, in the shadow of pines, he sawed his tangled locks off to the length of his little finger. The result, viewed in a slow stream under the pale sky of early summer, was less than reassuring. If the thing had been sharper he would have shaved his head entirely. Now he looked less like a mad seer and more like an evil-doer on the run. He would not travel openly; if he was seen and recognized, there would be offers of horses, and messages sent to White Hill that would bring out riders to meet him and escort him back. This was not merely a journey of the body, but a test of the mind and will; it must be undertaken at its true pace. Each step held its own learning; each sunset, each moonrise was a gift from the ancients, a message to be held and cherished.

Resting that night on a bed of bracken as birds hooted and screamed and cried above him, words crept back to him, words he had once held dear to his heart. *There is learning in everything.* How many times had he repeated that to Bridei after a frustrating lesson? How many times had he reminded himself of that wisdom when . . . Images slipped into the space that had been freed for them: himself wracked with illness after an enemy slipped poison in his food, and struggling to go on, to fulfill his duty; Bridei defying him, Bridei making him choose between public acceptance of Tuala and the loss of the perfect king he had dedicated fifteen years to preparing. That day, he had learned that Bridei was his own man.

But, he thought as stars appeared above him, one, three, seven, a scattering as generous as bluebells in a spring glade, that was not the only learning to be had that day at Pitnochie when his foster son came out of the forest, half drowned, with Tuala in his arms. There had been another layer; a layer none of them had recognized. The girl Bridei had made the price of kingship had been Broichan's own daughter.

He did not sleep that night. He lay quiet, watching the sky, as memories edged back one by one to repopulate his mind. As they came, he considered them in turn: Bridei's trust, as a child, replaced by a wary truce between them; Bridei telling him, in effect, that he would listen to his druid but, as a man and a king, would make his own decisions. Tuala cold and exhausted after her desperate flight from Banmerren at Midwinter, all alone. The way he had barred her from his house. Tuala more recently, cautious in his presence, delicate in her presentation of the unpalatable truth. Tuala trusting him, reluctantly, in a way Bridei no longer could. Fola, his old friend . . . Fola who had guessed at the truth, perhaps far earlier than any of them . . . He would like to see the wise woman. He would like to tell her about the winter and what he had experienced. He would enjoy hearing her acerbic voice, her sharp, wise comments.

When the sky began to lighten and the first birds made their brave small announcements that it was day again, he got up, wiped his eyes, and foraged for edible roots, fungi, and leaves to keep him alive a little longer. He had lost a night's walking. Today he must lie low; there was a small settlement close by and he would not risk being seen. At dusk, he would resume his journey.

§

"OH, BUT OF course you must not mind the children again tonight!" Tuala exclaimed. "You've already done more than your share today, and you should be there for the feast—there will be music and dancing."

Eile grimaced. "I've never done real dancing, only silly things with Saraid, just for fun. Are you sure?" The thought of the great hall thronged with all the grand folk who were staying at White Hill was momentarily overwhelming. She'd been taking most of her meals in the children's dining area with Saraid. Besides, what was she to wear? She had returned the clothes Tuala had lent her for the handfasting, and her others were surely not good enough for a king's celebration.

"Elda prefers not to go," Tuala said. "She gets tired easily with her baby due so soon, and Garth will be on duty. She says Saraid can sleep in her quarters with the twins, if that suits you, Eile. Derelei and Anfreda have their nursemaids. And I've found a gown for you. It should be just right: not too plain, not too showy. I've noticed you prefer not to draw attention to yourself."

"It's very kind of you, my lady—"

"It's nothing, Eile. Faolan is my husband's friend, not just a bodyguard. I view you as the same. Here, take this back to your chamber and try it on. If it fits well, and if you like it, you may keep it. Unless you really don't want to go . . ."

"Thank you, my lady. I will go." Eile took the folded gown, deep green with a tracery of gold thread at neck and wrists. In the face of such generosity, not to speak of forward planning, she could hardly say no.

"I would have put you next to Elda at the table," Tuala said. "I know how it feels to have nobody to talk to. I'll ask Dorica to seat you with Ferada, I think. She doesn't care to sit at the king's table, although she is entitled to by blood. And Wid—he can translate what you don't follow. He tells me you are showing great promise; a very quick learner, he said."

"Oh." Eile felt a flush of pleasure rise to her cheeks. "He's a good teacher. Rather strict, but he makes lessons fun. The time passes quickly."

"I know," said Tuala, smiling. "He taught Bridei and me, so long ago it sometimes seems like a different life. Make good use of Wid; he's a rare breed."

"I'm so grateful, my lady. There is no need to do all this for me—"

"Shh. We're happy to have the opportunity. I'm just sorry Faolan won't be here to see you in my green gown; I've always had a particular liking for it."

Eile felt obliged to offer a correction. "It's not like that with him and me. It's not the kind of thing he would notice, even if he were here." Then, unable to hold back the words, "Has there been any message from him? Have you heard when he may be coming home?"

"Nothing as yet. I hope it will be soon. There's a decision for Bridei to make regarding his chief war leader. He must announce it tonight. It would have helped him considerably to have Faolan's report before doing so, but it seems that's not to be." Then, with a searching look at Eile's face, she added, "You shouldn't worry unduly, Eile. Faolan has a habit of extricating himself successfully from the most perilous situations. This delay simply means his mission has become more complex or has taken him farther away than we anticipated."

Eile thought of Blackthorn Rise, and Faolan with a noose around his neck. He had not extricated himself from that; if she had not been there, he would be dead by now and his family bearing the weight of yet another tragedy. "Thank you for the gown," she said, "I'll try to keep it clean," and departed for her own quarters.

THE GREAT HALL at White Hill had seating for many folk, arranged tonight at three long tables with benches on either side. There was a shorter table on a raised platform at one end. This was for the king and queen and other persons of high status. Many lamps hung from brackets on the stone walls; here and there an expanse of richly colored weaving softened the stark surface. Although Eile could not put names to most of those present, Ferada on her left and Wid on her right were ready to point out who was who and to explain how the celebration would unfold, with the festive meal first, then a formal speech by Bridei recognizing his chieftains' contributions to last autumn's war against the Gaels. A presentation of gifts would be next, followed by the music and dancing Tuala had mentioned.

Garvan, the royal stone carver, was seated opposite Wid. Eile wondered if it was by chance or by intention that this allowed him and Ferada to exchange words and glances without being seen to be placed as a couple. Their friendship intrigued her. She thought of the three girls, Tuala, Ana, Ferada, all at Fola's establishment of Banmerren together, and the fact that each of them seemed to have flouted convention and bent rules to go her own way when she grew up. There was Tuala, an outsider, a child of the Good Folk, marrying Bridei and becoming queen of Fortriu. Ana had chosen a man of unusual qualities as the future father of her children, and had traveled far from home. And there was the matter of Ana and Faolan, which Eile still did not fully understand. Ferada was the most impressive of all: a woman who was determined to make her mark. Garvan made that picture still more interesting. No doubt a stone carver was not considered suitable for a highborn woman like Ferada. All the same, they looked at each other with the tender eyes of lovers. They gazed on each other with an expression that was a lesson in itself. Eile felt a pang of envy.

"Shining One preserve us," muttered Ferada. "Look who's here." Her eyes had moved to the king's table, where Breda had just appeared, golden hair dressed in an elaborate crown of plaits, shapely figure clad in a gown of vivid light blue, the color of her eyes. She looked interestingly pale and needed to steady herself with a hand on the chair back before she sat down beside Keother. Even he looked surprised.

"Too sick for her sister's wedding," Ferada murmured. "Too shocked for her friend's funeral. But well enough for this. I wonder if she'll get up and dance."

That was not the only surprise. There was an empty space beside Garvan at the table; Eile wondered who had decided not to attend the feast. Just as the first platters were brought in, baked fish with leeks and onions, Dovran appeared, not in the leather and iron of his daily work but in tunic and trousers of dark red wool, his hair tied back with a cord, and seated himself in the vacant spot, right opposite Eile. He offered his shy smile.

"Been given the night off?" inquired Garvan. He was indeed plain-looking, with a square, heavy-jawed face and big hands. It seemed a little unfortunate that he now sat beside the best-looking man in the hall.

Dovran gave a nod. "King's orders. Garth's on the job. I'll be happy when Faolan gets back; a night off is rare." Then, after a pause, "Green suits you, Eile." This was delivered awkwardly; his need to pluck up courage before speaking thus was plain.

"Thank you," Eile mumbled, avoiding his eye. "My lady, who is that very large man with all the tattoos? He seems to be wearing cat skins."

"A Caitt chieftain," said Ferada in Gaelic. "Umbrig.

He fought in the war, on our side. He lives in Dalriada now—you know where that is?"

"We passed through that region. Faolan and I."

"Of course. Umbrig took over a Gaelic fortress there; he oversees the former king of that territory who is in custody at Dunadd. The Caitt are ferocious warriors. Drustan is a notable exception."

"Who are the people in the very bright clothes?" Eile had spotted a woman, a boy, and several men at the next table, each wearing garments of a striking multicolored weave, all squares and stripes.

"Speak your new tongue," Wid ordered from his place beside her. "If you run out of words, we'll help you. Some baked fish? I detect garlic in abundance; we'd best all have a serving."

"Those folk are the wife and son of a chieftain who died in the war, Ged of Abertornie," said Ferada. "Several men of their household have come with them. Ged's people are intensely loyal; his death has only strengthened that. He was very close to Bridei. There were many deaths; many losses. Tonight cannot be all celebration."

"For you," Dovran ventured, looking at Eile, "this must be difficult. Confusing."

For a moment Eile was not sure what he meant. Then she realized, and struggled for words in the Priteni tongue. "I am a Gael, yes . . . But at home, I knew nothing of war . . . nothing of all this . . ." She felt obliged to smile, for his comment had shown a sensitivity that surprised her. "You fight in war?" she asked him.

"I did. Not as the king's guard. I was chosen for that afterward. He took only one of his bodyguards to Dalriada, and that man fell in battle."

Silently, Eile thanked the gods that Faolan had not been a part of it. Then she retracted it, since such a thought seemed to belittle the worth of the man who had died. War was stupid. A terrible waste. For every hero to be honored and rewarded tonight, there were probably fifty who had never come home.

. It was not possible to eat much, though dish followed sumptuous dish: beef, soup, pig's trotters, vegetables in aspic, puddings, and preserved fruits.

"You have an appetite like a little bird's, Eile," said Wid, who was taking full advantage of the spread.

She smiled but did not comment. She could hardly explain that when you had spent years and years on a diet of almost nothing you did not need a feast to satisfy you, only an amount that was enough. Her body had responded already to better feeding. The mirror showed her not a skinny girl but a slight, well formed woman. Her moon-bleeding, which she had not seen for years after Saraid's birth, had now come back quite regularly: a nuisance, but a good one, for it showed her bodily rhythms had survived that time of deprivation. Of degradation. With Dovran right opposite her, eyes admiring, she would try her best not to think of that.

When the feasting was over and the assembled crowd sat relaxed, goblets of ale or mead in hand and an array of sweetmeats set out before them, King Bridei rose to his feet, flanked by his chief councillors, tall, dark Tharan and gray-haired, weary-looking Aniel. "My friends and honored guests," the king began, "this is a night of light and darkness; of joyous celebration and profound sadness . . ."

Eile did not follow much of it, though Wid and Ferada whispered fragments of translation. Here and there she let her mind drift as Bridei's voice, warm, confident, sometimes almost intimate, as if he spoke not to a crowd but to each individual, held his audience in complete thrall. She watched their faces, seeing there the mingled joy and sorrow the king had mentioned, the acknowledgment that victory and death went hand in hand. After a while, she could pick out those faces that were less captivated by the king's undoubted gift for public oratory.

Keother, king of the Light Isles, seated at the top table: aloof, guarded, wary. Breda: bored and cross. Among the chieftains who sat in silence, eyes alight with the hope and loyalty Bridei's words conjured, were one or two who wore looks of skepticism or irritation or doubt.

"Who is that?" she whispered. "And that?" She received the names, and a look from Ferada that was entirely knowing.

"He does not have them all in the palm of his hand," Talorgen's daughter murmured. "Not yet. And he still has an announcement to make; they are waiting for that."

First, however, came a call for each of the chieftains to step forward in turn, to receive Bridei's thanks in person and be presented with a gift. Aniel held a coffer; Tharan stood by a small table where larger items were laid ready. In turn, items of jewelry, fine garments, or pieces of weaponry were bestowed. Eile liked it best when the brightly clad boy, with his mother beside him, went up to receive thanks on behalf of his slain father. He was perhaps twelve years old. Bridei kissed him on both cheeks, formally, and spoke to him as man to man. The gift was a pair of huge hunting hounds: formidable shaggy creatures with a noble grace of expression. The boy was dignified. He thanked the king in a few courteous words, bowing his head. It was only when he turned away that Eile saw him catch his mother's eye and grin with pure delight.

The massive Caitt warrior in his cloak of many small skins received a heavy arm-ring in silver. Many others went forth; each got his greeting, and to each Bridei spoke as to an old and dear friend. Eile's eyes went to Tuala, sitting at the high table in what was her first appearance before the full court since her daughter's birth. The queen wore dove gray. Her flyaway dark curls were part concealed by a short, gauzy veil; her large eyes were intent on her husband as he negotiated his long speech and went through the personal acknowledgments, offering each man the respect due for his courage and sacrifice. It seemed to Eile that Tuala lived each moment with Bridei; that she was somehow lending him her own strength so he could go on. She thought, again, of Faolan in despair, Faolan about to surrender to the darkness, and how her shout had saved him.

The gifts were given. Folk began to stir again; jugs and goblets chinked and conversation began to buzz around the tables.

"Silence for the king!" shouted someone with a big voice.

Bridei spoke, saying something about music and dancing which Eile could only half translate, and then Wid leaned toward her, murmuring, "I'll give you a rough translation as we go with the next part; it'll be an important speech. Stand up now; the king asks us to honor those fallen in last year's war."

They stood. The silence was so absolute that Eile thought she could hear her own heart beating.

"Thank you," the king said soberly. "And I have one last matter of which to speak. My kinsman, Carnach of Thorn Bend, who served with great heart as my chief war leader in our venture, cannot be with us tonight. It is evident he has encountered delays in returning to take up his responsibilities at Caer Pridne, where we retain the core of our fighting force, ready to move again should a new threat arise. I am aware that, in the wake of a great triumph, one must remain watchful. Fortriu has many enemies; we must keep our eyes open and our weapons sharp. For this reason, and because I cannot say when Carnach may be free to come back to us, I will tonight appoint another chieftain as war leader in his place."

A general sigh went around the hall. Wid whispered in Eile's ear, "They have awaited this a long time, since the rumors began of Carnach's defection and a possible rebellion. Bridei doesn't want to do it; it means publicly acknowledging that he believes the rumors may have some substance. But, failing news of exactly what Carnach is up to, the king must announce this tonight. To delay longer will make him appear less than decisive."

"Shh!" hissed a man farther along the table, and Ferada looked down her nose at him.

"Talorgen of Raven's Well has agreed to take up the position, on my invitation." Bridei spoke with quiet confidence. Eile was pleased to discover that she was understanding more than she had expected of his speech; she needed Wid's whispered translation only for the most complicated parts. "I have faith in Talorgen's abilities," the king went on. "He is a warrior of long experience. At his hand I honed my own skills in armed combat; under his leadership I took part in my first battle. I ask you to acknowledge my choice and I expect you to support it wholeheartedly. Talorgen will be training men at Caer Pridne over the summer, against certain possibilities. I thank him for his readiness to take up this onerous duty. After the bloodshed of last autumn, each of us holds strong hope for a season of peace and time to rebuild. But if war comes again, we will be ready for it."

Eile was startled when, instead of applause and words of approval, a chorus of shouts broke out around the hall, challenges, objections, men's voices raised in protest. "Why wasn't this done in open assembly?" "Why no vote?" "Choose a younger man!" "What about Morleo?"

The king's councillor Aniel, who was not a tall man, rose to his feet and held up a hand. The hall fell silent; Aniel's authority was widely respected. Talorgen was already standing; he was at the head of one of the long tables with his younger son by his side. Ferada had begun gnawing on her fingernails; across from her, Garvan murmured, "He knows what to say. It'll be fine."

"I should make it clear," said the chieftain of Raven's Well, "that I agreed to take up these duties on certain conditions. I trust that, when I explain them, your concerns will be laid to rest. Be assured that, when and if the position of chief war leader becomes available on a long-term basis, it will be contested in open session, and any man who thinks himself worthy of consideration will have the opportunity to put his name forward."

"Explain yourself!" someone shouted. Immediately, another voice rose across that, "Hold your tongue! Talorgen's the best choice anyway!" The first man hissed, and Eile saw Ferada turn pale. She put her hand over the other woman's on the table. Ferada might on occasion appear intimidatingly capable, but this was her father being publicly attacked.

"I've agreed to act in the position only until Carnach returns or King Bridei decides it is time to appoint a permanent replacement," Talorgen said. "Nonetheless, I will carry out my new duties with all the energy and dedication I have to give." He himself looked pale. Ferada's father was still a handsome man, for all the touch of gray in his russet hair, but tonight he was plainly ill at ease.

"He's worried about the boys," Ferada muttered. "Bedo in particular. This is a lot for my stepmother to handle. Father doesn't really want to do it."

"That's all very well," someone spoke up over a continuing rumble of unrest, "but where's Carnach? That's what we all want to know. The men need certainty, not short-term measures. We all do, in the aftermath of war."

"If you ask me," said another man, "there's no better time than now to appoint this permanent replacement."

"Shut up!" yelled someone from down the hall. "What are you trying to do, defy the king?"

There was an uncomfortable silence.

Keother of the Light Isles got to his feet; all eyes turned to the top table. "Indeed," said Keother, running a hand through his thatch of fair hair, "a celebratory banquet is hardly the occasion for such . . . robust debate. King Bridei has made his decision. Now is not the time to challenge it. If he has appointed Talorgen here, then I am certain Talorgen will do an excellent job."

Ferada said something under her breath.

"No doubt in time, perhaps in relatively little time," Keother went on smoothly, "due process will be followed and a new appointment made. We've all heard what folk are saying about Carnach of Thorn Bend. In times of such threat, what's required is a decisive leader. One who does not shy away from difficult choices."

"When does the dancing start?" A ripple of laughter followed this query, which had boomed forth in the sonorous voice of Umbrig of the Caitt.

"Thank you, Umbrig," said Bridei levelly, "for you remind us why we are here: principally for a celebration of victory and valor. There will be time to debate this other matter. That I promise you. And I assure you that it will not be debated before its due time. To choose a path on the basis of rumor and conjecture is the decision of an impulsive fool."

"Then why not cast an augury?" put in Keother, who was evidently not finished yet. "Let the gods advise you."

"That's a low blow," whispered Wid.

"You are a man of deep faith, my lord king," Keother went on. "Should not the Flamekeeper have the final word on this matter?"

Then an exceptionally bold, or foolish, man from somewhere at the third table called out, "Where's the king's druid, then? Where's Broichan? Ask him what he thinks!"

"Enough!" There was a quality in Bridei's voice that cut the interjection off as crisply as a sharp axe splits dry pine. "We are done here. Let the musicians commence their work, for it is time to put weighty matters aside awhile. Be assured that I will hear every man's concerns in due course. But not tonight. We have waited long to celebrate."

Folk got up; serving people began to move aside benches and tables. In the press of bodies, Ferada could be seen heading to her father's side to speak to him reassuringly, while Garvan hovered, far enough away for decorum. Wid rose to his feet more slowly; Eile offered him her arm. An instant later Dovran was on the old scholar's other side, doing the same.

"I'm not in my dotage yet, young people," Wid chuckled. "But it's true, I would prefer a comfortable seat; my capering days are long over. Put me beside Fola and her wise women over there in the corner. They should keep me entertained. Now go off and enjoy yourselves; that's what the king wants. Let's see you dancing, the pair of you. I'll wager you're light on your feet, Eile."

It's a challenge, Eile told herself grimly. *Let Dovran take your hand, let him touch your waist, convince everyone you're having a wonderful time. And hope you can convince yourself.* The music was good, not that she had much to compare it with. She thought she could remember a wedding or something similar at Brennan's in Cloud Hill. A long time ago. Maybe so long ago that her father had been there, and her mother had still been able to smile. There'd been a little bowed instrument that made a scraping sound, and a goatskin drum—she'd liked that—and a reed pipe, high and shrill. She thought she could remember getting up to dance and someone— Deord?—saying with an approving grin, "That's my girl." These musicians were as far above those as the sun is above a little yellow daisy in a field. The flute throbbed and sang, the drum set feet tapping. There was a harp as well. That Eile loved best of all, a magical kind of music like a voice from a fairy world. It made her think of Derelei and his visions in the water.

"Will you?" asked Dovran, holding out his hand.

"I . . . not know . . . steps. Never do . . . before."

"Nor have I." He grinned.

Eile was disarmed. "I suppose we'll have to tread on each other's toes, then," she said in Gaelic, then gave him a demonstration of her meaning, making him laugh. By the time that was done she had taken his hand and they were moving out into a swirling mass of couples. *It is possible,* she told herself, *to bear his touch. If I concentrate on other things, I can do it. Just. I wonder if Faolan knows how to dance?*

14

❦

IN THE AFTERMATH of King Bridei's victory feast, the household at White Hill began to shrink toward its usual number. Chieftains and their families rode for home and men-at-arms headed to Caer Pridne in anticipation of a season's training under the new leadership of Talorgen.

Bridei had made his decision and intended to stick by it, but he was uneasy. He had asked Fola to conduct an augury, in Broichan's absence, to obtain the wisdom of the gods as to the immediate future and the question of Carnach. Was it best to send a force southeast, to be ready to hold the border against armed insurgency from that quarter, or should he wait in hope of clearer information? How could he set strategies in place against an uprising when he did not yet know who Carnach's allies were?

The gods had provided no clear answers. It was not that Fola lacked skill in the interpretation of a pattern of birch rods cast on a stone table. She was a priestess of long standing, learned and deep. Bridei himself, raised in a knowledge of such tools, could see the message of the rods was obscure, hinting at one interpretation, then another. He had consulted Tuala, who had in the past proved more astute than anyone in her comprehension of the gods' messages. Even she had been unable to reach a conclusion. "We face confusion," she had said. "Challenges; fences and bridges. But we knew that already."

Late one afternoon Bridei called his inner circle to a meeting in his small, private council chamber. There were an oak table, two benches, a narrow window looking out over the forest below the parapet wall. A lamp stood in a niche, for the place was naturally dim. Otherwise the place was bare, stone floor swept clean, walls devoid of decoration. With the window set so high and the door both unobtrusive and effectively defensible by one man—currently Garth stood guard—it was a place where conversations on delicate matters could be held with confidence.

Talorgen had come early; it was plain he wanted to speak to Bridei before the others arrived. The king was alone in the chamber save for his dog, Ban, whose small white form was a blur under the table.

"I'm packed up and ready to go, my lord," the chieftain said. Talorgen's brow was, if anything, still more furrowed than on the night of the feast, and he paced the small chamber restlessly, setting Ban on edge. "We've decided, Brethana and I, that it's best if she takes the boys home to Raven's Well, for now at least. Because of Bedo's arm, they'll travel by water. That means they'll need to stay on here awhile without me, until passage is available."

"Of course," Bridei said, a little surprised that this need even be mentioned. "Your family is welcome at court as long as they want to stay."

"Uric wants to come with me. But he's young yet. I've told him if things go well he can travel to Caer Pridne later in the summer. It's Bedo who most concerns me."

"His arm is not mending?"

"Oh, the arm is all right; the physician's pleased with him. But Bedo's still acting oddly. He can't let go his suspicions about that day, the day he got the injury. They've gone quiet about it, he and Uric both; they won't tell me exactly what it is they believe happened. I know they're offended that we didn't seem to take them seriously when they first raised the matter. Now they're afraid we'll dismiss their fears as nonsense."

"I did have the events of that afternoon investigated, Talorgen. Nothing suspicious was uncovered, beyond the fact that a well-trained mare shied and bolted for no apparent reason. Some folk thought Breda screamed before the horse reared up; some thought she did so afterward, as one would expect. If your boys won't put this theory of theirs out in the open, I can't see any real grounds for pursuing this further, and nor would Keother, I'm sure. Where this matter is concerned, he's shared my own opinions. Indeed, he's been remarkably cooperative."

"A surprise in view of his performance at the feast," observed Talorgen, curling his lip. "I've never seen such a disgraceful attempt to belittle and undermine a leader as the exhibition he put on that night. What Keother's up to I don't know, but I'll be glad when he and his spoiled brat of a cousin are gone from here. Their visit has been disruptive and unsettling."

"Breda was quite blunt when asked to account for the behavior of her horse that day. In her mind it was a clear case of the animal's inadequacy. She considers herself entirely blameless. I spoke to her myself. The girl seems too naïve and childish to be the instigator of anything devious."

"Her uncle might have exerted pressure on her. Keother's powerful, and she's young. I hope you don't intend to retain her here as a replacement for Ana."

"Keother's outspokenness at the feast suggests some action may be required to keep him in check. If taking a hostage is the only option, then I will do it."

"You say she's too childish to be dangerous. I should tell you that Bedo's obsession seems to be centered on her. Of late, he's taken to sending his brother out on horseback to conduct some kind of search in the field where the accident took place."

"Search? For what? Surely all signs will be gone now; time has passed, and we've had rain."

"He wasn't exactly open about it, but I gather the search is for an implement that may have been used to startle Breda's horse. Once I'm gone from White Hill, my wife is not confident she can call a halt to this. My sons know they're due to return home shortly, but Brethana believes that when it comes to the point, if they haven't found what they seek, they may insist on staying at White Hill. They treat her with respect, but she's not their mother."

"I see. Very well; if required, I will assist your wife with the matter. It's awkward with Keother and Breda still here. Would Bedo talk to me now?"

"I doubt it, Bridei. I think it's best if—"

A knock on the door. Ban barked, a sound far more arresting than his size suggested was possible. Then Garth's voice: "My lord?"

Bridei nodded to Talorgen to open the door.

"My lord, I regret the interruption," said Garth from outside. "Faolan's back."

A LITTLE LATER, while the chieftain of Raven's Well waited tactfully outside, Bridei regarded his right-hand man across the table and tried to mask his concern. Faolan had limped in; his efforts to disguise the fact that he was in pain did not deceive Bridei. His face was pale under the marks of fading bruises; his dark eyes were shadowed, as if he had gone long without sleep. The little dog looked up at him but remained silent, for this was a trusted confidant well known to him. Of course, Faolan always drove himself hard. But Bridei had never seen him like this. His heart sank. It must be bad news; the worst news.

"Faolan, welcome back. Sit, please. I must ask for your report immediately. I have a council scheduled; the participants will be here soon. But I will hear from you first, before we decide what we can share."

Faolan did not sit. "The tale's odd, my lord," he said. "A long journey with nothing new to be gleaned, only the same rumors, and tales of activity on the road toward Circinn and within, armed men, parties of riders. Then I stumbled on Carnach in person."

Bridei leaned forward, hands clasped before him on the table. "If you did, you'll be the first man in all Fortriu who's clapped eyes on my kinsman since he went home for the winter. Where? In what company?"

"On the surface it looks bad, Bridei." Faolan abandoned

the more formal mode of address, falling into the common pattern of speech between friends. "He was in Circinn, and the man with him was Bargoit."

Bridei whistled. "Are you sure?" If true, this was almost worse than he could have imagined. It made Carnach a traitor of the basest level.

"I'm sure. They captured and interrogated me. Oh, nothing too bad," at Bridei's gesture of concern. "I managed to convince that stoat Bargoit that I was insignificant. The chief problem was that it delayed my return. Made me slow."

Bridei did not ask about the leg. He could see the uneven stance, the pain written all over his friend's well-governed features. "I take it from what you've said that Bargoit did not know who you were," he said, thinking hard. "So . . . ?"

"I believe this is not the ill news it appears to be," Faolan said. "Garth told me you've appointed Talorgen in Carnach's place. I curse myself for taking so long to get back. In the matter of your chief war leader, you could have afforded to wait."

"What are you saying? That Carnach is coming back? That he expects to step into his old position after consorting with the likes of Bargoit? Whatever he is, my kinsman is not a fool."

"Bridei," said Faolan, sitting on the bench at last and stretching out his leg before him with a grimace, "there's something you may need to take on trust."

"Yes?"

"Firstly, note the fact that Carnach showed not a flicker of recognition when his men brought me in. He played along with my assumed identity as a rather dull farmhand who'd wandered a little too far from home."

If the matter had not been so serious Bridei would have smiled at that. "You, a farmhand?" he said. "That must have been a challenge."

"They believed me; at least, Bargoit did. I had an odd conversation with Carnach. Let me tell you . . ."

Bridei listened, weighing it up: talk of going away, of turning one's back on a good home and a good job; of loyalty calling a man home. Something about opportunities in Circinn. Mention of Midsummer. Trust was a fine thing. All the same, what Faolan suggested required quite a leap of faith.

"If you're right," he said, "Carnach showed an amazing degree of quick-wittedness."

"Ask yourself if, before the day he took exception to your decision regarding the crown of Circinn and marched away home, you had any doubts at all about Carnach's loyalty."

"You know I had none, Faolan. But he was angry; bitterly disappointed in me. Can I risk believing that this conversation between the two of you, for which he cannot have been prepared, was indeed the passing of a cryptic message assuring me of his loyalty? What if I act on that belief and you're proved to be wrong? We could be caught perilously underprepared for an attack. Besides, nothing alters the fact that Carnach was in Circinn, in company with Bargoit. Bargoit has never been a friend of Fortriu. And he's powerful; more powerful than any councillor should be."

"All I can do is offer my own conviction that Carnach meant me to tell you his allegiances are unchanged, and that he will return to his position as war leader. I believe that when he ordered me to go home by Midsummer he meant you could expect him then."

"Do you have a theory concerning Bargoit?"

"Several; I have yet to decide which is the most plausible. I think it possible Carnach is luring Bargoit into a trap of some kind. It would be greatly to Fortriu's advantage if Bargoit lost his influence with the new king of Circinn. I'm certain my sudden appearance in the middle of it all was highly inconvenient for Carnach. However, he used his wits to turn my presence to his advantage. He'd have known you sent me to find out what was going on; he used me to respond to your concerns. To let you know he can handle the situation, whatever it is. That you haven't lost his support and that he'll be back."

"Flamekeeper aid us," said Bridei, "perhaps it really is good news. You know I trust you, Faolan. I wasn't there; you were. The question now is, shall we share this and, if so, how widely?"

"Who will be present at this council?"

"Talorgen. You may be relieved to know he accepted his new post somewhat unwillingly, and only on a temporary basis. Fola, who will be leaving soon for Banmerren, but agreed to stay for this. Aniel and Tharan. Perhaps Tuala, if she can be free."

Faolan nodded. "The decision is yours, of course. I believe you can inform that group of this matter. Do I take it that Broichan is not yet returned?"

"We've heard nothing. My next task for you may have to be seeking out news of these Christians; I hope their arrival is not imminent. Keother and his cousin are still here. I'd prefer to avoid the complication of dealing with both at once. He's dangerous and she's volatile. And there's a strong Christian presence in the Light Isles, which Keother is known to tolerate."

"Yes, my lord." Faolan's tone had changed, as had his expression; something in Bridei's speech had made him seek the protection of formality.

"I don't plan to send you off right away, friend," Bridei said, guessing as one usually had to do with Faolan. "Right now, you should go off and wash, change your clothes, and have a bite to eat. Then I'd be glad if you would return here to give your personal account to my council."

"Yes, my lord."

He was nearly at the door when Bridei said, on impulse, "By the way, that young lady of yours has settled in very well."

Faolan stopped as if hit by a crossbow bolt. He stood utterly still, half turned away from the king.

"Eile, I mean," Bridei added when it became evident

Faolan was not going to ask. "She's learning the Priteni tongue—we asked our old tutor Wid to help her—and making new friends. She's become quite a favorite here. Tuala says she has a rare touch with the children."

Faolan could be seen to breathe again. "She's still here?" His voice was odd; tight and strained. "Does that mean Ana and Drustan haven't left court? I thought—"

"Ana and Drustan were handfasted some time ago, Faolan." Bridei kept his tone neutral. He was perhaps the only person in whom Faolan had confided the truth about his impossible passion for Ana, and the complicated nature of the bond between the three of them, Ana, Faolan, and Drustan. "They are long since departed for the north. But Eile and her daughter stayed behind."

"I see." It came after a pause in which Bridei thought he could almost feel the turmoil in his friend's mind, such was the tension in the little chamber. "Where have you housed them? A rare touch, you said . . . Is Eile working as a nursemaid? That is not—"

"Why don't you go and ask her?" Bridei suggested. "She'll very likely be in our private garden at this time of day, pulling up a few weeds and keeping an eye on Derelei."

"Your council—"

"Go on, Faolan. We can wait a little. Remember you are human."

Faolan limped to the door and set a hand on its frame for support. "Oddly enough," he said quietly, "I no longer need reminding."

THE SUN WAS low; its rays slanted across the quiet little garden, warming the rows of herbs and the creepers on the stone walls, setting a yellow glint in the water of the pond. The place looked deserted. That was just as well; his heart was pounding like a war drum and his tongue was surely incapable of uttering a coherent word. She was here. She was still at White Hill, and he had to find the right things to say, the safe, reassuring things, while his body had leapt with desire at the sound of her name and his head was a mess of chaotic thoughts and jumbled emotions. The king's assassin and spy, cool and professional, was suddenly and completely unmanned.

Faolan made to turn back. He'd best clean himself up and present himself to the council. That, at least, he would be able to do efficiently. A sound froze him in place.

"One, two, three, buzzy bumblebee . . ."

Saraid, without a doubt. Her voice came from behind the lavender bushes where, he seemed to remember, there was a small patch of grass edged by flower beds.

"Four, five, six, beetle on a stick . . ."

Eile. Oh gods, Eile. He felt his blood surge. Then a new voice spoke, a young man's.

"Seven, eight, nine, berries on a vine . . ."

"Now Derry." That was Saraid again. A tiny voice said something, the words indistinct, the inflection copying exactly that of the other participants in this game, whatever it was.

"Very good, Derelei," Eile said. "We'll have you speaking Gaelic in no time. And you, Dovran."

Dovran. He would kill the man. No, he would turn and walk away quietly; he would go to Bridei and volunteer to travel down the Glen and find the Christians. She need never see him. She sounded happy; settled. And Dovran, a pox on the fellow, sounded as if he belonged there. Faolan edged back down the steps. On the second tread his foot slipped and he grasped at the bushes by the path to keep his balance. A moment later Dovran was at the head of the steps, spear poised to thrust; the king's bodyguards were all professionals.

"State your name and—Faolan!" Dovran's expression relaxed; he withdrew the weapon. "You're back! Welcome home."

But Faolan was not looking at Dovran. His eyes were fixed on the space behind the young guard, where one, two, three figures appeared: Saraid, clad in a little gown of pink wool, with Sorry under one arm; Derelei, big-eyed and solemn on the bodyguard's other side; and Eile. She wore a skirt and tunic of deep green and her fiery hair was caught in two little braids at the temples, then flowed down her back. His hands could feel how soft it would be to touch; his mind spanned the distance between them, imagining the myriad sensations of holding her in his arms. He saw a sequence of expressions cross the pale, neat features: surprise, shock, confusion, something else he could not interpret, something that might be good . . . He wanted to hold out his arms; to invite her embrace. Automatic defenses held his body still.

Then Saraid cried out, "Feeler! Feeler home!" and launched herself down the steps, and his defenses crumbled utterly. He knelt and caught her, and hugged her and Sorry both, blinking back tears. He murmured something that was both greeting and apology, feeling the child's peach-soft cheek against his, then rose with Saraid in his arms and turned a certain look on Dovran.

"I'd best be off," Dovran said in the Priteni tongue, not without delivering his own look. "I'll see you at supper, Eile."

"Thank you for playing," Eile said. Her accent had improved markedly.

"Any time." The young guard strode past Faolan and away across the garden.

"What's he supposed to be doing?" Faolan demanded, using Gaelic.

"Keeping watch. Keeping folk out of the queen's garden. Don't glare like that. Come up where I can see you."

The words were practical; why was her voice so shaky? Faolan mounted the steps and stood before her. He said not a single word. Eile scrutinized him, narrowing her eyes against the afternoon sun. "You look terrible," she said.

You look wonderful. "You're still here," Faolan said. "I thought you'd be gone. I thought Drustan and Ana . . ."

"As you see, I'm not so easily tidied away. There's

plenty for me to do here, and Saraid seems happy enough. I made my own decision. Come and sit down on the bench, Faolan. Your leg's worse, isn't it? What happened?"

He limped to the bench, unable to pretend before her perceptive eye. He sat, putting Saraid beside him. Eile squatted down in front of him, the silent Derelei close by, staring. Scrutiny from all sides: he felt as if he were being weighed in the balance. Only Saraid, snuggling against him without question, had evidently judged him satisfactory. He cleared his throat; found words. "Bridei said you've settled in well. I see that is so."

"You make it sound like that's a bad thing."

"No, of course not—I'm surprised, that's all. Taken aback."

"Taken aback that safety and kindness have made me almost content? Surprised that I've grown out of threatening intruders with pitchforks?"

"Dovran. That surprised me. A man you'd never met when I left here, sitting on the ground as if he was part of the family, playing games with you and your daughter; looking at you with ownership in his eyes. I haven't been gone so terribly long. It made me wonder if I'd misunderstood, earlier."

Eile's eyes darkened with anger; she rose to her feet. "We can't talk about this now, here," she said, glancing at the two children. "I'm not sure if I want to talk about it at all. It sounds as if you're saying I'm only of interest to you as long as I'm flawed; damaged. Things change. Sometimes they change despite us."

"You know that's not what I meant." He felt as if she'd struck him; how could she believe this of him? "I expected . . ." The image in his mind was clear as day, himself with his arms spread wide, laying his heart bare, and Eile running, her red hair flying, running to embrace him as if he were the only man in the world. It was farcical. "Forget it," he said. "I should get back to the king's council. I must clean myself up first; I stink." He got up, feeling the fire shoot through his knee, and before he could take a step, Eile had reached out and gripped him by the arms.

"Careful," she said, her tone quite different now. "I can see how much it hurts. Go on pretending there's nothing wrong and you'll find you can't walk at all soon. There are healers here; have it looked at. If you want, I can help you—"

She fell silent, still supporting him with her hands on his upper arms. He felt her touch warm every part of his body. For a moment, the thrill of it drove out all caution, and he bent his head and touched his lips to her temple, just for a moment, a wonderful, perilous moment. "I'm sorry," he said. "I'm going to get this all wrong. I think I should just turn around and go away again. That would be easier for both of us. I know it would be best for you."

Eile had not moved; she had neither flinched away nor made a sound. Her hands still held him, strong and un-wavering.

A little voice spoke up from beside him. "Feeler go away?" It was full of woe; when he looked, he saw silent tears streaming down Saraid's cheeks.

"No, Saraid," Eile said shakily. "Faolan's not going away again. No need to cry, little one. Shh, shh, you're starting Derry off, too." Then, looking up at Faolan, "You do stink a bit. No worse than either of us did coming up the Glen, but if there's a council you'd better take time to wash and change. Did you come straight here after seeing the king?"

"Yes, I . . ." It didn't seem possible to frame coherent words, nor to make a simple decision. "Where are you lodged?" he asked her. "Can I see you later?"

"We're in a little chamber next to Ana's old quarters."

"We?"

"Saraid and me. What else? You imagine a miracle has occurred, and I have a perfect young man in my bed already?" Then, after a little, "Faolan, are you blushing?"

Her tone was very sweet; it made his heart behave quite oddly.

"I suppose," he made himself say, "that if it were true—you and Dovran, so soon—it would be a good thing. Even though it would mean you had broken a promise. But . . . if it were true, it would . . . it would hurt me, Eile."

"You broke a promise," she reminded him.

"I know, and I am sorry for it. Bitterly sorry. The king made me go. I could not explain to him."

She had released him. Now she took Saraid's hand and Derelei's, as if preparing to leave.

"Don't go yet. Please."

"I don't want to, Faolan. But I have responsibilities and so have you."

"It's no excuse, is it? *The king made me go.* I wanted to leave you a message. I couldn't find the words."

Something hung suddenly in the balance; Eile's eyes held a question whose answer was all-important. "Can you find them now?" she asked quietly.

His heart thundered; his blood raced. It was akin to the most difficult challenge in the world. No, perhaps not the most difficult; he thought that was still to come. "I don't want to go," he whispered, "but Bridei needs me to do this. I put my arms around you, and around Saraid, and I beg you to forgive me. I will dream of you every night until I see you again." He felt cold sweat on his brow. If he had stood in the heat of a battle alone, naked and unarmed, he could not have felt more vulnerable.

There was a long silence. Saraid yawned; Derelei remained still, looking at Faolan.

Eventually Eile gave a stiff little nod. He had no idea at all if she was pleased or shocked or frightened. He could not say what was in his heart: *I love you. I need you.*

"All right." Her tone was constrained. "I have to go now, it's Derelei's suppertime and the queen wants to attend a meeting, probably the same one as you. This seems to have got complicated. We'll have to talk about it. Later. But you can't just march into my chamber. Not here at court. It's not like traveling through the forest, where it doesn't matter if you sleep side by side."

"I'm expert at coming and going unobserved," Faolan said.

"Faolan . . ." She was more hesitant now. "I didn't mean . . ."

"I know that. Farewell for now, Eile. I'll see you tomorrow, Saraid."

"Bye." Saraid's voice was plaintive.

"I know you didn't mean that kind of invitation, Eile." *Even though I want it so badly; even though my body aches with the need for you.* "We'll talk, then I'll leave. I promise nobody will see me."

"Farewell, then."

"Until later. Now if I can just persuade this leg to work . . ."

"I HATE YOU!" yelled Breda. "You're a stuffy old know-it-all, and you don't understand!" She dissolved into furious tears.

Her cousin Keother stood on the other side of the private meeting chamber in his allocated quarters at White Hill, arms folded, expression stern. "You're behaving like a child," he said. "It's becoming more and more difficult to believe you are almost seventeen years old, an age at which, cousin, many young women have already borne their husbands fine sons. Have you taken in a word I've spoken, Breda?"

Breda sniffed, flicking her fair hair back from her tear-stained features. "A big lecture about propriety," she said. "I heard it. It's stupid. The whole thing's stupid. What am I supposed to have done? Go on, tell me. Tell me! Who's been gossiping, I bet it was that Dorica, wasn't it, the dried-up old stick, she can't bear the way all the men look at me, even her husband who's fifty if he's a day—"

"Breda!"

Sometimes Keother used what Breda called his "king voice." This was one of those times. She fell silent.

"If you're not capable of understanding that your behavior is completely inappropriate, then perhaps my best course of action is to send you straight home," Keother said heavily. "I hardly know where to begin."

"You're not still harping on about the stupid horse thing, are you?" Breda glared at him. "That wasn't my fault. I was hurt and upset, and instead of being nice about it, everyone kept asking me questions."

"That episode is best forgotten," said Keother. "I've spent more than enough of my time and energy making excuses for you. Your complete lack of respect for Cella's family, your total absence of remorse could not fail to create a very unfortunate impression. I have work to do at White Hill before I return home, cousin. There's more hanging on this visit than an opportunity for you to parade your wares before a wider circle of young men."

A jug of bluebells stood on a side table; Breda's fingers stretched out to wrench a flower from its stem, then shred the petals.

"You've been seen more than once in the company of stable hands, kitchen men, others of Bridei's household. If you must insist on behaving like a cat in heat, then do me the favor of confining it to those of our own party who have already sampled what you have to offer. And for pity's sake show some discretion."

"It's your fault." The petals fell to the floor; she seized another stem. "You wouldn't let me bring Evard."

"I hoped you might be able to restrain yourself. To emulate your sister for a little."

"Oh, Ana. Boring, prudish old Ana."

"I'm told Ana conducted herself, as hostage here, with dignity and discretion. She's made a marriage that benefits both Bridei and myself. Allies among the Caitt are difficult to secure. A marriage for you may prove harder to arrange. It certainly will if tales of your escapades travel outside White Hill."

"I don't want to get married. A child in my belly every year and some oaf in my bed who imagines a quick fumble is going to satisfy me—I'd die of frustration. You have no idea—"

"You may have no choice. There's every likelihood Bridei will require you to stay in Fortriu when I go home. If that occurs, he's the one who will decide when and where to bestow your hand."

Breda stared at him then erupted into a peal of laughter. "Bestow my hand? You're so stuffy, Keother, you sound like an old man. I don't know how Orina puts up with you, I really don't. But then your wife's not exactly the lively, vivacious kind, is she? An illustration, in fact, of how quickly women lose their figures and their charm over those early years of marriage—"

"Hold your tongue!" Keother strode over to her and raised his hand. Breda took a step back and giggled. The sound fell somewhere between alarm and excitement. He lowered his arm. "You disgust me," he said. "Let me not hear a single concerned comment about your behavior from now until the end of our stay at White Hill. You're severely restricting my capacity to gain ground in my discussions with Bridei and his councillors; you're wasting my opportunity here. What's got into you? I thought you wanted a permanent invitation to the court of Fortriu. I distinctly remember you telling me how exciting it would be after the tedium of my own court."

"I was wrong," Breda said, crushing the last of the flower petals in her hand. "It's even worse than home. So many things just aren't right in this place. But I can deal with that."

Keother narrowed his keen blue eyes. "What do you mean, you can deal with it?"

Breda turned a guileless smile on her cousin. "Nothing," she said. "Nothing at all."

Back in her bedchamber, she lay flat on the quilt staring

up at the arched roof, and made some adjustments to the list in her head. No point in putting Keother on it; bossy and irritating as her cousin could be, she was forced to acknowledge that he did provide many things that made her existence more bearable. He was generous about paying for clothes and shoes, and plenty of attendants, and a good horse, not a mad one like that brute that had nearly thrown her.

Dovran; she was of two minds about Dovran. He'd disappointed her; not only had he been unbelievably slow at picking up her cues, he had actually begun showing interest in that pasty little Gael to the exclusion of anyone else. It was truly bizarre. It would be easy enough to lose Dovran his position of trust in Bridei's household. On the other hand, if Eile were out of the way, there would still be possibilities where he was concerned. Breda would enjoy the challenge of getting that tight expression off his face and making him sweat a bit. So, no punishment for the king's bodyguard, even if he had offended her. He'd change in time. They all did; Breda had a sure touch.

But Eile, ah, Eile was another matter. To think she'd come so close to bestowing her friendship on the wretched girl! To think she'd confided in her, done her best to help her, and all the time the skinny wretch was scheming to get Dovran for herself. Upstart.

Breda rolled onto her stomach, resting her fair head on crossed arms. What on earth had possessed Eile to refuse her offer of a privileged position as handmaid? The argument about the child was just silly. Anyone could care for a child. All they needed was feeding and cleaning. Eile was a fool if she thought herself indispensable. Well, she was a Gael, after all. They'd lost the war, hadn't they? Eile wanted too much. The girl had one bodyguard already, the mysteriously absent Faolan, another Gael, another loser. That hadn't stopped her moving in on Breda's territory while the fellow was away. Breda had seen them, her and Dovran, exchanging looks over the supper table, playing their silly little games with the children in the garden. She'd seen them dancing on the night of the feast. She could have put a stop to that quickly enough. All she'd needed to do was get up and dance herself; she had a number of techniques for ensuring the eyes of all the men went straight to her. But Keother had stopped her. She could still feel his hand gripping her arm—he'd bruised her—and his furious hiss, *No, you don't!* Wretched Keother. Maybe he should go back on the list after all. But at the bottom; others deserved their treatment first.

Eile at the top of the list; it would be quick work to discredit the girl. Let her see how easy it was to provide for her child when she lost the queen's patronage and got thrown out of White Hill. Let her see how much her lover cared about her then. Breda was sure the girl came from quite humble origins; Eile was moving far above her due place in society. All she planned to do was put the little Gael back where she belonged: at the bottom of the heap. It was very satisfying to be able to set things to rights.

The child: she'd be caught up in it, which was a pity because she was a pretty little thing, but if she survived she'd doubtless grow up like her mother, who must have conceived the infant when she was a child herself. Slut of a mother, slut of a daughter. White Hill was best rid of the two of them.

Breda sat up, easing her back against the pillows. They were lumpy and uncomfortable. Cella had been the only one of her maids who knew how to get them just right. Stupid Cella. If only the girl hadn't taken a liking to Talorgen's elder son. Bedo was young, certainly, but the fact was, he bore royal blood. He had possibilities Breda had not recognized when he first came bumbling in with his awkward introductions. If only Bedo in his turn had not shown an interest in Cella, with her too-innocent smile and her endless stories about her poxy terrier. Cella had made a bad mistake; Bedo had been caught up in it. Too bad for them. They'd never get in Breda's way again.

A sudden brilliant thought came to her, making her laugh out loud. She saw how it could be done; how not only Eile but the next on the list, that weird little child, could be handled in one bold move. They were always together, the three of them: the Gael, her daughter, and the queen's fey offspring with his scary eyes and his odd silences. The deformed baby was beyond Breda's reach. It was clear they didn't trust her, Tuala and Bridei; they had extraordinary measures in place to keep her out of the royal apartments and out of the garden, as if she had some filthy disease. And they let Eile in. They left her in charge of their son. It was wrong. It was an insult, and it was up to Breda to put it right.

WHEN THE KING and queen of Fortriu returned from their council, Derelei was sitting on the floor by the hearth, rocking to and fro. The nursemaid said he'd been that way awhile. Anfreda had woken, cried, had her wrappings changed and been soothed, and all the time her brother had done nothing but rock. His eyes had stayed fixed on the wall and when the nursemaid had knelt by him he had not seemed to see her.

Tuala told the young woman not to worry and dismissed her for the evening. Then she sat down to feed Anfreda and Bridei settled himself cross-legged a little way from their son. This did not seem the trance of a seer; the eyes were too blank, the small body too rigid. Equally, it was not a seizure, something that might be dealt with by the administration of a herbal draft. That Broichan's apparent defection had wounded and confused her son, Tuala knew well already. It had become evident that time was not healing that hurt. It seemed to her, tonight, that the damage done had been more grievous than anyone had realized. Derelei seemed shut off, unreachable. It sent a chill through her heart.

"I did ask Eile how he was earlier," she murmured to

Bridei. "She said he was quieter than usual. And apparently Saraid keeps saying he's sad. But this is new, this . . . withdrawal."

"Derelei," said Bridei quietly. "Derelei, Papa's here, and Mama, and Anfreda. You're safe."

The rocking continued. Bridei reached out a gentle hand to touch his son's shoulder. Derelei shrank away as if terrified, then began his steady movement once more.

Tuala saw the stricken look on Bridei's face. "He doesn't see you," she said. "I think he's not only sad, but frightened as well. The scrying bowl has not shown me Broichan for a long time. My confidence that he'll walk back into White Hill when it suits him is beginning to wane, Bridei. It's been too long. Something's happened to him; something Derelei knows but can't tell us."

"You believe Broichan is gone from us forever? A victim of the winter or of his own misguided attitude to the truth?"

"I cannot believe the revelation that I may be his daughter would drive him to complete despair. He is too strong for that. But perhaps, if it compelled him to seek solitude and he lost sight of the fact that he is of mature years, in indifferent health and not only druid but frail human as well, he might have fallen victim to the harsh season. All the same, I can't bring myself to accept that he'll never come back. I've had all kinds of feelings toward him over the years: distrust, anger, terror, concern. If he is indeed my father, it would be deeply sad if I never got the opportunity to show him a daughter's love."

The little white dog, Ban, had been watching the child from under a chair, wary-eyed. Now he crept out and went to Bridei; in the quiet of the family apartments the creature was prepared to forget his dignity awhile, to climb onto his master's knee, curl up and fall heavily asleep. Anfreda finished feeding. Tuala walked up and down awhile, holding her daughter against her shoulder. Eventually Derelei's rocking slowed and ceased, and he lay down on the mat before the hearth, thumb in mouth. When

Bridei, dislodging Ban, reached to gather up his son, Derelei made no protest. Bridei held him close, cradled like a baby.

"He's shivering," Bridei said.

Tuala could see a terrible fear in her husband's eyes. The touch of the Nameless God was everywhere: the god whose command Bridei had disobeyed long ago at the Well of Shades.

She put Anfreda to bed and came back with the little blanket Derelei liked to hug at nighttime. They wrapped it around him; he had turned his face into his father's breast now and clutched onto Bridei's tunic.

"You remember," Tuala said, fetching a jug of mead and two cups, then sitting down beside her husband, "when Broichan first went away and I said I thought I would be able to find him?"

"I remember." Bridei's tone was full of unease.

"Perhaps I should try. Derelei's really scaring me. I can't be with him all the time. I'm reluctant to trust his care to anyone but Eile. Elda is close to delivering her own infant; with the twins to watch over, she has more than enough to handle. But I think there will come a point when, if we take no action, even Eile's firm kindness and Derelei's attachment to Saraid will not be enough to keep this in check. Just now, he seemed . . . almost crazed."

"You know I've always respected your decisions. You know I'm as worried about him as you are; guilty, too, that other matters occupy me so much I cannot give you the support you need."

"You do very well, dear one; no need for apology. We always knew it would be like this. Kingship is a lonely road. Go on, finish what you were saying. I can sense what is coming."

"You just said you think Broichan may be dead. We performed the most thorough investigation and the most rigorous search; the only thing we didn't try was sending Drustan out to scour the forest from the air. How can it help even to talk about that other possibility now?"

"You're not saying what you really want to say, Bridei."

In his father's arms, Derelei now seemed asleep, lids closed, thumb plugged in mouth. Bridei moved a hand to stroke his son's soft curls. His voice was very quiet. It was not the strong, sure voice that had become so familiar to his chieftains and advisers. "The thought of your trying this fills me with utter terror," he said. "A transformation, becoming some other creature, then going off on your own into the forest with no idea if he's dead or alive, or even if he's there at all . . . I will not say, what about Anfreda? I will not ask what would happen to our son if he lost not only Broichan but his mother as well. I will not even point out that you've never tried this kind of metamorphosis before; that you do not know the risks. If you think you can do it, you probably can. But, Tuala . . . everything in me shrinks from the idea. Surely we can wait a little longer; seek the wisdom of the gods; give Derelei a chance to recover on his own. Perhaps I am selfish. I don't want to lose you. I don't think I could go on without you."

She met his eyes. "Would you forbid me to attempt this?" she asked him.

"You know I would not, despite my fear. You must make your own choice. I wonder at your capacity for forgiveness. Broichan has hardly shown you the same degree of concern. Not only has he never risked his life for you, quite the contrary: he was prepared to sacrifice you for what he saw as the greater good."

Tuala considered this. There were images in her mind, memories of those things the seer's craft had granted her over the long season of the druid's absence. "If he returns," she said, "I believe he will have recognized that error. I have forgiven him that." It was only as she said this that she realized its truth. The feeling of kinship had crept up on her, even though the bond was not proven. Now, when she thought of Broichan, she no longer thought, *Bridei's foster father*, or *king's druid*, but *my father.* "Yes," she mused, "and I've surprised myself. Maybe he got things wrong, horribly wrong on occasion, but he believed he was serving the goddess in the way she required. If my vision did represent truth, discovering he had offended her must have been hard for him. He always held obedience so high."

There was a lengthy silence. Then Bridei said, "If you did it, what form would you choose? When you were a little girl you told me once you dreamed you were an owl. Is that what you would do, take a bird form as Drustan does? I suppose that would allow the best capacity for a search."

Tuala leaned over and kissed him on the cheek. "I know how much you hate this. I hear it in your voice. I see it in your eyes. Thank you for being prepared to talk about it, at least. No, not a bird; even I think that is too dangerous. I would choose something closer and more familiar, I think. It's probably best that I don't tell you. Your imagination will conjure up more dangers to whatever creature I become than the real world could possibly hold."

"When—?"

Tuala shivered. "I don't know. I will be honest with you, the prospect frightens me. I haven't forgotten that Anfreda is dependent on me. This is not something I can do between dinner and suppertime. We'd need to find a wet-nurse for however long it takes. And we cannot do that without drawing attention to my absence. I know how perilous this is. I would not complicate matters by having half of White Hill know your Otherworldly queen plans to make a very personal use of deep magic. The whole thing requires a great deal of thought. And calm. It is so hard to be calm when Derelei . . ." She faltered, then drew a deep breath. "Perhaps we'll wait a little longer. Maybe you were right earlier. Maybe Derelei can come out of this by himself."

"I would welcome that delay. Each day a few more of our visitors leave, and that reduces the risk of unfortunate gossip. If we could wait until Keother was gone, I'd be happier. He seems in no hurry to move on."

"Very well, then, let's at least wait a few days. With Eile here, I do have one reliable source of support for Derelei. That young woman has quite a gift. Saraid is a sweet child; I can see she's been brought up with love. I often wonder what Eile's background is. She's very reticent on everything that happened before she reached White Hill."

"It's Faolan who interests me," said Bridei. "I don't think I can send him out again; not for some time. Underneath that cool exterior he's a bundle of nerves."

Tuala smiled. "Let us hope Eile's sure touch can be extended to your right-hand man. I'd like to see Faolan happy at last. I wonder what happened when he went home?"

"I don't suppose he'll ever tell us," Bridei said.

There was a discreet tap on the door; both Tuala and Bridei started. Ban was instantly alert, ears pricked, body tense. Since Dovran was on guard outside, the visitor must be one of the familiar, trusted circle. Nonetheless, Tuala gathered up Derelei and retreated to the sleeping quarters while Bridei called, "Who is it?"

"Ferada. I have some news I think will interest you."

When Tuala had returned from putting Derelei to bed, and more mead had been poured, Talorgen's daughter gave her account to the two of them. The news was startling. A man had come in a short time ago, after ferrying a load of wood up Serpent Lake from beyond Pitnochie. A boat was on its way, and in it a group of Christian monks, nine or ten in number. There was talk of them all the way down the Glen. That much Bridei had expected, if not quite so soon. But there was more to come. The party had put in at a settlement on the shores of Maiden Lake where a young man lay on the point of death. Accounts varied as to the cause of his illness: the flux, an ague, a scythe wound turned foul. At any rate, a visit by the local healer had achieved nothing, another by one of the forest druids had proved fruitless, and the victim's kinsfolk had resigned themselves to lighting candles and waiting for Bone Mother's arrival. In such a state of despair, they'd probably decided it didn't matter one way or another if they let the Christians in, Ferada commented, since things could hardly get any worse.

"And then," she said, "apparently the leader of these monks, none other than this Colm we've heard mention of, laid his hand on the dying man's brow and spoke a powerful prayer to his own deity, whereupon the fellow opened his eyes, sat up, and greeted his family. He was completely cured; a bit shaky on his feet, but in good health. The father and mother, the sister and brother fell to their knees, but Colm raised them up and bid them turn their hearts to the new faith, the power of which they had just witnessed with their own eyes. It sounds a fanciful tale, I know, but the man who brought it here said he heard versions of it, and stories of other such miraculous feats performed by this cleric, in several different settlements along the lakes. There's a lot of talk, and it centers on this Colm's power and influence. It seems to me it hardly matters if the substance of the tale is true or not. What's important is that folk believe it. I thought you'd want to know promptly."

"If he's already come beyond Maiden Lake," Bridei said, "his party could be here in a matter of days. Do they go under sail or oars?"

"That I can't tell you. I did hear that your old friend Brother Suibne is among them. It was his task to translate his leader's words for the local populace. It seems folk's initial distrust melts away like snow in summer when they hear these wonder tales."

"I see. I will speak to this boatman myself after supper. Have you mentioned this to Fola?"

"I haven't seen her since this morning. I've been packing up to return to Banmerren tomorrow; it's past time that I paid my students some personal attention. Fola was thinking of traveling with me."

"It seems we may need her here a little longer," Bridei said. He was pale; Tuala saw the signs of an approaching headache of severe proportions. Her husband was plagued by these at times of great pressure.

Ferada nodded. "It's evident the court of Fortriu will not be able to call on its powerful druid at this critical time," she said. "I wonder how Colm and his brethren will react to a woman as the king's chief spiritual adviser."

"Fola can be formidable," Tuala said, "for all her diminutive size. She will do a better job of standing up to this visitor than, say, Amnost of Abertornie would. We'd have been obliged to ask him to stand in for Broichan if he hadn't already left for home. A shy sort of man; he was most uncomfortable in the confines of White Hill."

"Fola doesn't like it, either," Ferada said. "She'd much rather be outdoors with oaks as her walls and the sky as her roof. Bridei, I have another reason for coming here. I have a request from my brother."

"Bedo?"

"No, it's from Uric. Since the boys are not permitted in the royal quarters anymore, and since this is apparently deeply private, he's made use of his elder sister as go-between."

"Deeply private?" queried Tuala. "Should I absent myself?"

Ferada smiled. "That shouldn't be necessary. Uric wants to borrow Ban for the day tomorrow."

Bridei stared at her. "Borrow my dog? Now that I didn't expect. May I ask for what purpose?"

Ferada was abruptly serious again. Tuala, who knew her friend very well, could see the reddish tinge around her eyes and the pallor of her cheeks. Garvan had commissions at White Hill. If Ferada was leaving, that meant a difficult farewell. "Father has told you, I think, that Uric and Bedo are on some kind of quest. Uric has been spending a lot of time out riding. He wants to take Ban with him next time. I assume he thinks this particular dog can sniff out whatever it is they're looking for. They're being quite mysterious about it all." She eyed Ban skeptically.

"We have hunting hounds in the kennels. They are trained to track by scent. Ban is just . . . a dog."

"Whatever he is," Tuala said, looking down at the small white creature who sat at Bridei's feet, "Ban cannot be described as *just* anything. He's a being with a complicated and very long history."

"Even so," Bridei said, "what Talorgen told me suggested this particular scent has long gone cold."

"It can do no harm," said Tuala. "As long as Ban is prepared to go."

Ban was a one-man dog. Since the day when he had first appeared by the scrying pool at Pitnochie, a creature from a vision made suddenly flesh and blood, he had shadowed his master with a loyalty that was as complete and absolute as a dog's can be. Left behind when Bridei rode to war with the Gaels, Ban had been the saddest being at White Hill; on Bridei's return, the most joyous.

"Tell Uric I'll meet him at the stables in the morning," Bridei said. "A run won't hurt Ban. I may well make my permission contingent on your brothers' agreeing to limit their activities to this one last venture before returning home with their stepmother. My belief is that the episode they're concerned about is best forgotten. As for Ban himself, if I bid him go, he'll go. I hope he's not too much of a disappointment to Uric. Rabbits, he's got a talent for flushing out. But I doubt very much that that's what your brothers are looking for."

EILE DIDN'T KNOW quite what she felt. After taking Derelei back to his nursemaid, she went to her quarters with Saraid and found herself straightening the blankets for a third time and taking one gown then another out of her storage chest and putting them away again. Both she and Saraid were far better clothed now, for the kindly

Queen Rhian had sent them garments from a household
store of good, plain wear, and Tuala had made a gift of
several of her own old gowns. As Eile's hands worked
automatically, folding and smoothing the clothes, feelings were churning away inside her, a monstrous jumble
of feelings she could make little sense of.

"Mama sad?" inquired Saraid, who was seated on the
green mat doing up the fastenings of Sorry's gown. At
Cloud Hill, she had been trained to call her mother Eile,
so as not to draw attention to the irregularity of her
parentage. Here, where the twins and Derelei all used
Mama and Papa, Saraid had fallen into the same habit. It
made Eile smile.

"No, I'm not sad. I'm happy that Faolan's back." That
was true, but much too simple. She was more than happy,
she was joyful. She was also confused and afraid. When
she'd asked him to put in words the message he should
have left them, she'd expected a simple apology. Not a
declaration. She tried to make sense of it. What had he
meant, exactly? The words had been almost . . . tender.
But a father could speak thus to a daughter, or a brother
to a sister. Had he really dreamed of her and Saraid
every night? What kind of dreams?

That was not something she could ask him. By speaking thus, by looking at her the way he had, by showing
his jealousy of Dovran so plainly, he had changed things
between them. He had indeed made this complicated.
And now she was so mixed up she wasn't even sure she
would be able to go to supper in the hall, with many eyes
on her, if Faolan was there. As for afterward and talking
to him alone, here in her bedchamber, she feared it and
longed for it. One glimpse of him had brought their journey vividly back, the nights in makeshift shelter, the eas-
iness of their talk as they grew accustomed to each other,
the memory of how wonderful it had felt to have a true
friend at last and to know he would keep them safe. The
fact that she had found a haven at White Hill and now
had new friends did nothing to weaken that bond.

She got out the plain blue gown again, the one Líobhan had given her. "Maybe I should have supper with you, Saraid," she muttered. The White Hill children usually had their meals in a small area off the kitchens, under the supervision of a senior maidservant. "I think I'm too much of a coward for this." Nonetheless, she fetched water, stripped and washed first Saraid then herself, trying very hard not to think of Dalach. *Clean yourself up. I don't want your stink on me.*

Saraid sat quietly, clad in a little skirt and blouse of dove gray, while Eile put on the blue gown and brushed her hair with such vigor that the fiery strands crackled. She put on her stockings and the good indoor shoes she'd been given at Blackthorn Rise. That seemed so long ago; so far away. They had come a great distance, a distance that could not be measured simply in miles.

Eile paced nervously. Saraid watched her. After what seemed an impossibly long time, the sound of a metal plate being struck with a wooden spoon out in the courtyard indicated supper was imminent.

"Here we go," Eile said.

When Saraid was settled with Gilder and Galen and a small clutch of other children deemed old enough to sit up at a table to eat, but not yet ready for the adult meal, Eile wavered a moment. She could make do with a bowl of the soup the maidservant was giving the little ones, then go quietly back to her chamber. Then, if he decided to come, she'd deal with it.

"Bye, Mama," Saraid said, blowing a kiss.

"Bye," Eile said, deciding she must be brave. "Enjoy your supper." It was possible, she thought, that she wouldn't even see him in the hall anyway. Despite so many folk packing up and leaving court, there were still fifty or more at the table every night, a press of people, and the only ones she got to talk to were the folk seated near her.

Hovering in the children's dining area had made Eile later than usual. She scanned the hall but could not see

Faolan. Dovran was guarding the king; he stood behind Bridei's chair, stern and watchful. Bridei looked tired. Tuala, seated beside him, was pale and drawn. Eile knew the queen was worried about Derelei. He'd been behaving increasingly oddly in recent days, not that he wasn't always an unusual child, but he'd been much harder to cajole out of his fits of melancholy. Eile resolved to offer her services for tomorrow morning. She would take Saraid and Derelei for a really long walk, an exploration of new parts of White Hill. She would tire them out so they had a good sleep in the afternoon. That way, Tuala could at least get some rest. She was feeding a baby, after all.

Garth was holding up a hand, beckoning Eile. The usual assortment of folk sat close to him: Elda, Wid, Garvan, and Ferada, these last two tonight seated almost side by side; there was one empty place between them. Eile made her way to the table and sat in the spot they had kept for her, between Garth and Wid. A surreptitious glance up and down; she couldn't see him. Perhaps she'd been braver than he had tonight.

"Did you hear about the Christians?" Ferada was asking the old scholar.

"Mm," murmured Wid, applying himself seriously to the barley broth. "Expected, of course. That they'd make their way to court with a request or a petition or suchlike. They want the king's permission to spread their doctrines throughout Fortriu, as others of their kind are doing in Circinn. I suppose Bridei should be pleased that they're taking the trouble to ask. What nobody expected was an arrival attended by miracles. Folk like feats of magic. That kind of thing gets their attention. This Colm is astute."

"You think it's true, then?" Garth asked. "That this priest raised a fellow from his deathbed?"

"Who knows? Perhaps the man wasn't as sick as everyone thought."

"Even Broichan could not perform that feat," said Elda. "Raising the dead."

"The almost dead." Wid broke off a chunk of oatcake and dipped it in the soup. "Then we have to ask ourselves, was it magic or miracle, and what is the difference between the two?"

"You need Fola to debate that question," Ferada said, then turned her head. "Ah, someone's even later than you, Eile."

There he was, walking down the hall toward them between the tables. He was clean-shaven now and dressed in fresh clothes, blue and gray, the anonymous kind of garb he favored. He was trying not to limp. And it seemed to Eile that, once she set her eyes on him, there was nothing else in the hall worth looking at. She did not smile or nod or offer a greeting; she simply fixed on his well-schooled features, his dark, guarded eyes that held, tonight, the same expression she had seen when he uttered those words: *I will dream of you every night.*

"Sit here, Faolan," Ferada said, indicating the place between herself and Garvan. "You nearly missed the soup."

Faolan halted, standing behind the bench, gazing at Eile across the table. For a moment she wondered if his knee was so painful he could not perform the maneuver required to scramble over the bench and sit. Then his eyes moved to Garth and he gave a little jerk of the head. Garth sighed, slid his own bowl, knife, and spoon across the table and put the untouched ones from the empty spot in front of him. He got up and moved around the table, which involved edging behind a large number of folk and drawing considerable attention to himself. Elda, Wid, Ferada, and Garvan watched with undisguised interest. Faolan came the other way. If the leg hurt, he disguised it well. Eile felt him settle beside her. As he sat down, his hand brushed hers and she felt the blood rise to her cheeks. She reached for the ladle and spooned soup into his bowl; it was something to do.

After that, although the talk went on, lively and at times combative, about the Christians, the threat they posed and what the king should do about it, Eile heard it without comprehension. The awareness of him beside her, so close, the new feeling that engendered, something sweet and good and at the same time deeply unsettling, robbed her of the ability to take in anything else at all.

"You two not eating?" inquired Garth with a smile.

Faolan had consumed barely a mouthful of the soup. Now he had a small piece of tonight's pie on a platter before him, but he had not picked up his knife. Eile found herself unable to speak; she could not even manage an inconsequential remark that might make this more like any other supper. To divert herself she looked up toward the king's table, and was surprised to find two pairs of eyes fixed intently in her direction: Dovran's, somber and questioning from where he stood guard and, more alarmingly, Breda's, narrowed in apparent fury before Ana's sister turned pointedly away. Eile knew she had displeased Breda with her entirely reasonable refusal to become a handmaid. But that look seemed quite out of proportion. Maybe she'd done something else wrong, something she didn't even know about. Well, at least this had put a topic of conversation into her head. Faolan had seen Dovran's stare and was returning it in kind.

"Don't forget you have to work together," said Garth.

Eile spoke to Faolan in Gaelic, keeping her voice low. "While you were away, I had the opportunity to assist at the wedding, Ana's and Drustan's. Ana's sister was unwell that day and I was invited to take her place. It was beautiful, Faolan. A druid came from the north to conduct the ceremony. It was at dusk, out of doors. I know they will be happy together. If you want, I can tell you all about it."

Faolan nodded absently. His hand was right beside hers on the bench.

"I know it's a little difficult for you," she went on, "but I think it would be good for you to hear it. What I saw, and what I know of Drustan, convinced me that she will be loved and looked after for the rest of her life." She hoped the babble of talk around them would prevent those of their neighbors who understood Gaelic from hearing too much of this rather personal statement.

After a moment Faolan said, "If you wish, tell me."

"I . . . It was not so much my wish to tell it . . . More your need to hear."

He was looking down at his platter. His reply was little more than a whisper. "It was not of Ana that I thought while I was away."

Eile drew a deep, steadying breath. "Perhaps we should talk about something else," she said.

"I cannot tell you where I have been or what I have been doing. I regret that, but it's the nature of my work for the king." His hand had edged closer; it touched hers for a moment. It was extraordinary how such a little thing could make a flush rise to her face; how it could set her heart racing thus.

"I could tell you what I have been doing. It's not very interesting."

"I want to hear it."

"Eat up that pie and I'll tell you. You look tired and I know you're in pain. Good food will help you mend more quickly."

"Does what you've been doing include ordering small children about?" Faolan cut his pie, then used the knife to convey a morsel to his mouth.

"Not ordering. Usually they just do as I tell them. Actually, it's Saraid who's taken to issuing orders . . ."

"Use your new language, Eile," put in Wid, a look of mock ferocity on his craggy features. Eile and Faolan turned their heads toward him in unison. Something in their faces made the old man say, "Ah, well, maybe not tonight. The return of friends merits some relaxation of the rules, I suppose. Your young lady there has proven to be quite a scholar, Faolan. She's apt; very apt."

"I don't suppose Eile likes to be called my young lady," Faolan said. "She is her own woman. If you've been spending time in her company, I imagine you know that already."

"Fortriu abounds in women who know their own

minds." Wid chuckled, glancing at Ferada. "It must be something in the water."

"I am not a woman of Fortriu," Eile said in the Priteni tongue. "He means well," she added in Gaelic, finding that, without any real decision at all, she had moved her hand just far enough to curl it around Faolan's on the bench between them where nobody else could see. She saw the color rise in his face; his fingers tightened on hers, and she felt warm all through.

"I heard that," said Wid, grinning. "Best watch her, Faolan; now she's got two languages she's becoming dangerous."

"You should see her with a pitchfork," said Faolan. His voice was entirely calm. The tension in his hand told Eile a different story.

Over the pie and the pudding that followed it, she gave him an account of her daily routines at White Hill; of Saraid's blooming confidence, of the bond between her daughter and Derelei, of the trust Tuala had placed in her. She even described the clothes she had been lent and the wedding dress she had constructed for Sorry. "But," she said eventually, "I don't imagine this is really of much interest to you. Apart from being reassured that I did quite well without you."

"I did not do so well without you," said Faolan. "It's difficult to talk here. I find myself not at all in the mood for eating, nor for making conversation in public."

They were keeping their voices low; their companions at the table were now involved in a debate about the nature of miracles, and if they were listening to the soft flow of Gaelic they gave no sign of it.

"I'm going soon anyway," Eile said. "I have to collect Saraid and get her to bed. You need to remember . . . You shouldn't . . ."

"I understand, Eile. I know people see things and jump to conclusions. I'll wait awhile here. All the same . . ." His hand tightened around hers once more.

Dovran was still looking at them, and Eile did not

much care for what she saw in his eyes. Perhaps, after all, she should have been entirely honest with Dovran from the first. If she had told him she thought he was a nice young man, but that she still had to work very hard not to flinch when he touched her, he would likely have turned his attentions elsewhere. It had been unfair to be friendly when she knew she could never meet Dovran's expectations. As for what was between herself and Faolan, there was a barrier to surmount before the true nature of that would become apparent. Perhaps the talk of miracles was apt. No, best not think that way. She was in danger of setting her expectations too high; of wanting the impossible. That was to invite disappointment. It had been an early and hard-learned lesson, and she'd best not lose sight of it now. Causing your own heart to break was surely the ultimate stupidity.

"I'd best be going," she said with artificial brightness, and rose to her feet, her hand still in Faolan's. "I must fetch Saraid. Good night all. Ferada, good wishes for your journey."

"Thank you." Ferada was somber now. "You should come and visit us at Banmerren some time, Eile. I think my work would interest you."

"I expect it's all singing and fine embroidery," Eile said, grinning. "Not my sort of education at all."

Ferada gave an uncharacteristic snort of laughter. "I hope you will come. I have hopes for Saraid, in a few years' time. Perhaps her calming influence on small boys may extend to girls as well."

"Thank you. I don't know how long we'll be staying here. But I'm grateful for your kindness."

Faolan's hand clung to hers a moment longer. She felt his fingers brush hers in a slow farewell before he relinquished her touch altogether. Then Eile turned and left the hall, not looking back.

15

SHE MUST HAVE been waiting. When he scratched on her door, she opened it immediately. Faolan slipped through; Eile closed the door without a sound.

Saraid was still awake, bolt upright in bed with her big eyes fixed on him. "Feeler sing a song," she ordered.

"I'm sorry," Eile said. "I told her you were coming, and she was too excited to go to sleep. We generally have a song before bed, or a story. I've tried to keep that up." Then, to Saraid, "I'll sing it, Squirrel—"

It seemed to Faolan there might be a number of tests presented and that he must do his best to pass every one. "What kind of song is it to be?" he asked the child as he moved to sit on the bed.

"A song about Sorry." At a look from her mother, Saraid added, "Please."

For a man who had once been a bard, albeit a long time ago, this was not a difficult challenge. He gave a tale of Sorry's exploits, cast in the form and style of a mythical adventure, while the little girl stared, enthralled, and Eile, seated on the storage chest, spoke not a word. He had Sorry suffer a terrible accident and endure surgery in stoic silence; he had her ride in a boat over monstrous seas; he had her gifted with new clothes that made her the loveliest creature anyone had ever clapped eyes on. This seemed a good place to stop; he put in one final chorus. By now Saraid's small voice could be heard joining in the fa-la-la's and fol-de-riddle-o's.

"Time for sleep now," he told her.

"More?" asked Saraid hopefully.

"No more tonight. Of course, this song has many, many verses. Enough for any number of nights."

"How many?"

"Lots and lots. As many verses as Sorry has adventures. But we'll save the rest for later."

"Ah, now you've started something," observed Eile with a smile.

He smiled back, hearing the nervous edge in her voice, which echoed an uncomfortable sensation in the pit of his stomach. This had not been allayed by the need to concentrate on the music.

"Mama do story now," Saraid said, keen to take advantage of a sociable bedtime.

"Just a short one, and you must lie down and close your eyes while I tell it."

Saraid snuggled under the green blanket with Sorry beside her and squeezed her eyes shut. "House on the hill," she said. "Please."

Eile seemed a little reluctant. Faolan saw something cross her face like a swift shadow, and the green eyes changed. "All right," she said. "Once upon a time there was a little girl who lived with her mother and father . . ."

". . . in a house on a hill." It was clear Saraid knew this tale word for word.

"That's right. It was not a big grand house, but a neat small one made of stones and thatch. As well as the girl and her mama and her papa, three chickens lived there . . ."

"One black as coal, one brown as earth, one white as snow."

"There was someone else who lived in the house on the hill . . ."

"A cat!" Saraid's eyes snapped open.

"Close your eyes," Eile ordered. "A striped cat who followed the girl around everywhere and curled up to sleep on her bed every night."

"Had the cat a name?" Faolan kept his voice quiet, not sure if he was permitted to participate in what was obviously a long-practiced family ritual.

"Fluffy." Saraid's voice had faded to a murmur.

"Every day the girl fed the chickens with mash and

grain, and she gave Fluffy his dinner, and she helped her mother weed the garden and tend to the vegetables that grew there."

"Cabbages, leeks, and beans."

"And she grew all the plants she loved, the ones with beautiful smells: lavender, rosemary, chamomile. Thyme, sage, calamint, and briar roses."

Saraid sighed, shifting the doll in her arms.

"When her father came home she cooked eggs for him, with fresh herbs stirred in. And he gave her a hug and said, *That's my girl.* When he did that she knew her mama and papa loved her, and that she was the luckiest girl in the world."

A long silence, then Eile said, "Good night, Squirrel," and bent over to kiss her daughter on the cheek. "She's almost asleep," she said, sitting down beside him on the bed. "She was actually quite tired, but she insisted on waiting for you. Consider it an honor."

"I do," said Faolan, getting up and moving to sit on the storage chest, for his need to touch was compelling, and he knew he must tread carefully. There was too much to lose if he got it wrong and frightened or offended her. There was everything to lose.

"Well," said Eile, eyeing him across the two arm's-lengths that separated them. The blue gown suited her; it enhanced the creamy pallor of her skin. "I don't know how to start this. I don't know what to say. You surprised me earlier. What you said. I'm not sure I understood."

"I was so certain you'd be gone. It was a shock to see you. I had . . . I had come to recognize that . . ." He stared at the mat on the floor, his tongue refusing to negotiate a suitable set of words.

"Why did you want me to go away?" Eile was doing better than he was. "To go with Drustan and Ana?"

"It seemed better for you. And for Saraid. Safer. More . . . settled."

"And better for you." Her tone was flat.

"I thought it would be. In some ways, that is still so. I don't know if I can . . . I don't think I can be . . ."

"If you still think that," Eile said, "why are you here?" She had stood up, folded her arms, and walked over to the little slit window overlooking the garden; the summer night filtered in, eerily blue-white. "I mean, here in this chamber, breaking convention."

A deep breath. "Because, when I was away, I couldn't stop thinking about you. Part of me said, yes, it was the right thing to do, for your sake; part of me recognized the kind of man I am, the kind of work I do, the utter impossibility of it. But the other part of me . . . I felt your absence like a wound. Saraid's, too. I knew I'd made the worst mistake of my life. I'd thrown away something irreplaceable; something I thought I could never get back."

She stayed at the window, her back turned. Faolan heard the change in her breathing. His palms felt clammy; his heart was racing.

"What about Ana?" Her voice was tight. "It's not so very long since you gave me the tale of that journey; less than a year since it took place. You love her. I know how important she is to you. I saw the way you looked at her, Faolan." She turned now, hands clutched together, eyes dark. "That kind of love doesn't just vanish away in a season. It's forever, the way they tell it in stories. You're just . . . confused and lonely. Or worse, you're saying this out of pity, because I chose to stay at White Hill and now Saraid and I have no protector."

His feelings welled up, breaking the precarious barrier he had held around them. "Dovran seems all too ready to step into that role, from what I saw. If not him, then another man. I would be a fool if I believed you needed me for that."

"Stop it, Faolan!" He heard the hurt in her voice; saw the twist of her mouth; fought the urge to take two steps forward and fold her in his arms. "Don't say those things! I can't help it if Dovran likes me. Besides . . ." Her voice trailed away.

He had risen to his feet; he made himself sit down again. "Tell me," he said.

"I suppose we have to talk about it sometime." Eile came back to sit on the edge of the bed, one hand on the curled form of Saraid. "For some reason it's even harder to do than it was before. You remember what I asked you to do for me, the thing you refused to do. You know why I asked." She was not meeting his eyes; her voice was very quiet.

"I remember."

"In some ways, all that has changed. I've learned some things here at White Hill."

Things Dovran has taught you. He swallowed the comment. "What things?"

"I used to think it was a falsehood, that women could enjoy lying with men, enjoy giving their bodies and having . . . that . . . done to them, even when it was a man they cared about. After Dalach, I couldn't believe that was possible. But I've seen folk look and touch with such love and tenderness in their eyes and such care in their hands that I have to believe it can be so. Bridei and Tuala; Ferada and her friend Garvan. Most of all—I'm sorry if this hurts you—Ana and Drustan. It's not just friendship and closeness, it's . . . passion. Something deep and wonderful. I saw it."

He nodded, holding his breath.

"You have nothing to say." She had her eyes on him now.

"I would ask . . ." He cleared this throat. "I would ask if this means you no longer need a man to share in a certain . . . experiment."

"Are you saying," she asked, plainly choosing her words with care, "that you would do it now, if I still wanted you to?"

"Tell me first."

"That's not fair, Faolan. This is difficult enough. You tell me first."

He met her eyes. "If you wished me to attempt that test," he said, "I would offer you my best effort, yes."

"Test?" She frowned. "I wouldn't see it as a test. Isn't that sort of thing easy for men?"

"I would consider it one of the most difficult challenges I had ever faced, Eile."

She stared at him. "After what you've said—half said—I can't believe that's because you shrink from the idea of sharing my bed, though that's what I thought when you refused, that first time. It's a challenge for me. But what's so difficult for you?"

"I don't know if you will want to hear an honest answer."

"You think I'm the kind of woman who likes reassuring lies? Tell me. Say it."

"Very well." He found that he had wrapped his arms around himself as if in defense; he stood, holding them by his sides. "First I want to make it clear that I don't . . . expect anything from you. That if we do this, the when and where and how of it will be your choice and yours alone. Then I must tell you that I lived this in my dreams, night after night, while I was away. Lived it as both delight and . . . and as bitter failure. Desire was a constant companion; desire not for Ana, but for you, Eile. I did love her, yes, I will not lie about that; I suppose I still do. But what possessed me that season was like a thing in a story, the passion of a lonely, flawed man for an impossible ideal, a perfect woman forever beyond him. You are . . . real. You are best friend, trusted companion, and . . . and if you would be, most passionately desired lover. Every time I look at you I want to touch you, to put my arms around you. To protect you, to confide in you, to spend my days with you. And to lie by you at night; to have you. I feared to confess this. Please don't be frightened. I'll leave if you want."

"I see." She sat there on the bed, looking away from

him. "A lonely, flawed man needs a lonely, flawed companion, then? That's why you've fixed on me."

"I didn't mean—" He stopped himself halfway through the automatic denial. "Maybe," he said. "Maybe that was what drew us together; made us friends. At least, I think we are still friends."

"I want to tell you something," Eile said. "But I'm going to ask you something first."

He waited.

"I want you to come and sit next to me here, and hold my hand." She looked across at him and his heart turned over at the mixture of warmth and wariness on her face. "Is that all right?"

He did as she asked. Her hand was cool in his.

"Yes," she said, "it is different. It was at suppertime and it still is. I think that's probably a good sign."

"What's different?" He was trying not to consider the effect of her thigh against his.

"I danced with Dovran," she told him. "Holding hands, letting him touch me. It didn't feel like this."

Breathe in; breathe out. "What did it feel like?"

"I didn't like it. It made me afraid. It's the same with other men, Garth, for instance, or Garvan, if one of them passes me the salt and accidentally brushes my hand. It's different with Wid, but he's a very old man. The others, even though I like them, their touch brings Dalach back. I've tried to get over it. I did use Dovran a bit for that. Letting him help me down the steps and that sort of thing. I'm sorry if that makes you cross or hurt." Her voice had gone small and tentative.

"And holding my hand feels different? Should I take it that puts me in the same category as Wid? A father figure?"

After a moment she said, "No, Faolan," and laid her head on his shoulder. "It feels good. Nice. I'm not afraid to touch you. And you don't seem at all fatherly; you never did, even at the start. But I am still afraid of lying with any man. That includes you, even though I wonder if . . . if it might be all right, the two of us. I'm scared of doing it because if it doesn't work, if I can't enjoy it with you, I know it will never be all right. And I want it to be, I want that, my little house and garden, the cat and the chickens and the warm kitchen, and I want Saraid to have a proper family. Perhaps a little brother or sister. She'd love that. Without this, that's not going to happen. It's never going to happen."

"Shh, shh," Faolan whispered, touching his lips to her hair, lifting gentle fingers to brush her cheek. "Is this all right?" he asked, feeling her tremble. "Tell me. Anything I do, if it scares you, anything at all, you must tell me . . ."

"Not this. This is nice. It makes me feel safe. But I will be afraid of the other. I know that."

"I'm afraid, too. Afraid that my ardor will not allow me to go slowly; that desire will make me selfish."

"I don't think you would be selfish about it, Faolan. You have such strength."

He took her hand and lifted it to his lips. "You, too. You're the strongest person I know. Perhaps even stronger than your father. Eile, we need not rush into this." She must surely be able to see how his body belied his calm words; he was hard with desire now, ready for action, and his breath was coming quick and unsteady.

"Not here," Eile said. "Not now. But we should do it soon. It's like a bridge to be crossed, a scary bridge; the sooner you get it over the better. Tomorrow night. That's what I want." She glanced at the sleeping child. "But not in this chamber. The one next door, through there, is empty. Nobody used it after Ana and Drustan left. It's got a hearth and a bed. If we're doing it, I want it to be . . . nice. Not off in a corner somewhere, furtively. I hope that doesn't sound unreasonable to you."

"All the choices are yours," Faolan breathed. "The yes or no, stop or go on. I'll do whatever you want. Eile, I have something I want to ask you. About the future. I should have said it right at the start of this—"

"No!" she said quickly. "Not now. Afterward. After we find out if it's all right or not."

"If that's what you want." *Will you marry a man who looks at least five and thirty, with an injured leg and a tendency to disappear for long periods without explanation?* Better, perhaps, that he did not ask. "I suppose I should go now."

"Will you stay?"

Gods be merciful. "I have to be honest, Eile. If I lie on this bed with you and have to keep my hands off you, I won't get a wink of sleep. And I imagine I will need rest if I'm to meet your challenge tomorrow."

"Oh. I didn't think of that."

"I could sleep on the floor. Is there a spare blanket?"

"You'll get cold. And what about your leg?"

"I'll be fine. Could I kiss you good night?"

"If you want." He heard the anxiety in her voice.

"I do." He touched his lips to hers, parting them only slightly, keeping it gentle. Her hand came up to his cheek; for a brief moment her lips returned the pressure, then she drew back.

"Good night, Faolan. Are you sure the floor is all right?"

"I've slept on harder beds, as you well know. Good night, Eile." He found the blanket and settled himself on the green mat; at least he need not lie directly on the flagstones. Eile moved about, bringing the candle to a small shelf by the bed, changing into a nightrobe—she made him close his eyes—then slipping under the blanket beside Saraid.

"I'm blowing out the candle now," she said, and did so.

The pale light from outside began slowly to enter the chamber, rendering all dreamlike and strange. Faolan wondered if he would wake tomorrow in his bed in the men's quarters and find that this had been another cruel dream.

"Faolan?"

"Mm?"

"Tomorrow might be a bit difficult to get through. Don't you think? Even suppertime today was awkward."

"It was. Yes, I agree. It will seem a very long day."

"I think it might be easiest if we keep busy and see each other as little as possible," Eile said. "It's not that I don't want to see you, and Saraid will, too, but . . . well, you know what I mean."

"Just don't spend the day with Dovran." As a joke, it was not his best effort.

"If he's on duty I can't avoid seeing him, Faolan."

"Will you be looking after Derelei again?"

"Probably. He's not a happy boy these days, and his mother needs time for the baby. I plan to keep him as busy as I can. What about you?"

"I think I'm officially off duty until this leg mends. I'll find a job that keeps me out of your way until suppertime. But . . ."

"Mm," said Eile. "I'll miss you."

"Will you tell me something?"

"What?"

"That story, the house on the hill; is that how it was when you were a little girl of Saraid's age?"

"That's how I remember it."

"Poor Deord," murmured Faolan.

"Why do you say that?"

"If that's what he had, and after Breakstone he came back and he couldn't be part of it anymore . . . What a terrible decision, to walk away before he destroyed it." Deord's heart would surely have broken. No wonder he had never spoken of his wife and child later, in all the long years at Briar Wood.

"He destroyed it anyway." Eile's voice was cold. "Without him it could never be whole again. Who do you think was going to be strong enough to keep it together? Not my mother. She loved him as if he were the sun and the moon and the stars, and he turned his back on her. Not me. I was only eight years old when he left. I bet Dalach had his eye on me even then."

"I'm sorry. I shouldn't have spoken of this."

After a little she said, "It's all right. It's part of what we share now, you and me. Good things and bad things. I liked what you said before, Faolan. When you called me real. Maybe what that means is that I've got bad bits as well as good bits. Weaknesses and strengths. It might be why we seem to suit each other. You're very real. I knew that when you told me my father was dead, even though you so much didn't want to. I knew it when you didn't even consider turning me in to the authorities; when you burned my clothes and told lies for me. I know it tonight because you were jealous, and because you sang a song, and because . . ." Her voice drifted away.

Faolan had thought he would not sleep. His leg ached, there were little drafts coming in under the door, and his mind and body were stirred by restless anticipation, heightened by the presence of Eile lying there in her nightrobe, almost close enough to touch. But sleep claimed him quickly and thoroughly, and he awoke to find dawn light streaming in the narrow window, and Saraid sitting up in bed regarding him owlishly. He realized that, as far as he could recall, he had slept the whole night without a single dream.

(from Brother Suibne's Account)
Our leader being somewhat weary from the miraculous act of healing that God, in His grace, worked through him, he agreed reluctantly to stay one night in a small settlement on the shore of this long, lonely waterway the Priteni call Serpent Lake. The place had a simple jetty and one or two huts; a little farther up the hill was a more substantial dwelling (in this account, all must be taken as relative) and there we were afforded space to sleep. Colm they lodged in the house; the rest of us shared the straw with a sow and a clutch of piglets. The forest nearby, our host informed us, provided

*generous fruits for porcine browsing. We took his word
for it.*

*Colm finds it difficult to admit to weakness. God's
flame burns so brightly in him, it drives him on despite
his human limitations. At such times as these it seems to
me that fire comes close to consuming the man who
bears it. Perhaps that is God's will. Far be it from me to
gainsay the Lord's intention for His servant. Even after
that night, Colm was worn and pale. We persuaded him,
after much debate, that we should remain in that place a
second night, then set sail for the upper margin of the
lake and the king's stronghold of White Hill.*

*The second day, after our morning devotions, we en-
joyed the quiet of the place. The man had taken his pigs
into the forest. The day was fair, with a westerly breeze,
and three or four small boats were out on the lake fishing
with nets. I sat on the jetty with two of my brethren, a
peaceful sensation deep within me, a wonderment at the
beauty of God's creation. I thought of King Bridei,
whom we would soon encounter. I had met him briefly at
the time of his victory over our people in Dalriada. Earlier, when he first became king of Fortriu, I had known
him better and admired him greatly. I wondered how
much kingship would have changed him. He had ever
been strong in his faith, misguided as its tenets are. Perhaps he would close his gates to us, pack us off back to
our home shore.*

*A shout from across the water; I and my brethren
stared in horror as a strange wave arose, rocking one of
the small boats violently while the others, farther away,
remained still. The man on board the affected craft
could be seen tugging at his net; his screams were full
of terror. I felt my gut clench tight. We saw something
swimming around his boat, something so huge we gaped
and blinked and muttered prayers, our hands moving in
the sign of the cross. "God in heaven," muttered Brother
Éibhear. "Can it be . . ." whispered Brother Lomán, who
had gone ashen white. "Fetch Colm," I said, not knowing*

what else might be done, for the thing—a monstrous snake, a dragon, a serpent—had coiled itself around the craft and looked fit to crush it to splinters. The fisherman clung to the mast, mouth stretched wide in terror, but not a sound issued forth now, such was the degree of his fear. The lake was calm, save for that one spot where the water roiled around the scaly monster. It was an uncanny sight.

Then Brother Colm was by my side, tall, grave and calm. With his eyes fixed on the dreadful scene before us, he stretched out his arms so that his body was like a cross, and uttered these words: "God's peace on these waters and on all who ply them. In His name I banish all evil demons, all mischievous creatures, all devilish whirlpools, waves, and currents from this place. Lord, spare Thy servants from the wrath of monster and serpent. We are obedient to Thy will."

As we held our breath, the heaving waters subsided and the creature submerged itself once more. One last flip of its tail, iridescent blue-green in the morning light, and it was gone. With that final, defiant salute, the serpent capsized the boat and the occupant was thrown into the lake.

He yelled for help. We could see him thrashing about in the water. The ability to swim is rare, even among fishermen, and he was already frightened out of his wits. The other sailors could be seen to begin maneuvering their craft closer; it was clear the man would be drowned before they could reach him.

Brother Éibhear stripped off his habit and dived in. I should record here that these waters are particularly cold, even in summer. The lake is chill, dark, and deep year around. I had wondered at the iron amulets I saw around the necks of returning fishermen the previous night; now I understood their purpose. Such superstitions abound among our own people at home. Iron offers protection against what they see as Otherworldly forces. It had not kept the serpent from this hapless fellow.

We prayed; the fisherman splashed and flailed and shouted; Brother Éibhear swam.

"God will not let this poor soul go," declared Colm. "His net will catch the man and gather him safely home."

It was so. The net, in the form of our stalwart Éibhear, reached the drowning man just in time and, not without some difficulty, for the fellow was beside himself with terror, towed him safely to shore. His boat was gone, reduced to a few scraps of timber floating in peaceful waters, but his life was saved by the grace of God and the intervention of His servant Colmcille.

"That was brave," I said to Éibhear, who stood shivering on the shore, dripping wet from tonsured head to sandaled feet. "What if the thing had come back? You saved that man's life."

"Not me," said Éibhear, glancing at Colm. "If I hadn't known his prayers would keep me safe I'd never have dived in. No serpent has the strength to stand up to him. He's like a mouthpiece of God Himself."

As I helped him get dry and dressed while others tended to the half-drowned fisherman, I pondered this. If a great serpent could not prevail against our leader, I wondered if a heathen king might do so. Tomorrow we head for White Hill, and there, I suppose, I will find out.

SUIBNE, MONK OF DERRY

GARTH HAD BEEN looking for him, early as it was. Faolan narrowly avoided being seen coming up a flight of steps close by Eile's quarters. By the exercise of certain skills he managed to meet his fellow bodyguard in a neutral spot near the upper courtyard.

"Faolan! Where have you been? The king wants to see you."

"Now?"

"Now, yes. He's in the stable yard. I won't ask where

you spent the night. You'd best go and see him right away. I think there's a job for you."

"Thanks. And thanks for not asking." They had worked together a long time and understood each other well.

"Any time," said Garth.

In the stable yard Faolan found the king with Talorgen's two sons and a pair of saddled horses. Ban was sniffing about, anticipating an outing. Bridei came over to speak with Faolan outside the young men's earshot. The mission was a surprise: ride out with Uric on some kind of search, take the dog, try to find an unspecified object which the boys seemed to think vitally important. Bedo could not go; he had his arm in a sling. It was plain from the scowls on both young men's faces that they resented Bridei's decision to send his bodyguard with Uric.

"Will you do it?" Bridei asked after his sketchy outline of the job.

"If I can get up on a horse with this leg, then yes." It was something to do; a useful distraction to get him away from White Hill and out of Eile's way until tonight.

Bridei frowned. "I didn't forget your injury. I wouldn't have asked this of you if I hadn't needed your particular skills on the job. Talorgen needs this settled. You've heard about the ill-fated hunt by now, I assume, on which a young woman was killed?"

"Garth told me, yes."

"This is related to that. It was in the same accident that young Bedo broke his arm. The boys have been conducting this search for many days. This is their last chance; I've made that clear. Uric!" He raised his voice. "Faolan has agreed to ride out with you. He's not a watchdog; I'm sending him to help you. There's the added advantage that Ban knows him well and will obey his commands. You're to be back before sunset."

"Yes, my lord." Uric's voice was truculent, but he swung into the saddle with style.

"As for you, Bedo," the king said, "I imagine your stepmother will be worrying about you."

"I'm not a child, my lord king." The young mouth was set tight, the skin pale in the morning light.

Bridei sighed. "I know that all too well. I see your compulsion to solve this puzzle, believe me; I know your feelings are those of a man. But your father is my friend, and he's concerned about you. Sometimes it can be best to let go. To move on."

Bedo gave a curt nod, turned his back and left. Whatever that signified, it was certainly not agreement.

Faolan managed to mount the spare horse without assistance, though not without cost. His leg was protesting at requirements that had, not long ago, been everyday. When he got back he'd have to get some advice on it. "Well, then," he said brightly to the stony-faced Uric, "we'd best be on our way. Where exactly is it we're going?"

BREDA HAD FOUND the perfect place. Bridei's stronghold was well maintained, with a substantial number of folk to keep everything in working order. One would constantly come across people mending thatch or oiling hinges or fixing pumps; not much was forgotten or neglected, nor was there any wasting of space. But she'd found what she needed in a corner down a narrow way below the quarters Keother's party occupied. Exploring one day when she was terminally bored, she'd seen the door and expected a dungeon or torture chamber or other exciting discovery. The place was shut up with a heavy chain through a hole in the door and around a post. The fastening had been moved around to the inside, safe from prying fingers.

Breda had small hands; she was often complimented on their daintiness. It had been a simple matter to ease the thing open and slip inside, then loop the chain loosely shut behind her. A narrow chamber lay within, lit dimly through a low opening at the foot of the outer wall, a space hardly large enough for a cat to use. Perhaps that was why the gap had not been blocked up; no invader was going to get in here unless he stood only knee high. In the chamber was a well. A dry well; Breda had tested it with an amber bead she had in her pouch, from a broken necklace she intended to ask one of her handmaids to restring. She'd heard it land, after a little, not with a splash but with a minuscule thud. She understood why the narrow space had been chained shut. The well rim was low, barely two handspans off the ground, and the place was so dim it would be all too easy to fall in. Especially for a child. Children were easy to lure, even peculiar ones like what's-his-name.

The idea took form in her mind. Any little story would do it, a lost kitten, a treasure accidentally let drop . . . Would this be deep enough? She crouched to peer down, but it was too dark to see. It was perhaps three or four times a tall man's height. A fall might achieve a fair bit of damage. Would he make a noise? Maybe that wouldn't matter. This was quite an isolated corner of White Hill. It seemed to Breda that, with the heavy door closed and chained again, the cries of a little child were unlikely to penetrate far. Of course, the fall might actually . . . No, she wouldn't think of that or she might lose her nerve. This wasn't about the boy, it was about Eile. If Eile let this happen, she didn't deserve her position of trust. That was simple truth.

The opportunity came earlier than Breda had expected. The day after Faolan returned to White Hill, Eile was out and about with the two children, Saraid and the boy. She wasn't staying in her usual haunt, the queen's garden, with Dovran hanging about, but wandering around all over the place. They seemed to be playing a kind of game, with the children hunting and making a collection of things, a feather, a white pebble, a dead moth. Disgusting. Breda watched them surreptitiously as they made progress around the general garden, the small upper courtyard, the steps down to the passageway by Eile's own quarters. Own quarters: that in itself was an irritant. Why was it the little Gael and her offspring got housed in the chambers once allocated to Breda's own sister, a woman of the royal line of the Light Isles? Eile should be in the kitchens scrubbing pots and pans. She should be in the stables forking dung. No, she should be gone. The Gael should not be here at all.

"Eile!" Breda stepped out from behind a pillar, greeting the three of them with an exclamation of surprised delight. "How good to see you! I was hoping you'd forgiven me for being so churlish the other day. I was disappointed, I confess, but not so much that I couldn't understand your reasons for saying no. You look different today. You seem . . . happy." *And it had better be your boring Faolan who's put that look in your eye, because if it's Dovran, believe me, wretch, it'll be short-lived.*

"It's a fine day," Eile said. "That's enough to make me happy. I'm glad I'm forgiven."

"Why don't you bring the little ones along to my quarters for a visit? It would help pass the time. I have some sweetmeats." She saw the look in Saraid's eye; food always worked.

"Oh, well, we were on a kind of expedition," Eile said. The other child hung back, trying to hide in the shadows. Too bad, thought Breda, if he did not care for her. The feeling was entirely mutual.

"That sounds serious. Explorers need sustenance. Why don't we pack the sweetmeats up in a cloth and take them to eat out of doors somewhere? Come on!" Breda held out a hand to Saraid; the little girl took it—she was a lot more trusting than the other one—and they headed off for Breda's quarters.

It was not easy to collect what she needed and get out without a bevy of girls in attendance. All the handmaids wanted to make a fuss of Saraid, who did look sweet in her rose-colored gown. They gave her a ribbon to put on her hideous scrap of a doll and another for her own hair. It was Eile who got them out, saying Derelei was becoming tired and they should be thinking of going back.

The next part would need careful timing. How would she snatch a moment on her own with the boy, who clung so close to Eile, right by her skirts? Or could she actually do it with Eile present, and make it look like an accident? Even if Eile saw, who was going to believe her over Breda? Hearing the account of it, the king and queen must recognize instantly how flawed their judgment had been to entrust their son to a virtual stranger, and a Gael at that.

"Oh, don't go yet," she said as sweetly as she could. "We haven't had our treat. Bring the bundle, Saráid. I have something very interesting to show you. A secret place. I only just found it myself. Come and see; it's down here."

"I don't think—" Eile began, but Saraid trotted ahead at Breda's side and, short of grabbing her daughter and pulling her back, there wasn't much she could do.

Breda unfastened the chain, eased open the heavy door, and went in, Saraid beside her. "Careful," she warned; if the little girl fell first, there would be no way of making this work. "Come, sit down here, Saraid. You can unwrap the sweetmeats if you like."

"Breda." Eile's voice was sharp; she stood in the doorway, eyes still adjusting to the dim light within the narrow space between inner and outer walls. "This doesn't look a very safe place—come, Saraid, Derelei—"

The weird little boy was beside her. Now he would wander across, curious, and Breda would give one quick, sharp push, and . . .

Derelei moved so fast none of them had time to stop him. He was across the chamber and out through the tiny space at the foot of the wall before Breda could suck in a startled breath. Out. Outside the wall, by himself.

"Derelei!" shouted Eile, flinging herself across the

chamber and down to peer through the little gap. "Derry, come back! Oh, gods . . . Saraid, come here, quick! I can't see him at all, can you see where he went? Breda, we have to fetch help!"

Saraid crouched down by her mother, looking out to the sloping hillside, the deep shade under the thickly clustered pines that cloaked White Hill below the fortress walls. "Derry's gone," she pronounced.

"Don't fuss," Breda said, her heart racing with excitement. The plan had changed. The new one in her head was even more thrilling. "He's little; he can't have gone far. You can go up and fetch Dovran, can't you? Send him out and the queen need never know—"

"Don't be stupid!" Eile jumped to her feet. "Of course I must—"

Breda lifted her hand with the bunched-up chain in it and struck the Gael on the temple, hard. Eile had obliged her by standing in the perfect position. Her green eyes went wide with shock and she crumpled neatly into the well.

Saraid stood immobile, clutching her wretched doll, eyes round.

"What are you staring at?"

The child took a step back.

"It's all right," Breda said, realizing there was an element in this new plan that she had not fully thought out. "Come here, Saraid. Come closer. Nice sweetmeats."

The child backed farther, until she was pressed hard against the outer wall.

"Don't be afraid. I won't hurt you." Breda tried to put honey in her voice, but it wasn't coming out right. She saw the terror in the big brown eyes. "Come on, poppet. Come here."

Saraid crouched, backed, wriggled out through the hole in the wall. She did not flee like the other one, but stood just beyond. Breda could hear her sniffing.

"All right, then!" Breda called through the tiny aperture. "Go, if you want. Go and look for your little friend.

I'm sure he's out there somewhere; you'll find him just down the hill."

Saraid began to wail. Gods, it was loud! How was it tiny children had such big voices?

"Hold your tongue!" Breda hissed. "I mean it! You make a noise, you say one single word about this, and your mother will never, ever come back! Do you understand me, Saraid? *Don't tell anyone.* If you want to see your mama again, stop that noise *right now!*"

The crying subsided to a woeful sniveling; the child was still visible through the chink, a swathe of pink skirt, a pair of small feet in kidskin boots.

"Go on, now! Find your little friend! And don't forget, no telling *or else.*"

The boots moved, running, running away. All was silent, save for the thudding of Breda's heart, the thrill of her blood coursing, the gasp of her breathing. She'd done it. She'd done it so neatly she could hardly believe her own cleverness.

She did not look into the well. What was there might be unsightly. She slipped through the door then fastened the chain anew, rotating it so the closure lay inside the shadowy chamber. She made sure nobody was around before making her way not to her own quarters but up to the general garden. There she found a bench under a wild rose heavy with buds, and sat down where nobody was likely to see her. Farther up, Dovran was pacing up and down at the margin between this garden and the smaller one; through the screening fronds of a rosemary bush she could watch him unseen. She unwrapped the sweetmeats and selected one. Then she let her imagination run free.

16

❧

I T WAS AN odd sort of day. Faolan decided early that, if he let his thoughts linger too much on Eile and on what was to come, the time would pass unbearably slowly. Better to try to establish some rapport with this keyed-up boy and do what he was best at: performing the mission Bridei had entrusted to him.

Perhaps it was the knowledge that today was a last chance; perhaps it was all in the way Faolan asked his carefully chosen questions. At any rate, by the time they reached the open ground near the shore where the unfortunate hunt had taken place, the boy had revealed that the item they were looking for was a small, sharp thing, a pin or knife.

"Something that was used to goad the mare," Uric mumbled. "I thought I saw a flash of metal at the time. I went to the stables to check, after we came home, but the horse was covered with scratches; there are bushes and rocks all over that area she crossed. There was no way of picking out a single injury." He had not yet said whom it was he suspected, and Faolan had not asked.

"Mm-hm," Faolan said, thinking the theory, though tenuous, was not far-fetched.

They tethered their mounts beneath a shady tree. Ban stood by Faolan, awaiting instructions. Uric had brought a piece of red cloth, perhaps a lady's scarf, as a scent for the dog. He held it for Ban to sniff.

"You're in charge," Faolan said to Uric. "I gather you've already searched the area quite thoroughly, but not with dogs. Where do we start?"

"Up here first, where we were gathered with our birds. Then down in that direction, toward the water. That's where the mare went, and the king and Dovran after her."

No mention of Breda by name. That alerted Faolan to a possible reason why the boys had kept this so quiet. One did not accuse a royal personage of ill-doing without good proof. "It's been raining," he said. "And it's a long time since this happened."

"I heard Ban has . . . uncanny abilities," said Uric. "I'm hoping that's true. Otherwise I'd have asked for one of the king's hunting dogs."

"All we can do is put him to the test." Faolan gazed down the tree-scattered slope to the marshlands by the shore, and across the broad expanse of undulating ground studded with clumps of vegetation and great stones. It was a big area to search in one day.

They covered the higher part before the sun was at its midpoint. Ban worked busily but unearthed nothing beyond a scrap of cloth and a broken buckle with no sharp edges. Uric wasn't saying much. Faolan observed the pallor, the tension in the young shoulders, the grim eyes. "This must have been difficult for you," he said quietly.

"I need to prove this before our stepmother packs us off home," the young man said. "If Bedo and I are right, there's a person at court who's not just dangerous but completely mad. Someone who has no idea about right and wrong; someone who doesn't understand what it means to kill. We can't walk away and leave things like that."

For a little Faolan made no comment. Then he said, "If that might be true, perhaps you should have come right out with your suspicions to the king."

"Bedo did say something to Father, and I think Father spoke to King Bridei, but all we had was a theory. I suppose it did sound mad. They didn't take us seriously. There's still no proof. And there are powerful folk involved, folk the king won't be wanting to offend."

"You've started to worry me, Uric. I think we'd better head down the hill toward the water. We need to be sure we've covered the whole area before dusk. Earlier, if we can manage that. I have my own pressing reasons for wanting to get back."

"We have to find it," Uric muttered as they set off again with Ban trotting ahead, alert and purposeful.

"Uric," Faolan said, "even if we don't, you should voice your suspicions to Bridei. He must know that, as Talorgen's sons, you and your brother are unlikely to be given to wild suspicions and ill-founded theories."

"You forget," the young man said flatly. "We're also our mother's sons. They kept it quiet, but Bedo and I aren't stupid. We know she was banished because she plotted to murder Bridei."

"As the king's protector, I am aware of that." *And of more; I know the intended assassin was your eldest brother, Gartnait, and that he died not in a heroic attempt to save Bridei's life but through an eldritch intervention by the Good Folk.* Bridei had been able to conceal that cruelest element of Dreseida's plot from Talorgen's family. Ferada had been the only one of them who had come close to the full truth. Best that these young men never knew. They had more than enough to deal with. "I'm certain that makes no difference to the king's opinion of you. It would not affect his response, should you explain your suspicions to him. Bridei never judges a man on who his parents were or on what lies in his past. He looks at a man's true merits and at what is possible for the future."

"Was it like that for you?" The question was tentative; Faolan was well known at court as a man of whom one did not ask personal questions.

"If it had not been so, I would not now be in his employ and under his patronage," Faolan said. "If you wished to confide in him, he would listen without prejudice. Consider it, at least."

They walked on. Ban seemed tireless, moving here and there behind rocks, under bushes, through deep furrows and over small rises. The sun moved across the sky. A flock of geese passed over, honking calls and responses among themselves; down on the wetlands ducks floated and dived and long-legged waders foraged. The buzzing of crickets made a counterpoint to the peeping and chirping of smaller birds in the grassland around the two men and the dog.

Ban was working hard. Once or twice he went off in a rush, raising the men's hopes, then returned with nothing. Time passed, and Faolan found it increasingly difficult to keep his thoughts from Eile and what loomed tonight. If he had been the kind of man who gave credence to gods or spirits, he would have prayed: *Let me get it right. Let this be the right time for her. Let me not lose the two of them over this.* But he knew it was up to him and to Eile, and to whether they might be strong enough, together, to overcome the shadows of the past. If he failed to carry out Eile's mission perfectly, would she give him a second chance? Was their friendship sufficient to allow him that, or would the damage wrought by initial failure be too devastating to mend? *By tomorrow,* he thought, *I will know if I have a future.* For it had become quite clear to him that, without her by his side, the future dwindled to a pointless nothingness. He could no longer form a picture of it at all.

"Faolan?" Uric was holding his voice quiet, but the intensity of the tone alerted Faolan instantly. The dog was off, sniffing hard, ears pricked, his gait one of purposeful pursuit. The two men followed, striding fast, then running as the small, white form bobbed ahead of them through the long grass. After a time Ban halted, pawing at something, then raised his head to look at the approaching men as if to say, *Come on, then.*

Faolan let Uric get there first. The boy crouched to touch, then pick up what Ban had found. His eyes were fierce with some dark emotion: vindication?

"Look," he said, holding the little item out on his palm.

It was a long, jeweled pin, ornate, silver, the decoration a twining tangle of limbs and tail and strange snout, a red stone for the eye. The creature on it was recognizable as the sea beast, one of the ancient kin tokens of the Light Isles. The ornament was the kind of thing a lady would use to skewer her plaits atop her head, so they'd sit high and elegant. Or to keep them out of the way while she was riding.

"You recognize this?" Faolan asked.

Uric shook his head. "I couldn't swear I've seen a particular person wearing it. But there are others who would know. I can ask." His voice held a dangerous edge; it was clear he had scented vengeance.

Faolan crouched down to give Ban a congratulatory scratch behind the ears. "You should take this to Bridei now," he said. "The nature of this jewel narrows its possible ownership considerably. I'm assuming Lady Ana did not take part in the hunt?"

"She was not there; nor was her betrothed."

They began to walk back up to the horses. Faolan was unsettled by the look on Uric's face, though he understood it well.

"I know the temptation," he told the young man mildly. "You have the clue, you've worked for it and suffered for it, and now you're all afire to rush in and make the kill—so to speak—all by yourself. I advise caution. If my guess is correct, you face very powerful opponents here. A clever man, a devious man, would have no difficulty in standing up before the king and making a mockery of your evidence. The presence of this item in the field where the hunt took place does not in itself equate to foul play. Folk drop things all the time."

"I know what I heard," Uric said. "Others heard it, too, but they chose to disregard it. And I saw. Half saw."

"Tell me."

"A flash of something metallic in a certain person's hand; at the same time, the scream. Then the horse rearing up and . . ."

"I see. You must tell Bridei about this, Uric. You should do so as soon as we get back to White Hill."

"Not before I talk to Bedo. We agreed to do this together. He needs to know what I found. This is more his quest than mine. That girl, Cella: my brother liked her. He really liked her."

"I understand brotherly loyalty, but you should talk to Bedo straightaway. If you prefer, I will accompany you when you speak to Bridei. My instincts tell me this is no fanciful overreaction to the sudden loss of a friend."

After a little, Uric said, "Thank you. I didn't expect you to be so helpful. Or to believe me."

"All in a day's work," said Faolan lightly, realizing the sun was descending into the west and that, remarkably, the difficult day would soon be over. How had Eile filled in the long time of waiting? He supposed running around after two small children consumed a lot of energy and left little time for dreaming. He imagined her in the garden, sitting cross-legged on the grass in her blue gown; he thought of her up on the walkway, clutching the hands of her small charges to keep them safe, perhaps looking out over the wall toward this very part of the shore, her hair streaming in the wind. He pictured her back in her chamber, brushing Saraid's long brown locks, telling her daughter that he would be back again tonight and would be sure to sing the next installment of Sorry's adventures. He tried not to think too far beyond that.

They were very quiet riding home. Uric had stowed the silver pin in the pouch at his waist, well wrapped in the red cloth. Ban kept pace, a steady, short-legged warrior. Pines stretched long dark shadows across their way, like warnings of change. Faolan shivered. He had been afraid of tonight, possessed by an uncomfortable mixture of hope and dread. Now, he thought of the chamber with the green blanket as sanctuary; he imagined her arms as home. It would be all right. It must be.

By the time they reached the approach to White Hill, along a thickly wooded way where undergrowth fringed the path and the tree-clad hillside ahead loomed dark against the sky, daylight was fading. Shadows hung around the bushes and the canopy of trees was full of the evening cries of birds, harsh and unsettling.

Faolan was not sure what it was that made him halt, a little sound, a glimpse of something not quite right. "Uric!" he called quietly. "Wait!" He dismounted and walked back a few paces, Ban at his heels.

"What is it?" Uric called.

"Wait there; no need to get down."

Something; a hint of color where so bright a shade did not belong. Yes, there it was, a vivid blue, down under a bush by the track, a blue he had seen before not long ago. He crouched, peering in. From under the prickly branches of a thorn, a pair of black, unwinking eyes stared back at him. The blue was a little gown, with a strip of delicate embroidered ribbon for a sash. It was Sorry.

Faolan's heart seemed to flip over. Wrong; all wrong. Not here, so far beyond the safe walls of the king's stronghold, and almost dark. What had happened? He reached in to take the doll by its limp cloth arm and draw it out. He listened. Only the cries of the birds, the rustle of the foliage.

"Uric!" he called. "Get down and come here!" Then, keeping his voice soft, "Saraid? Eile? Are you there?" No reply. "Call out, Saraid! It's Faolan. Where are you?" It was evident the doll had not been dropped by accident or cast aside, but placed there by loving hands, its pose one of watchfulness. Waiting. Waiting for what? His heart was a fierce drum. In his head, one awful possibility after another played itself out.

"What is it?" Uric was beside him.

"Saraid's doll. Here, in the bushes. They wouldn't have been outside the walls. The child wouldn't leave this behind. It's like another self."

"Maybe they went out walking. Maybe she just dropped it." Uric was trying to be helpful.

"Eile was looking after the king's son. They wouldn't come out. Saraid! Saraid, make a sound so we can find you!" Gods, what a choice; stay here and search as it grew ever darker, or ride for the fortress and risk leaving the child on her own in the woods at night. Eile would never, ever have left her daughter alone out here.

"I heard something," Uric whispered. "Listen."

There it was; not a sob, exactly, but breathing, the stifled, desperate breathing of a terrified child.

"Saraid?" Faolan was on his feet, moving through the undergrowth, going carefully despite his fear, for the child was only three; a crashing, dramatic rescue would only frighten her further. "Where are you, Squirrel?"

It was Ban who found her, running ahead, then announcing success with a single sharp bark. By the time Faolan reached the spot, a little hollow at the foot of an oak, Saraid had her arms around the dog and her face pressed against his hairy coat.

Faolan crouched by her, Uric a pace behind him. "Saraid? It's all right, Squirrel, we've come to take you home." He reached to touch the bunched-up figure and felt her flinch. Her whole body was quivering with tension. "Saraid, look at me. It's Faolan. I've got Sorry here; she found me. Look up, sweetheart. That's it. See, it's me and my friend Uric." She looked like a little pale ghost, eyes hollow, cheeks wet with tears. She made not a sound. "Here's Sorry. She was worried about you." Saraid reached for the doll. Ban turned his head to lick her face. A moment later she was in Faolan's arms, clinging as if she would never let go. Silent sobs racked her body.

He stood up, holding her. "Saraid," he said quietly, "where's Eile? Where's Mama? Is she here in the woods?"

There was no reply; the little face was pressed against his shoulder, the hands clutching his shirt. Sorry was wedged between his body and hers.

"Faolan," murmured Uric, "it will be dark soon. She's too scared to talk."

It was plainly true. Faolan carried the child to his

horse and got Uric to help him mount with Saraid in front of him. She wanted to keep holding on; to bury herself in him. Uric surprised him by talking to her quietly and calmly, explaining she needed to sit up like a proper horsewoman, and that Faolan would hold on to her and make sure she did not fall. She, in her turn, must hold on to Sorry. That way they would all be safe.

"Want me to go ahead and find out what's happened?" the young man asked diffidently.

"No, stay with me. We'll go as quickly as we can. And if you believe in gods, pray that this is not as bad as it seems."

THEY CAME IN through the gates, after the usual challenge from the men on duty. As soon as they rode into the lower courtyard it was apparent something was afoot. Men were assembling, collecting torches, heading off in every direction within the walls. Garth was issuing orders. At the sight of Faolan with Saraid mute and still before him in the saddle, the big bodyguard froze, staring, then hastened over to lift the child down.

"Where was she? Where did you find her?"

"On her own in the woods near the bottom of the hill. What's happened? Where's Eile?" He was cold; cold all through.

"We can't find her or Derelei. We thought Saraid was with them. Nobody's seen them since this morning."

"This morning? And you're only searching now?"

"Eile had the two children; folk just assumed they were safe within the house and gardens somewhere. Faolan, I need to—"

"How can nobody have seen them? This is ridiculous—" He heard the panic in his own voice and made himself breathe.

"The king is speaking to folk now, questioning them. It's being done properly, Faolan, I promise you. But if you found this little one outside the walls, we're going to have to change our tactics. Gods, what a turn-up."

"Saraid won't talk," Faolan said. "She can't tell us what happened." He could feel the little hand holding on to his tunic; the little form by his side, pressing herself closely against his leg.

"She must be able to tell us something." Garth eyed the child, who turned her face away, burying it against Faolan's thigh. "Would she talk to Elda? You'd best take her to our quarters, anyway. We must be able to get something out of her, some sort of clue. Maybe once she's warm and fed and with friends, she'll be prepared to talk. Tell Elda it's urgent."

Faolan nodded, picking Saraid up and wondering if he could bear to surrender her, even to Elda, whom he trusted completely. He was going to have to ask Garth's wife to undress the child and check for injuries; to find out if anyone had molested her. The very idea filled him with a white-hot anger. "I'll be back here as soon as I can," he said, setting a well-practiced veneer of calm on his features. *Eile, Eile . . .* "I'd suggest you get the men organized to search down the hill before the light goes; if Eile and the boy were in the house or garden surely they'd have been seen by now. Uric, our other business must wait. I won't forget."

FAOLAN HAD NEVER seen Bridei looking so white, or so old. This seemed to have sucked something out of the king; it was clear what an immense struggle it was for him to remain calm and composed. He had Aniel with him as he interviewed, in turn, each member of the household who might possibly have seen Saraid or Derelei or Eile that day. Faolan made his report, doing his own hard work to remain in control of his voice and expression. "I don't think Saraid's been hurt," he said at the end. "But she's frightened; whatever has happened, she seems too scared to talk, even to me. Elda's checking to make sure she's unharmed, then she'll try to get something useful out of her."

"We need to know if Eile and my son went outside the walls; whether they went out walking, or were taken by someone. Abducted. Couldn't you question the child yourself?"

"I did try, Bridei. Saraid's closed up as tight as a limpet. She seems determined not to speak."

"Try again." Bridei's tone was uncharacteristically sharp. "I cannot imagine how this has happened. Such a lapse in security here in the heart of White Hill seems unthinkable. You believe they've gone outside the walls, don't you? I hear it in your voice."

"Eile would never leave her daughter alone in the woods. She'd never allow Saraid to go beyond the fortress without her. If Saraid was out, so must Eile be, and Derelei with her."

"They'd have had to go through the gates. None of the men on duty has reported seeing them."

"Indeed. And Eile knows, as all your people do, that Derelei does not leave White Hill without guards in attendance. There's some kind of foul play here, Bridei. We need to move the search out into the woods. Folk can't just disappear within the walls of a place like this. Especially not a little child like Derelei." Faolan did not voice one obvious exception to his own theory; that once a child was dead he no longer made noise when hungry or thirsty or tired. He would not say it; Bridei was strung tight enough already. "I'll lead a search party outside, if you agree."

"It's almost dark. There's no point going beyond the base of the hill before dawn tomorrow; you could easily miss them. Garth has already sent men to the settlement. They'll scour that thoroughly. Yes, by all means institute a search of the woods around the hill, and take dogs. Faolan—" Bridei hesitated.

"What is it?" Faolan was barely listening; his mind

was concentrated on how the search might most effectively be done, how to deploy men and dogs, which were the likeliest spots for a child to conceal himself in. Which were the routes a man, or men, might take if they wanted to abduct a woman.

"You'll hear some talk around the place." It was Aniel who spoke, his grave features even more serious than usual. "Theories about what has occurred and why. It's foolish talk, but folk tend to want to accuse at such times, to find a culprit."

"What are you saying?"

"Eile's a Gael. She's had a position of trust with Derelei. It's inevitable that people will jump to the conclusion that this is a kidnapping engineered by disaffected Dalriadans or by Gabhran's powerful kinsmen in your home country. There's talk that she was planted here in order to do precisely this; to win the king's and queen's trust, then spirit away their son to be held for ransom. Our enemies would have much to gain from such a plot. To some it seems entirely plausible."

Faolan's fists tightened with fury. "You're not telling me you believe this filth?"

"No, Faolan," Aniel said wearily. "I know the girl and I know you. If Eile was given trust, it was because she merited it. Others look at her and see only the enemy. It is not so long since we and the Dalriadans were at one another's throats. These folk have lost fathers and brothers to the Gaels."

"You need to know this," Bridei said, "if you're to take control of the search, in part or in full. We've already had Dovran take to a fellow with his fists for making a remark about Eile. All of us need to keep calm. That is the best way to do this. It is the best way to find them." The king's voice shook on the last words.

"I'm sorry, my lord," Faolan made himself say. "Garth and I will arrange this together. Saraid was close enough to the base of the hill. With luck we'll find the others quickly."

"I want to come with you," Bridei said. "I want to find my son. He's only two, and it's cold out there. Aniel and Tharan say I must not. There is a possibility this whole thing is designed to draw me out of the protection of White Hill by night and to separate me from my personal guards. An assassination attempt. Dovran will remain on duty here with us. Do what you can, you and Garth; know that I rely on your courage and expertise. I'm sorry this has come so close to you. That Eile is involved."

Faolan managed a brief nod, then turned on his heel and left them. The sooner he got back to Garth, the sooner they changed the orders to get the searchers outside with dogs and torches, the better chance they had of finding Derelei before he perished from cold, and of reaching Eile before . . . before something happened to rob her of her newfound happiness and confidence. Before something plunged her back into the nightmare of Dalach.

AT A CERTAIN point, before the sky began to brighten, they called off the search and sent the men home to rest. Almost the entire manpower of White Hill had been out; Faolan had seen Talorgen's sons among the searchers, Uric intent and focused, Bedo doing his best with his arm still strapped in a sling. For now, their other quest must take second priority. Even King Keother had joined the search, attended by his own guards, his shock of fair hair and impressive stature making him clearly visible among the darker, shorter forms of the men of Fortriu. Once or twice the dogs had caught a scent and the search had taken on a new dimension, but each time it had petered out, the hounds losing the trail to mill about in confusion.

With every moment that passed Faolan felt a new

tightening of the heart, a new clutching at the gut. He fought to keep his mind from seeing her in peril, hurt, cold, afraid. To do this job well, he must banish his own feelings entirely. The time was coming when the men must sleep or be unfit to resume this task by daylight. He caught up with Garth and agreed on the order, though his own urge to keep searching was hard to deny.

They went home and the men dispersed quietly to their various quarters; only a token guard was left atop the walls and in the courtyard.

"I'll report to the king," Faolan said to Garth. "I won't disturb Elda at this hour, but it would please me if, before you rest, you would check that Saraid is well and sleeping. If she's awake and asks for me, call me. Please."

"Of course." Garth was showing signs of exhaustion, stalwart and strong as he was. "We recommence at first light, yes?"

"The men must be fed; once that's done, we'll talk to them in the yard. The search must go wider once it's day. I have a plan."

"Good, you've done better than I have; my head's incapable of another rational thought. Make sure you catch some sleep, Faolan. Nobody can go on forever."

It was evident to Faolan, on entering the royal apartments, that nobody was expecting him to announce success. Bridei sat with his head in his hands; beside him was Tuala, calmer than her husband, but with a look in her eyes that stopped Faolan in his tracks. Not sorrow, not fear, not anger, though all three were present there. It was an expression of implacable determination. By the hearth was Aniel, a reassuring presence in his councillor's robe, gray hair rumpled, eyes maintaining calm. A flask, cups, a platter of food stood on the small table. All were untouched.

Faolan had already passed Dovran in the hallway. A glance had gone between them conveying, on both sides, apology, distress, understanding. "I want to search," Dovran had said. "At dawn, when they go out again, I want to be there."

"Someone has to guard the king."

"Let Garth do it. I need to go out. I need to find her."

"That's not my decision," Faolan had told him, swallowing his first reaction. "If you've energy to spare, put it to planning. They could have gone a long way by now. How do we cover the territory with the resources we have? Apply yourself to that. It doesn't matter who finds her, as long as the two of them are found before it's too late."

Now, within the king's quarters, the atmosphere was tense. Faolan reported what had been done; apologized for not doing better. He was feeling quite odd. It was not just the ever-present pain in his leg, but a vagueness, a disassociation, as if his mind did not quite belong to his body. Dimly he was aware that Garth was right. He needed to rest. But who could rest at such a time?

"Thank you," Bridei said. "You should go and lie down awhile. It's not long until sunrise."

"Before you go, Faolan," Tuala looked up from her position kneeling on the floor beside her husband, with Ban close by, "we need to tell you something. Fola! Come through."

The wise woman emerged from the inner chamber. Of them all, she looked the least exhausted, her silver hair neatly caught back, her strong old features serene, though the dark eyes were troubled. "Anfreda's stirring," she said.

"That is good," said Tuala. "Best if she feeds just before . . . Faolan, there's a certain matter you need to know. It's to be kept confined to a very small group of people. Those of us present now, with Tharan and Dorica, already know about it. We'll extend that to Garth and Elda, and also Dovran. Faolan, I . . . I have a way to reach my son. I believe it is possible. I'm not speaking of scrying, of attempting to see him in a vessel or mirror.

We need more than that now. Derelei possesses powerful abilities in the craft of magic. As great, perhaps, as Broichan's, but only partly formed; lacking in the expert controls required to channel such skills to wise use. Derelei is only a little child. His speech is limited; his physical skills are those of any two-year-old boy. He may be a budding mage, but at the same time he's a vulnerable infant with little knowledge of the world and its dangers. I need to bring him home, and fast. There's only one way I can do that. It involves . . . going away."

"Going where?" Faolan asked, but the truth was already creeping up on him, weary as he was.

"Changing," Tuala said. "Assuming another form. I do not believe our son will be found by an ordinary search, however persistent and brave your men may be. His skills in magic will make him hard to track. I know what I intend is dangerous. But it's unthinkable that I risk Derelei's life simply because I lack the courage to do this."

Bridei was saying nothing. Faolan read the king's reluctance in the set of his shoulders and the tightly clenched hands. His heart bled for him. It was a terrible choice. The cost of rescue—possible rescue—for Bridei's son was risking death or worse for his wife. The transformation she suggested would be fraught with peril.

"It goes without saying," put in Aniel, "that this must be kept secret. We all know the possible consequences of drawing undue attention to the queen's special abilities. Dorica knows of a woman in the village who can take on the duties of wet nurse for Lady Anfreda. She'll go down to fetch her first thing in the morning. Offered sufficient incentives, the woman can be persuaded to adhere to the official story, which will be that Queen Tuala is so distressed by her son's disappearance that she can no longer feed the infant herself."

"I intend to remain within the royal quarters and oversee this wet nurse," said Fola. "We'll also explain the truth to the most trusted of Anfreda's nursemaids. Tuala's

illness will be given as the reason for keeping others out.
One of the three of you, yourself, Garth, and Dovran,
will be on guard outside at all times. All of us will keep
our mouths shut until the queen returns." She spoke with
brisk confidence.

"I see." Faolan eyed Tuala with a certain wonderment.
"Your courage impresses me, my lady," he said. "I wish
you success with your mission and a safe return. Meanwhile I will ensure the other search continues. When will
you go?"

Tuala fixed her large, uncanny eyes on him. "After I
feed Anfreda one last time. By sunrise I'll be on my way.
I hope I find my son, and I hope I find Eile for you,
Faolan. She is a courageous girl, and deeply loyal. She
and Derelei will be together, surely." On her son's name,
her voice faltered.

"Go and rest, friend," Bridei said, raising his eyes.
The look of pain on his face left Faolan without words.
"We know you share our fear. I do not expect you to seek
comfort from the gods. But know you are in my prayers,
as is Eile. May the Shining One keep her safe from
harm."

FAOLAN DID NOT go to his own pallet in the men's quarters, but to the chamber with the green blanket. He shut
the door behind him and stood with his back to it as his
eyes accustomed themselves to the dimness. A trace of
light seeped in through the little window. Torches in the
garden outside? Or was it the first predawn blush? Let it
be so, for he needed to be out, he needed to be on the
track; how could he waste a moment while she was still
lost? And Derelei. Derelei's safety had always been his
job since the tiny child first arrived in the world. It was
for Faolan to order the duties of the king's guards; to
oversee the security of the king's person and of his fam-

ily. The fact that he had been gone from court when this happened, gone on the king's mission, made no difference to that. If there was a danger, he should have seen it and been ready for it. If there was a threat, he should have set safeguards. He had failed Bridei and Tuala, and he had failed Eile.

Faolan lay down on the bed, staring up at the shadows in the thatch. *Be strong,* he willed her. *Hold on to hope. Soon it will be day again, and I will find you.* And in his heart, silently, he spoke to her every endearment and every tenderness he could find, such as *sweetheart* and *beloved* and *heart's dearest;* words that, a season or two ago, had not been in his vocabulary. He did not allow himself to weep, for that was an admission of defeat, and if he wished her to be strong he must exhibit that same strength himself. No matter that this cut like a knife; no matter that he felt his heart fraying and coming apart with fear for her and for the child. He would lie still. He would rest. That was the king's order. At the first real hint of light he would get up and organize the men once more, and by sunset Derelei would be back in his father's arms and Eile would be safe. To give her hope, he must find hope within himself.

As THE SKY paled toward dawn, Tuala sat with her baby at the breast, breathing slowly, making herself calm. She hummed a little tune, committing to her memory her daughter's ivory skin, her long dark lashes, her startling pale blue eyes, and her sweet bud of a mouth. Anfreda was hungry; she sucked and swallowed, sucked and swallowed, one minuscule hand patting busily at the curve of her mother's breast.

Aniel had gone away to rest before dawn; Fola was asleep in the inner chamber. Outside, Dovran remained on guard.

Tuala glanced across at her husband, who had gone unusually quiet. She could see the distress in his fine blue eyes. He didn't want her to go, that much was plain to her. He didn't want her to risk the peril of changing. But he would not say so, not now. This was her choice, not his. All the same, she saw in his face that his heart was full of fear, for her, for his children. At every turn, he anticipated the dark god's retribution. All his life, he would bear that burden beneath the assured mask of his kingship.

"Anfreda will do very well," Tuala made herself say, while every movement of the small body, every little snuffle, every glance of her daughter's fey eyes was telling her, *Farewell. Perhaps forever.* "She'll have plenty of folk to tend to her. As long as she's fed and warm and dry, and people don't forget to hold her and talk to her, she'll be perfectly happy. That's all they need at this age." Then, after a little, "Bridei?"

"Mm?"

"Trust me."

He bowed his head. "Always. You must know I do."

"Don't forget, then. No matter what happens."

"Can you tell me where you will go? Which direction, at least?"

She shook her head. "I won't know until I become that other creature. I think I will find the way by scent; by instincts a man or woman possesses only weakly. But I don't believe the tales of abduction and holding for ransom. My heart tells me our son has gone of his own free will. Gone on a mission."

"At two years old?"

"This is not just any two-year-old, remember. This is Derelei. I'm certain he's gone to find Broichan."

EILE WOKE TO pain. Pain in every part of her body, her legs, her arms, her neck. Her head was on fire, her temples throbbed. Her throat was dry; she ran her tongue over her lips and tried to swallow. Cold. So cold, like deepest winter. Where was her cloak, her shawl? Why was it so dark? Where was . . . where was . . . She sank down again, down into oblivion.

⁂

TUALA MADE HER husband stay at the bottom of the steps with Dovran. Fola, whom she would almost have welcomed by her side, had remained indoors with Anfreda. It had been hard for Tuala to put her sleeping daughter back in the basket; hard to turn her thoughts away from all the things that could go wrong and to fix on the Shining One with a prayer: *Whatever happens, keep Anfreda safe.* A finger to the pale, downy cheek; lips touching the rosebud mouth lightly, a promise: *I will be home soon, little one.*

Now, in the small upper courtyard where Broichan had been wont to cast his auguries for good or for ill, Tuala stood alone under a sky touched by violet and gray and pink, closed her eyes, stretched out her arms, and called into her mind a powerful image of what she needed to be. The charm had no words. It came from deep within her, a gift of the Good Folk from whom she was descended, her mother's people. She had not needed to learn this; it was already part of her. She turned once, twice, three times, a slender, pale figure in her plain gray gown, her dark hair plaited down her back, her feet treading noiselessly in their kidskin slippers.

The light changed; a bird flew over, crying a tentative greeting to the dawn. The flagstoned surface of the upper courtyard was bare; the stone table was empty. No woman stood there to greet the new day. Only a small shadow moved at the foot of the wall, a pair of bright eyes, a long tail. A whisk and a leap and it was atop the parapet; in the blink of an eye the creature vanished over the wall and away into the darkness of the woods.

SHIVERING, SHIVERING so hard she could no longer sleep, if sleep it had been, that dark, deep unconsciousness from which she'd fought her way out once again. Where was she? She stretched cautiously, one arm, the other—there was something there, stones, they bruised her hand . . . She tried to move and pain lanced through her shoulder. Gods, it hurt! Her knee would not bend properly. It was dark. It was too dark. Why was it so dark still, as if night went on forever?

She got to her feet, her legs close to buckling under her weight. She reached out one way, the other way; turned, touched, reeled in disbelief. Where was she? What were these walls, so close, shutting her into a tiny space? Memory stirred.

"Saraid?" Eile whispered, her voice rasping and dry, the single word an immensity of effort. "Saraid! Where are you?" If she could have, she would have screamed, but there was something wrong with her voice. Her shout came out as a murmur, her desperate cry a whisper. "Help!" she yelled, and felt the word shrink to a little weak thing before it left her lips. "Saraid," she whimpered, crouching against the wall, hugging her arms around her shivering body. "Saraid, be brave. It'll be all right. Be strong, Squirrel. Mama's coming."

TUALA WAS GONE. Bridei had told her he would accept her decision, and he was always true to his word. Now, holding his daughter in his arms as Dorica showed the wet nurse the alcove where she and the nursemaid would sleep, the way to the privy, the places where clean clothing and fresh water and spare blankets could be found,

Bridei wished he had no need to move before Tuala came home again. If he could just stand here by the window, watching the sky, cradling the warm bundle that was Anfreda, it might be possible to endure the time of waiting without breaking apart.

The wet nurse was called Tresna; she was the wife of a blacksmith. Apparently she had milk enough to feed her own babe, a strapping, rosy-cheeked girl, and Anfreda as well. As for keeping silent about the queen's absence, Dorica had dealt with that in her usual manner, discreetly and effectively. Certain improvements would be made at the smithy. There would be a place at court for an elder daughter, now coming up to thirteen; a good place, not as a kitchen maid but in the sewing room or, if she proved apt, as a nursemaid. Tresna was calm and quiet. She took Anfreda from Bridei's arms and bore her away, making little soothing sounds.

Then he had nothing to do; nobody to hold. He bent to pat Ban and fondle his ears. Then he called Aniel and Tharan and, as the men of the search party gathered in the yard after an early breakfast, the king and his councillors settled to another bout of questioning.

They had followed an order of priority. First interviewed, soon after Derelei's absence was discovered, had been those most likely to have seen him or Eile: the bodyguards, Elda, the royal nursemaids. Fola and Wid; Garvan and his apprentice. Next they had questioned the guards who had been stationed in the outer court and on the walkways, with a good view of comings and goings. By then it had been dark, and Faolan had returned, and the search had gone beyond the walls. All the same, Aniel had continued to speak to the kitchen men and women, and to other folk with children who might have played with Saraid or with Derelei. Faolan had already interrogated the guards at the main gates. They had seen nothing at all.

This morning it was necessary to begin questioning White Hill's guests, those who had for their own reasons lingered on far beyond the time of the victory feast. This was awkward, especially when the guests were people of a certain status, folk who would believe themselves above suspicion.

Still, both Aniel and Tharan were old hands at diplomacy, and they had invited Wid to assist them. The ancient scholar had a wealth of experience in the halls of powerful men. He had used it effectively to school the young Bridei in such matters, and after him Tuala.

They came, at length, to Breda of the Light Isles and her four remaining handmaids. Dorica had provided the information that Breda had at first been friendly toward Eile and that of recent times things had cooled between the two of them. Indeed, once or twice she had overheard Breda making quite cutting comments about this outsider who had so quickly insinuated herself into the queen's favor. Dorica had dismissed it as foolish talk; it was well known that Breda lacked her sister's maturity.

It was not possible to have Keother present during his young cousin's interrogation. The king of the Light Isles had surprised them all by volunteering his services for the search once again. In a way that only added a complication, since Fortriu's royal guest could not be allowed to venture forth without personal guards. To have Bridei's vassal king suffer an accident or be attacked while under White Hill's hospitality would be unthinkable; the political ramifications would be enormous. However, Keother's readiness to help was disarming, and he rode out with his two guards and several of his own courtiers, following Faolan's orders like everyone else.

They called Breda in. The princess of the Light Isles was on her best behavior this morning. She curtsied to the king, then inclined her head to the other men. Eyes on Bridei, she said, "I'm so sorry, my lord. Your son . . . You must be very upset. If there's anything I can do . . ."

"Thank you," Bridei said. "We'd like to ask you a few questions, then speak to your maids. A formality, you understand; we need to talk to everyone who was at White Hill yesterday. As no doubt you've heard, we don't know when Derelei and Eile actually went missing, or how. That makes an effective search much more difficult to mount."

"Oh." Breda waited, hands prettily folded in her lap. In recognition of her status, they had given her a padded stool to sit on.

"How did you spend your day yesterday, Lady Breda?" Tharan asked politely.

"*My* day? You don't mean—What are you saying?" Her blue eyes went round with shock.

"We simply need to find out who saw either Derelei or Eile and her daughter, and when," said Aniel. "And where folk were, so certain possibilities can be ruled out."

"Certain possi—You can't mean—oh, well, it's easy, anyway. I was in my own quarters in the morning; my attendants brought me breakfast. Later on I went out and sat in the garden. I was there a long time. Then I went in to supper. By then everyone was running about with torches."

"What part of the garden?" Aniel asked, narrowing his eyes.

"The main part, of course. I'm not allowed in Queen Tuala's *special* garden." She glanced at Bridei. "I was sitting on a bench near a rosebush. I was there all afternoon."

"Just sitting?" Wid eyed her, his expression one of incredulity.

Breda flushed. "I had my embroidery with me. To tell you the truth, I get sick of my handmaids. They giggle and chatter so."

"Can anyone vouch for your presence here?"

"If you're accusing me of something, why not come right out with it?" Breda's voice went up a notch. She turned once more to Bridei. "My lord, this is—"

"Just answer the question, please," Bridei said quietly.

The girl seemed unusually defensive; she was an odd creature, her manner at the same time naïve and knowing. He did not know what to make of her.

"Of course people can vouch for where I was. My attendants will back up my story. And Dovran was there, in the garden. I don't know if he saw me; he's very intent on his duty. But I certainly saw him."

"Lady Breda," Aniel said, "what is your theory on this disappearance? What do you think most likely to have occurred?"

Breda shrugged. "I have no idea. It's all terribly sad. That sweet little girl; I hate to think what might happen to her. I find it hard to believe Eile would be so wicked; I quite liked her, myself."

"You believe in this tale folk are putting about, do you?" Wid's voice was calm. "A kidnapping, perhaps on behalf of Dalriadan interests?"

"She's a Gael, isn't she? And only lately come here. Nobody knew a thing about her."

"Lady Breda," Tharan said, "I'm not sure if I understood correctly. Can it be that you have not yet heard the news that little Saraid was found safe in the woods last night and is back at White Hill?"

The oddest expression crossed Breda's face; it was too complicated to read. "Oh." She looked down, then up again, then to the door as if she wanted to flee. "Oh, really? Well, isn't that wonderful? Such a dear little thing. I'm so glad. So didn't she say what happened? Where the others are?"

"Not thus far," said Bridei. "She's too upset to speak."

"Oh. How sad. Where is she now? Who is looking after her?"

There was a pause. Then Wid said, "She's being well cared for. I don't think we need detain you any longer, my lady."

"For now," said Tharan.

"For now? You mean I may have to go through this again?"

"There's a child missing," Aniel told her flatly. "And a young woman. A little inconvenience is surely a small price to pay for finding them more quickly."

Breda rose to her feet. She clasped her hands before her. "There's just one thing," she said in a small voice, a child's voice.

The four men looked at her. Suddenly the silence in the council chamber was full of tension. "Yes?" said Tharan.

"I didn't want to say . . . I mean, this talk of kidnapping, of treachery, it's all so distasteful. And I may have got it wrong, misinterpreted what I saw . . ."

"Whatever it is, tell us now and in plain words." Bridei was on his feet, his face white.

"I . . . I did see her. Them. It was when I was outside, going up to the garden. Eile was in her outdoor clothes, and she had the two children, Saraid and little . . . and your son, my lord. They were going out the gate, the small gate at the side of the main entry."

The men stared at her.

"You saw this, and you have waited until now, until they have been missing a whole night, before thinking to tell us?" Aniel, an expert in composure, could not keep the fury from his voice.

"It . . . it seemed so unusual, so unlikely, I began to wonder if I'd made a mistake." Breda's features were a picture of girlish confusion. "I thought maybe it had been someone else. Besides, even if it was Eile, the guards wouldn't have let them out if it hadn't been authorized, surely? I just supposed she had been allowed to take the children for a walk. Everyone knows how much Queen Tuala trusts the little Gael. Trusted, I suppose that should be."

Bridei drew a deep breath and sat down at the table. "Be seated, Breda," he said. "I very much regret that you did not make this known as soon as you saw Eile leaving; you could have mentioned it to Dovran or Garth, to any member of my household, and thus have allowed us to bring back my son and the other two straight away.

Everyone knows Derelei does not go beyond the walls without armed guards. Everyone. I cannot understand why you have kept this to yourself for so long."

"Nobody asked," said Breda in her little voice, hunching her shoulders.

"Go through it again, please. We need to fix on a time of day, a direction."

"I do want to help, as much as I can. It was around midday, I think. A direction? It was hard to see, but I am fairly sure they were headed toward the western track, the one that leads down to Serpent Lake. I'm sorry, my lord. I didn't want to get Eile in trouble . . ." A single tear flowed down the flawless cheek.

"What do your handmaids know of this?" Wid asked.

"Nothing. I told you. I decided I must have got it wrong. I didn't tell them anything. You know how girls gossip and build up something from nothing."

"Very well. We will speak with these young women now, one by one. You may go, Lady Breda. Think hard about the consequences of your decision to keep this to yourself. Telling this tale to someone, anyone, could have saved lives."

"But I *have* told you," Breda said, eyes wide. "I've told you everything I know."

The handmaids all told the same story. Breda had spent the morning in her quarters and the afternoon in the garden. Most of them had stayed indoors sewing, playing games or practicing the harp. Nobody had seen Eile or Saraid or Derelei. Aniel sent them away.

"I can't believe it," Bridei said shakily. "Breda must be weak-witted. How could she not understand how important that was? I can understand, perhaps, her reluctance to speak straightaway, not comprehending why it was so vital. But surely, once Derelei was found to be missing, anyone should have known to speak up?"

"That last young woman seemed on the verge of tears," Aniel commented. "All of them were quite edgy; nervous out of all proportion to the situation."

Wid managed a wintry smile. "For girls of fourteen or so, being questioned by four grim men, one of them a king, is enough to bring out either tears or defiance. They're far from home, and this is a troubling matter."

"Unfortunately," Aniel said, "this has come too late to be of much assistance to us, except that it lends credibility to the unlikely story that's going around the household, that Eile was deliberately planted here in order to carry out a kidnapping. Indeed, it would appear she's done so with remarkable efficiency."

"I cannot believe it," Bridei said. "I know Tuala wouldn't."

"I hate to say this," said Tharan soberly, "but that may merely reflect the fact that whoever is behind this chose his agent with particular cleverness. What now? What action do we take?"

"If there's a man to be spared," Bridei said, "send him out to find Faolan and pass on this new information, which will not be welcome. He needs to know. For ourselves, I do not think there is any more we can do until the search party reports back."

"It seems our only option is to entreat the gods for a good ending to this, and to await the return of Faolan and the other men," said Aniel. "And that of the other emissary who went out this morning. Bridei, if you need our company, we are here. I think this will be a long day."

☙

THERE WAS A slight paling of the gloom in the small, deep place where Eile was trapped. Not day; not unless the sun was a long, long way away. She had slipped in and out of consciousness more times than she could count. At each waking her prison seemed smaller, the air colder. At each opening of her eyes, at each new return to the nightmare of *now, here,* her body ached more fiercely and her will grew weaker.

She fought for recollection of what had happened, of

where she was and how she had come to be here. She remembered getting up and dressed, Saraid in her pink gown and Sorry in the celebration blue. Faolan . . . Faolan had slept in her chamber, and had been gone when she woke. They were going to . . . They would have . . . How long had she been here? Why hadn't he come to find her? Why had nobody come, nobody at all?

Calm; she must stay calm. Breathe. Think it through. Eile rubbed her arms and legs, moved and bent them, trying to get warm. Derelei. She had been with the two children, Saraid and Derelei. Exploring; finding little treasures. Up in the garden first, greeting Dovran, feeling odd about that after last night and Faolan's words of sweetness and promise. Saraid happy, running ahead. Derelei withdrawn and quiet. Then . . . then what? Then darkness, and waking in this shadowy hole.

It had been a long time, she judged. Her bladder was full, and she had to squat and relieve herself by the wall. She was thirsty. How long? Where were the children? Saraid would be frantic without her . . . And Derelei, what about Derelei? She was supposed to be looking after him; the queen had trusted her . . .

She made herself examine her surroundings. Above her, a circle of dim light revealed that she was at the bottom of a shaft, a well shaft, probably. Mercifully, it held no water now, though the walls had a crumbling dampness that was not reassuring. It looked a long way up, perhaps three times a tall man's height, maybe more. Could it actually be daytime, and the shadowy darkness caused by some barrier at the top? Could she really have been down here from one day's midpoint to the next morning? How could they have left her here so long? How could they not have found her? And if they had not thought to look here by now, did that mean . . . No, she would turn her thoughts from the possibility that she was in some place quite unknown, a place nobody could find. Of course someone would be searching. Faolan at least would be searching . . . He would keep on looking until he found her. Trust. Hope. Without those she would never have come to White Hill; she would never have begun to break free of the shadows that clung to her: her father, her mother, Dalach . . . They hovered close now, in this little dark place. Perhaps she would always carry them, like a burden never to be put down. Perhaps she had been foolish to presume it could ever be different; that Faolan could help her escape the shades of the past.

She huddled against the wall, willing her tears back. Weeping was a waste of energy; she must save what little she had. She must survive. No matter what else happened, there was still Saraid. But it was cold, so cold her bones ached with it. She did not think she had broken anything in her fall, though there was crusted blood on her face, by the temple, and something in her shoulder was not quite right. There should not be such pain when she moved it. She wondered, vaguely, how long a person could stay alive without water.

Fight. It was her father's voice; she could see him, dimly, seated against the opposite wall, not the young Deord with his red hair and calm smile, but the older one, after that place, the man who had been almost, but not quite, broken. *You must fight. Take control. Save yourself.*

"I can't," she whispered. "How can I?" The shaft was too wide to allow a climb with legs braced against one side, back against the other, even assuming she had the strength for that. The stone surface looked slippery and treacherous. "My shoulder's hurt and my legs feel weak. I'm thirsty and I'm tired. I can't even shout for help."

You're strong, daughter. Get up. Climb.

Eile struggled against the urge to lie down, to weep, to give up. She made herself think about her father's words. Perhaps his ghostly voice spoke simple truth. Always, in the past, she had indeed been strong. She had endured Dalach, protected Saraid, taken action, in the end, to get herself and her daughter out of that place. It was only when Faolan had come that she had learned what it was like not to have to carry the whole burden herself. And even Faolan had been saved by her strength. Without her he would be dead by his own hand.

Her father's image had faded, but she had no doubt he could hear her; that he watched her, willing her to succeed. He loved her; he wanted her to live. "I have to," she muttered. "If I don't do it now, soon I won't be able to do it at all. I must do it. For Saraid. And for myself. And for Mother and Father, to show them the story need not end like this." She rose to her feet, ignoring the pain. She tucked up her skirt, gritted her teeth and began to climb.

17

(from Brother Suibne's Account)
We arrived at King Bridei's new fortress in the afternoon. We were tired; it is quite a walk from the lake shore to the tree-blanketed hill that now houses the court of Fortriu. The dramatic events attending Colm's progress up the Great Glen had renewed our faith in God's grace and our hope for the mission, but our bodies were weary. Here, I thought, at least we had a good chance of sleeping in a bed and not a pigpen.

At the gates of White Hill came a shout of challenge: "State your name and business!"

I translated. Colm announced us as men of God; he gave his own name quietly, but such is the natural power of our leader's voice that the word rang forth as if it were the peal of a great bell: Colmcille.

"Drop your weapons! Turn around, kneel down, both hands in the air, and don't move until I say so!"

These warriors were not accustomed to dealing with

clerics, that much was evident. Maybe we should have dressed as druids. I could not imagine that powerful mage Broichan submitting gladly to such abrupt treatment.

I explained the commands to my brethren and we knelt, all but Colm.

"Didn't you hear me, fellow? On your knees or you'll get an arrow through the chest!"

"These are warlike folk," Lomán whispered when I murmured the translation.

Colm walked calmly across to the gates. An arrow was trained on him from above; I was obliged to disobey the command to turn my back, so I could watch. It was safe enough. Nobody was looking at me.

"Open in the name of God!" Colm cried out in our own tongue. "We come in peace, with the light of faith to lead us! Open, I say!"

There was no miraculous swinging apart of the great gates that spanned this stronghold's main entry. That is the kind of detail that attaches itself, later, to tales of such momentous events as the visit of a great Christian leader to a powerful pagan king. It was the little side gate that opened, the one designed to let folk come in or out without the need to expose the place by spreading wide the main portal. A man came out, leading a donkey. Colm beckoned and, to a chorus of outraged shouts from the guardpost above, we arose and went in. I did not look up. God was merciful; it was not my day for an arrow in the heart.

After a certain initial confusion, we were greeted cordially enough by one of Bridei's senior councillors, a tall man named Tharan, whom I remembered from my visit to the court of Drust the Bull. He had, I recalled, been hostile to Bridei in the early days; he'd have preferred to see Carnach of Thorn Bend take the throne of Fortriu when the old king died. Perhaps he'd had a strategic change of heart; he was, after all, still here.

Tharan found us quarters. There were beds with blankets and pillows. He apologized on behalf of the king.

White Hill was in disarray. Bridei's son, a mere infant, had been missing since the previous day, along with his Gaelic nursemaid. Most of the men were out searching. The queen was indisposed, overwhelmed by fear for her child.

Colm told Bridei's councillor that we would pray for the boy. Tharan appeared less than impressed by the offer. Although the hospitality had improved since my last visit to the court of Fortriu, I suspected the attitudes of the king's retainers would be no warmer than before.

I thanked Tharan on Colm's behalf. I am the only one of our group fluent in the Priteni tongue, and it falls to me to translate and to act as go-between. I reminded him that I was personally known to King Bridei. I asked him to arrange an audience for Colm at the king's convenience, and I told him it was our preference that Broichan be present. Colm had requested this. He has never been one to seek the easy path, preferring to confront difficulties as if breasting a fearsome wave, full on. His flight from our homeland has been the only exception to this rule. And that, in its way, was far from an easy choice.

Tharan said he would convey our requests to the king. He advised us which parts of the court we were welcome to visit. The place sprawls across the entire hilltop, an imposing construction surrounded by high walls, impressively fortified. The view, out over the pine-clad slopes to the sea, and the other way to the hills of the Great Glen, is most wondrous. Within the formidable barrier of stone are many chambers and all amenities as well as extensive gardens, both large and small. We were allocated not only our sleeping chamber but an adjoining room suitable for prayer, though, of course, nobody specified this. I well remember Broichan's frozen horror at the sight of me conducting a Christian rite at Caer Pridne at the time of the last election. Tharan showed us a small patch of garden adjoining our quarters, where we might sit and enjoy the sun. Refreshments would be brought to us, he said, and water for washing. There was a privy close by, which we might use. Supper would be announced in due course. It would be served in the great hall.

"We live a frugal existence," Colm said after I translated this. "Our day is woven around prayer." He glanced at me, indicating I should render his comment for Tharan.

"Thank you," I told the king's councillor. "This is most generous. Apart from the official meetings with King Bridei and his spiritual adviser, it is likely we will keep ourselves to ourselves."

Tharan's haughty features were fleetingly softened by a smile. "You forget, Brother Suibne," he said. "You, at least, are already known to us. I do not think you are capable of visiting any court without wishing to put a finger in whatever pie is to hand."

"What is he saying?" asked Colm.

"That he hopes we will avail ourselves of supper, at least," I told him. "That way, King Bridei will be reminded of our presence, and of the need to offer us an audience. He suggests that this evening's fare may include a pie." Occasionally my tongue does run away with me a little. It is an inevitable consequence of working as a translator. Juggle languages enough, and one can become drunk with words.

SUIBNE, MONK OF DERRY

AFTER HIS NIGHT spent out in the woods searching fruitlessly for Derelei, Bedo was unable to conceal from his stepmother that his arm was troubling him. Brethana ordered him to stay back in the morning when the others went out, his brother among them. For once Bedo obeyed her without question, though he chafed at the restriction. The physician had made it quite clear what would happen if he overtaxed the mending limb. The thought of little Derelei freezing to death or coming to some other harm filled him with the urge to help, to take action.

Common sense told him there were many men searching, capable men; it told him that his own small contribution was of insufficient worth to justify risking his future as a warrior chieftain. He stayed behind and won his stepmother's smile and words of praise.

Then there was another tedious day to fill, a day which, like every other since the hunt, seemed endless and empty. He'd never been much of a scholar, though he'd worked hard enough at his learning while Ferada was bringing them up, him and Uric. He'd had to; his sister had been no easy taskmaster. After their mother went away, Ferada had applied herself to the job of overseer and tutor with all her formidable strength. As a result, he and Uric were competent in the branches of learning a young man of noble blood required. Still, it had been a relief when their father had wed Brethana and Ferada had gone off to Banmerren to start her experiment in the education of young women. Bedo had never really enjoyed cramming his head with history, geography, astrology, and languages. He was happier taking his horse over a difficult jump or wrestling with his brother. Until this arm mended, he would find his days hard to get through.

Today was a little different. He did have a task to accomplish. The pin Uric had found was in Bedo's pouch, well concealed. With Uric gone out again on the search, it fell to Bedo to discover whether their theory was correct, and to do so without arousing their quarry's suspicion.

Girls seemed to like to travel in packs. It was exceptionally difficult to separate one out without the others noticing and coming after their friend. Of course, today most of the men were absent from court, for the search area had widened, taking them well away from the wooded slopes of White Hill and out across the flat lands beyond, up toward the coast, down toward the dark, deep lake, over to the rising ground in the southwest that eventually became the Great Glen. Court was quiet. The arrival of the Christians created a small drama; Tharan handled it with his usual competence, shepherding them away to somewhere secluded. Another thing for the king to deal with.

The absence of so many folk made Bedo's quest more difficult. It made him more visible. The morning had been useless, the girls coming out only once and staying together the whole time. In the afternoon he hung about in the garden a while, exchanging desultory talk with Dovran. Later he found temporary occupation with Garvan the stone carver and his assistant. Garvan was touching up some of the small decorative carvings along the courtyard wall, little creatures mostly, cat, badger, squirrel, owl. With one arm in a sling Bedo couldn't do much, but there were times when an extra hand to hold bracing timbers in place or reach for a particular chisel came in useful. Besides, Garvan seemed to welcome the company.

Breda and her handmaids came past twice and Bedo watched them without being too obvious about it. They kept close together like a gaggle of geese, Breda a little in front, the others in her wake. Not a chance of singling one out. Not a hope. None of them was like Cella, who had stood out for her wit and independence, quiet girl as she was. He still found it hard to accept that Cella was dead, Cella with her soft brown hair and her shy smile. It was wrong that she should have been taken thus, and this heartless princess still walking about as if the world owed her humblest allegiance. These other girls seemed all too ready to give it; they clung as close to her as burrs in a dog's coat.

The day wore on and the light began to fade. Garvan packed up his tools, thanked Bedo and the assistant, and left. Curse it, Uric would be back soon and Bedo would have to report that he'd achieved absolutely nothing. There must be some way to do this. He went to the privy and sat awhile thinking, the jeweled pin like a leaden weight in his pouch. He thought about girls, and the way they always needed their friends with them for some reason. They probably even went to the privy in a group. Or did they? What about washing? Breda would be the kind of girl, like his sister Ferada, who could not attend supper without washing her face and hands, dressing her hair, and getting into a fresh gown even if the old one was perfectly clean. With that bevy of handmaids she wouldn't have to lift a finger. They'd bring warm water and take the leftovers away again. He'd wager the ordinary household serving people of White Hill never set foot in Lady Breda's private quarters.

It was getting on for suppertime now, though the king would doubtless delay it until the search party returned. That there had as yet been no sign of them foreshadowed bad news; if they had found Derelei or Eile, a message would have come back swiftly. A plan suggested itself to Bedo. He must find a spot from which he could watch the entry to Breda's apartments, but in which he could not be seen. Gods, to think that not so long ago he'd been practically panting for the opportunity to speak to her. It shamed him to recall it.

Most of the guards were away. That made it easier for Bedo to conceal himself without drawing attention. It wasn't the subtlest of hiding places, behind a pillar at the foot of some steps, but it did allow a clear view of what he needed. It was a test, he thought. A warrior's test: keep silent, stay alert, be ready to strike at a moment's notice. *Strike* being used figuratively, of course. *I'm doing this for you,* he told the shade of Cella. *I hope you know how much I cared about you.* Then he leaned against the wall, narrowed his eyes and waited.

ELDA DECIDED SHE would have supper with the children. Saraid could not be left on her own, even with Gilder and Galen and the familiar maidservant. The child had barely moved all day. The twins, boisterous even at their quieter moments, had been tiptoeing around her, unnerved by her hunched silence.

It wasn't that Saraid had lost the power of speech. She had accepted the breakfast offered her on a tray with a whispered *thank you,* testimony to Eile's rigorous training in good manners. She had murmured to Sorry on and off during the day, little songs and rhymes. Elda took the three children out to the garden in the afternoon, thinking it would not hurt Saraid to stretch her legs and breathe fresh air. The twins were more than ready for some exercise and ran off along the paths with their ball. Elda sat down on a bench, easing her back. It would not be long before her baby arrived. Gods, she hoped it was a girl.

Saraid climbed onto the bench beside her. The little girl sat close, right up against Elda's side, her doll pressed tightly to her chest. Elda could feel her shivering as if chilled to the bone. She put her arm around the child. Down the garden, Gilder and Galen were trying to skip stones across the pond, as they'd once seen Dovran doing. She kept a watchful eye on them, not wanting to deal with wet clothes.

"Are you all right, Saraid?"

"Mm."

"Sure?"

"Mm."

"You know last night? When Faolan found you in the woods?"

"Feeler find Sorry."

It was more than she'd offered all day.

"That's right, sweetheart. Faolan found Sorry under a bush. She was in her lovely blue dress, the one Eile made for her."

Elda felt the small body tense; looking down, she saw Saraid's lips tighten. She knew the signs. This was a child holding back a secret, something she dared not tell.

"Saraid, do you know where Eile went? And Derelei? Will you tell me?"

The lips pressed together. There was the smallest shake of the head.

"It might help your mama, Saraid, if you can tell us what you know. If Mama's hurt or lost or . . ." It did not bear thinking about, the possibility that Eile—*Eile*—might be a traitor, a spy. "Or if Derelei went off somewhere and he's cold and tired and wants to come home . . . You should tell me, Saraid. You could help Derelei come home." Privately, Elda was holding out less and less hope of that occurring as the time passed. Alongside her own sturdy boys, Derelei was like a single violet growing next to a pair of thorny rosebushes. A breath of wind might carry him away. How could such a waif survive even a single night out in the woods alone? "Saraid?"

But Saraid's lips remained firmly shut. They sat a while longer; Dovran came down to greet them and went away again on his patrol. He looked drained and weary. Then the twins began to argue about the ball, a frequent cause of disagreement, and it was time to go in again.

On the way to her own quarters, Elda stopped by the chamber Eile shared with Saraid, for the little girl would need a nightrobe, clean smallclothes, her own comb and mirror, and there might be other familiar items she would find comforting.

"Don't touch Eile's things," Elda warned the twins. "Sit on the bed, the two of you, and wait until Saraid and I have what we need." She opened the storage chest, looking through its meager contents, hoping Eile would not mind.

"Other dress," said Saraid. She had a little box of her own; it rested on the small table by the bed. She opened it and lifted out a minute pink gown and a length of silk ribbon. The twins clambered along the bed, craning to see.

"Yes, of course, fetch Sorry's things, too," Elda told Saraid. "You'll be sleeping in our chamber again tonight. Do you want your gray gown . . . ?" Her voice faded while, in the background, the twins kept up a commentary on the pros and cons of Sorry's wardrobe. Elda rose to her feet. She looked around the chamber. The story had got about quickly, spread by those girls who were attached to King Keother's cousin. Eile had been seen going out. She'd actually been seen taking the king's son beyond the gate and down the track toward Serpent Lake. It was difficult to believe; they'd have needed to travel fast to evade the search. They'd probably have had to go by boat, down the freezing waters of the lake. Yet there, hanging neatly on a peg, was Eile's outdoor cloak. And there, placed precisely together in a corner, were Eile's outdoor boots.

Elda felt suddenly cold. "Saraid?" she asked. "Where is your warm cloak?"

Saraid scrambled down from the bed and came over to point into a corner of the chest. There it was, tidily folded, a brown woollen garment Elda had seen many times before. "Of course. What about your boots?"

Saraid looked down at the soft kidskin boots she was wearing, which were stained from their journey on the forest floor.

"Not those, sweetheart, your big boots, the outside boots."

Saraid went to the bed, peered underneath, reached and drew out a pair of sturdy small boots in good leather. "Going outside?" she asked. Her voice was suddenly small and shaky.

"No, Saraid, not now. It's nearly suppertime. I just needed to know where to find them. Now, I've got your nightrobe and comb and a fresh gown for the morning. Gather up Sorry's things and we'll go and put them away in our chamber. I expect Papa will be home soon, boys. And Faolan." She glanced at Saraid.

"Feeler home." The little girl spoke on a sigh.

Thank the gods, Elda thought, that Garth would be back by suppertime, whether with good news or bad. It had been hard to take in the possibility that Eile was not what they'd thought her. Perhaps that was not because Eile had cleverly duped them all, but because it simply wasn't true. Maybe she should go now, and let the king know what she'd discovered. She eyed the three children, Saraid pale and withdrawn, Gilder and Galen grubby from their adventures in the garden and starting to get fractious with hunger. They were in no fit state to go anywhere but into a bath and then straight to supper. Out in the hallway, she looked about for someone to call, someone who could take a message to the king, but there was nobody in sight. With a sigh, Elda headed back to her own quarters; this would have to wait.

AT LAST A girl came out on her own, with a big ewer in her hands. She was short, dark, timid-looking; Bedo struggled to remember her name and got it just in time.

"Cria," he said, stepping out into her path and causing her to flinch in fright. "I need to ask you something."

"Oh—oh, no I can't—I have to fetch water—"

"It won't take long. See this?" He had the jeweled pin ready; now he displayed it on his hand and saw her eyes widen. "Do you know who it belongs to?"

Cria eyed him warily.

"It's important," Bedo said.

"Where did you find it?"

"That doesn't matter. I'll return it to the owner, once I know who she is."

Cria lowered her eyes, hugging the ewer to her chest. "It's Lady Breda's," she mumbled. "I can give it to her—"

"No, that's all right, I'd like to return it in person. Are you sure?"

She flashed a glance at him, suddenly annoyed. "Yes, of course I'm sure. See that emblem, the sea beast? It's a royal kin token in the islands. Breda's the only woman here at White Hill who's allowed to wear that, now her sister's gone."

"I've got another question."

"I have to go. She gets angry if we're late."

"Was Breda wearing this on the day of the hunt? The day Cella was killed?"

The girl's features tightened. Her eyes narrowed. "Why would you ask that?"

"Why would the question frighten you?" Bedo countered. "You're scared, aren't you? It's written all over you. I don't mean you any harm. I need your help."

There was a silence. "This is about how she died, isn't it? Cella?" Cria's voice had changed. Her whisper was furtive, almost conspiratorial.

"An innocent girl was killed. I broke my arm. I just want to find out what happened."

"It was an accident. A tragic accident. And it's over now."

"In that case, it's safe to answer my question."

"I've really got to go." She glanced nervously back toward Breda's door. "Yes, she was wearing it. But don't say I was the one who told you."

"Why not?" He pretended bewilderment. "If it was an accident, I mean?"

"Listen." Cria took hold of his sleeve and drew him up the steps with her. "Keep walking. I need to go to the well up by the kitchen. It's not just this, it's all the time. If we don't say what she tells us and keep quiet when we're ordered to, we get punished. If she even saw me talking to you, I'd get a beating later. What happened that day—it's not worth thinking about. Cella's gone now. All the questions in the world won't bring her back. And none of us is in a hurry to be next."

They were walking along the path to the well. Bedo's heart had begun to race. "Why would she punish you for talking to me? And what do you mean, next? You can't mean next to die?"

"Shh! I shouldn't have said anything. Leave me alone, you've got what you wanted and it's nearly suppertime. I'm going to have to run."

"Tell me! What's wrong with talking to me?"

"She gets jealous. That's what Cella's offense was, talking to you."

"*What?* But Breda never even noticed me; she hasn't the least interest in me. This can't be true."

Cria gave a grim little smile. "She's all mixed up. There's no logic to what she does or who she takes a like or dislike to. Somehow she's identified you as of interest, and that means nobody else touches you or looks at you or exchanges a word with you. She can change in an instant. Take that girl Eile. Breda liked her at first, but when she drew Dovran's attention it was a different matter."

Bedo drew a shaky breath and released it. "Cria," he said, trying to keep his tone calm and controlled as his father might in such a situation, "Eile's gone, as you know. Disappeared with the king's son. Might that be in any way connected with this other matter?"

She looked miserable, like a wan moth caught in a trap. "I don't know," she said. "All I know is that if you offend Lady Breda, you pay the price. All of us were questioned about Eile and the child. We said what we'd been told to say."

"You mean you lied? You lied, even though a two-year-old had been missing overnight out in the woods?"

"Haven't you ever lied because you were terrified of what would happen if you told the truth?" Cria whispered.

"I'd be more afraid, now, of what could happen if I kept on lying," Bedo said, hearing the chill judgment in his own voice. "You and the other girls could have a child's death on your conscience. Maybe Eile's, too, depending on what's happened to her."

"Eile's a spy," Cria said, setting her ewer on the rim of the well and reaching for the handle that turned the lifting mechanism. "Everyone says so. It was a kidnapping. Why would we care about her, when she wormed her way into King Bridei's house and stole his son?"

"You speak as if that were a certainty." Bedo felt suddenly much older than he had this morning.

"They were seen. And Eile's a Gael. Nobody can argue with that, she never tried to hide it."

"Oh, that's right," Bedo said. "They were seen. Going out the gate, in full view. And yet, somehow, all the guards missed them. Really odd. But I understand that's the story that's going around."

Cria flushed, turning the handle to lift the bucket. "It was Breda who saw them, not us." Her tone was defensive.

"Cria," Bedo said, "I know you need to get back quickly with that water. If I speak up later about this," touching the pin, "and about yesterday and what Breda did or didn't see, and did or didn't ask you to say, will you back me up? Will you tell the truth?"

"I can't," she muttered.

"So you'd let an infant perish out there, all alone, because you're afraid of a beating?"

"I feel terrible about the little boy, but I don't think I can do it." Cria drew aside the neck of her tunic to reveal the start of a heavy welt across her shoulders. "She uses a strap with knots in it," she said, her tone flat, resigned. "It hurts a lot."

Bedo had thought that, in this affair, he was past shocking, but he'd been wrong. "You should tell King Keother about this," he said. "She must be stopped."

"She likes power. She has that here; we can't go home. The more control she gets, the trickier her little games. I don't want to end up like Cella." The bucket reached the top of the well; she heaved it onto the rim, ready to fill the ewer.

"Let me help you."

"With one arm?"

"I can hold your jug, at least, while you pour."

"Bedo?" Her voice had shrunk to a conspiratorial whisper.

"What?"

"If you told everything, all of it, to King Keother and King Bridei, could you make her stop? You're only young. They wouldn't listen, would they?"

Perhaps he had misjudged her. Her fear was no girlish fit of the vapors; it was real. "I will do my best to make them listen," he said grimly. "And I will ask Keother to protect you and the other girls. I'll do that whether you help me or not. I hope very much that you'll change your mind. Cella deserves our best efforts. She deserves the truth."

The ewer was full. Cria picked it up and, with a glance over her shoulder, scurried off in the direction of Breda's quarters. And here he was, heart thumping, blood rushing, not sure where to turn first. Should he take this straight to Bridei, or wait until his brother came back, adhering to their agreement to do this together? Uric had said Faolan would support them. Faolan would likely be back soon, along with Uric and the others. Bedo could hardly demand that the princess of the Light Isles be dragged out to answer his questions. He might be the son of Bridei's chief war leader, but he was only fifteen years old, untried in the arena of battle or that of diplomacy. Even now, his case was heavily dependent on the word of others, on surmise and on guesswork. He wished his father were still at court. Common sense said wait until Uric got back and use what little time that allowed him to plan exactly what to say and how to say it. And pray that, by taking this brief delay, he was not adding himself to the list of those who had lengthened Derelei's time alone out there, and increased the chance that he would perish before they found him.

Gods, it was unthinkable. Bedo remembered Derelei's grin of delight as they'd given him his first ride in the little cart they'd brought from Raven's Well; the way his pale features had lit up when they'd shown him and the twins how to slide down a certain bank while sitting on a wooden tray. He recalled Derelei riding on his shoulders, pretending Bedo was a horse, while Galen sat atop

Uric and they raced across the courtyard whinnying, with Gilder in pursuit. Derelei was only little. Whatever this new game was, it was the cruelest thing in the world to make such a tiny child a pawn in it.

IT HAD BEEN a fruitless, heartbreaking day. The dogs had picked up nothing at all. The search parties had scoured a wide expanse of land in all directions spreading out from White Hill, but no trace of infant or young woman had been found, and nobody in cottage or small settlement or farmhouse had seen them. At midday a messenger had come for Faolan, telling him about yesterday's sighting of Eile and Derelei leaving White Hill quite openly through the gates. The messenger had made the mistake of advising Faolan that the king and his councillors thought this lent strength to the kidnapping theory, and Faolan had come perilously close to hitting the man. They were all on edge, short of sleep, knowing the more time passed without finding something, anything, the closer they were to having to acknowledge that the king's son was probably dead.

And Eile. Folk tended to mention her as an afterthought, as if she were only of interest because Derelei had vanished while in her care. It was another reason to be angry; another reason to lash out. Faolan held on to his temper, but only by a thread.

Some of the men stayed out; they would snatch a few hours of rest at a temporary camp, then move on to search a new area at first light. Most returned to White Hill when dusk fell, the king's bodyguards among them. Even Garth admitted he would have to get some real sleep to be able to go on in the morning.

Faolan devised a roster that would allow other capable men, Aniel's guard Eldrist and Tharan's Imbeg, to stand in for Bridei's personal guards so they could sleep more than a brief snatch. Dovran had been on duty almost continuously for two days and a night. It would be folly to let him go on.

He set these arrangements in place while Garth went to the king with the news of another day's unsuccessful search. Then Faolan made his way to Elda's quarters, where the twins were being bathed in a large shallow tub before the hearth, while Saraid watched gravely from the pallet the children would share. The room was blissfully warm. Elda, sleeves rolled up, face flushed, was crouched awkwardly by the tub, scrubbing a twin's back.

"Faolan!" she exclaimed, looking up at him with a little frown. "Where's Garth? Is he home?"

"Reporting to the king. No news, I'm afraid." His eyes were not on Elda and the boys. "I've just looked in to see how my girl is doing."

"She's—"

There was no need for Elda to finish. Dropping Sorry unceremoniously on the coverlet, Saraid flew across the chamber, dodging bath and kneeling woman, and straight into his arms where she clung as tightly as a young marten to its mother.

"She's been quiet," Elda said. "Very quiet. I'd be happier if she shed tears; let some of it go, whatever it is. She hasn't told me anything. I did try."

Faolan murmured to the child, stroking her hair, feeling how hard she held him, how tightly strung her small body was. "There, Squirrel, there. My good girl; my dear little one. I'm here, *mo cridhe.*" He felt the thunderous beating of his own heart; heard, in his mind, words he could not speak, not here, not now: *my daughter.* "If you want," he said to Elda, "I will stay with her while you go to supper. It's a lot for you to handle, the three of them all day."

"Good practice," Elda said, helping one twin out of the bath and beginning to scrub the other. "I'll have three of my own before the moon's waxed and waned again. Faolan—"

The door opened to admit a weary-looking Garth. His

appearance was greeted by screams of delight from the twins.

"Come here, Gilder, you're dripping on the floor." The big guard seized the nearest twin and began to dry him vigorously. In the general hubbub, Faolan could not make out what Elda was trying to tell him; something about cloaks and boots. After a certain time, Gilder and Galen were quieter. Faolan sat on the bed with Saraid on his knee and asked her to say it again.

"Everyone's talking about this sighting, Eile taking Derelei out the gates; everyone thinks it means she was placed here to abduct him, Faolan. I'm not talking about the usual silly gossip, the sort of thing that dies down as quickly as it springs up. After this, even Aniel and Tharan were expressing misgivings, wondering if they'd read the situation wrongly before."

"I got the message." It still made him furious. "We searched the path to the lake with no success. A boat did leave late yesterday, but nobody saw a woman and a child on it. This is a pernicious rumor. I hope you're not giving it credence—"

Saraid made a little sound and he realized how tightly he was holding her. "It's all right, Squirrel. I was angry, but not with you. What has Sorry been doing today?"

"Walking." The tiny voice was doleful. "Getting clothes. Waiting."

"Faolan," Elda said, "when I went to Eile's chamber to fetch Saraid's things, I noticed that Eile's outdoor clothes were still there, her warm cloak and heavy boots. She's only got the one set. She'd have worn them, surely, if she were taking Derelei right away from White Hill. Besides, the way I heard the story, Breda said she saw Eile wearing her outdoor clothes when she went out the gate. It doesn't add up."

"Breda," muttered Faolan, his mind putting a puzzle together in a number of different ways and liking each one less than the last. "You're telling me it was Breda who came up with this tale of Eile walking out of White Hill deliberately? Who else saw them?"

"I don't know, Faolan. Maybe nobody. But Breda's maids were talking about this as if it were fact, and the whole household picked it up."

His body was tense; his hands wanted to form fists, but he was holding Saraid and he forced himself calm. "Breda must be questioned again," he said. "Now. Maybe we've been wrong; chasing a scent that doesn't exist. Maybe Eile never left White Hill. Gods—"

"Faolan," said Garth, who was putting a little shirt on a wriggling twin while his wife dried the other, "Bridei was going straight into a meeting with Keother and the councillors, and after that it will be suppertime. You know what a burden the king's carrying right now, with Tuala gone as well as his son. It's been complicated still further. The Christians are here and demanding an audience, preferably with Broichan in attendance. Fola's with Anfreda; she can't quit that responsibility to take the druid's place."

"Eile's life could depend on this. It has to be now."

"He's asked this Brother Colm, the one we've heard so much about, to sit in on the meeting. I imagine it's to offer an apology in person and to request that they accept a delay before their official audience. He'll probably tell them Broichan isn't here. You must at least wait until after that. A council of that kind is not something you can burst in on. Especially not if you plan to level some kind of accusation at Keother's kinswoman. This is difficult enough for Bridei."

"Feeler?" whispered Saraid. "Sing a song?"

"Later, Squirrel. You need your supper first." He bent to kiss her cheek. His gut was churning; wrong, they'd got it wrong, he could feel it.

"I'm not coming to supper in the hall," Elda said. "I'll eat with these three, then bring them back here. If you're quick, Faolan, Saraid may still be awake after you've eaten, and you can come and sing her a song. I didn't know you had a talent for music." She managed a smile. "Garth, you must sleep tonight. If the king asks you to stand guard, tell him I said you're dead on your feet."

Garth yawned widely. "The rate I'm going, I'll be first to bed. Faolan, you and I need to eat, after such a day. I'll come with you; wait for your moment, is my advice, and remember the king's juggling more balls than a man can reasonably manage right now. He won't want Keother offended."

"If that girl's lied and put Eile at risk, I'll . . ." *I'll kill her.* He remembered, just in time, that there were children in the room. "Squirrel," he said, "I have to go and wash; I smell of horse." Saraid sniffed at his sleeve and wrinkled her nose. "Saraid . . ." He hesitated, not sure whether to attempt the question again. She seemed prepared to talk now, and calmer than last night, but the look in her eyes troubled him. "Saraid, can you remember where Eile went? Can you tell me what happened yesterday, when I found you and Sorry in the woods?"

She gazed at him, solemn as an owl, then very deliberately shook her head.

"It would help Mama if you did tell. It might help us find her and Derelei. How did you get out there? Through the big gate or somewhere else?"

Her gaze did not waver. Her lips were pressed tightly together. At that moment, he saw Eile in her so strongly it made his heart turn over. Faolan sighed. "It's all right, Squirrel," he said. "Go and have your supper with the twins. I'll be back as soon as I can. If you get tired, don't try to stay awake for me. I'll come and see you in the morning, before I go out again."

"Sorry song? House on the hill?"

She was ready enough to speak of other things today. What was it that held her silent on the very matter he most needed to know? A threat of some kind? The child was only three. "I'll sing the Sorry song," Faolan told her. "House on the hill is the one Mama does." His throat went tight. "When she comes home, she'll tell it for you."

"Promise?"

He could not look at her. "Promise," he whispered, then set her down on the pallet and, like a coward, fled.

"I'M BALANCED ON a knife edge," Bridei said to Fola. "Every day I give these Christians house room, every time I listen to their arguments, every concession I grant them offends the ancient gods of Fortriu more deeply; the gods in whose hands rests the fate of my little son. Every step I take in that direction puts Tuala at further risk. You know what I did when I stopped the ritual at the Well of Shades. I set my whole family on a path of constant peril."

"But?" Fola was standing by the hearth, serene in her gray robe. She watched Bridei, who was pacing up and down with Anfreda in his arms.

"But I know, in practical terms, that change is coming. One of the reasons Keother is here is to make an argument on behalf of the Christian elements in his own kingdom. And he wants to rebuild bridges with me after his woeful failure to support me against the Gaels. For all his bluster, he cannot afford to do otherwise. His territory is isolated; he'd be a fool to detach himself still further. Where matters of faith are concerned, he'll put his position still more strongly with these emissary clerics here at court. As king of Fortriu I must at least hear him. If Faolan's wrong about Carnach, I could have a powerful new enemy on my doorstep. I need Keother fully on my side."

"So you cannot placate the gods by sending these Christians packing. But you do not want to listen to them now."

"How can I turn my full attention to anything while Derelei's gone? And Tuala; I'm frightened for her, Fola. She's never tried this before. The gods could snatch away the two of them so easily. What have I wrought here?"

The wise woman regarded him levelly. "Keep on in this vein," she remarked, "and that baby will be fretful and unsettled all night. If you insist on holding her, use the skills Broichan taught you to make yourself calm. You can't walk into this meeting looking wild-eyed and jittery. Sit down. Now let us imagine we are back in the past: living again the night of the Gateway sacrifice, the only one you ever witnessed. Think of the moment when you decided that, should you become king, you would bring an end to that particular rite and take the burden of the Nameless God's wrath on your own shoulders. You knew you would wed and likely father children. You knew the risk. If you could live that moment again, would your decision be different?"

There was no need to consider this. Bridei shook his head. The dark images of that night, the bleak echoes of the Well of Shades and a girl drowning, a white-clad girl whose long hair had floated out on the black water, were never far from his thoughts. He could hear Broichan chanting, his voice full of a terrible, Otherworldly power; he could see the blanched faces of the men; he could feel his own hands helping to ensure the death of the innocent. "I wish only," he said, "that for their retribution the gods would choose me and me alone. Not Tuala; not Derelei. They are blameless."

"The Shining One loves Tuala," said Fola. "And Derelei, so small and so prodigiously gifted, is surely marked out for a special path in life. I cannot think the gods would let that go to waste. You must not give up hope, Bridei. Your wife is a strong woman. She seemed to have faith in her ability to achieve her mission. You, too, should have faith."

"I do," he said, not quite sure if he believed this. "And yet I fear the dark god's vengeance. I fear the choices that lie before me. As king, there is a path I wish to follow, a path of compromise, of conciliation. My love for the gods is sure and unwavering. That will never falter, not in all the nights and days I walk this earth. I intend to keep the ancient ways strong in Fortriu. But I must also rule with a view to political change, Fola. There are powers at work all around us: a new king in Circinn; a precarious peace in Dalriada; the mysterious and change-able influence of the Caitt. I do not forget the Uí Néill chieftains, full of ambition and only a day or so's sailing from our western shores. I cannot take a strong and wise path forward for Fortriu if I am constantly fettered by fear for my loved ones; by terror of the darkness that re-sides within me, and within any man who walks the lands of the Priteni. The Nameless God is part of us all. We cannot escape him. Tonight, all I want to do is stay here in this chamber, holding my daughter and hoping Tuala and Derelei will walk in the door, safe and sound. I do not want to speak to Keother or to these missionary Christians. I don't even want to see Tharan and Aniel, staunch supporters though they have been. Tonight, I am not much of a king."

"And me?" she asked wryly.

Bridei smiled at her. "For being here to watch over my daughter, I can never thank you enough," he said. "I hope you know you are always welcome with Tuala and me. I was going to say you are like a mother to us, but I know you would dismiss that. It's not quite right, anyway. You are both respected teacher and beloved friend. Your wis-dom and honesty help keep us on a straight path."

Fola said quietly, "I'm not sure I merit such praise, but it warms me. In my turn, I would tell you that it is at times such as this, when you feel wrenched apart and helpless, that you discover what it means to be a king. You are a king to your very core, Bridei, strong of heart, wise and brave. And human. That's part of what makes you so good at the job. Now it's time for you to go. If it will reassure you, I will fetch out Tuala's scrying bowl once the baby's been settled for the night and see what the gods can tell me. You know, of course, that they may have ill visions for us, or none at all."

"I know." He transferred the drowsy Anfreda to the

wise woman's arms. "Thank you, I would welcome that."

"I can do it soon enough. This one's due to be fed shortly, then I'll let Tresna go to her supper. I may have some wisdom for you before you sleep." Her tone was full of compassion; she had known Bridei since he was a lad of twelve.

"I won't sleep, not tonight. Not with the two of them in peril. Eile, too. I intend to keep a vigil. To pray."

"Alone?"

"My men are exhausted. You must stay here; Broichan is gone. Yes, alone."

"Bridei, do you credit this tale of Eile, which seems more plausible as time passes? Do you believe she would do such a terrible thing out of zeal for a cause, or from desperation?"

Bridei shook his head. "I know circumstances drive folk to extremes. But there is one aspect of that story I cannot believe: that Eile would go away and willingly leave her daughter behind. The bond between them is iron-strong. The truth does not lie in this tale of kidnap but elsewhere. Besides, I have unshakable faith in Faolan's good judgment. I know Tuala would agree with me."

"As do I. Once or twice in my life I've encountered a soul who is good through and through; such folk shine like lamps in a morass of doubt and uncertainty. Eile is one such individual. In time, I suspect her daughter will become another. Your Faolan is a fortunate man."

"That's if he finds her," said Bridei grimly.

THE MEETING WAS awkward. Keother, weary after the day's search, was quieter than usual. He greeted Colm with deference and answered the cleric's queries as to the state of the monastic settlements in the Light Isles, a topic Bridei had hoped would not be aired until the formal audience. Colm was an impressive man, perhaps forty years of age, tall, ascetic in appearance, with the unmistakable stamp of his Uí Néill breeding, the eyes bold, the nose jutting, the jaw firm. The high frontal tonsure served to emphasise the Gael's strong, domed brow. His innate authority was clear in his every gesture. His voice was somehow both stern and beguiling, a powerful tool of influence.

Bridei had a sound grasp of the Gaelic language and could speak it with reasonable fluency, thanks to Wid's tuition in his early years. He seldom revealed this ability, and never in such situations as this. Had Faolan not been off rearranging the night guards, he'd have used his right-hand man as both protector and translator. As it was, Keother's two men-at-arms were the only minders present, and it was Brother Suibne who rendered the conversation into Gaelic and back again. Bridei knew him of old. An astute man, clever, subtle, and possessed of a dry sense of humor. For all their differences, Bridei liked him. But you could never trust a Christian, not fully. Bridei listened closely to both original and translation, knowing how slight the nuance required to cause a major misunderstanding. That, too, was something he had learned from Wid.

Aniel, well prepared, proposed a day and time for the formal audience and suggested all parties give him an idea, in advance, of what matters they wished discussed there. He stressed that, although the delay might inconvenience the brothers, all the amenities of White Hill would be open to them in the interim.

"On the understanding, of course," Bridei put in, "that there will be no public prayer or religious teaching within these walls. We have tolerated your progress across Fortriu, word of which has reached us by various messengers. A journey attended by dramatic encounters and wondrous deeds, we are told. It is a long way; a taxing experience. It seems to me it would be wise of you to allow for recovery before you must repeat it. Eat, drink, rest. Take time for yourselves."

Brother Suibne altered this subtly on relaying it to Brother Colm. Somehow, the opportunity for recovery became less a matter of good beds and fine food, and more one of time to pray and reflect in this season of change. Perhaps that was a wise mistranslation. Colm agreed, with visible reluctance, to the delay.

"Also," said Aniel, "should this matter of the king's son develop in any way unexpectedly, Bridei may need to delay the audience longer or to cancel it."

Colm raised his brows as Suibne rendered this.

"The fact is," said Tharan, "we don't know if we're dealing with a mishap or an abduction. If your own countrymen are involved and we need to exert pressure to have the child returned, you may find yourselves enjoying White Hill's hospitality for longer than you intended. King Bridei has authorized me to tell you this."

Suibne translated Colm's reply. "We do not condone the abduction of children. We appreciate your candor and will pray for the boy's safe return. If King Bridei wishes, Brother Colm says he will keep vigil by the king's side tonight and offer up prayers for the child. What is his name?"

"Derelei." Bridei found it hard to get the word out. "Thank Brother Colm from me. I know he means well. There is no need for him to lose sleep over this."

They spoke of other matters. It was clear Colm wished the formal audience to cover assurances of safety for the Christian hermits of the Light Isles, not just from Keother but from Bridei as Keother's overlord. Then there was a question of Gaels whom Colm had seen among the serving people at White Hill. He wished to know the fate of last autumn's captives, those of the defeated Dalriadans who had come here in Priteni custody. How many were slaves? What would their future hold? What of the fate, in the longer term, of Gabhran, deposed king of the Dalriadan Gaels, now locked up in his own old stronghold of Dunadd?

The list was thorough. Bridei remembered that this

man, as an Uí Néill, was kin to Gabhran. It was powerfully apparent to him, even through the fog of exhaustion
and anxiety, that when the formal audience did take place
it would range far beyond matters of religion. He began
to revise his idea of exactly why this Colmcille had made
his arduous journey all the way to the heart of Fortriu.

"And lastly," Brother Suibne said, "there will be a
matter of which you already know; the matter central to
our mission. It concerns the island of Ioua, in your west-
ernmost territory. We visited that place. It is beautiful,
remote, and wild, with few inhabitants. We have hopes
you will reconsider those words you spoke at the moment of victory over Gabhran's forces last autumn. We
have hopes you may, after all, grant us sanctuary in that
place." It was a more poetic, and humbler, rendition of
his superior's closing speech.

"You are a clever translator, Brother Suibne," Bridei
said.

"And you an astute listener, my lord king." Suibne
smiled. "I'm so sorry about your boy. How is your wife
taking it? I remember her from Caer Pridne. A fey, small
thing, but strong-hearted. I assume it is the same."

"Tuala. Yes. I cannot speak of this here. But I thank
you for your concern."

They were seated in a chamber not far from the Great
Hall, in order to be able to continue talking until the
meal was about to be served. Bridei had become aware,
over the course of the last few interchanges, that there
was a level of disturbance outside well beyond anything
one might have expected: shouts, scuffling, many voices
raised. He thought perhaps one of them was Faolan's.

"Tharan," he said calmly, "you'd best go out and discover what that is about. Take one of the guards." Then,
turning to his guests, "We'll go to supper shortly. I regret
that my court druid, Broichan, is unable to be with us tonight. He is currently away from White Hill. I hope he
will be able to join us for our official discussions. It is
another reason a delay will aid us."

"You hope?" Colm raised his brows. "Cannot you command his return? I'm told Broichan wields great power within Fortriu and strong influence here at your court. My belief is that he should be present."

"I am my own man," Bridei said quietly, using one of Broichan's techniques to set his anger aside. "Broichan is one of those who advise me. Where the welfare of my people is concerned, the final decisions are mine. Does the high king in your homeland command your movements, Brother Colm?"

The translation provoked a wintry smile. "What can I say?" was Suibne's rendition of the reply. "He is in Tara, and I am here in heathen Fortriu."

It was at that moment Bridei decided that either Suibne was too clever for his own good, or Colmcille was no different from the rest of them: for all his miracle-working, a real human being.

"Then welcome to Fortriu," he said. "Now let us go to supper—"

The door opened and Tharan came back in, his features carefully arranged into an expression of calm. "My lord king," he said, "there's something of a . . . spirited discussion taking place among those in the hall awaiting their meal. It involves Lady Breda and certain accusations. And also—"

Keother was on his feet. "I'll deal with it," he said, "if I may be excused."

"—the matter of Eile, and the search," Tharan went on. "This requires your personal intervention, my lord king."

Bridei could hear Faolan shouting. "Very well, we'll go through," he said, wishing he could achieve Tharan's self-control. "Brother Colm, Brother Suibne, it will be best if you remain here until this is dealt with. I regret the inconvenience." He nodded to the remaining guard to stay with the Christians. The shouts were getting louder; he could hear Breda, her voice rapidly rising. And one of Talorgen's boys. Abandoning protocol, the king of

Fortriu strode out the door and down the passageway to the Great Hall.

There was no way to tell exactly what was going on. The hall was full of folk, and ale had been served while they waited for their supper. Most were seated, but Faolan was on his feet, pointing an accusatory finger at Breda. He was enraged; his face was flushed, his scowl thunderous. Whatever this was, it must be serious to rob Bridei's self-disciplined spy of his well-known equanimity in public. At the king's table Breda, too, was standing, hands on hips, head high, her elegant attire a stark contrast to the shrillness of her voice.

"What are you saying?" She was glaring at Faolan. "Are you calling me a liar? *Me?*"

All around the hall voices were buzzing and eyes were turned on this battle with keen interest. For entertainment, it seemed it far surpassed what could be achieved by a bard with a harp.

"Sit down," Bridei said, aiming his command halfway between his right-hand man and the princess. "You, too," he added as he noticed both Bedo and Uric standing at the front of the hall, beside the dais that held the high table. "If there is a dispute to be settled, it should be behind closed doors, not here in the hall as if you were a mob of brawling drunkards."

"My lord—" Faolan began. Bridei heard a note in his friend's voice that sent a chill through him. This was something serious.

"I won't just let this go!" Breda snapped. "You can't expect that, not after the vile things you've been saying!" The big blue eyes turned to Keother, a step behind Bridei. "Cousin, this man—this *Gael*—is trying to accuse me of some kind of misdemeanor. I want him thrown out of the hall. I won't tolerate this." She tossed her head; the artful curls at her temples quivered.

"Cousin, take your seat." Keother moved to stand beside her. Something in his tone made Breda obey. Her eyes were venomous; there was no telling if that look was all for Faolan, or half for Keother himself.

"My lord—" Faolan tried again, and this time his voice cracked.

"Let us take this to a council chamber," Bridei said. "Who is party to the dispute? Lady Breda? Uric? Bedo?"

"No, my lord." The uncharacteristic flush in Faolan's cheeks had faded; now he was white. "The matter concerns Eile and this story that's being put about. I need it resolved straightaway. It's possible we've been searching in the wrong place, based on misleading information. This must be settled now, quickly and publicly. I won't have Eile made the subject of lying gossip."

"I see." Bridei moved to his place at the royal table and sat. The hubbub died down. Keother seated himself between the king and Breda; Aniel and Tharan took their seats on Bridei's other side. Faolan made no move; nor did Uric and Bedo.

Out of the corner of his eye, Bridei could see the two Christians entering the hall with an irritated-looking guard behind them. It was not possible to order them out. "Seat them at the end of this table, one on each side of Queen Rhian," he murmured to Aniel. "I don't want Suibne to do too much translating." He turned to Faolan. "Very well," he said, "I will hear the matter of this dispute now. Keep it brief and to the point. If it concerns my son and Eile, we need it set out quickly so we can take appropriate action. Who will speak first?"

"Talorgen's sons." Faolan was in better control of himself now, his voice level, his eyes grim. "There are two stories here, my lord, and the one feeds into the other."

"Step forward, Bedo, Uric. What is this?"

"It relates to the hunt, my lord king . . ." The two boys told their tale well, with calm logic, plain though it was to Bridei that they were strung up with tension. For all his own nervous anticipation, he was struck by their maturity and self-control. Talorgen would be well pleased if he could see them now. Bedo related how, at the moment before Cella was struck, there had been a scream, and that the horse then reared up and descended in a flurry of lethal hooves. Uric related the same sequence: the scream, the movement of the mare, and added one more detail. There had been something flashing in the sunlight, something Lady Breda had been holding in her hand. Then the mare had bolted and taken Lady Breda with it.

"This is stupid—" Breda began.

"Please be quiet, Lady Breda," Bridei said. "You will be given the opportunity to speak."

"But—"

"Hush." Keother's tone was a hiss of rage. Glancing sideways, Bridei was alarmed by the expression in the other man's eyes. He read there horror, shame, and something that suggested this was perhaps not as much of a surprise as it might have been.

"I don't see the relevance to the other matter, the search, Eile, my son," he said to Faolan.

"It will become apparent, my lord," Bedo said. "My brother and I had certain suspicions as to what had made Lady Breda's horse shy. A scream might have done it. A scream and a sharp goad would certainly have frightened the most placid of creatures. Uric thought he saw something flash downward just before the . . . accident. He has been searching the place of the hunt for that item. A day or two ago he found it." The hall was completely silent.

Uric held up a jeweled pin. "The mare sustained no major injuries that day, but she did come back with many scratches and abrasions from her headlong flight," he said. "If one of them was a deliberate wound, inflicted by this silver hair ornament, the grooms would not have singled it out for particular notice. I found the pin—or, at least, your dog found it—in a part of that field where only Breda and the two men who rescued her had ridden that day. This ornament bears the royal insignia of the Light Isles. It belongs to Lady Breda."

"Nonsense!" She was on her feet again, hands clenched. "Yes, maybe it is mine, but what you say is just silly! Why would I do that? Anyway, I wasn't wearing it that day. Ask my attendants. I had quite another hair clasp on, the gold one with little chains. You're just making this up!"

Keother looked down toward the table where Breda's handmaids were seated in a huddle. "Who can support my cousin's version of events?" he asked. "Do you recall what she was wearing on that day? The young men's story is somewhat flimsy, there's no doubt, but we owe it to them to respond to their questions. A girl died."

The young women looked into their ale cups, at their hands, at the floor.

"We require an answer," Bridei said. "Faolan has indicated lives may be at risk. Does this silence mean yes or no?"

A fair-haired girl half rose to her feet. "Lady Breda was wearing what she just said. Gold, with chains."

"That's right," muttered a second girl.

The third girl stood up slowly. She was a little thing. Her face was white as linen. "No, it's not," she said in a shaking voice. "Breda was wearing the silver pin. I know because I did her hair that morning. I'd swear to it. Amna helped me."

After a moment the fourth girl got up to stand by the third. "Cria's right." Her voice, too, trembled. "She was wearing that one. The sea beast. It's her favorite."

"I never did anything!" Breda burst out, hitting her fists on the table and making the spoons rattle. "It was the poxy horse! It's not my fault if you give me a creature that shies and bolts at the slightest thing! If Cella had kept her wretched merlin under control—"

"Hold your tongue!" Keother shouted. His cousin fell silent, but Bridei sensed it would not be for long.

"The theory you propose is that, for some reason, Lady Breda deliberately caused the mare to shy, then to bolt," Bridei said levelly, knowing this could not be pursued much further in public, not if there was any chance at all that it was true. It was for himself and Keother to resolve behind closed doors. "I cannot imagine any possible motive she might have for such an irresponsible action. It set her own life at risk. It killed a young woman and wounded you, Bedo. This is a very serious accusation. To do what you suggest would be an act of insanity."

"We're told," Uric said, "that Lady Breda is subject to fits of extreme jealousy. That, in this case, the friendship between my brother and Cella had made her angry. I'm sorry, my lord," he inclined his head in Keother's direction, "but we have one, maybe two young women who can testify to that. They prefer not to speak here before the whole court."

"*What?*" Breda glared at her handmaids, her lovely face suffused with rage. "Which of you's been telling tales? How dare you? By all the gods, you'll wish you'd never opened your filthy mouths—" She stopped dead, suddenly mindful that the entire court of Fortriu was sitting there staring, horrified, in her direction. "My lord, this is . . . unseemly. Distasteful. These boys have got it all mixed up. Not so long ago they were trying their hardest to impress me; these accusations are the result of sheer pique. Besides, Cella's gone. What is the point of raking over old ground?"

Keother muttered something. Perhaps it was a prayer of thanks that the dead girl's father had already departed from White Hill and need not hear this.

"Faolan," Bridei said, "what is the relevance of this matter to our present crisis? Be quick, I beg you."

"I'm told, my lord king, that it was Lady Breda who reported seeing Eile and your son walking out of White Hill yesterday, clad in their outdoor clothing as if for a journey."

"That is correct," said Aniel.

"The tale of the hunt must, at least, raise questions over Lady Breda's reliability," Faolan said. "I'm a bodyguard, not a nobleman; I say these things in an open forum only because lives are at risk and time is short. Lady Breda, if Eile was planning to spirit Derelei away as a hostage, why did she go out of White Hill without her warm cloak and boots?"

Breda stared at him as the assembled folk hushed anew. "But she didn't—I mean, she did go out, but she was wearing them, of course she was, and so was the boy. I saw them. I said so."

Garth rose to his feet; he came to stand by Faolan's side. "That's not true, my lord king. My wife can vouch for it. Eile's warm clothes are still in her chamber."

"Eile would never leave Saraid behind," said Faolan. "Anyone concocting a lie about abductions would need a story to cover that. I don't believe Lady Breda's tale. Eile couldn't have just wandered off. She wouldn't have. And if that was a lie, perhaps both Eile and Derelei are still somewhere inside White Hill."

Bridei felt the blood drain from his face. "Breda," he said, "could it be you were mistaken?"

"No, of course not! If I saw something, I saw it. Unless it was someone else, not her. I mean, there are other women here and other little children, after all. With a hood on, and her back turned . . . perhaps it wasn't her. I may have mixed it up . . ."

"I need an answer." Bridei could not keep the edge from his voice. Derelei, oh gods, Derelei here all the time, here somewhere, and silent . . . "Was your account of how you spent that day true or wasn't it? Did you see my son or didn't you?"

"Of course it was true. Ask my handmaids." She fixed them with a ferocious glare. "They wouldn't lie, would they?"

The smallest girl, Cria, stood up again. This time she held herself straight. "My lord king, may I speak?"

"Please do."

"This might be best in private," Keother muttered in Bridei's ear, but it was too late.

"I'm not proud of this," Cria said. "Lady Breda asked us to lie and we did. There were reasons for that, reasons I'm not saying here. We all saw Eile and the children yesterday."

A gasp ran around the hall, and Bridei clenched his fists until the knuckles were white. "Go on," he said.

"Eile came down to our quarters with Breda. They fetched some sweetmeats. Amna gave the little girl a ribbon and she put it on her doll. It was one of those lavender ones, the ones Amna's got in her hair. Then they all went off together, Lady Breda and Eile and the two children. Lady Breda told us we couldn't come."

"She said something about a secret place," Amna said softly. "She was going to show little Saraid."

"When did Lady Breda come back?" Faolan's tone was a reminder of why so many folk feared him.

"Not until much later," Cria said. "When she came back she told us what to say. Then, today, she told us about Eile going out and taking Derelei, and that was what we had to say. I'm truly sorry, my lord." She was crying.

Keother had risen to his feet. "You others," he said, "what tale do you tell now? Is this an accurate account? Did all of you indeed see King Bridei's son and his attendant and say not a word, even when the child's life was in jeopardy?"

"My lord," Bedo spoke up, "there were reasons why these girls did not speak up earlier; reasons best set before you in private."

Keother ignored him. "Speak up!" he commanded. "Who is telling the truth, Cria or my cousin?"

"This is outrageous!" Breda's voice had risen still further; it was approaching a shriek. Tharan's wife, Dorica, got up quietly and went to stand behind the young woman's chair. She put a hand on Breda's shoulder, whether to reassure or restrain her was not clear, and the princess of the Light Isles shook it off with some violence.

"Cria's telling the truth," the fair-haired handmaid said. "We all just said what Breda told us to say. I'm sorry, I really am."

"She's right," said the fourth girl. "Lady Breda didn't like Cella, not after . . ." She glanced at Bedo. "And she didn't like Eile. She said it was wrong that a Gael was given so much trust; that she shouldn't be left in charge of the king's children."

"That's a lie! I liked the little Gael!"

"Breda," Keother said, "there's to be not another word. Not one, understand. My lord king—"

Faolan was suddenly on the dais, confronting Breda across the king's table, breaking every rule of court protocol. "Where is she?" he demanded, and Breda flinched backward. "And where's Derelei? What have you done?"

Before Bridei could say a word, Garth was taking hold of Faolan's arm, drawing him away, speaking calmly. "Come, we'll search again. I'll help you."

"By all that is sacred," Faolan hissed at Breda, as his fellow guard half dragged, half supported him from the dais, "if you've harmed either of them I will make you pay!"

Breda gave a little squeal of fright.

"I remind you," Bridei said sternly to his right-hand man, "that you are in the presence of the king and of his guests. Curb your anger." It was the first time he had ever had to reprimand one of his personal guards in public. The look on Faolan's face made him wretched, for he felt its twin in himself, a powerful compulsion to rush off and search, and a fierce anger that this erratic young woman had, through sheer foolishness, prevented them from reaching their lost ones quickly. He reminded himself that he was king, and turned to address the assembled household. "Many of you have searched long today on little sleep. You're weary and supper is late already. Tharan and Dorica will preside over the meal. Please eat and rest. King Keother and I will excuse ourselves to pursue this weighty matter in private. I ask you to remember that my son is still missing, as is Eile. I ask you not to spread tales that may be untrue. Do not increase the distress of those close to this terrible unfolding of events by passing on rumor and gossip. We of Fortriu are strong people. Lend one another your strength. Garth has offered to assist Faolan. Any man who is prepared to help them will be welcome. Any man who prefers to eat and then sleep must do so with a clear conscience. Unless we find our lost ones tonight, or gather further information that can help us, the main search goes on tomorrow outside the walls as planned."

Keother was standing beside the now-sobbing Breda, his hand firmly around her arm. Farther down the table, Brother Colm was looking on with a little frown on his brow.

"My lord, I should be present at your discussion," Faolan said. "I need to know—"

"Go, begin your search," Bridei told his friend quietly. *Get out that door, search high and low until a miracle occurs and you find the two of them safe and well in some forgotten corner. Go now.* "If we discover information that can help you, we will bring it to you promptly. Go, Faolan."

A small knot of men was gathering around Garth and Faolan: Talorgen's two sons, an exhausted-looking Dovran, Garvan the royal stone carver and his assistant. Wid, leaning on his staff. No more. Perhaps the rest of them were simply exhausted. Garth could be heard telling the group to eat something quickly, then take torches and meet him in the lower courtyard.

Bridei retreated toward the council chamber where his earlier meeting had taken place, with Keother beside him, shepherding the weeping Breda. Aniel came behind, followed by a guard.

"Gods, Bridei," muttered Keother, "if this is what it seems, I don't know what to say to you. I should be out there with them, searching."

"I ask only one thing of you tonight," Bridei said.

"Keep your cousin in check. If Lady Breda's lies have caused my son to be harmed in any way, it is not just Faolan who will be seeking vengeance. If Derelei is hurt, if he is dead, your kinsmen will pay for it in blood. Make no doubt of that. Harm my child and you will know what it means to offend the king of Fortriu."

INSTINCT SERVED TUALA well. The creature whose form she had borrowed went with speed and caution, padded feet soft on the forest floor, the journey a dance of light and shade, of concealment and swift, calculated exposure. Scent offered the path; sharp vision helped her avoid trouble. On the fringe of the great wood that cloaked the slopes by Serpent Lake, a wild dog gave chase. She climbed for safety, claws and bunched muscle carrying her up the trunk of a young oak before there was time to think. Crouched between branches, every hair standing on end, she willed her human understanding back with some difficulty, and marveled at how quickly instinct had served her in her borrowed shape. She must be more wary; she must remember how small she was, how vulnerable to hungry predators. When the sun was low in the sky, she caught a new scent, a sweet, familiar one, though her animal senses found it confusing. There were marks in the soil here and there; she thought they were the prints of little feet shod in soft leather.

The part of her that was still Tuala, the part that was exercising all its strength to remain in control, was desperate to change back then; to be human, to call out to her son, to run after him. The day was passing quickly and it was dark here in the forest. She longed to find him, to scoop him up in her arms and hug him tightly, to weep with relief that he was safe at last. The other part, the instinctive, animal part, held back, sniffing the alien scent, cautious yet. She crouched there, hesitating, her mind torn two ways, and as she did so there was a rustling in the bushes behind her. She sprang up and turned in one movement, tail bristling, as the presumptuous fox hurled itself across the small clearing toward her.

She snarled and struck with claws extended. With a yelp the fox retreated, blood streaming from its nose. And Tuala fled, deep into the cover of the trees, to hide awhile under a clump of ferns and remind herself that she had changed her form for both speed and safety. If she was to reach Derelei unscathed, she must follow her instincts every step of the way. No confusion. No lapses.

Dusk came, and the woods grew darker. Her vision changed with the light; she found that she could still follow the tracks she hoped were her son's. Perhaps he would be asleep by now, curled up in the bracken somewhere; perhaps she might go past and not know he was there. No; the scent would guide her.

There came a need to cross water, a thing she didn't like, not in this form; the human part of her consciousness tried not to think too hard about Derelei and the fact that he did not understand *deep* and *shallow* yet. On the far side, the need to stop and lick her body tolerably dry was not to be disregarded. She did so with ears pricked for sounds of danger, but all she heard was birds crying and a small scuttling in the undergrowth. The urge to chase gripped her, but she held back. If this took much longer, she would have to hunt and eat. But not yet. Not unless she must.

The scent grew stronger. Before it was quite dark, she emerged between elders onto the bank of a broader stream, and there was Derelei sitting on a flat stone. She stood very still a moment, watching him with love and relief flooding through her. There were biting insects all around, and his small hands slapped ineffectively at these unwelcome companions. Tuala could almost hear her son thinking; she could see the conflict on his face. Weary to the bone, his body was telling him it was sleep time, time for cuddles and songs and a last kiss before being tucked into bed. Hungry and thirsty, he was wondering where his supper might be. She saw him yawn, then get to his feet, ready to walk on along the bank. His mouth was quivering. His eyes were stoical. And he was not alone; as soon as he had moved, two others had emerged from nowhere to take their places beside him: a tiny, eldritch girl with snow-pale skin and a garment made of what looked like wood smoke; a sturdy small boy with nut-brown skin and ivy twists for hair. Derelei glanced at them and started to walk; it was plain they were his accepted companions on his lonely journey.

Tuala released the breath she had been holding. As she sidled out from under the trees in her animal form, the fey boy and girl turned as one, gazing at her, and their faces were not those of children, but of far older creatures, all too familiar from her past. *Gossamer,* Tuala thought. *Woodbine.* They *led him here* . . .

There was a tinkle of laughter like a peal of little bells; the pale-skinned girl tossed her threads of silver hair, but spoke not a word. The boy raised fingers like twigs and greeted Tuala with a kind of salute. She seemed to hear his thoughts: *We are only companions on the journey. It's your son who is the leader.* A moment later boy and girl had faded away to nothing.

Tuala came forward, feet rustling in the leaves, and her son turned at the little sound. The droop of his mouth changed to a beaming smile. "Mama!" he exclaimed.

Tuala effected the change to human form and took him in her arms. "You clever boy," she murmured, tears starting in her eyes. She'd done it; he was safe. "I might have known you would see through that straightaway! I've come to help you, sweetheart. Help find Broichan? That's what you're doing, isn't it?"

"Bawta," said Derelei, his arms around her neck, then yawned again.

"Sleepy time first. Let's find somewhere warm to curl up."

There was a hollow under an oak. Bracken formed a bed, and Tuala's cloak covered the two of them. Derelei was hungry and thirsty. The queen of Fortriu unfastened her bodice and let her son drink the milk that should have been Anfreda's, and he took it like the weary infant he was. Falling asleep under a sky washed with pale stars, Tuala thanked the Shining One for delivering him safely back to her. She considered what part the two fey companions of her own childhood might have played in this, and whether they would start to appear more often now, seeking a part in Derelei's growing up. Perhaps it was he who had summoned them. She pondered the fact that a child of such astonishing powers was, at the same time, every bit as fragile and vulnerable as any other two-year-old. What would he be if he managed to grow safely to a man?

18

FAOLAN AND GARTH stood waiting for the rest of the search party. For a moment a stillness seemed to come over the courtyard; the moon was dark, the stars barely perceptible in summer's long, eerie twilight, and even the night birds were hushed. It was cold. Wherever Eile was, she didn't have her cloak. Faolan knew he should be planning how to do this, using logic, but logic had abandoned him completely. Suddenly, he understood faith; the compelling desire to trust in a power beyond the knowable, a benign and loving deity. Or maybe what he needed was the instinct of a wild creature, the ability to seek and find by scent, by subtle sound, by changes in the air that caused the hackles to rise, the breath to catch in the throat.

"Do you think—" Garth began.

"Shh. Just a moment." Faolan held himself still and closed his eyes. In his heart, he cried out to her, a great shout of faith, hope, instinct: *I love you! Where are you?* Then silence. Silence save for the desperate drumming of his heart.

He sensed a change in the light and opened his eyes. The other men were coming with torches: Garvan, Wid, Uric, one or two more now, among them the unassuming figure of Suibne with two of his brethren.

"Brother Colm has given us approval to help you," the translator said in Gaelic. "Meanwhile, he and the others will pray that we find your wife and the king's son safe and well."

"Wife?" Garth raised his brows.

"It's a long story," Faolan said, nodding thanks to the priest.

"Bedo's been called in by the king," Uric said. "That girl, Cria, as well. Aniel promised to send us a messenger if they got anything useful. May I make a suggestion?"

"Be quick," said Garth.

"We should start down by Breda's quarters. That's the last place anyone saw them apart from Breda herself."

Garth glanced at Faolan. "That's the section we were starting on last evening when you came in with Saraid," he said. "Some of it's only been covered sketchily. Very well, break up into pairs and head down that way. One torch to each team. Faolan with Brother Suibne. Dovran with Wid. Garvan with Uric." He paired them all, experienced man with less experienced, stronger with weaker, older and wiser with younger and fitter. "Cover every chamber top to bottom, no matter if the occupant is a court guest. Open storage chests, look in privies, don't leave a thing unexamined. The least sign of anything untoward, report straight to me or Faolan. Understood?" He shielded a yawn. "And stay alert," he added.

"I DON'T KNOW what you want me to say," protested Breda, wiping her eyes with a delicately embroidered handkerchief. "Everyone's telling me different stories, even my own maids are saying the cruelest things, and I'm terribly confused. And scared. That man, your body-guard, my lord, he didn't need to threaten me like that. He should know better. Anyway, he's a Gael, too. Didn't Eile come here with him? Hasn't it occurred to you that he could be part of the whole thing?"

"Breda," said Bridei with hard-won patience, "we just need you to tell the truth. This was only a day ago. You can't have forgotten. It seems you don't realize how serious these matters could be for you. Your status, your royal blood, those things don't render you immune where charges of this kind are involved."

She stared at him. "Charges? What do you mean?"

They had been in the small council chamber for some time. Cria, her halting narrative growing steadier as she realized the men believed her, had told a grim story of jealousy, resentment, and retribution, of small omissions and errors punished by severe beatings and by subtle cruelty. She had advanced a theory, long shared in secret by all the handmaids, that Breda had caused the accident at the hunt partly in a deliberate attempt to injure Cella and partly out of sheer mischief. It was well known by the girls that the princess of the Light Isles could not tolerate a day without drama. If things got too boring, Breda took action to liven them up.

Bedo had related what he'd been told about jealousy and how that might have made Eile a target. All the while, Breda had watched him under her lashes.

"You are on the verge of finding yourself held responsible for Cella's death," Bridei told her. "If you would not have further accusations of unlawful killing leveled at you, tell us where you went with Eile and the children yesterday morning and where you left them. And let me add, in support of Faolan, who is an old and trusted friend of mine, that I was a hair's-breadth from taking hold of you myself and shaking the truth out of you. Now speak. The question is simple."

"I don't like this." Breda's voice was small and tight. "I don't think I want to say anything more. It sounds as if I'm being accused of . . . murder." She turned her eyes toward Keother. "You're my cousin," she said on a plaintive note. "You're supposed to protect me."

"I'm a king, as Bridei is. And yes, I am your kinsman. That allows me to do what he cannot." Keother strode over to where she was standing, the candlelight illuminating her wan, tear-stained cheeks, her brimming blue eyes, her cascade of golden hair. He seized her by the shoulders and shook her hard. "Tell the truth!" he roared. "Tell King Bridei what you saw! I will not have innocent blood staining the hands of my family!"

Breda blanched. "We took the sweetmeats down to a . . . a . . . storage place," she said in a whisper. "There were some locked-up chambers, old dark musty areas. The little girl said she wanted to explore. It was part of a game Eile was playing with them, having an adventure, collecting things. I said I didn't think it looked a very suitable place to be in, especially with children, and I went back to my chamber and then up to the garden."

Perhaps, at last, she had told plain truth. Keother sighed. "Why didn't you say this before? Why all the lies?"

"Aniel," Bridei said quietly, "will you send a man to convey this to Garth or Faolan immediately, please?"

"I was scared," Breda said, her tone one of misery. "When I heard they were lost, I thought . . . I thought I'd be blamed. And it wasn't my fault. I wasn't even there. Not after that. They were fine when I left. Really."

"My lords," said Bedo, "may I be excused? I've told you all I know, and I want to join the search. I could convey the message."

"Go," Bridei said, "and the gods go with you. Remind Garth that within that part of White Hill there is a disused well." His stomach was tying itself in knots. The well. The well that was behind a chained door, so secure that, almost certainly, nobody had considered it a danger. Perhaps they had not even checked it, for it lay at the far end of that long walkway below Breda's quarters, a place the search might not have reached at all before it was diverted to the wooded hill outside the walls. *Thus you take your vengeance. You give me my very own Well of Shades.* He thought he could hear the bitter laughter of the Nameless God. In his mind, Derelei lay down there in the darkness, a broken doll, limbs sprawled, fragile skull smashed. "Keother," Bridei said, "I cannot go on with this tonight. I think it's best if Lady Breda remains here until the area close to her quarters has been searched. I would suggest her handmaids sleep in our women's quarters from now on; Dorica will find them beds, and will provide a serving woman for your cousin. Will you excuse me?"

"Of course, my lord."

"Bridei," said Aniel, dispensing with formality, "you should not join the search. We must be mindful of security. I'll have supper sent to your private quarters. And I will come myself the moment we have any news."

Bridei managed to nod politely and leave the chamber before he began to shake. He managed to walk to his own apartments before the tears spilled from his eyes. Then, because he was not just husband and father but also a king, he did not seek out Fola or go to watch his baby daughter sleeping. Instead he knelt in the corner he had set aside for his devotions, quieted his breathing and began to pray. But tonight, for the first time in his life, no matter how deeply he searched within himself he could not summon obedience to the gods' will.

૪૭

THEY FOUND THE door before any message reached them. Brother Suibne held the flaring torch; by its shifting light Faolan examined the chain that held the portal shut. It could not be readily unfastened; the holes through which the chain passed were too narrow to admit his hand. It seemed unlikely Eile would enter such a place. It was not possible a small child could have opened this door. Yet he felt suddenly cold, as if chill fingers had gripped his heart. "Hold the torch closer," he said. "There's something on this chain, it's sticky. Can you see?"

"Oil?" suggested Suibne.

But Faolan already knew what it was. He wrenched at the heavy door with some violence, trying to heave it bodily open.

"Take the torch," said Suibne. "I may be able to get a hand through."

"She's in there," Faolan muttered. "I know it. I feel it. Eile!" There was no sound save for a muted rattle as Suibne sought to maneuver his hand through the hole and unfasten the chain blind.

"Almost got it . . . Stay calm, Faolan. God will aid us. Ah, that's it . . . Now, I need to draw it through . . . God help us, is this blood?"

The chain was off. Faolan thrust the torch back in Suibne's hand and pushed open the door. And there she was, a limp form on the ground, gown rent and filthy, face corpse-pale, eyes shut, limbs sprawled. He fell to his knees beside her, forcing himself not to take her up in his arms but to put his ear to her lips, his fingers gently to her neck. In his mind was a desperate plea, to whom he did not know: *Let her be alive. Let me not lose her.*

"God have mercy," murmured Brother Suibne, then stuck his head back out the door to shout, "Down here!" in the Priteni tongue. He moved back in, lifting the torch to illuminate the raised stones encircling the shadowy pit; to reveal the narrow gap at the foot of the outer wall.

For an interminable few moments, Faolan's own heart forgot to beat. Then he felt the weak whisper of her breathing, the slow pulsing of her blood. He stripped off his tunic and laid it over her, touching his lips to her brow as his eyes filled with tears. "She's alive," he said, and they were the sweetest words in the world.

"Faolan." Something in Suibne's voice alerted him. "There's a well."

He made himself get up; forced himself to take a step across and look in. The torch showed the two men evidence of a cruel climb. Eile had left her blood on the crumbling wall of the pit, her clawing final effort marking the moss-crusted rim with desperate red trails. It was clear that, once she was safely up and over the edge, she had collapsed into unconsciousness before she could call for help. Suibne held the torch out to illuminate the bottom of the pit. Heart in his mouth, Faolan looked down. The well was empty.

"Merciful God," said Suibne quietly. "I had expected the child to be there, and this a heroic attempt at rescue. What has happened here?"

"Come and look at this." Faolan, crouched once more by Eile's side, was examining her hands. The torchlight played on the broken nails, the abraded palms, the fingers whose flesh was raw and torn. Her soft indoor boots were ripped and holed, her feet a mass of cuts and blisters. Her knees were deeply grazed, dirt worked hard into the wounds.

"She has an injury to her temple," Suibne said. "Look, there. Best touch her cautiously, there may be hurts we cannot see. It is a long way to fall. A perilous and terrifying climb. Here, take my cape, she's freezing."

"Garth!" Faolan shouted from where he knelt. "Get

down here now!" And, disregarding the cleric's good advice, he gathered Eile into his arms.

"Faolan?" Suibne's voice was soft. "Is it possible, I wonder, that a small child might slip out through a chink such as that appears to be over there? If that were to occur, a woman would not be able to get through to bring him back before he wandered. She'd need to raise the alarm. Folk would need to go out by the gates, then around the wall to find him. The trees grow thickly on those slopes."

"Mm," said Faolan, holding Eile close, wondering if he could be sure her heart was beating.

"Might she slip and fall in her haste to run for assistance?"

"Not Eile. Besides . . ." He reached a gentle hand to touch the crusted blood on her head wound. "Suibne?"

"Yes?"

"Take that chain, coil it up, put it in your pocket or conceal it elsewhere. I don't want anyone tampering with evidence. If that's her blood on it, I need the truth out in the open. I need justice."

"One might say, of course, that we are the ones who are tampering. In fact I already have the item in question secure. I admire the young lady immensely, Faolan, whether she is your wife or something else entirely. I saw her courage and sweetness on our voyage to Dalriada. I saw her devotion to her child and her trust in you. I will pray for her recovery."

Torches; voices; running footsteps. Garth was there, and behind him the bulky form of Garvan, with Uric close by. More men followed: Wid making remarkable speed, Dovran gray-faced with dread.

"She's here. She's alive. No sign of Derelei. Garth, I need to get her inside quickly. She's been hurt and she's icy cold."

Exclamations of concern, of shock; a warm cloak—Wid's; Garvan offering to carry Eile. It was wrenchingly hard to give her up; Faolan did so only because he knew

the brawny stone carver would get her to shelter more
quickly than he could. He had already demanded more
of his knee than it was fit for, and he feared it might give
way on him at any moment.

"Garth," he said quietly, "seal up this chamber for tonight, and don't let anyone tramp about in here. It could
be important."

"Of course. We should take Eile to the women's quarters, yes? And call for Fola."

"I'm not letting her out of my sight," Faolan said.
"Take her to her own chamber. I will watch over her, at
least until morning. If that's considered improper, too
bad. We do need Fola; will you tell Bridei what's happened and ask him if she can come?" They began to
walk up the pathway, Garvan leading with Eile in his
arms, Dovran beside him with a torch.

"Garth?" Faolan murmured.

"What, friend?"

"Bring Saraid. Even if she's asleep."

"You are both healer and nursemaid now?"

"Please."

"Very well. I think you need a healer yourself. I've
never seen you shed tears in public before."

"This merits more than tears," Faolan said. "Derelei is
still lost. We don't know what damage has been done to
Eile. I am beginning to see answers. But I won't do anything until Eile's hurts are salved and she is safe and warm
again. And you must sleep. I promised you rest. Instead,
this. It is no life for a man with a wife and children."

HE WANTED TO stay by Eile every moment, to do everything that was needed, to watch over her constantly, to
ensure he would be by her side when she regained consciousness. He wished to be there to allay her fears and
soothe her hurts. He wanted to tell her what he had not
dared to put into words before.

Fola, however, had other ideas, and before her formidable will and indubitable competence Faolan retreated to the smaller chamber, the one with the green blanket, biting his nails. In the chamber which had once been Ana's, a fire was made up on the hearth and candles lit; he watched through the half-closed connecting door. More blankets were fetched. Under the wise woman's calm instructions, men brought warm water for bathing and a supply of plain food and drink. Elda arrived bearing a basket of salves and lotions and a clean nightrobe. Then the two women shut the connecting door and Faolan was left to pace alone.

As time passed he thought he might go mad. They were taking so long; what was wrong? He imagined her slipping away from him between one breath and the next. He thought of her waking, confused and terrified. He thought of her not waking at all. He imagined the chain and the hand that had wielded it, a wicked, arbitrary hand. He was on the point of bursting through into the other chamber to say he knew not what, when there was a tap at the outer door, then Garth's voice.

"We're here."

Saraid was not quite asleep. She was in her little nightrobe with a blanket around her and Sorry in her arms. "Mama?" she said in a tiny, doubtful voice.

"I told her Mama was back, but sleeping," Garth said.

Faolan nodded, taking the child in his arms. "Thank you. You've spoken to Bridei?"

"I've told him what we know. I understand Fola has seen something, too; something suggesting Derelei is indeed outside the walls and may still be alive. You know what that means, Faolan."

"Another day's searching tomorrow."

"Will you come?"

Faolan looked down at the solemn face of Saraid. He listened to the soft, capable voices of the women from the adjoining chamber. He was Bridei's chief bodyguard; he was responsible for the king's family. "I'll face that choice in the morning," he said. "I take it you've decided not to continue the search inside these walls tonight?"

"The king says no. He believes Fola's vision to be accurate."

"You'd best go to your bed, then. Thank you for everything. You're a true friend."

Garth nodded. "You'd do the same for me," he said.

When Garth was gone, Faolan and Saraid sat side by side on the bed and he sang her the Sorry song. In the newest verse, Sorry was put on guard in the forest, watchful and silent, and when Faolan passed she alerted him and the brave dog Ban to peril. Thus Saraid was rescued and brought home. He spun it out, wanting the child to see her mother before she went to sleep, but they reached the end and still the door remained closed.

"Mama?" Saraid asked. "House on the hill?"

"Mama's too tired to tell a story tonight. I will tell it. We'll wait till Mama's ready. We'll do it all together."

"Faolan?" The door opened a crack, and Fola was there. "Oh." She glanced at Saraid. "Can I speak in front of the child?"

He was chill again. "It's ill news?"

"Not so ill, though Eile has not yet regained full consciousness."

"Then tell me now. May we see her?"

"Sit down, Faolan. You can go in shortly. I can't remain with her overnight, and nor can Elda. As you've refused other help, I must explain to you what is required. I know you won't listen once you're in the other chamber. Go on, sit. That's better." She came in to seat herself on the storage chest. The sleeves of her gray robe were rolled to the elbow. "We've warmed Eile up and tended to her cuts and bruises. She seemed to respond to the bathing and the heat of the fire; she managed to swallow a few drops of water. It's important that you keep offering her something to drink each time she comes to herself sufficiently to swallow. But not too much at once.

There's plain bread and a little broth there; you can warm the pot over the fire. It doesn't matter if she takes that or not. Tomorrow will be soon enough for eating. But she must drink."

"Will she—"

"Let me finish. We've examined her closely to see what harm has been sustained. Apart from the blow to her head, it seems there's been some damage to the left shoulder; she didn't like us touching it. I don't think anything's broken, or she couldn't have climbed so far. She'll lose a few fingernails." Fola glanced at the round-eyed Saraid. "There is no sign of abuse. I can't tell you how she sustained the wound to her temple. Perhaps in the fall. On the other hand, it could be that blow caused her to fall. There are certain markings . . ."

"Yes," said Faolan. "What damage has been done by that, apart from the flesh wound?"

"I can't tell you. There may be no long-term damage. It's astonishing that she sustained no broken bones, Faolan." The wise woman regarded him gravely.

"You saw the mark on her head. I believe she was rendered unconscious before she went into the well. That can reduce the damage caused by a fall. I don't want to make the particular details of the head injury public until I've asked a few more questions."

"If you're saying what I think you're saying," Fola commented, eyes shrewd, "you'd best not take too long over your investigations. Tonight, you'll need all your energies for Eile. She'll be confused and distressed when she wakes fully. Keep her calm. Elda's left you a salve for her hands and feet. Apply it often. And call one of us if there's the slightest need, Faolan. I will come back in the morning."

"We'd like to see her now."

Fola smiled. "You've been patient. Don't expect much sleep tonight."

"Garth said you saw something. About Derelei. Can you tell me?"

"I do not generally share my visions with the world," the wise woman said, getting up. "But I see a difficult choice for you at dawn; love in conflict with duty. I saw Derelei, yes."

"Where? Was he safe?"

"He was walking through deep, dark woods, all alone. He made his way with utter confidence. It seems to me his mother's theory was correct. Derelei has not been abducted. He has not run away or wandered off and become lost. At two years old, he's gone on a mission."

"Derry's gone," said Saraid, nodding sagely.

"Where did he go, Squirrel?" Faolan's heart was in his throat, but he kept his tone light.

"Derry's gone. Gone in the woods. All dark."

He looked at Fola; she regarded him calmly. A decision was made, without need for words, that no more questions would be asked tonight.

"Saraid," said Fola, "Mama's very tired. She's having a big sleep. You can go in and see her, but don't wake her up. Good luck, Faolan. Don't hesitate to ask for help if you need it. I sense that doesn't come easily to you."

But he had already moved to the other chamber, where Eile lay tucked up in the big bed, a slight form beneath layers of woollen blankets. The flickering fire, its light playing on woven hangings depicting trees, flowers, and creatures, gave the room a good feeling, bright, safe, cozy. Saraid climbed onto the bed and wriggled in under the covers, as close to her mother as she could get. "Mama's home," she said. A moment later she started to cry, a small, repressed sound that soon grew to unrestrained sobbing as she clutched on to Eile and buried her head against her mother's breast.

Faolan did not allow himself time to think. He lay down on Eile's other side, on top of the covers, and wrapped his arm over the two of them. "Hush, Saraid," he whispered. "It will be all right. I promise. Everything will be all right." A terrible weariness came over him, made up not simply of the ache in his leg, the gritty feeling in his eyes, the weight of too many sleepless nights. He sensed how small and powerless they were before the violent and arbitrary acts of destiny. It took him back to Fiddler's Crossing and the night his whole life had changed.

Saraid's weeping died down. He stroked her hair, and Eile's, and felt his own tears flowing anew. After a while a little voice said, "Story now. Please."

He drew a shuddering breath and let it go. "All right, I'll try. You'll need to help me. I don't know it as well as Eile does. Once upon a time there was a girl who lived with her mother and father . . ."

"In a house on a hill."

"It was a little house, just big enough for three."

"Chickens," said Saraid. "Cat."

"It was just the right size for everyone. Three chickens, one black as coal, one brown as—as mud . . ."

"One brown as earth."

"And one white as snow. And a cat. Fluffy, is that right?"

"Mm. Garden."

"She . . . she pulled up weeds and staked up beans and in between she stared into the pond, dreaming."

Eile stirred, making a little sound.

"I think Mama's waking up." He lifted his arm away, slowly so as not to startle her; he eased himself off the bed.

"More story. Papa away. Eggs."

He watched Eile as she raised a hand to touch her temple; as her eyelids fluttered and she tried to swallow. "When her Papa came home she cooked eggs for him," he whispered, "and put in all the good herbs she had grown in her garden; I can't remember the names."

"Thyme, sage, calamint," said Saraid sleepily.

"And when she gave it to him, he said, *That's my girl.* Then she knew her mama and papa loved her, and that she was the luckiest girl in the world. Eile, are you awake?"

"Faolan?" Her voice was a croak, dry and painful. "What's happened? My head hurts. And I'm thirsty."

He fetched water; put an arm behind her shoulders to help her sit up; held the cup while she drank. "Not too much."

Eile looked at him over the rim of the cup, her eyes shadowy in a face that seemed that of a ghost, pallid and shrunken.

"You had a bad accident; we didn't find you straight-away," he said carefully. "You got very cold. We need to take things slowly." He set the cup aside; moved away again to sit on the very edge of the bed.

"What happened? I can't remember anything. What day is it? How long—?" She began to shiver.

"Mama fell. Down, way down."

"Oh gods, Faolan. Was Saraid hurt?" Eile drew her daughter closer.

"She's not hurt. She was missing for a little, but no harm's been done. She can't tell us what happened. Eile, you were with the two children that day, Saraid and Derelei, out and about in the grounds. Then you vanished, the three of you . . ." He told her what he knew, without mentioning Breda. "And we found you, just now, by the rim of the well. Look at your hands, Eile. Can't you remember?"

She stared at her hands, slathered with salve and wrapped in bandages. Her eyes were confused.

"Mama's hurt," said Saraid.

Eile's shivering became convulsive, fierce bursts racking her body.

"Lie down again. Under the blankets. Let me . . ."

"I'm so cold, Faolan. I don't think I'll ever be warm again."

He went to lay more wood on the fire. The chamber was warmer than was entirely comfortable. When he turned, Eile was sitting up again.

"You were lying here before, weren't you, with your arm around us?" she said. "I wasn't so cold then. And I felt safe. Who else is here, Faolan? I thought I heard some women."

"Fola was here, with Elda. Now it's nighttime and it's just the three of us."

"Come and lie down next to us. Keep us warm."

So he did, staying on top of the covers, and very soon Saraid was asleep, cheeks pink, one arm around her mother's and the other around Sorry. But Eile and Faolan stayed awake. *It is like the dream,* he thought. *The good dream, where I wake with her in my arms. But cruelly changed. What will she say when she knows the truth: that Breda tried to kill her?* For he knew in his heart what had happened; instinct and the evidence matched too neatly for there to be any other explanation.

"Faolan?"

"Mm?"

"Thank you."

"For what?"

"For being here. For looking after me. For coming to find me. Faolan, I . . . You said the top of the well. I think I can remember climbing up. Did I just imagine that?"

"No, *mo cridhe.* You climbed to the top. It was a feat of matchless courage. But when you got there, I think your strength gave out. Don't thank me for finding you. It was my error that brought us there so late."

"What error? How long was I there?"

"Almost two days and a night, Eile. It's no wonder you're thirsty."

He felt sudden tension run through her body. "Derelei? What about Derelei? Is he safe?"

It had to be the truth. "We don't know. We think he's outside the walls, but our search has found no trace of him. Fola saw a vision, and in that he was alive and well, somewhere in the forest. We're hoping very much that it was accurate."

Eile said nothing for a little. Then her voice came, shaky and faint. "I was looking after him. This is my fault. Why can't I remember? A well. Why would I go anywhere near a well with the two of them?"

Faolan's lips were against her hair; his arm lay loosely across her, careful not to jar her injured shoulder. Quietly, he told her about Tuala's search, and the arrangements that had been made to keep it secret.

"I can't remember anything," she whispered. "Except . . . I think my father was there. Down in that place. I just wanted to lie there. Everything hurt. He said, *Fight*. He wouldn't let me give in."

"So you climbed up."

"I suppose I did. My hands are a mess, aren't they? Why does my head hurt so much, Faolan?"

"You've got a lot of cuts and bruises. You're lucky you didn't break anything." He got up, moving to the hearth. "Do you want some soup?"

She shook her head, wincing with pain. "I don't want anything. I feel sick. I should have kept him safe. They trusted me and now he's lost. He's only little—"

"Shh, Eile. We'll talk about this in the morning. Lie down now."

"Faolan?"

"Mm?" He was banking up the fire; he must not let her get cold.

"You look exhausted."

"I'm fine. I don't need much sleep."

"Rubbish. Leave that, come and lie down."

"I can sleep on the floor."

"I need you here, next to me. Please."

There was no chance at all, in his current state of exhaustion, that desire would create any kind of difficulty before morning. All the same, the only items of clothing he removed were his boots. When he was lying down, Eile shifted so her head was on his shoulder. She curled against him. The fire set a rosy glow on the tapestry at the foot of the bed, a piece of Ana's making, an image of a plum tree in full spring bloom with a family of ducks foraging beneath.

Faolan held Eile closer; his fingers twined in her hair.

"I don't think I'll be able to sleep," she said. "I can't get it out of my mind, Derelei all alone out there. It's so cold at night."

"Tuala may already have found him."

"But—"

"Do I need to sing a song and tell a story to get you to sleep?" he asked her.

"You can if you want," she said, and there was a smile in her voice.

There was a silence. "I'm worried that I'll fall asleep halfway through. And there's a thing I have to tell you. I—"

"Shh. Not now."

"A story, then. Once upon a time there was a man who had lost his way. When he was young he'd had a blow, and for a long while, years and years, he'd been following wrong paths, and all that time the world had been rushing by him, and he'd never bothered to stop and do little things. Hugging a child. Sitting quietly with a friend, talking. Singing songs. He'd gone so far down a track to nowhere, he hardly knew who he was anymore, and although he was not yet thirty, he was told he looked old."

"I never said that."

"Not in so many words, maybe, but it was what you meant. Anyway, to cut things short, he met someone— two someones—who suddenly made his life very complicated. They were always doing things that surprised him. Sometimes they scared him. Sometimes they brought tears to his eyes, tears he could not shed, because he had forgotten how. It became impossible to lead the life he had before. They were a nuisance and a hindrance and they made it necessary to throw away his carefully devised rules, the rules that held him safe, the ones that stopped him from feeling. He tried to let the two of them go, thinking they'd be better off without him; thinking it would be easier for him without them.

Then he felt something odd, as if a part of him long closed had at last been exposed, raw and painful beyond belief. He thought maybe that was the sensation of his heart breaking."

She said nothing. He wondered if the story had worked all too well; perhaps she had fallen asleep.

"Remarkably, he got another chance. She gave him that; she was wiser than he was. This time he determined to tell her how he felt; how she had opened him up and let light into his life. But she kept saying, shh, no, not yet, and he held his tongue. Until the time he nearly lost her again. Then he told her, even though she tried to stop him, because he knew that if anything happened and he hadn't said it, he could never forgive himself."

A silence. Then she murmured, "I suppose you'd better say it, then."

"I love you," he whispered. "I'll take as much or as little as you're prepared to give me. I'll give you and Saraid everything that's in me."

The fire flickered; the birds on the tapestry moved in the draft; the silence lengthened. At last Eile's voice came, hesitant and sweet: "That was the best story I ever heard, Faolan. Will you sing the song now?"

He did not tell her where and when he had last sung this lullaby. He did not speak of Deord lying in Briar Wood with his head on Faolan's shoulder as his eyes grew slowly more tranquil and his face paler, and his lifeblood drained into the dark soil of the forest floor. But he sang it for the three of them, father, daughter, granddaughter; a trio of souls whose courage was a beacon, lighting the way forward. The melody wafted around the sleeping form of Saraid and wove its way across Eile's body lying against his as if it belonged there. It moved out through the fire-lit chamber where maybe, just maybe, Deord, too, could hear it. By the time Faolan got to the last lines his own lids were drooping, and a sweet warmth was stealing through his aching body. "Rest tired limbs and weary eyes," he murmured, "and to a bright new day arise." And, holding her close, he slept.

UNDER THE SPREADING canopy of an ancient oak, in a hollow partway up a wooded slope some miles from White Hill, the druid sat cross-legged on the ground. He felt the heartbeat of Bone Mother in the earth that supported him; he smelled the myriad scents in the air, the tiny, subtle differences he had learned to recognize over the long years of his training. The sounds of the woodland were a wild, soft music, balm to the ears, telling a wisdom deep beyond human knowing, old and unchangeable. *I endure. I am strong.*

His eyes were closed, his back straight, his hands loose against the tattered garment that covered his nakedness. Soon he would slow his breathing, clear his mind, enter deep meditation. As he had come closer to his destination, he had heard the goddess bid him slacken his pace and take time for reflection, for a task awaited him that would tax his newfound strength hard. Daily he had sat thus awhile, fixing his mind on the gods and on obedience.

Often, in the visions his trance brought him, he would see a figure climbing the hill, feet soft on the forest path, face dappled with sun as the Flamekeeper's light sought to penetrate down between the leaves. Sometimes it was Bridei, a strong, square-shouldered man in his prime with steadfast blue eyes and curling hair the color of ripe chestnuts. Sometimes it was Tuala, his daughter, a slight, graceful girl whose form seemed both ethereal and strong, both eldritch and dearly familiar, with her snow-pale skin, her cloud of dark hair, and her deep, knowing eyes. And sometimes, as today, it was the child: Derelei, his little student, his frail, precious infant mage. Broichan's vision showed him the tiny figure clad in nothing warmer than shirt and trousers, his feet in indoor boots that were fraying and mud-coated. The child's face was grubby, too. Beneath the grime of his journey, the soft mouth was set in iron-strong determination. The large eyes gazed straight ahead.

Ten paces away, Derelei halted, looking up the hill. At that moment the druid realized that this time it was not vision, but reality. It was indeed his dear one who stood there on the track between the trees, his light, odd eyes lifted, unwavering, to examine the seated figure of the druid. Broichan held his breath.

"Bawta!" exclaimed Derelei and, opening wide his arms, ran forward, his small face illuminated with joy. Broichan's heart performed a somersault. Tears flooded his eyes. He rose to his knees, spreading his own arms, and caught his grandson in a strong embrace.

"Derelei," he murmured against the child's hair. "Have you come all this way to find me?" Even as he spoke, he knew it was so. There was no need to consider how such a journey had been made; the fragility of the infant, the long distance and rough terrain, the fickle nature of the weather and the threats attending the path. With this particular child, such considerations had no relevance. Broichan held the boy close, feeling Derelei's arms tight around his neck, and knew this for a moment of deepest change. He was made whole at last, and now he would go home.

After a little he opened his eyes and observed that, after all, the child had not made his journey quite alone. Sitting neatly at a slight distance, using a paw to wash behind its right ear, was a small gray cat with a tail like a brush. It looked vaguely familiar.

A druid did not leap to conclusions. He did not ask questions unless absolutely necessary. Life was a series of puzzles. A druid's skill lay in choosing from a range of solutions, each of which might be correct in one way or another. Broichan studied the creature. When the cat had completed washing to its satisfaction, it fixed its large, fey eyes on him in solemn examination. The druid smiled.

"Welcome, daughter," he said, and the cat was gone. In its place stood the queen of Fortriu, regarding him with something of the same calm scrutiny.

"Father," said Tuala. "We've missed you. You're needed at home."

Not a word about his sudden departure. Not a sign that she was shocked or alarmed at the change in his physical appearance. Her cool self-discipline was the twin of his own demeanor as it had once been, hard-learned, hard-practiced, a shield and defense.

"Then we should go," he said, and heard his voice tremble like a leaf in autumn. He stood with Derelei in his arms and found that he was weeping.

"You may be the king's druid," said Tuala, "and I a queen, but I think we can allow ourselves to forget that for a little. There's no one to see us out here."

She moved across to him and Broichan saw that, although her gait was as neat and smooth as that of the creature whose form she had assumed for her journey, the hand she stretched out toward him was not quite steady. There was a shadow of uncertainty in her eyes.

"I'm sorry," Broichan said, shifting Derelei to his hip and wrapping his arm around his daughter. "Tuala, I'm so sorry."

"Shh." Tuala hugged him, and he saw the tears glinting in her eyes. "That's all past. What have you been eating, grass? I can feel every one of your ribs."

"Tuala—your child—is all well—?"

"A fine daughter. We named her Anfreda."

He felt another wide, uncontrollable grin spreading across his face; it was an odd sensation. In the days of *before,* he had not been a man who smiled. "Anfreda. That pleases me. You'll be needing to get home to her. Quickly. Perhaps we should—?"

"Derelei is too little for a transformation. No doubt he could do it, but we shouldn't allow that. He lacks control. I can carry him."

"I will carry him, Tuala."

She did not question his fitness. "Very well. And as we go I will give you the news from White Hill. Much has occurred in your absence. We needed you. We still do. I hope you will stay this time."

"If I am needed, I will stay," he said. "It seems to me you have taken a great risk for me." He knew how much she feared making her Otherworldly powers public knowledge.

"For my father, yes. And for my son. When we are nearly home I will use that other form again."

"I remember the little cat Fola gave you when you were a child. Mist, wasn't it?"

"I loved her dearly. A true friend in lonely times. I don't think she would be offended to know I copied her form. Remembering her so well made the transformation easier."

"It's a rare gift," said Broichan. "I hope, in time, you will show me more. I think we could learn from each other."

"YOU SHOULD GO," Eile said. "I know that's what you would be doing if it weren't for us. Saraid and I will be perfectly safe here. We can spend the day with Elda or up in the garden with Dovran to guard us, if you're really concerned. Derelei's at terrible risk. The king needs you." She scrutinized Faolan where he crouched by the hearth, remaking the fire so she and Saraid could dress in warmth. Already he had fetched them breakfast while Garth hovered in the hallway and, to oblige him, Eile had made herself swallow a few mouthfuls. She still felt odd; there were aches and pains everywhere and a curious dizziness when she tried to stand up. But she would not admit this to Faolan. The men were even now assembling out in the yard, ready for another day's search. She knew that if she held him back, guilt would torment him all day.

"Of course," she added, "if your leg's not up to it . . ." She would not say how badly she wanted him to stay. It had been sweet indeed to wake in his arms and realize she was not afraid. The anticipation of a wondrous change in herself had stirred her to the core.

"I'm not leaving you on your own. You must stay where you can be adequately guarded. We still don't know what happened to you. It's possible your fall wasn't an accident."

"I know what you think. It sounds . . . crazy."

"Eile, I'm deadly serious. If I'm not here, the best place for you is the royal apartments. Fola is there, and at least two other women, and Dovran will be on guard during the day. I'll carry you up there before I leave. You mustn't try to walk about. You need complete rest. I want you to stay with Fola until I get back."

Seeing his tight jaw and his pallor, Eile bit back a remark about giving orders. "All right," she said. "I suppose you do know about these things. Maybe I could help Fola with the baby."

"You must rest, Eile. Don't try to do anything. You can't expect to be instantly well again; you need time to recover."

"If that's what you think. Resting is something I'm not very good at. Faolan, I hope you find Derelei. That's the most terrifying thing, not knowing if your child is lost or found, dead or alive."

Faolan nodded, then bent to pick her up in his arms.

"Faolan?"

"Yes?"

"Before we go up there, I want to tell you . . . What you said last night . . . those things . . . They were good to hear. Very good."

He said nothing; his eyes spoke for him, making her catch her breath.

"And . . . waking up this morning with you there, your arms around me, that was good, too. Surprising, but good. I wanted you to know that before you left."

Faolan smiled. It was like watching a ray of sunlight break forth in a dark place. "Thank you," he said.

☙

FOLA SEEMED UNPERTURBED to find herself overseeing Eile and Saraid as well as the queen's baby daughter and her wet nurse. She made Eile lie down on a pallet, refusing to take no for an answer. Anfreda's trusted nursemaid tried to take Saraid out to play in the garden, but the child stood firm, refusing to leave her mother's sight.

"Maybe it's best," Fola said. "Until Faolan gets to the bottom of what happened to you, he's wise to suggest the two of you remain within safe walls."

"I think he believes someone did it on purpose," Eile said, glancing at Saraid, who was on the mat playing with Derelei's wooden animals. She would not use the words *hurt, injure, kill* in her daughter's hearing. "I think he's hoping I'll remember without prompting, so he can prove his theory. Or that Saraid will say something. But why would anyone want to do that to me? I'm nobody."

"Can't you remember anything?" Fola asked.

"Not between earlier in the day and waking up in that place. Faolan said there was a narrow opening to the outside; that the children might have got out there. But why would I take them to a well? That's so foolish, when they're little and curious. What must people think?"

"I suggest you ignore what they think, Eile. Those of us who know you at all well would never believe you capable of negligence where children are concerned."

"So folk *do* think it's my fault that Derelei is lost. Oh, gods . . ."

"There's talk. So I'm told. At such times of crisis folk tend to gossip. Bridei trusts you. You should be reassured by that."

"Gossip, what gossip? What exactly are they saying?" Eile sat up on the pallet, trying to disregard the way her head reeled.

Fola was at the table, grinding something efficiently with a small mortar and pestle. A pungent odor filled the chamber. The wise woman turned shrewd dark eyes on Eile, but said nothing.

A sudden suspicion came to Eile. "Did Faolan ask you not to tell me?"

Fola smiled. "You know each other pretty well, don't you?"

"Tell me, please. I need the truth, woman to woman. What is it people are saying about me?"

"I heard a theory," said Fola with some reluctance, "that you'd been placed here for the purpose of kidnapping Derelei. That you were a spy, a very clever one who won the queen's trust with astonishing speed. In some people's eyes, that makes Faolan guilty, too, guilty by association. Bridei stood up at supper last night and ordered the entire household to stop spreading such tales. He was right; the whole idea is sheer nonsense."

Eile's stomach tightened with a feeling that was part misgiving, part fury. How dare folk turn on Faolan, who had been with the king since Bridei first came to the throne? "But they know Faolan," she said. "They must know how loyal he is; how stupid it is to suggest he could be a traitor."

Fola had finished pounding her dried berries to powder. Now she transferred the result from the mortar into a tiny stone jar. "Faolan is a particular kind of man," she said. "He may have been at court for years, but few folk really know him. He's ever been less than open to friendships. He's been guarded about his past. He is by no means universally liked, Eile. And he's a Gael who, by choice, has attached himself to a Priteni king. That in itself must arouse suspicion. Those few who do understand the man at all well know he is flawlessly loyal to Bridei even when out there playing some contrary role, as his work often requires him to do. But ordinary folk may well look at him, and look at you and what has happened to you, and leap to an unpalatable conclusion."

Eile made herself speak, though she feared her voice would betray too much. This hurt far more than the gash she bore on her head. "But nobody knows what happened to me," she said. "If I fell or was pushed; if I was stupid enough to take the children into that place of danger. Whether I sent them outside the wall; whether someone took Derelei with or without my approval. There were no witnesses except Saraid, and she won't talk about it even to me. If I can't remember, how can I defend myself? How can I defend Faolan? He's been the best friend I ever had and all I've brought him is trouble."

"Lie down, Eile. You've been through an ordeal. It's essential that you rest. That's a severe head wound, not to speak of the chill you sustained. Take my advice and set these rumors aside. Don't let them bother you. In time the truth will come out." She corked the little bottle and set it on a shelf. "I hear that baby stirring. I'll ask Tresna to bring her out here to be fed; we could do with a distraction."

Obediently, Eile lay down and closed her eyes. She listened to the sounds of the two women changing Anfreda's wrappings; of Tresna feeding her while her own baby kicked on the mat, cooing happily. She listened to Saraid singing to Tresna's infant and examining its tiny fingers and toes. All the time the feeling in her belly, a cold stone of uncertainty, grew heavier and the images in her head grew darker. How could she set this burden on Faolan, who had been so good to her? It wouldn't just be today. If she stayed with him, if she let him take responsibility for her, it would be one thing after another. She was trouble; he'd more or less said so, even as he'd spoken his sweet words of love. She would create problem after problem for him without even trying. Besides, tied down by her and Saraid, how could he continue with the special duties he performed for the king, the duties he excelled at, the secret ones nobody else could carry out? He'd never be home. She'd constantly be worrying about him, out there in danger. They'd both be unhappy. Common sense suggested she should walk away; leave White Hill and let him get on with his life. She pictured him coming back and finding her and Saraid gone; his voice sounded in her heart, saying, *I'll give you and Saraid everything that's in me.* "No running away," she murmured to herself. "Not anymore."

The day wore on. In the early afternoon, when it became apparent both Eile and Saraid were chafing at the restriction of staying indoors, Fola allowed them to go out and sit in the queen's private garden. With Dovran on guard it was deemed safe.

"But don't venture any farther," the wise woman warned. "I'm under orders to keep you more or less in sight. If you need anything we'll send someone to fetch it. And don't talk to anyone except Dovran."

Out by the long pond, Eile watched Saraid running along the path, then stopping to show Sorry something she had found. Her daughter's hair was glossy, her skin rosy; she looked neat and pretty in her gray gown with a little embroidered cape over it, a gift from Elda.

Dovran hovered close by; he seemed keen to talk. "How are you feeling? You looked so limp and white last night. And your head . . . That's a nasty injury."

"I'm well enough. Don't waste your time worrying about me."

"I do worry," Dovran said, the words rushing out. "I care about you. If I could—"

"Dovran," said Eile, "tell me what folk are saying about what happened to me. What stories are they telling?"

"It might be better if you disregard that." Dovran stood leaning on his spear, brown eyes troubled in his handsome, open face. "Folk talk a lot of rubbish."

"I want to know. I expect my friends to be honest with me."

"Can you really not remember what happened?"

"Nothing. What have you heard?"

"The talk should have died down now you've been

found; now it's clear you were trapped in that place and too weak to call for help. But I heard the men talking this morning; I rearranged one fellow's face for him." Dovran eyed his right fist. "He was suggesting you didn't fall down the well at all, just waited there to give your accomplice time to get away undetected with the child. That it was an elaborate cover for a kidnapping. He hadn't seen your hands, or your head. You should be resting, Eile."

Eile folded her arms tightly, pushing her bandaged hands out of sight. "What about Faolan? Did anyone say anything about Faolan?"

Dovran gave a grim smile. "Faolan's more than capable of looking after himself. A person would be a prize fool to get on his wrong side." Then, at her look, he added, "There's been a rumor or two. A Gael at the court of Fortriu, a regular traveler; it's inevitable. How *did* you two meet?"

He saved me from the worst place in the world. He came for me: a wondrous friend in the guise of an unprepossessing stranger. "On the road," Eile said.

"You sound sad. Eile, you know how I feel about you. I want you to be safe; I want to help—"

"You've been kind to me," Eile said. "I value your friendship, Dovran." She saw in his face that he had understood the unspoken message, *but we will never be more than friends.* She could not find any words to make him feel better. He was a nice man; he would meet someone else soon enough.

Saraid was sitting by the pond, refastening a ribbon around Sorry's head. It was an unusual color, a delicate lavender. Someone must have given it to Saraid; it was new. Eile felt an odd sensation, a prickling at the back of her neck, somewhere between memory and premonition. "Saraid?" she called. "Who gave Sorry the ribbon? Was it Elda?"

Saraid shook her head, small face solemn.

"Who was it, Squirrel?"

"Lady."

"What lady, Saraid? Ferada? Red-haired lady?"

But Saraid was hugging the doll tightly now and had closed in on herself; her pose told Eile there would be no more said on this subject today. Her stance reminded Eile, uncomfortably, of the old days at Cloud Hill, Saraid sitting hunched and silent on the front step while, in the hut, things happened that were no fit sight for a child. "You'd best be off, I suppose," she told Dovran.

"I can watch the garden and talk to you at the same time."

"We should be going in."

"Oh. Very well, then. I don't suppose I will see you at supper tonight."

"No, I don't imagine I will be there. Farewell, Dovran."

"Farewell, Eile. Bye, Saraid."

"Bye." It was wistful. Nobody had offered games today.

19

THE SEARCH PARTY returned to White Hill well before the light began to fade. The men were tired and dispirited. They had not found Derelei. Faolan and Garth had made the judgment that the child could not have gone outside the broad area already covered unless someone had spirited him quickly away. Either the king's son had been conveyed beyond the reach of an ordinary search or he was already dead.

Faolan reported this to the king. Bridei took it calmly,

but the look in his eyes was desperate. "Go," he said. "You'll be wanting to see Eile. I will not give up hope, Faolan. There is still Tuala."

Faolan refrained from mentioning that the search parties had seen no more sign of the queen than they had of her son. He supposed it was possible they had in fact seen her in the form of beetle, bird, or vole, and passed her by unthinking. Strange indeed. "I should stay with you," he said to Bridei. "But I am concerned for Eile, it's true. Have you learned any more about what happened?"

Bridei shook his head. "Keother says Breda is distraught. He believes she has nothing more to tell. We may never learn the truth."

"It will come out," said Faolan grimly. "I'll make sure of that."

"Doubts and theories do not make up a convincing case. It does seem Breda has played a dark part in the matter of the hunt and her handmaid's death. Where the issue of my son is concerned, and indeed that of Eile, there is no real evidence against her. I know what you're thinking. You must cool your anger. One cannot accuse a person of Breda's status without being sure of the facts. I know it's difficult. Go on, now. Go and see your sweetheart. I'll do well enough."

Privately, Faolan doubted this. Bridei was linen pale and had all the signs of one of his monumental headaches. Here in the small private meeting room, the king had been sitting alone without so much as a candle to illuminate the gloom. His usual supports were gone, Tuala on her perilous journey into the forest, Broichan who knew where. And now he, next closest to the king, was walking off to tend to his own business. "You need someone with you—" he began.

"And Eile needs you. Go on. I'll seek out Aniel or Tharan if I decide I must have company."

Faolan made his way down to the apartments he had already begun to think of as *theirs*: the three of them, himself, Eile, and Saraid. He tapped lightly on the door of the smaller chamber and went in.

Saraid was on the bed, sorting out the contents of a little box, with Sorry beside her. Eile was sitting on the floor with her back to him. She, too, was sorting. There was a neat pile of garments beside her; he spotted the blue gown his sister had given her and a carved comb that had once been his. *This is what I'll be taking.* Spread over the storage chest was an old tunic and skirt, the things she'd worn at Blackthorn Rise as a servant, and by them the boots in which she'd journeyed by his side, all the way over the sea and up the Great Glen. *This is what I'll be wearing.* In another heap, over by the wall, were her best clothes, the ones she'd been given here at White Hill. The green gown; the soft slippers; the little cape Elda had made for Saraid. *And this is what I'll be leaving behind.* He stood just inside the door, calming his breathing, as Eile turned her head to look at him. He could not read her expression.

"What are you doing?" he asked, willing his voice calm.

"It's all right," Eile said, her bandaged hands continuing, awkwardly, their task of folding. "We're just . . . going over things. Don't look like that. We wouldn't go away; not without giving you the choice. But you do need to think about it, Faolan. You need to be sure this is all right, me and Saraid, I mean, here at White Hill with you, depending on you, perhaps being a burden you don't really want or need."

He moved swiftly to kneel beside her, to take her hands in his. His voice came out ragged and harsh despite his best efforts. "What has prompted this? I thought you trusted me, Eile. I thought you knew . . ."

"I do." Her voice was tight, constrained with some emotion he could not identify. "But you need to know what folk are saying: that I betrayed the king's and queen's trust. That I'm a spy. And they're saying vicious, horrible lies about you. That you were in collusion with me all along, that we arranged a kidnapping together. I won't have them saying those things. It's so wrong. As if you would ever act against King Bridei . . ."

"I see." He got to his feet. Watching his face, she had stilled her hands. "And you think going away would make it better?"

A tear trickled down her cheek; she mopped it with a swathed hand. "I'm trouble for you, Faolan. You know how difficult things will be for you if I stay. I need to be sure you are prepared to face that; that you think it's worth it. I don't want you to keep us here just because of duty. Or worse still, from pity."

Saraid had lain down on the bed, her head buried in the pillow. Half under her, Sorry was barely visible.

"Eile," Faolan said, his heart hammering, "please believe what I tell you. If you were to go away, I would follow you to the ends of the earth. I'd leave White Hill and Bridei in an instant rather than lose you. I can't do without you and Saraid. It's as simple as that. As for the rumors and gossip, we'll find a way to deal with them."

For a little she simply stared at him, green eyes assessing. Then she whispered, "Good, that's all right, then," and he saw her shoulders begin to shake and tears begin to spill in earnest. He knelt by her again, putting his arms around her. "It's the truth, *mo cridhe*," he murmured. "The desperate truth. I would not lie to you. Where you go, I go. If you left this place, I would come after you without a second thought. Saraid, come down here and give your mama a hug." And, after the child had settled by him and he had done his best to enfold the whole of his small family within his embrace, "I think I've discovered something. I'm home at last. You, me, Saraid . . . this is it. This is home. Don't go away."

"Feeler go away?" He could feel Saraid's small hand clutching his shirt up by the shoulder, and the damp warmth of her tears soaking through the fabric over his heart.

Eile drew a shuddering breath. "No, Squirrel," she whispered. "Nobody's going anywhere. Oh gods, I can't stop crying, this is ridiculous. You really do mean it, don't you? You really do mean you'll stay with us, no matter what?"

He stroked her hair, his fingers close to the place where the ugly wound disfigured her temple: the imprint of a regular pattern resembling the links of an iron chain. "Forever and always," he said. "As long as I breathe."

She sighed. He felt her arms come around him. "I want to tell you something," she said.

Faolan waited.

"You said you learned where home is. I've learned something, too. I've learned why my father did what he did. Why he left us; why he walked away and never came back. And I've learned that I'm not going to repeat what he did. I can't do that to the people I love best in the world. It might be bad for you if I stay. But it would hurt you far more if I went away, and it would hurt Saraid, too. And I can't make you leave White Hill, the work you love, the folk who depend on you. Faolan, I think I've forgiven him. My father. His choice was far harder than mine."

His heartbeat was quick but steady. He did not ask Eile to clarify what she had said about love. It was enough, for now, to hold those words close; to feel them sink within him, a force of profound strength. "Come," he said, "you're still an invalid and my knees are feeling the effects of a day's riding. We'd best get up off the floor, rekindle our fire, and dry our tears. Squirrel, will you go next door and see if there's kindling in the basket?"

"Faolan," Eile said as he helped her up, "there's still the question of gossip and mistrust; the vicious tongues that keep so busy. I won't have you subject to that. If you stay with me, I'll attract those tales to you."

"Come through here and sit down, Eile. I need to see you drink something; that's better. I do have a solution to the problem. You won't like it. It presents a challenge every bit as taxing as scaling the sheer side of a well."

Eile sipped the water he had given her, as he knelt with flint and tinder to make the fire anew. Saraid, all sign of tears gone, was busily sorting out the wood.

"What?" Eile asked.

"The rumors are based on how we met, how long we've known each other, who might have recruited us," he said, wondering if he was being a prize fool for even suggesting this, yet seeing a curious rightness in it, as if their tale was making a neat full circle. "So we tell them the truth. We tell them our story. All of it."

"*All* of it? You mean Cloud Hill and . . . and Dalach . . . and what happened afterward?"

"And Blackthorn Rise. And Fiddler's Crossing."

"I can't . . . how can I . . . Faolan, what are you saying? That we should get up in front of *everyone* and talk about those things? I'd be so ashamed I wouldn't be able to get a word out." The cup shook in her hand, spilling droplets on her skirt.

"Ashamed?" He looked up at her as the fire began to catch. "Why? You haven't a single thing to be ashamed about, Eile. Your actions have been selfless. Heroic. You are your father's daughter. What advice do you think Deord would offer right now?"

Eile gave a wan smile. "*Fight,*" she said. "But I'm afraid, Faolan. This is a great deal to ask."

"I'll be there. I'll stand by you; I'll help you tell it."

"I don't know enough of the language yet. And if you translate for me, people will say you can twist the story any way you want."

"Then we will ask for another translator. I know one who will do very well."

"When? When would we do it?"

She looked frail and wretched, her hands shaking, the wound fresh and livid on her temple. Faolan would have given much to be able to say, honestly, that he did not care if she never told; that all he wanted was to wrap her up, hide her away, keep her safe. But when he looked at her huddled there by the fire, it was not an injured woman he saw. It was the daughter of Deord; Deord who had only once in his life run away, and who had paid a terrible price for it. Deord who, he sensed, was still watching over them.

"Tonight," he said. "We should do it tonight."

EILE ALREADY KNEW that Faolan's self-control was formidable. She did not think she had ever been so impressed by it as she was that evening. Saraid had gone to her supper with Gilder and Galen; brows had been raised when Faolan and Eile appeared in the Great Hall to take their places, but he had acted as if there were nothing untoward about her attending supper so soon after what had happened.

Garth was on duty, guarding the king. Faolan and Eile were flanked at table by Wid and Garvan. Dovran had placed himself opposite, next to Elda. Beyond that small circle of safety lay the unknown. Eile saw the looks, observed folk whispering to one another, and wondered if they were discussing her probable guilt, though it seemed to her the wound on her head should be some indication of innocence. She could hardly have inflicted it on herself. Her stomach was churning; she could not touch her food. Faolan ate his roast meat and pudding, and chatted to Wid about navigation and to Dovran, guardedly, about the finer points of swordplay.

At the high table Bridei sat ashen-faced, contributing the occasional word to a conversation between his councillors and King Keother. Another day, another fruitless search. Eile had seen how much the king of Fortriu loved his children, how close he was to his wife, and her heart bled for him. She had Saraid. She had Faolan. Against what the king must be feeling, the trepidation that now gripped her, making her dizzy and nauseous, was nothing at all.

"Not eating?" Wid asked her. "You look as if you

should still be in bed, young woman. Faolan, what were you doing, letting her get up?"

"I'd rather be here than in my chamber," Eile said. "Besides, we have something to do."

"Oh?"

She did not elaborate. Most folk had finished eating; Faolan was looking over toward the second table, where Brother Colm sat with his brethren, a small sea of brown robes topped by gleaming tonsured heads.

"Are you ready?" he asked her in an undertone.

I could never be ready for this, not in all my days. "If you are," she said.

It was customary, before or after the meal, for Bridei to say a few words to the household. In good times it might be thanks for certain work done or news that could affect them. Bridei's speech might be followed by music; there was usually a court bard in residence. Or, if anyone had a matter of general interest to raise, Bridei might invite him to air it. In bad times folk expected little. Faolan had told her that tonight the king would wish to advise his household that the full search for his son was to be called off, leaving the task of tracking Derelei to a few specialists rather than taking so many of the household's men away.

"I won't wait for him to speak," Faolan whispered to Eile. "I see on his face that he can't bear to declare the full search over." He rose to his feet, took Eile's hand and led her out to the open area before the dais.

Folk took some time to notice. Talk buzzed around them until the king stood and raised his hand.

"You wish to speak, Faolan?" Bridei's voice was level and quiet.

"If you permit, my lord."

"Of course."

"My lord king, I wish to start with an apology for my breach of protocol last night. It will not happen again."

Bridei inclined his head in a spare indication of forgiveness.

"With your approval, I will speak to the household about today's search. After that, Eile and I have a matter to set before all present. We have a tale to tell."

"You have my approval."

Dizziness came over Eile again. The walls were moving about; the torches went double. The sea of faces around her was turbulent, the hum of voices strangely remote.

"Eile?" A concerned voice: it was Dovran, beside her with a stool. She sat; Faolan nodded to the other man, expression somber, then put a reassuring hand on her shoulder.

"Tell me if you feel faint," he murmured. Then, raising his voice again, he said the words Bridei had not been able to get out. "You will all know by now that today's search was unsuccessful. That is not through any lack of effort or of heart on the part of those who have worked so tirelessly these last days and nights, both those who went out to search and those who performed extra duties here at court so that could happen. Garth and I have concluded, with great reluctance, that there is no longer any chance a search of this kind will be successful. It seems likely King Bridei's son has been taken far beyond those territories that lie within a few days' reach. We will not require the men of the household any longer for these duties." Muttering had broken out and he raised a hand to silence it. "That doesn't mean we've given up. We'll be adopting a more strategic approach. We may call on some of you as required."

"Who's we?" someone called out.

"Garth and I will handle the practical arrangements. Decisions will be made in consultation with the king and his councillors." His tone was coolly controlled, his hand steady on Eile's shoulder.

Another voice came from the rear of the hall. "You say the boy's been taken away. That's no surprise; everyone knows children don't wander off from places as well fortified as White Hill. What does come as a surprise is to find a Gael taking charge of the search, giving orders, telling us what's what. It's no wonder we've hunted until we're dead on our feet and not found a trace of the lad, even with the dogs on the job. You were perfectly placed to allow his abductors time to get away." A hubbub of talk broke out as the man, invisible to Eile, got into his stride. "It makes me wonder how you've got the gall to stand up there with your woman beside you. My lord king, surely you must see the likeliest explanation here—"

"Stand up," Bridei said, his eyes like flint. "Identify yourself before the court."

"Mordec, my lord king. I have a holding south of Mage Lake. No offense intended. I simply want to put in the open what many folk are saying in private: that Gaels at the heart of a Priteni court are trouble, unless they're hostages or slaves."

"Very well." The king's grim expression did not change. "Your suggestions offend me, but at least you are prepared to speak out openly. I will not have the court of Fortriu polluted by gossip."

Eile found herself unable to keep quiet. "My lord king, it is wrong for folk to accuse Faolan of treachery. He's completely loyal. If it weren't for me, nobody would be saying these terrible lies."

"Faolan," Bridei said quietly, "do I guess correctly that you stand before us tonight not only to assist your king with a difficult duty but also to defend yourself and Eile against such accusations?"

Eile put her hand up to cover Faolan's.

"Yes, my lord," Faolan said. "We know of the rumors. They are hurtful untruths. I won't have Eile subject to that kind of foul suggestion. We come before you tonight to tell our story; to show every man and woman here present that our journey from our homeland to White Hill had nothing at all to do with the struggle of Priteni against Gaels. It was unrelated to political machination or strategic plotting. We made a journey into the past and back again; we followed a long path through pain and endurance, blood and hurt."

"A path from darkness to light," Eile said in the Priteni tongue. "My lord king, I wish to tell my part. But I lack sufficient words . . ."

"Faolan can translate for you." Bridei was leaning forward now, forearms on the table, clearly both surprised and intrigued.

"Oh, yes?" could be heard in the crowd, and, "I know what sort of translation that'd be."

"My lord," said Faolan, "with your permission I will ask another man to do so; one who may be judged as impartial. That way nobody can accuse me of twisting Eile's words."

"Whom did you have in mind?" the king asked.

"Er . . ." Brother Suibne was on his feet. "I'll volunteer my services, my lord king."

"He's a Gael, too," commented one of the lesser chieftains. "We're overrun with them."

"Brother Suibne is indeed a Gael." Aniel spoke calmly from his place beside the king. "You have a short memory if you have forgotten the part he played in Bridei's election to kingship. It was Suibne's impartiality and impeccable sense of fairness that made him abstain from casting the vote he was entitled to as spiritual adviser to the king of Circinn. That was the vote everyone expected would win the kingship of Fortriu for Drust the Boar. That, and the late arrival of Umbrig there," he nodded toward the huge Caitt chieftain who sat along the table from the Christians, "secured the crown for King Bridei. Let Suibne do the job tonight. There are few men here fluent in both Gaelic and our own tongue, and the rest of them must be judged less than unbiased, I believe. Eile has many friends at White Hill."

"Thank you, Brother Suibne," Bridei said as the priest came forward. "Once again you prove indispensable."

Eile prayed the Christian would not mention that he

knew her well already; that she and Faolan had spent a good part of winter lodged near Brother Colm's house of prayer at Kerrykeel, and had shared with these selfsame clerics the perilous sea voyage to Dalriada. She cleared her throat, glancing up at Faolan. "Should I begin?" she asked, her voice coming out as a strangled whisper, now the time was actually here. She could not believe she had agreed to this; she must have been crazy.

"Begin, dear heart," he murmured. "I'm with you."

IT WAS INCONVENIENT that the little Gael had survived her sojourn in the well without serious damage. Fortunately, Eile could remember nothing of what had happened; at least, that was what folk were saying. The child was another matter. Now that her mother was back safe and sound, there was nothing to keep her from blabbing out a story that included Breda and an iron chain and a certain threat. Saraid must be silenced.

Breda made her plan with care. The little ones ate their evening meal in a separate area, and there were only a couple of maids to watch all of them. As long as Breda was quick enough, she could get Saraid out and away before the stupid servants even noticed they had one child less at the table. It would be nearly dark. Most folk would be at their own meal in the hall. She could get it over with and be back in the isolated chamber that witch Dorica had allocated her before the alarm was raised.

She only had one guardian: a hag chosen by Dorica to watch her. The woman was sour-faced and fat, with a bloated stomach and sagging breasts. Why did old people have to be so ugly? Her minder's constant presence was intolerable. They could at least have let her have one of her own maidservants who, although tiresome and disobedient at times, did not offend the eye and needed only a whipping to keep them in order. But Breda hadn't seen a single one of them since Cria—wretched girl—

had led them in their ill-considered and embarrassingly public revolt. What her attendants hoped to gain from that, Breda couldn't imagine. They owed their positions at Keother's court to her; without her, they wouldn't be here in Fortriu. Indeed, without Breda they'd be nothing at all.

The hardest part of the plan to work out had not been how to deal with Saraid who, after all, was only little and not very strong. The real challenge had been how to get out of her poky chamber long enough to do the deed. The place was like a prison. It was so unfair; she hadn't even done anything wrong. Indeed, she had done her best to put things right; to make them the way they should be. She did not deserve punishment, but a reward. In time, people would come to see that.

She'd been working on the hag ever since they made her stay in here, after that horrible supper with everyone making cruel accusations. Breda hadn't been honey-sweet, for overdoing things would only make the woman suspect she was up to something. Instead, she'd done her best to seem calm, friendly, and cooperative, while forcing down her fury at the way she'd been treated and her disgust at the crone's double chin and wrinkles. Breda promised herself she would not grow old. Not ever.

She'd pretended so successfully the woman was getting quite trusting now. Even Dorica, who had come in for a bit in the morning, had made some comment about how helpful Breda was being. Once Dorica was gone, Breda had tested the water by asking politely if she could visit the privy on her own, as long as she came straight back. The minder had allowed it, but she'd come out of the chamber and hung about within sight of the privy door. There was a guard within shouting distance. Not good enough. This must be done tonight, before Saraid decided to talk.

Fortunately, one of Breda's talents was her ability to seize opportunities when they presented themselves. The gods had sent her one on her way back from the privy, in the form of the man on duty, who came right past her on his patrol up and down the walkway outside her chamber. After yesterday's search, the king must have been desperate for guards that weren't going to fall asleep on the job; Breda knew this man, knew him very well indeed, and he was a few straws short of the full haystack, but had other qualities that compensated for it. The fellow's eyes had lit up when he saw her; Breda had glanced and smiled and murmured a very specific set of instructions she made sure the old woman could not hear. She'd yet to meet a man who was prepared to refuse what she had to offer.

It worked. Her invitation had allowed enough time for the guard to get his reward; Breda was feeling a certain itch herself, one she wanted satisfied before the real business of the evening took place. The fellow knocked on the door a bit before suppertime, and when the crone opened it he stammered out a version of what Breda had instructed him to say, something incoherent that included Dorica and stables and supervision.

"Oh, thank you!" Breda made her voice suitably girlish. "My sister asked me especially to go every day to visit her pony, the one she couldn't take with her. I've been feeling so sad and guilty; I really want to spend some time with Jewel and give her a treat. This is so kind of Dorica. And I'm sure you could do with a little rest." She turned a winsome smile on her keeper, hoping very much the woman would not seize the opportunity to go and talk to Dorica. "It should be fine, shouldn't it, as long as this man escorts me all the way there and back?" Before the woman had too much time to think, Breda swept out of the chamber and off to the stables, her guard behind her.

In a little alcove with various harnesses of polished leather and shiny silver hanging on the wall, she gave the fellow his reward. He took her the way she liked it, with rough vigor and minimal conversation. Breda shifted slightly, putting out her tongue to lick the sweat trickling down the man's chest. She wished he wouldn't grunt so;

it made the whole thing a little like rutting a boar. She let her mind drift onto that for a few moments, then brought her attention sharply back as a wave of pleasure spread through her body, making her dig her nails into the man's shoulders. She arched her back, clenched her teeth, attained her climax in silence as her partner thrust once, twice, thrice and emptied himself inside her. Messy. She'd need to bathe again, then take the herbal potion just in case. If there was one thing she never, ever wanted in her life, it was a child.

"You can go," she told the guard, who had withdrawn his now flaccid manhood and was endeavoring to refasten his trousers. His performance had been a little perfunctory. The fact was, Evard had spoiled her for other men. She couldn't wait to get home. "Keep your mouth shut or there'll be no repeat performances. If that old woman asks where I am, say I'm still at the stables and another guard is watching me." He gave her a look; she glared back. "Go!" she snapped. "I mean it. Do as I say or I'll tell the king you walked off the job. Go on!"

When he was gone, Breda sought for a clean rag on which to dry herself and found nothing but old cloths impregnated with oil; no wonder the harness was gleaming. Sighing, she used a fold of her shift. That old witch had better provide a decent supply of hot water tonight; she could swear there'd been a sly, self-satisfied look on the crone's face last night when a pitiful three tepid buckets had arrived. How on earth did Keother think she could manage without her handmaids? She could hardly be expected to do everything herself.

Breda emerged from the stables into semidusk, hoping the hag was still unaware she'd been given the slip. There would be a certain satisfaction in turning up in her quarters once the deed was done, smiling sweetly and telling a tale of becoming lost in memories of home and her sister so that she'd quite forgotten how late it was.

The place was deserted. There wasn't a guard in sight, except the ones on the walls, who were busy staring out over the forest. No sign of the old woman. Lights blazing from the hall indicated supper was in progress, but it was uncannily quiet. Perhaps the king was making one of his boring speeches. Even that did not generally create this kind of hush. The only voices she could hear were coming from the small room off the kitchen, the one where the children had their supper. Children never ate quietly.

It was time. If she didn't do it now, it would be too late. Quite apart from the likelihood the little girl would talk, King Bridei was on the track of something, and Keother, who was Breda's own flesh and blood, was treating her as if she were some kind of miscreant. As for the Gael, Faolan, he'd looked as if he'd wanted to throttle her then and there. In another man, that would have excited her. In him it was plain scary.

She moved across the courtyard quietly, her kidskin slippers noiseless on the flagstones. This must be quick. She knew how Eile watched over her daughter like a hen with a lone chick. If folk began to spill out of the hall before Breda was done, and someone saw her, it could lead to disaster. Breda shivered. Her heart raced. Her blood pumped. This was thrilling. It made her feel like a goddess, with life and death in her hands. It made up for all the years of her growing up, the years of cruelty, the years of loss, the years of loneliness.

All that could be set aside. She, Breda, was in control now. She was strongest of all. Wherever she went, she would order things to her satisfaction. The king's son was almost certainly dead. A freak like him did not deserve to live; most certainly did not merit the privileges he had enjoyed. Eile's daughter must be next because of what she had seen. Breda would ensure Saraid's silence.

"AND SO," FAOLAN was saying, "we came to White Hill; I first, Eile and Saraid soon after. It was almost the last step on a very long journey."

The household had sat spellbound throughout the lengthy tale. Now the story was all out. Everyone knew about Dalach, and that Eile had knifed a man who was her kin by marriage. Everyone knew she'd packed up and walked away from that. They knew about the *éraic*: that she was Faolan's bond-slave. It was odd; that had once loomed so large in her mind, the unwelcome feeling of obligation, the humiliation of belonging to someone else, the crushing debt. Now it seemed of little consequence. That was how much things had changed between them. So she had got her story out, and now she felt as if she'd been wrung dry, yet at the same time she felt light, as if a weight had been lifted from her shoulders. She had known how hard this would be, like stripping her own flesh bit by bit from her body and standing exposed to the elements. What she had not understood was that Faolan would take a full share of the burden. She had not expected him to identify himself as of the Uí Néill, and kin not only to the high king in Tara, but also to the deposed king of Dalriada, Bridei's opponent in last autumn's war. That had seemed a dangerous truth to make known. But his story had shown why, though he was of the same family as the powerful chieftains of Ulaid and Tirconnell, he would be the last man ever to aid them against Fortriu or any other foe. He had told the tale of Fiddler's Crossing. The household knew Faolan had killed his own brother when he was only seventeen and had been paying for it ever since. They knew it was an Uí Néill chieftain who had engineered that. They knew Faolan's own sister had held him prisoner. They knew, as well, that Eile had saved his life. He had told that with quiet satisfaction. At the end, although he still stood tall before the king, Faolan's voice was shaking. Eile sat by his side, holding his hand. The hall was so quiet, she could hear the faint sound of the children's voices as they played in the supper room, awaiting the arrival of parent or nursemaid to take them off to bed.

Bridei afforded the narrators a few moments' silence; it was clear to Eile that this was a gesture of deep respect for their honesty and courage. Then the king rose to his feet. "I am full of amazement," he said quietly, "as, I believe, are all who have heard this tale tonight. We expected, perhaps, a story of intrigue and adventure, of hardship and struggle. Some may have anticipated revelations of a political nature. And indeed, many of those elements were contained in this extraordinary account. But I think, above all, that what we have just heard was a stirring and revelatory tale of love. Faolan, you said coming here to White Hill was almost the last step in the journey. May I ask you what is the last?"

Faolan met the king's eyes. His own face was pale; his hand was tightly clasped in Eile's. "I cannot tell," he said. "That is yet to be determined by Eile and me. Perhaps also by you, my lord king. I hope . . . I very much hope that this account has cleared the air for those folk who distrusted the two of us. My loyalty lies with you and, through you, with Fortriu. Eile wants only to enjoy peace, to provide a safe home for her daughter, to work and live as other folk do, without constant fear. It is a simple enough request."

Before Bridei could respond there was a disturbance at the side door of the Great Hall. A serving woman came hurrying in, her face tight with anxiety, and made her way along the tables to Elda. Words were exchanged. Elda went suddenly white. Dovran got up, heading for the door at a sprint, careless of whom his elbows knocked on the way.

"What is this?" the king asked.

Elda was on her feet, threading a path between the tables, slowed by the swell of her pregnancy. She looked back to answer. "My lord, there's a child missing. It's Eile's daughter. Please excuse me. Faolan, you'd best come."

Eile's heart went cold. She should never have left

Saraid with the others for supper. She should never have let her out of her sight, not for one instant. She sprang up, and the hall wavered and rolled around her. "Run!" she said. But Faolan was already gone.

20

I T WAS WID who helped her out to the courtyard; Wid who, despite his advanced age, was steady enough on his feet if he used a staff. By the time they reached the open, folk with torches were everywhere. Eile's head was devoid of thought; it held only a blank gray wash of utter terror. Her heart was jumping about, her skin clammy with sweat. *Saraid, Saraid . . .* Saraid who knew something and wouldn't tell. Saraid whom Faolan had said needed guarding until the truth came out. Saraid whom they'd judged it safe to leave with the twins, just for tonight, under the supervision of the serving woman the children knew well, the one who gave them supper with calm and loving competence. The one whose face had been drained of color as she brought the news.

"She can't be far off, Eile," Wid said quietly. "Breathe slowly."

The light was not good for searching. The sky still held the blue pallor of a late summer evening; beyond the walls, the forested slopes of the hill would be dark, save for the area before the great gates where torches burned on poles. But Saraid would not be outside the walls. Not unless someone had taken her. Why? Why?

Folk were moving about gardens and walkways, lanterns in hand, calling. The Great Hall emptied. Now

Bridei was in the courtyard, and King Keother, and Brother Colm with his brown-robed brethren. Curse this weakness! Saraid was out there somewhere, in danger, and Eile could hardly take two steps without losing her balance. "Saraid!" she shouted, hearing how feeble her effort was against the voices of the men, the scurrying footsteps, some new outcry from the guard post at the gate. "Saraid, where are you?"

She'd spotted Faolan vanishing in the direction of the lower court, which lay directly inside the main entry to White Hill. She followed, leaning on Wid's arm. It was something to do. There was a general movement of folk toward the gates. Elda, a twin's hand in each of hers, came up beside her. "Oh, Eile, I'm so sorry, the woman says she only turned her head for a moment, just long enough to cut up some cheese, and when she turned back Saraid was gone. She must have timed it exactly between guards . . ."

It passed Eile by as meaningless gibberish. They reached the lower court, where the great double gates stood closed, heavy bolts locking them secure. Atop the high parapet walls torches flared at intervals and men-at-arms paced between. Dimly, Eile registered the voices of the guards above the gate, raised in their usual challenge: "Halt! State your name and business!"

Faolan was running, Dovran a pace or two behind him. He was running up a steep set of stone steps, at some distance from the gates. The steps led to the parapet wall that circled the fortifications. It stood two arm's-lengths above the walkway where the guards patrolled; a man standing could look out and see the winding track that led up the slopes of White Hill to the gates. Faolan was hurling himself up the steps, heedless of his injured leg. Another man, one of the guards, had seen whatever it was Faolan had and was running along the walkway from the gates, a torch in his hand.

And there, illuminated by its approaching glow, was Saraid, standing right up on the parapet, so high her feet would be level with a man's shoulders. She was wobbling a little, her feet shifting on the narrow stone edge. She could not put her arms out for balance; she held Sorry clutched to her chest. In the flickering light Eile made out another figure, this one standing safely on the walkway right beside the child. She felt a surge of relief. Someone was already there; someone need only reach out and lift Saraid to safety. The torchlight gleamed on a swathe of golden hair, a drapery of fine silk fabric. Breda. *Breda.* Suddenly Eile was seeing it: Breda with something bunched up in her hand, Breda hitting her, then the fall, down, down into the darkness . . . *Breda had tried to kill her.* And now Breda was going to kill her daughter.

Eile opened her mouth to scream, and Wid said softly, "No. Don't startle Saraid. Look, Faolan's almost there."

He was at the top, not running now but moving with caution around the walkway, Dovran behind him.

"He's trying not to scare her," Wid said. "Faolan knows what he's doing, Eile."

The scream she had not released built up inside her, threatening to rip her apart. He was close, only a few strides in it. On the other side, the guard with the torch had halted, waiting. Faolan seemed to be saying something, perhaps telling Breda to step back and let him get to Saraid, lift her down. It was almost over.

Breda reached out a hand. It looked as if she was trying to pull Saraid back, to stop her from falling. Faolan abandoned his careful approach and lunged toward the fair-haired woman. And in that instant, Saraid flinched away from the reaching hand, lost her footing and fell. One moment she was there, the next gone.

Eile sank to her knees. It was dark. It was the darkest it had ever been: perpetual night. Nobody could fall so far and survive it. The scream broke free, ringing around the courtyard like a summons from Black Crow herself.

Someone was saying, "Lord have mercy; Christ have mercy." Garth was shouldering his way through the crowd, rushing for the steps. Why? It was too late. Too late. Night had fallen. Up on the wall, Breda was shrieking, "Get him off me! I didn't do anything! I was trying to save the stupid child! Get him off, he's hurting me!"

The noise kept on, a harsh, primitive howl of grief. She couldn't seem to stop, even though there were folk around her now, Elda, Garvan, Brother Suibne, all making meaningless sounds and trying to comfort her. Her body was bursting with anguish; there was no holding it in.

"I said, state your name and business!" The guard at the gate repeated his challenge, but his tone had changed. He would have seen; in the light of those torches set beyond the gate, they must all have seen the tiny figure descending to lie broken below the wall.

A voice spoke from outside, the kind of voice there was no ignoring. "I am Broichan, the king's druid and foster father. If you do not know me, Kennard, your memory is short indeed. I have not been away so very long. With me are the queen of Fortriu and her son. I trust you will not ask them to turn around, kneel and throw down their weapons before you let them in. We've come a long way."

"Open the gate!" It was Bridei who spoke, and when Eile looked up, gasping for breath, she saw him striding across the courtyard with his blue eyes ablaze. "Quickly!"

Then Faolan was by her side, crouching to enfold her in his arms, his face drenched in tears, his eyes full of a grim fury. She could not see Dovran or Breda, though King Keother was crossing the court with a face like thunder. "I was so close," Faolan was saying. "So close . . ."

The small side gate swung open. Through a mist of tears, Eile saw three travelers walk in. One was a tall, austere-looking man with oddly cut gray hair and only a ragged shirt to cover his gaunt form. In his arms was Derelei, head on the man's shoulder, thumb in mouth, just like any two-year-old who has missed his afternoon

nap. Beside them walked Tuala, making no attempt at
concealment. She was carrying something between her
hands; she conveyed it with great care, as if it were precious and fragile. Eile found herself holding her breath,
though why this should be, she did not know.

Bridei was weeping openly. So many tears. He threw
his arms around the tall man, encompassing his son in
the same embrace. But Tuala walked over to Eile and
Faolan and stood before them, grave and quiet. Eile
struggled to her feet; Faolan rose with her, his arm
around her shoulders.

Tuala opened her hands. Nestled on her palm was a
tiny brown bird, perhaps a dunnock, fully fledged but un-
naturally small. Eile felt a strange prickling at the back
of her neck; Faolan's arm tightened around her. Wid
muttered something and, on their other side, Eile saw
Brother Suibne make the sign of the cross.

"It's all right," Tuala said. "I caught her in time."
Then, with an odd little flick of her fingers, she released
the bird. It fluttered toward Eile. In the space of a single
breath, as Eile reached out a hand, the creature was gone
and there was Saraid, eyes wide, hair rumpled, a shaky
smile on her lips. "Mama?" she said. "I flew."

"God be praised," said Brother Suibne mildly. But
Eile was not listening. Her arms had closed around her
daughter, and Faolan's around the two of them, and for a
moment she cared nothing for the rest of the world.

It was a sudden stiffening of Saraid's body that made
Eile release her convulsive grip on her daughter. She
raised her head. Saraid was staring across the courtyard,
which was now full of chattering folk, movement, and
lights. Bridei stood by Broichan with Derelei clasped in
his own arms now. Tuala had vanished; Eile assumed she
had gone to see her baby. She realized she had not even
said thank you for what the queen had done; for the wondrous, unexpected gift of her daughter's life. Saraid was
staring, staring between the people to a corner of the

yard where Breda stood, a strangely impassive look on her lovely features, with Garth on one side and Dovran on the other, and King Keother in front of her, his face all shadow and bone.

Saraid pointed. "Lady pushed me," she said in the penetrating voice of her three years. "Lady pushed Mama down. Way down."

"Dear God," muttered Brother Suibne. Behind him was the imposing figure of Brother Colm. He appeared to be murmuring prayers of his own.

"Saraid." Faolan was kneeling now, his arms around the child from behind as if he were both protecting and restraining her. "Tell me again, just so we can all be sure. A lady pushed you?"

Saraid nodded. "Lady hit Mama. Mama fell down."

"Which lady? Show me again."

The accusatory finger pointed once more. Saraid was starting to wilt now, shock beginning to replace excitement. "Yellow hair lady," she whispered.

They'd all heard: Gaelic priest and Priteni scholar, Gaelic guard and Priteni herbalist. Eile saw the look in Faolan's eye; felt the tension coursing through his body, like that of a wildcat poised to spring. She saw his unspoken intention in every corner of his being: *And now I will kill her.*

"No, Faolan," she said. "You're a father now. You have responsibilities. Leave others to deal with this." And when he looked at her, the wildness still in his eyes, she added, "We've got our daughter back. Our own miracle. You've got your evidence. King Bridei will see justice done. You don't need vengeance in blood as well."

He drew a deep breath; let it out in a shuddering sigh. Then he put his hands over his face. "Gods, so close," he muttered. "I feel as if my heart has been shredded."

"Faolan, Eile." The king was beside them, still holding his son. Behind him stood Broichan who, for all his unkempt appearance, emanated power from every part of his emaciated form. His eyes were obsidian dark, their depths full of secrets. If he had not come in with Derelei cradled in his arms, Eile would have been afraid of him. "Is Saraid unharmed?" Bridei asked.

"She seems all right, just a bit shaken. I don't really know what happened," Eile said. "My lord, I'm so glad Derelei is home. He looks exhausted."

"He's made a long journey." Broichan's voice was deep and authoritative; it seemed to swallow the listener. "He needs rest."

"There will be questions to answer," the king said, his eyes passing over the figures of the Christian clerics and the openly curious faces of his own courtiers. "I will speak to the household in the morning. Tonight is for glad reunions and, as my foster father suggests, for sleep."

A voice cut across the yard, brittle as fine glass. "Didn't anyone see that? The little girl fell, I was trying to stop her but she lost her footing. Then, halfway down the wall, she turned into a bird. And as if that wasn't enough, the queen . . . She came up the hill as a creature, walking beside the king's druid, and a moment later there she was with her white face and her strange big eyes, Queen Tuala in her blue gown standing there as if she'd never worked magic to change the child, and to change herself . . . Your queen is something uncanny. That's wrong. It's all wrong, like everything else here at White Hill." Keother could be seen trying to stop his cousin's gush of words, but to no avail. Eile felt Faolan ready himself to intervene; his eyes met Bridei's, and the king gave a little shake of the head. *No, let her spit it all out.*

"Gaels in trusted positions, a queen who everyone can see isn't fully of humankind, royal children who look like . . . like something else, something all wrong, a king who doesn't even care what folk think about that . . . It just isn't right. But nobody bothers to try to fix it. Everyone's afraid to speak up. Well, I'm not afraid. If I see something wrong, I do something about it. You don't put people in high places if they don't deserve it. Queen

Tuala's one of the Good Folk. Everyone knows that and they just turn a blind eye—"

"Be silent!" Whether Broichan merely spoke the words or whether he accompanied them with a druidic charm was not clear. In any event, Breda's pretty mouth snapped shut as effectively as if the druid had delivered a swift uppercut to the jaw. "Hear this now, all of you, and heed it well. The queen of Fortriu is my daughter, born of a union sanctioned by the Shining One herself."

There was a universal gasp of astonishment around the courtyard; it seemed to Eile that nobody, save for the druid and the king, had known this. As Broichan moved forward, Tuala herself appeared from the direction of the royal apartments with Anfreda in her arms and Fola walking behind in her gray robes. At the sight of Broichan, the wise woman's face was transformed by a broad smile.

"Most of you know me," the druid went on. "You know I possess a power gifted by the gods themselves. You know my authority, which I owe to the king. The acts of transformation you have seen tonight have saved the life of a child. I hear the poison tongue that seeks to find ill in this. Those of you with wiser judgment must see it for what it is: a thing of wonder. Ask the guards on the wall what they just witnessed; ask those on duty above the gate. Which of them will say the queen of Fortriu should not have used the god-given power she possesses to let this innocent one fly safely down to waiting hands?

"I ask you, would you challenge my own right to perform such a deed? I think not. Then do not seek to criticize the queen's act of mercy, for I tell you now, once and forever, that any man or woman who seeks to harm my daughter by word or deed will be answerable to me. Let no mischievous hand, no venomous tongue reach out toward the king or his family, which through Tuala is my family, while I live and breathe upon this earth. For should a man seek to hurt them, the gods of Fortriu will surely smite him."

Utter silence. Nobody moved a muscle. Then Suibne began to mutter a Gaelic translation, and Colm stopped him. "I need no words to get an understanding of this," he said. "Come, we are out of place here." He ushered his brethren away. The place was hushed, as if folk needed time to take in the immensity of what had occurred. Then a small voice spoke out.

"Feeler? I dropped Sorry."

"I'll fetch her," said Faolan, rising to his feet with a certain difficulty. "She did this on purpose, you realize, Squirrel, just so we'd have a new verse to put in the song. Eile, perhaps you should take Saraid indoors. Don't wait for me." He limped off toward the gate.

Bridei raised his voice. "In the morning we will meet and consider this; a night of wonders and of horrors, too much to take in quickly. The gods have been kind. I thank them from my heart." Tuala had come down to his side, her large eyes clear and steadfast in the uneven light of the torches. Above the wall the moon appeared, framed by light clouds. It was a sliver, new and fragile, a harbinger of hope. "We will retire now," Bridei said. "Take Broichan's good advice and think long on this before making it the subject of idle talk. Ask yourselves if you would rather watch a little girl fall to her death than accept difference in this community. The gods have spared two precious children tonight. Whatever the immediate causes of their loss and their recovery, we should give thanks to the Shining One and to the Flamekeeper, and indeed to Bone Mother, guardian of the final gate, that both Derelei and Saraid have been restored to us. Good night, my friends."

Breda was gone already, led away by her cousin with Dorica on her other side. Walking up toward the garden between Tuala and the rather alarming Broichan, Eile said, "Thank you, my lady. I don't know how you did that, but you saved Saraid's life. I can never repay that. I let Derelei go out of the fortress; I betrayed your trust . . ."

"Shh," Tuala said. "You can tell us the whole story to-morrow. I'm sure it's not your fault. Derelei had a mission to fulfill; he was only waiting for his moment. He'd have slipped away eventually whoever had charge of him. And all's well; he's found his grandfather and brought him home."

"I thought you were in another form; that you would not return openly." Eile was hesitant, not sure if she should speak of this, but full of questions. By her side, Saraid walked steadily, but her earlier excitement was gone; her hand clung tight.

"I did not intend to do so. It became necessary the moment I saw Saraid topple from the wall. To transform her, I had to be in my own form. Once she was secure it was too late to change back; I'd been seen. Besides, it wouldn't have been safe."

"Why not?" asked Bridei, who was walking on the druid's other side.

"Cats and birds don't mix," said Tuala.

EILE AND FAOLAN could not bear to let Saraid out of their sight. They tucked her up in the middle of the big bed and lay down one on either side. Faolan sang the Sorry song and Eile told the story of the house on the hill. They reminded Saraid how brave she'd been, and how lucky she'd been to fly like a bird, and that Derry would be there to play with her in the morning. Then they kissed her good night and she fell asleep.

"Faolan?" said Eile.

"Mm?"

"You can sleep under the covers tonight. I don't want you catching cold."

"You mustn't feel obliged—"

"I don't. I offer because I want to."

"Thank you," he said.

"For sharing my blankets?"

"For the blankets, and for letting me be a man with family responsibilities. For everything, Eile."

"You, too. You were so brave tonight. Telling your story, and then rushing up there to try to save her, even though your leg was hurting so much . . . I wish Breda wasn't still here at White Hill. I can't believe she would do such wicked things. Who would want to harm a child?"

"Shh. Don't think of that now. Remember what you told me: Bridei will see justice done. I don't imagine Breda will ever face charges here in Fortriu. That would be too damaging to Bridei's relationship with her cousin. I think Bridei will have a stern word with her, and then Keother will convey her swiftly and quietly back to the Light Isles. It's an ignominious end to his efforts to strengthen his alliance with Fortriu."

There was a little silence. Then Eile said, "You know, this makes me understand why the folk of White Hill, Garth and Elda, for instance, are prepared to live all together within these walls; to give up the privilege of having their own cottage, their own piece of land. I suppose this allows them to keep their children safer."

"But," Faolan ventured, "you would not want to do that, I imagine? To reduce the house on the hill to a thing that exists only in tales and in dreams? The cat, the chickens, the little dog?"

"Dog? What dog?" She raised herself on one elbow to look at him across the sleeping form of Saraid.

"I did wonder," he said, "if there might be a dog, provided the cat would tolerate it. When I was a boy in Fiddler's Crossing we always had a dog."

Eile had laid her head back on the pillow. When she spoke, he heard incipient tears in her voice. "It's too hard, isn't it? How can you do your job if we don't live at court? How can we bear to have you away so much of the time?"

"Shh," Faolan said. "We're both too tired to work this out now. But we will. If I'm to be a father, I want to do it properly. If I'm to be a husband, I want to be the best one I can be. Do I still have to wait until a certain event takes place before I ask you?"

Her voice was small. "No, Faolan. You don't need to ask at all. I can't imagine any other ending to the story now. Didn't the king call it a stirring tale of love? You know my answer must be yes, for me and for Saraid. Never mind the house on the hill. We can let that go, as long as we have you."

"Such power," he whispered. "At a snap of your fingers you can make a grown man weep. And you're such a little thing, *mo cridhe*."

"Sleep now," said Eile. "Rest that knee. As for the certain event you mentioned, I expect that will happen soon enough. But not tonight. I feel as if I've been pummeled and pounded and shaken, like a garment washed in a mountain stream. Every bit of me's tired. Shall we hold hands while we fall asleep?"

FAOLAN WOKE EARLY, well before dawn. He did not open his eyes, for that was to lose the dream, the loveliest of dreams in which he felt the whisper of her long hair against his skin, and the warmth of her next to him, and the gentle, tantalizing movement of her hands as she explored his body, stroking here, brushing there, until he felt desire pulsing through him. The chamber was warm; she was sitting beside him on the bed, her slender form clad only in a fine lawn nightrobe. Blind still, he reached to touch; his hand brushed her breast, small, high, perfectly round, and the tip hardened under his fingers.

"You can open your eyes," Eile murmured.

He did, and it was real. She had remade the fire; set out the jug and goblets. Through the open doorway he could see Saraid asleep in the other room, under the green blanket, a candle on the little table surrounding her with flickering shadows.

"I moved her," Eile whispered. "She was so tired she didn't even stir." Then she lay down next to him, her head on his shoulder, her fiery hair soft against his lips, her hand still working its irresistible magic, making his breath come quickly, bringing his manhood to sudden, urgent readiness.

Slowly, he ordered himself. *Slowly, carefully. Don't get this wrong.* "Say no," he whispered, "if there's anything . . . anything at all . . ." And he began to touch, with fingers, with lips and tongue, remembering all the while how dear she was to him, and although desire made it difficult, love made it easy. Eile helped him. He had not expected she would play her own part, caressing his body as if it were a whole new world to explore. He had not expected she would untie his shirt and trousers, helping him to shed them, so they could lie heart to heart. He cupped her buttocks with his hands, pressing her close; she did not tense or flinch away, but relaxed against him, her own breath coming faster. He kissed her, using his tongue, tasting her, and with his hands he rolled her body against his, this way, that way. Perhaps not such a good idea; he wanted her so fiercely it was a physical pain.

Eile was still wearing her nightrobe. Its delicate fabric lay between them, a last flimsy barrier.

"Will you take this off?" he asked, his lips against her shoulder.

Eile's cheeks flushed. "I know it sounds silly, but I feel shy," she said. "As if I were doing this for the first time. Like a wedding night."

"It is a wedding night, *mo cridhe,*" Faolan said. "Our first time; yours and mine. I just hope I can match up to the required standard. It's a long time since I last—"

She kissed him, letting him know without words that

she had no doubt at all he would fulfill this mission perfectly. She sat up a moment; took hold of the nightrobe's hem and drew the garment over her head, discarding it. He watched her, loving the perfect smallness of her body, the lily-pale skin, the gentle curves, the neat triangle between her legs, the same enticing red as the long hair that fell across her shoulders and down over her rose-tipped breasts.

"You're the loveliest thing I've ever seen," he whispered. "And that from a man who's done more than his share of traveling. I'll wait. Tell me when. Or, if you want, we can just . . ." Just what? Lie here together while desire drove him out of his mind? Gods, he wanted her.

"Now," Eile said, moving to lie over him, her legs parted, her hands on his shoulders. "Do it now."

"Are you sure?" He couldn't breathe. He felt how open she was, moist and ready. *Let this be real. Let this not be the dream.*

"Of course I'm sure." She touched his cheek, a gesture of tenderness and trust, and then they moved together, and whether it was he who entered her, or she who received him, all at once their bodies were locked tight, and they were breathing hard and moving in a dance of passion and wonder, and Faolan knew it was going to be all right. It was the good dream that had been the truth, not the other one after all. He tried not to thrust too hard, not to release himself too soon; he held back, using his hands to help her, murmuring words of reassurance, listening to her breathing, hoping she would tell him if, suddenly, she was afraid. He took himself to the brink; knew that if he must wait much longer the battle would be lost, for he had desired her long, and even a man of iron-strong discipline has his breaking point. Then Eile's body tensed, and she made a little sound, an astonished sound of pleasure, and after it she gave a sigh, and an instant later his control was utterly lost, and he felt his seed pump deep inside her as the moment of fulfillment drove out all thought.

He lay spent, wordless. She curled against him, her head on his shoulder, her hair a soft shawl over his chest. He felt her breathing gradually slow. After a little she pulled up the blankets to cover the two of them. Then came her voice, a tentative murmur. "Was it all right?"

"You ask *me* that? It was wonderful, Eile. I have no words to describe it. I don't know if I dare ask you the same question."

She was silent long enough to set him worrying that he had misinterpreted the signs and sounds. Then she said, "It was . . . it was completely different. Not at all like . . . there were so many things I didn't know about. I can't believe . . ."

"Give me a simple answer, dear one. My mind is not capable of much right now."

"Faolan, it was . . . lovely. You were lovely. It makes me wonder why I was so afraid. Only . . . I think it did take all that time, you and me, the journey, the things we shared, good and bad . . . Without that, this couldn't have been what it was. With you, I wasn't afraid at all. That's what love does."

He held her closer. "You never quite said it. About love."

"I don't need to, do I? You must know how much I love you, Faolan. More than the moon and stars; more than flowers and trees and all the beautiful things on earth. You must have seen it."

"A man likes to hear it, all the same."

"Then I'll keep on saying it. I'll say it when we're old and wrinkly and Saraid's a grown-up woman with children of her own. Faolan?"

"Mm?"

"I don't know about you, but I'm starving."

"You didn't eat your supper. Shall I go and see if there's anyone up yet? Procure some supplies?"

"Not yet," Eile said. "I don't think I can bear to let go. Will you fetch me a drink of water? Then come back to bed so I can hold you while we wait for dawn. When Saraid wakes up, we'll all go in search of breakfast."

BRIDEI CALLED HIS formal audience with Colmcille for three days after Broichan's return. Now that his court druid was home and his wife and son restored to him, there seemed no reason for further delay. Besides, there was Keother to consider. When the king of the Light Isles, summoned to a private meeting to discuss his cousin's shocking misdemeanors, confessed that he had long known the girl to be somewhat unstable, Bridei was filled with a fury beyond what he had believed himself capable of feeling. To have set little children and young women at risk, to have brought to Fortriu a force of such amoral mischief was unthinkable as the act of a responsible leader of men. Bridei was a king; he controlled his anger. He made his opinion known to Keother nonetheless.

There was little the king of the Light Isles could say in his defense, and nothing at all in Breda's. He offered grave apologies. He did not make excuses. He mentioned that he had anticipated, on setting out from home with his cousin and their entourage, that Bridei would require a hostage in place of the now-married Ana.

"Perhaps I do," Bridei told him. "But whoever that may be, it most certainly will not be Breda. I'm counting every moment until your cousin is gone from White Hill. You'd best act quickly on that score. I cannot guarantee her safety after what has happened here." Garth had spoken to him in confidence earlier, advising that while Eile provided a strong moderating influence on Faolan, his own opinion was that if Faolan happened to find himself face to face with Breda he might prove unable to refrain from physical violence. Both Garth and Dovran had seen Faolan's hands close on Breda's neck up by the parapet when Bridei's right-hand man had believed his little girl pushed to her death. The look on his face would have turned the strongest man's bowels to water.

"I understand," Keother said, "and will take steps to remove my cousin from White Hill almost immediately. I had hoped very much to be a part of your audience with Colmcille. It's plain that strategic matters relating to my own kingdom will be included in the discussion. To have traveled so far and to miss that opportunity . . ."

Bridei forbore from the easy answer: *You should have thought of that before you unleashed your cousin on my court and on my family and friends.* The fact was, it would be useful to have Keother present at the audience. On the other hand, three more days of Breda at White Hill, even watched over by enough guards to deal with the most difficult prisoner, was three days too many.

"I thought," Keother said, "I might dispatch two boats tomorrow, with my cousin and a suitable number of guards and attendants. I've asked my advisers to set that in motion. The remainder of our party, myself included, could follow after your audience with the Christians. If you agree. Bridei, this is a sorry end to what I intended as a mission to build bridges between us."

"In fact," Bridei said calmly, "I would welcome your presence at the audience with Colm. I understand that Breda's actions are her own, not yours. Nonetheless, you brought her here and are in part responsible. I have no great desire to speak with her again, after what happened with my son, but I believe it's necessary that I do so. I must explain to her the significance of what she has wrought here."

"In full council?" Keother's voice was tight.

"I've no desire to make this any more public than it need be, Keother. We'll have someone make a record of what is said. I'll need you there, and Dorica, and a couple of guards, neither of which will be Faolan. Perhaps one of your senior advisers and one of mine. We can do it this evening before supper. Whether Breda is capable of understanding what I have to say, I don't know, but I must say it. As to what occurs once you reach home, that is not for me to determine. Your cousin will never again be welcome in Fortriu. I will be dispatching messages to her sister and to Drustan of Dreaming Glen, letting them know what has occurred. I imagine Breda will not be accepted as a guest in that household."

"Yes, my lord king." Keother was pale and drawn; he seemed to have aged ten years in the space of a few days. "If I may be excused, I will go now to attend to the arrangements for her departure. This is a cause of great shame for me, Bridei. I thought my cousin only a little wild, a little wayward. I believed a sojourn at Fortriu's court would settle her. This terrible lapse in judgment will haunt me long."

Bridei nodded. "As king and as her kinsman, you retain responsibility for Breda. That is a burden you may well bear for the rest of your life. You'll need patience. You'll need judgment beyond the merely human. I wish you luck."

ॐ

LAMPS WERE SET about the small council chamber, and there was a jug of mead on the table, with fine glass goblets. The room looked warm and inviting, not at all like a place of judgment. Breda herself, when she came in with Dorica, seemed to have dressed for a grand supper, not for an accounting. Her hair was plaited elaborately and piled up on her head, with artful wisps escaping around the brow, and she wore a gown of palest cream with embroidered borders. The color in her cheeks was high; the blue eyes dared anyone to challenge her.

Keother and Bridei were already seated at the table, with Tharan and one of Keother's councillors, Dernat. Tharan's personal guard, Imbeg, stood behind the two kings; Garth came in with the women and took up a position by the door. At the far end of the table sat the old scholar Wid, with parchment and ink before him and an expression of studied neutrality on his face. The meeting must be recorded, in view of the delicate nature of the matter in hand.

Once they were all seated, Breda opposite the men with Dorica beside her, Bridei made the speech he had prepared, listing Breda's misdeeds in order. It was a statement of fact, plain and unadorned. He had sought advice from Broichan as well as Tharan and Aniel in preparing it, wanting to be certain his love and fear for his family were nowhere in evidence, for as king and arbiter he must be entirely fair and impartial, with emotion weighing nothing in the balance of his judgments. The list spoke for itself: the goading of the mare, which had led to Cella's death and Bedo's serious injury; the coercion of Breda's handmaids on pain of further beatings; the cruelties she had inflicted on them, day by day and night by night, terrifying them into blind obedience. The injury to Eile and the abandonment in the well. The lies that had led to two children being left alone and helpless beyond the walls. The blatant attempt to murder Saraid, just three years old.

Breda sat impassive, hearing him out. Or perhaps not hearing; when he was finished Bridei asked her if she understood the gravity of her actions, and the girl simply stared through him. She was toying with an empty goblet, turning it absently around on the tabletop.

"Breda," said Keother sharply, "this meeting has not been called to pass the time. I explained this to you; didn't you take any of it in? It is important that you acknowledge your wrongdoing and express gratitude to King Bridei. As I told you, it is only his generosity that is allowing you to return home rather than face formal charges here in Fortriu. He's under no obligation to exercise such discretion."

Breda's gaze turned to her cousin. It was startlingly without expression; looking at her, Bridei felt a prickle of unease at the back of his neck.

"If there's been any wrongdoing, it hasn't been by me," Breda said crisply. "This place is ridiculous. I came here expecting a real court with everything done properly, but White Hill's full of freaks and Gaels. All I did was try to make it the way it should be; to put things in their right places. I've explained that already. I have nothing at all to apologize for, and if you had any sense you would see that, Keother. Gratitude, well, I suppose I can say I'm grateful to King Bridei for sending me home. In fact, I can't wait to get out of here. The only thing is," she turned a new expression on Bridei, widening her eyes and smiling sweetly, "I am going to need my maids on the voyage, some of them at least. Not Cria; she's really offended me. But one or two of the others. Keother says they can't come with me. Will you speak to him, my lord? I'm sure you understand a girl can't do without her attendants, not if she's to endure a long trip and look half presentable."

Bridei could not summon anything to say.

"You'll have a woman to attend to you, Lady Breda." It was Dorica who spoke, disapproval written all over her severe features. "That's been explained to you already."

Breda tossed her head. "Some shriveled-up old thing, yes, I heard that. It's not good enough. I want Amna or Nerela."

"Your maids have no wish to serve you further," Keother said. "The girls are all afraid of you. You must know why. They'll be returning home with my own party somewhat later. This meeting is not for the purpose of discussing your traveling arrangements, Breda. I want to hear some words of contrition from you or, at the very least, some recognition of the gravity of what you have done. If you cannot understand the importance of that, I fear for your future."

Breda's glance darted down the table to Wid. "What's the old man doing?" she demanded. "What's all that scribbling?" Her fingers tightened around the goblet; a note of unease had entered her voice.

"Wid is making a record of what is discussed here," Bridei said. He was starting to feel a deep longing for this to be over and the girl dispatched away from his kingdom forever. "That's important. I know Keother has told you that, if you were not of royal blood and from beyond the borders of Fortriu, you would face a very serious penalty for what you have done here. The record is a safeguard against the future."

"It could be all lies. How do I know what he's writing?"

"If you wish, Keother's scribe can read it to you when the account is finished."

"Never mind. I'll be gone tomorrow. I can get new maids back home. The trip will be tedious, no doubt, but I can endure it. When I reach the Light Isles I intend to forget all this completely. Thank the gods I didn't end up like my sister, condemned to stay in Fortriu more or less forever. That would be quite unbearable. Worse than a death sentence. I can't wait to see my favorite horse, and my court musician, and . . ." Breda had detected something in her cousin's stare. "What?" she demanded.

"Bridei," Keother said quietly, "I don't think we are going to get very far here. Breda, I did explain to you. When we get home, things will not be the same for you. After what has happened here, you cannot simply step back into your old life. You must pay a penalty for what you have done."

Breda's voice shrank to a whisper. "I thought you were joking," she said. "I thought you were saying that just to frighten me, because you were cross."

"I was entirely serious, cousin. I'll set it out again now, for King Bridei and his advisers to hear. Your behavior makes you a danger to others. It cannot be allowed to continue. There is no way you can be permitted to go free among folk, at least until we can be sure you comprehend the fact that you have committed several heinous offenses, crimes that go against all human decency."

"Oh, I do," said Breda hastily. "Comprehend. Of course

I do. I won't do it again. I promise." Her head turned quickly to look at each of them, her eyes wide and innocent.

What Bridei felt most powerfully then was pity for Keother, pity and respect, for the king of the Light Isles rose to his feet, addressing his young cousin in a tone that was both weary and authoritative.

"Such a monumental lesson is not learned quickly," Keother said. "You'll go home under guard and, when you get there, arrangements will be made to convey you to a place of isolation where you can do no more harm. Not a prison, since we do not possess such a facility on the islands. I plan to ask your aunt if she will take responsibility for you again, since she stood in place of mother to you until you came to my court. There will be other watchers. There will be no horses, no musicians, no finery and trinkets. No maids. This is the future you have earned for yourself, Breda. Be grateful for it. It is a chance to redeem yourself. There are those here who would have wanted you dead."

For a few moments the girl simply sat there staring at him, eyes wide, mouth slightly open. It was plain that, until now, she had not believed this prospect would ever actually come to pass. Then she whispered, "My aunt— you didn't tell me that—no, not that, cousin, please, you can't!" For the first time, there was a note of genuine feeling in her voice; what it conveyed was pure panic.

"It sounds an entirely suitable arrangement to me," Dorica said.

"There is no choice in the matter," said Keother. "It's decided. Bridei, do you wish to continue, or shall we conclude this now?"

"I—" Bridei did not get the chance to formulate a reply. There was a smashing sound, and a moment later Breda was standing over Dorica, the jagged edge of a broken goblet held at the older woman's throat.

"You can't do this," the girl said, eyes on her cousin, whose face had blanched. "Promise I don't have to be locked up, and I won't cut her throat. Say it, go on, say it!"

Dorica was keeping very still; her breathing came in gasps. The glass had nicked the skin of her neck, and a trickle of blood ran down to stain the pale wool of her tunic. Tharan was on his feet, staring horrified at his wife; Imbeg was edging around the table.

"Don't move!" Breda snapped, and the guard stood still. "Anyone tries to take this off me and I'll do it. You think I care about her? She's nobody. Say it, Keother! Hurry up and say it! I'm not going anywhere near my aunt and I'm not going to be locked up, I'd go crazy! Say it!" The glass dug deeper, and Dorica made a little whimpering sound.

"In the name of the gods, Bridei," whispered Tharan, "do something."

Bridei summoned one of Broichan's techniques for calm. He carefully avoided looking at Garth, who was advancing extremely slowly from his position by the door, behind Breda. "Put the glass down, Breda," Bridei said quietly. "Hurting Dorica cannot help your case. Come, just set it down on the table—"

Garth lunged forward, using his full weight to knock Breda sideways and sending jug and goblets flying. Things crashed onto the flagstoned floor, and for a moment everyone seemed to be moving. Imbeg vaulted across the table toward Garth. The others leaped to their feet, dislodging pieces of glass from their clothing. Dorica got up and backed to a corner where her husband gathered her into his arms.

"No!" Breda's voice had become a shriek. "Don't touch me! I'll cut you! I mean it!" Garth had spread his hands wide, palms forward; facing him, Breda still clutched the broken goblet by the stem, moving it toward the bodyguard's face in little jerking stabs. To grab her effectively, he must risk having that jagged edge thrust in his eyes or swept across his neck. The only person in position behind Breda now was Wid.

Keother opened his mouth and shut it again. Breda was beyond reason.

"Garth, back off," Bridei said quietly. Let this not end in another senseless death, a woman widowed, children fatherless. Perhaps, after all, they had needed Faolan here. "Tharan, go for help." Imbeg was in the wrong position to aid Garth; all he could do was stand by and wait for an opportunity.

"No!" screamed Breda. "Nobody move! No help, didn't you say this was going to be private?" The goblet stabbed out and up; Garth moved back out of range. "Say it, Keother! Why don't you say it? What's wrong with everyone?"

A river of ink spilled down over her brow and into her eyes, blinding her. Wid was a tall man, and had moved in silence. Breda screamed, putting both hands up and dropping the glass. Garth took a decisive stride forward, grabbing her by the shoulders as the old scholar stepped back out of the way. "No! No! No!" Breda's voice was high and wild. "I'm not going, I can't—" and she twisted and turned, struggling to evade Garth's grip.

"This is over, Breda," said Keother shakily.

Bridei's bodyguards were good at what they did. They seldom made mistakes, even in the most challenging of situations. Garth's error was to remember his captive was a young woman and to moderate the degree of force he used. Breda wrenched herself free and, in doing so, lost her footing on a floor treacherous with broken glass, mead, and spilled ink. She fell hard. There was a moment's silence, then Bridei saw first Garth, then Wid kneel down on the far side of the table. Imbeg said, "Oh, gods." And there was a sound from Breda, a bubbling, terrible sound, then nothing at all.

Bridei knew, even before he moved around to look, that she was dead. He felt it in his belly, a dark inevitability. Wid had taken off the warm wrap he had around his shoulders and held it pressed tightly against Breda's neck; the gray wool was already crimson and oozing. There was a growing pool of blood on the floor.

"The goblet," Imbeg said shakily. "She fell on the glass. You'll never stop the bleeding from such a wound, I've seen it before."

Bridei knelt by the girl; it was plain she was beyond help. The blue eyes were already growing filmy in a face stained dark with ink. Imbeg was right. If that vessel in the neck was punctured, even a big man would bleed to death almost before a prayer could be spoken over him. "May Bone Mother gather you gently," he murmured. "May she guide you safely on your journey. May you find forgiveness in the next world." He rose and gripped Keother by the shoulder. "I'm sorry," he said. For the moment it was the best he could do.

Keother crouched down and took his cousin's limp hand, on which four silver rings glinted. A moment later, he set it down and reached to close Breda's sightless eyes. "I could have lied," he said blankly. "I could have stopped her. All I had to do was tell her she could have what she wanted."

"There have been enough lies," Bridei said. Other folk were coming into the room now, summoned by Tharan. There was no way this could remain private. Breda had made quite sure of that. He wondered how the goddess would receive her; what journeying the young woman's spirit must do now, to earn a new place in the earthly realm. There would surely be a time of penitence far more exacting than anything Keother could have required. Well, there were certain things to be done here, and he must do them; he was king.

"Garth," he said, "go and find Faolan. Tell him what has happened. I don't need him here; I want him to listen to your story and give you his counsel. You are off duty from now until I need you again. This was a simple accident. You acquitted your duties with your usual good judgment."

"Yes, my lord." Garth was ashen-faced. Bridei knew

his bodyguard would see this as a personal failure. With luck, Faolan would be able to talk him out of that and, if he could not, maybe Elda could. Now there was Keother to deal with, and the arrangements that must change to encompass yet another funeral rite. Gods, he was weary. There must be some learning in all this, but with the girl lying on the floor in her blood and the king of the Light Isles crouched blanched and shaking by her side, Bridei was hard put to discover what it was.

"I will deal with this." A voice spoke from the doorway, deep and authoritative. It was Broichan, with Aniel a step behind him. "If you permit."

"Thank you." Bridei felt relief flood through him. "Wid will explain the sequence of events to you. Dorica needs a healer, and we're all shocked. I will accompany King Keother to his quarters myself, with Dernat's help, and return when we've broken this news to the party from the Light Isles. You should speak to Tharan, and—"

"Bridei," said Broichan, "I will deal with it. When Keother is attended to, I suggest you retire to your quarters awhile."

Aniel was already advancing into the chamber, giving quiet orders to the serving people who had accompanied him. Folk moved to cover Breda with a blanket, position a board to convey her out, sweep up the broken glass. Bridei took Keother's left arm and Dernat his right. "Come then," Bridei said. "We are no longer needed here. Let us see what wisdom two kings can gain from such a cruelly arbitrary event. For, as my foster father has so often said to me, there is learning in everything."

"The gods intervene," Keother said, "when men are too weak to act."

THE AUDIENCE WITH Colm was delayed to allow time for a funeral rite. After consultation with Broichan and with Fola, Breda's remains were taken to Banmerren for burial; it was considered the goddess might view this gesture favorably, and besides, Bridei found that he could not stomach the idea of having her laid to rest at White Hill. Since there was now no need for Keother's party to travel in two groups, they stayed at White Hill to wait for him. There was much unspoken; things that could not be put in words, but which were strong in people's minds.

After the burial, Fola did not return to court. She needed a time of peace and quiet, the wise woman said, to hear the voice of the Shining One with true clarity. Besides, she had missed Ferada. To Bridei, in private, Fola expressed concern about Broichan. He looked like a walking skeleton, a man who had been tested and tried to the very limits of his strength. He would not admit to any weakness, Fola said. In that, his season away had not changed him at all.

Bridei came back to White Hill as early as he could. The place was returning to normal under the capable hands of his councillors and of his wife. With all that had happened, there had hardly been time for Bridei and Tuala to speak of her journey into the forest, her transformation, how she had found her son, and how the two of them had discovered Broichan. Those were matters of deep mystery, matters that could not be lightly dealt with, not even between a husband and wife who shared a bond of perfect trust. He was proud of her. He feared for her. The future held so much that was unknown, and this added a new layer of uncertainty.

The day after he came back, he emerged from a meeting with his councillors and went out to find her in the garden. The day was sunny; Anfreda's basket lay in dappled shade under a plum tree, and the queen of Fortriu sat by it, watching as Broichan and Derelei floated leaf boats on the pond. There was no obvious exercise of magic in what they did. They could have been any grandfather and grandson spending a fine summer afternoon at play together.

Bridei sat down beside his wife. He made himself observe his foster father with dispassionate eyes, the eyes
of the king, not those of the man.

"Fola's right," he said. "He looks too frail even to play
with Derelei, let alone stand up to a man like Brother
Colm. That fellow may be a Christian priest, but he's Uí
Néill through and through, combative, powerful, ruthless. Broichan looks as if he's been tried to the breaking
point."

"I believe he has." Tuala's tone was as tranquil as her
eyes, those strange, clear eyes Bridei had so loved since
the moment she opened them to gaze on him, when she
was an infant of Anfreda's size and he a lonely boy of
six. Broichan had been a force to reckon with in those
days; no mere Christian could have stood up to his authority.

"Has he confided in you?"

"A little. I suggested he might perhaps go home to Pitnochie awhile to recover his strength. He won't hear of
it. In your absence he has dealt with your affairs as capably as he would have in the old days. He says he feels
young, alive, full of energy to do the will of the goddess.
His reflection shocks him; I can see that in his eyes. But
I see also a core of iron. The Shining One has tested him
severely. She has forced him to confront his weaknesses
and to set them aside. She has scoured his mind and
cleansed it of all that was holding him back. She has a
particular purpose for him, I am certain. Maybe it's to
stand up against Colmcille. Maybe it's to continue watching over Derelei and teaching him. Perhaps both. I did
not tell you . . ." She shivered suddenly.

"What?" Bridei was alarmed; her eyes had gone distant, their serenity vanishing.

"In the woods, when I found Derelei, there were . . .
there were folk with him, accompanying him on his
journey. They were the same that used to appear to me
as a child, but in a different guise. I believe they chose

a shape that would not alarm Derelei; he seemed to accept their presence as an everyday thing. The Shining One is moving us along, Bridei; she continues to shape our destiny. Even Derelei's, little as he is. She uses the Good Folk as messengers, as helpers. But I think sometimes they decide to do things their own way. They like to make mischief. Broichan will guard our son against that."

The druid was kneeling by the pond now, a sleeve rolled up, a hand in the water. Derelei, lying on his belly, was copying him. Around their submerged fingers a school of little fish swam.

"He cannot do it if he pushes his tired body beyond the limits of human endurance," Bridei said.

"He's home now," said Tuala. "Love will mend him."

"My lord!" Aniel's voice sounded from across the private garden. "You have an unexpected visitor. One you'll want to see."

Under his breath the king of Fortriu muttered an oath. "Is it so urgent?" he asked his councillor. Even as he spoke he was rising to his feet, knowing Aniel would not disturb him unless it were so.

"It's Carnach," Aniel said quietly. "He rode in just now with a small escort of four men. I've taken him to the council chamber off the Great Hall."

"Flamekeeper preserve us," said Bridei. "Everything at once; the gods test all of us. I'm sorry, dear one, I must go. Aniel, will you find Faolan for me? I want him to be present for this."

∽

"I owe you an apology, my lord." Carnach was clad in his riding clothes, his blue cloak discarded on the bench beside him. Ale and cakes had been brought, but the chieftain of Thorn Bend was too full of news to eat and drink just yet. "I knew what you must have been thinking. As spring and summer wore on your suspicions must only have increased that I had turned against you. I was angry that day; I made no secret of my fury at your decision not to contest the kingship of Circinn. I've seen Talorgen; I left the rest of my men at Caer Pridne and rode on to report to you. Talorgen told me I was almost replaced as chief war leader; that you relented sufficiently to appoint him on a temporary basis only."

"That was all Talorgen wanted," Bridei said. "And you may well find that, if you want your old position back, you'll have to stand up and contest it against a number of other contenders. Only my closest advisers were told of Faolan's encounter with you. There have been rumors sweeping across all the territories from here to Circinn." He glanced at Faolan, who had a particularly relaxed look about him today, though his eyes showed his keen interest in what their visitor might have to say. "Tell me your story, kinsman. I trust your willing return here bears out my faith in you."

"It does, my lord. It took me some time to work my anger out; to understand that your decision was a sound one, based on a longer vision than mine. I spent the winter with my family, tending to neglected work on my own holding. Then I decided to travel to Circinn; to see the newly appointed king for myself and to take his measure. That put me in the path of certain surprising information. It gave Bargoit the opportunity to approach me with an offer; an offer that will quite probably shock you."

"Go on."

"Bargoit's acquired a perfect puppet in King Garnet. The fellow's weaker than his brother was. Bargoit serves his new master in the same way as he did Drust the Boar, by whispering constantly in his ear and convincing him that Bargoit's decisions are his own. And Bargoit has a new plan, one he would never have dared attempt during Drust's reign, for although Drust was malleable, he was not a fool."

"Bargoit wants to strike out on his own?" Faolan, though officially present as Bridei's bodyguard, was unable to refrain from joining in the discussion.

"Of course, he can never be king," Carnach said. "But he can be a kingmaker, and through his puppet wield immense power in our region. When he saw me nosing about Garnet's court, he seized on what seemed a golden opportunity to persuade me to his cause. He knows how much influence I have among the chieftains of Fortriu; he knows I am your kinsman, my lord king."

"I'm astonished that a man like Bargoit would not realize how futile such an approach must be," Bridei said.

"I acted gradually." Carnach was not meeting the king's eye now, but looking down at his hands. "That is why I was absent from court so long, and unable to send a plainer message of reassurance than the cryptic one Faolan brought you. Bargoit thought he was wooing me. He saw an opportunity to destabilize your rule, my lord, by turning your staunchest allies against you one by one. If I changed my allegiance, and I played along by letting him believe I was considering that, then it was only a matter of time before he gained the loyalty of Wredech, of Fokel, even of Talorgen. So he believed; I started to think the man's mind had become addled with the grandeur of his plans."

Bridei's head was reeling. The news of Bargoit's plotting was troubling in itself, but there was something else here; something missing. "Why stay so long?" he asked Carnach. "Why drag it out until most of Fortriu had started to think you a traitor?"

"Information," Carnach said simply. "I encouraged him to expose full details of his plot by pretending to consider seriously what he suggested. That took time; I had to make it convincing. He believed me, and as a result I've come back with vital intelligence for the future. I have the details of Circinn's armies, its strongholds, the will of its people; insights into King Garnet's character that will serve you well at the council table. Names of certain allies we did not know about; plans for certain meetings at which you'll want a listening ear in place."

Bridei eyed him; it was at moments like these that he remembered why he had given Carnach the position of chief war leader. "A perilous path," he said. "How did you extricate yourself? Does Bargoit still believe you a traitor to your king?"

"He believes I'm considering his offer, which included certain privileges for me and my family. In time, I'll let him know I've changed my mind."

"You'll have made a powerful enemy," Faolan observed.

Carnach smiled. "I'll take my chances with the weasel," he said.

"So Faolan was right," Bridei said. "You did make use of him to send me reassurance of your loyalty. I did wonder if the whole thing was in his head."

"He made an unlikely farmhand," Carnach said, grinning. "You'll wish to consider this before we speak further, I imagine. I can provide detailed information when you are ready."

"These are grave matters," said Bridei. "Bargoit's ambitions seem unrealistic, but we need to discuss what you've brought us and the possible consequences of his plans. Not one of us wants war with Circinn, but if Bargoit and his new king try to undermine my authority and turn my chieftains against me, I'll be obliged to take decisive action. We can wait a little before we decide how to meet this new challenge. We've had an eventful time here at White Hill, Carnach. You'll find this household's news strange and disturbing. But that's for later. You should eat and drink, then go to rest awhile. We are indeed glad to see you back at court, kinsman. You were sorely missed. Faolan, you may leave us now if you wish. I thank you again for your part in this, which was bravely and cleverly acquitted. You need time with your family."

When Faolan was gone, Carnach poured ale for the king and for himself. They were close kinsmen and, when alone, did not stand on ceremony. "Family?" Carnach queried.

"It's a complicated story," Bridei said. "Faolan's undergone more changes in recent times than anyone would have believed possible. But he'll never lose that ruthless quickness, that uncanny nerve, that keen-eyed determination. Or the mask he can slap on to cover whatever he's feeling."

"Faolan's quite exceptional," said Carnach. "I saw him put to a severe test when I encountered him in Circinn. He passed it with flying colors. I believe he's underutilized. If I were you I'd be employing him not as a guard or even a spy but as a strategic adviser. The fact that he's trained himself to kill at a snap of the fingers wouldn't be a disadvantage. That man's too clever to be wasted on spear-throwing and fancy horsemanship."

"IT IS STRANGE," said Broichan to his daughter, "how, in the light of such dramatic events here at White Hill, the very thing you feared most, a public exhibition of your extraordinary skill in magic, passed with remarkably little fuss. Folk do speak of the child's fall and how she was saved by a transformation. They mention that some of the guards saw a cat, and then a woman. Nothing at all about the queen of Fortriu and her sorcerous powers. Breda's sudden death seems to have taken that right out of their minds."

"They are also afraid of you," Tuala said. "You did speak up rather strongly in my defense. You surprised me."

Broichan changed the subject. "I heard folk debating whether Bridei will make concessions to Brother Colm and his brethren," he said. "The parties were divided on whether the king and his druid would come to blows over it all."

Tuala smiled. They were still in the garden, and Derelei had now been joined by Saraid, demure in her pink gown. The children were sitting under a bush, collecting twigs in a little cup and talking in whispers. On the sward was Eile, watching over them, her face wreathed in dreams. Tuala and Broichan had moved a little way off to a stone bench where they sat in conversation.

"And will you?" Tuala asked the druid. "Come to blows, that is? Has Bridei told you what he intends?"

"We've yet to speak of it. There will be no dispute between us. I anticipate our being out of step where this matter is concerned. I will make my position known to him. In council, I will support whatever stance Bridei decides to take. I will not weaken the king of Fortriu before his enemies."

Tuala nodded. "He was afraid to tell you of his choice where the kingship of Circinn was concerned," she said. "He will hesitate to speak to you on the matter of Ioua and Brother Colm."

"Afraid? Bridei? The only time he was ever in fear of me was the first time he clapped eyes on me at four years old, and even then he did his best to master it."

"He was afraid of distressing you; concerned that you would believe he had deserted your common goal, to see all Priteni lands united under the old gods. He felt disloyal even as he knew his choice was right strategically."

"He wants a time of peace," Broichan said, his tone soft and dark. "After the winter, I understand that. He wants conciliation. He will give the Christians their island. He has his family back; he is full of joy. That will make him generous."

"Maybe so. But not so generous that he loses his strategic grasp. He never forgets that he is king. Not for a moment. You should trust him."

Broichan was watching the two children, deep in their

secret world. The harvest of twigs had been placed in Sorry's lap; Saraid was making the doll pick up each in turn, examine it and utter some grave pronouncement. Derelei was laughing. "You realize," the druid said quietly, "that at some point I'll need to take the boy away. When he's older. His talents can only be developed to a certain point here at White Hill. There are so many distractions."

"He's an infant, for all his intrepid journey into the wildwood," Tuala said, but she did not snap out a denial as she might once have done, for what he said had now begun to ring true for her. Derelei's abilities were frightening. The forest druids would nurture them to maturity while keeping him safe. But . . . "I don't think Eile would be happy to hear her daughter called a distraction," she murmured. "Saraid is good for Derelei. She lets him be a child. He needs that. He needs friends."

"Up to a point. The stronger his childhood friendships become, the harder it will be for him to go away. Remember that."

Tuala looked at the two little heads, bent close in concentration. Saraid's cascade of dark curls, her limpid brown eyes; Derelei's pallor, his delicate neck like the stalk of a tender plant. His strange, deep gaze. A chill went through her, a premonition of future sorrow. "We need not face this yet," she said. "We've only recently become a whole family. Let us enjoy that a little. Father." She smiled. "It feels very odd to say that."

"It feels odd to hear it, daughter. Odd, but good."

(From Brother Suibne's Account)
It has been a time of wonders. I saw the miraculous feats worked by our own Colmcille through his faith in God. We came to the court of Fortriu, and here we witnessed a phenomenon still more astounding: the transformation of a bird into a child at the hands of Bridei's queen. In

*private, Colm called this an act of sorcery and con-
demned it. I felt bound to say that, by whatever art it was
she used, Queen Tuala had saved the life of an innocent.
I'd seen that shadowy well. I'd seen how pale and
bruised Faolan's young wife was when we found her, and
the look in her eyes when she thought her daughter dead.
I knew that if godless evil lurked within the walls of
White Hill, it was not in the fey form of the queen, nor in
the powerful druid who, they say, is her father—that was
apparently as much of a surprise to the folk of Bridei's
court as it was to me—but in the hands of the woman
who wrought havoc among these people on no better
grounds than a jealous whim. That night, Faolan nearly
killed the princess of the Light Isles. I saw his hands
around her neck, until his fellow guards pulled him
away. That I did not mention to my brethren. Now she is
dead, not at the hand of an assassin, but by pure mis-
chance. May God rest her soul, for although she performed wicked acts, she was still young. If she had lived,
perhaps in time she might have learned to tread a better
path.*

*There is another mystery within this tale. How was it
Tuala appeared outside the walls of the fortress, accompanied by the long-absent Broichan and her own missing
child? She was said to have been unwell; to have remained in her quarters looking after her newborn infant
all through the time of Derelei's absence. Yet there she
was that same evening, down below the gates, and ready
on an instant to halt the little girl's terrible fall by changing her. Miracle or sorcery? We discussed it long within
the enclosing walls of our private quarters at White Hill.
It seemed to me that the question of which priest spoke
the prayer that preserved Saraid's life, which deity chose
to exercise compassion that night, was almost immaterial.
I had only to see the look on Eile's face and on Faolan's
when their daughter was restored to them to know that an
act of great goodness had taken place. Perhaps, I said to
Brother Colm, wishing to move away from talk of Tuala's*

sorcery, it was an Act of Grace. We had all been praying hard that the king's son would be restored to him. God had heard our prayers. At the same time, in His wisdom, He had seen the fall of a tiny sparrow and out of His great compassion spared her.

SUIBNE, MONK OF DERRY

"I AM COME as an emissary," said Brother Colm, dark eyes intent in his pale, lean face. He had the appearance of an aesthete, but that was deceptive, Bridei thought. The man was strong as iron and every inch a leader. They sat now in the grand council chamber at White Hill, which was set about with lamps and hung with tapestries on which the ancient symbols of the Priteni bloodlines were embroidered: the twin shields, the broken rod and crescent moon, the eagle that was his own sign of kingship. The images gave Bridei strength; they kept him in mind of who he was and what he must do here. Today, he and Carnach both wore their blue cloaks, the particular dye of the cloth signifying that they were descended from the royal line of the Priteni. The preliminaries of the audience were over. Bridei had acknowledged the Christians and made an apology for the delay in receiving them formally. Colm had expressed sadness that there had been yet another death at White Hill, and thanked the king, coolly, for his hospitality. That done, Bridei had invited him to state his purpose at the court of Fortriu.

"You have a secular master, Brother Colm?" inquired Broichan, who was seated on Bridei's right. "Would that be a petty king of the Uí Néill? Close kin, perhaps?" He was wearing his customary black robe, and his eyes equaled it in darkness, deep-set in a face that seemed these days all bone. He had scraped his cropped hair back, tying it in a cord at the nape of the neck. His voice was resonant and strong.

"The Lord God is my only master," Colm replied, meeting the druid's eye. "I am His messenger. Those matters on which I wish to address King Bridei concern the safety of our brethren within Priteni territories, and the promise of a safe haven for myself and those men who accompanied me to this shore. My purpose is God's purpose. I follow the path He sets before me."

Faolan and Brother Suibne were sharing the duties of translator, since the discussion would be complex. Wid and Keother's scribe sat side by side with quills in hand, taking it in turns to record the proceedings. Colmcille had chosen to bring only Suibne to the audience with him and, in his turn, Bridei had limited his party to Keother, Carnach, and Broichan, along with the necessary translator, scribes, and guards.

"We understand this," Broichan said now. "Yet we have heard that your reasons for leaving your home shore had more to do with a territorial struggle than with a grand endeavor of faith. Is this not so? Were you not cast out of Erin for interfering in the course of a battle? If that is true, the king wonders at your temerity in approaching him here in the heartland of Fortriu, when less than a year ago his folk defeated yours in the great war of the west."

Colm turned a gaze on him that would have shriveled a lesser man. "I could examine your own past here and now, before these listeners," the Christian said. "But I choose not to do so; it has no relevance to the matters under discussion. Should you do me the courtesy of exercising equal forbearance, I will think the better of you for it." The penetrating look turned toward Bridei. "My lord king, let me set this out for you plainly. I know it is your practice to keep hostages at your court as surety against the compliance of your vassal king. King Keother is here with us today; his own cousin spent years as a captive at Fortriu's court. In his kingdom dwell many Christian hermits. They are tolerated there, allowed their patch of land and freedom of worship. I seek your assurance that our brethren in the Light Isles will continue to be offered that freedom; that you intend them no harm now or in the future. I know you have outlawed the practice of our faith in Dalriada. I would not see that restriction put in place for your northern islands as well."

"Tell me," said Carnach, "if King Bridei were to send Broichan to your own homeland, and our druid and his fellows were to teach the ancient faith of the Priteni to all in Erin who would hear them, would you expect that practice to go on unchallenged and unimpeded?"

"His teachings would fall on deaf ears," Colm said simply. "Erin is fast becoming a Christian land, as is your own southern realm of Circinn. Even a king's druid cannot stand firm against such a tide."

Bridei caught a particular look on Faolan's face, swiftly masked. Faolan was present as a translator, not as a participant in the meeting. Nonetheless, Bridei said, "Faolan, will you give us your opinion on this matter, since you are not long returned from that shore? Do Brother Colm's words give an accurate picture of the lie of the land in Erin?"

"I am not a man of faith, my lord. From my observations, I would say two modes of belief exist side by side in my homeland, the old and the new. In some regions one is more prominent, in some the other. Folk cling to the traditions of their ancestors, the trusted and true, even in the face of a tide such as Brother Colm mentions. On the other hand, the missionaries of the Christian faith have been astute in their teachings. They are expert at blending old and new in a way that draws folk in."

Colmcille had fixed a stern gaze on Faolan as he spoke. "We made you welcome among us at Kerrykeel, and on the voyage to Dalriada," he said. "Were you sent among us not as a messenger but as a spy?"

"An emissary only, as you are," Faolan said lightly. "But old habits die hard."

"Have you an answer for me on the question of the Light Isles, my lord king?" Colm asked, now ignoring everyone but Bridei himself.

Broichan rose to his feet. He was a tall man; his eyes were level with the Christian's. "If your intention is to run through a list of demands and obtain the king's approval for each in turn," he said coolly, "you have sorely mistaken the nature of this audience. You are a supplicant. You represent a faith that has been outlawed in Fortriu. When our own wise women and druids spoke out against those who spread the Christian teaching in Circinn, they were cut down or banished, their houses of prayer destroyed. Be glad that King Bridei treats your party with respect, and moderate your tone."

Colm's gaze had remained on Bridei. "What do you say, my lord king?" he asked.

Bridei drew a deep breath. "Broichan speaks for me," he said quietly. "We are of one mind. I will give you my decisions when all the business of this audience has been presented. You mentioned only in passing the matter which I know to be your strongest reason for making this arduous journey up the Glen to my court. Now is your opportunity to tell us of Yew Tree Isle, and a promise made by a man who no longer has the authority to honor it."

He wondered if Colm would choose to berate him for banning the practice of the Christian faith in Dalriada, or make a speech about folk needing to move with the times, or comment that, if the court at White Hill represented Bridei's kingdom in miniature, Fortriu must be a place where murder, plotting, and sorcery ran rampant. Instead, the priest made a simple statement of his heartfelt desire for a safe haven, a place where he might establish a house of prayer and contemplation amid the wonders of God's creation. Ioua was such a place; he had felt the breath of God in the west wind and heard the whisper of holiness in the waves on the shore. For now, should Bridei agree to fulfill the promise made by Gabhran of Dalriada, Colm and his twelve brethren would do no more than establish their monastic house.

"A man such as yourself is incapable of stopping at that," said Broichan flatly. "I see it in your eyes; I hear it in every word you speak. You're on a mission. If you are given Ioua, you will not long be content with it. Your teachings will spread like a creeping plague over all Fortriu, even to the eastern coast and down to the borders. Give us an undertaking that none of you will travel beyond Yew Tree Isle and the king might perhaps give your proposal some consideration."

"Are you afraid," Colm asked, and his tone was a battle cry, a ringing challenge, "that you must hedge yourselves about with restrictions thus? How can a man's faith be true faith if it has not been fully tested? To shut your ears entirely to our doctrines, to prohibit all Christian prayer on your home soil, is to admit that your own gods cannot stand up to the comparison. If your faith in them is stalwart and sure, where is the harm in learning the message of Our Lord Jesus Christ? Weigh the two against each other, as in a scale, and if your old convictions remain unshaken, perhaps you are justified in clinging to them with some degree of certainty. I know you will not do this, Druid. It is plain to me that your ears are forever closed to the word of God; that your eyes are blind to the light. You dare not test your faith in the way I suggest. But I challenge you to do so, King Bridei. Experience the opening of your heart and soul to the light of the one true God. His is a path made not by fear but by love. I see in you a man born to tread that path."

"I have been tested," Broichan said. His voice was like winter, spare and cold. The dark eyes blazed with feeling. It came to Bridei that he and Colm were a pair; not so much the two sides of one man, as the same man cast in two different molds. "And King Bridei has been tested more rigorously than your kind can ever understand," the druid went on. "There will be no spreading of the Christian faith within Fortriu." For a moment, the air around him seemed to crackle with energy, as if the anger of the gods inhabited him, lending him an Otherworldly power. "The king is the gods' representative on earth; he is obedient to their will."

"You are refusing to honor King Gabhran's undertaking?" There was no mistaking the tone of Colm's voice; the anger was undisguised. Suibne translated, looking at the floor.

"Are the matters of your petition set out in full?" asked Carnach. "As the king told you, we will hear all of them before any answers are given."

Colm gave a stiff nod. "For now, this is all," he said. "King Bridei, your druid asks that we remain on Ioua. There are practical considerations; questions of supplies and the fact that we might offer certain services to folk living on the nearby islands. I don't speak of prayers; we have a healer among us, and men with other useful skills."

Carnach glanced at Bridei. They had discussed this at length before the meeting began; their answers had been determined before the questions were formally presented. "Such activities as those would be deemed acceptable," the red-haired chieftain said. "As long as they are not accompanied by the telling of Christian tales and the conduct of Christian ritual. Those practices are banned throughout Dalriada. That extends to the western isles. Should the king decide to allow you shelter on Ioua, what you did within your own walls would be your own business. You are priests, after all. Should the practice of your ritual creep beyond the shores of the island, you would find yourselves bundled onto a fast boat back to Erin."

Colm waited.

Bridei rose to his feet. He knew, as did Broichan and

Keother and Carnach, what the decision was to be. All the same, his heart was pounding and his head beginning to throb in a familiar way. Stating this aloud before the Christians made intention fact. He had made difficult choices before, taken paths that had surprised his people and stretched the goodwill of the gods almost to breaking point. So he believed; and he knew that as soon as he had spoken, he had once again set his dear ones at risk. The shadow of the Nameless God hung over all of them. He could hardly have said why he was doing this; only that, after this season of fear and hurt and loss, it felt right.

"On the matter of your brethren in the Light Isles, King Keother offers you his assurance that they will remain safe," he said. "He and I are in agreement on that issue. I understand these hermits are quiet folk who are well accepted among the people there." He did not add another fact that he had been told, which was that the number of conversions to the Christian faith had been extremely small. The island people had a tendency to resist change. "We do not wish to see their number greatly expanded."

"They are few," Colm said, "and likely to remain so. They go for the sea and the silence."

Bridei glanced at Keother, who sat quiet and pale on his left side.

"You mentioned hostages," the King of the Light Isles said to the priest. "That situation is for King Bridei and myself to handle; we are kinsmen, and understand each other."

There was a little silence, during which Bridei looked across the chamber and met Brother Suibne's eye. The translator gave a little, crooked smile; it seemed to Bridei the Gael knew exactly the mixture of conviction and trepidation he felt in his heart.

"On the matter of the island," Bridei said, "we will allow you tenancy there for two years. Build your house of prayer; open your ears to the silence. Go no farther than the neighboring isles, and then only if your men's skills may serve the community. No prayers beyond Ioua; no ritual, no teaching. We have a powerful chieftain in control of the west; his name is Umbrig. He will be instructed to deal with any breach of those rules promptly and decisively."

"And after two years?" It was Suibne who asked the question; it seemed to Bridei that Colmcille had not heard anything after the first words, for the granting of his dream had rendered him temporarily wordless.

"After two years," Bridei said, "we'll look at this again. No promises. I'm not a fool. I don't for a moment believe Brother Colm capable of restricting his activities to a single island. If I decide to pack the lot of you back home, believe me, I'll do it. You'll be watched. Don't forget that."

Suibne nodded; neither he nor Faolan rendered this speech into Gaelic.

There; the words were out, and there was no going back, at least until the two-year trial was over.

Colm had regained his equanimity. "Thank you, my lord king," he said gravely. "I sense that your druid is not in full agreement with you on this matter, and I congratulate you on standing firm."

Bridei felt Broichan stiffen beside him, then heard the druid controlling his breathing, holding back words of anger. "You read us incorrectly," Bridei said. "Broichan and I are of one mind where these matters are concerned. Here in Fortriu, the will of our gods is woven into the long history of our people. They are older than time, knitted fast in the rocks and waters of the Glen. They are nourished by the love we offer them; we are blessed by the great web of life they wrap us in. It may be that the voices you hear in the wind and waves of your island are not so different from those that guide us. But it is not through a desire to know more of your own doctrines, or to see them advance like a shadow across my beloved land of Fortriu, that I grant you this favor. I think you are a good man; a man of integrity. I find myself in a position to offer you safe haven from certain powerful enemies we happen to share. As a man of honor, I believe it is my duty to do so."

"You have two years to prove yourself, Brother Colm." Broichan's voice was like an iron blade. "Break the restrictions we have set you and the king will banish you forever from this shore. Do not doubt his word."

"In two years," Colm said, "I will build my house and sow the seeds of my community. Then, God willing, I will return to White Hill and we will talk again."

(from Brother Suibne's account)

On the eve of our departure, seeing that Broichan looked pale and weary at supper, Brother Colm drew him aside and called me to translate for him. He offered the king's druid a cup of water. "I wish to leave you in a spirit of good faith," our leader told Broichan. "I see that you are not in the best of health. Whether this ailment is of the body or of the spirit, I cannot tell. But I have certain healing gifts. Drink of this cup, over which powerful prayers have been spoken, and your sickness will leave you."

I was somewhat surprised that Broichan did not dash the thing to the floor. "I need no Christian prayers," he said coldly. "What is this? I see a little stone in the cup. Would you feed me a charm to suck out my life?"

"The pebble is from Ioua; from the loveliest, most remote part of that seashore, where the waves roll in straight from Ulaid," Colm said. "The white stone holds great healing power. Place it in any cup and he who drinks from that vessel is well again. God is good. I offer this in . . ." He hesitated, the word friendship *refusing to leave his lips.*

"In deepest respect," I said in the Priteni tongue. "Carry it away unspilled, at least. Consider it. Good

health is an essential tool for a man with missions still to accomplish. Go in peace, brother."

Colm raised his brows at me, unable to understand, but Broichan took the cup and bore it away. His expression did not provide any assurance that he would make use of it.

I heard, later, that he had been on the point of tipping it out in the garden when his daughter, the queen, persuaded him to drink it. The argument she used related to her son, the odd little child Derelei, and the fact that Broichan must remain well and strong for a good fifteen years to see the lad become a man. So he drank. The next morning we left White Hill for our long voyage to the west and our new home on Yew Tree Isle. I cannot say whether the white pebble's miraculous healing powers were effective on a recalcitrant druid. I hope that, at some time in the future, I have the chance to find out.

It has been an adventure; a time of miracle and magic, sorrow and joy, grievous loss and wondrous finding. I thank God for giving me the opportunity to be part of it. I sense this is not yet finished. Colm held himself quiet during that meeting, but I know his zeal; it is a thing to be reckoned with. He is a bright beacon, a powerful force for change. Once we are settled on our peaceful isle, a new tide will flow across this land, and the dark practices of the past will struggle to stand up against it. That is my belief.

Bridei is no fool. Perhaps he sees what I see and is following a longer and subtler path than any of us can guess at. Or perhaps the joys and terrors of these last days have blinded him to the true force of Colmcille's mission. One thing I do know. There will be work for me yet at the court of Bridei, king of Fortriu.

SUIBNE, MONK OF DERRY

"WE HAVE SOMETHING to ask you, my lord king."

Faolan's tone was diffident. He and Eile had come

hand in hand up to the walkway where the king was standing alone save for Ban, with Dovran on guard at a distance. The formal manner of address alerted Bridei to some awkwardness in the matter to be raised.

"Speak openly, Faolan. Dovran's out of earshot and Ban can't repeat what he hears. What's troubling you?"

It was night, and the waxing moon was veiled by clouds. A chill wind from the northern sea whipped the torches into fiery banners and set the men's cloaks billowing.

"I'm wondering," Faolan said, "if you remember a conversation we had on the night you were elected king. It's a long time ago. Chances are you have forgotten it. You offered me a new position in your court and I refused it."

"Councillor, adviser, and companion."

"You do remember."

"Indeed. And you, I think, told me you did not have it in you to be a friend. Even then I knew you were wrong."

Faolan nodded. In the fitful light his expression was hard to read. "Eile and I have been discussing the future," he said. "I wondered whether that offer might still be open."

Bridei felt a smile creeping over his face. "It might," he said. "You are weary of travel? You no longer wish to exercise certain special skills?"

"That life mixes poorly with the duties of husband and father, Bridei. Besides, my knee isn't what it was. Eile hasn't asked me to do this. I want that to be clear. It's my decision to change the path of things. I can't inflict my old life on her and Saraid. I need to be here for them. If I keep on with these duties I'll be constantly worrying and so will Eile."

"If I said no, what would you do?"

"I'd leave," Faolan said bluntly. "Seek employment elsewhere. Provide for my family as best I could. I can turn my hand to a few trades."

"No doubt."

"But it would break my heart to do it, Bridei. I want to stay here; to work under your patronage. That's if you believe I can still fulfill the role you had in mind."

"I've no doubt at all that you can." Bridei put his arms around Faolan's shoulders and embraced him; after a moment, Faolan returned the gesture.

"Thank you, my lord," Eile murmured. "The truth is, I know Faolan will miss the adventure and the challenge. I think it's possible he may be available for an assignment here and there. Just as long as he's not away too often or for too many days. It would be unfair for him to have to change so much, just because of us."

Faolan smiled. "I already have changed," he said. "The man I was last summer would never have put such a request into words."

"I'm glad the two of you have come to see me," said Bridei, considering how to frame his next speech. What he knew of Eile meant the offer he intended to make must be expressed just right, or her pride would make it imperative that she refuse. "This will indeed be a major change for you; for all three of you, I believe. Eile, Tuala and I owe you compensation for the near-fatal attack you suffered while in our service. You were doing a highly responsible job of caring for our son when Breda took it into her head to make an attempt on your life."

"Oh, but I let Derelei go off—I didn't keep him safe—"

Faolan put his arm around her shoulders.

"Nobody could have foreseen what would occur," Bridei said. "Besides, as my wife tells it, Derelei was determined to get out, and he is a child of unusual abilities. I hope you will accept what I have to offer, Eile. It is customary to do so under such circumstances."

"I don't need any sort of reward, my lord. I have everything I want." She glanced up at Faolan, her eyes bright with love.

Bridei smiled. "I had in mind a modest patch of land with a cottage; there's a vacant holding situated near the settlement below the walls of White Hill, a smallish place set by itself on rising ground. Should the three of you decide to take it on, Faolan could still come up here to perform his duties as a councillor, but you could retain some independence and privacy as well. I sense the communal life of court is not entirely to your liking, and I see a difficulty in folk making undue demands on Faolan's time if he continues to dwell here once his role changes. We're all so used to having him on call night and day. For a married man, that's not reasonable; I'm sure you've heard Elda say so many times, and she's right."

Eile appeared to be speechless.

"I'm told the place needs a bit of work," Bridei said. "It's a little rundown and the garden's overgrown. Tuala tells me that should not be a problem for you."

"I—" faltered Eile. "I—"

"I expect I can add mending thatch and digging drains to my existing skills," Faolan said. "And Eile has the garden already fully planned in her head, I think. I imagine she would still come to visit court. Saraid and Derelei have formed a friendship."

"Tuala hopes very much that both Eile and Saraid will be frequent visitors."

"Thank you, my lord," Eile managed, looking as if she would as soon burst into tears as anything else. "I hope this isn't just—just charity—I mean, we couldn't accept that—I'm sorry, that's so discourteous—you can't know what this means to me, a garden, my own garden, and a little house . . . How did you know? How did you know that was what I wanted more than anything? Almost anything." She leaned her head against Faolan's shoulder. Then she lifted it again, peering into his eyes. "You didn't say something, did you?"

"Me? Not a word. I may have mentioned to the king that we would prefer to live outside the walls, but no more than that, I swear."

"Believe me, Eile," Bridei said, recalling a certain tale Faolan had confided about a house on a hill, "a gift from the king under such circumstances is entirely the usual practice. Think of it as part compensation, part wedding gift. I am assuming you two plan to allow Broichan to regularize your alliance?"

"If he's prepared to marry a pair of godless Gaels, yes." There was a new note in Faolan's voice.

"By the Flamekeeper's manhood, Faolan," Bridei said, "it does me good to see you so content at last. I welcome you gladly to the number of my councillors. To tell you the truth, both Aniel and Tharan are getting on in years, and it's past time a younger man joined them."

There was a silence, then Faolan said, "Thank you," and Bridei wondered if there were tears in his friend's eyes.

"My lord," Eile said softly, "we're so happy this has worked out well for you and the queen; that Derelei is safely home at last, with his grandfather. I thought, when I first came here, that kings and queens were grand people whose lives were quite unlike mine; folk who lived in a different world. But at heart we're all the same, aren't we? We all have the same love and the same fear. The gods set the same blows on us, and help raise us up when we are in despair. At least, that's how it seems."

Bridei smiled. "You've found a rare prize there, Faolan," he said. "Or maybe she found you. Perhaps you understand, now, what drove me along the shore to Banmerren by moonlight all those years ago in search of the girl they'd taken away from me. Back then, you found my behavior incomprehensible."

"Some things take a long time to learn. Good night, Bridei. Our gratitude is too strong to be put into words."

"No need for words. Besides, I'm the one who should be offering thanks to the two of you. Good night, Faolan. Good night, Eile. May the Shining One guard your dreams."

Then Faolan and Eile went back to their quarters, arms entwined, feet light with hope, ready to begin the next part of their lives. But Bridei walked the walls of

White Hill awhile longer, his loyal dog at his heels and Dovran on watch, silent by the stone steps. The clouds parted; the Shining One revealed herself in her cool, pale perfection.

What lies in store? the king of Fortriu asked her. *Have I done right? Have I led my people on a path of truth?*

The goddess gazed down on him, bathing his form in silver. And it seemed to him she whispered, *Walk on, my loyal son. Step forward with faith and with courage. Your people need you; they look to you. Do not fail them.*

AUTHOR'S NOTE

As with the other books in The Bridei Chronicles, *The Well of Shades* is a blend of historical fact, informed guesswork, and pure invention. The broader political and military framework of the story is loosely based on the small amount we know of Pictish history in the latter half of the sixth century. There are few written records, none of them Pictish, and all of them were set down well after Bridei's time.

The major players in this story were real historical figures: King Bridei, his druid Broichan, Gabhran of Dalriada, Drust the Boar of Circinn and his brothers, and the powerful Uí Néill chieftains in Ireland. The account of the battle of Cúl Drebene and its aftermath is on historical record. Brother Colm, better known as Saint Columba, did have to leave Ireland under unfortunate circumstances, and is recorded as making a journey up the Great Glen to Bridei's court and performing a number of miracles on the way, several of which make an appearance in this book in somewhat altered form. Columba was promised the island of Ioua, or Yew Tree Isle, by the Gaelic king of Dalriada, and later had to negotiate with Bridei to ensure permission for his monastic base to be founded there. Ioua gained its later and much better known name of Iona as the result of a slip in penmanship. The details of Columba's progress up the Great Glen, and such additional gems as the story of the white pebble by means of which he scored points against Broichan, we owe to Adomnan's *Life of St. Columba,* written about a hundred years after the saint's death. It is a far more starry-eyed account than Brother Suibne's.

Adomnan's chronicle tells us that Bridei kept hostages from Orkney (the Light Isles) at his court to ensure the loyalty of his vassal king, and that such hostages were at court when Columba came to visit, as was the Orcadian king himself.

The Well of Shades includes much that is fictional, although I have always tried to base the story on what might have been possible in the context of the beliefs and culture of the highlands in Pictish times. The Good Folk arise from the folklore of the region, and the religion followed by Bridei and his people blends together a number of earth-based spiritual beliefs. My Priteni are probably a little further down the path toward equality of the sexes than is altogether likely for that period, but the matrilineal succession is a plausible theory that has long been attached to Pictish culture, and it seemed to me that indicated a respect for women that might well flow more broadly into the attitudes and practices of the people. Hence the highly influential wise woman, Fola, the determined educator, Ferada, and a spiritual practice in which three goddesses (the Shining One, All-Flowers, and Bone Mother, sometimes known as Black Crow) are revered alongside the warrior deity, the Flamekeeper.

The geography of The Bridei Chronicles is that of the Scottish Highlands. In the interests of good storytelling, I have taken some liberties with some of the locations and distances. White Hill is located at Craig Phadraig in Inverness; Caer Pridne is Burghead. I placed the house of the wise women at Banmerren around Burghead Bay, where the spiritual center of Findhorn can now be found. For the Irish section of the book, I chose a location at

Kerrykeel in the north for Colm's temporary dwelling while he is waiting to leave for Fortriu. Faolan's home at Fiddler's Crossing and Eile's at Cloud Hill are somewhere in County Armagh.

Breakstone Hollow is an invention, but I expect that during those tumultuous times of internal warfare, such places of arbitrary imprisonment existed, just as they do now.

For more on the culture of the Picts and the historical background to The Bridei Chronicles, visit www .julietmarillier.com.